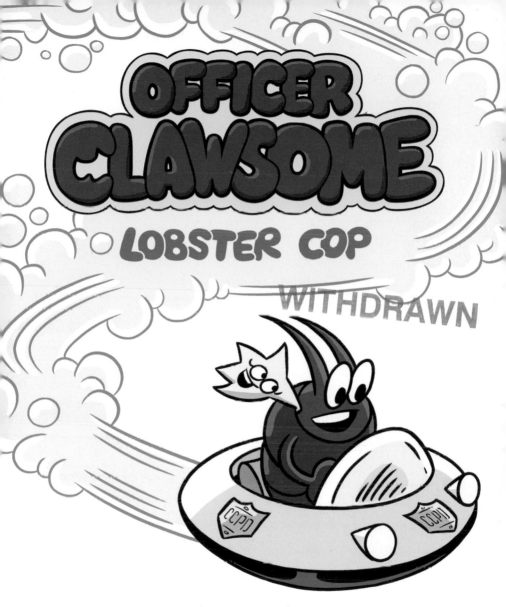

OFFICER CLAWSOME

LOBSTER COP

BRIAN "SMITTY" SMITH

CHRIS GIARRUSSO

HARPER alley

An Imprint of HarperCollins*Publishers*

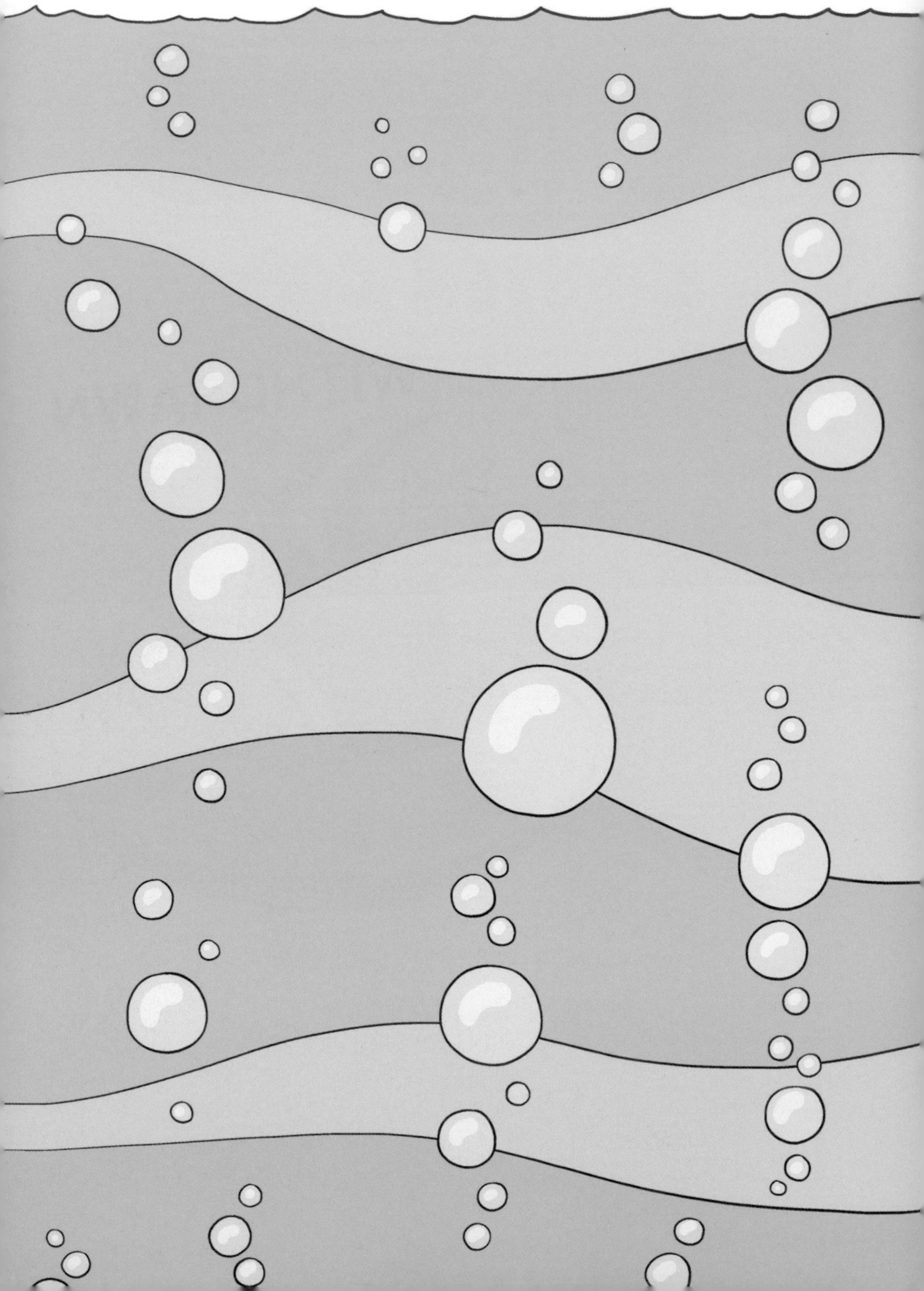

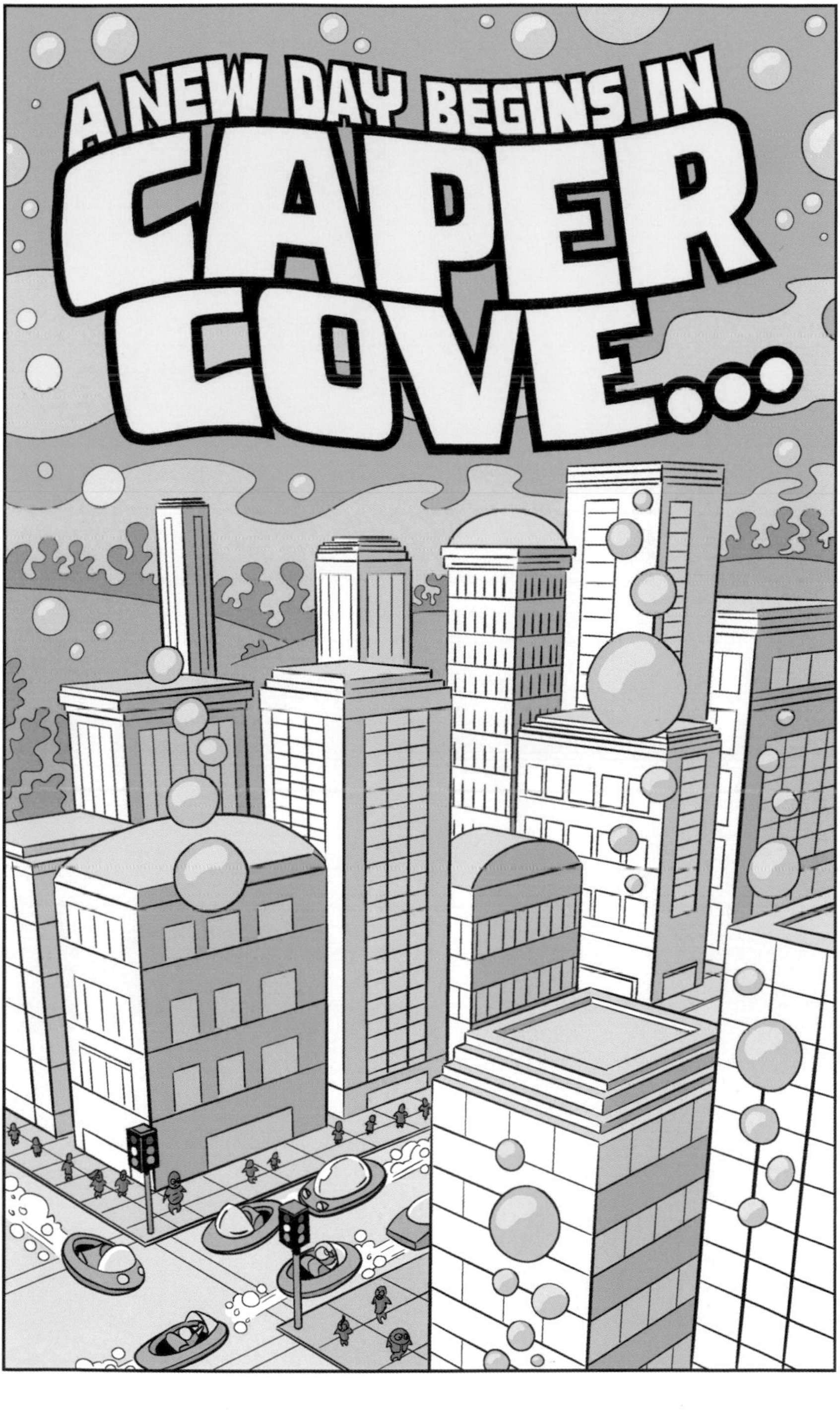
A NEW DAY BEGINS IN
CAPER COVE...

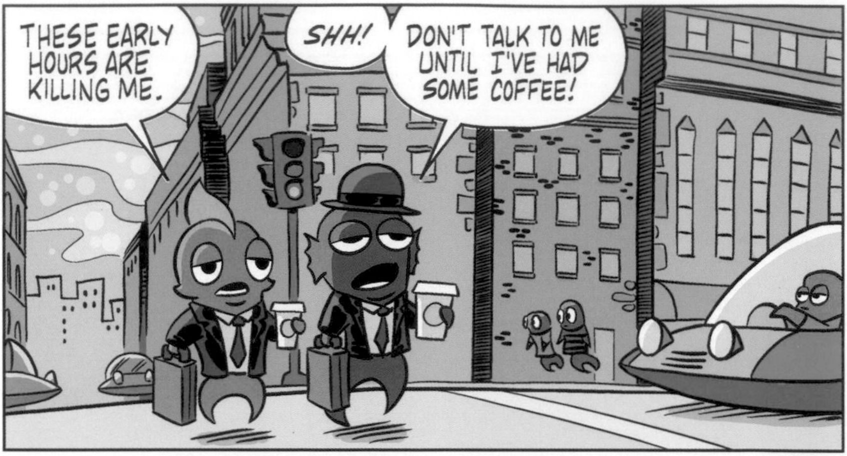
THESE EARLY HOURS ARE KILLING ME.
SHH!
DON'T TALK TO ME UNTIL I'VE HAD SOME COFFEE!

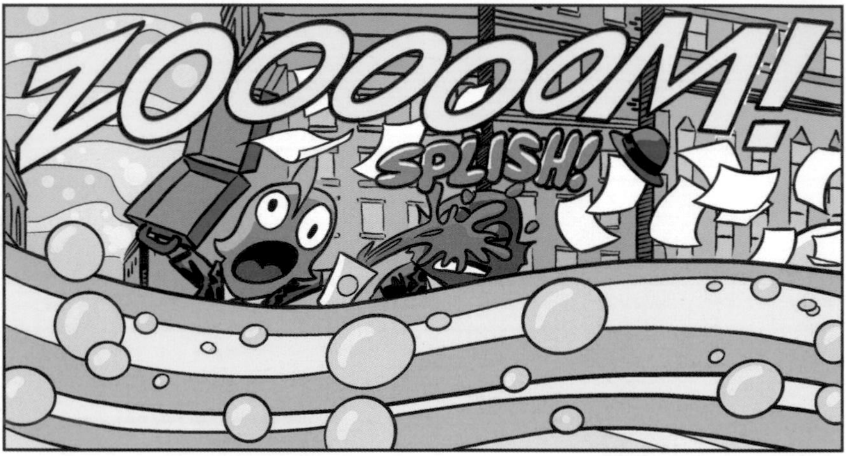
ZOOOOOM!
SPLISH!

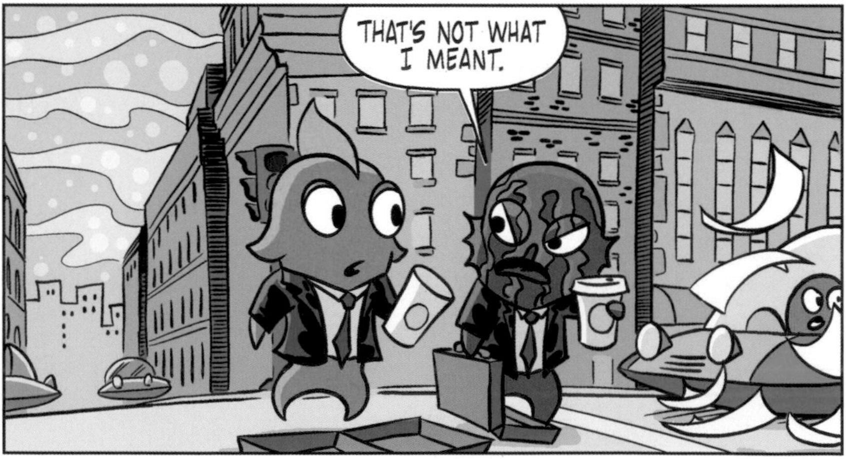
THAT'S NOT WHAT I MEANT.

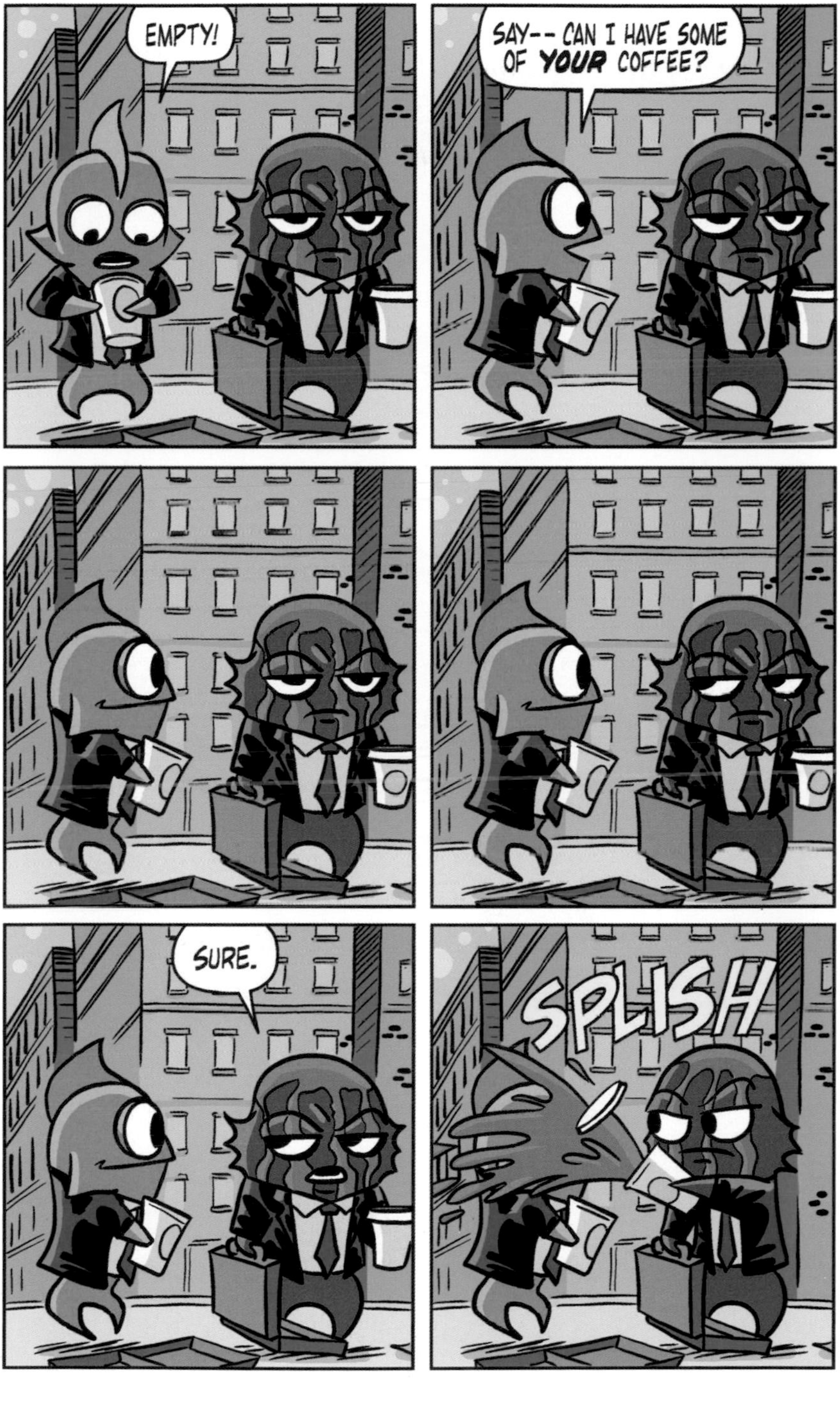
EMPTY!
SAY-- CAN I HAVE SOME OF YOUR COFFEE?
SURE.
SPLISH

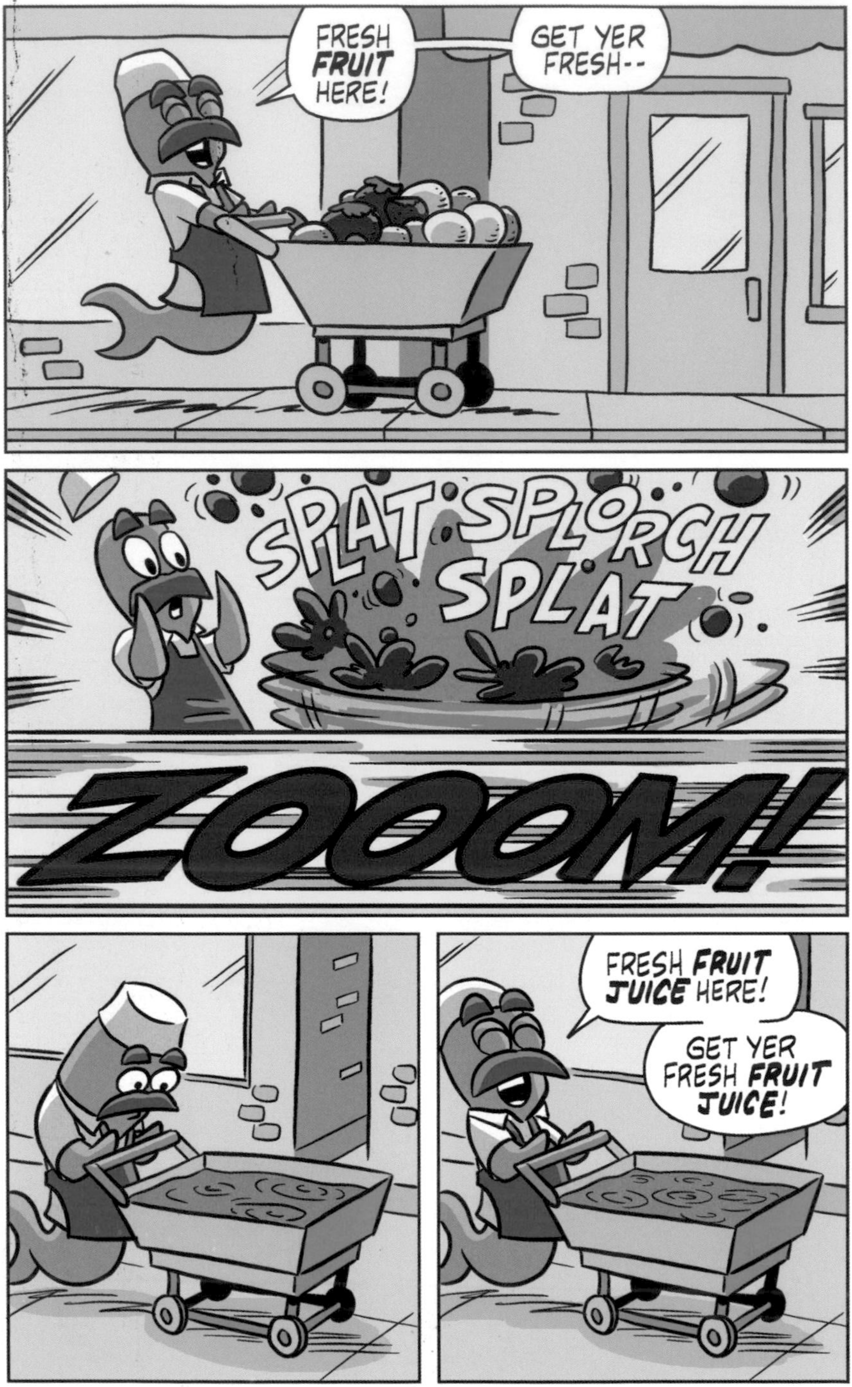

FRESH FRUIT HERE!
GET YER FRESH--
SPLAT SPLORCH SPLAT
ZOOOM!
FRESH FRUIT JUICE HERE!
GET YER FRESH FRUIT JUICE!

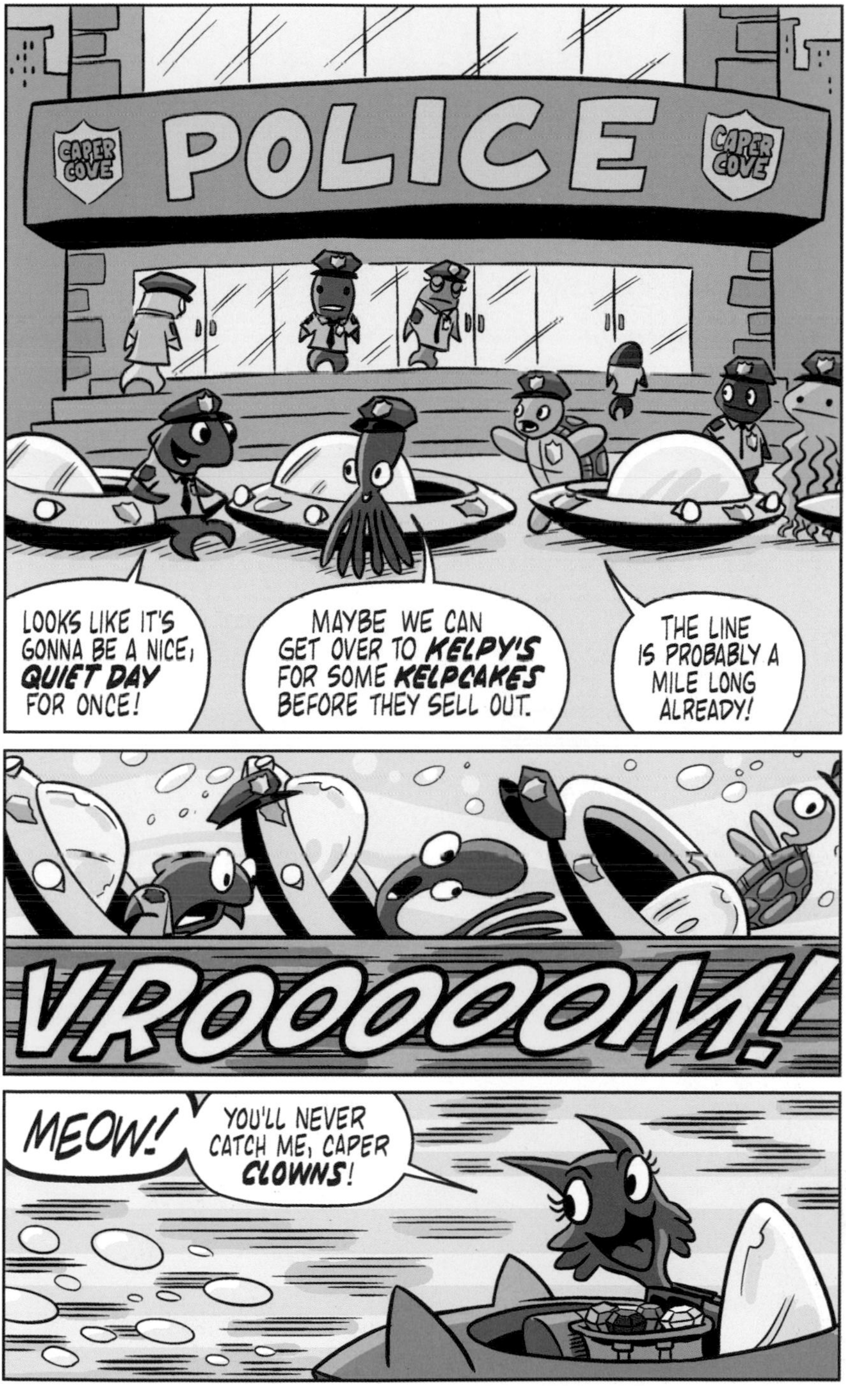
POLICE
CAPER COVE
CAPER COVE
LOOKS LIKE IT'S GONNA BE A NICE, **QUIET DAY** FOR ONCE!
MAYBE WE CAN GET OVER TO **KELPY'S** FOR SOME **KELPCAKES** BEFORE THEY SELL OUT.
THE LINE IS PROBABLY A MILE LONG ALREADY!
VROOOOOM!
MEOW!
YOU'LL NEVER CATCH ME, CAPER **CLOWNS**!

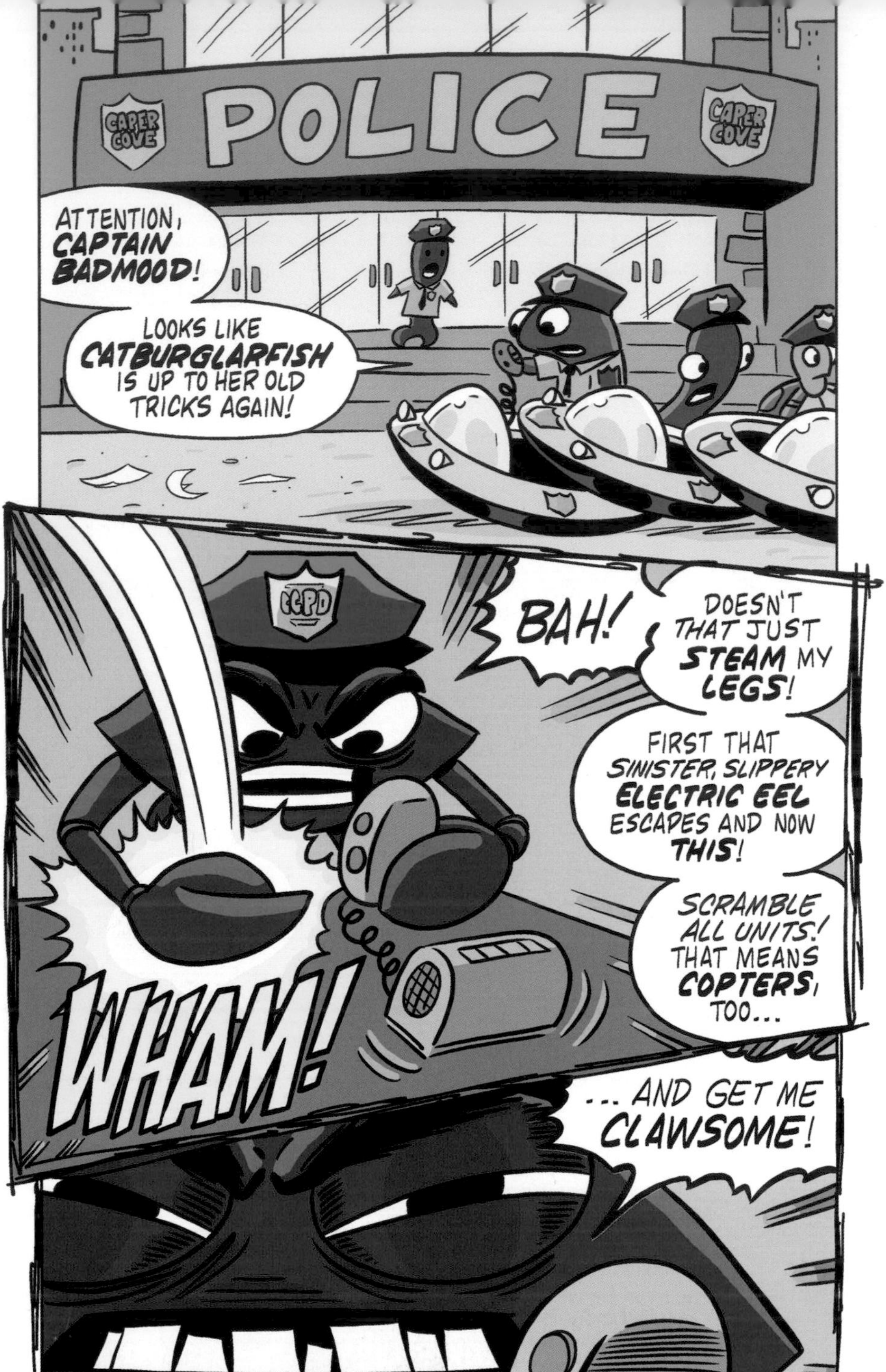
POLICE
CAPER COVE
CAPER COVE
ATTENTION, CAPTAIN BADMOOD!
LOOKS LIKE CATBURGLARFISH IS UP TO HER OLD TRICKS AGAIN!
CCPD
BAH!
DOESN'T THAT JUST STEAM MY LEGS!
FIRST THAT SINISTER, SLIPPERY ELECTRIC EEL ESCAPES AND NOW THIS!
SCRAMBLE ALL UNITS! THAT MEANS COPTERS, TOO...
WHAM!
...AND GET ME CLAWSOME!

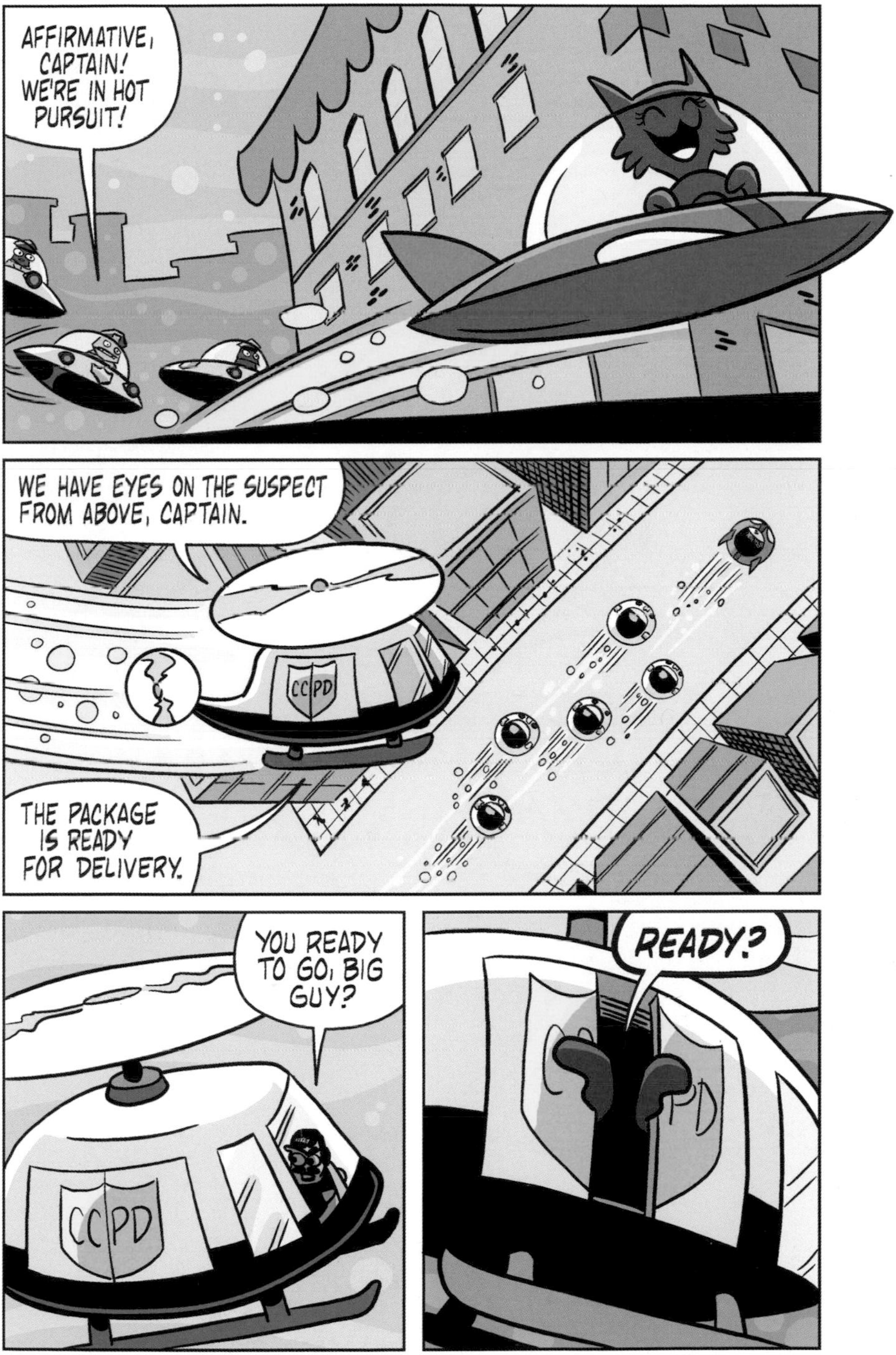
AFFIRMATIVE, CAPTAIN! WE'RE IN HOT PURSUIT!
WE HAVE EYES ON THE SUSPECT FROM ABOVE, CAPTAIN.
CCPD
THE PACKAGE IS READY FOR DELIVERY.
YOU READY TO GO, BIG GUY?
CCPD
READY?

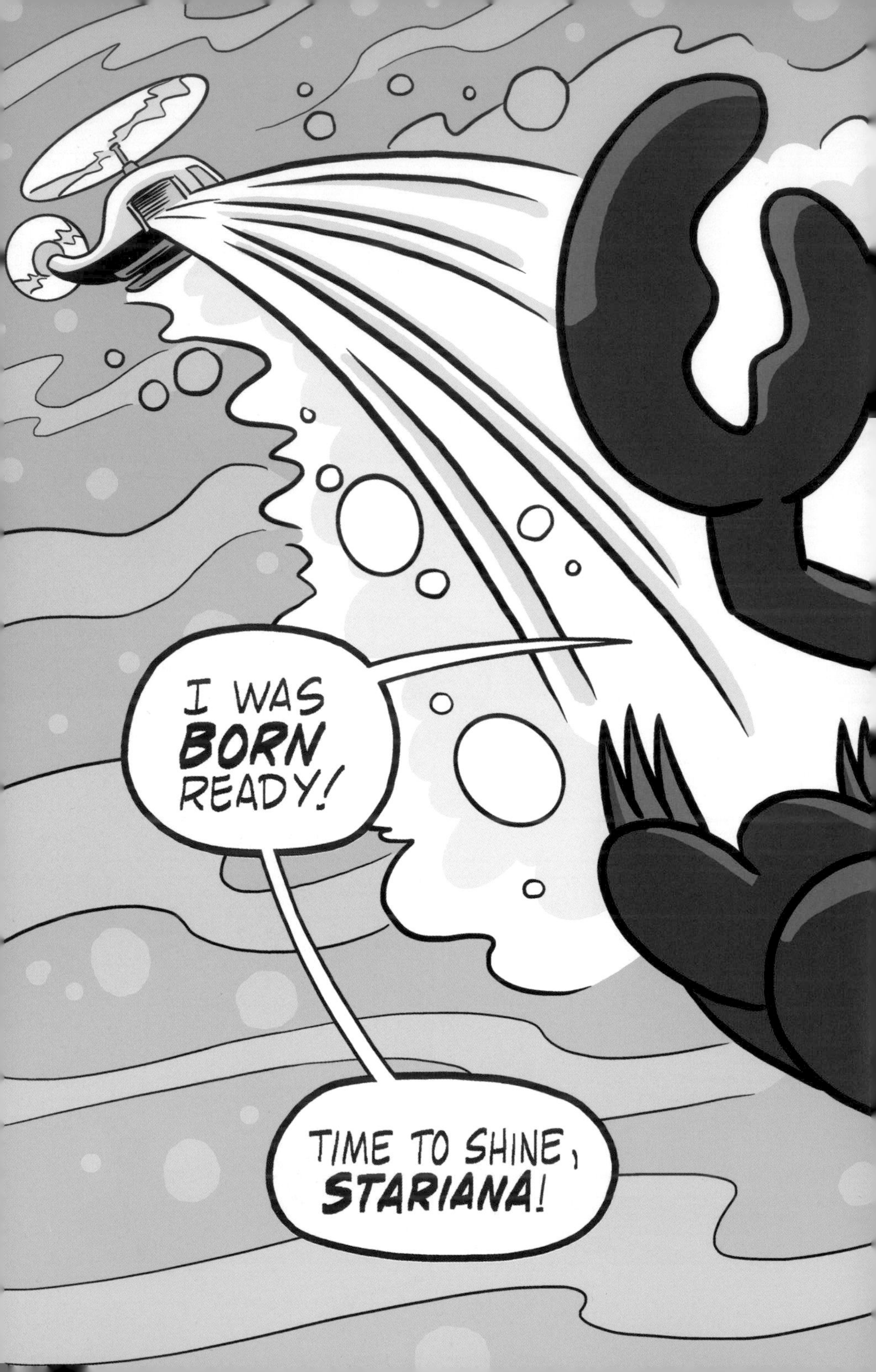
I WAS BORN READY!
TIME TO SHINE, STARIANA!

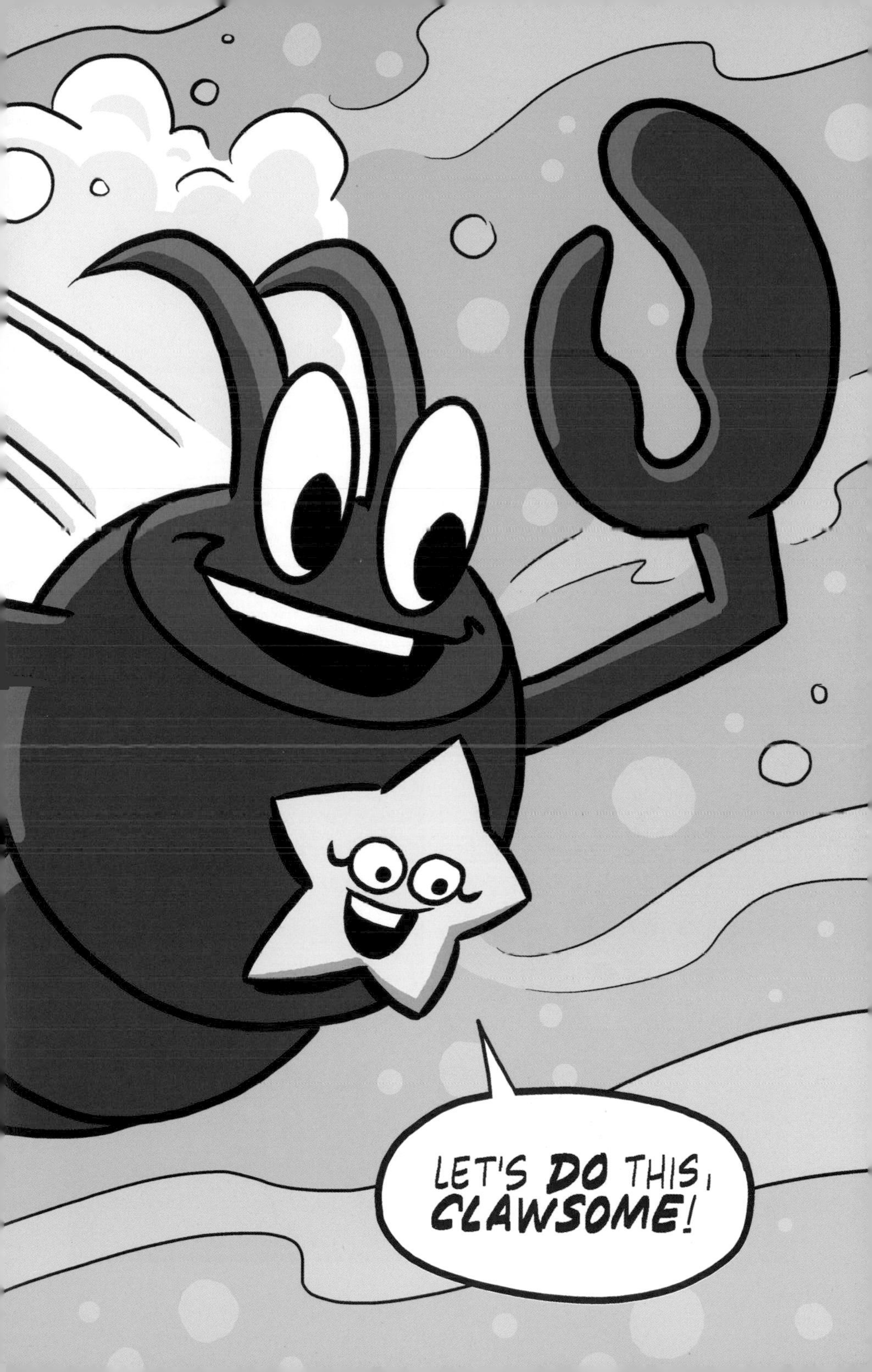
LET'S **DO** THIS, **CLAWSOME**!

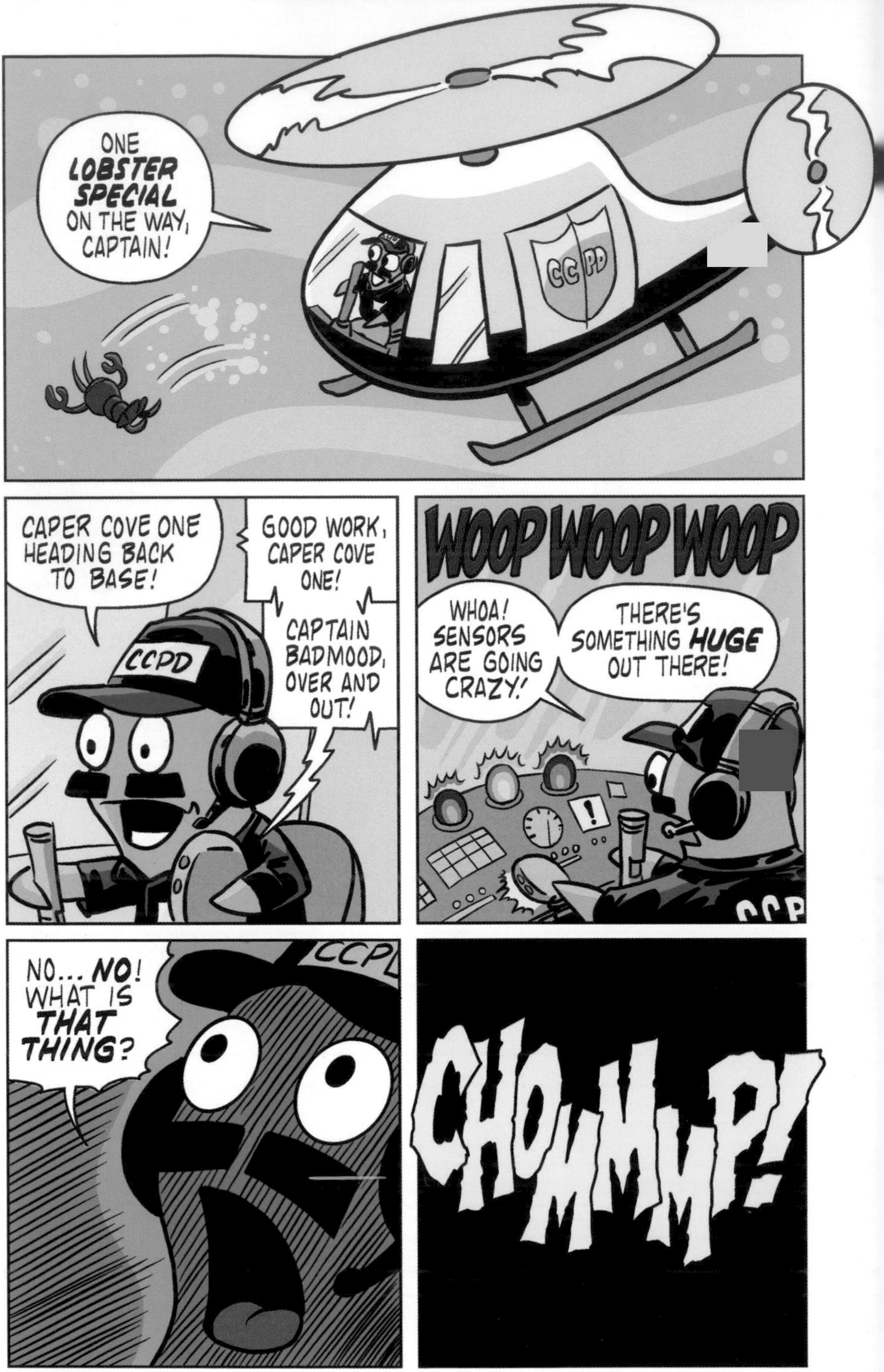
ONE LOBSTER SPECIAL ON THE WAY, CAPTAIN!
CCPD
CAPER COVE ONE HEADING BACK TO BASE!
GOOD WORK, CAPER COVE ONE!
CAPTAIN BADMOOD, OVER AND OUT!
CCPD
WOOP WOOP WOOP
WHOA! SENSORS ARE GOING CRAZY!
THERE'S SOMETHING HUGE OUT THERE!
NO... NO! WHAT IS THAT THING?
CHOMMMP!

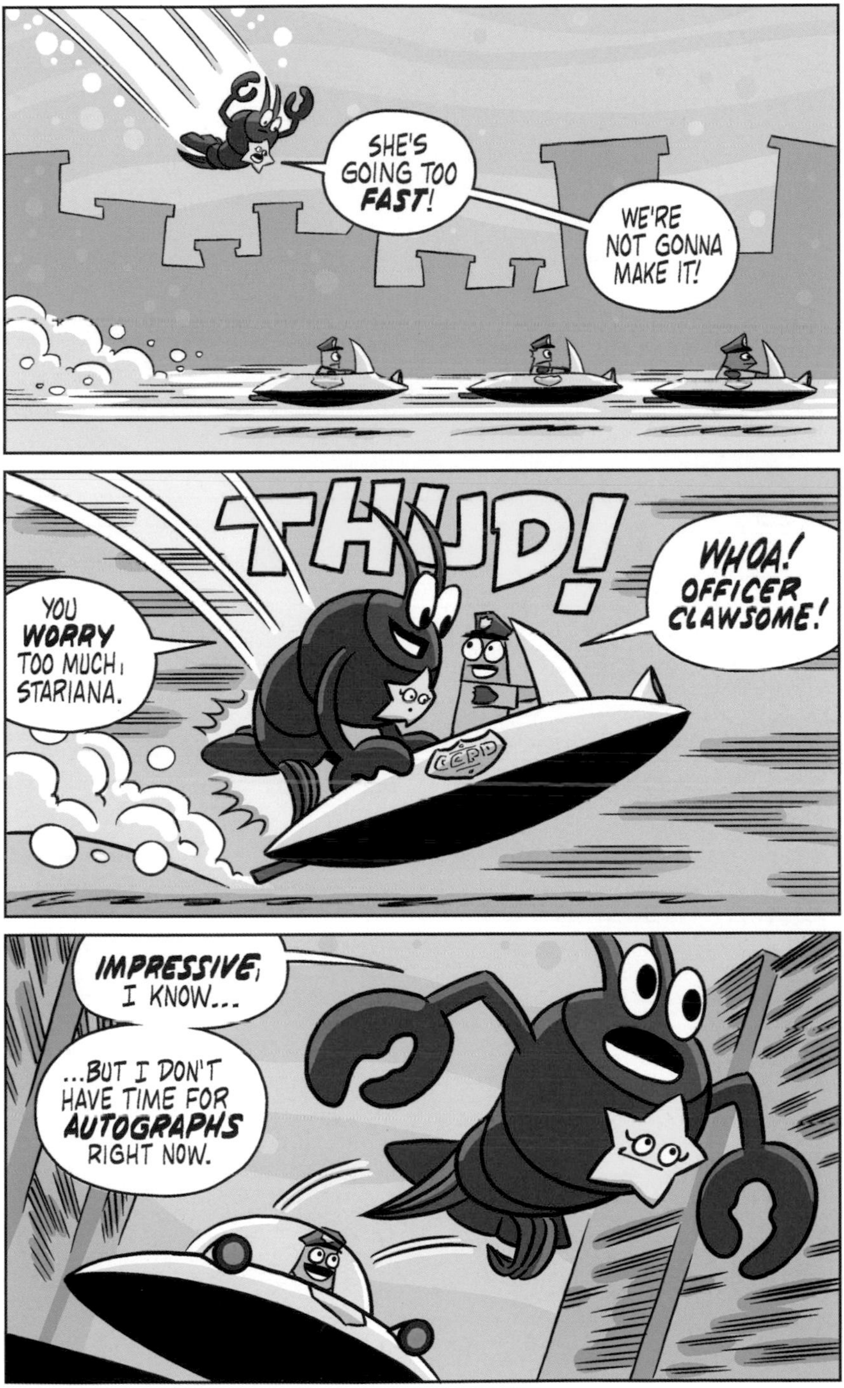

SHE'S GOING TOO **FAST**!
WE'RE NOT GONNA MAKE IT!
THUD!
YOU **WORRY** TOO MUCH, STARIANA.
WHOA! OFFICER CLAWSOME!
IMPRESSIVE, I KNOW...
...BUT I DON'T HAVE TIME FOR **AUTOGRAPHS** RIGHT NOW.

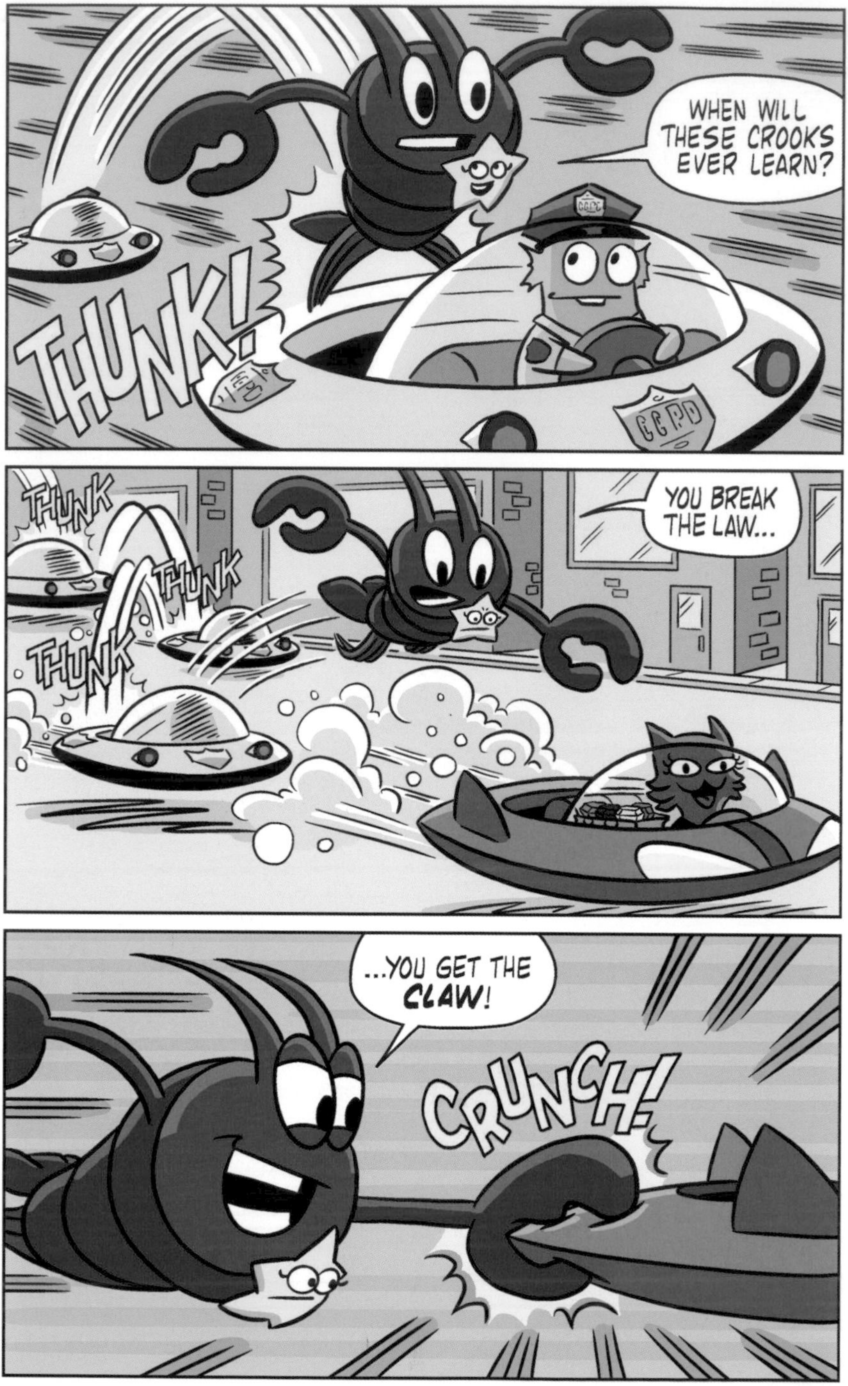
WHEN WILL THESE CROOKS EVER LEARN?
THUNK!
CCPD
CCPD
THUNK
THUNK
THUNK
YOU BREAK THE LAW...
...YOU GET THE CLAW!
CRUNCH!

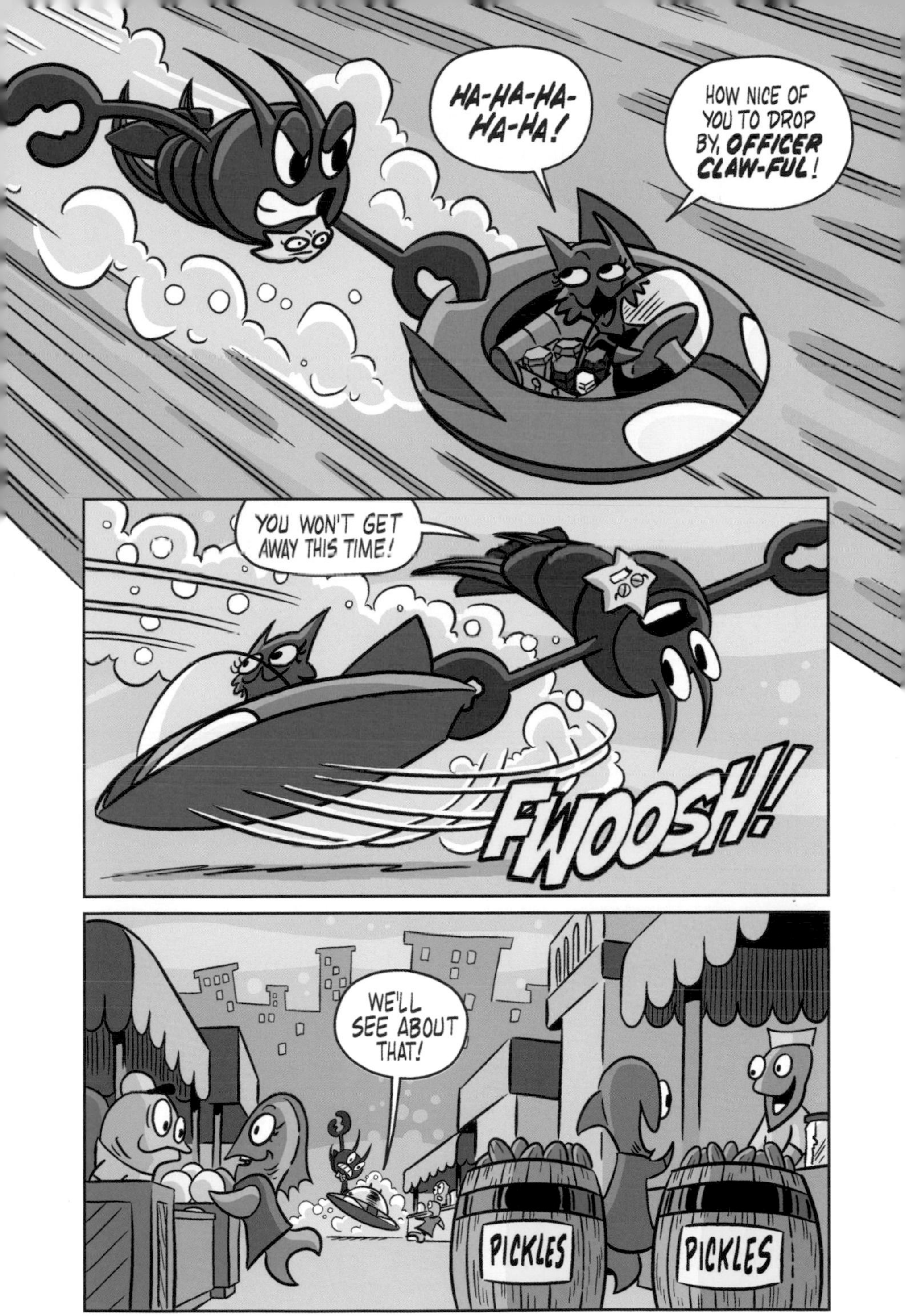
HA-HA-HA-HA-HA!
HOW NICE OF YOU TO DROP BY, OFFICER CLAW-FUL!
YOU WON'T GET AWAY THIS TIME!
FWOOSH!
WE'LL SEE ABOUT THAT!
PICKLES
PICKLES

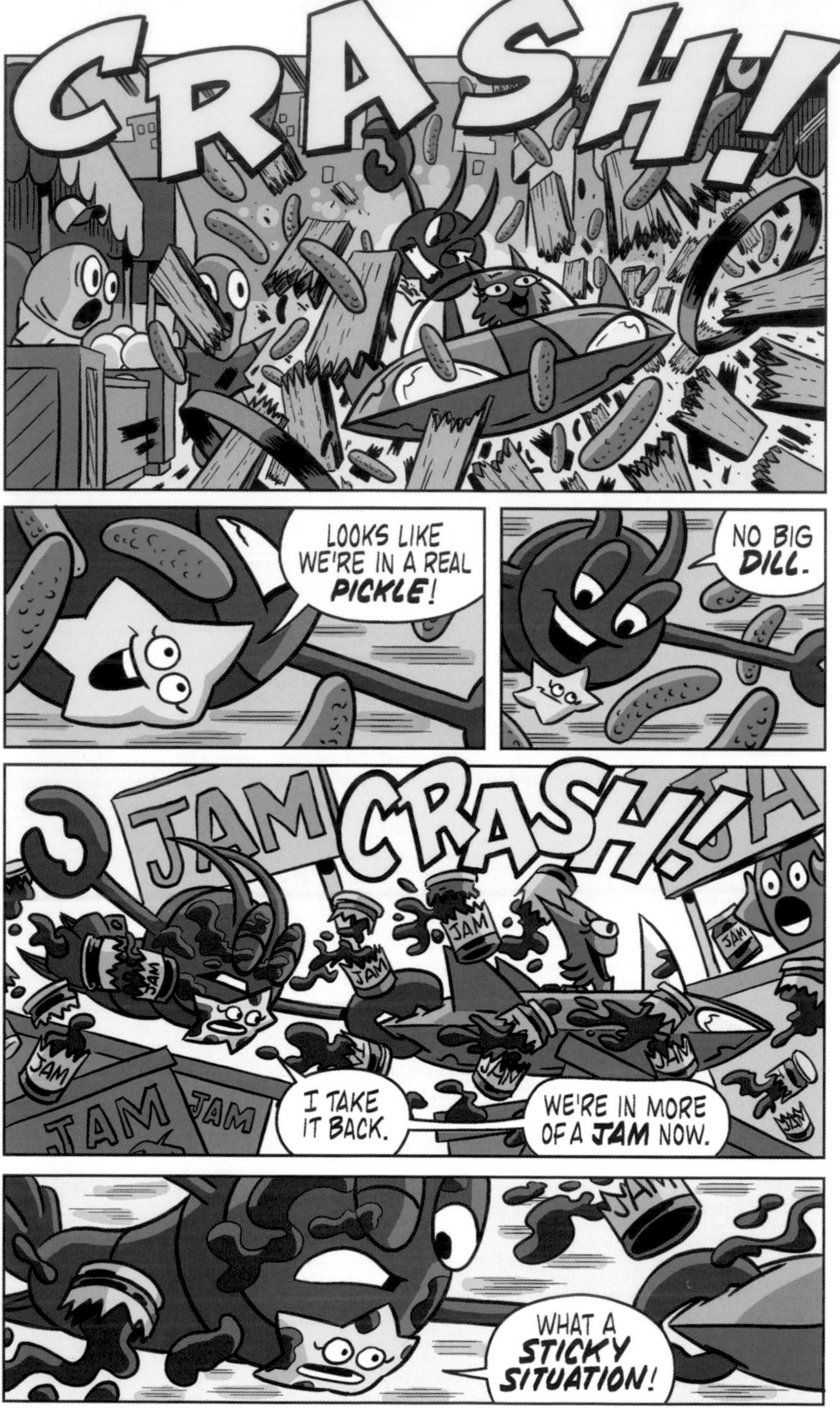
CRASH!
LOOKS LIKE WE'RE IN A REAL PICKLE!
NO BIG DILL.
JAM
CRASH!
I TAKE IT BACK.
WE'RE IN MORE OF A JAM NOW.
JAM
JAM
WHAT A STICKY SITUATION!

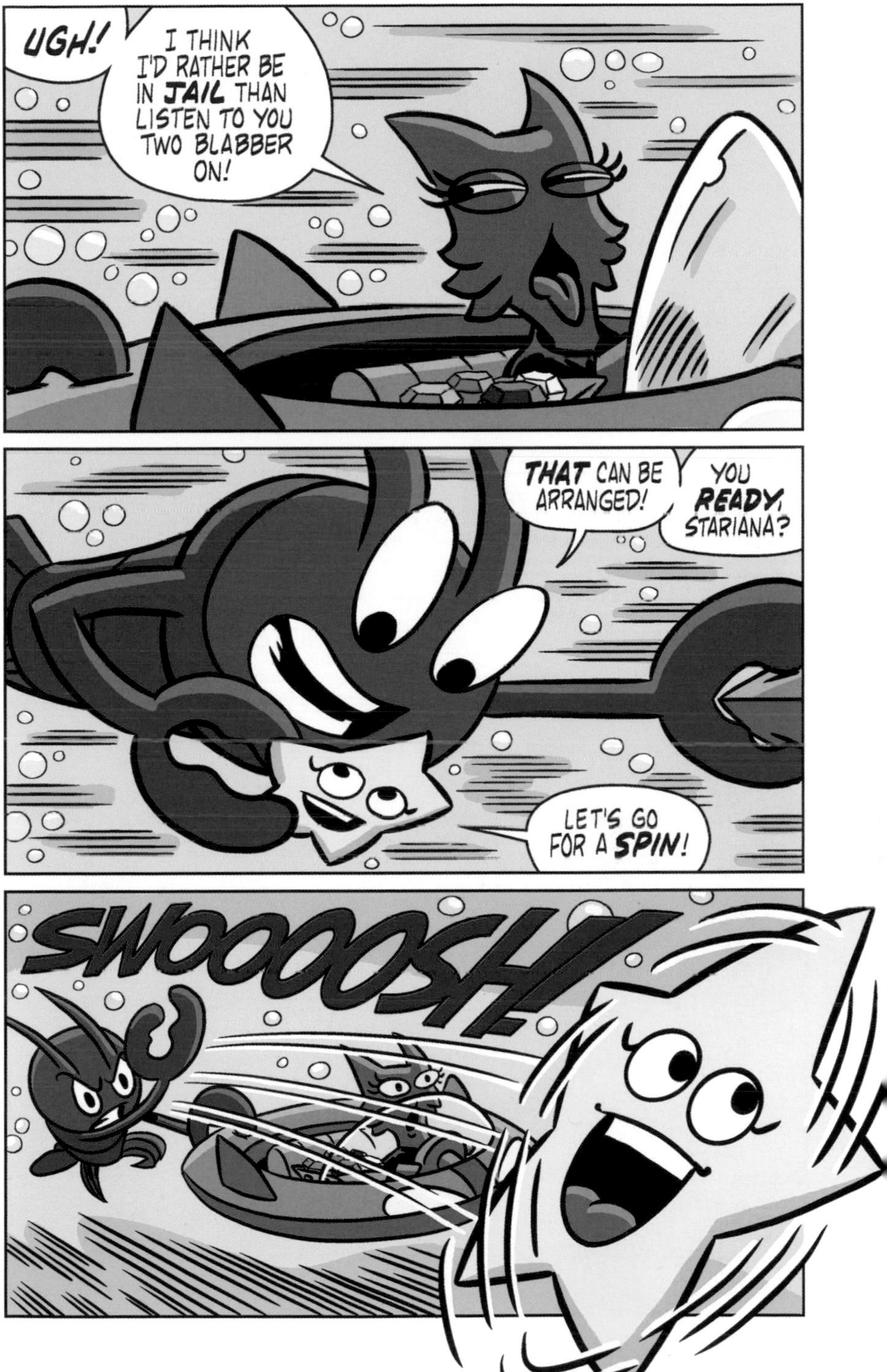
UGH!
I THINK I'D RATHER BE IN JAIL THAN LISTEN TO YOU TWO BLABBER ON!
THAT CAN BE ARRANGED!
YOU READY, STARIANA?
LET'S GO FOR A SPIN!
SWOOOOSH!

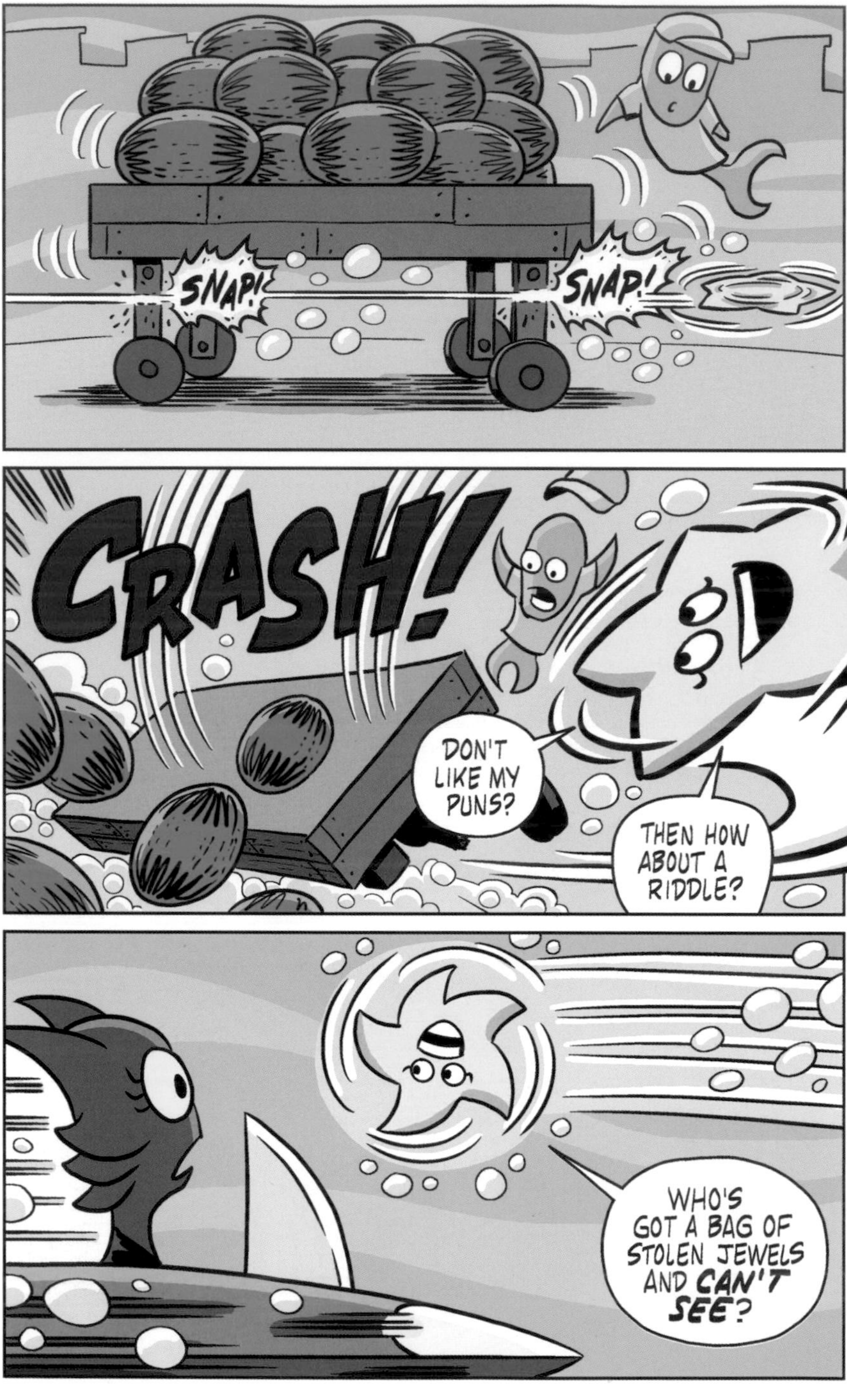

SNAP!
SNAP!
CRASH!
DON'T LIKE MY PUNS?
THEN HOW ABOUT A RIDDLE?
WHO'S GOT A BAG OF STOLEN JEWELS AND CAN'T SEE?

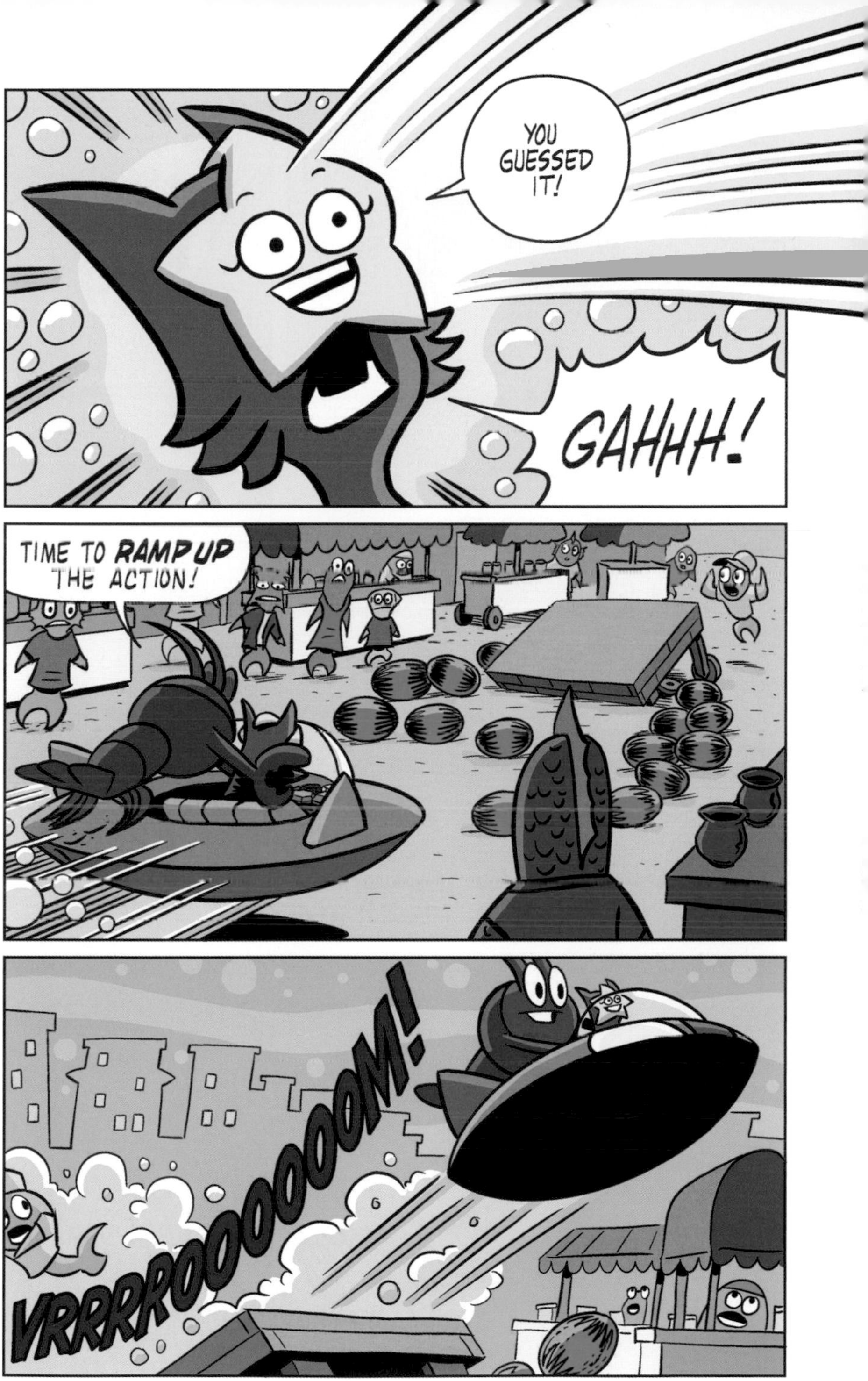
YOU GUESSED IT!
GAHHH!
TIME TO **RAMP UP** THE ACTION!
VRRRROOOOOOOM!

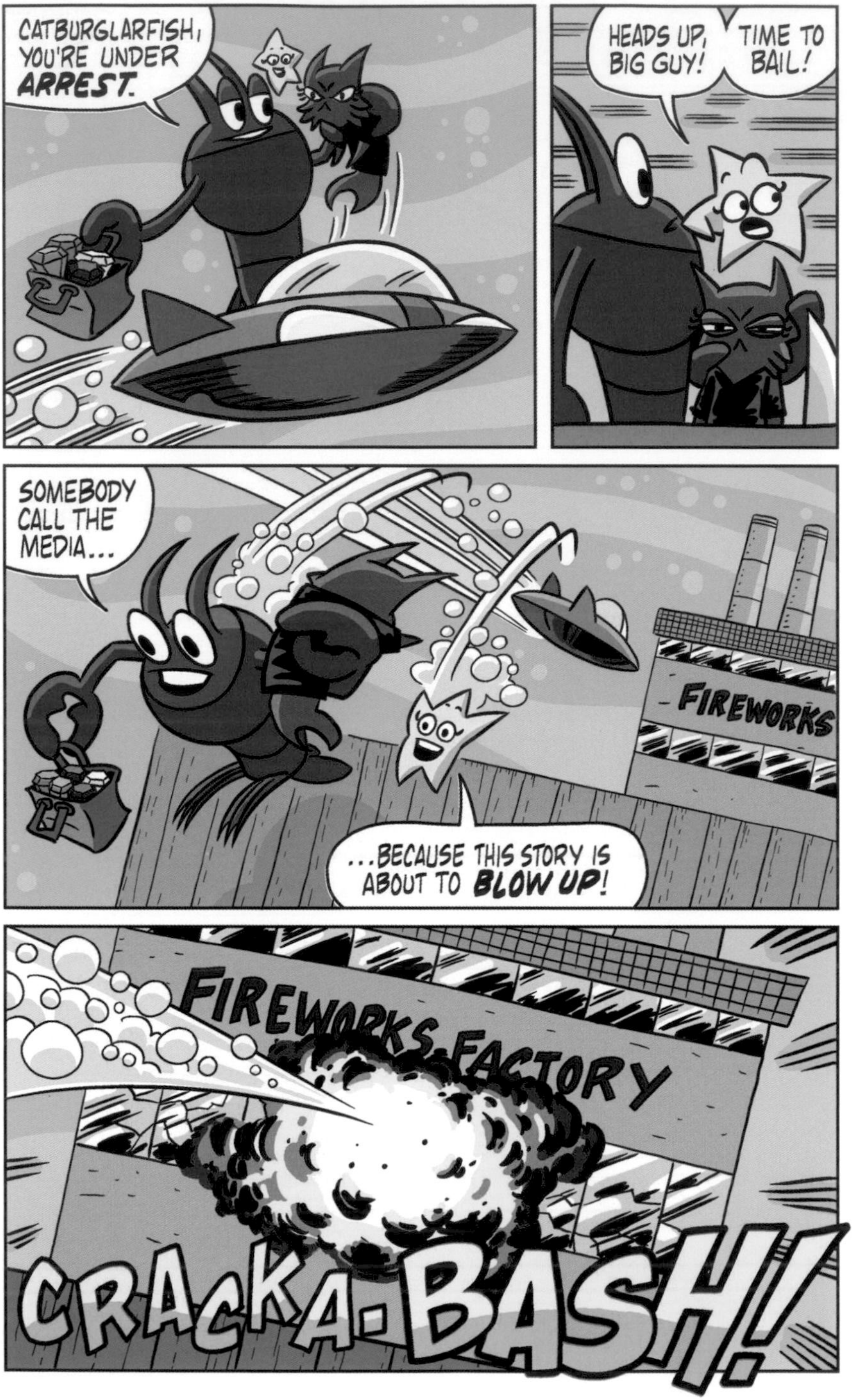
CATBURGLARFISH, YOU'RE UNDER ARREST.
HEADS UP, BIG GUY!
TIME TO BAIL!
SOMEBODY CALL THE MEDIA...
FIREWORKS
...BECAUSE THIS STORY IS ABOUT TO BLOW UP!
FIREWORKS FACTORY
CRACKA-BASH!

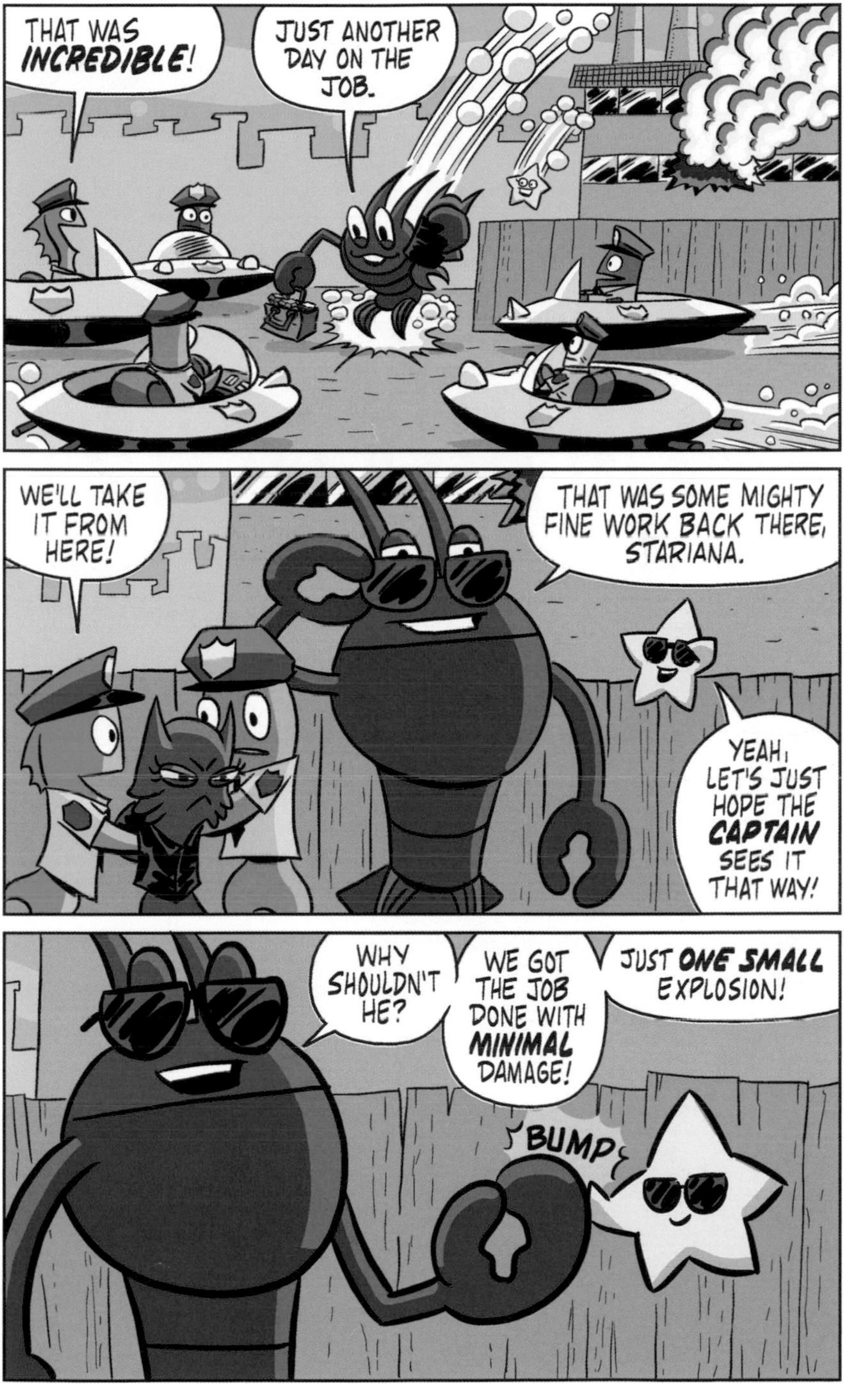

THAT WAS INCREDIBLE!
JUST ANOTHER DAY ON THE JOB.
WE'LL TAKE IT FROM HERE!
THAT WAS SOME MIGHTY FINE WORK BACK THERE, STARIANA.
YEAH, LET'S JUST HOPE THE CAPTAIN SEES IT THAT WAY!
WHY SHOULDN'T HE?
WE GOT THE JOB DONE WITH MINIMAL DAMAGE!
JUST ONE SMALL EXPLOSION!
BUMP

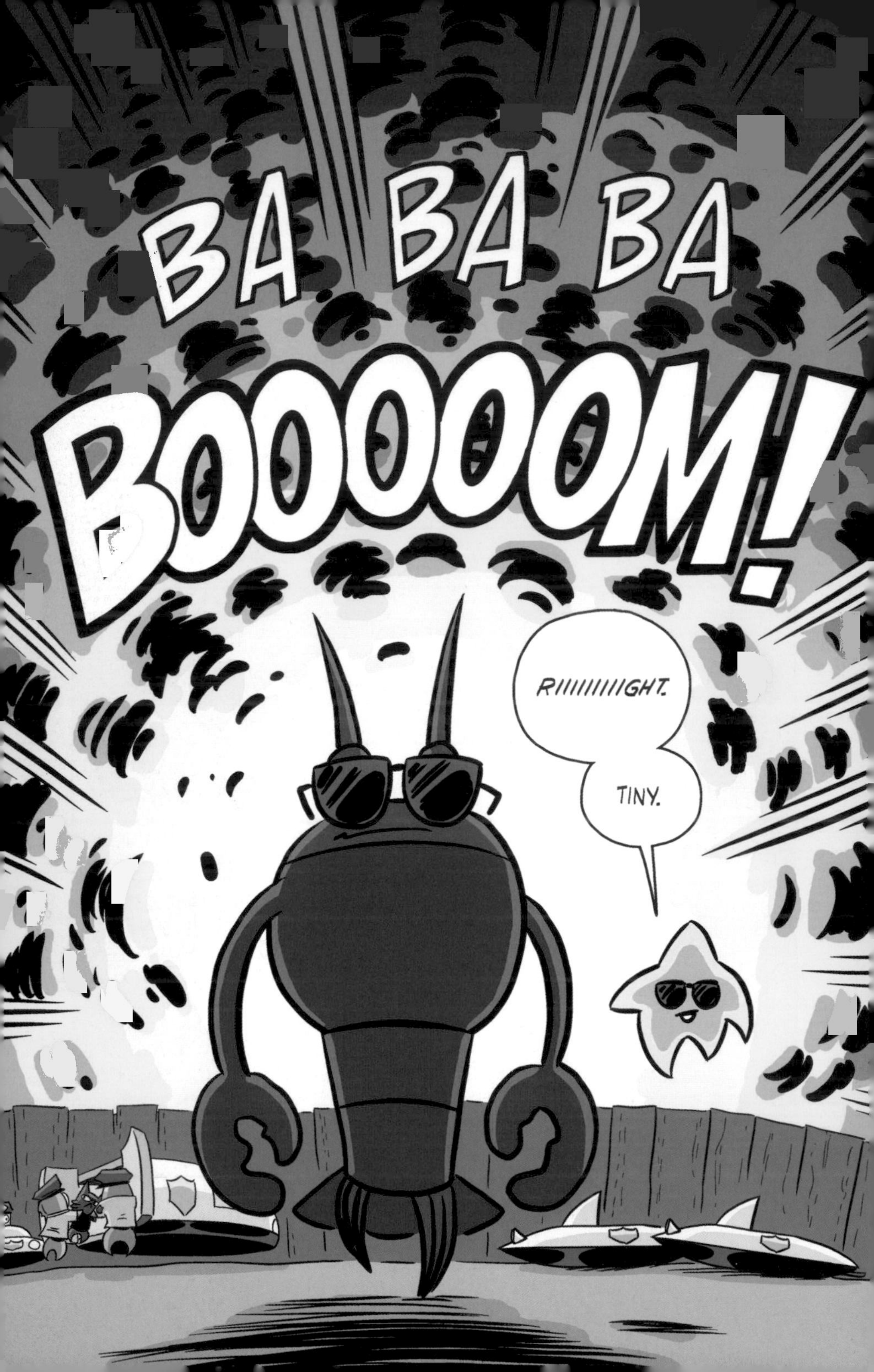
BA BA BA
BOOOOOM!
RIIIIIIIIGHT.
TINY.

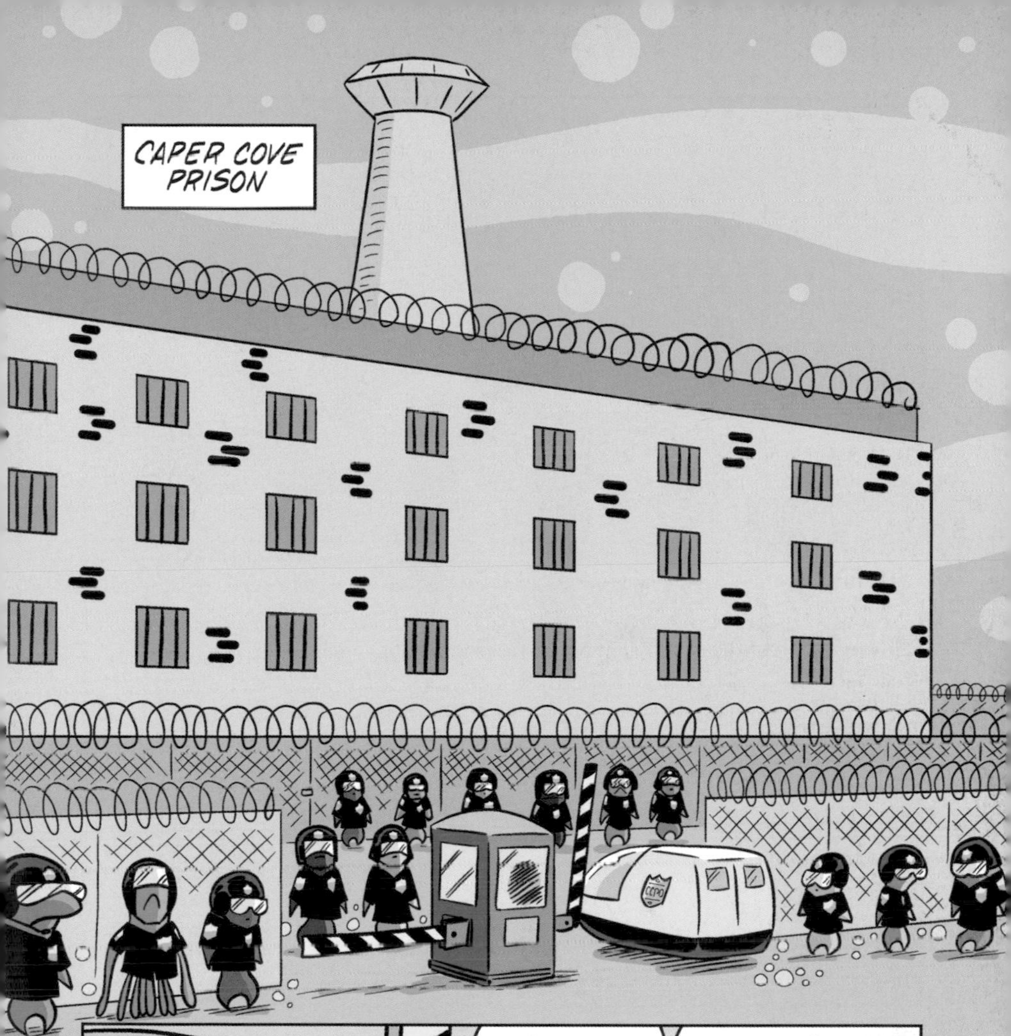
CAPER COVE PRISON

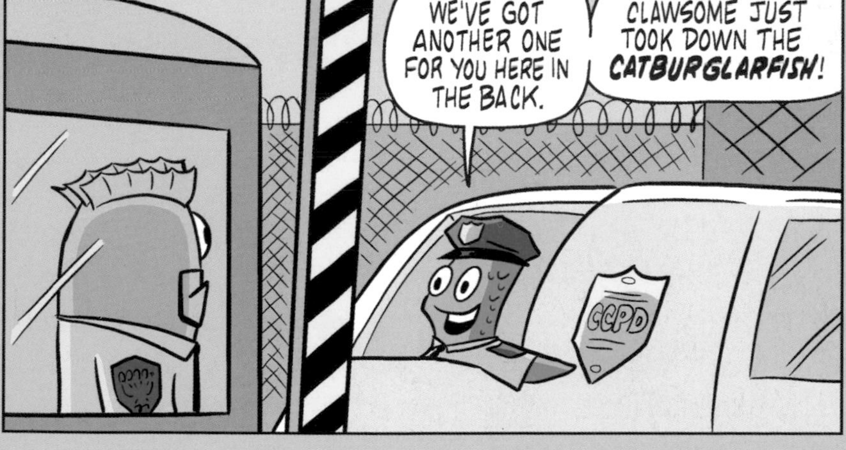
WE'VE GOT ANOTHER ONE FOR YOU HERE IN THE BACK.
CLAWSOME JUST TOOK DOWN THE CATBURGLARFISH!
CCPD

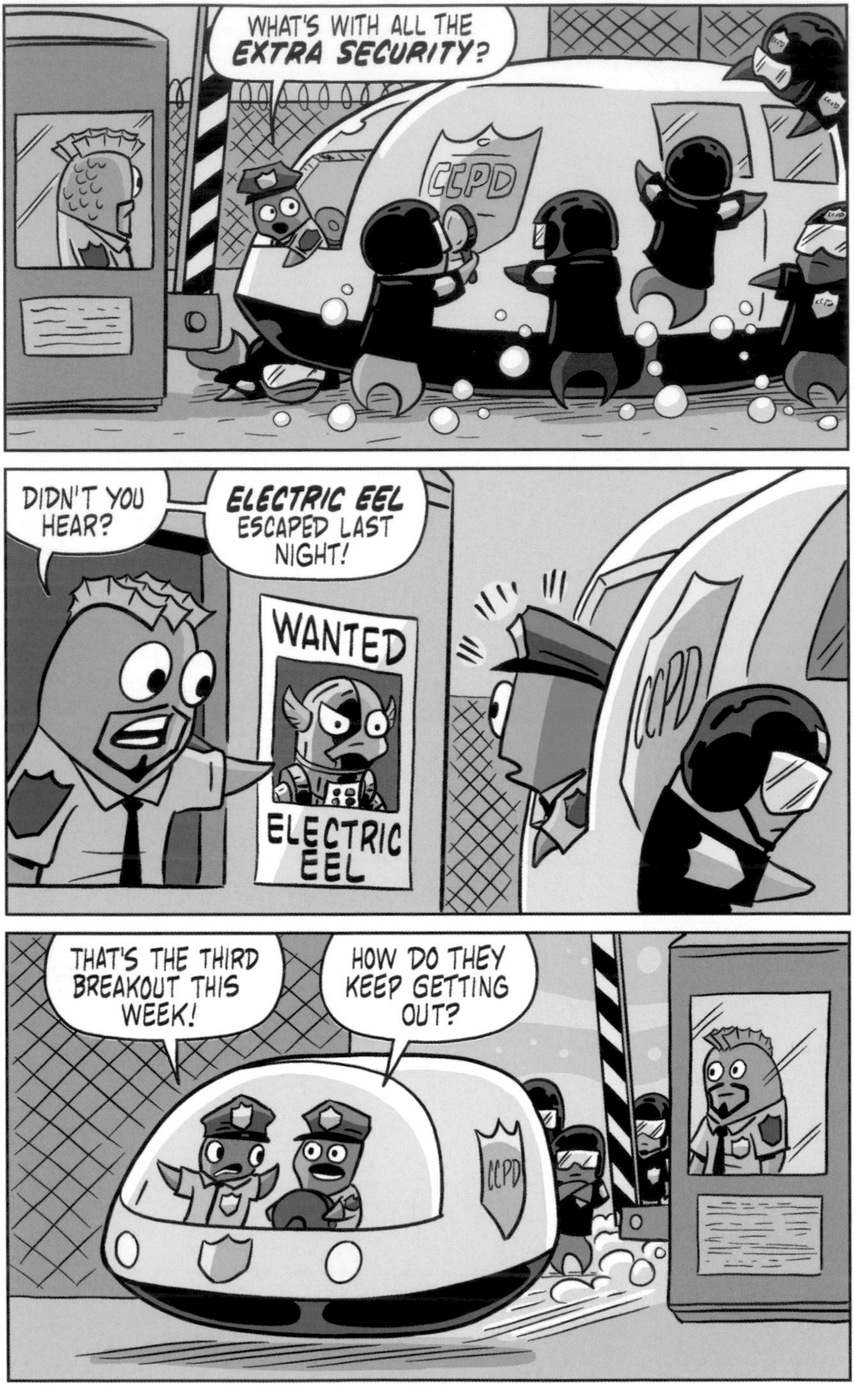
WHAT'S WITH ALL THE EXTRA SECURITY?
CCPD
DIDN'T YOU HEAR?
ELECTRIC EEL ESCAPED LAST NIGHT!
WANTED
ELECTRIC EEL
CCPD
THAT'S THE THIRD BREAKOUT THIS WEEK!
HOW DO THEY KEEP GETTING OUT?
CCPD

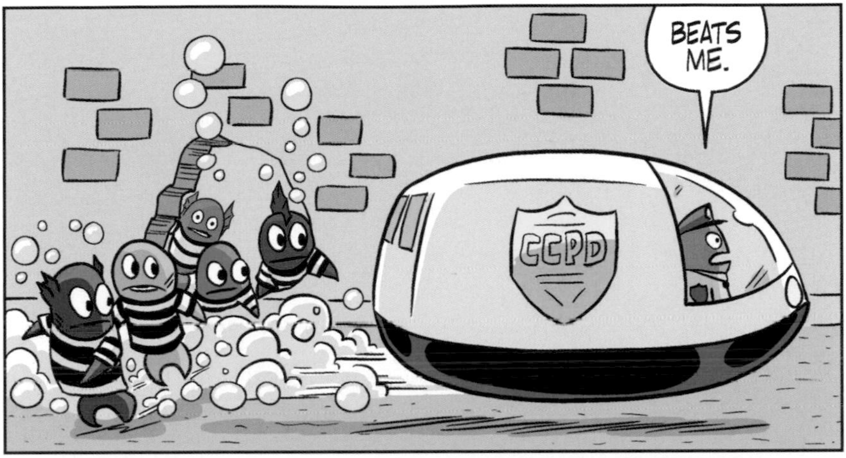
BEATS ME.
CCPD
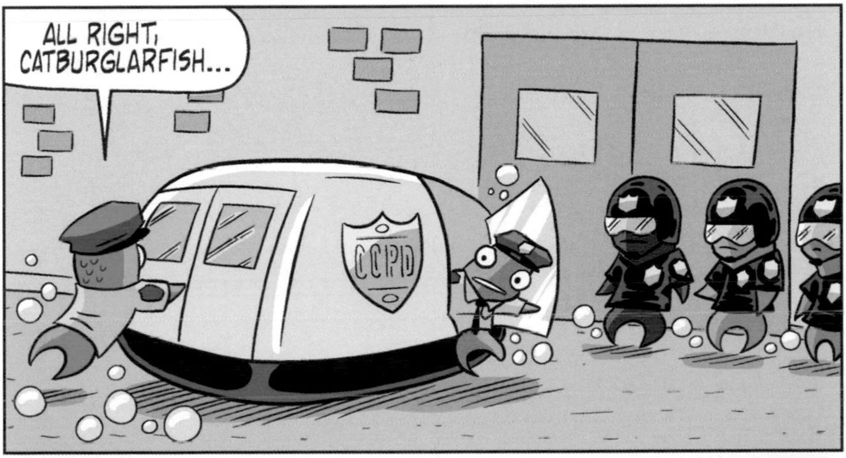
ALL RIGHT, CATBURGLARFISH...
CCPD
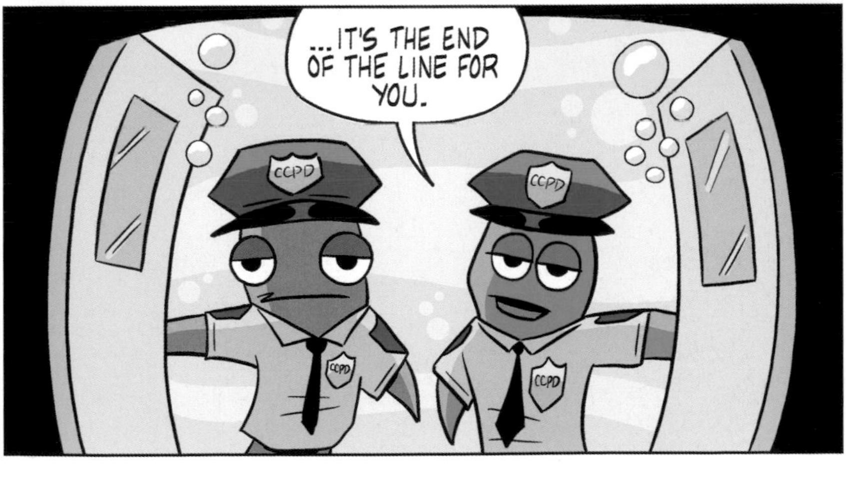
...IT'S THE END OF THE LINE FOR YOU.
CCPD
CCPD
CCPD
CCPD

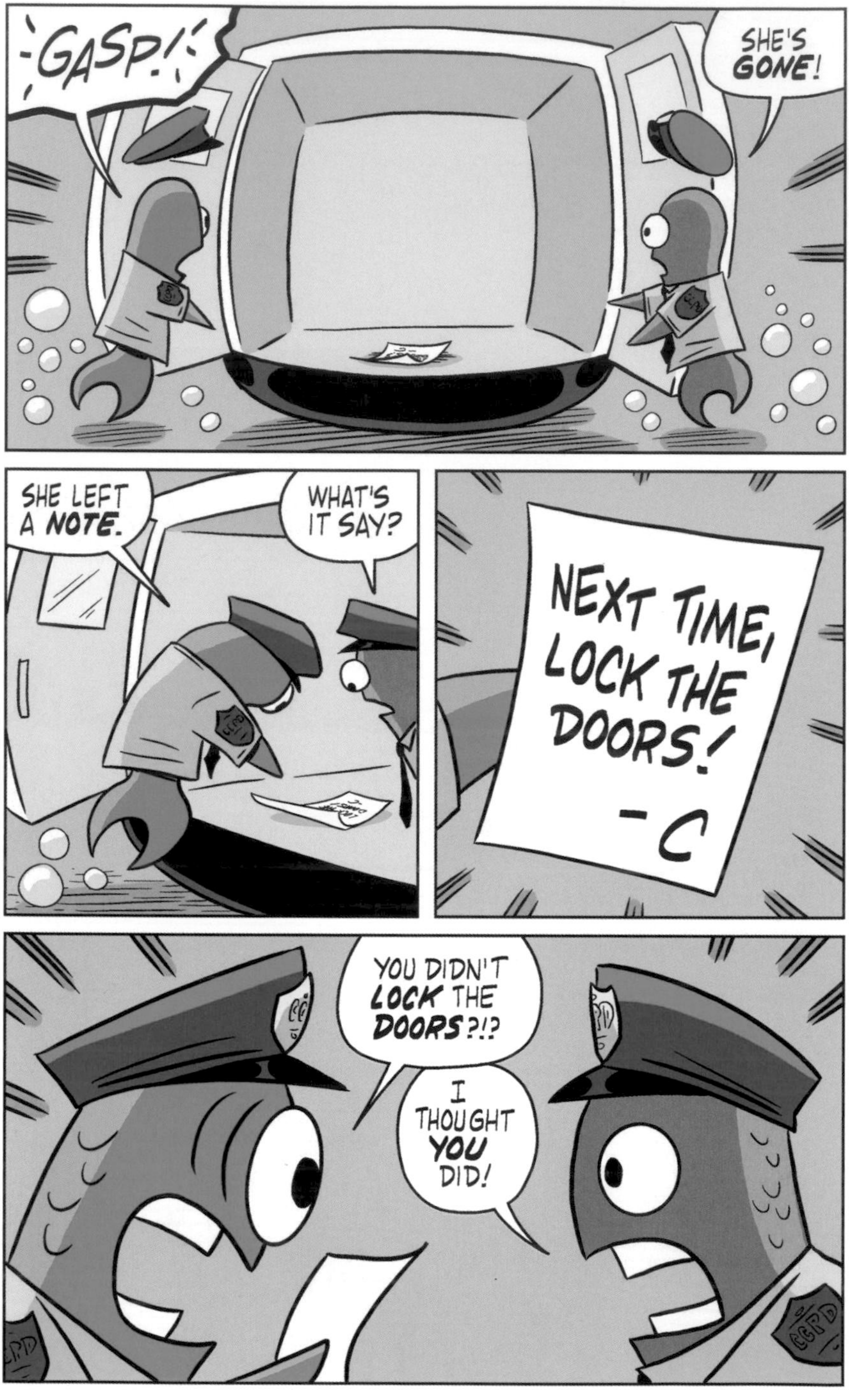
GASP!
SHE'S GONE!
SHE LEFT A NOTE.
WHAT'S IT SAY?
NEXT TIME, LOCK THE DOORS! - C
YOU DIDN'T LOCK THE DOORS?!?
I THOUGHT YOU DID!

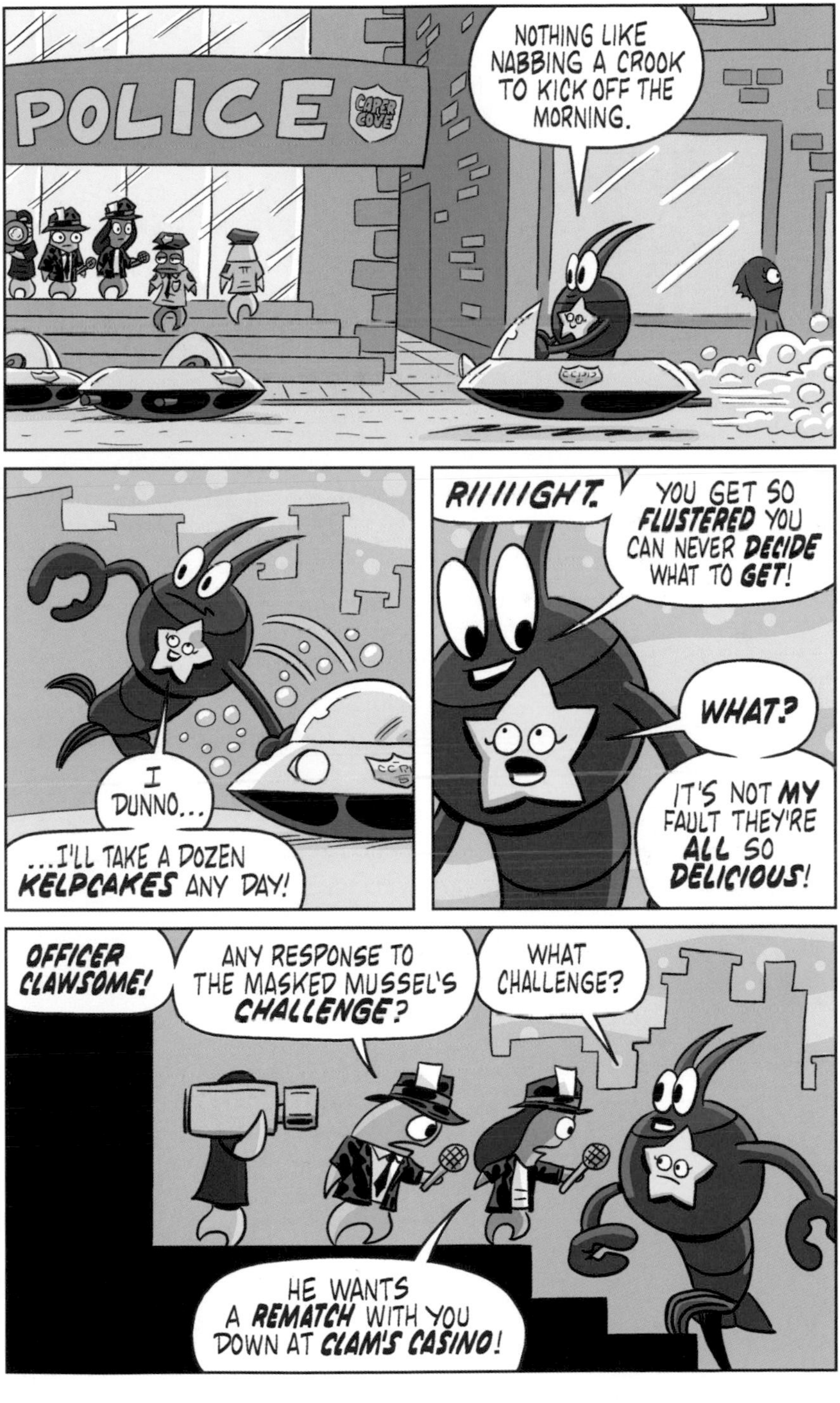
POLICE
CAPER COVE
NOTHING LIKE NABBING A CROOK TO KICK OFF THE MORNING.
CCPD
I DUNNO...
...I'LL TAKE A DOZEN **KELPCAKES** ANY DAY!
CCPD 5
RIIIIIGHT.
YOU GET SO **FLUSTERED** YOU CAN NEVER **DECIDE** WHAT TO **GET**!
WHAT?
IT'S NOT **MY** FAULT THEY'RE **ALL** SO **DELICIOUS**!
OFFICER CLAWSOME!
ANY RESPONSE TO THE MASKED MUSSEL'S **CHALLENGE**?
WHAT CHALLENGE?
HE WANTS A **REMATCH** WITH YOU DOWN AT **CLAM'S CASINO**!

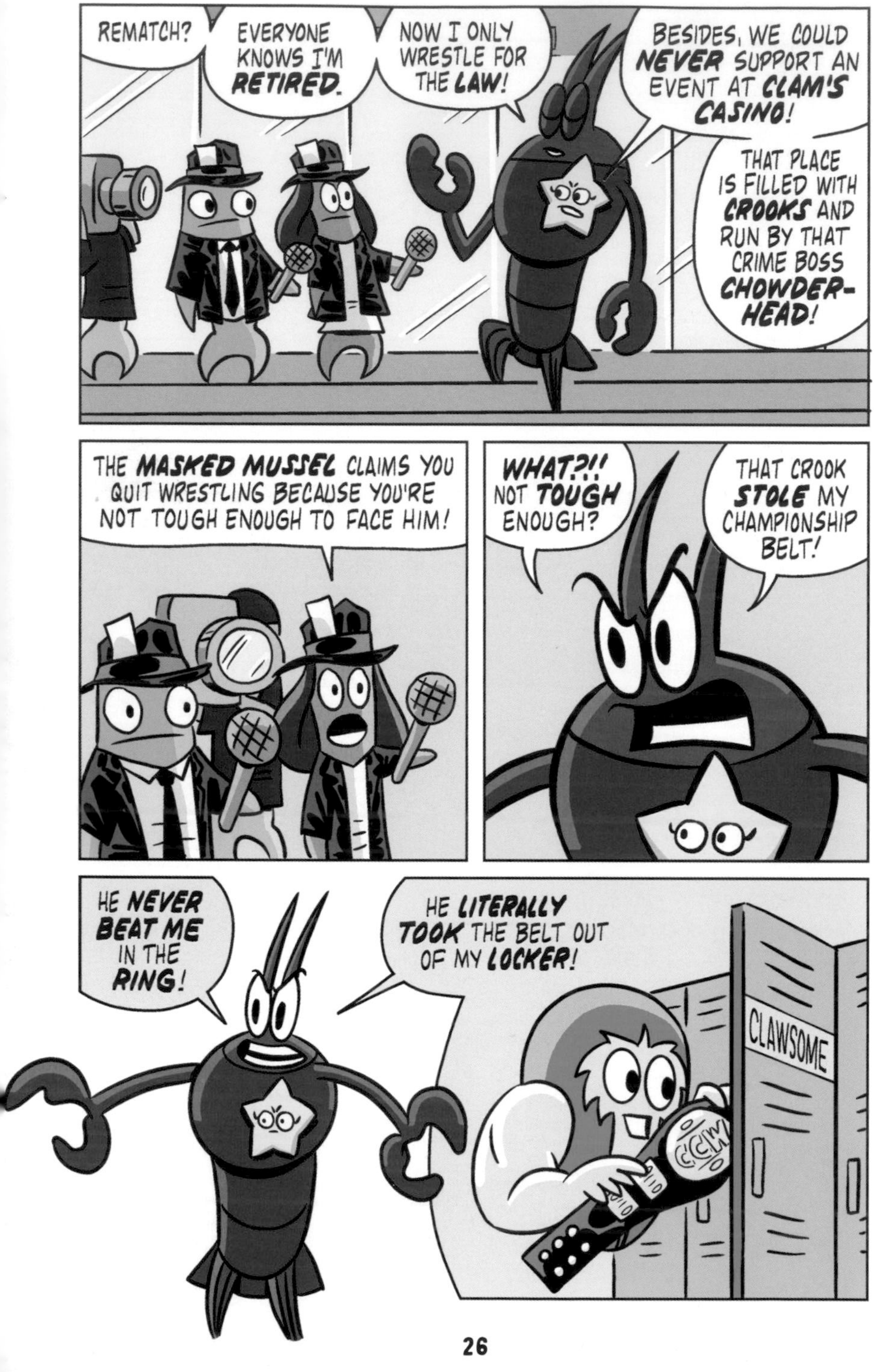
REMATCH?
EVERYONE KNOWS I'M RETIRED.
NOW I ONLY WRESTLE FOR THE LAW!
BESIDES, WE COULD NEVER SUPPORT AN EVENT AT CLAM'S CASINO!
THAT PLACE IS FILLED WITH CROOKS AND RUN BY THAT CRIME BOSS CHOWDERHEAD!
THE MASKED MUSSEL CLAIMS YOU QUIT WRESTLING BECAUSE YOU'RE NOT TOUGH ENOUGH TO FACE HIM!
WHAT?!! NOT TOUGH ENOUGH?
THAT CROOK STOLE MY CHAMPIONSHIP BELT!
HE NEVER BEAT ME IN THE RING!
HE LITERALLY TOOK THE BELT OUT OF MY LOCKER!
CLAWSOME

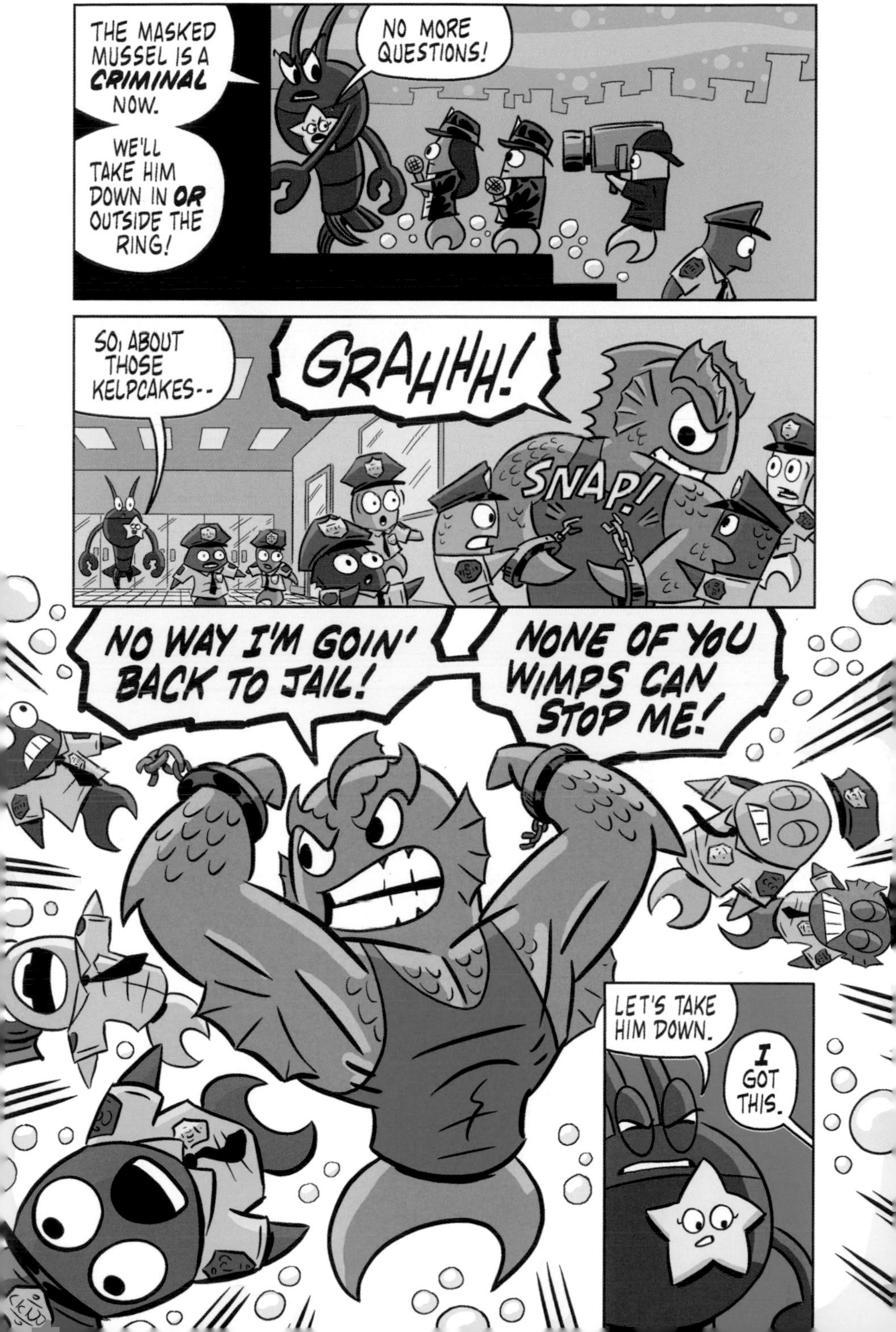
THE MASKED MUSSEL IS A CRIMINAL NOW.
WE'LL TAKE HIM DOWN IN OR OUTSIDE THE RING!
NO MORE QUESTIONS!
SO, ABOUT THOSE KELPCAKES--
GRAHHH!
SNAP!
NO WAY I'M GOIN' BACK TO JAIL!
NONE OF YOU WIMPS CAN STOP ME!
LET'S TAKE HIM DOWN.
I GOT THIS.

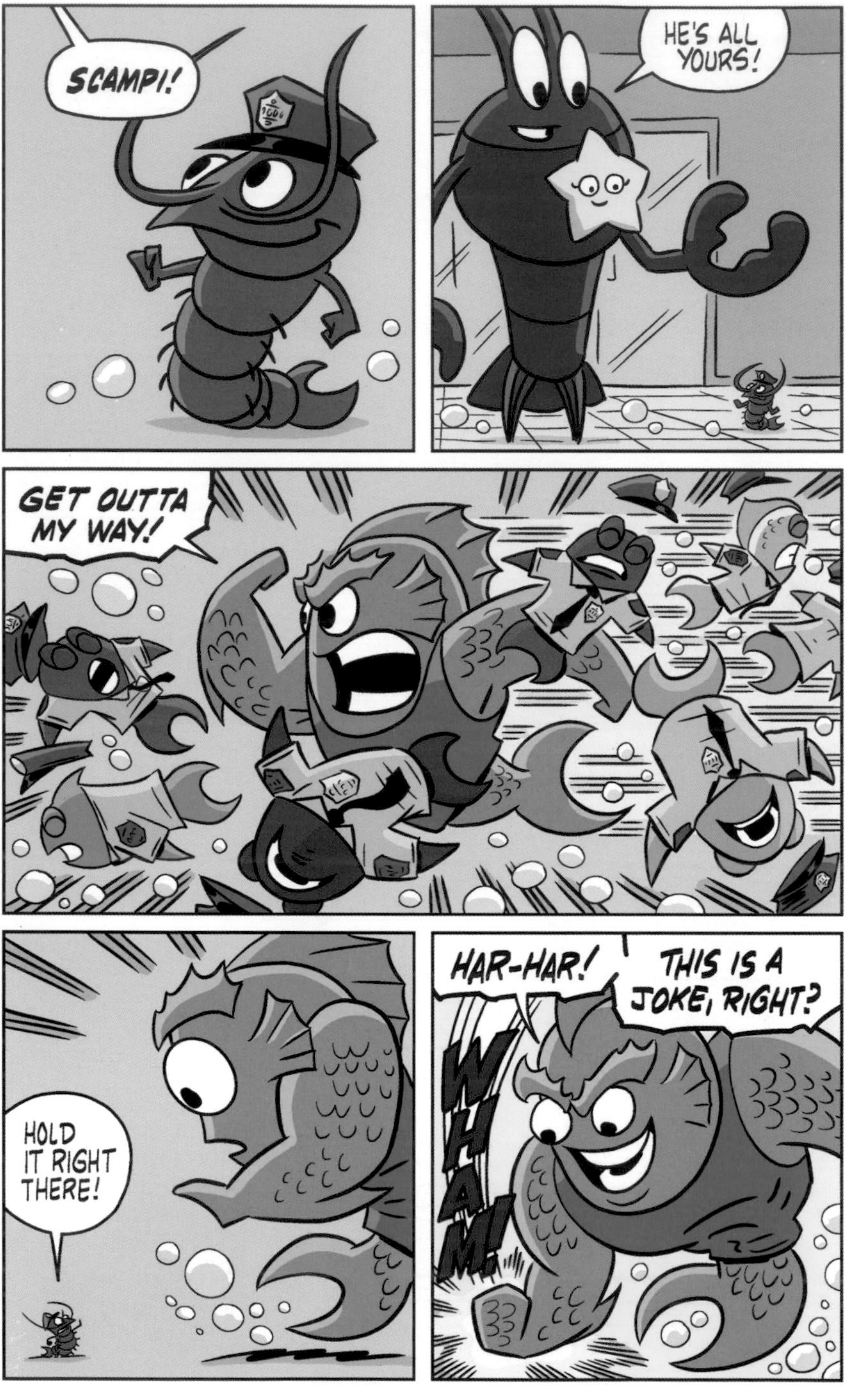
SCAMPI!
HE'S ALL YOURS!
GET OUTTA MY WAY!
HOLD IT RIGHT THERE!
HAR-HAR!
THIS IS A JOKE, RIGHT?
WHAM!

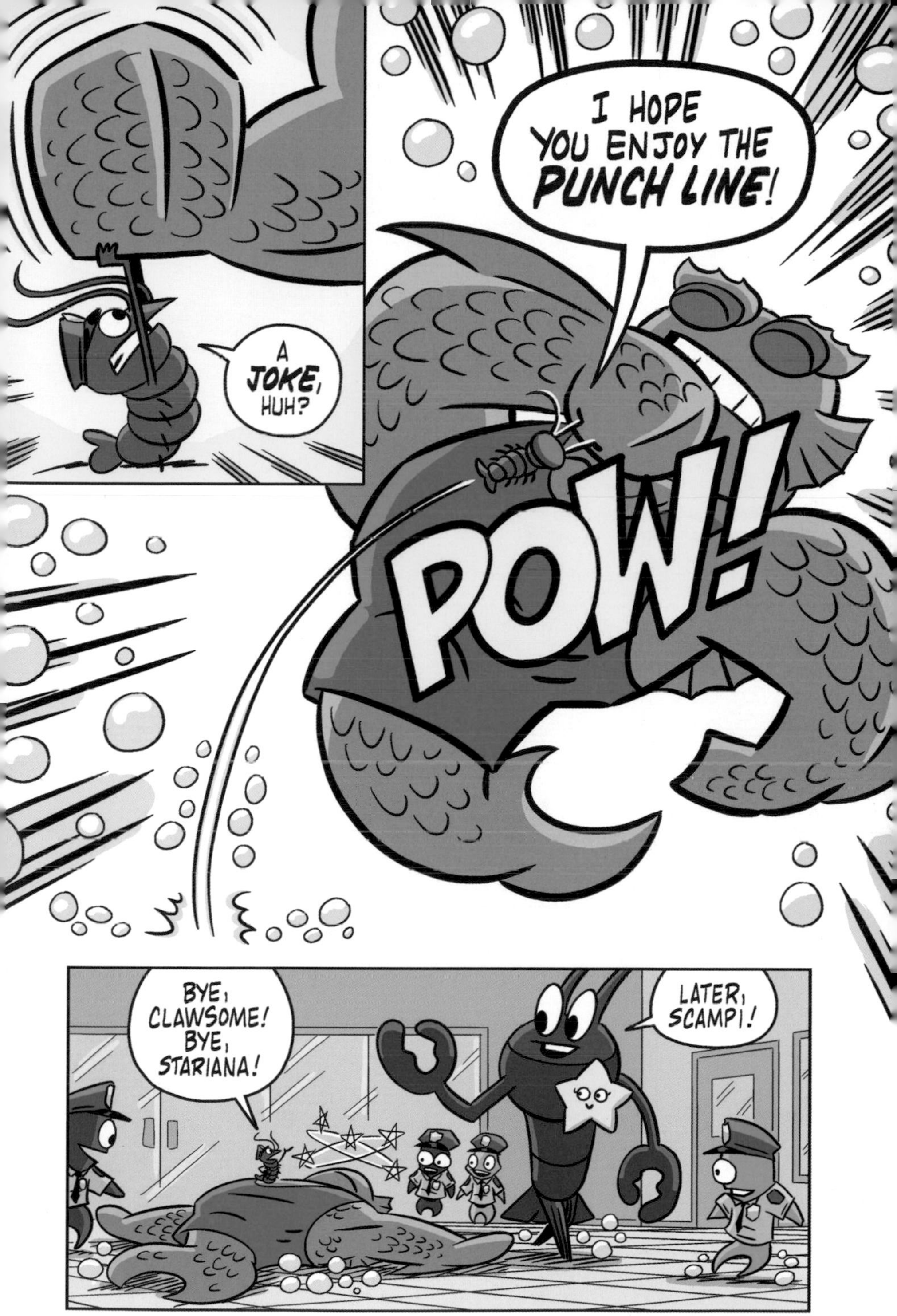
A JOKE, HUH?
I HOPE YOU ENJOY THE PUNCH LINE!
POW!
BYE, CLAWSOME! BYE, STARIANA!
LATER, SCAMPI!

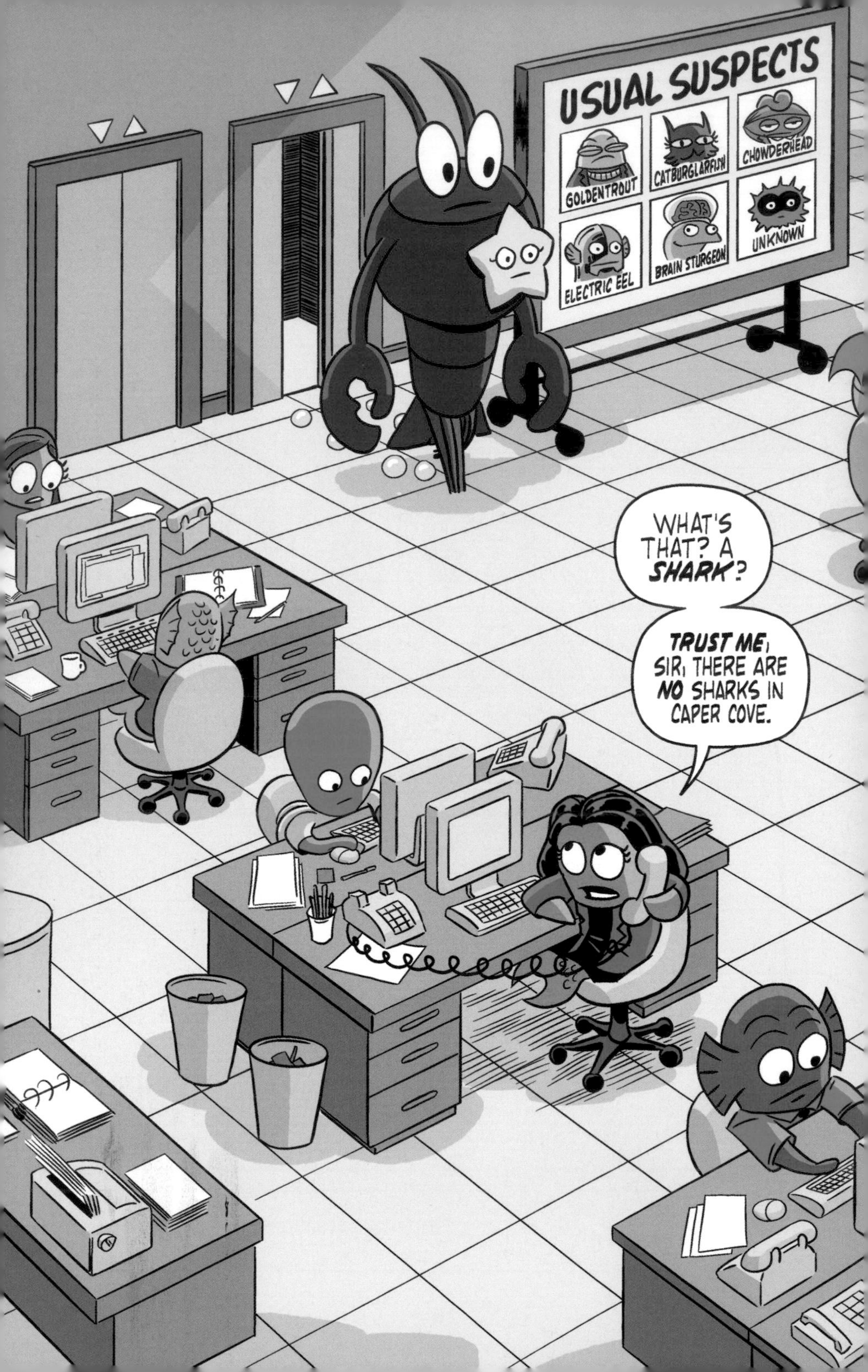
USUAL SUSPECTS
GOLDENTROUT
CATBURGLARFISH
CHOWDERHEAD
ELECTRIC EEL
BRAIN STURGEON
UNKNOWN
WHAT'S THAT? A SHARK?
TRUST ME, SIR, THERE ARE NO SHARKS IN CAPER COVE.

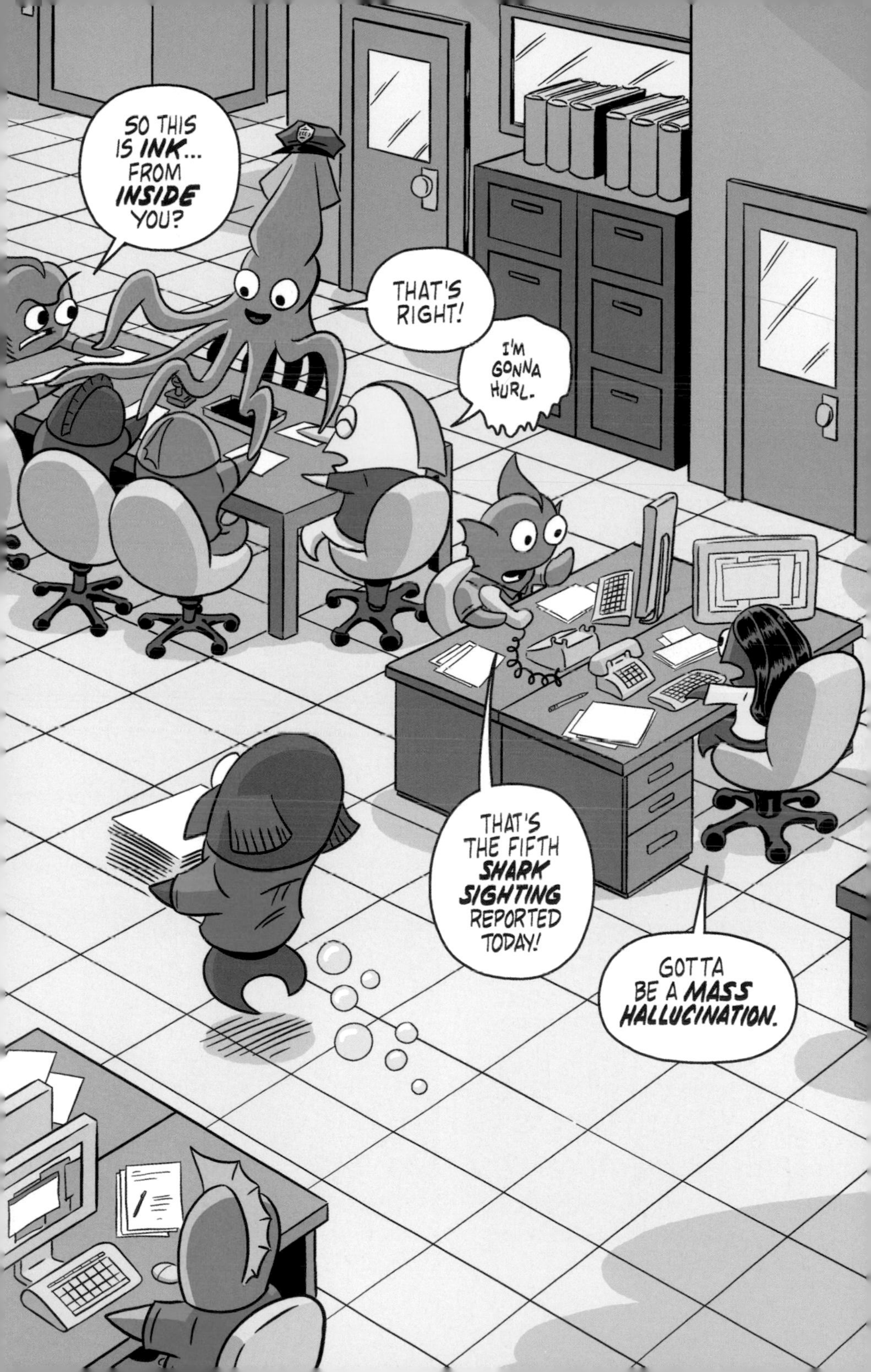
SO THIS IS INK... FROM INSIDE YOU?
THAT'S RIGHT!
I'M GONNA HURL.
THAT'S THE FIFTH SHARK SIGHTING REPORTED TODAY!
GOTTA BE A MASS HALLUCINATION.

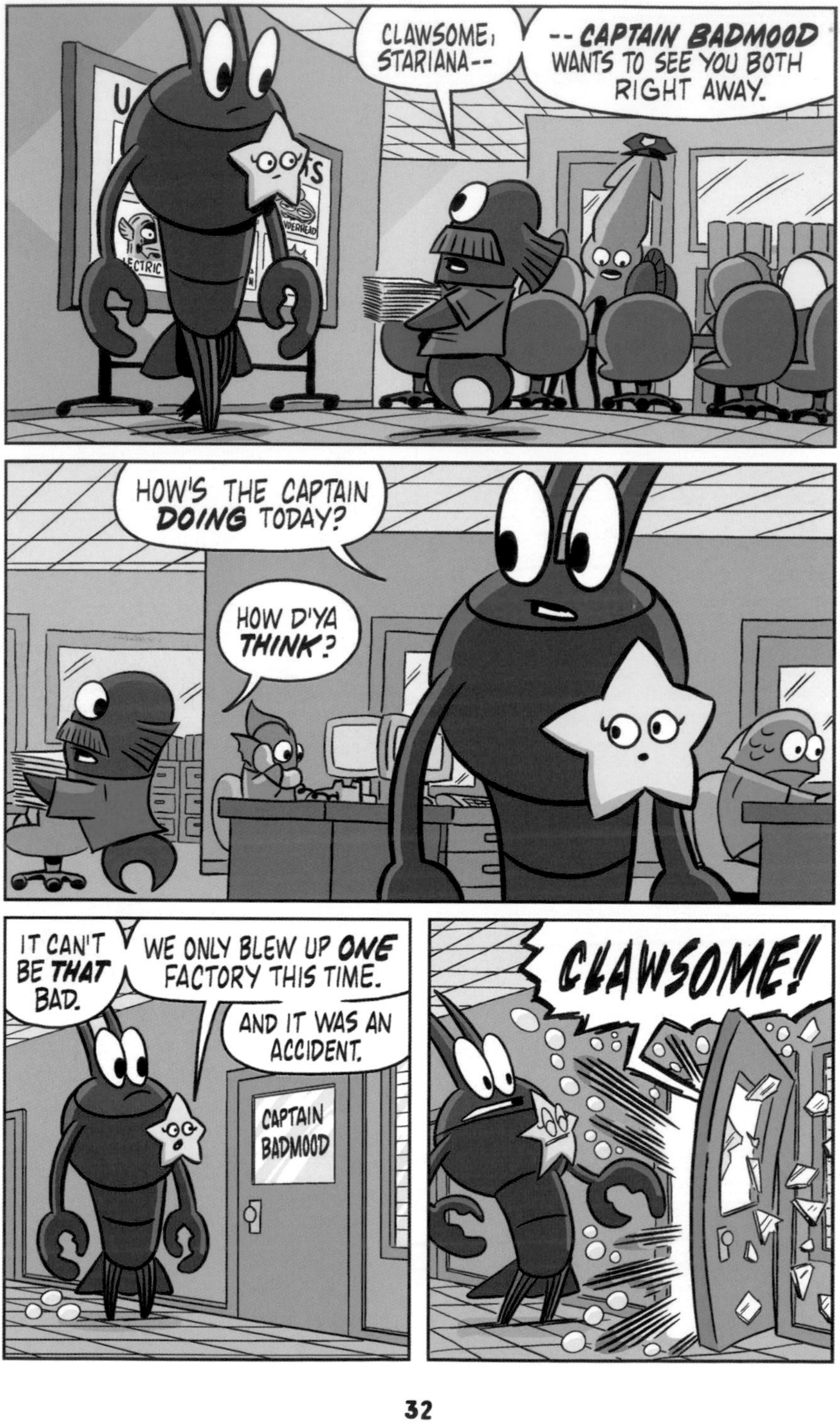
CLAWSOME, STARIANA--
--CAPTAIN BADMOOD WANTS TO SEE YOU BOTH RIGHT AWAY.
HOW'S THE CAPTAIN DOING TODAY?
HOW D'YA THINK?
IT CAN'T BE THAT BAD.
WE ONLY BLEW UP ONE FACTORY THIS TIME.
AND IT WAS AN ACCIDENT.
CAPTAIN BADMOOD
CLAWSOME!!

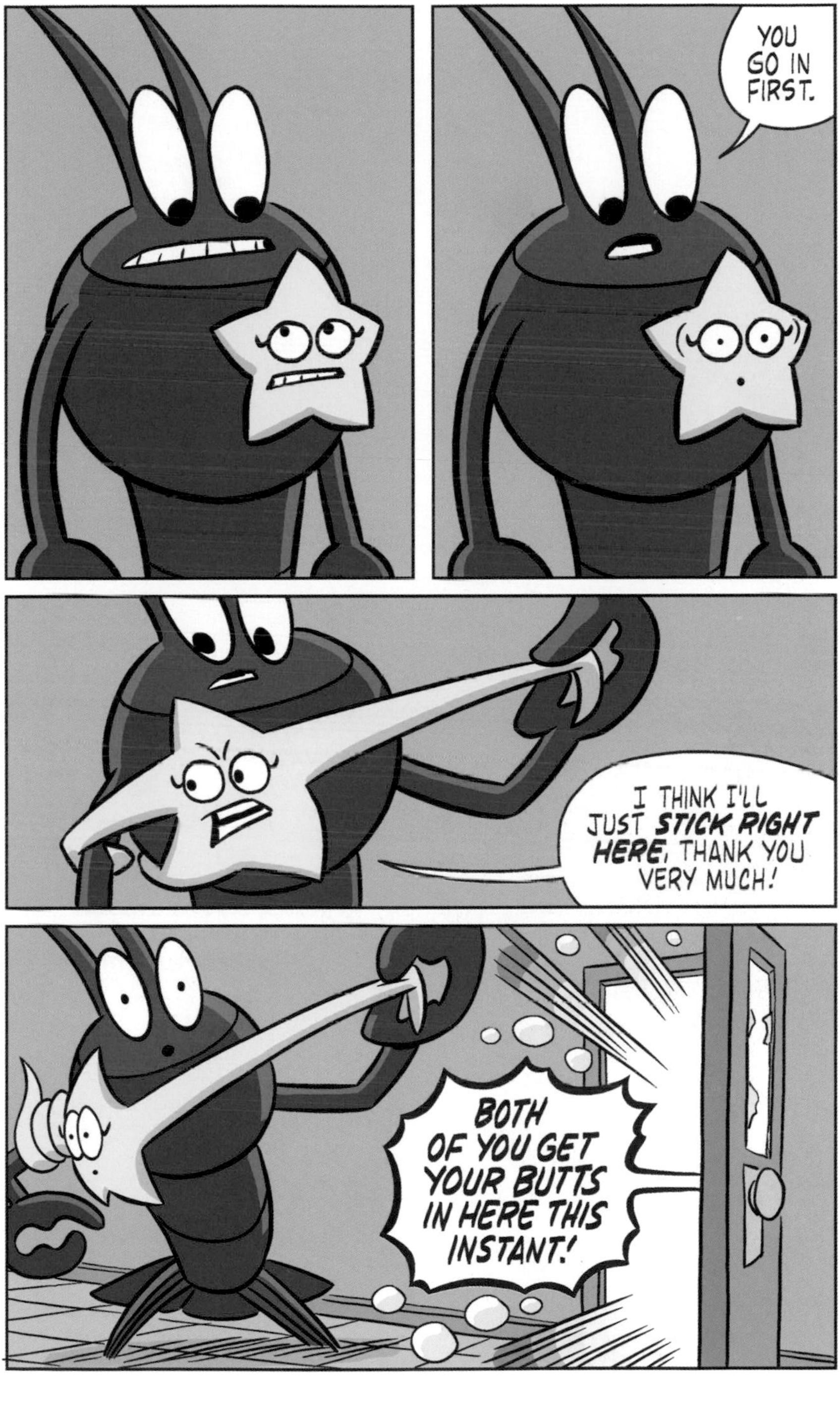
YOU GO IN FIRST.
I THINK I'LL JUST **STICK RIGHT HERE**, THANK YOU VERY MUCH!
BOTH OF YOU GET YOUR BUTTS IN HERE THIS INSTANT!

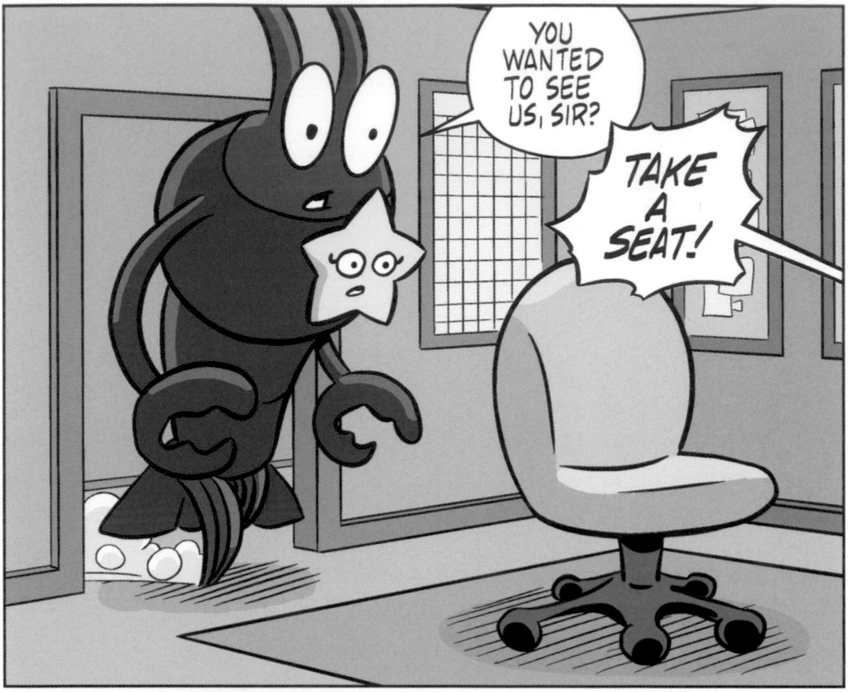
YOU WANTED TO SEE US, SIR?
TAKE A SEAT!

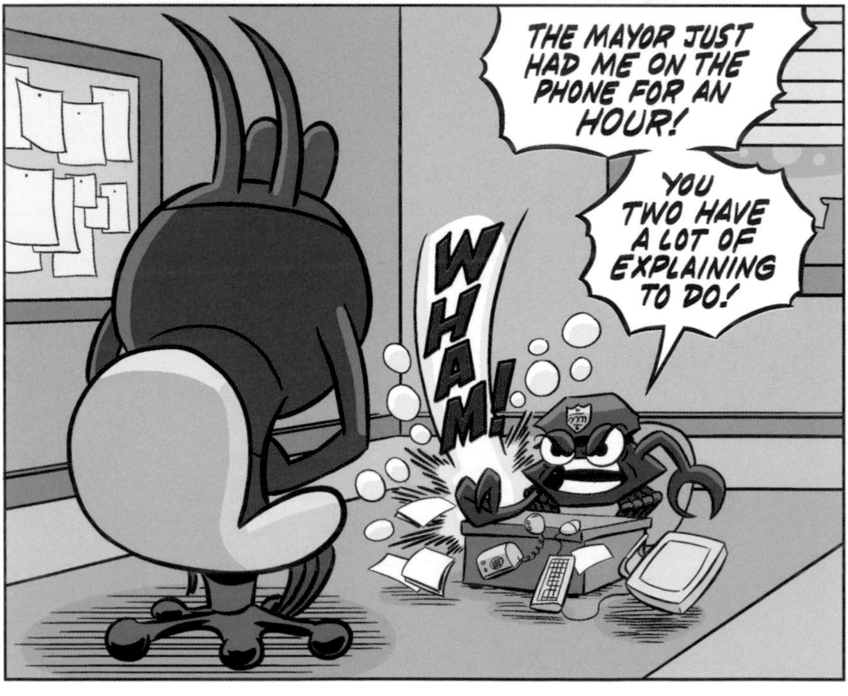
THE MAYOR JUST HAD ME ON THE PHONE FOR AN HOUR!
YOU TWO HAVE A LOT OF EXPLAINING TO DO!
WHAM!

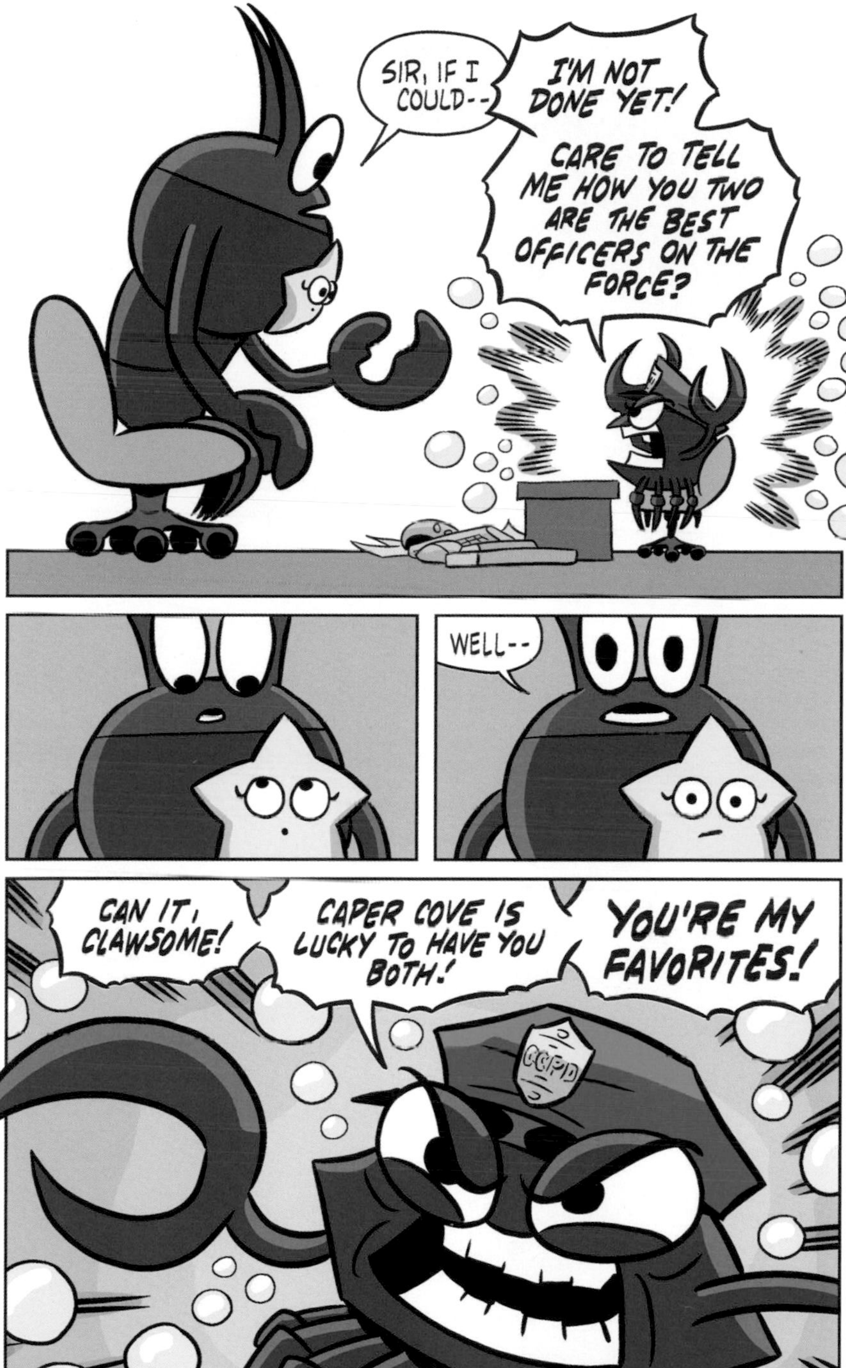
SIR, IF I COULD--
I'M NOT DONE YET!
CARE TO TELL ME HOW YOU TWO ARE THE BEST OFFICERS ON THE FORCE?
WELL--
CAN IT, CLAWSOME!
CAPER COVE IS LUCKY TO HAVE YOU BOTH!
YOU'RE MY FAVORITES!
CCPD

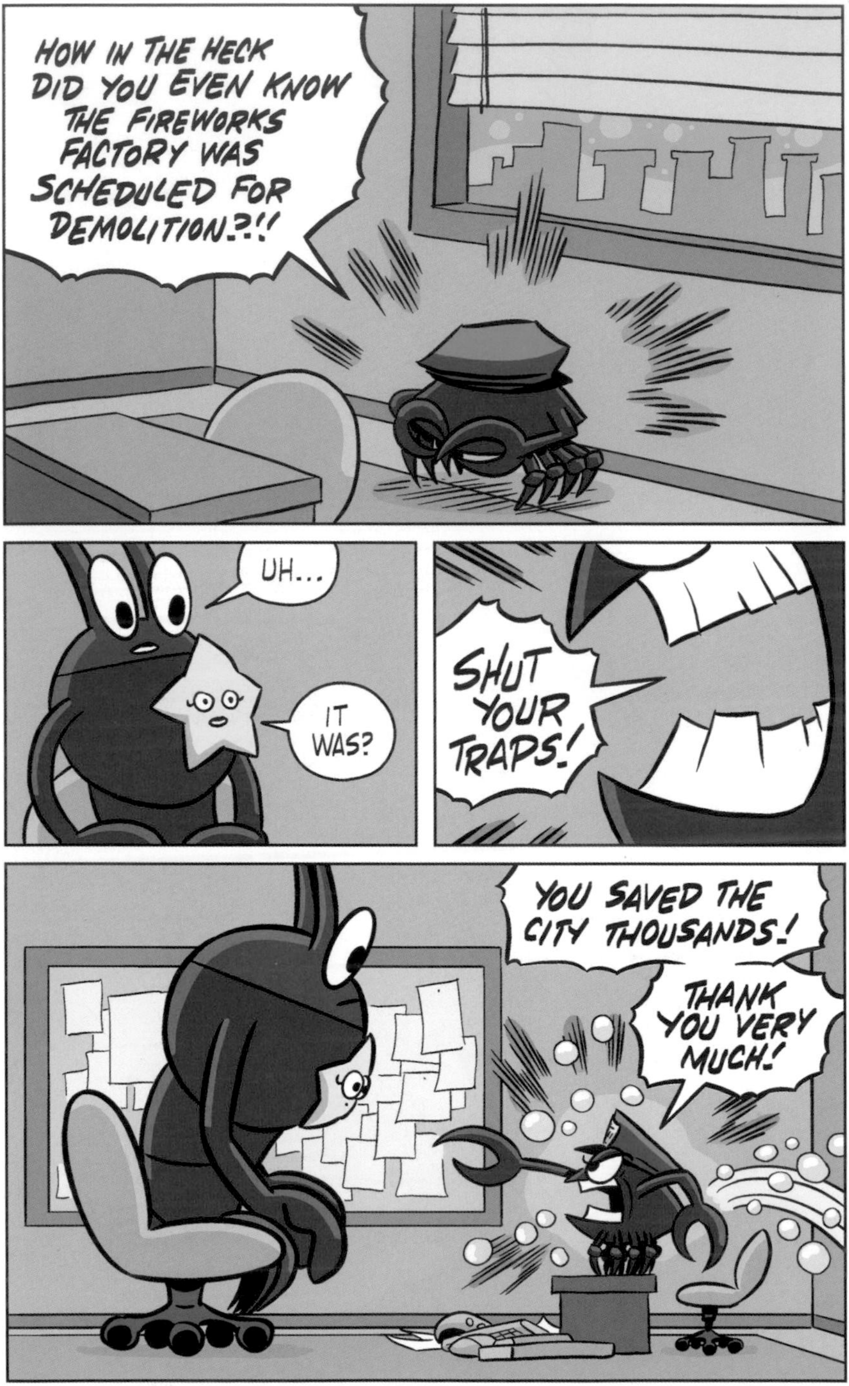
HOW IN THE HECK DID YOU EVEN KNOW THE FIREWORKS FACTORY WAS SCHEDULED FOR DEMOLITION?!!
UH...
IT WAS?
SHUT YOUR TRAPS!
YOU SAVED THE CITY THOUSANDS!
THANK YOU VERY MUCH!

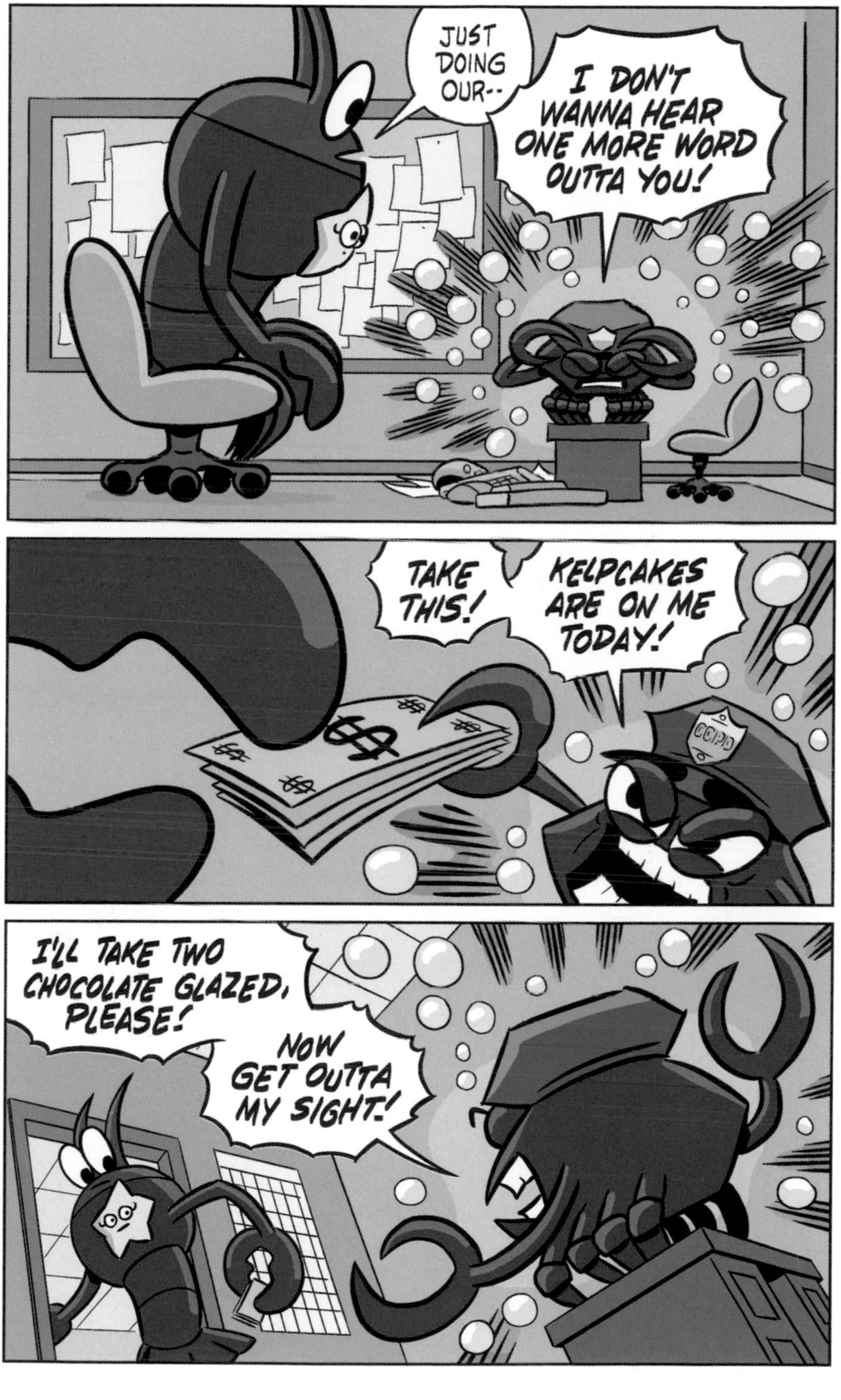
JUST DOING OUR--
I DON'T WANNA HEAR ONE MORE WORD OUTTA YOU!
TAKE THIS!
KELPCAKES ARE ON ME TODAY!
CCPD
I'LL TAKE TWO CHOCOLATE GLAZED, PLEASE!
NOW GET OUTTA MY SIGHT!

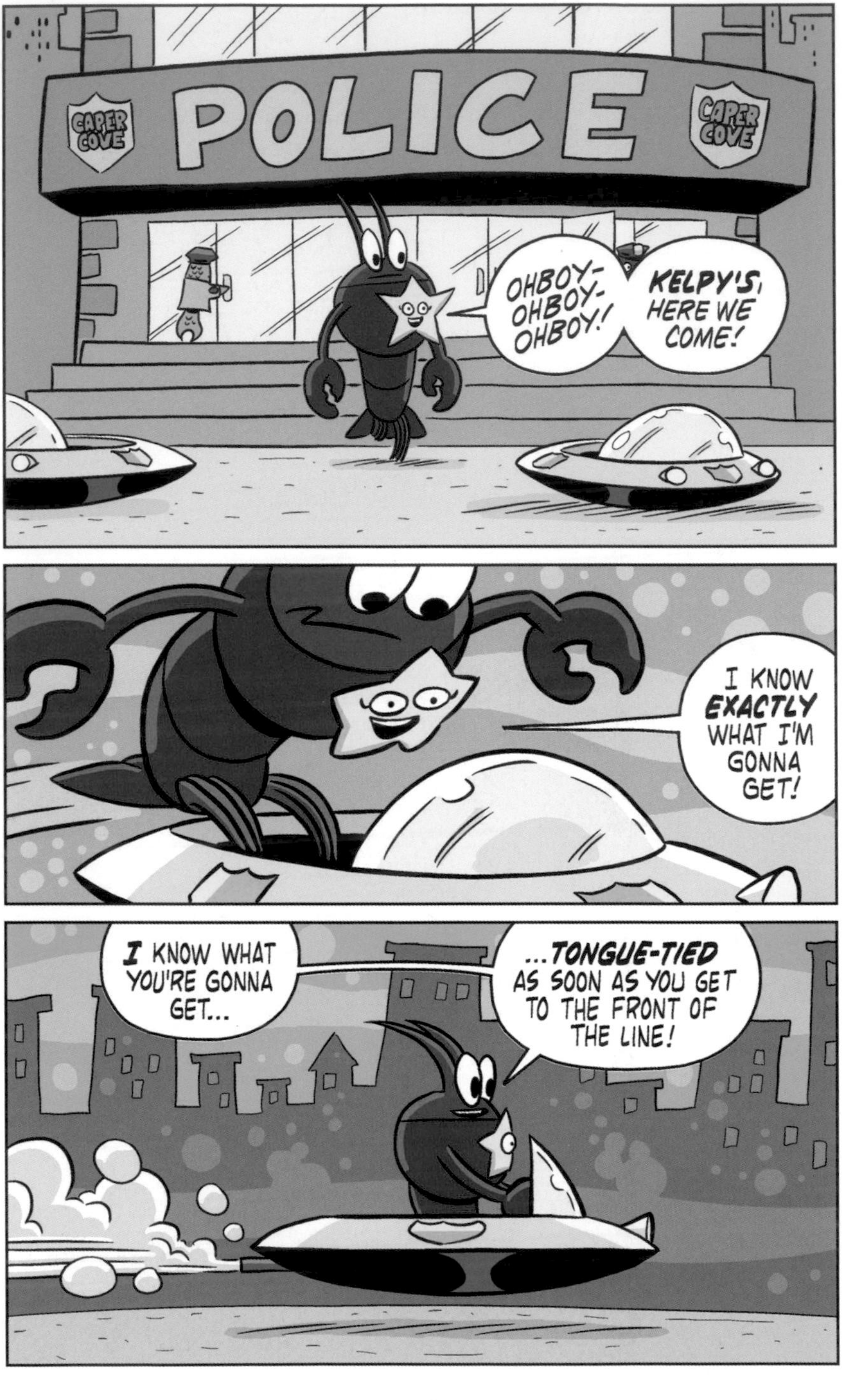
POLICE
CAPER COVE
CAPER COVE
OHBOY-OHBOY-OHBOY!
KELPY'S, HERE WE COME!
I KNOW EXACTLY WHAT I'M GONNA GET!
I KNOW WHAT YOU'RE GONNA GET...
...TONGUE-TIED AS SOON AS YOU GET TO THE FRONT OF THE LINE!

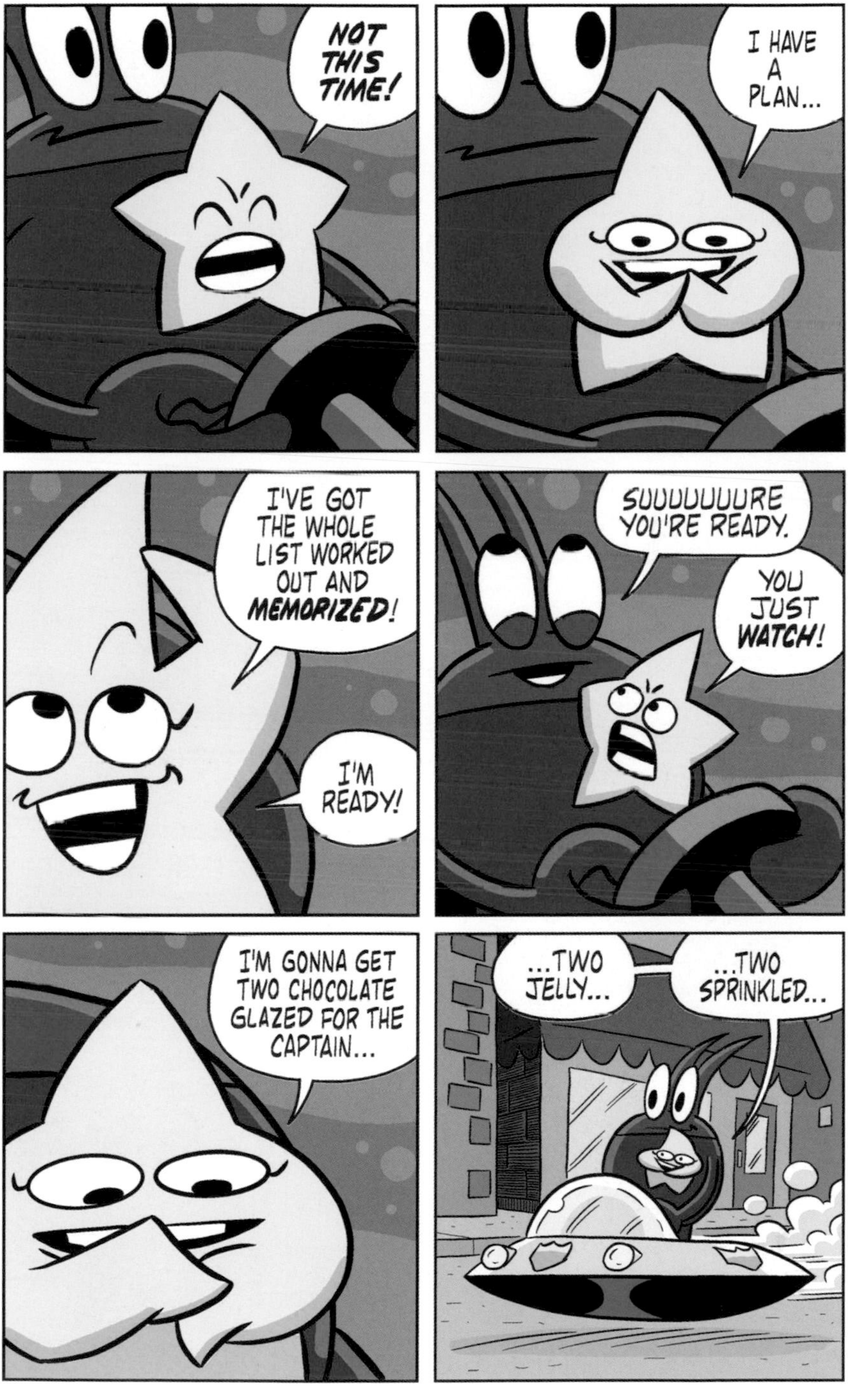
NOT THIS TIME!
I HAVE A PLAN...
I'VE GOT THE WHOLE LIST WORKED OUT AND MEMORIZED!
I'M READY!
SUUUUUUURE YOU'RE READY.
YOU JUST WATCH!
I'M GONNA GET TWO CHOCOLATE GLAZED FOR THE CAPTAIN...
...TWO JELLY...
...TWO SPRINKLED...

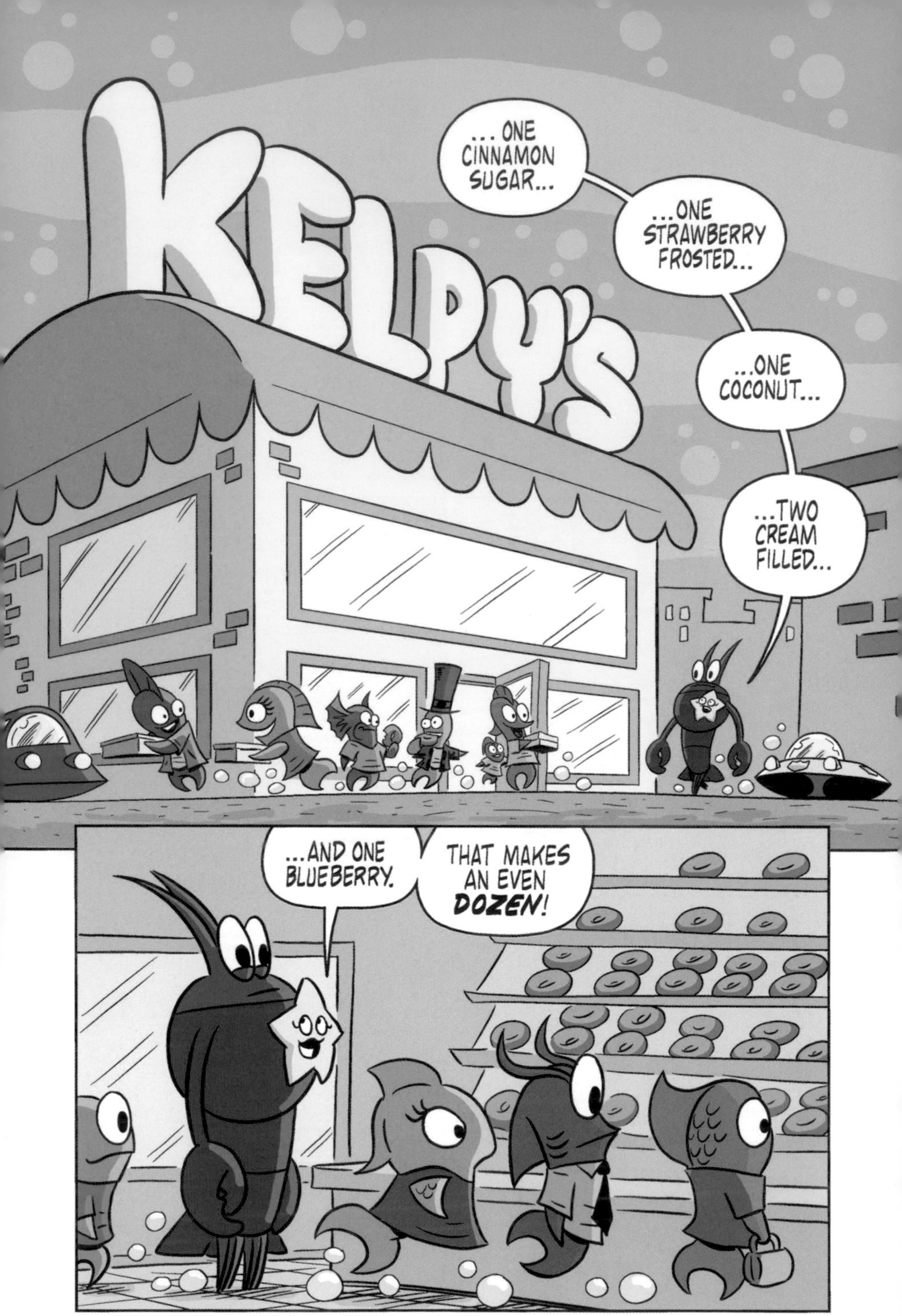
KELPY'S
... ONE CINNAMON SUGAR...
...ONE STRAWBERRY FROSTED...
...ONE COCONUT...
...TWO CREAM FILLED...
...AND ONE BLUEBERRY.
THAT MAKES AN EVEN DOZEN!

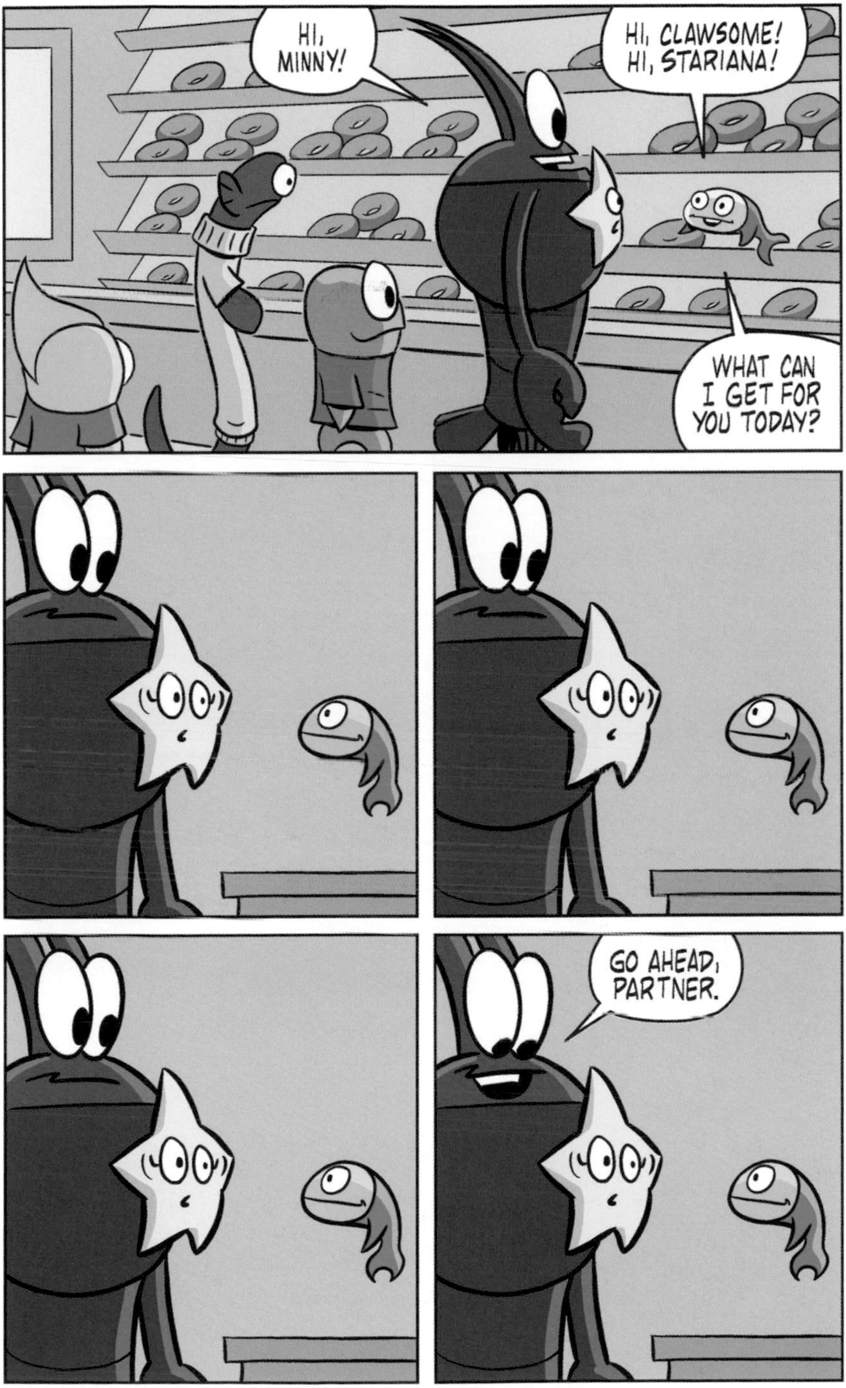
HI, MINNY!
HI, CLAWSOME! HI, STARIANA!
WHAT CAN I GET FOR YOU TODAY?
GO AHEAD, PARTNER.

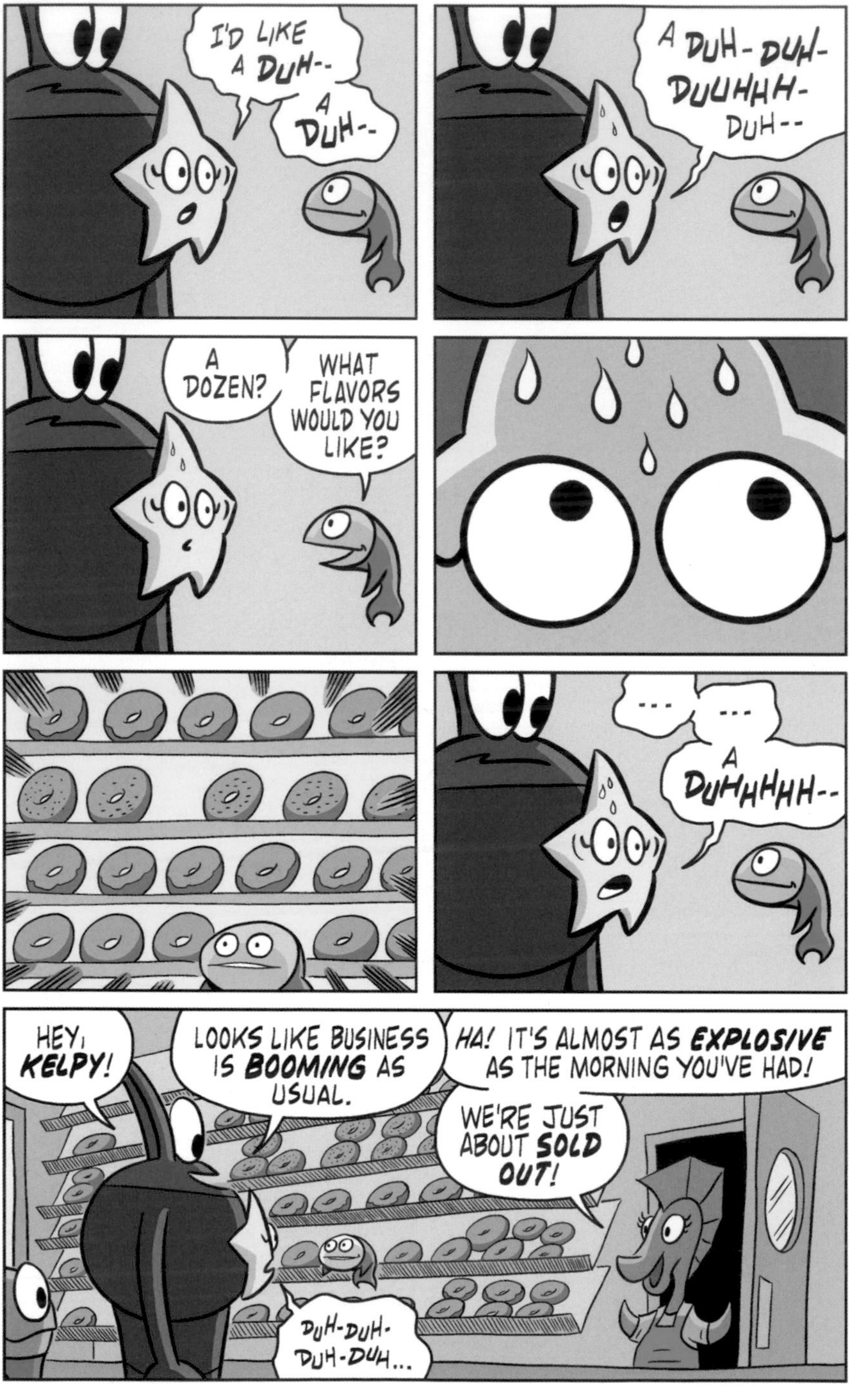

I'D LIKE A DUH--
A DUH--
A DUH-DUH-DUUHHH-DUH--
A DOZEN?
WHAT FLAVORS WOULD YOU LIKE?

A DUHHHHH--
HEY, KELPY!
LOOKS LIKE BUSINESS IS BOOMING AS USUAL.
HA! IT'S ALMOST AS EXPLOSIVE AS THE MORNING YOU'VE HAD!
WE'RE JUST ABOUT SOLD OUT!
DUH-DUH-DUH-DUH...

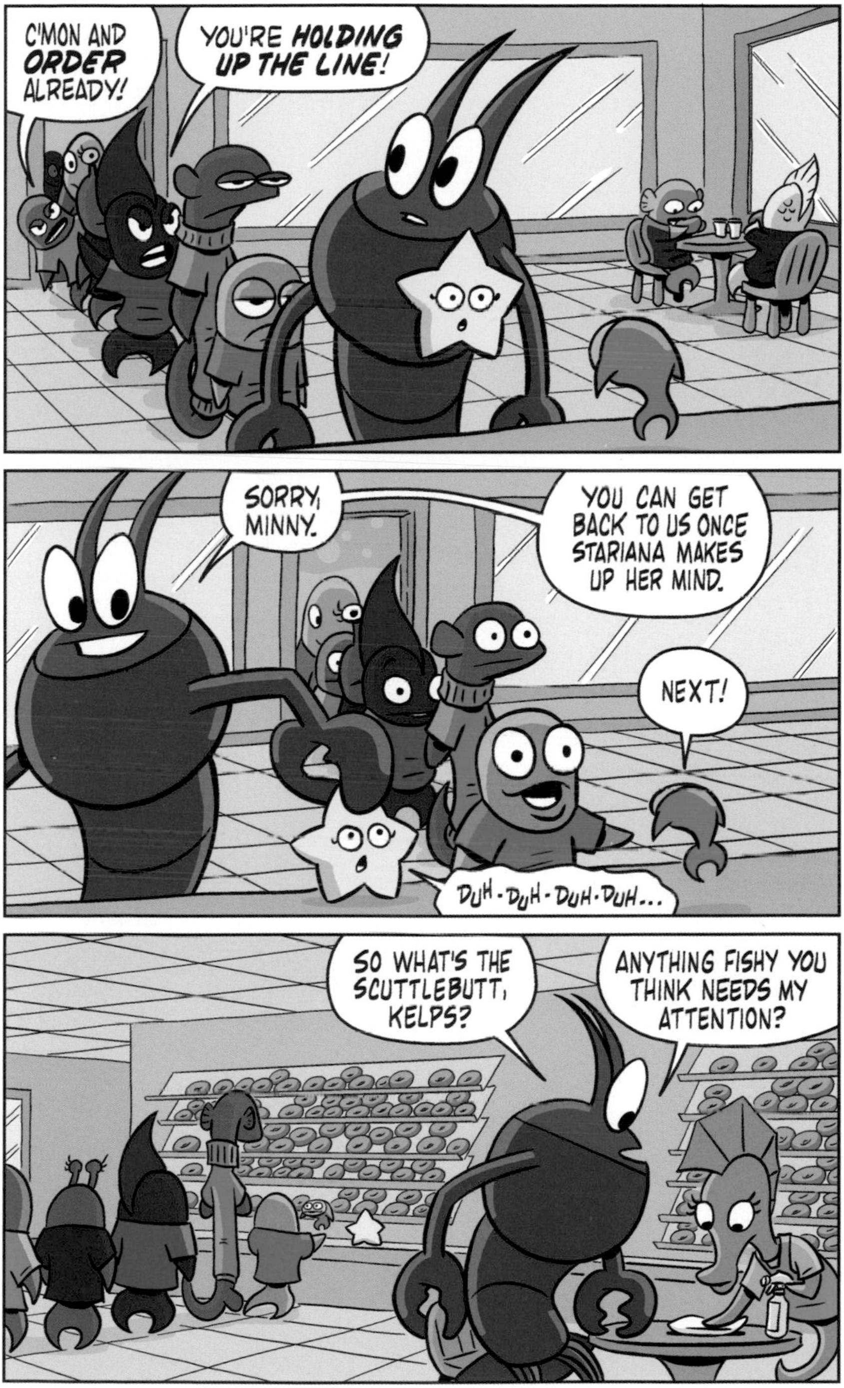
C'MON AND **ORDER** ALREADY!
YOU'RE **HOLDING UP THE LINE!**
SORRY, MINNY.
YOU CAN GET BACK TO US ONCE STARIANA MAKES UP HER MIND.
NEXT!
DUH-DUH-DUH-DUH...
SO WHAT'S THE SCUTTLEBUTT, KELPS?
ANYTHING FISHY YOU THINK NEEDS MY ATTENTION?

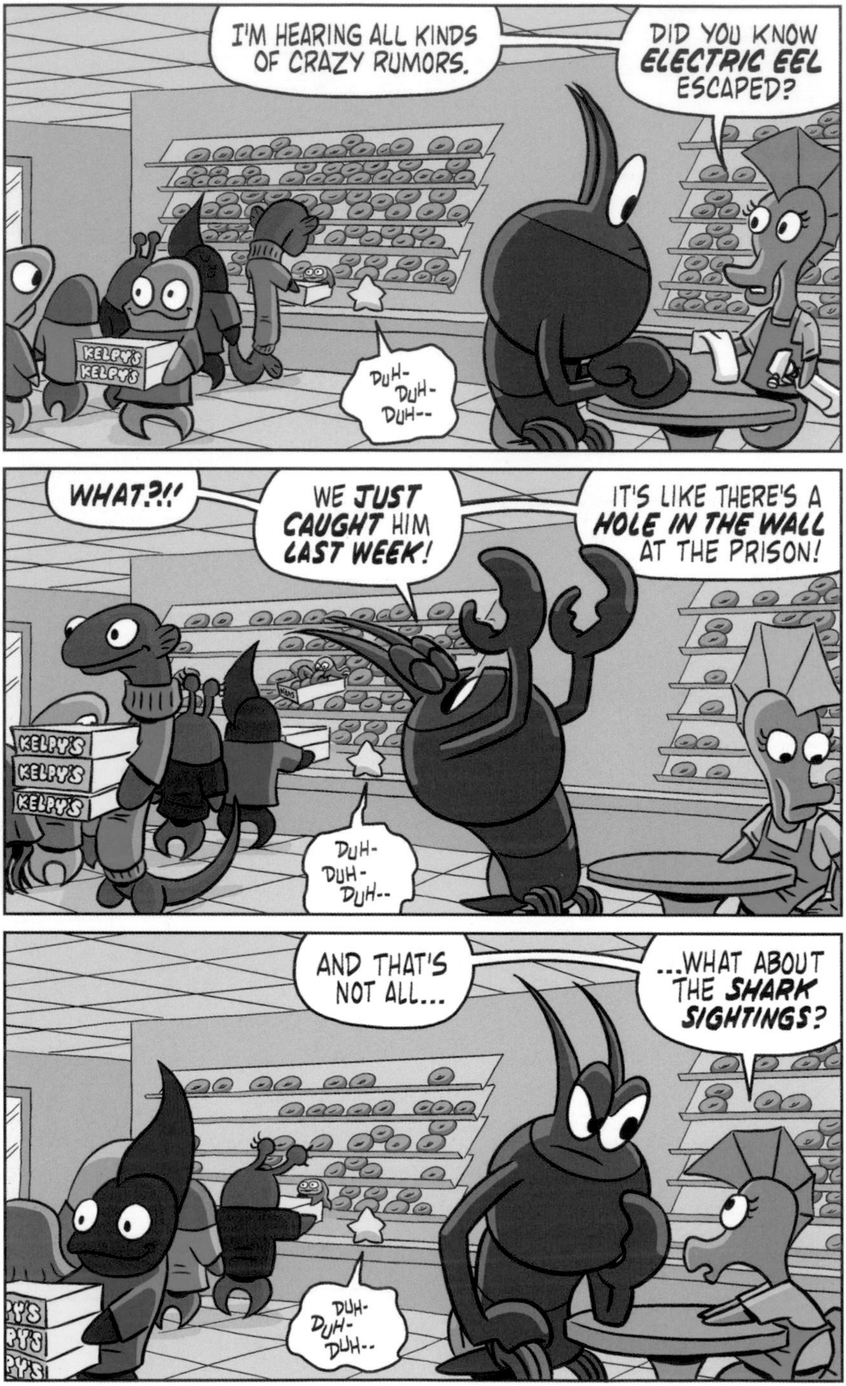
I'M HEARING ALL KINDS OF CRAZY RUMORS.
DID YOU KNOW ELECTRIC EEL ESCAPED?
KELPY'S
KELPY'S
DUH- DUH- DUH--
WHAT?!!
WE JUST CAUGHT HIM LAST WEEK!
IT'S LIKE THERE'S A HOLE IN THE WALL AT THE PRISON!
KELPY'S
KELPY'S
KELPY'S
DUH- DUH- DUH--
AND THAT'S NOT ALL...
...WHAT ABOUT THE SHARK SIGHTINGS?
DUH- DUH- DUH--

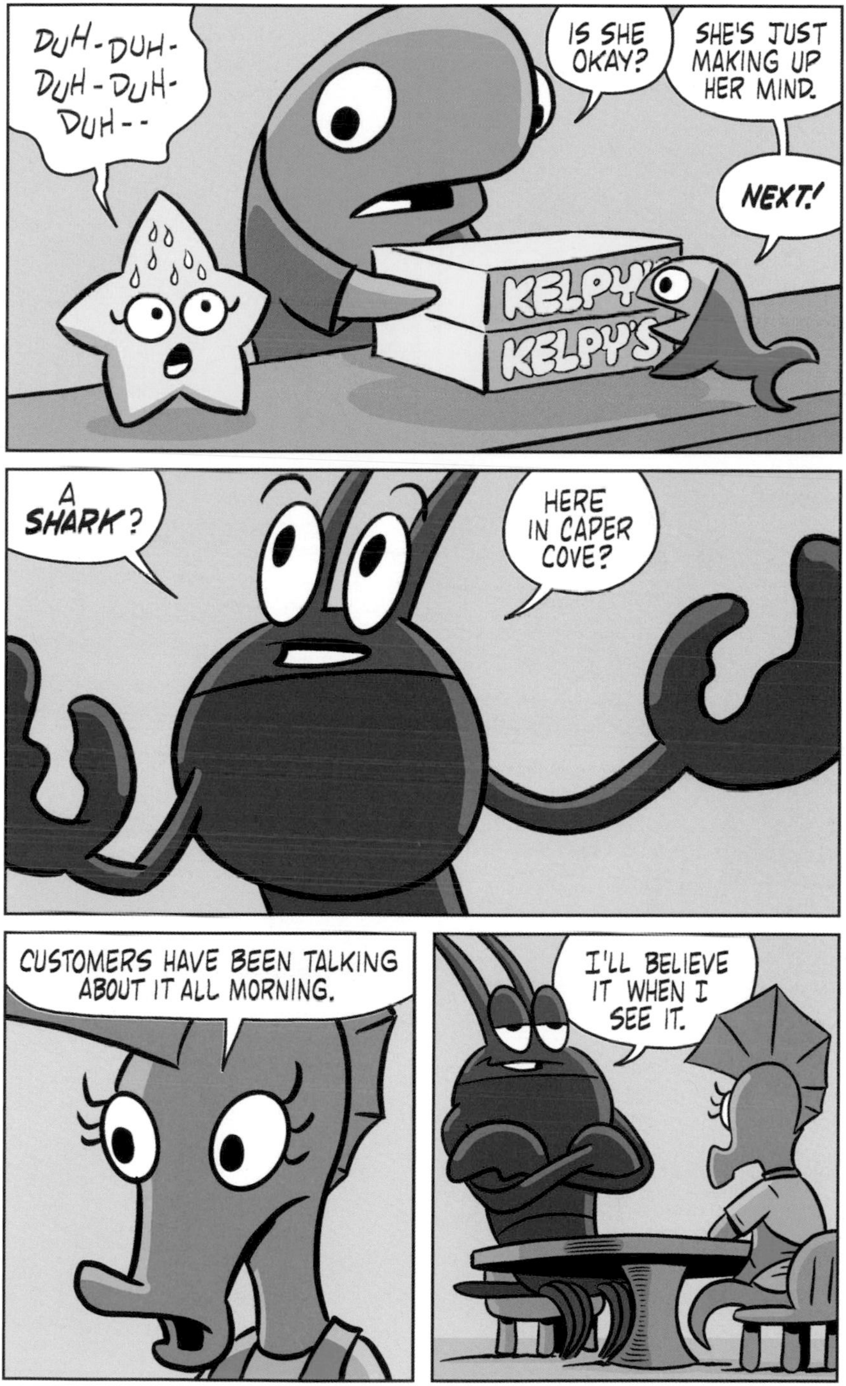
DUH-DUH-DUH-DUH-DUH--
IS SHE OKAY?
SHE'S JUST MAKING UP HER MIND.
NEXT!
KELPY'S
KELPY'S
A SHARK?
HERE IN CAPER COVE?
CUSTOMERS HAVE BEEN TALKING ABOUT IT ALL MORNING.
I'LL BELIEVE IT WHEN I SEE IT.

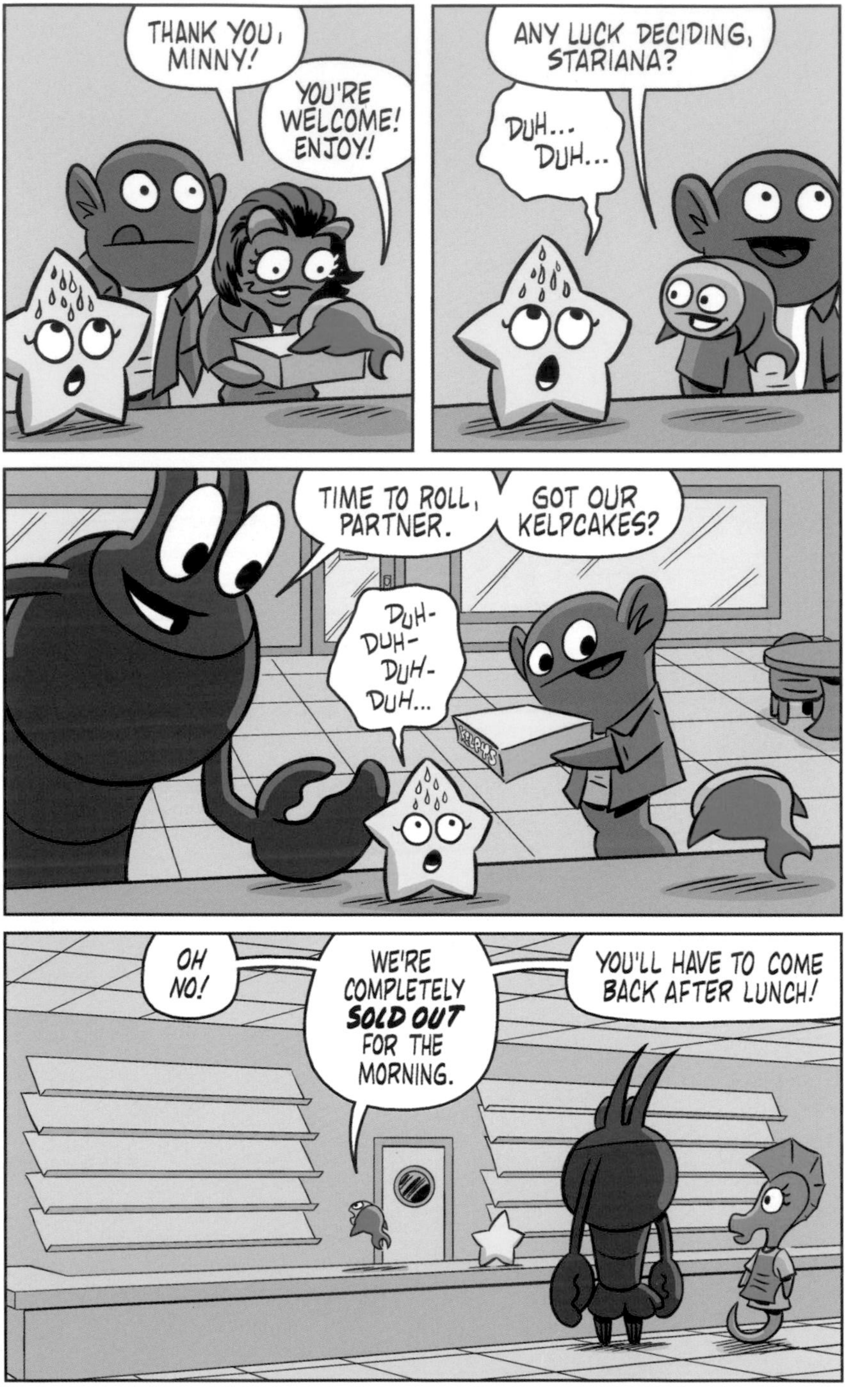
THANK YOU, MINNY!
YOU'RE WELCOME! ENJOY!
ANY LUCK DECIDING, STARIANA?
DUH... DUH...
TIME TO ROLL, PARTNER.
GOT OUR KELPCAKES?
DUH- DUH- DUH- DUH...
KELPY'S
OH NO!
WE'RE COMPLETELY **SOLD OUT** FOR THE MORNING.
YOU'LL HAVE TO COME BACK AFTER LUNCH!

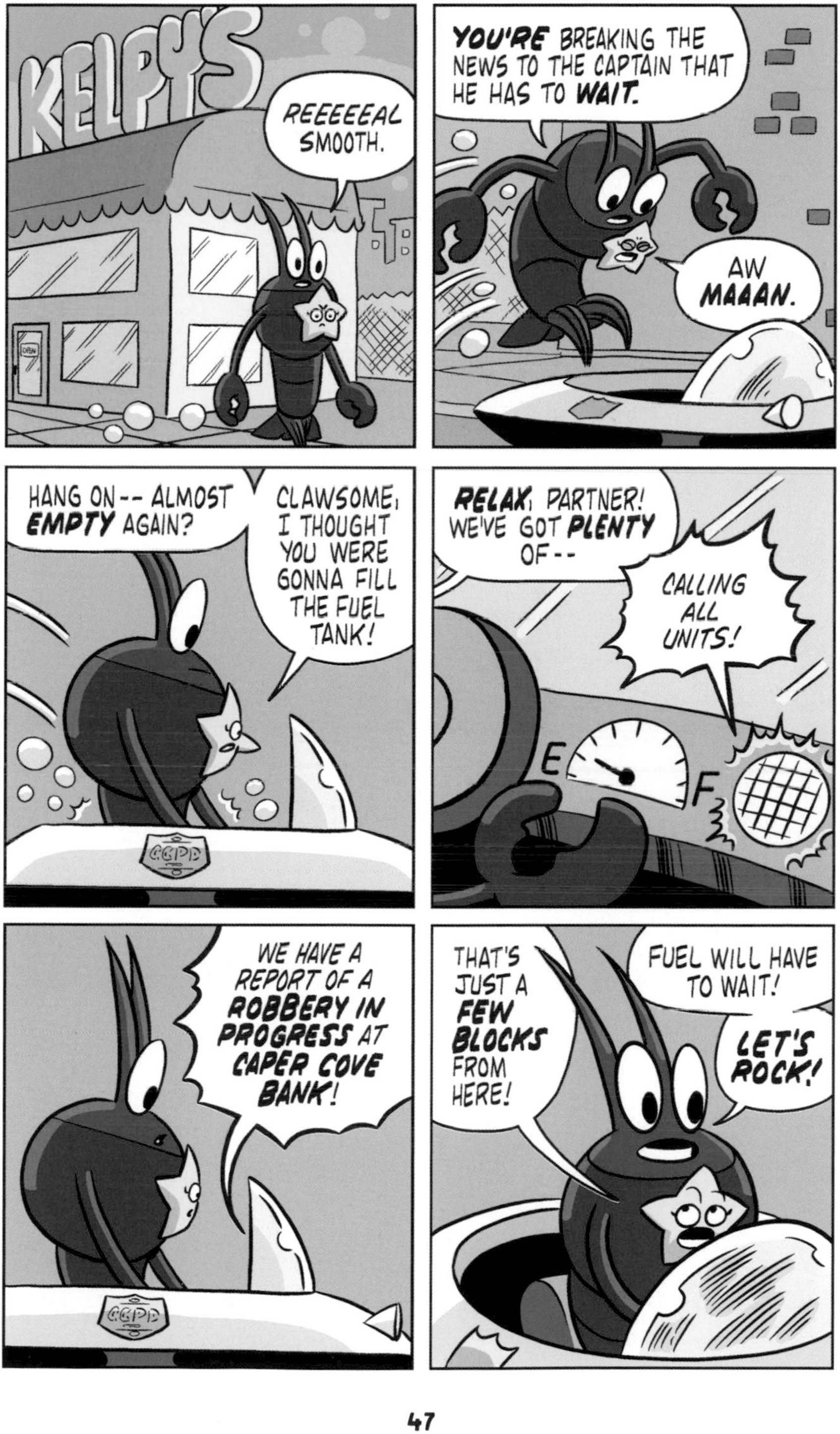
KELPY'S
REEEEEAL SMOOTH.
YOU'RE BREAKING THE NEWS TO THE CAPTAIN THAT HE HAS TO WAIT.
AW MAAAN.
HANG ON-- ALMOST EMPTY AGAIN?
CLAWSOME, I THOUGHT YOU WERE GONNA FILL THE FUEL TANK!
CGPD
RELAX, PARTNER! WE'VE GOT PLENTY OF--
CALLING ALL UNITS!
E
F
WE HAVE A REPORT OF A ROBBERY IN PROGRESS AT CAPER COVE BANK!
CGPD
THAT'S JUST A FEW BLOCKS FROM HERE!
FUEL WILL HAVE TO WAIT!
LET'S ROCK!

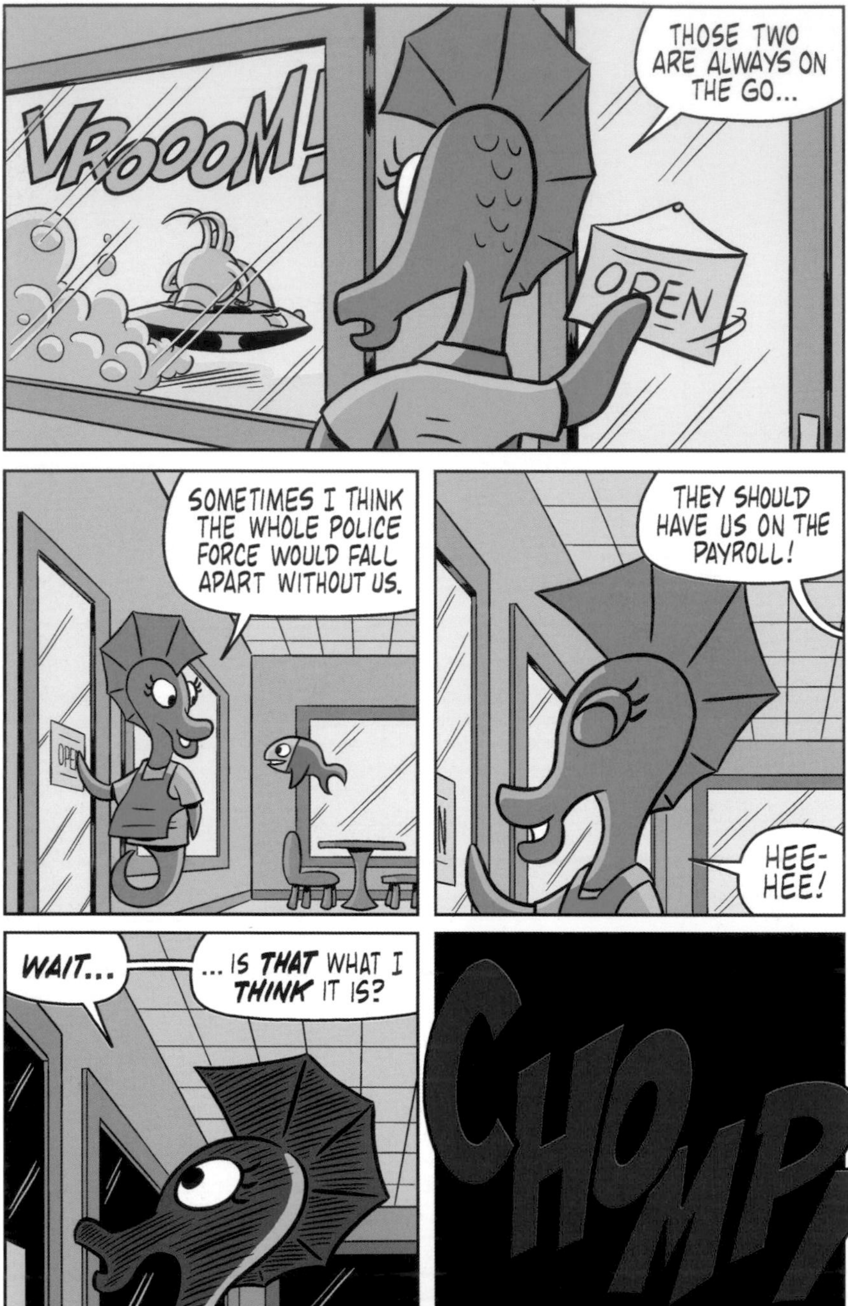
VROOOM!
THOSE TWO ARE ALWAYS ON THE GO...
OPEN
SOMETIMES I THINK THE WHOLE POLICE FORCE WOULD FALL APART WITHOUT US.
THEY SHOULD HAVE US ON THE PAYROLL!
HEE-HEE!
WAIT...
... IS **THAT** WHAT I **THINK** IT IS?
CHOMP!

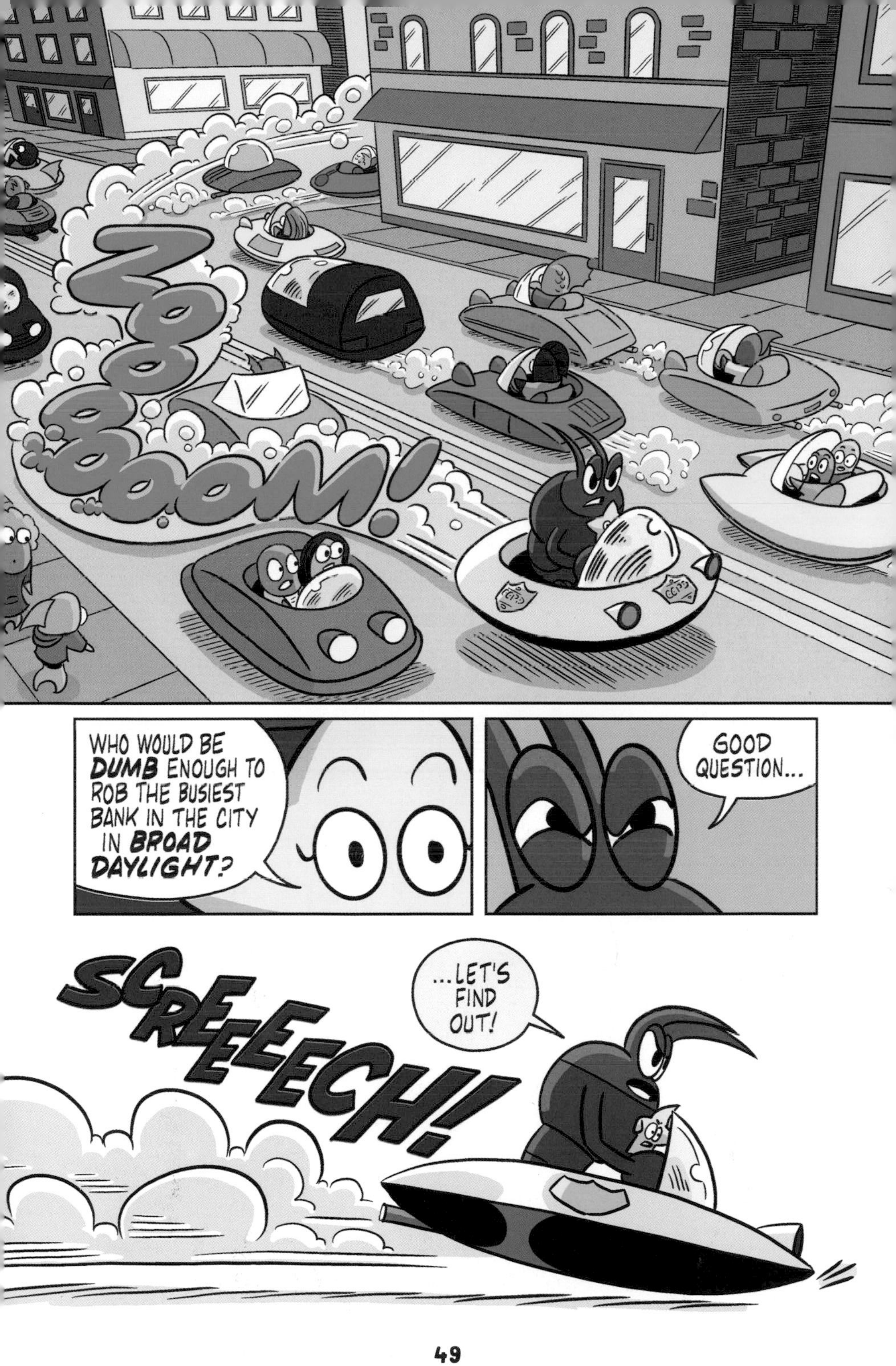
ZOOOOOM!
WHO WOULD BE DUMB ENOUGH TO ROB THE BUSIEST BANK IN THE CITY IN BROAD DAYLIGHT?
GOOD QUESTION...
SCREEEECH!
...LET'S FIND OUT!

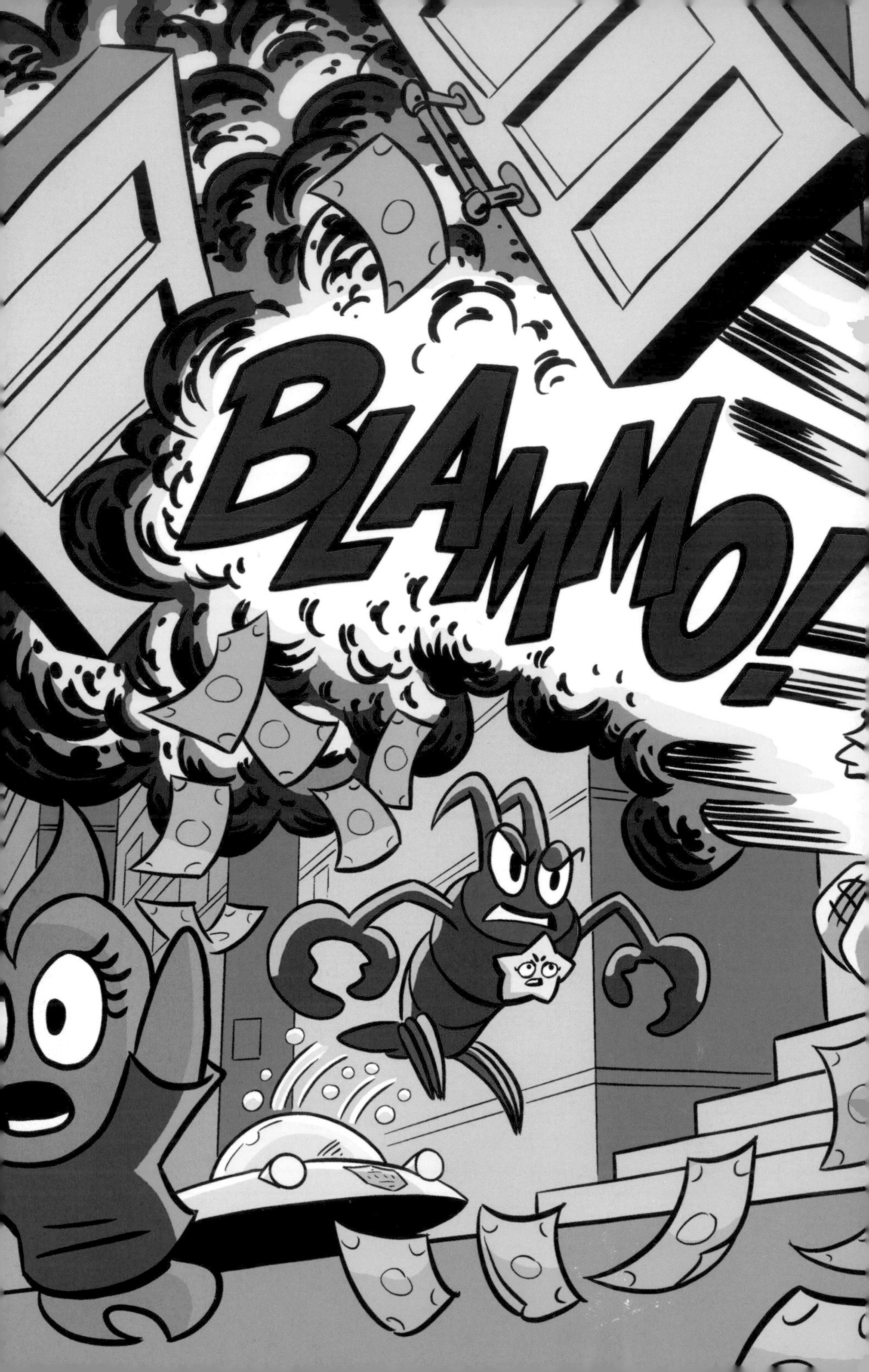
BLAMMO!

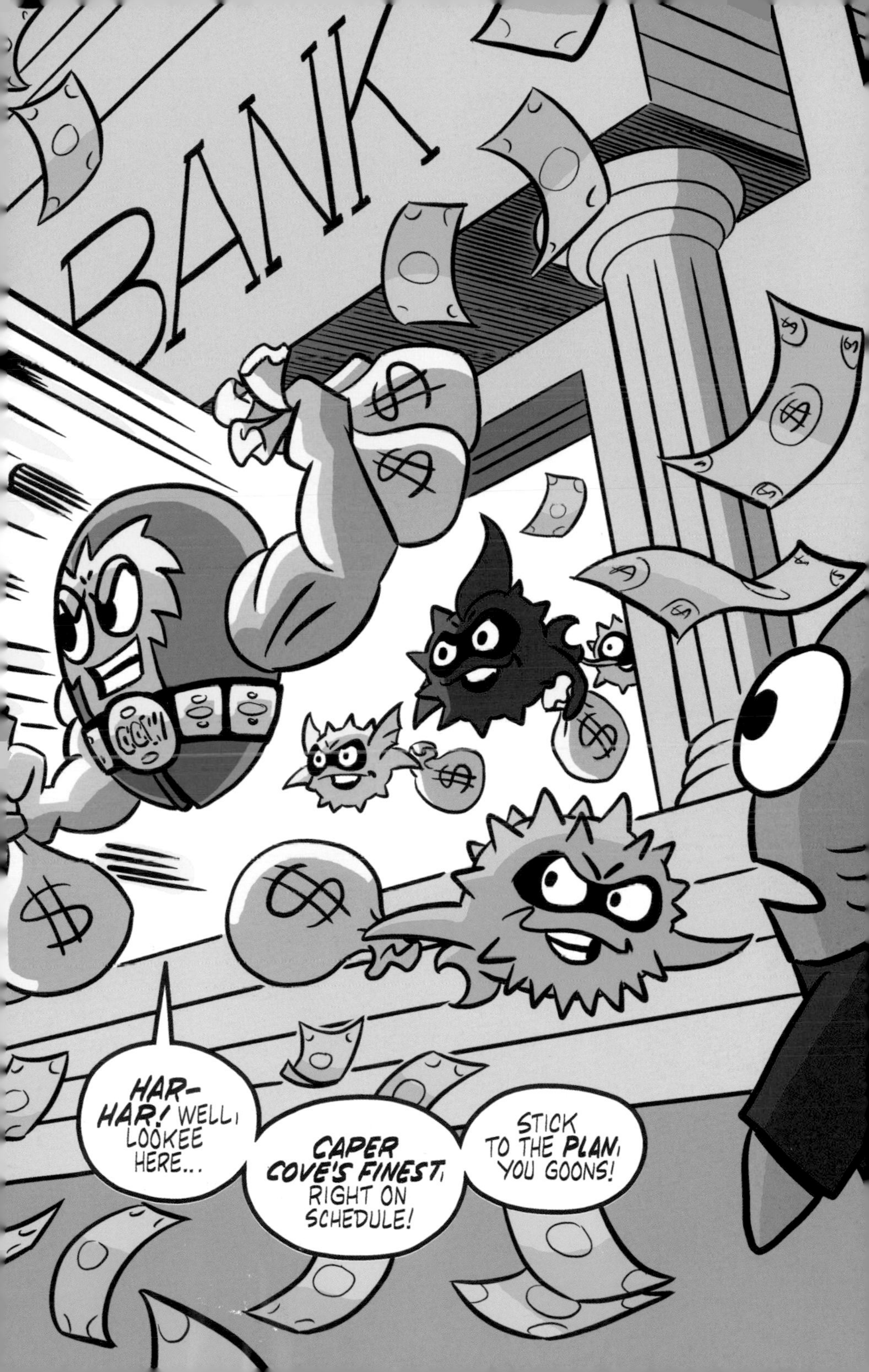
BANK
HAR-HAR! WELL, LOOKEE HERE...
CAPER COVE'S FINEST, RIGHT ON SCHEDULE!
STICK TO THE PLAN, YOU GOONS!

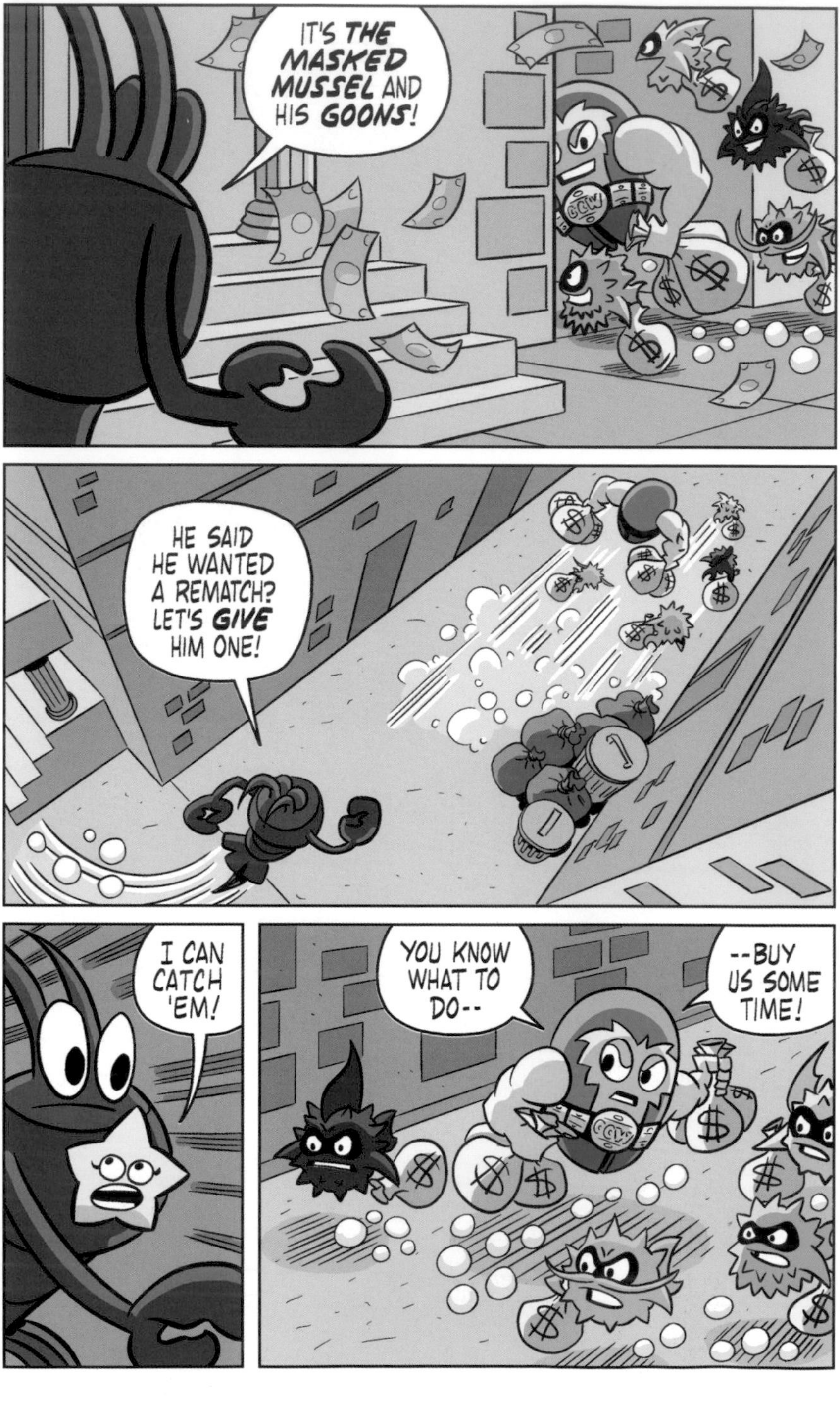
IT'S THE MASKED MUSSEL AND HIS GOONS!
HE SAID HE WANTED A REMATCH? LET'S GIVE HIM ONE!
I CAN CATCH 'EM!
YOU KNOW WHAT TO DO--
--BUY US SOME TIME!

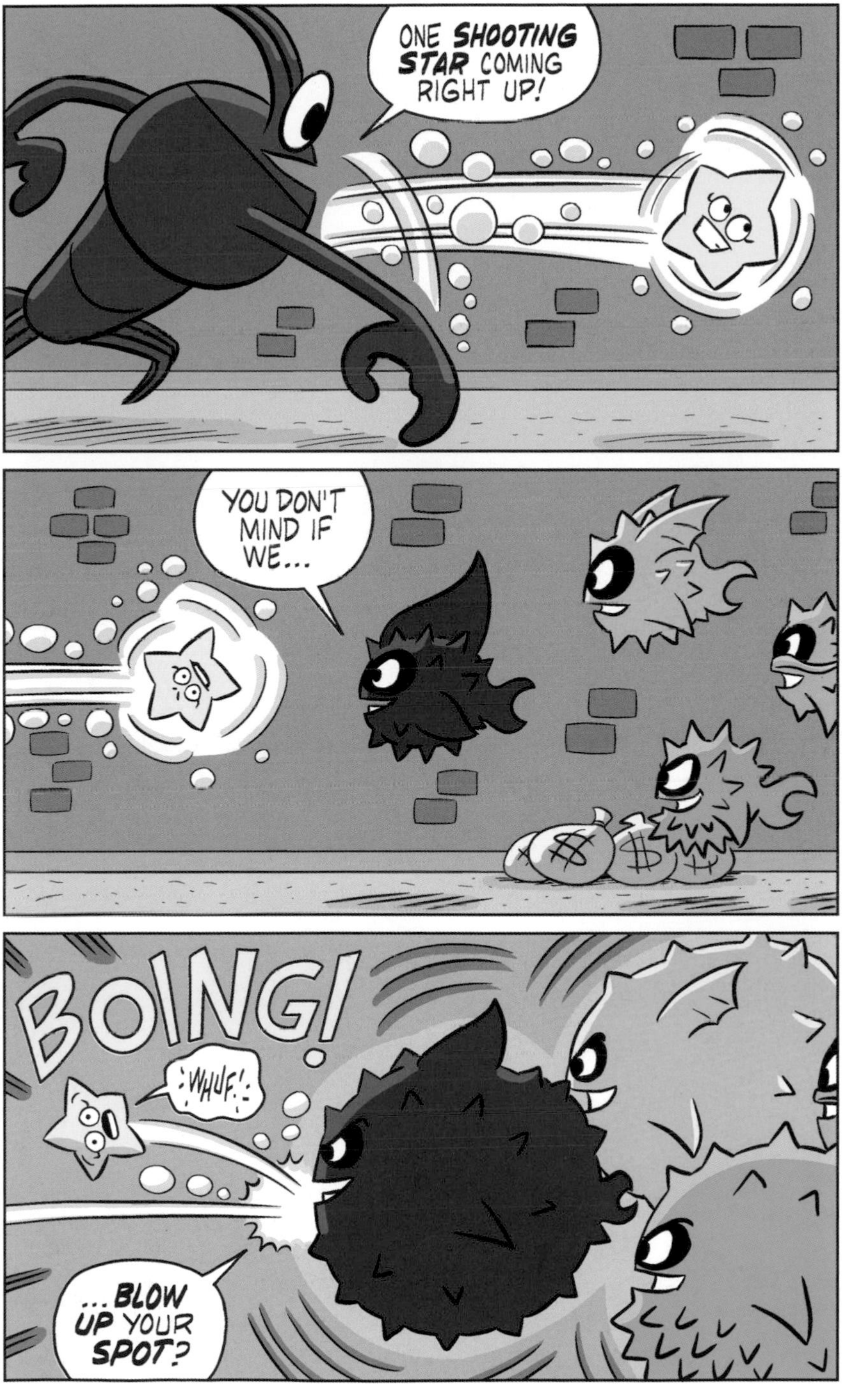
ONE SHOOTING STAR COMING RIGHT UP!
YOU DON'T MIND IF WE...
BOING!
WHUF!
...BLOW UP YOUR SPOT?

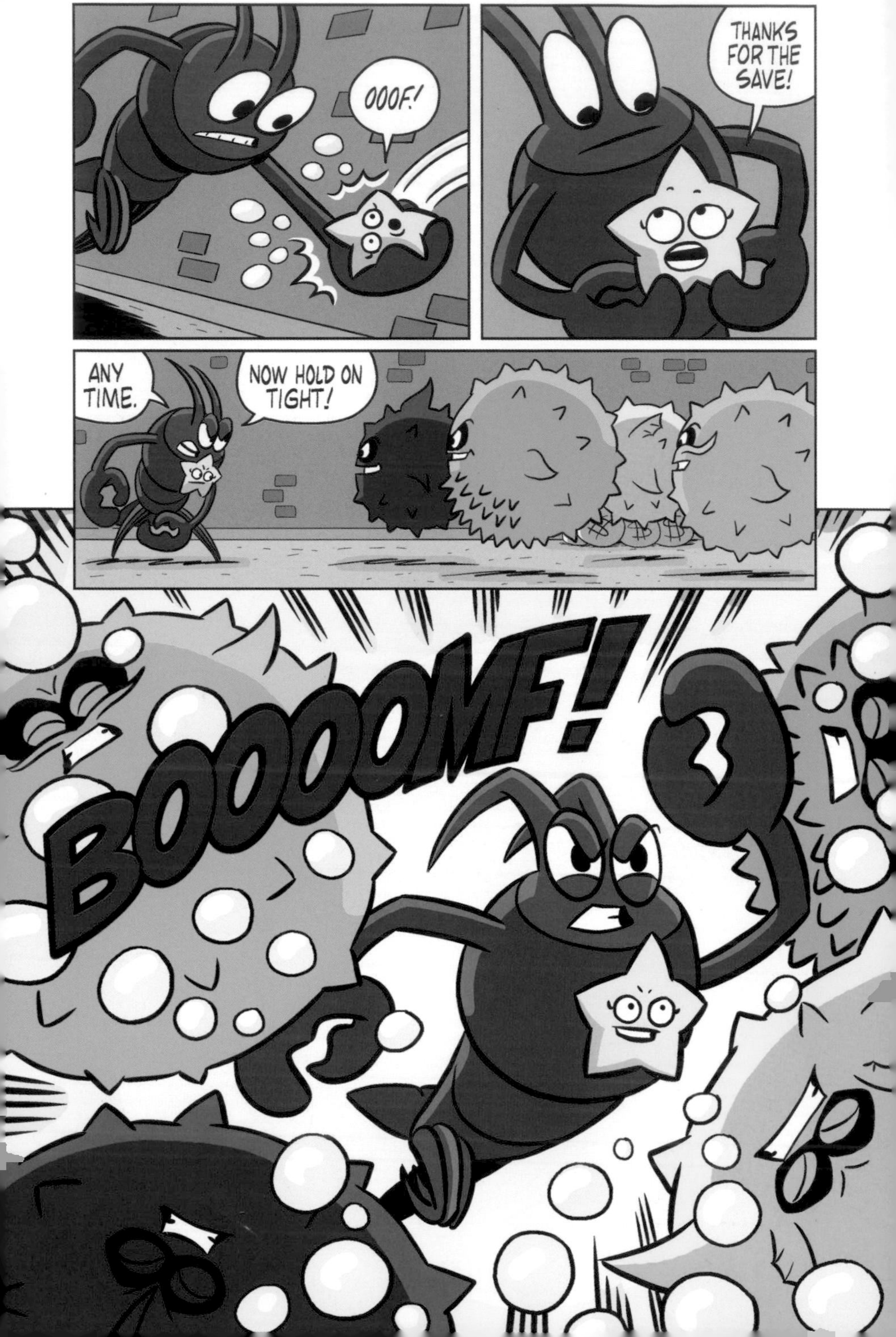

OOOF!
THANKS FOR THE SAVE!
ANY TIME.
NOW HOLD ON TIGHT!
BOOOOOMF!

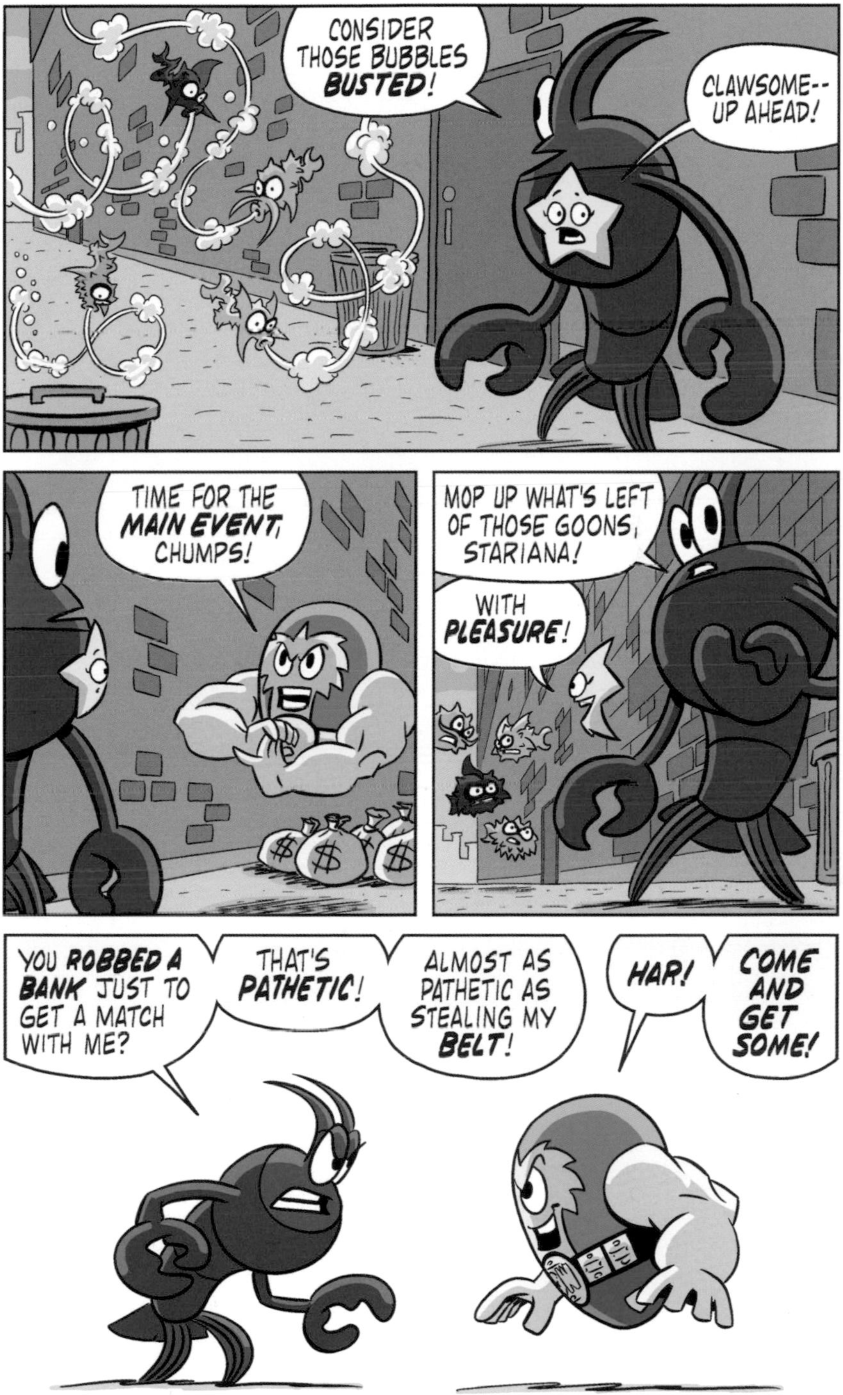
CONSIDER THOSE BUBBLES BUSTED!
CLAWSOME-- UP AHEAD!
TIME FOR THE MAIN EVENT, CHUMPS!
MOP UP WHAT'S LEFT OF THOSE GOONS, STARIANA!
WITH PLEASURE!
YOU ROBBED A BANK JUST TO GET A MATCH WITH ME?
THAT'S PATHETIC!
ALMOST AS PATHETIC AS STEALING MY BELT!
HAR!
COME AND GET SOME!

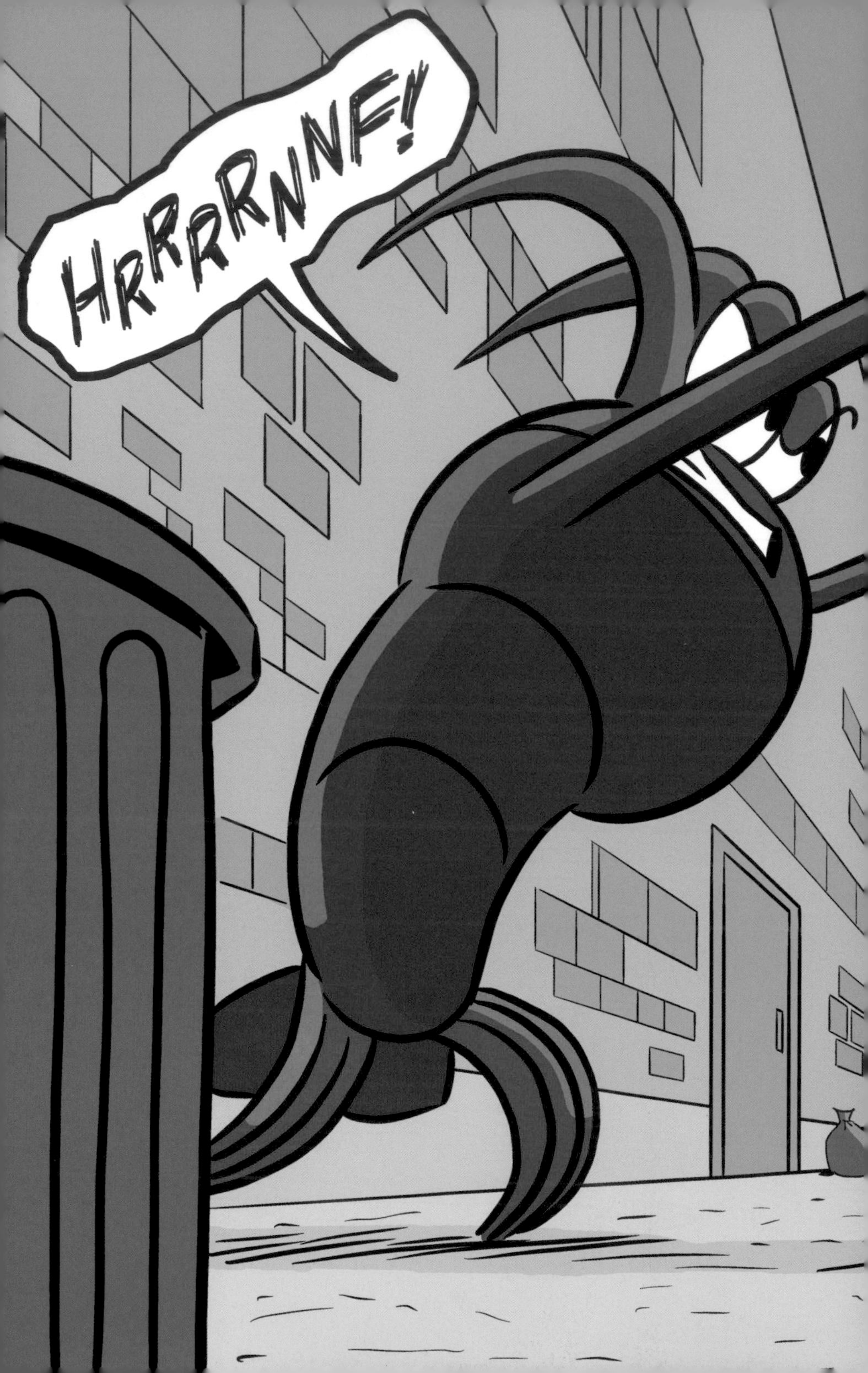
HRRRRNNF!

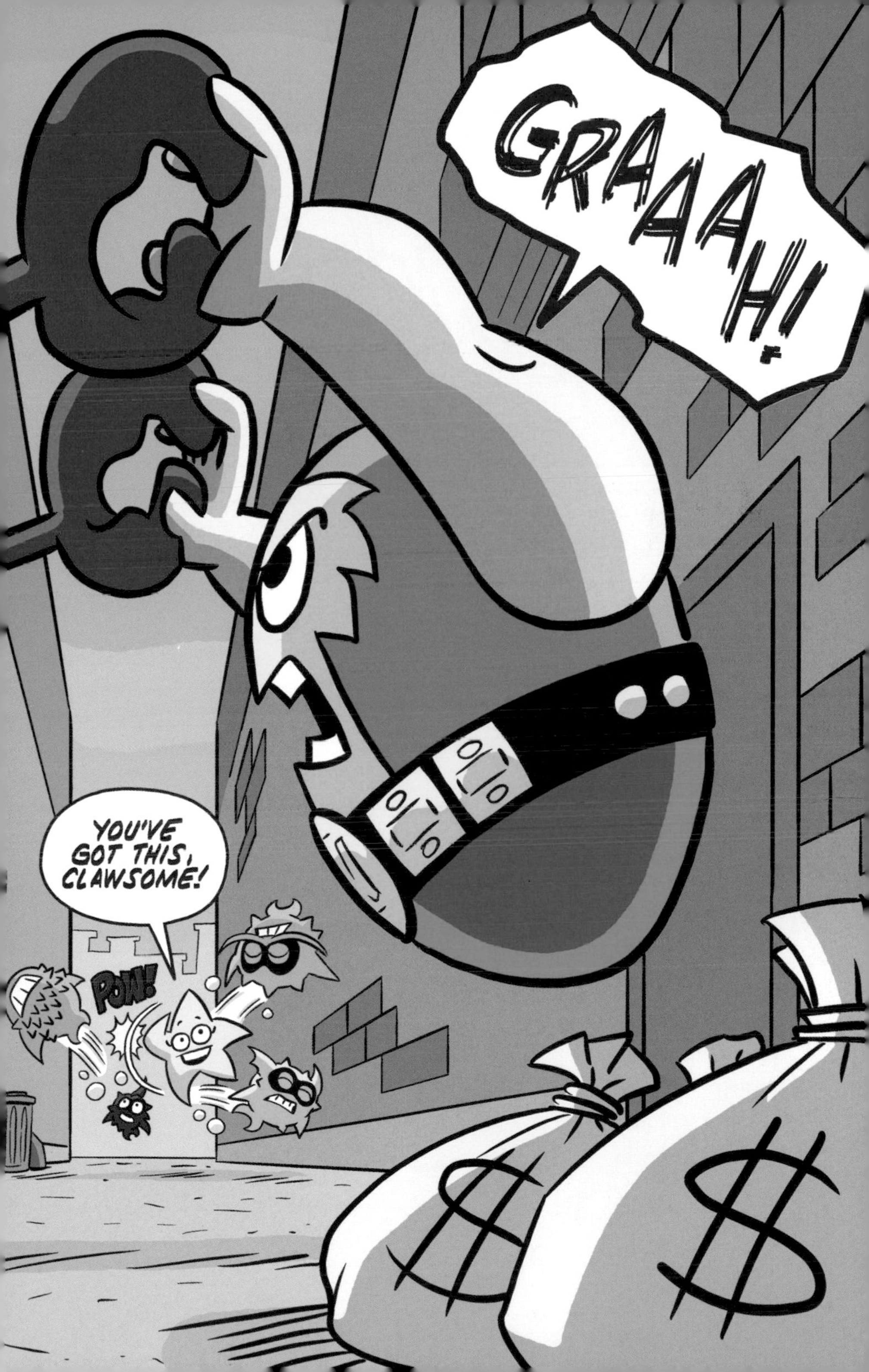
GRAAAH!
YOU'VE GOT THIS, CLAWSOME!
POW!

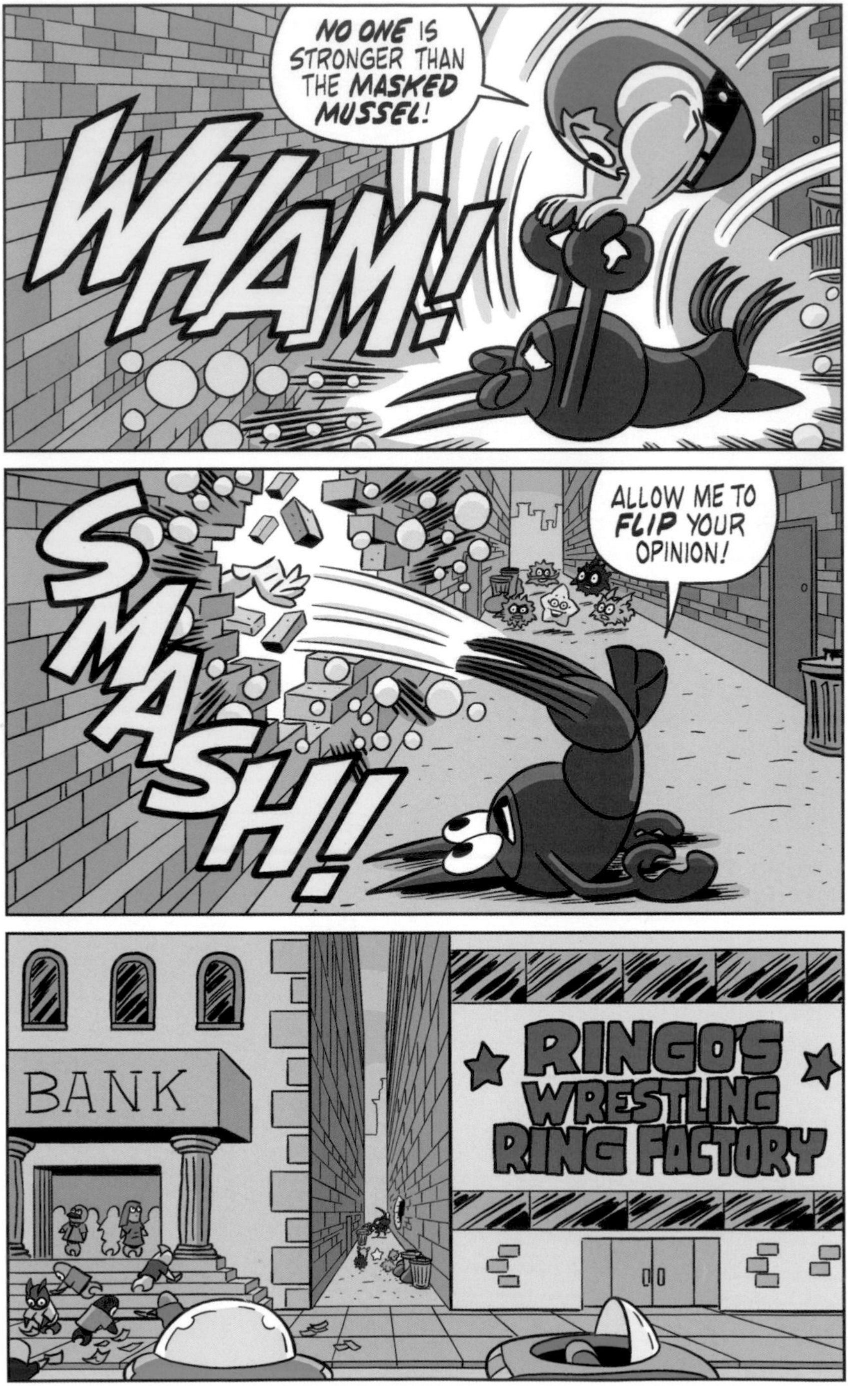
NO ONE IS STRONGER THAN THE MASKED MUSSEL!
WHAM!
ALLOW ME TO FLIP YOUR OPINION!
SMASH!
BANK
RINGO'S WRESTLING RING FACTORY

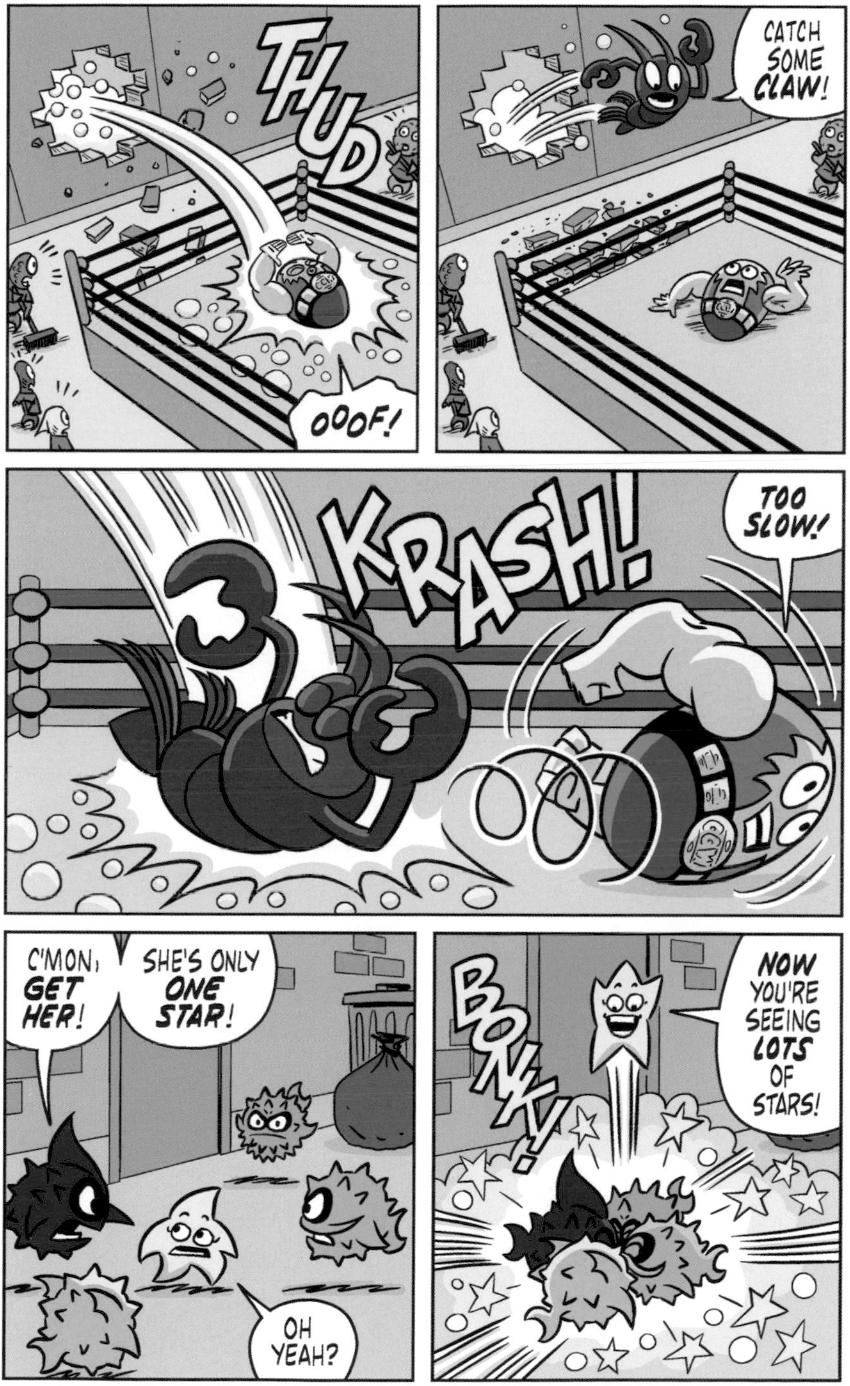
THUD
OOOF!
CATCH SOME CLAW!
KRASH!
TOO SLOW!
C'MON, GET HER!
SHE'S ONLY ONE STAR!
OH YEAH?
BONK!
NOW YOU'RE SEEING LOTS OF STARS!

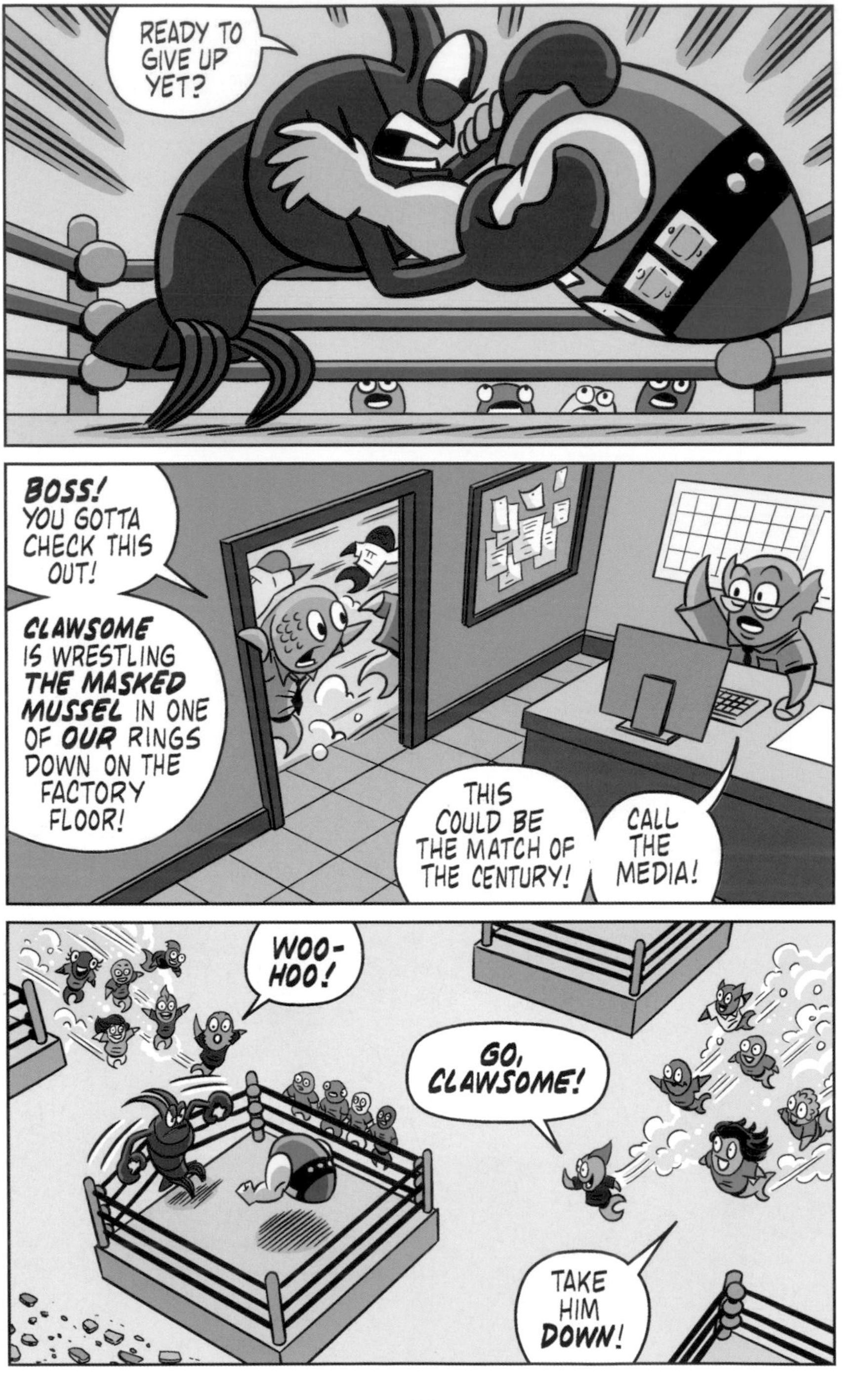
READY TO GIVE UP YET?
BOSS! YOU GOTTA CHECK THIS OUT!
CLAWSOME IS WRESTLING THE MASKED MUSSEL IN ONE OF OUR RINGS DOWN ON THE FACTORY FLOOR!
THIS COULD BE THE MATCH OF THE CENTURY!
CALL THE MEDIA!
WOO-HOO!
GO, CLAWSOME!
TAKE HIM DOWN!

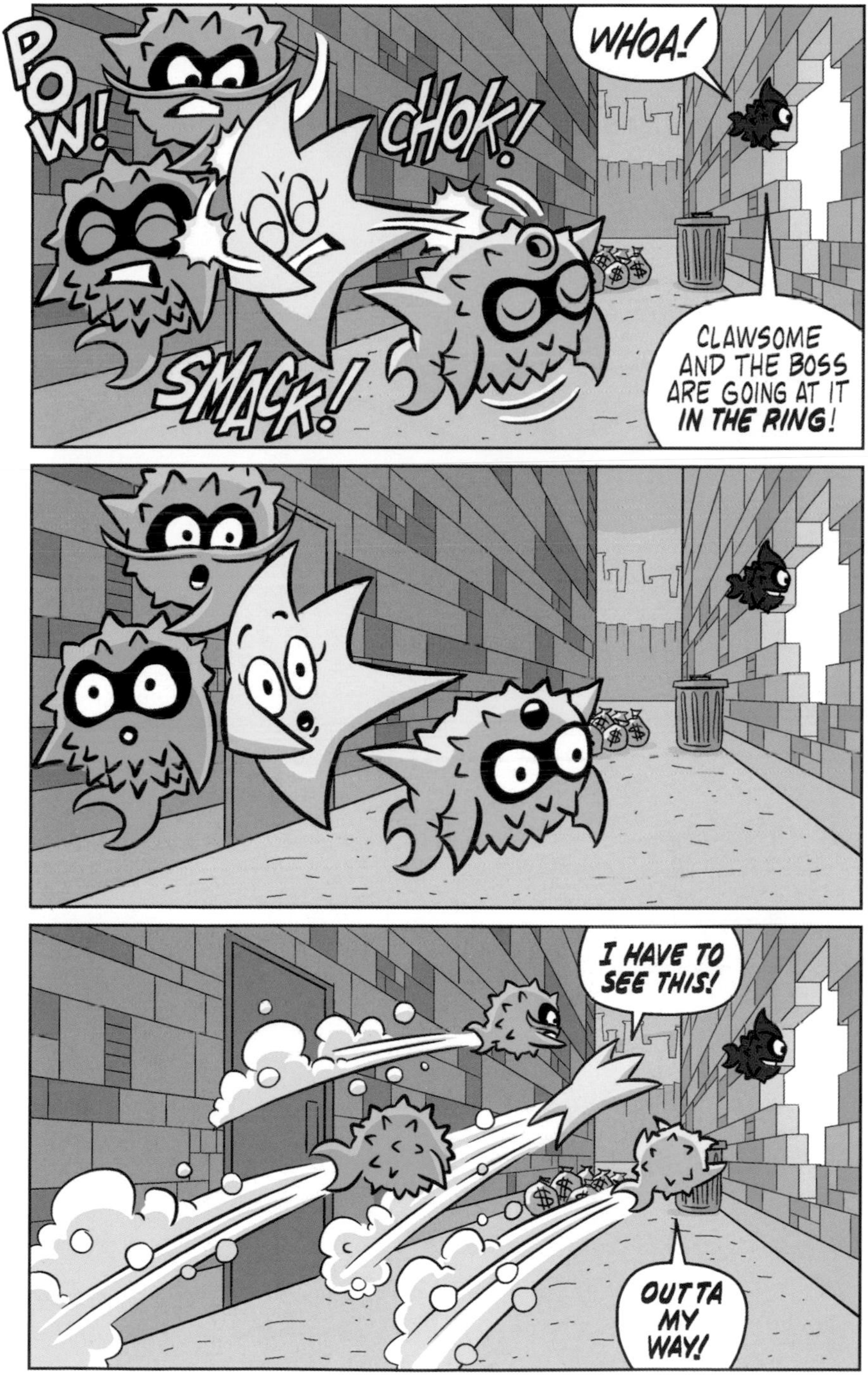
POW!
CHOK!
SMACK!
WHOA!
CLAWSOME AND THE BOSS ARE GOING AT IT IN THE RING!
I HAVE TO SEE THIS!
OUTTA MY WAY!

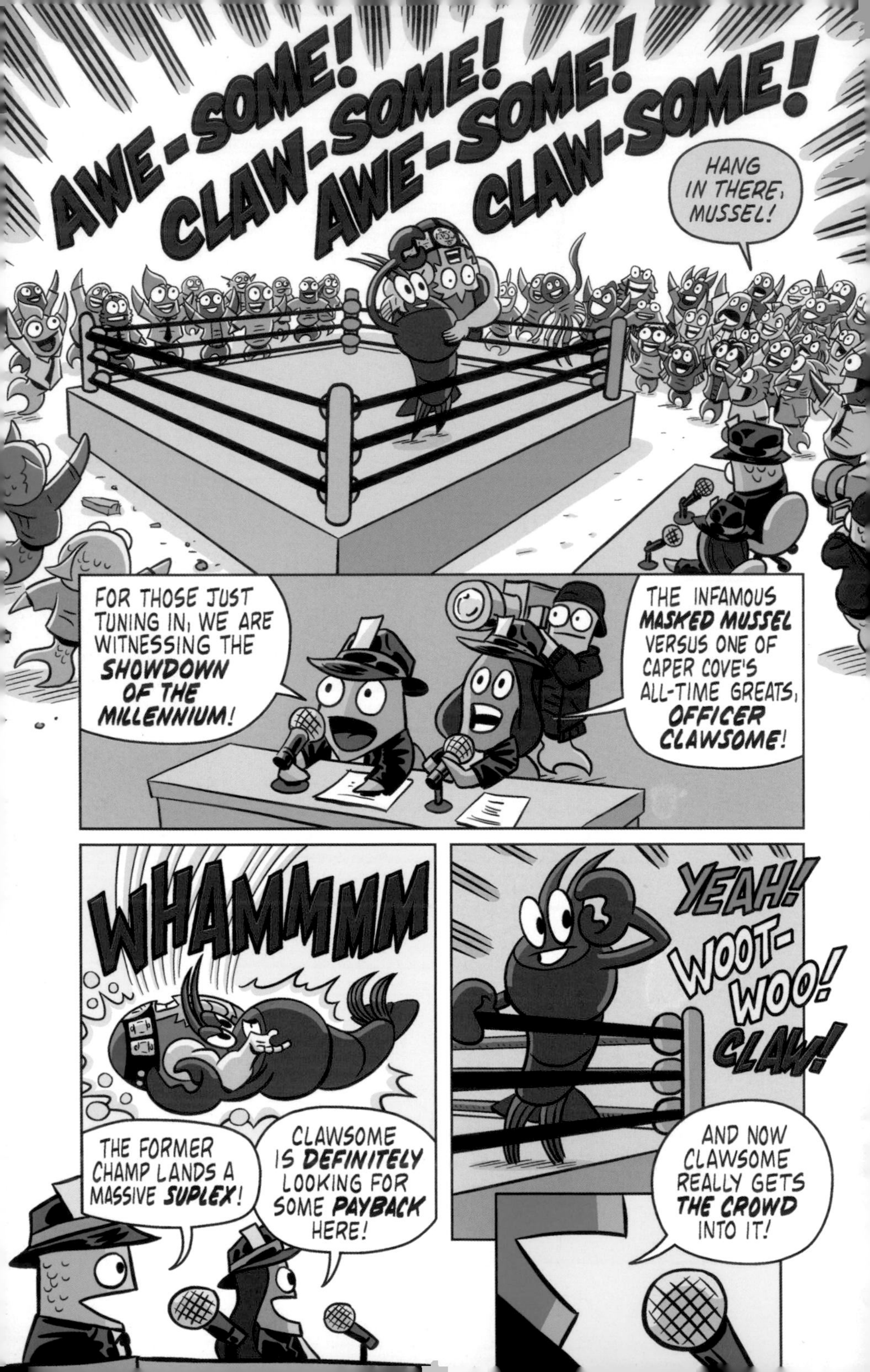

AWE-SOME! CLAW-SOME! AWE-SOME! CLAW-SOME!
HANG IN THERE, MUSSEL!
FOR THOSE JUST TUNING IN, WE ARE WITNESSING THE SHOWDOWN OF THE MILLENNIUM!
THE INFAMOUS MASKED MUSSEL VERSUS ONE OF CAPER COVE'S ALL-TIME GREATS, OFFICER CLAWSOME!
WHAMMMM
THE FORMER CHAMP LANDS A MASSIVE SUPLEX!
CLAWSOME IS DEFINITELY LOOKING FOR SOME PAYBACK HERE!
YEAH! WOOT-WOO! CLAW!
AND NOW CLAWSOME REALLY GETS THE CROWD INTO IT!

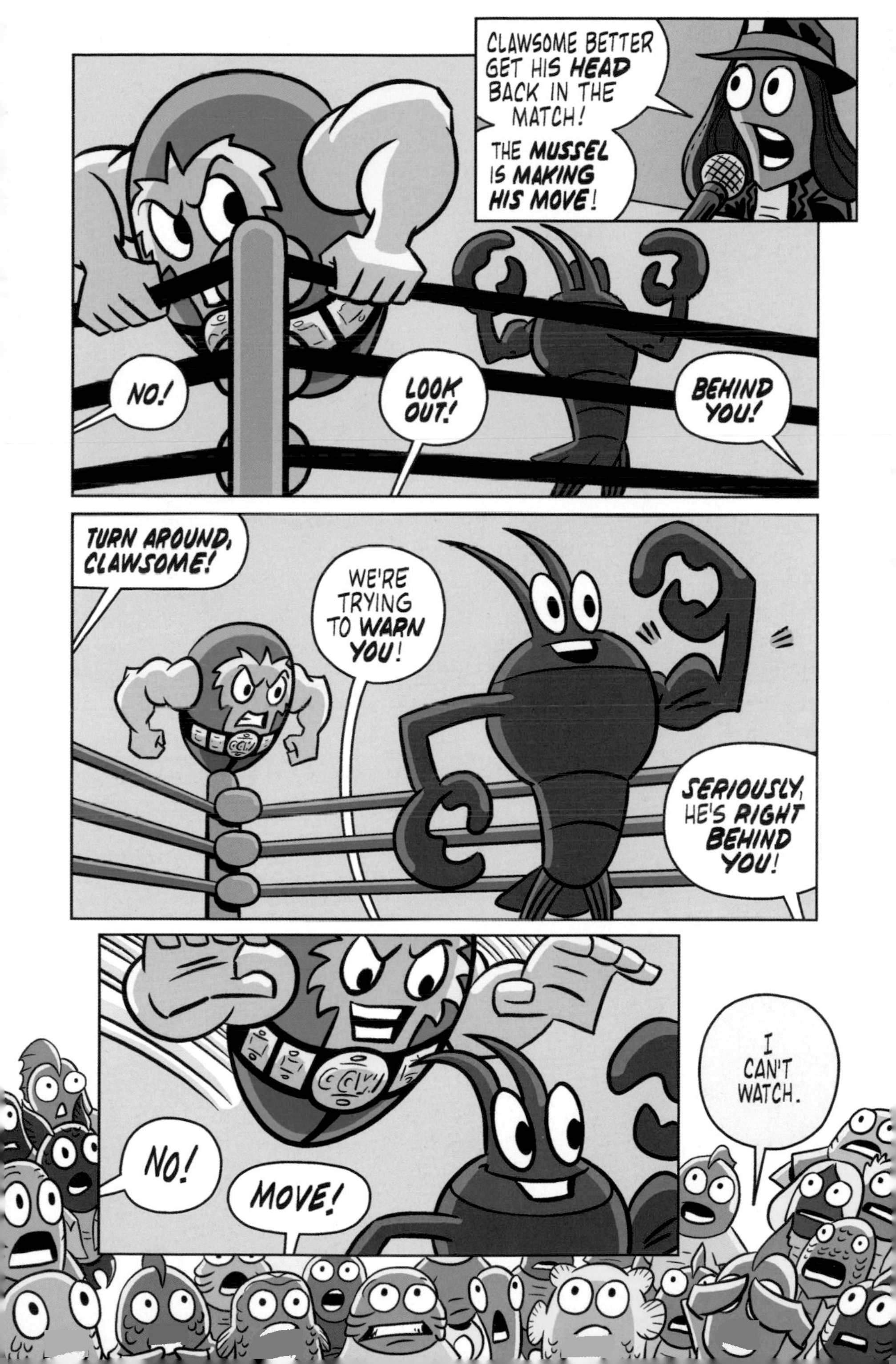
CLAWSOME BETTER GET HIS HEAD BACK IN THE MATCH!
THE MUSSEL IS MAKING HIS MOVE!
NO!
LOOK OUT!
BEHIND YOU!
TURN AROUND, CLAWSOME!
WE'RE TRYING TO WARN YOU!
SERIOUSLY, HE'S RIGHT BEHIND YOU!
NO!
MOVE!
I CAN'T WATCH.

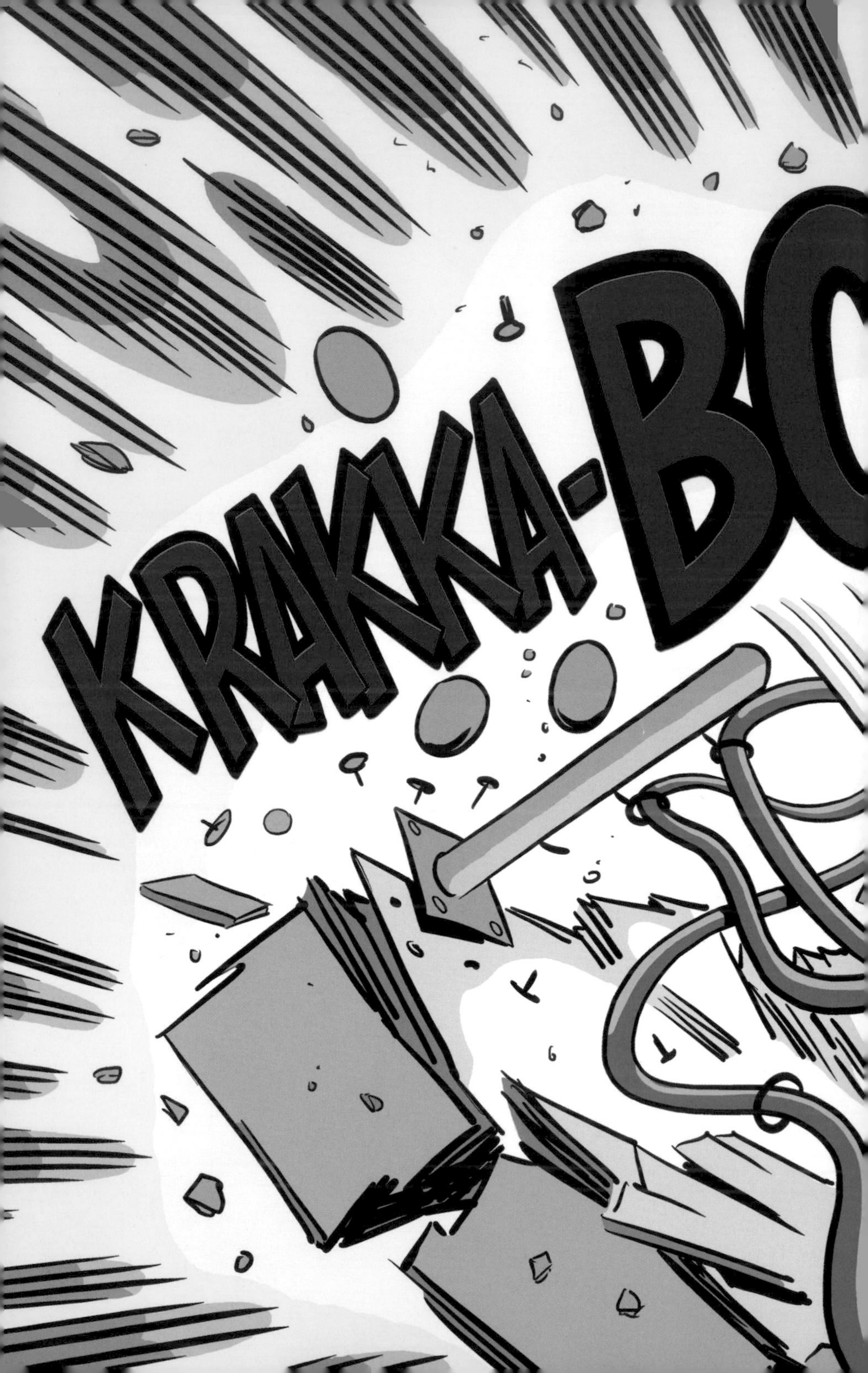
KRAKKA-BO

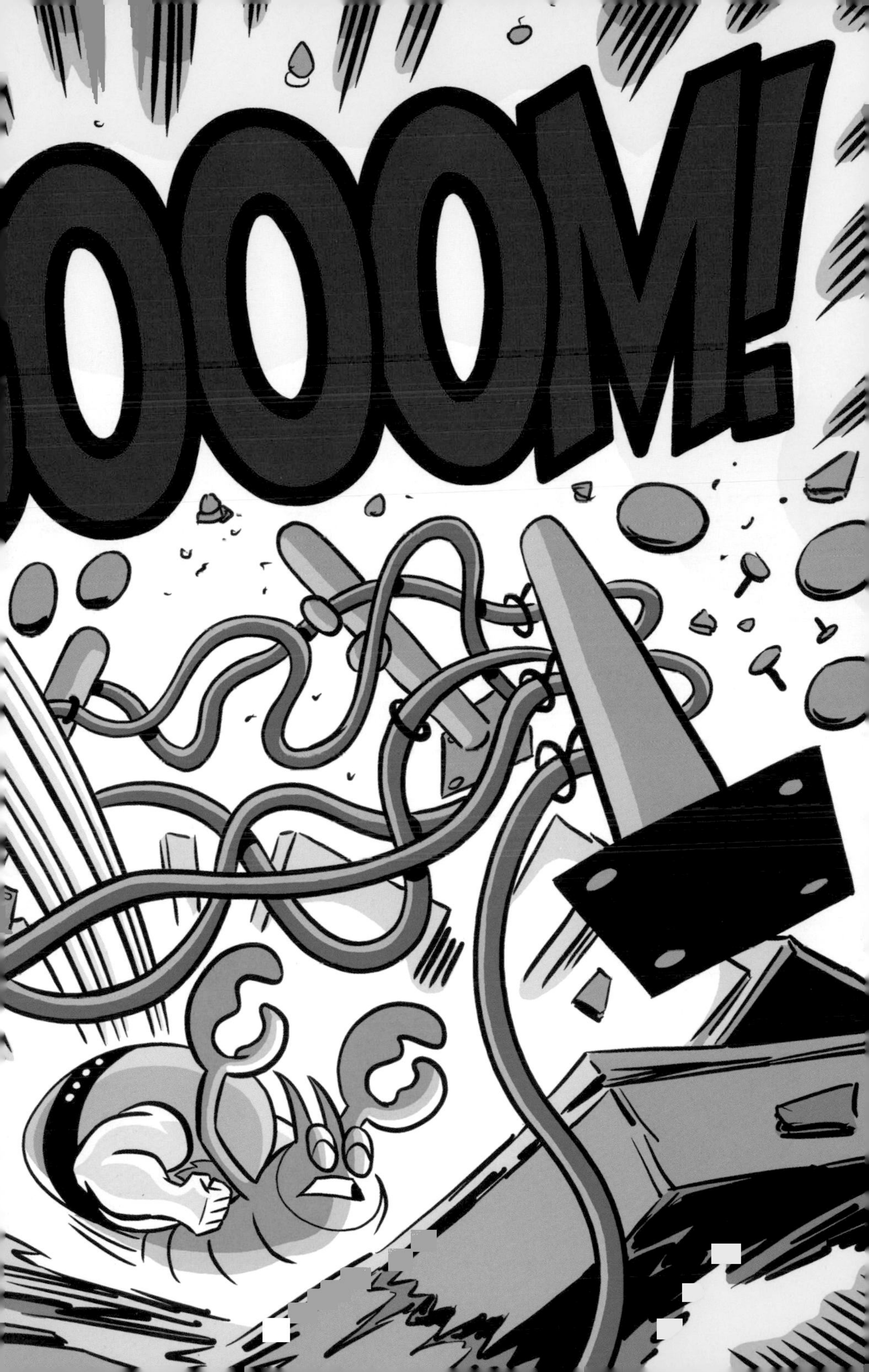
OOOM!

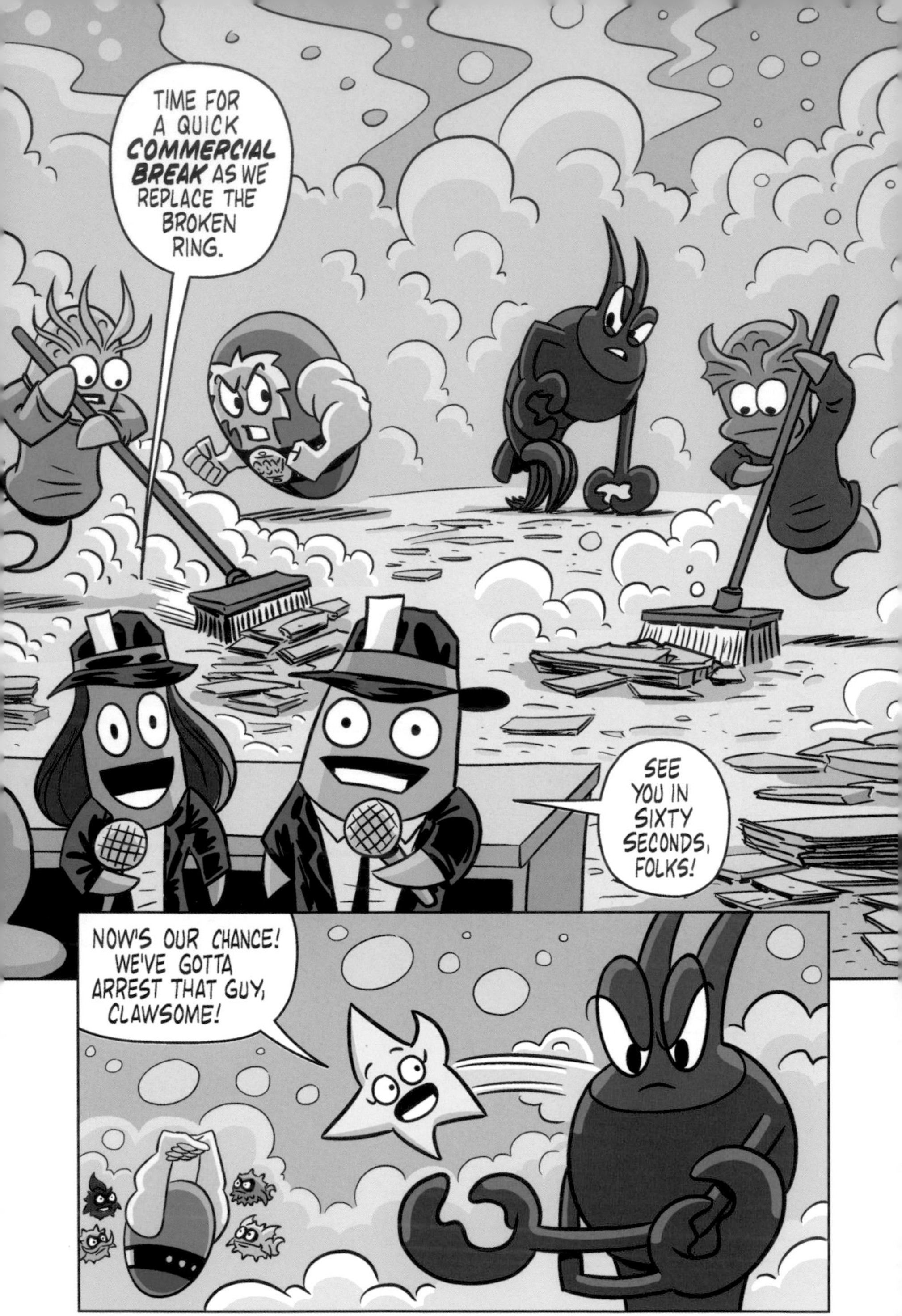
TIME FOR A QUICK **COMMERCIAL BREAK** AS WE REPLACE THE BROKEN RING.
SEE YOU IN SIXTY SECONDS, FOLKS!
NOW'S OUR CHANCE! WE'VE GOTTA ARREST THAT GUY, CLAWSOME!

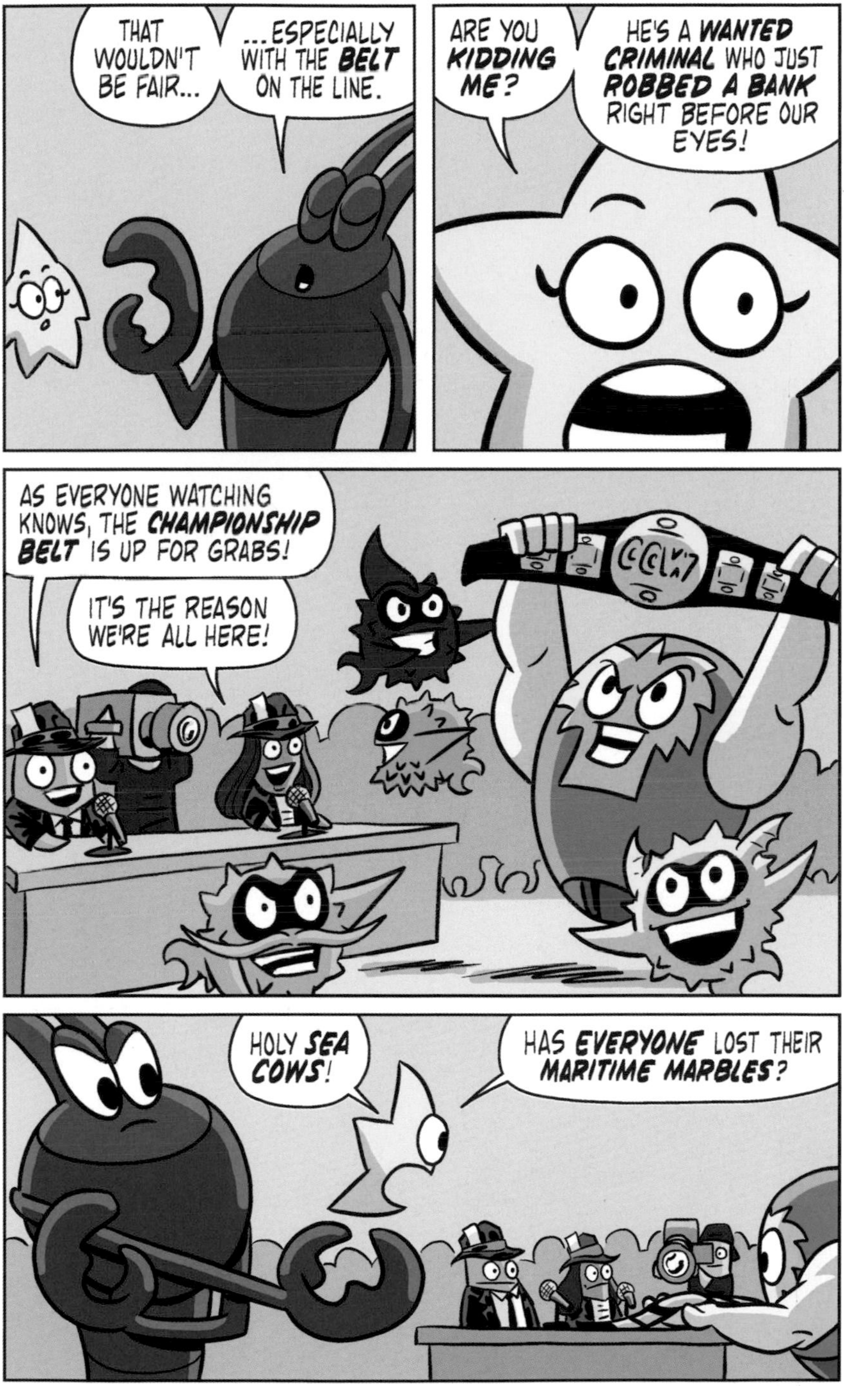
THAT WOULDN'T BE FAIR...
...ESPECIALLY WITH THE BELT ON THE LINE.
ARE YOU KIDDING ME?
HE'S A WANTED CRIMINAL WHO JUST ROBBED A BANK RIGHT BEFORE OUR EYES!
AS EVERYONE WATCHING KNOWS, THE CHAMPIONSHIP BELT IS UP FOR GRABS!
IT'S THE REASON WE'RE ALL HERE!
HOLY SEA COWS!
HAS EVERYONE LOST THEIR MARITIME MARBLES?

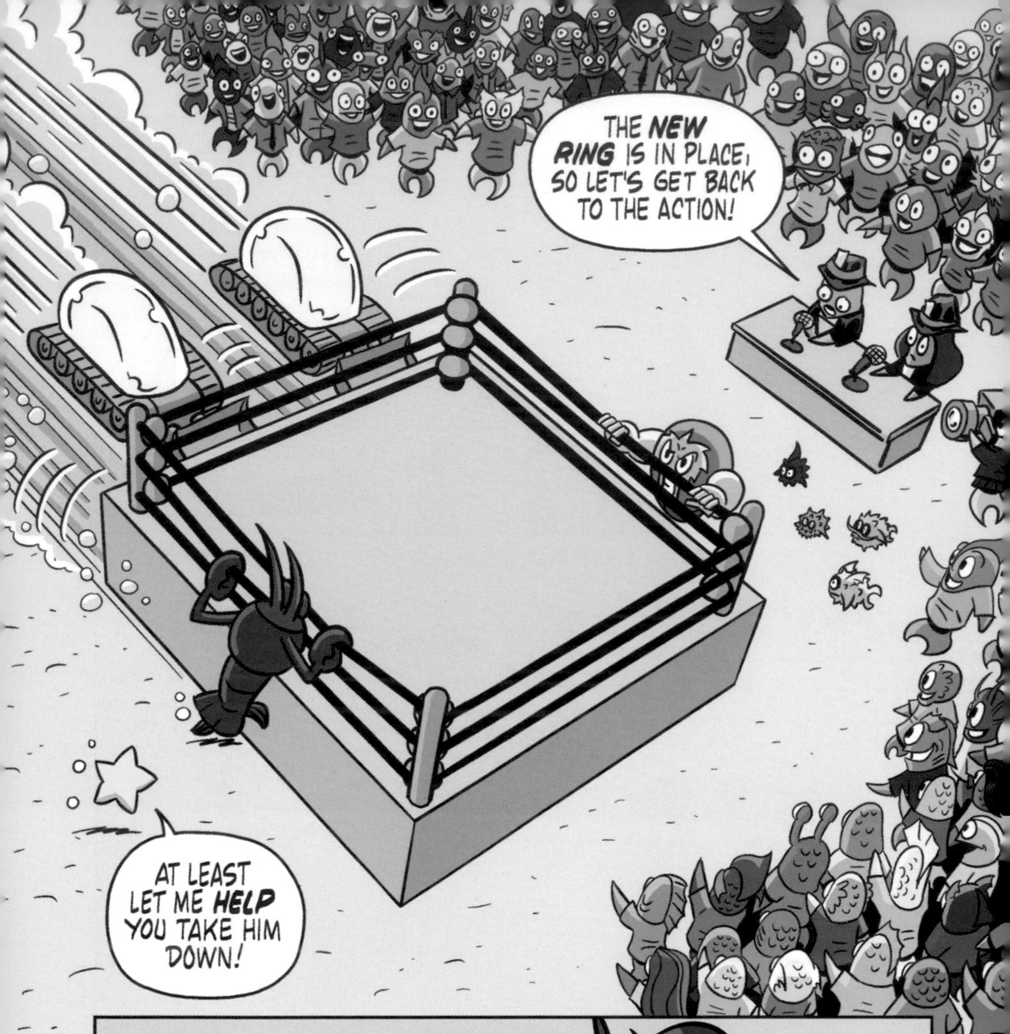
THE **NEW** **RING** IS IN PLACE, SO LET'S GET BACK TO THE ACTION!
AT LEAST LET ME **HELP** YOU TAKE HIM DOWN!

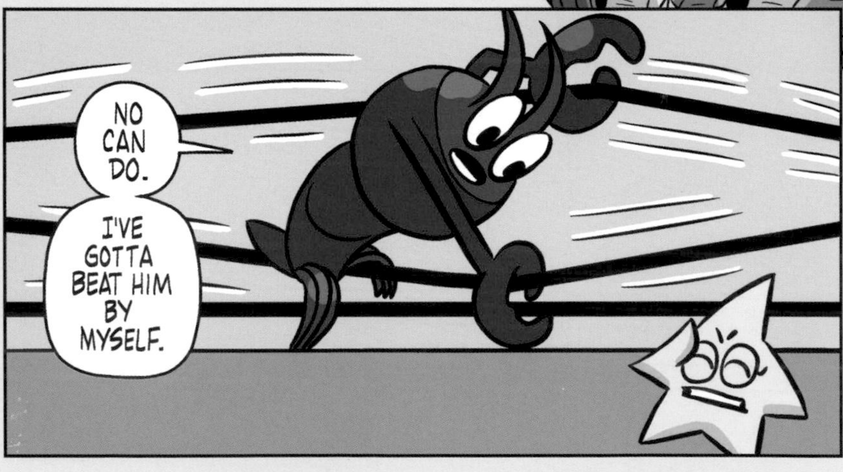
NO CAN DO.
I'VE GOTTA BEAT HIM BY MYSELF.

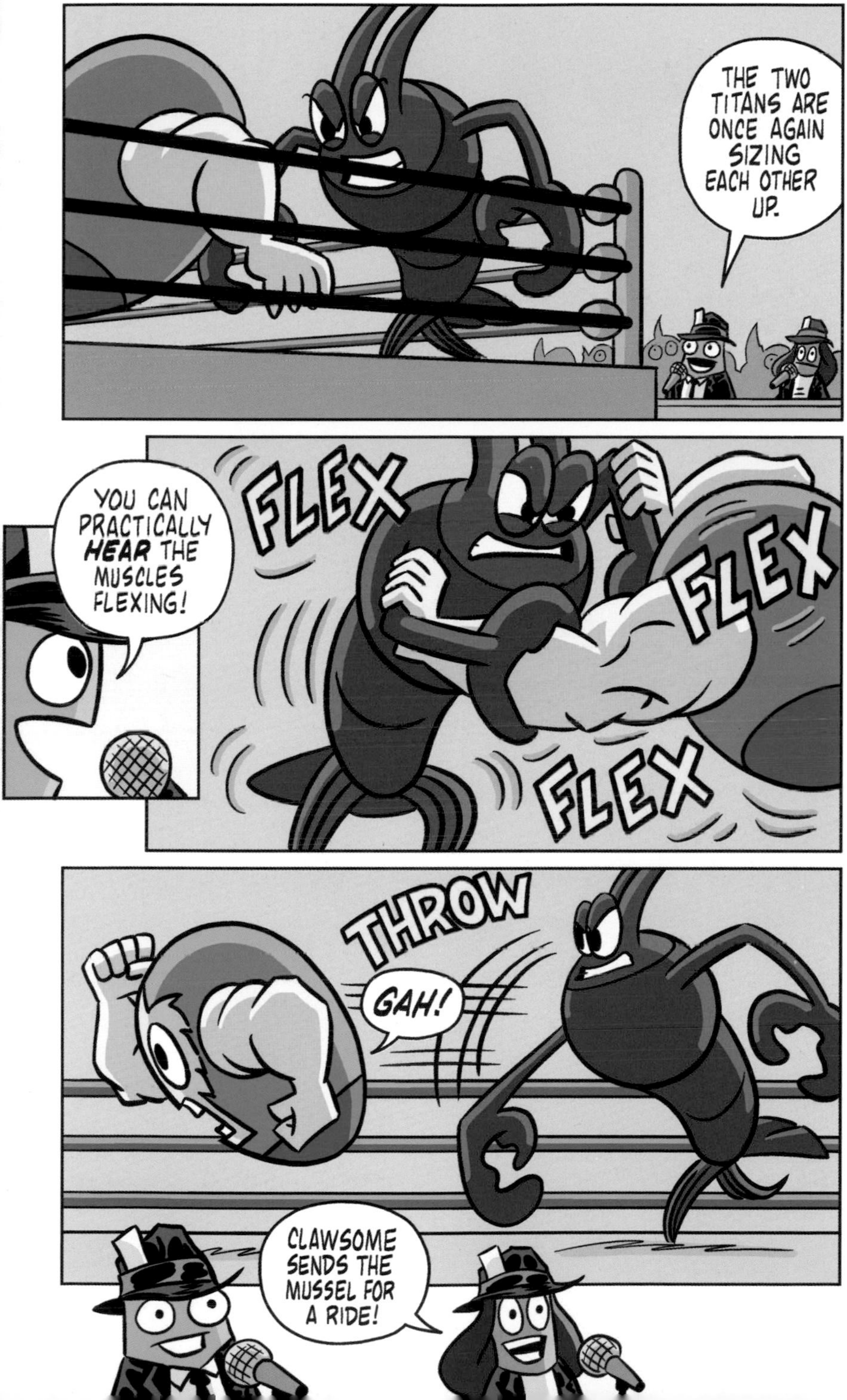
THE TWO TITANS ARE ONCE AGAIN SIZING EACH OTHER UP.
FLEX
YOU CAN PRACTICALLY HEAR THE MUSCLES FLEXING!
FLEX
FLEX
THROW
GAH!
CLAWSOME SENDS THE MUSSEL FOR A RIDE!

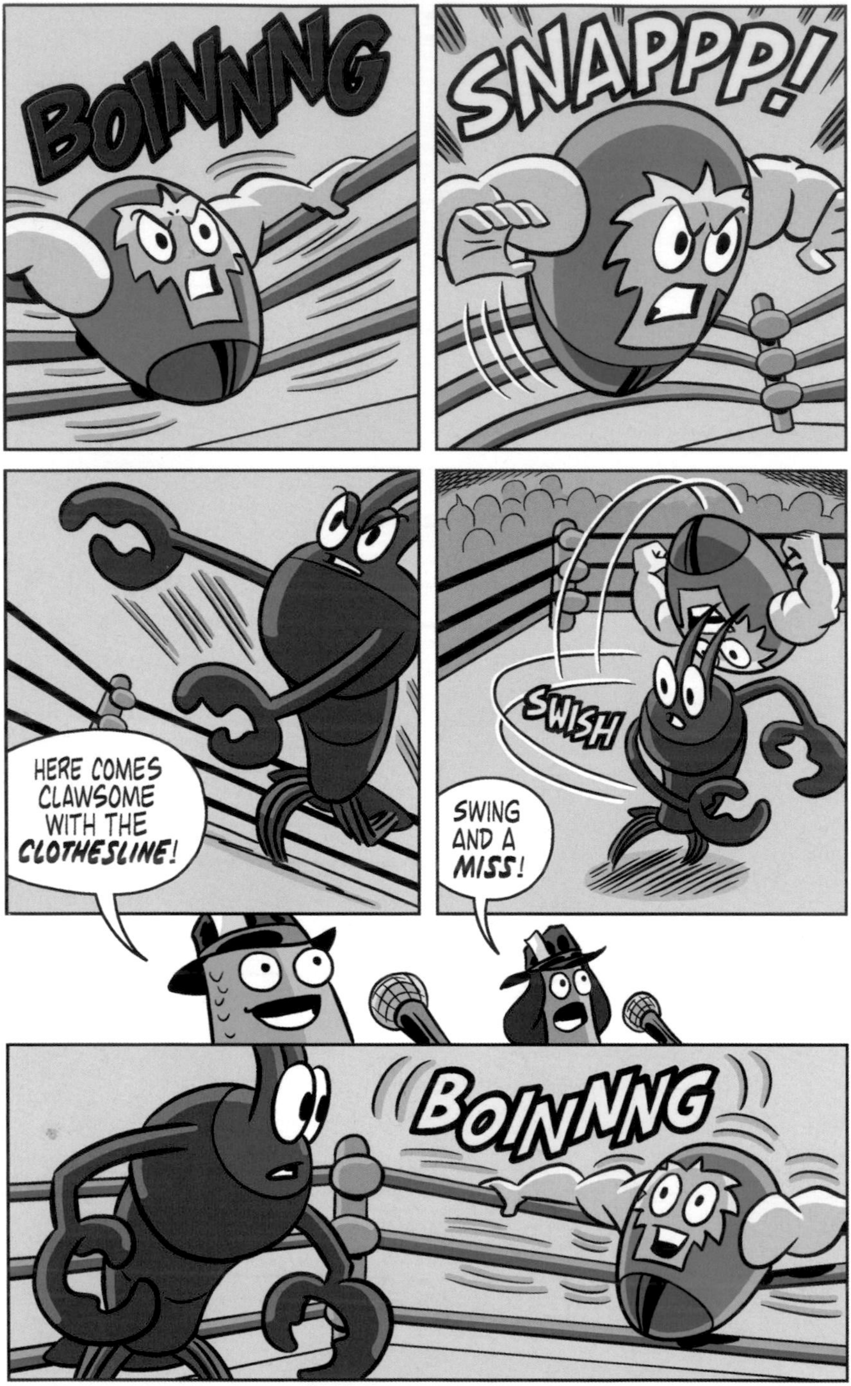
BOINNNG
SNAPPP!
HERE COMES CLAWSOME WITH THE CLOTHESLINE!
SWISH
SWING AND A MISS!
BOINNNG

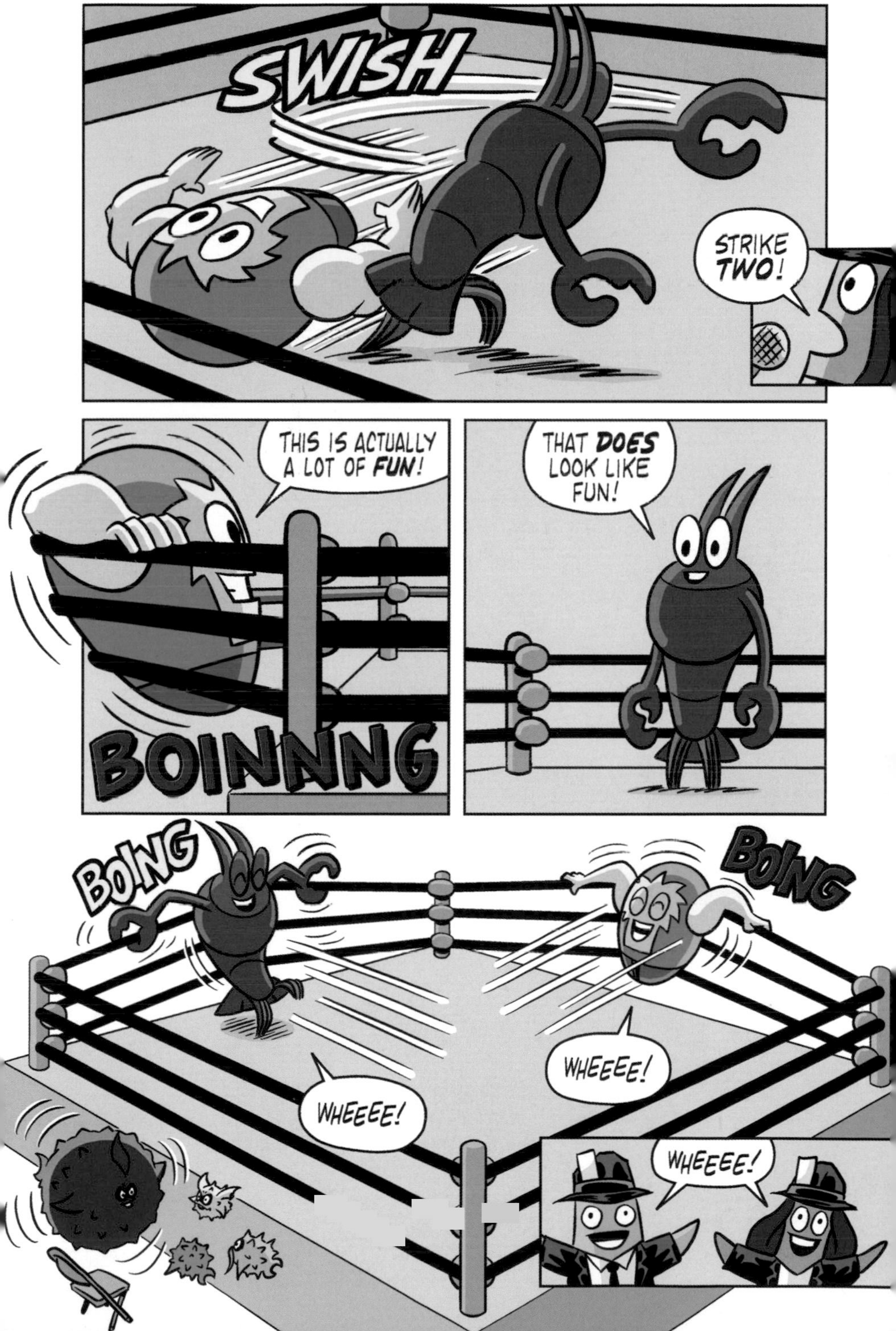
SWISH
STRIKE TWO!
THIS IS ACTUALLY A LOT OF FUN!
BOINNNG
THAT DOES LOOK LIKE FUN!
BOING
BOING
WHEEEE!
WHEEEE!
WHEEEE!

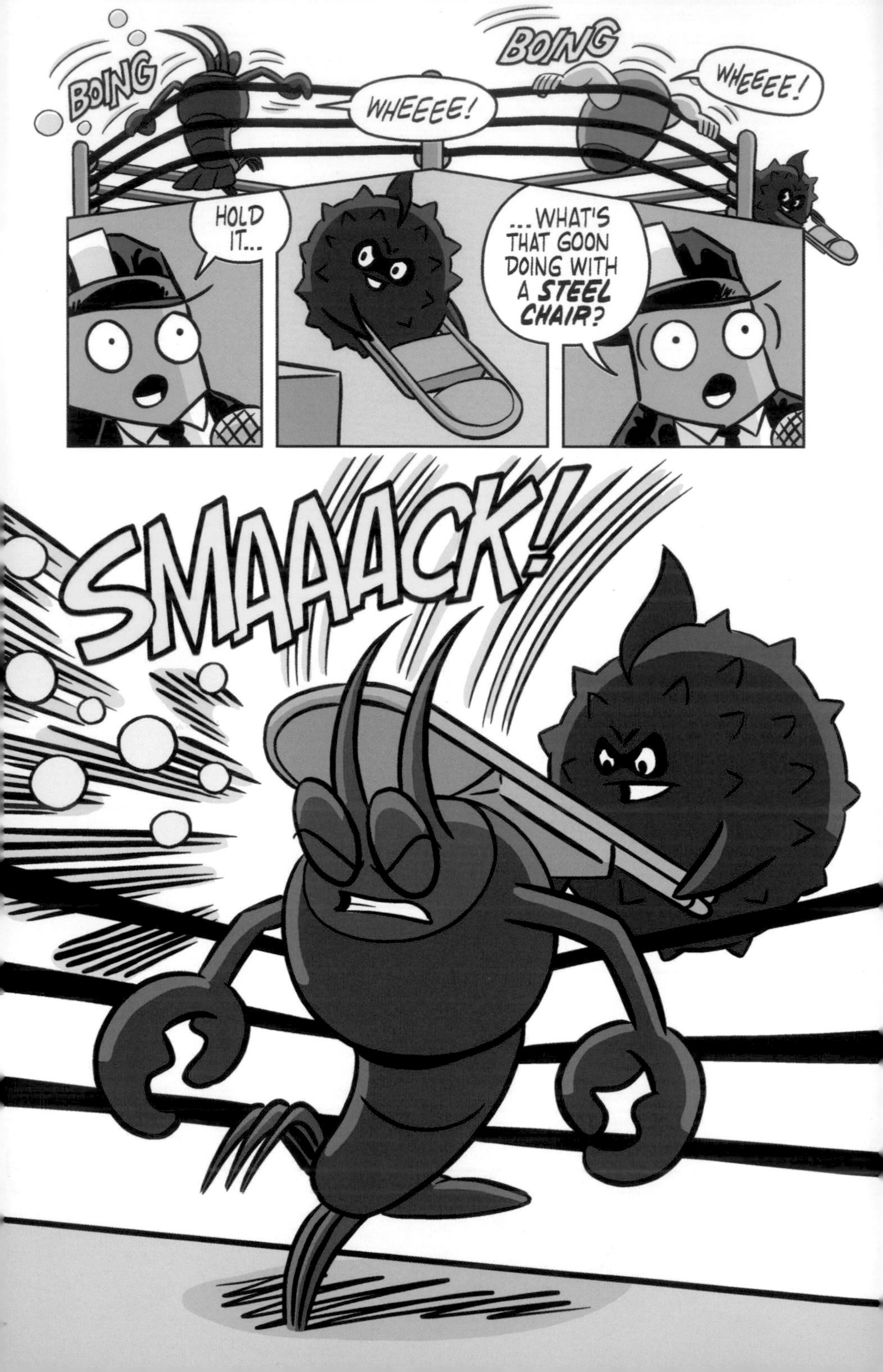
BOING
WHEEEEE!
BOING
WHEEEEE!
HOLD IT...
...WHAT'S THAT GOON DOING WITH A **STEEL CHAIR**?
SMAAACK!

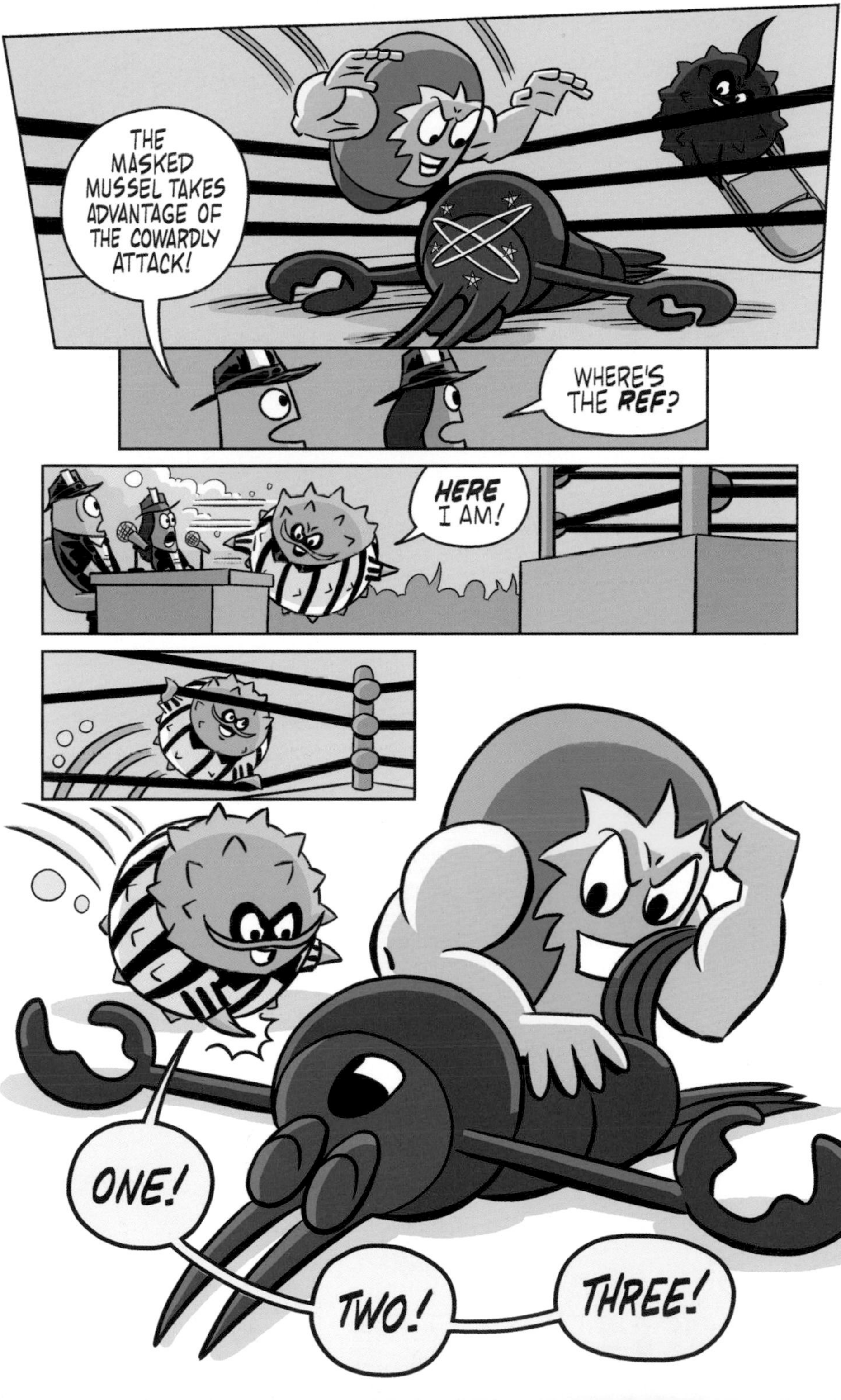
THE MASKED MUSSEL TAKES ADVANTAGE OF THE COWARDLY ATTACK!
WHERE'S THE **REF**?
HERE I AM!
ONE!
TWO!
THREE!

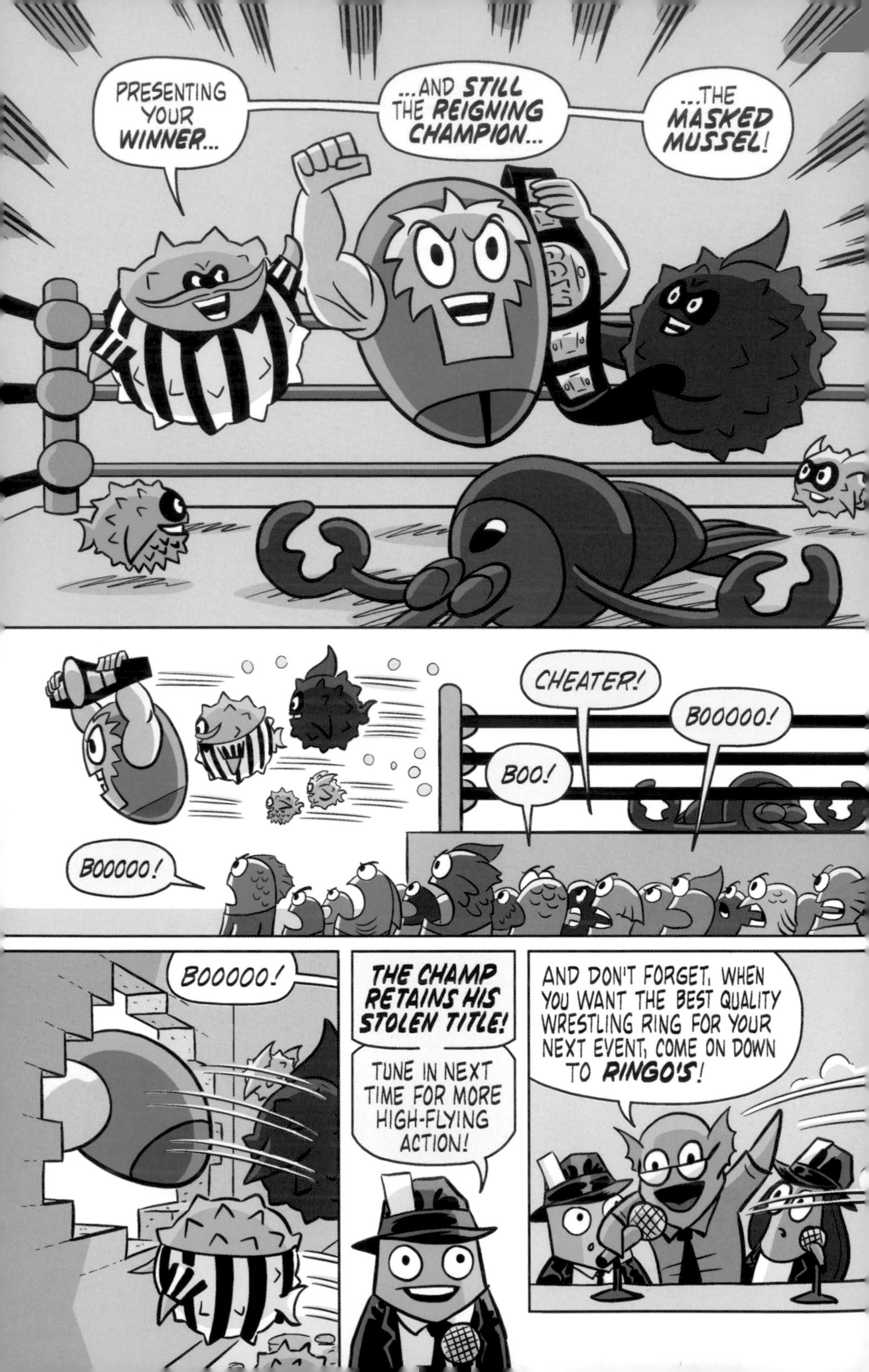
PRESENTING YOUR WINNER...
...AND STILL THE REIGNING CHAMPION...
...THE MASKED MUSSEL!
CHEATER!
BOOOOO!
BOO!
BOOOOO!
BOOOOO!
THE CHAMP RETAINS HIS STOLEN TITLE!
TUNE IN NEXT TIME FOR MORE HIGH-FLYING ACTION!
AND DON'T FORGET, WHEN YOU WANT THE BEST QUALITY WRESTLING RING FOR YOUR NEXT EVENT, COME ON DOWN TO RINGO'S!

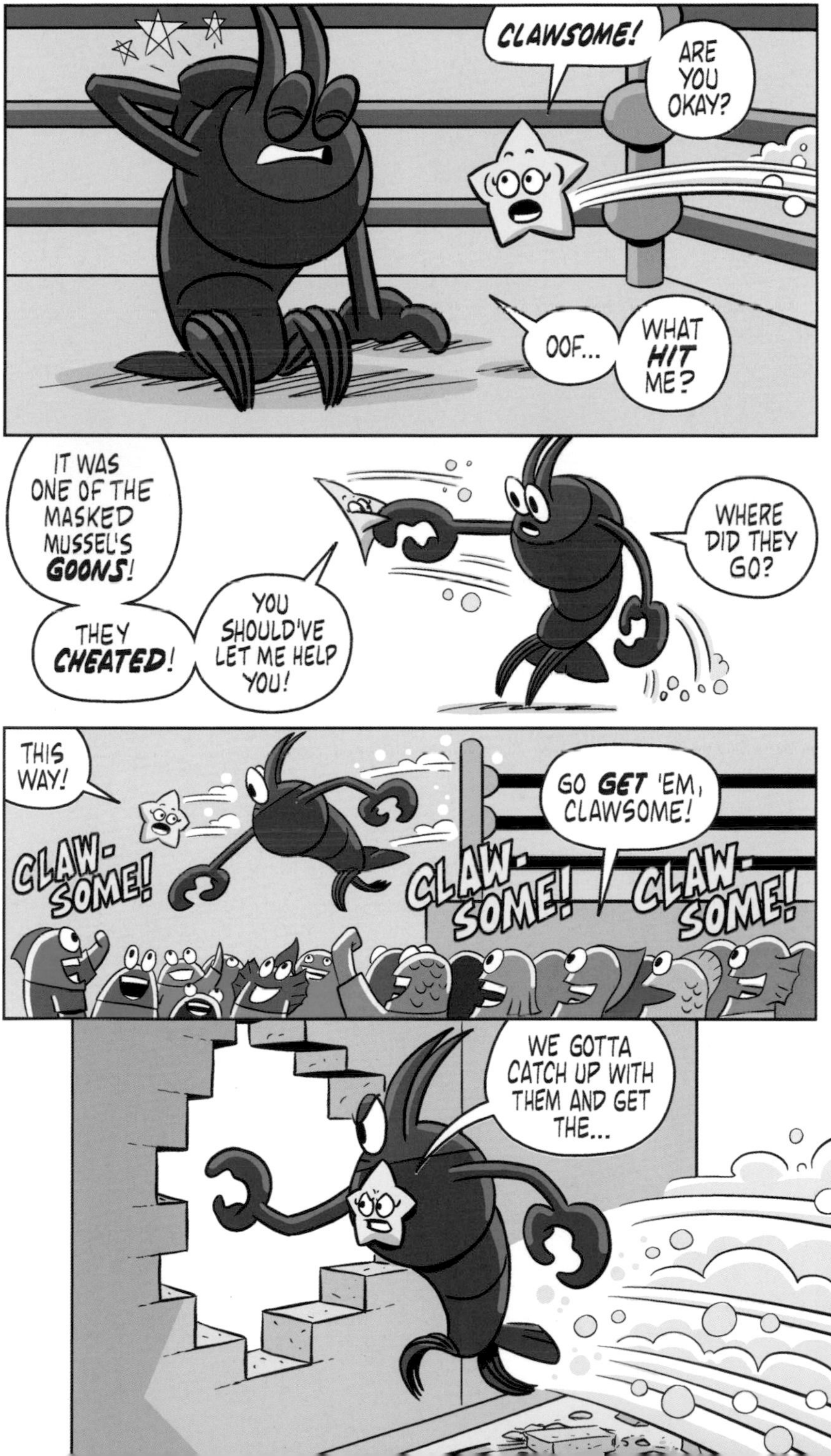

CLAWSOME!
ARE YOU OKAY?
OOF...
WHAT HIT ME?
IT WAS ONE OF THE MASKED MUSSEL'S GOONS!
THEY CHEATED!
YOU SHOULD'VE LET ME HELP YOU!
WHERE DID THEY GO?
THIS WAY!
GO GET 'EM, CLAWSOME!
CLAW-SOME!
CLAW-SOME!
CLAW-SOME!
WE GOTTA CATCH UP WITH THEM AND GET THE...

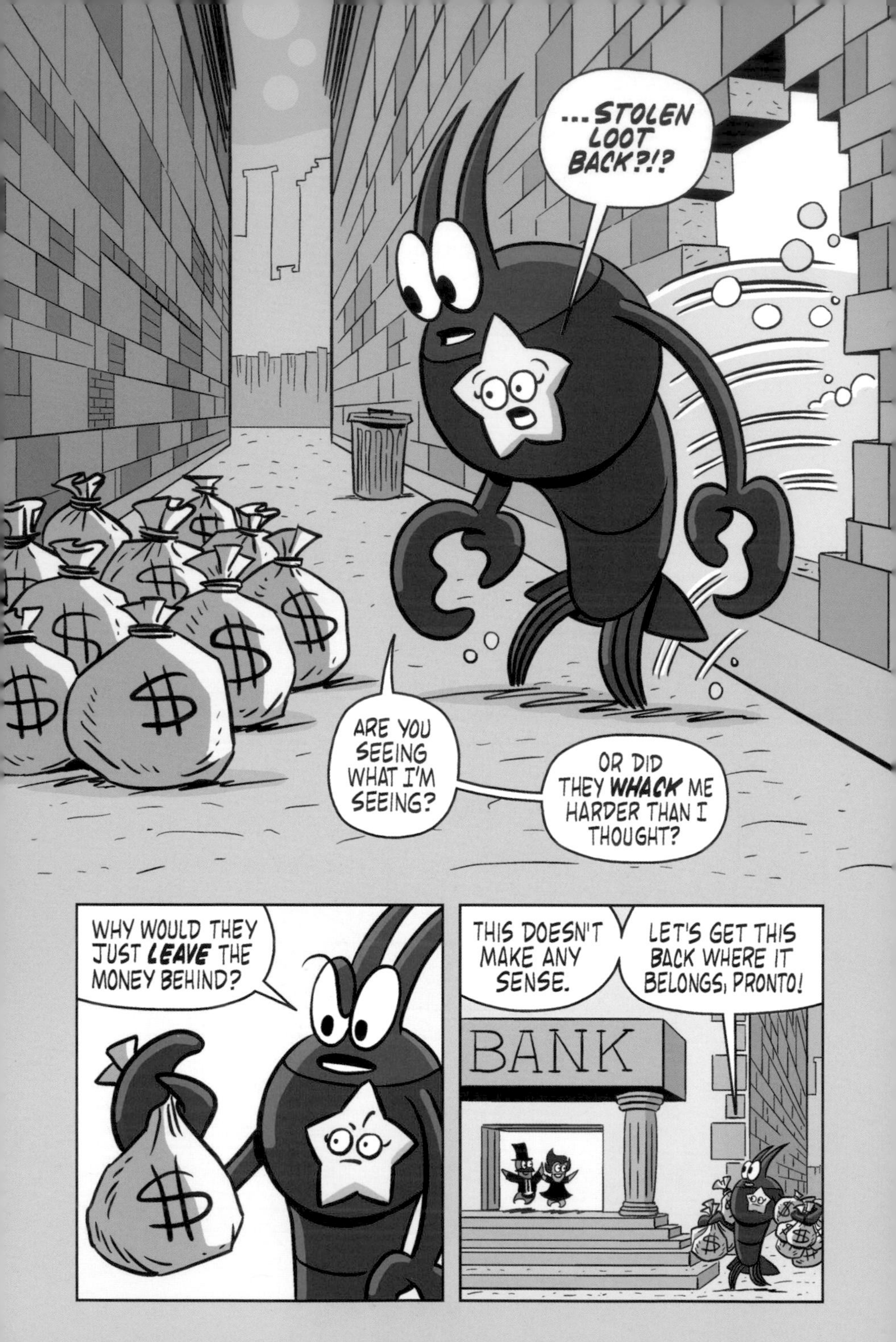
...STOLEN LOOT BACK?!?
ARE YOU SEEING WHAT I'M SEEING?
OR DID THEY WHACK ME HARDER THAN I THOUGHT?
WHY WOULD THEY JUST LEAVE THE MONEY BEHIND?
THIS DOESN'T MAKE ANY SENSE.
LET'S GET THIS BACK WHERE IT BELONGS, PRONTO!
BANK

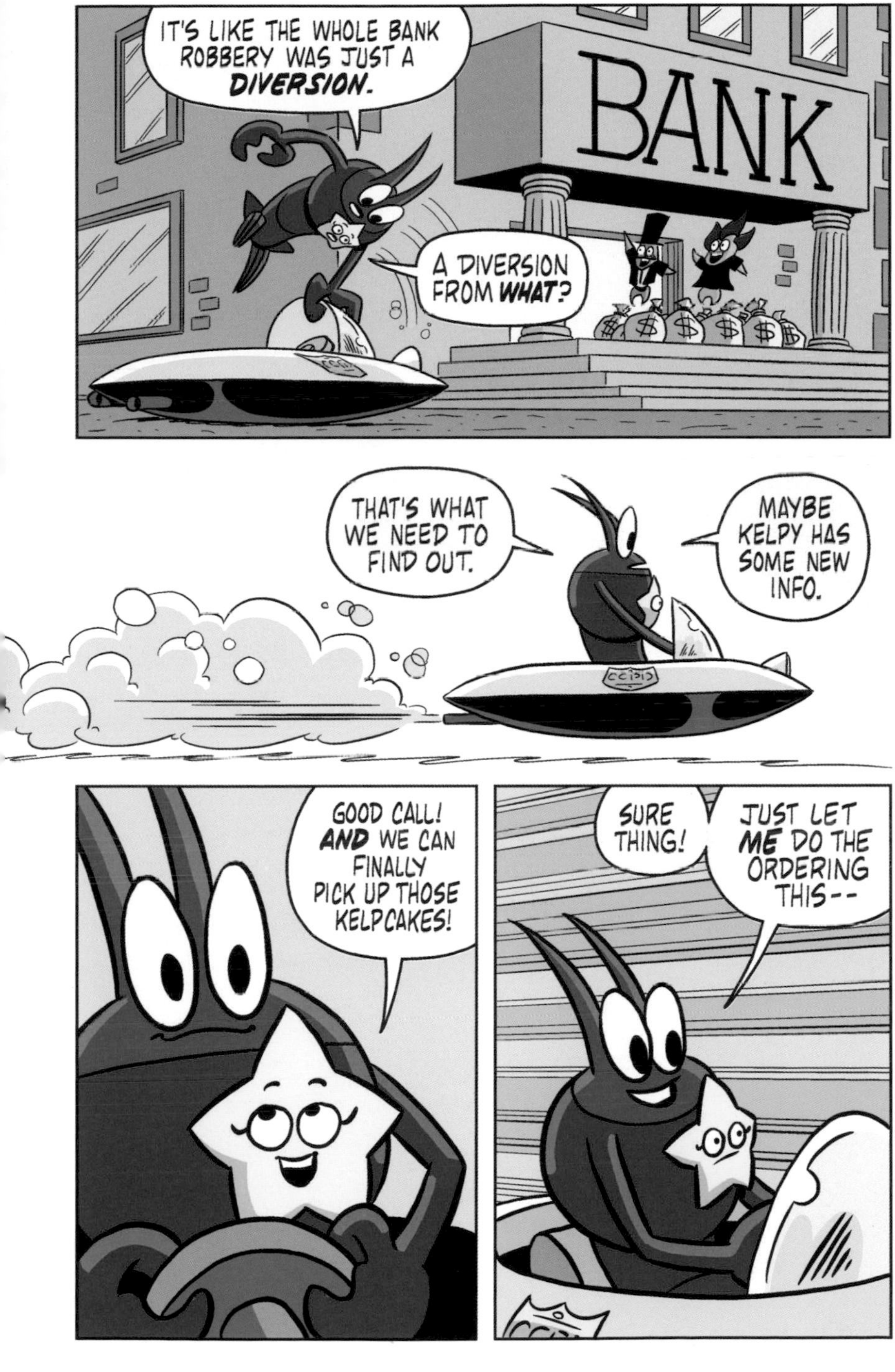

IT'S LIKE THE WHOLE BANK ROBBERY WAS JUST A DIVERSION.
BANK
A DIVERSION FROM WHAT?
THAT'S WHAT WE NEED TO FIND OUT.
MAYBE KELPY HAS SOME NEW INFO.
GOOD CALL! AND WE CAN FINALLY PICK UP THOSE KELPCAKES!
SURE THING!
JUST LET ME DO THE ORDERING THIS--

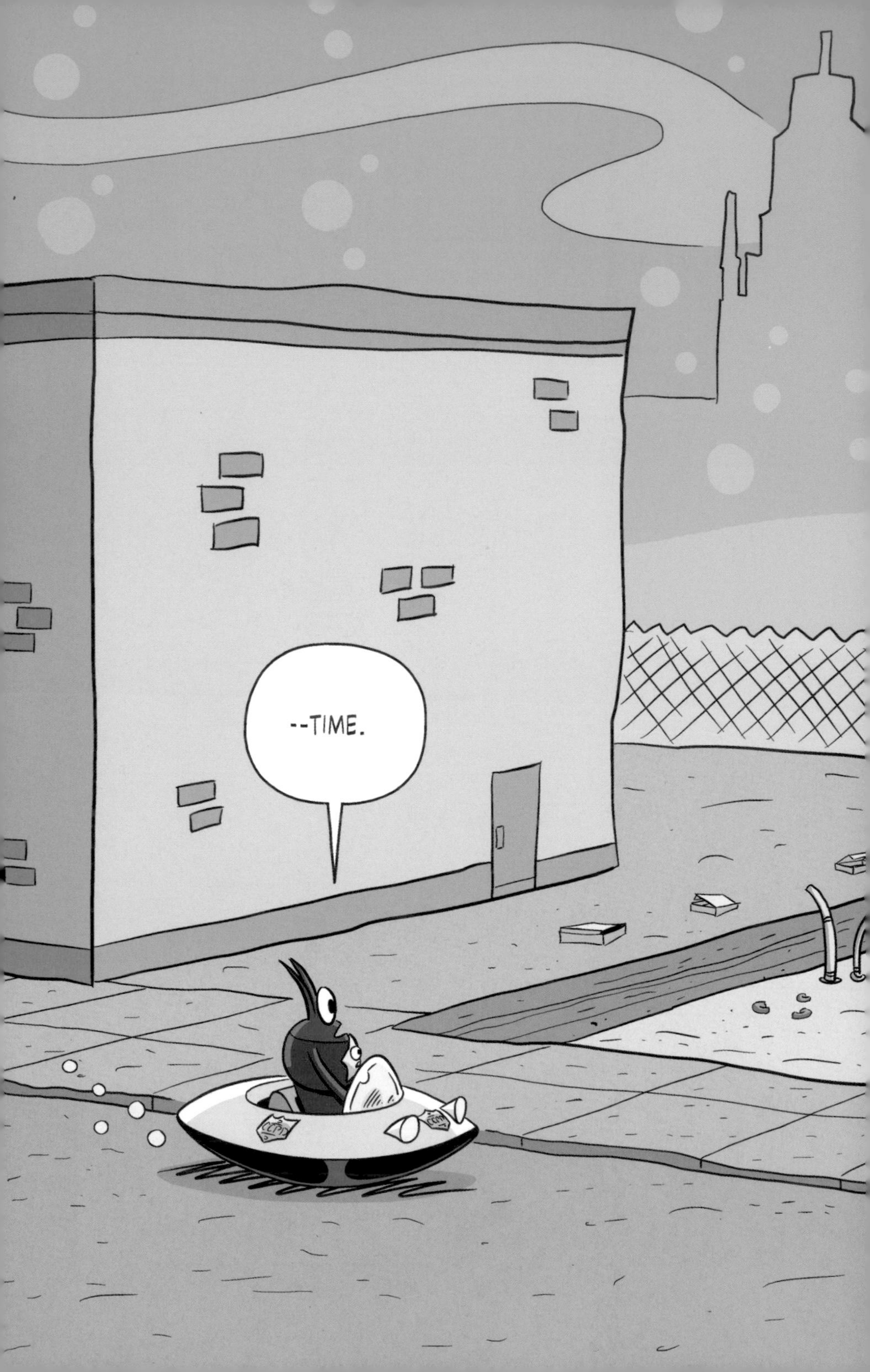
--TIME.

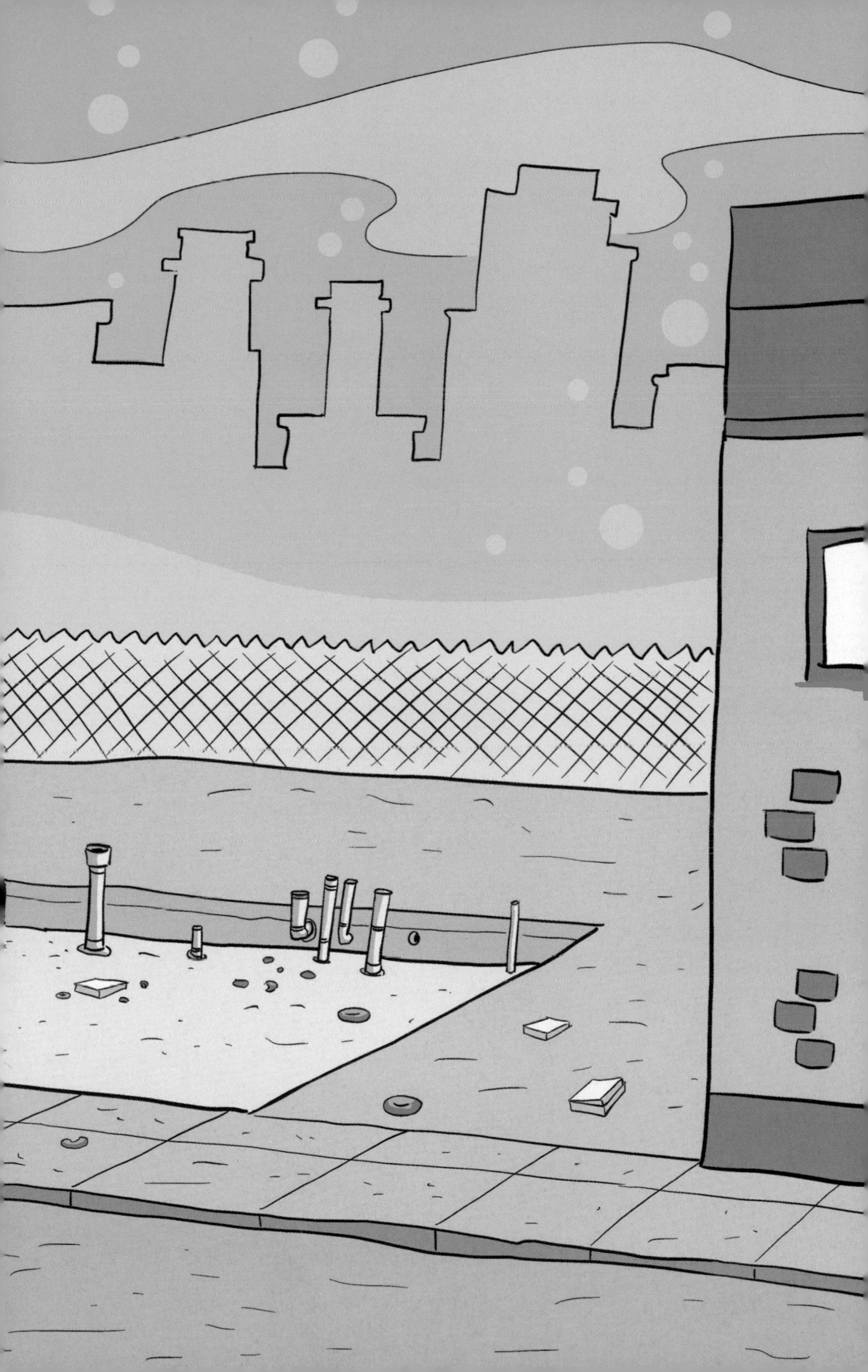

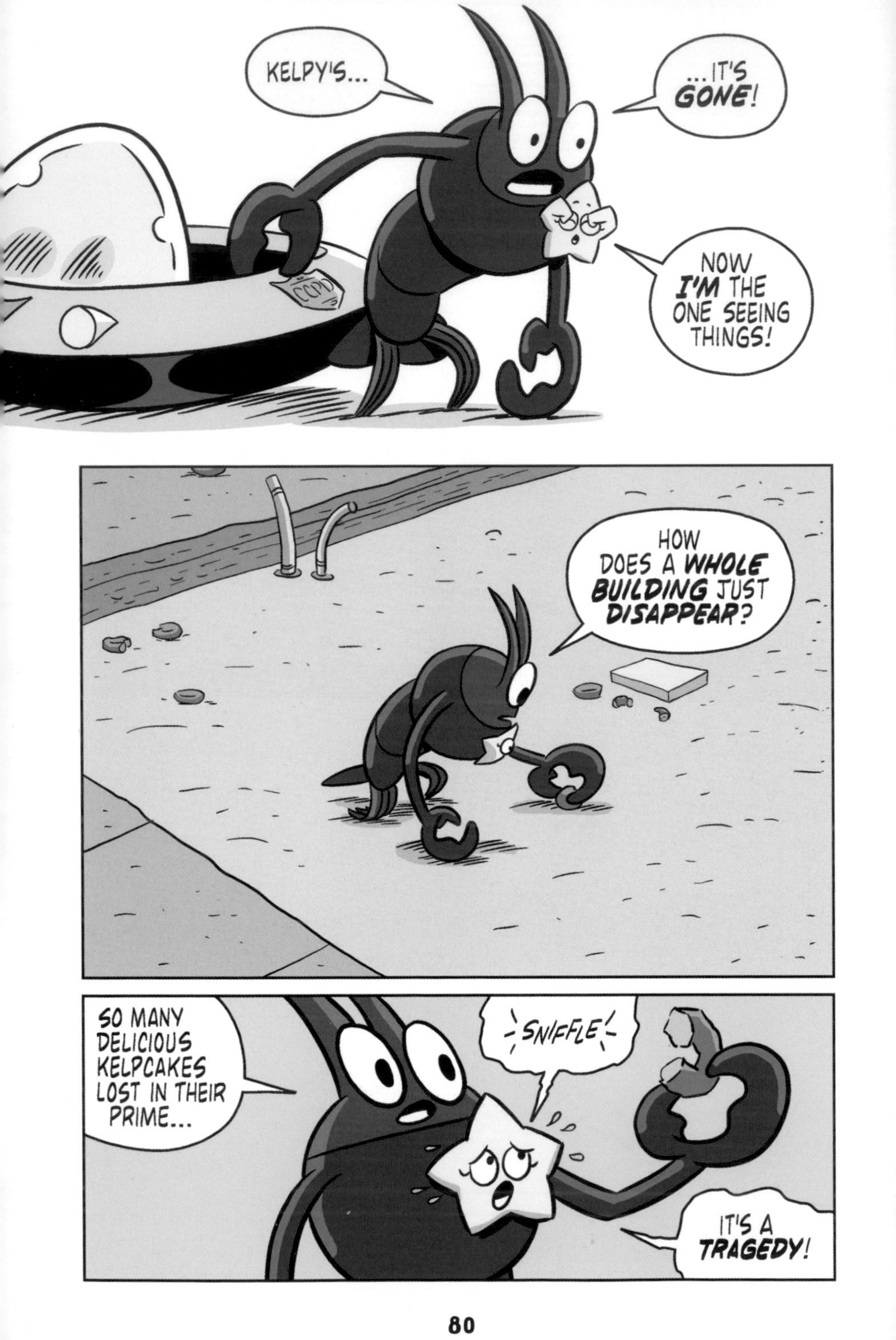
KELPY'S...
...IT'S GONE!
NOW I'M THE ONE SEEING THINGS!
CCPD
HOW DOES A WHOLE BUILDING JUST DISAPPEAR?
SO MANY DELICIOUS KELPCAKES LOST IN THEIR PRIME...
SNIFFLE
IT'S A TRAGEDY!

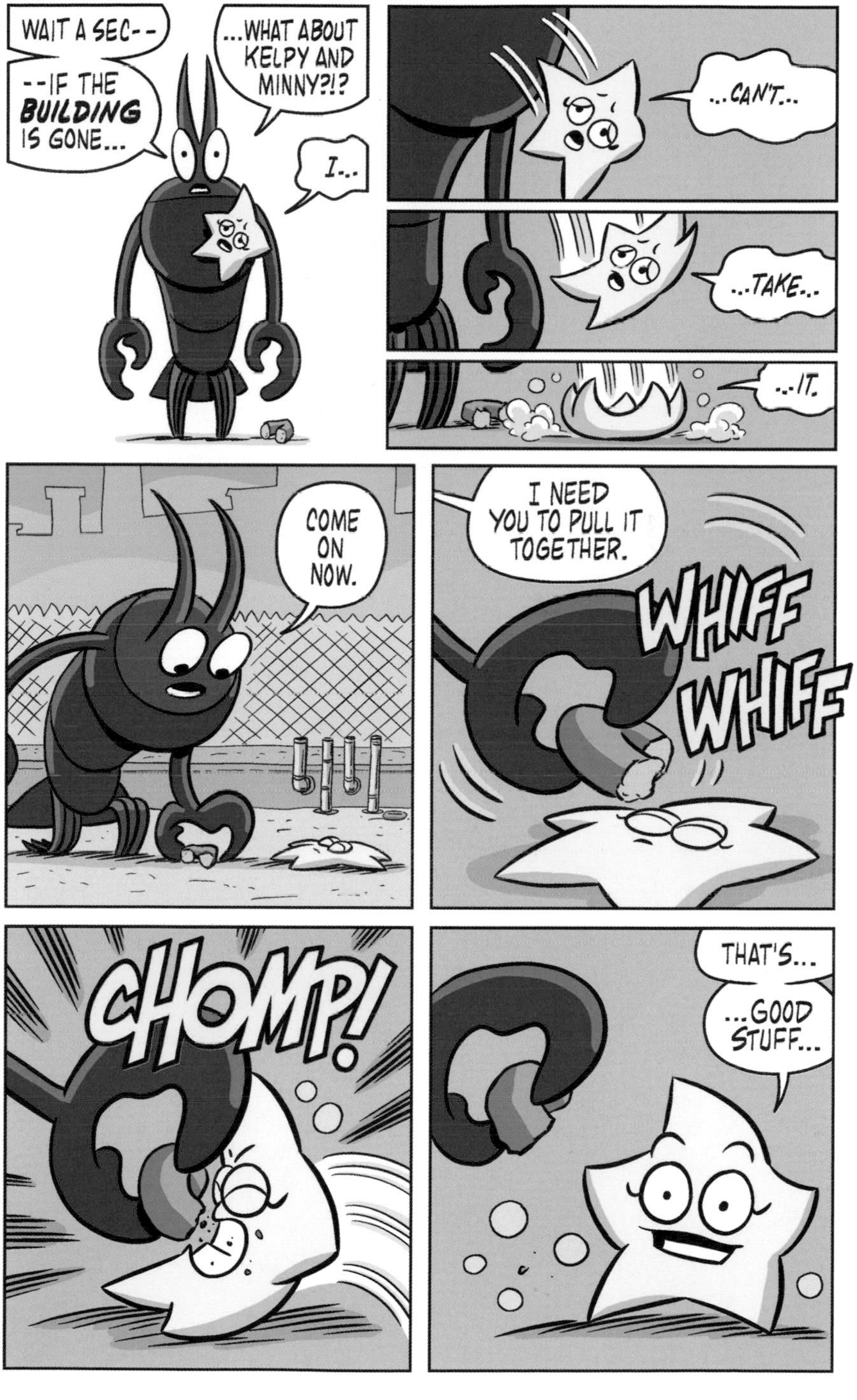
WAIT A SEC--
--IF THE BUILDING IS GONE...
...WHAT ABOUT KELPY AND MINNY?!?
I...
...CAN'T...
...TAKE...
...IT.
COME ON NOW.
I NEED YOU TO PULL IT TOGETHER.
WHIFF
WHIFF
CHOMP!
THAT'S...
...GOOD STUFF...

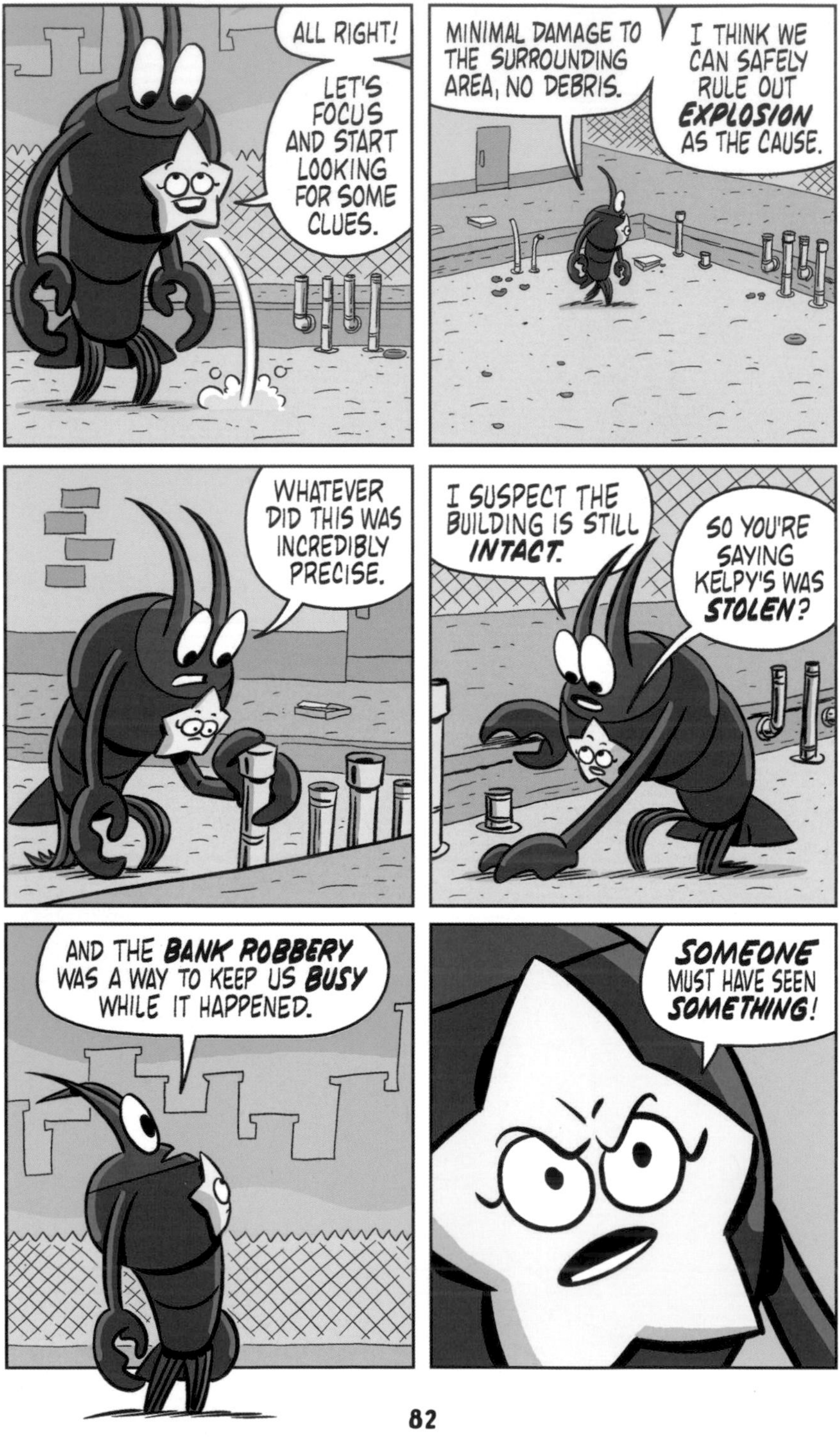
ALL RIGHT!
LET'S FOCUS AND START LOOKING FOR SOME CLUES.
MINIMAL DAMAGE TO THE SURROUNDING AREA, NO DEBRIS.
I THINK WE CAN SAFELY RULE OUT EXPLOSION AS THE CAUSE.
WHATEVER DID THIS WAS INCREDIBLY PRECISE.
I SUSPECT THE BUILDING IS STILL INTACT.
SO YOU'RE SAYING KELPY'S WAS STOLEN?
AND THE BANK ROBBERY WAS A WAY TO KEEP US BUSY WHILE IT HAPPENED.
SOMEONE MUST HAVE SEEN SOMETHING!

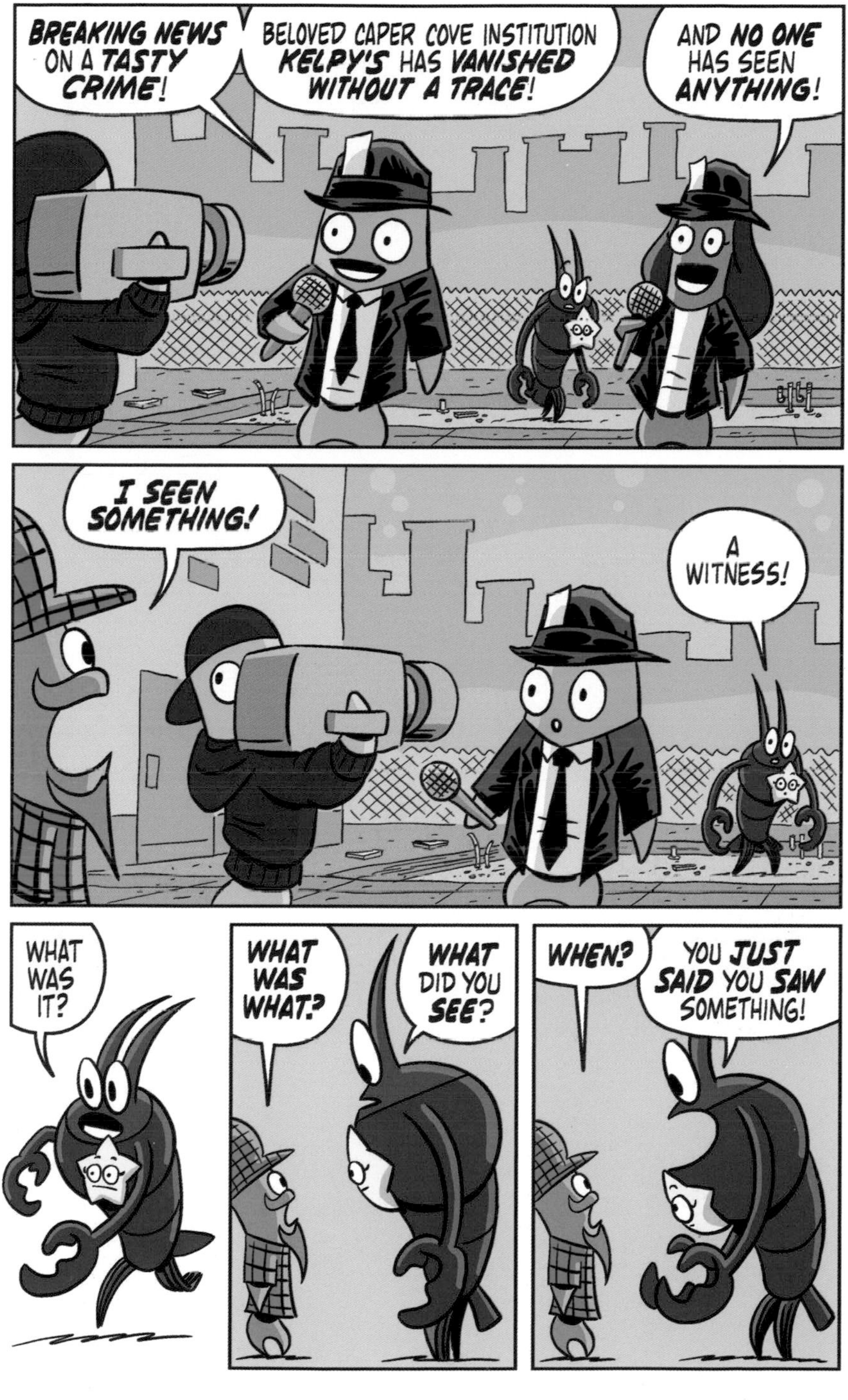

BREAKING NEWS ON A TASTY CRIME!
BELOVED CAPER COVE INSTITUTION KELPY'S HAS VANISHED WITHOUT A TRACE!
AND NO ONE HAS SEEN ANYTHING!
I SEEN SOMETHING!
A WITNESS!
WHAT WAS IT?
WHAT WAS WHAT?
WHAT DID YOU SEE?
WHEN?
YOU JUST SAID YOU SAW SOMETHING!

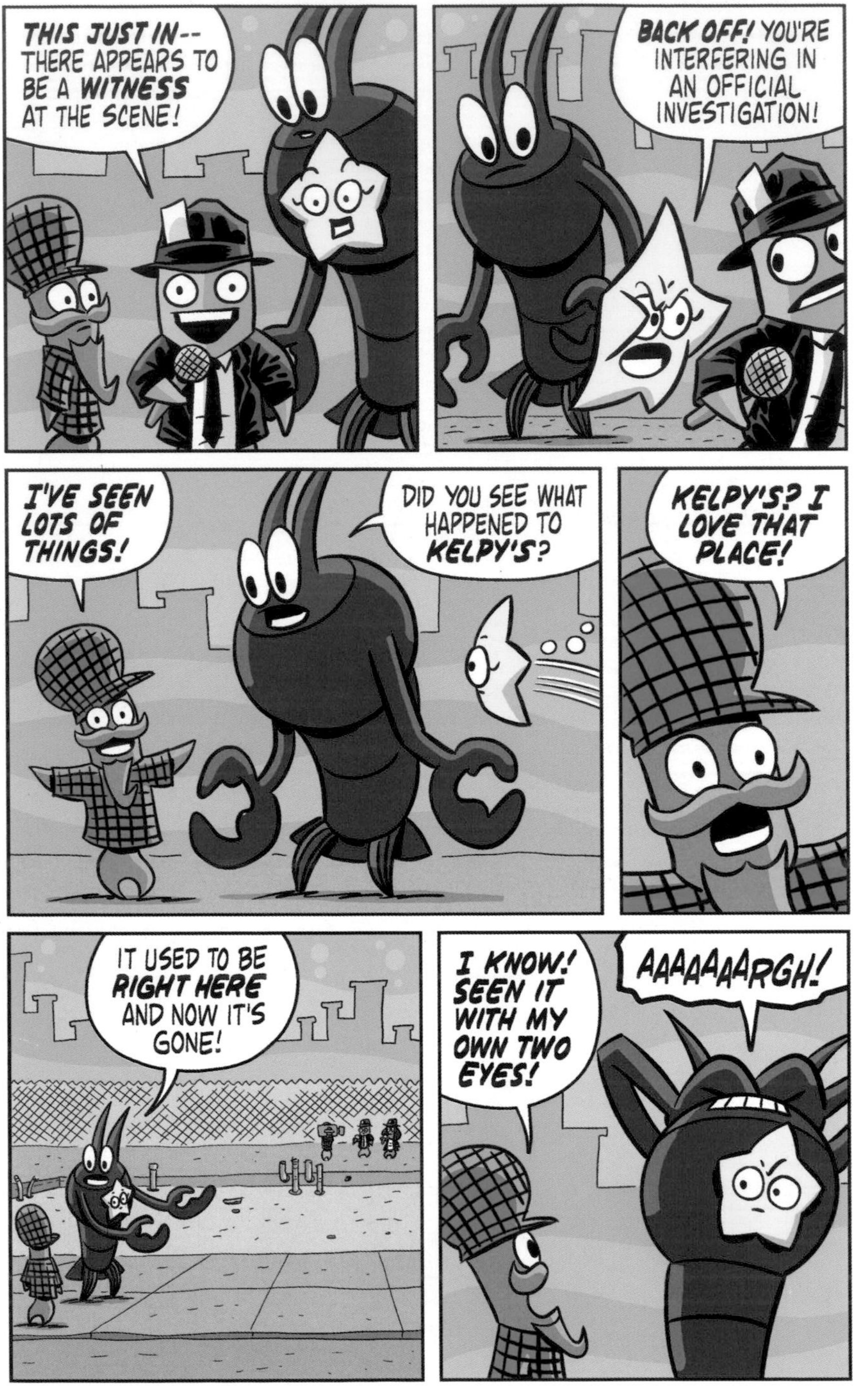
THIS JUST IN-- THERE APPEARS TO BE A WITNESS AT THE SCENE!
BACK OFF! YOU'RE INTERFERING IN AN OFFICIAL INVESTIGATION!
I'VE SEEN LOTS OF THINGS!
DID YOU SEE WHAT HAPPENED TO KELPY'S?
KELPY'S? I LOVE THAT PLACE!
IT USED TO BE RIGHT HERE AND NOW IT'S GONE!
I KNOW! SEEN IT WITH MY OWN TWO EYES!
AAAAAAARGH!

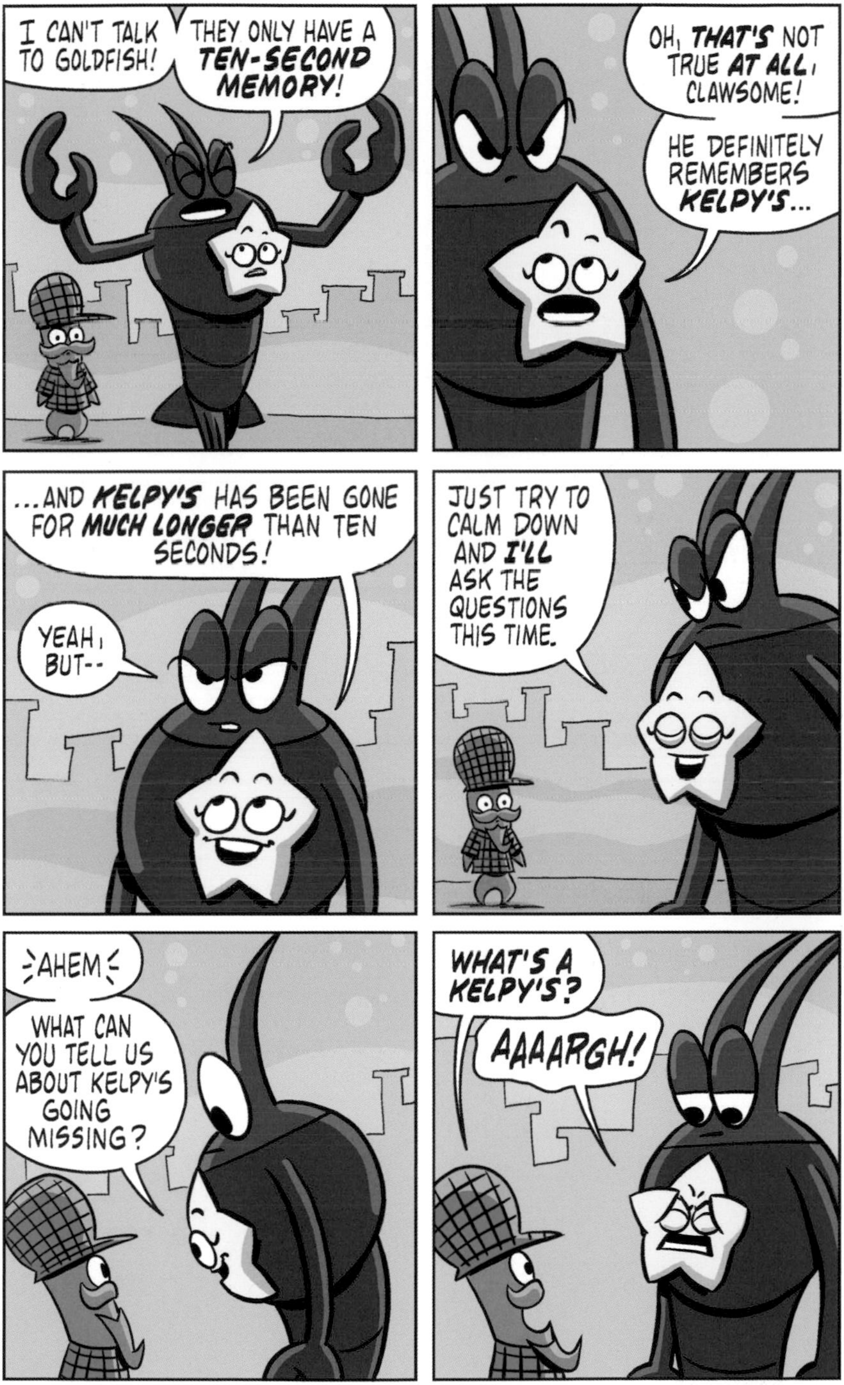
I CAN'T TALK TO GOLDFISH!
THEY ONLY HAVE A **TEN-SECOND MEMORY**!
OH, **THAT'S** NOT TRUE **AT ALL**, CLAWSOME!
HE DEFINITELY REMEMBERS **KELPY'S**...
...AND **KELPY'S** HAS BEEN GONE FOR **MUCH LONGER** THAN TEN SECONDS!
YEAH, BUT--
JUST TRY TO CALM DOWN AND **I'LL** ASK THE QUESTIONS THIS TIME.
AHEM
WHAT CAN YOU TELL US ABOUT KELPY'S GOING MISSING?
WHAT'S A KELPY'S?
AAAARGH!

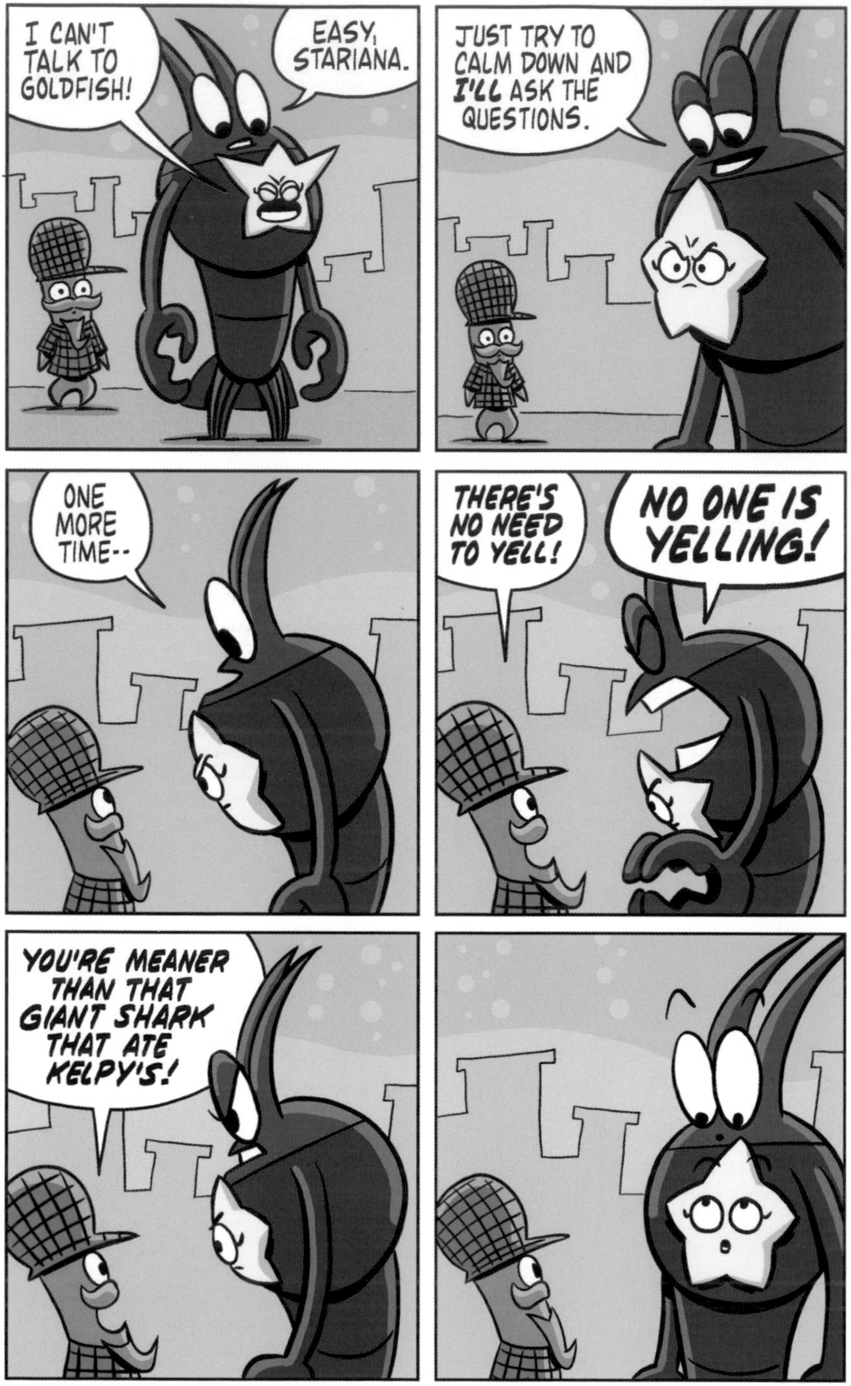
I CAN'T TALK TO GOLDFISH!
EASY, STARIANA.
JUST TRY TO CALM DOWN AND **I'LL** ASK THE QUESTIONS.
ONE MORE TIME--
THERE'S NO NEED TO YELL!
NO ONE IS YELLING!
YOU'RE MEANER THAN THAT GIANT SHARK THAT ATE KELPY'S!

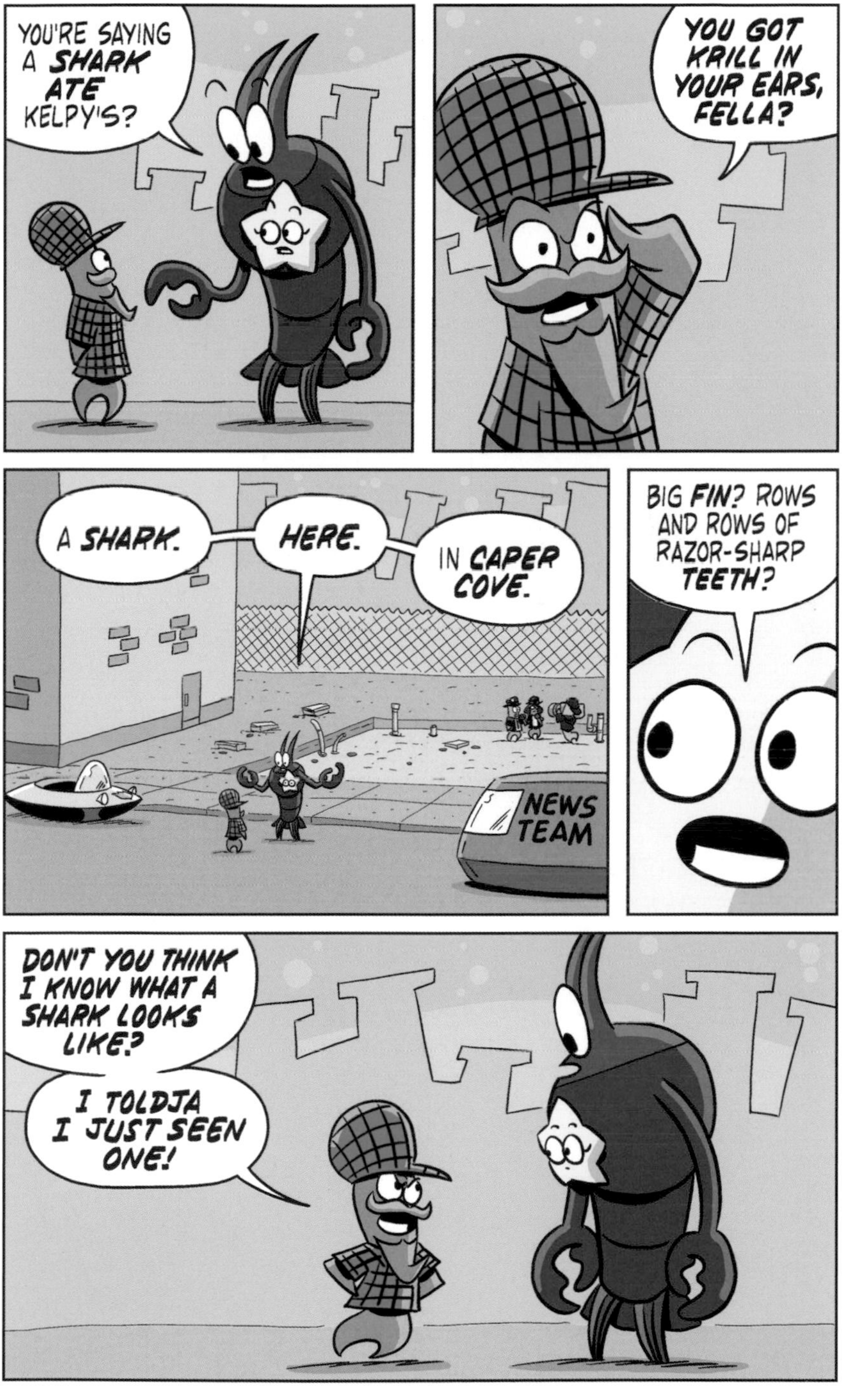
YOU'RE SAYING A SHARK ATE KELPY'S?
YOU GOT KRILL IN YOUR EARS, FELLA?
A SHARK.
HERE.
IN CAPER COVE.
NEWS TEAM
BIG FIN? ROWS AND ROWS OF RAZOR-SHARP TEETH?
DON'T YOU THINK I KNOW WHAT A SHARK LOOKS LIKE?
I TOLDJA I JUST SEEN ONE!

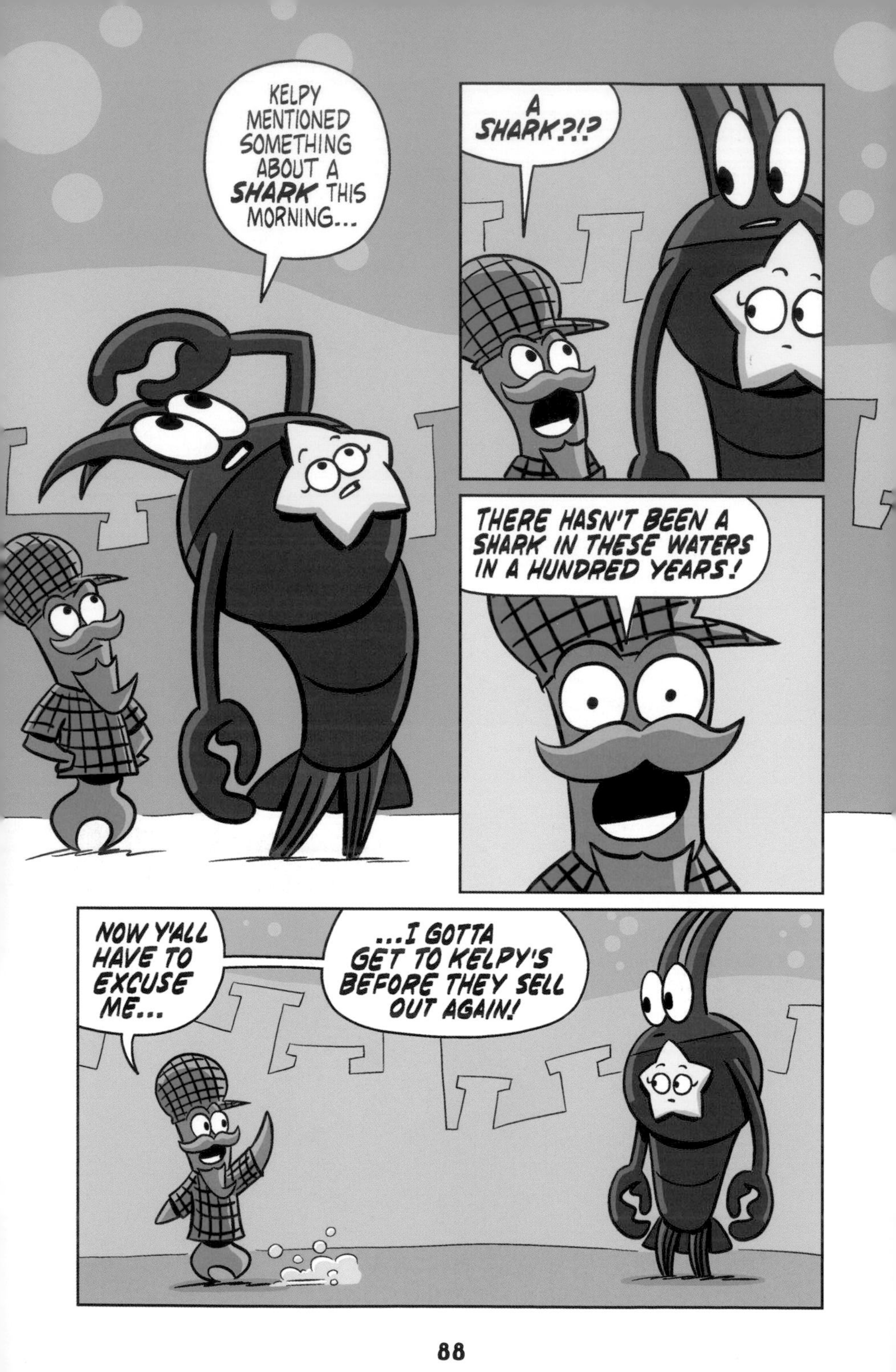
KELPY MENTIONED SOMETHING ABOUT A SHARK THIS MORNING...
A SHARK?!?
THERE HASN'T BEEN A SHARK IN THESE WATERS IN A HUNDRED YEARS!
NOW Y'ALL HAVE TO EXCUSE ME...
...I GOTTA GET TO KELPY'S BEFORE THEY SELL OUT AGAIN!

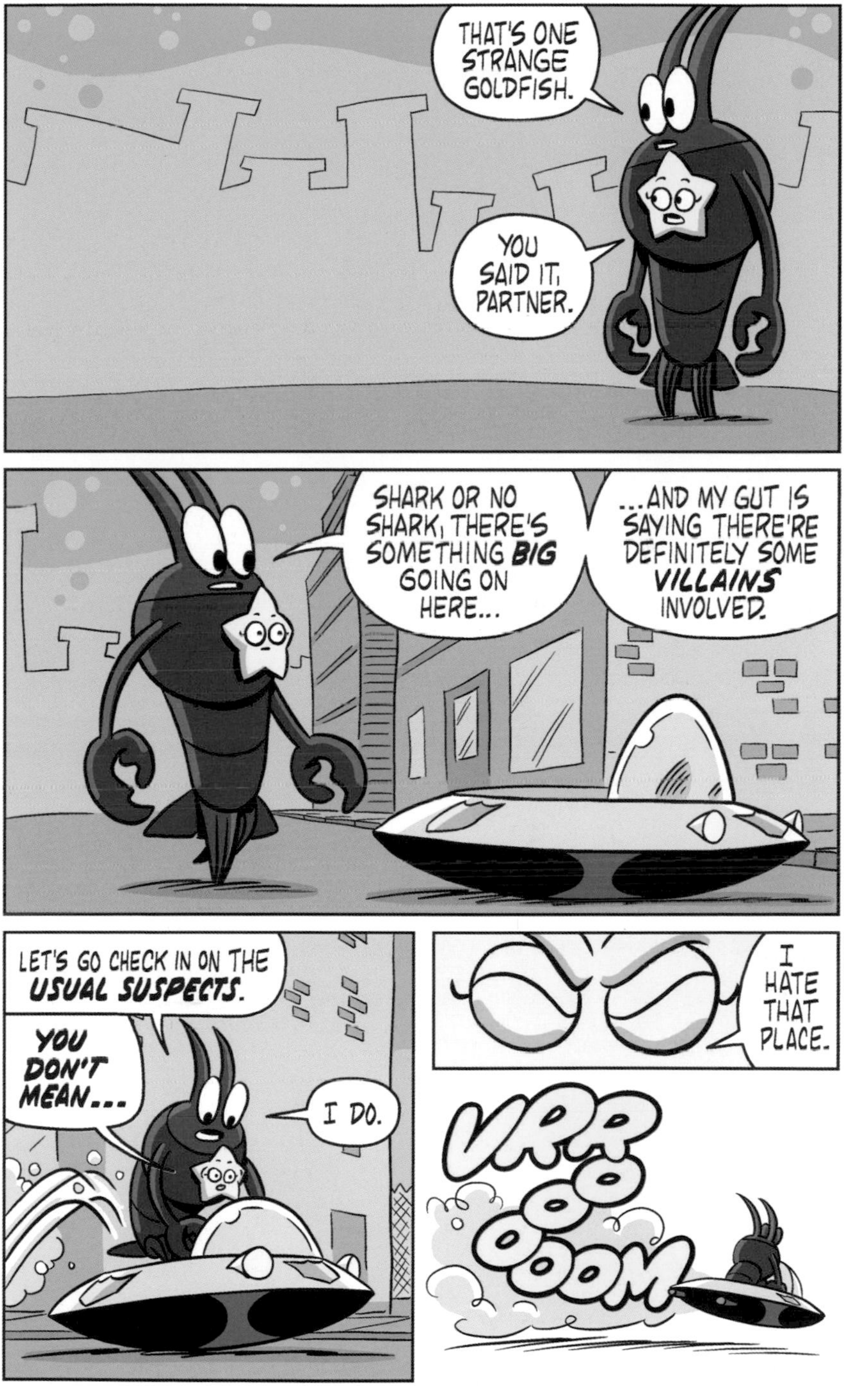
THAT'S ONE STRANGE GOLDFISH.
YOU SAID IT, PARTNER.
SHARK OR NO SHARK, THERE'S SOMETHING BIG GOING ON HERE...
...AND MY GUT IS SAYING THERE'RE DEFINITELY SOME VILLAINS INVOLVED.
LET'S GO CHECK IN ON THE USUAL SUSPECTS.
YOU DON'T MEAN...
I DO.
I HATE THAT PLACE.
VRROOOOOOM

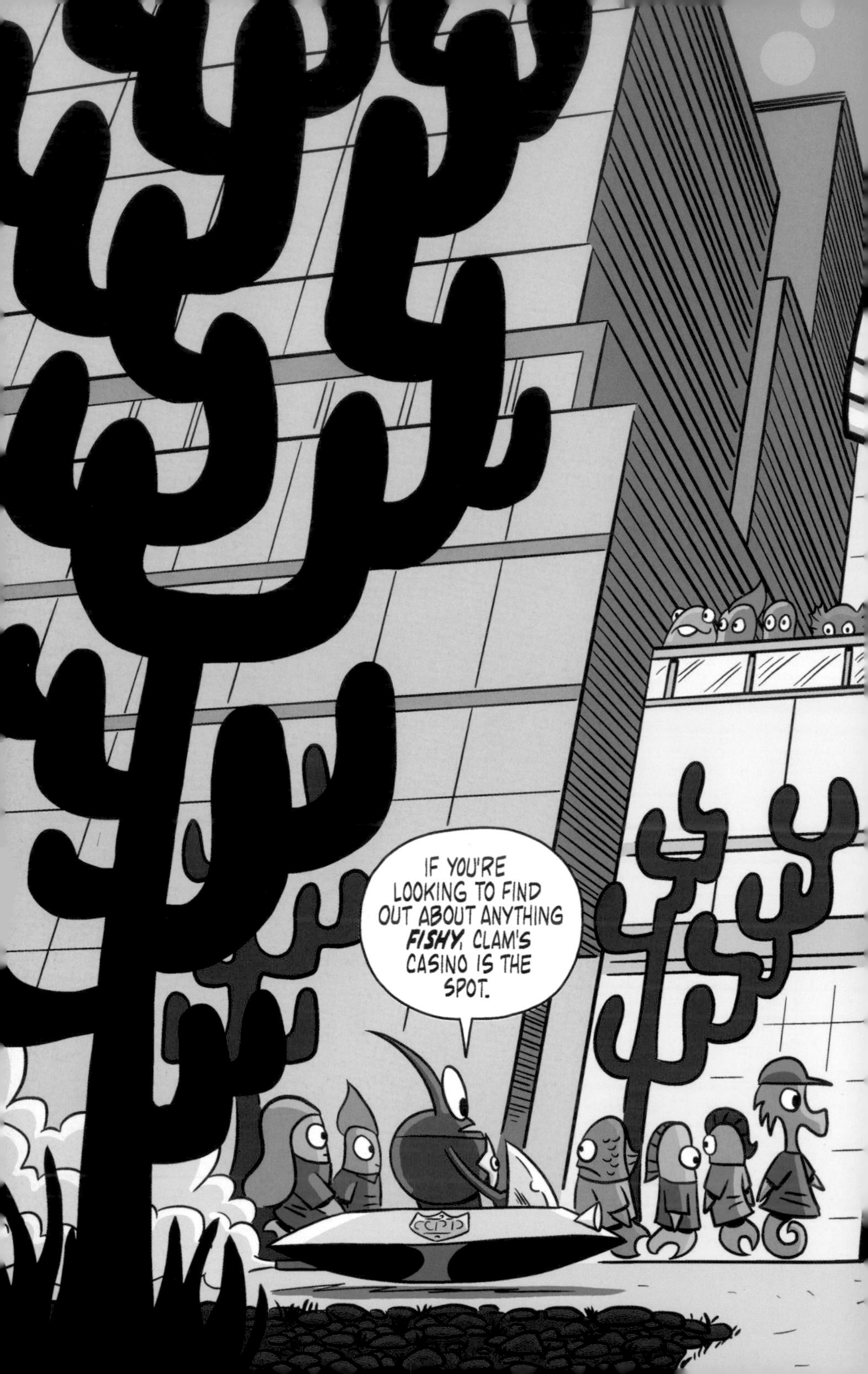
IF YOU'RE LOOKING TO FIND OUT ABOUT ANYTHING *FISHY*, CLAM'S CASINO IS THE SPOT.

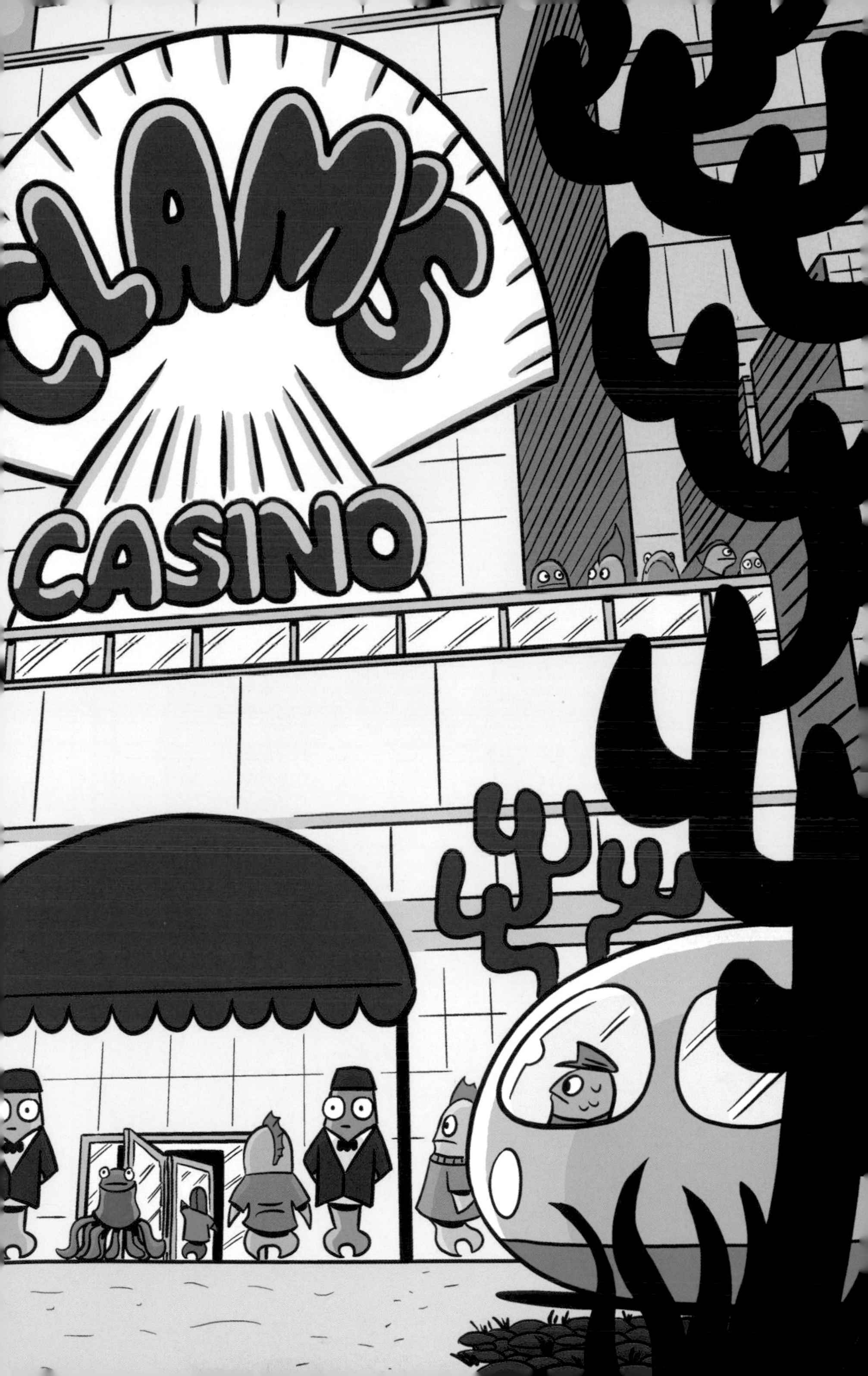
CLAM'S
CASINO

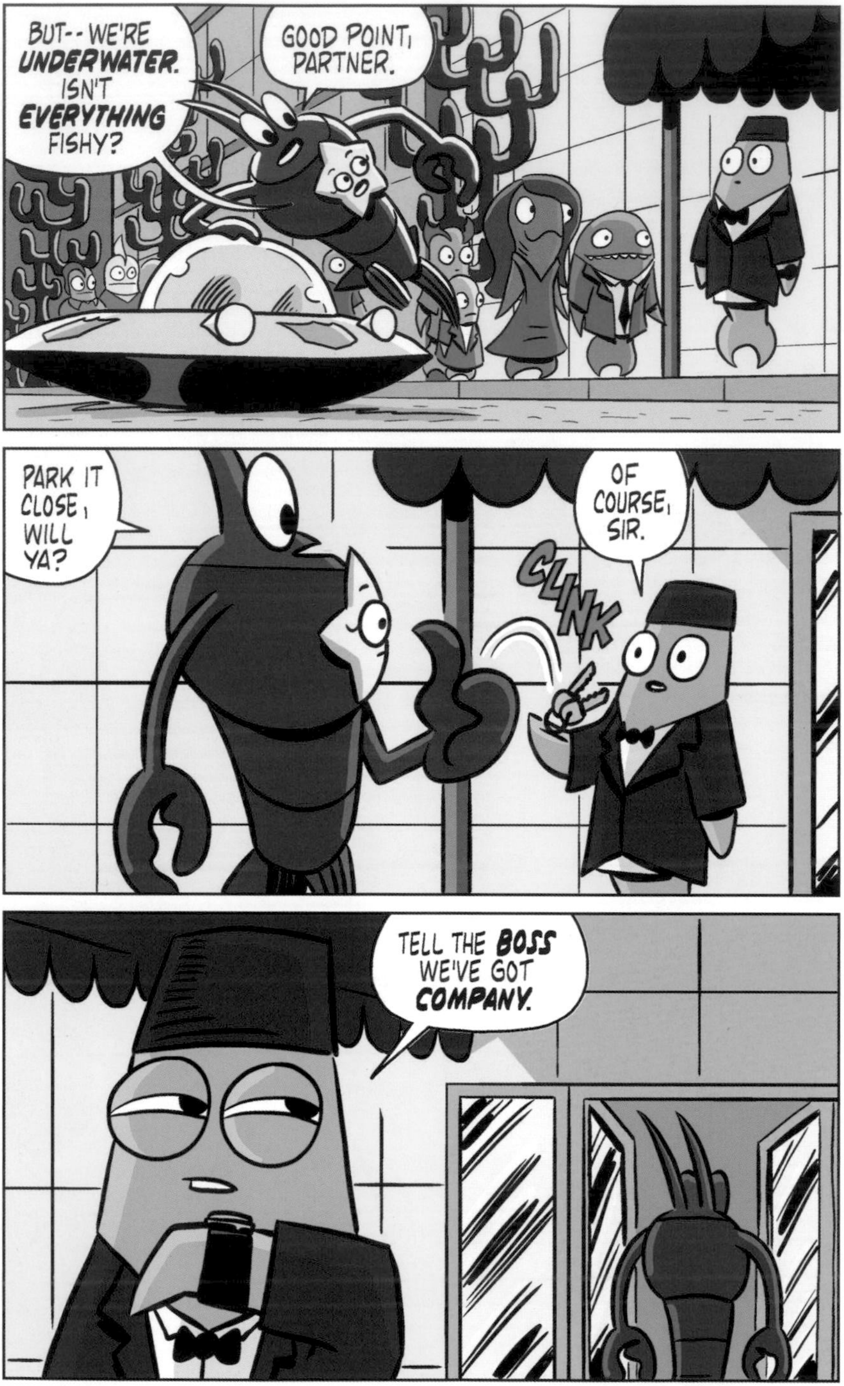
BUT-- WE'RE UNDERWATER. ISN'T EVERYTHING FISHY?
GOOD POINT, PARTNER.
PARK IT CLOSE, WILL YA?
OF COURSE, SIR.
CLINK
TELL THE BOSS WE'VE GOT COMPANY.

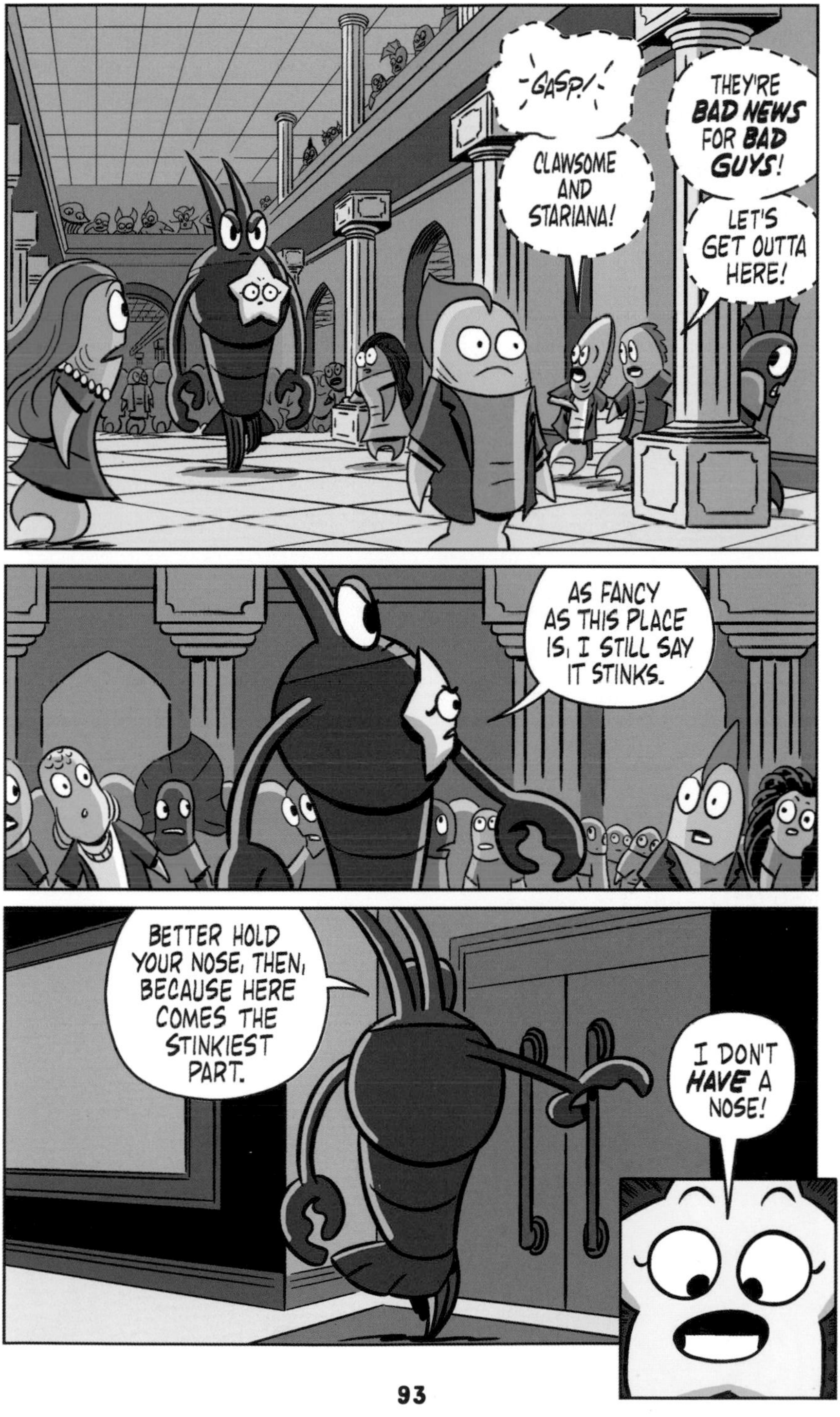
-GASP!-
CLAWSOME AND STARIANA!
THEY'RE BAD NEWS FOR BAD GUYS!
LET'S GET OUTTA HERE!
AS FANCY AS THIS PLACE IS, I STILL SAY IT STINKS.
BETTER HOLD YOUR NOSE, THEN, BECAUSE HERE COMES THE STINKIEST PART.
I DON'T HAVE A NOSE!

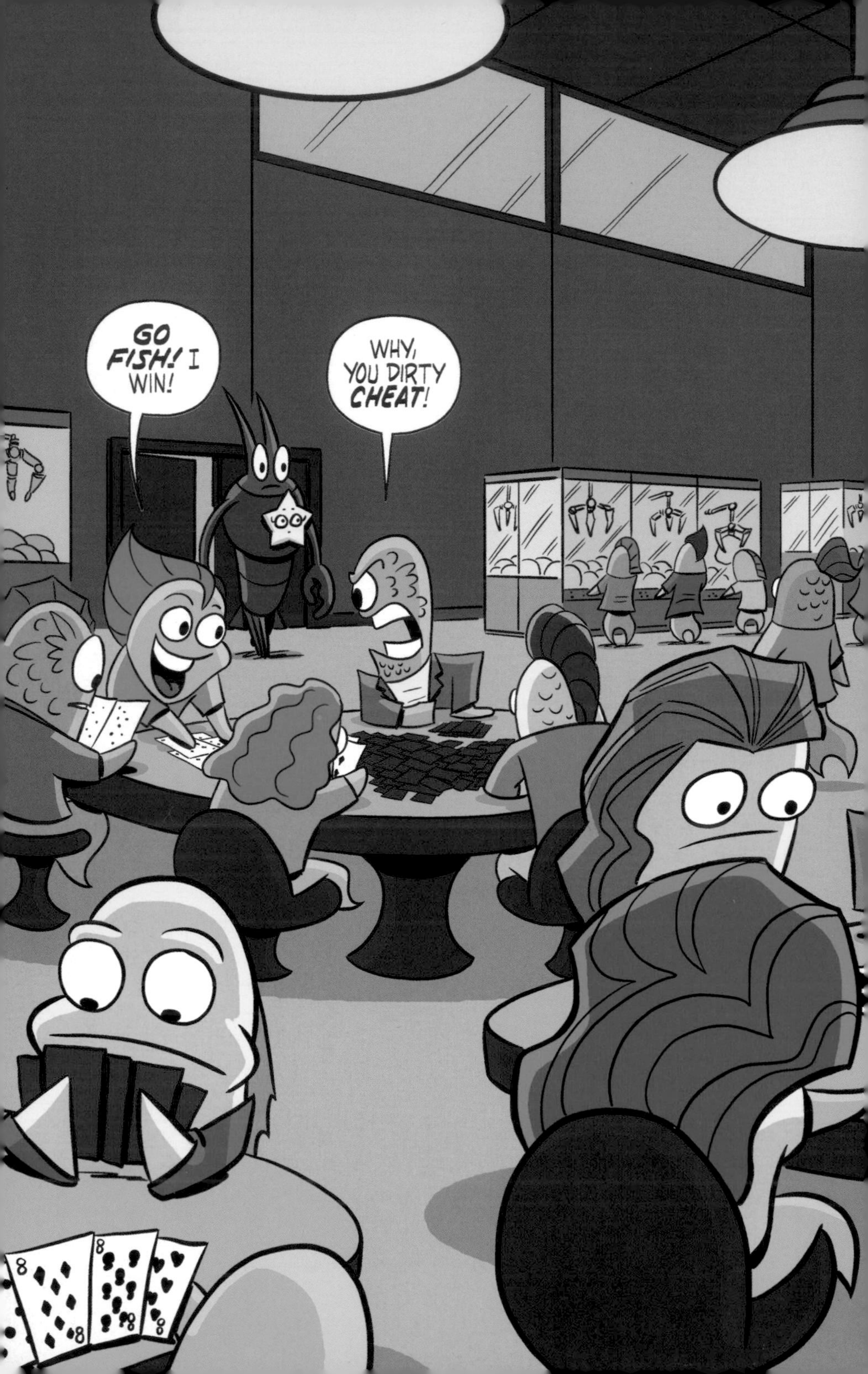
GO FISH! I WIN!
WHY, YOU DIRTY CHEAT!

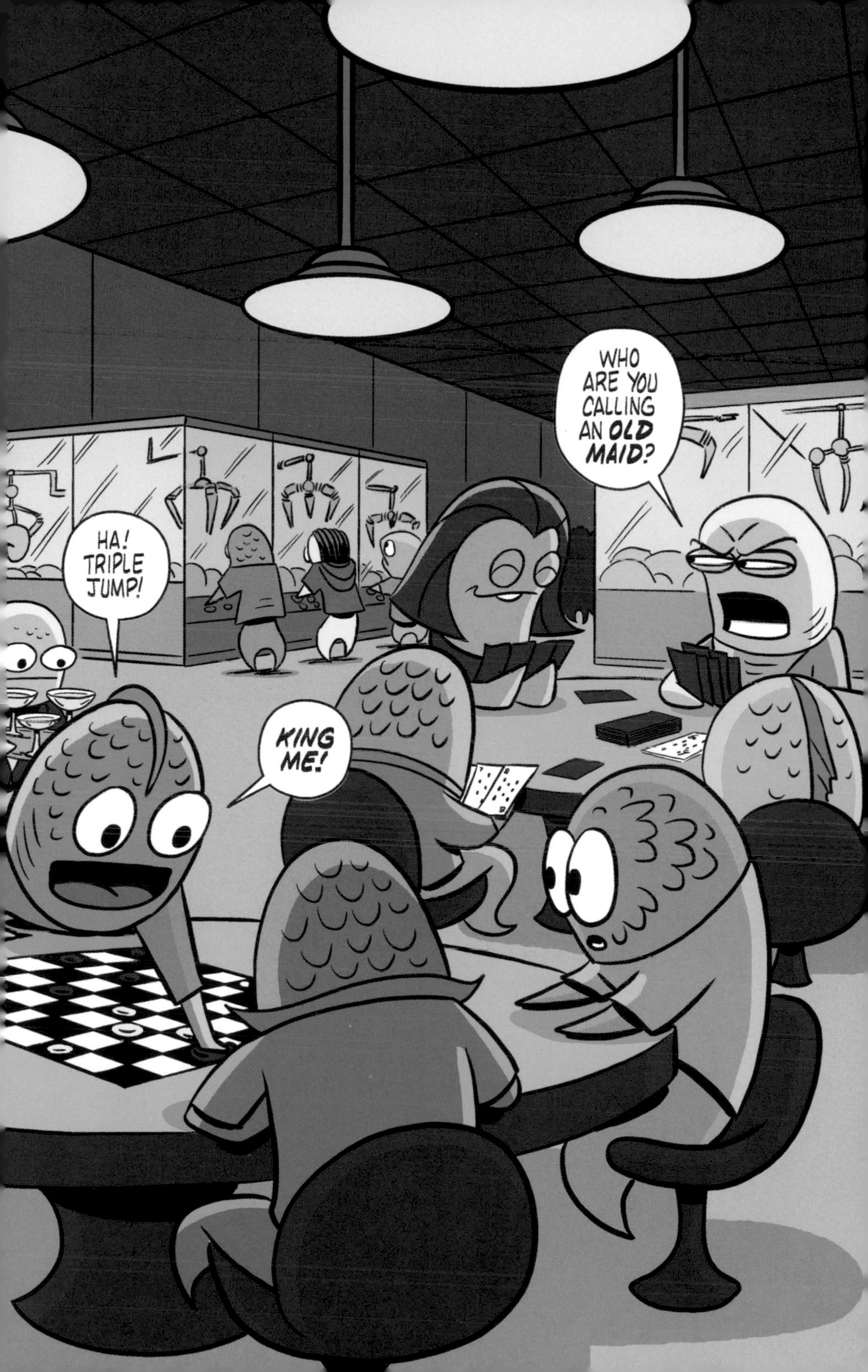
WHO ARE YOU CALLING AN OLD MAID?
HA! TRIPLE JUMP!
KING ME!

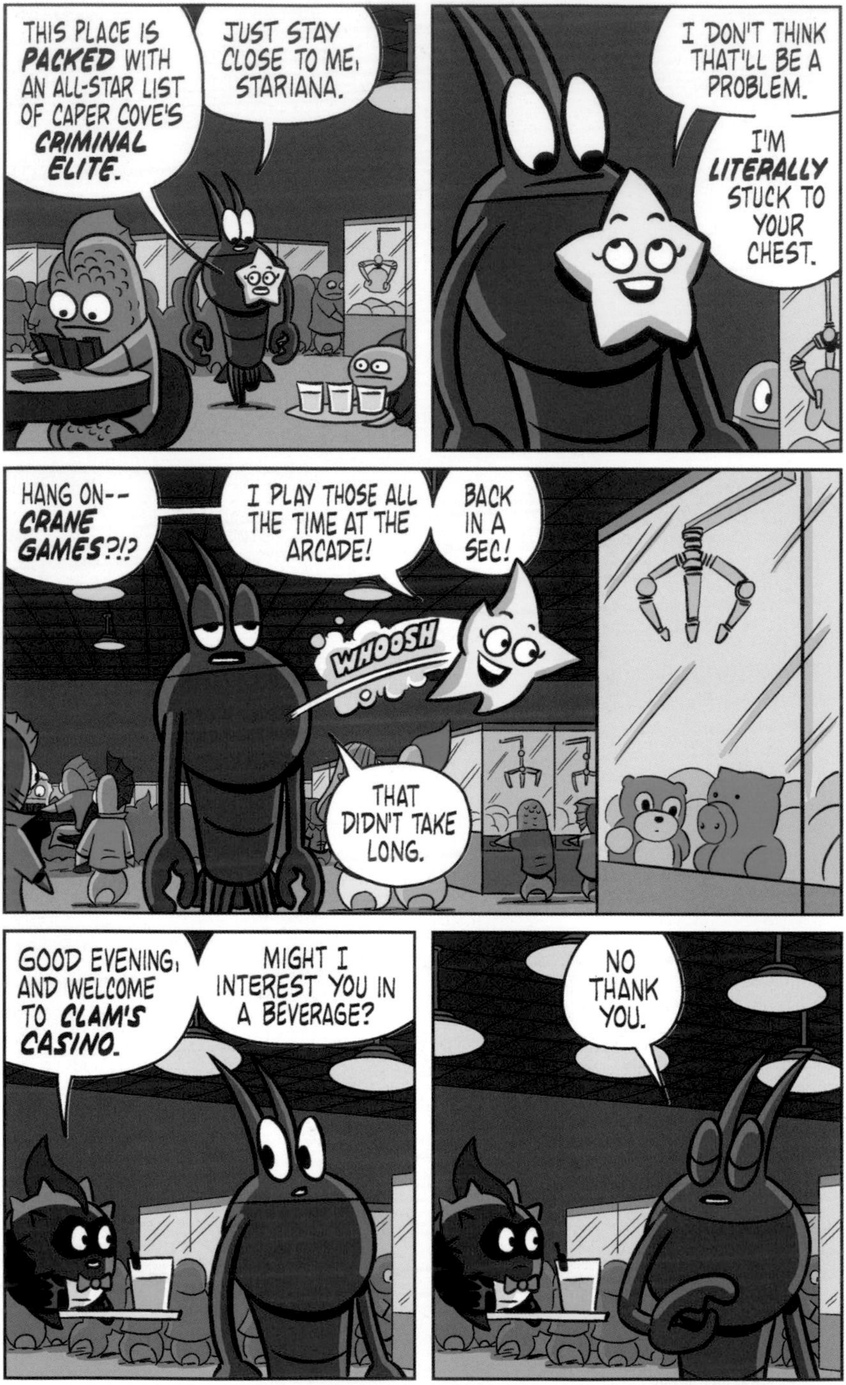
THIS PLACE IS PACKED WITH AN ALL-STAR LIST OF CAPER COVE'S CRIMINAL ELITE.
JUST STAY CLOSE TO ME, STARIANA.
I DON'T THINK THAT'LL BE A PROBLEM.
I'M LITERALLY STUCK TO YOUR CHEST.
HANG ON-- CRANE GAMES?!?
I PLAY THOSE ALL THE TIME AT THE ARCADE!
BACK IN A SEC!
WHOOSH
THAT DIDN'T TAKE LONG.
GOOD EVENING, AND WELCOME TO CLAM'S CASINO.
MIGHT I INTEREST YOU IN A BEVERAGE?
NO THANK YOU.

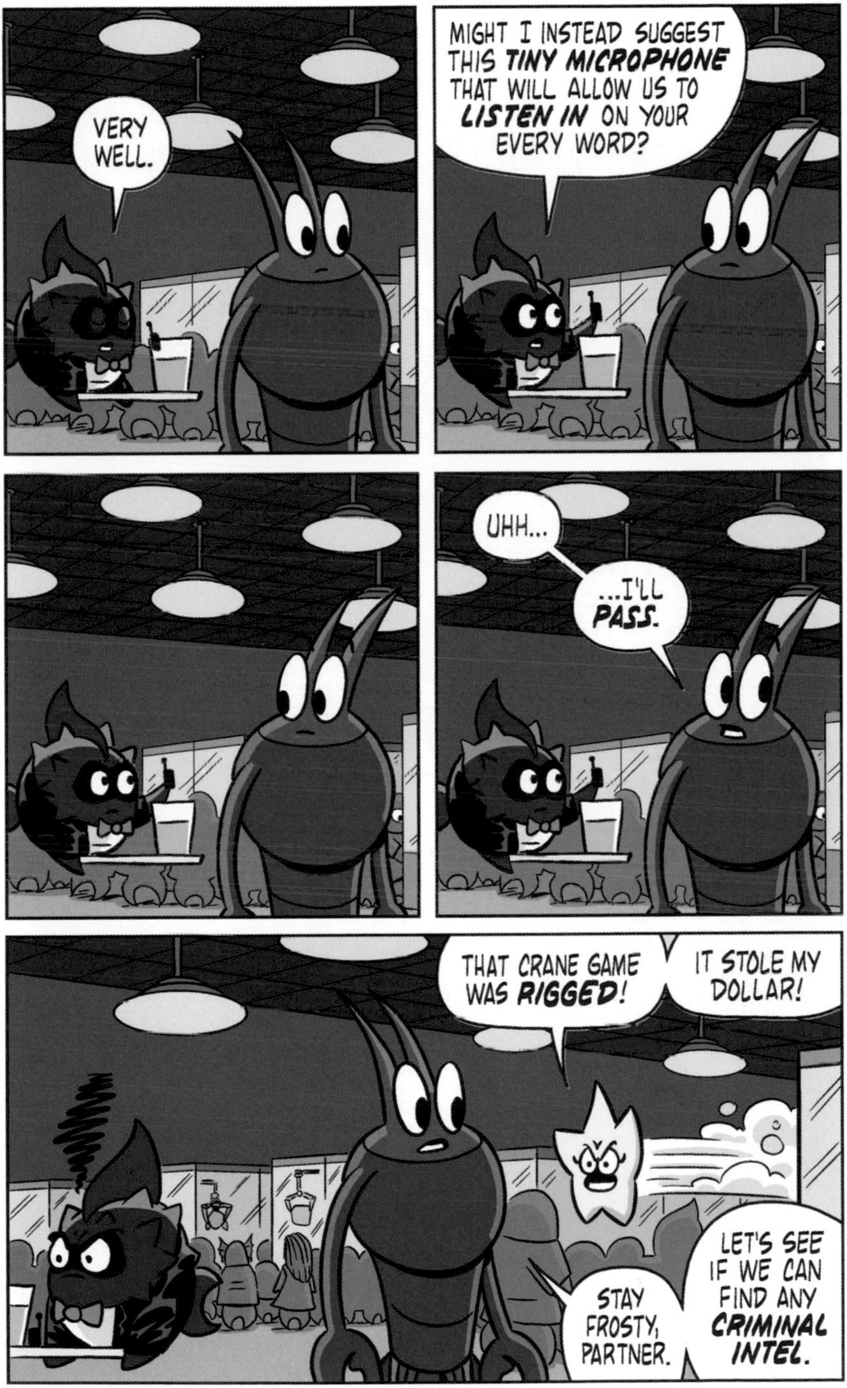
VERY WELL.
MIGHT I INSTEAD SUGGEST THIS **TINY MICROPHONE** THAT WILL ALLOW US TO **LISTEN IN** ON YOUR EVERY WORD?
UHH...
...I'LL **PASS**.
THAT CRANE GAME WAS **RIGGED**!
IT STOLE MY DOLLAR!
STAY FROSTY, PARTNER.
LET'S SEE IF WE CAN FIND ANY **CRIMINAL INTEL**.

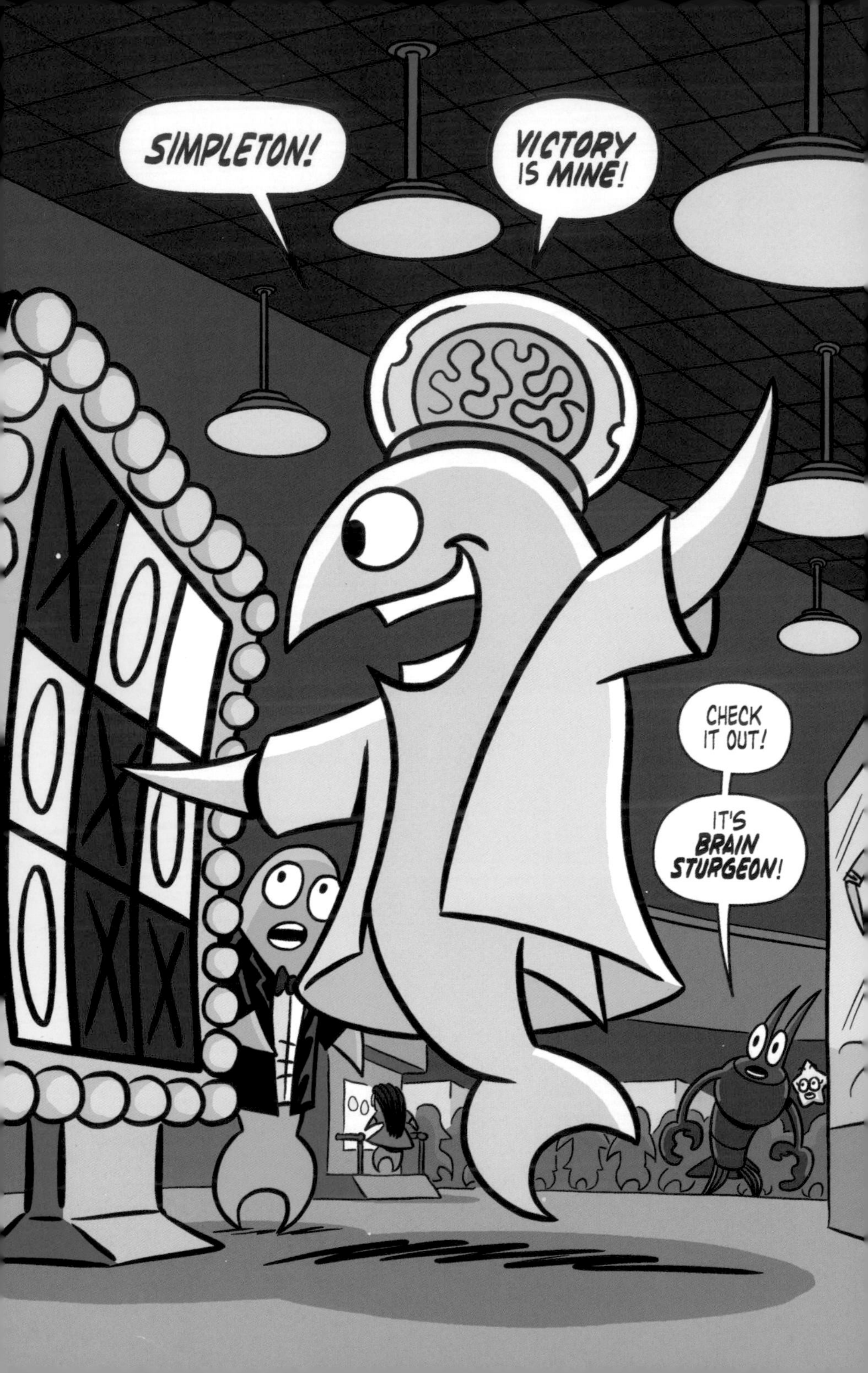
SIMPLETON!
VICTORY IS MINE!
CHECK IT OUT!
IT'S BRAIN STURGEON!

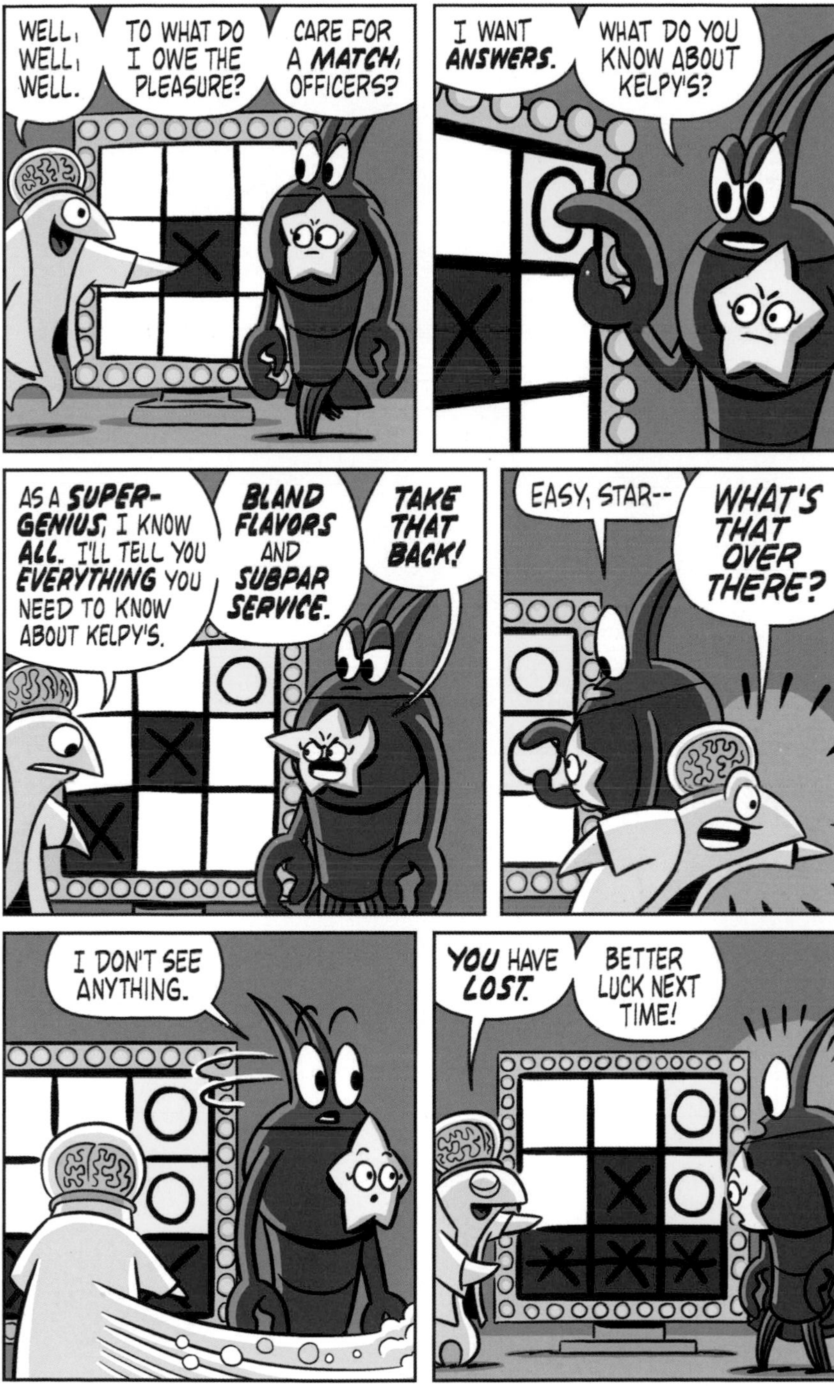
WELL, WELL, WELL.
TO WHAT DO I OWE THE PLEASURE?
CARE FOR A MATCH, OFFICERS?
I WANT ANSWERS.
WHAT DO YOU KNOW ABOUT KELPY'S?
AS A SUPER-GENIUS, I KNOW ALL. I'LL TELL YOU EVERYTHING YOU NEED TO KNOW ABOUT KELPY'S.
BLAND FLAVORS AND SUBPAR SERVICE.
TAKE THAT BACK!
EASY, STAR--
WHAT'S THAT OVER THERE?
I DON'T SEE ANYTHING.
YOU HAVE LOST.
BETTER LUCK NEXT TIME!

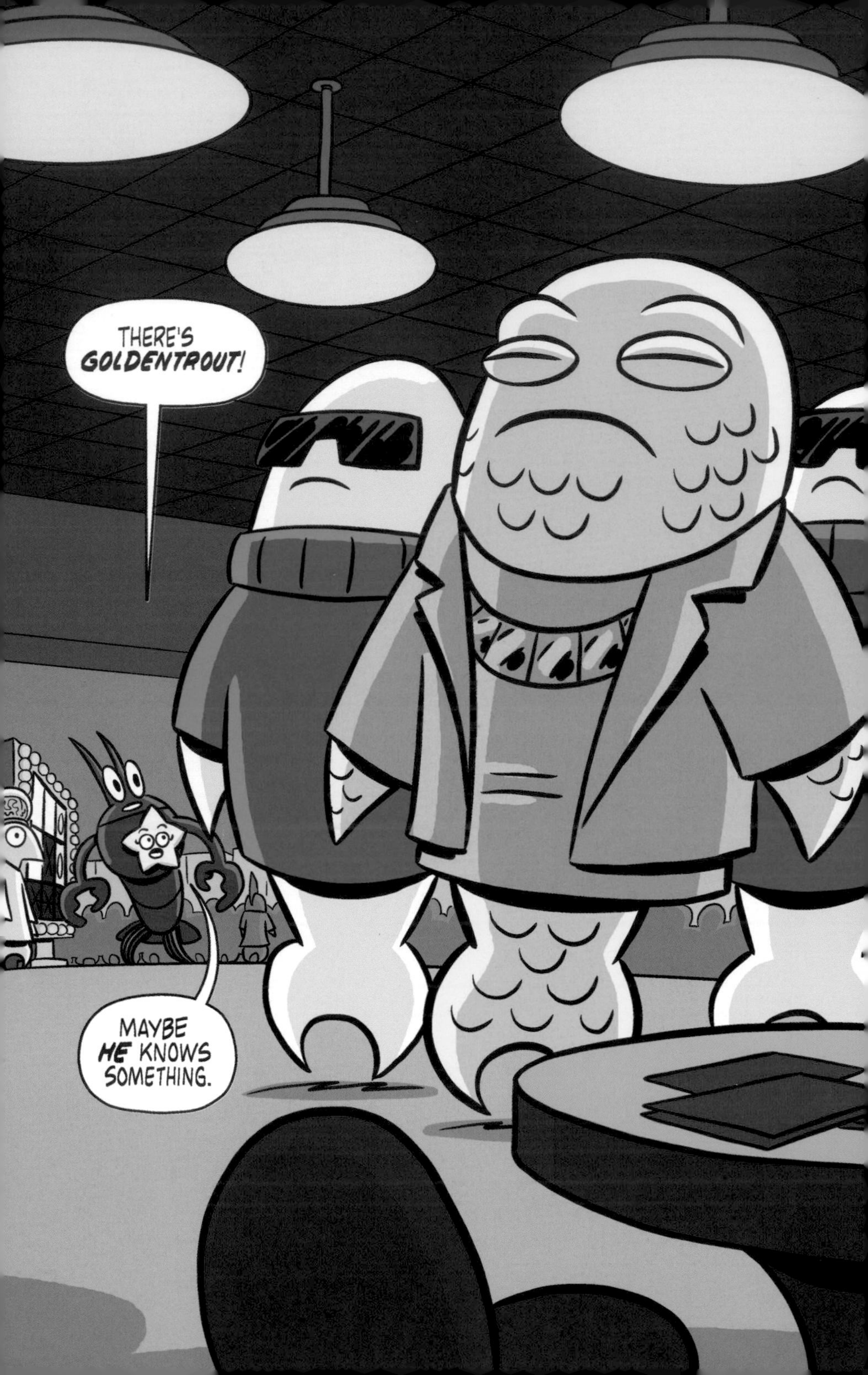
THERE'S **GOLDENTROUT!**
MAYBE **HE** KNOWS SOMETHING.

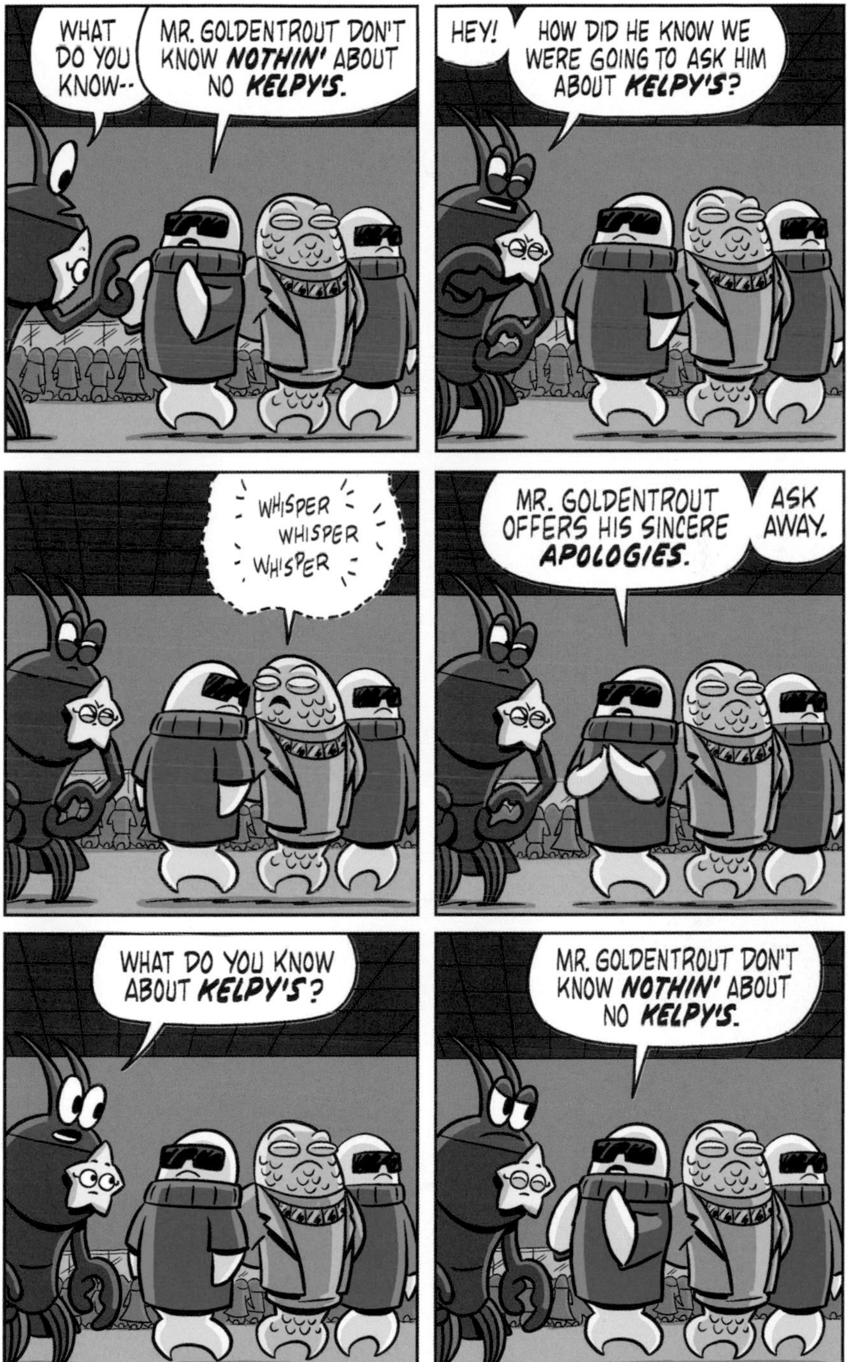
WHAT DO YOU KNOW--
MR. GOLDENTROUT DON'T KNOW NOTHIN' ABOUT NO KELPY'S.
HEY!
HOW DID HE KNOW WE WERE GOING TO ASK HIM ABOUT KELPY'S?
WHISPER WHISPER WHISPER
MR. GOLDENTROUT OFFERS HIS SINCERE APOLOGIES.
ASK AWAY.
WHAT DO YOU KNOW ABOUT KELPY'S?
MR. GOLDENTROUT DON'T KNOW NOTHIN' ABOUT NO KELPY'S.

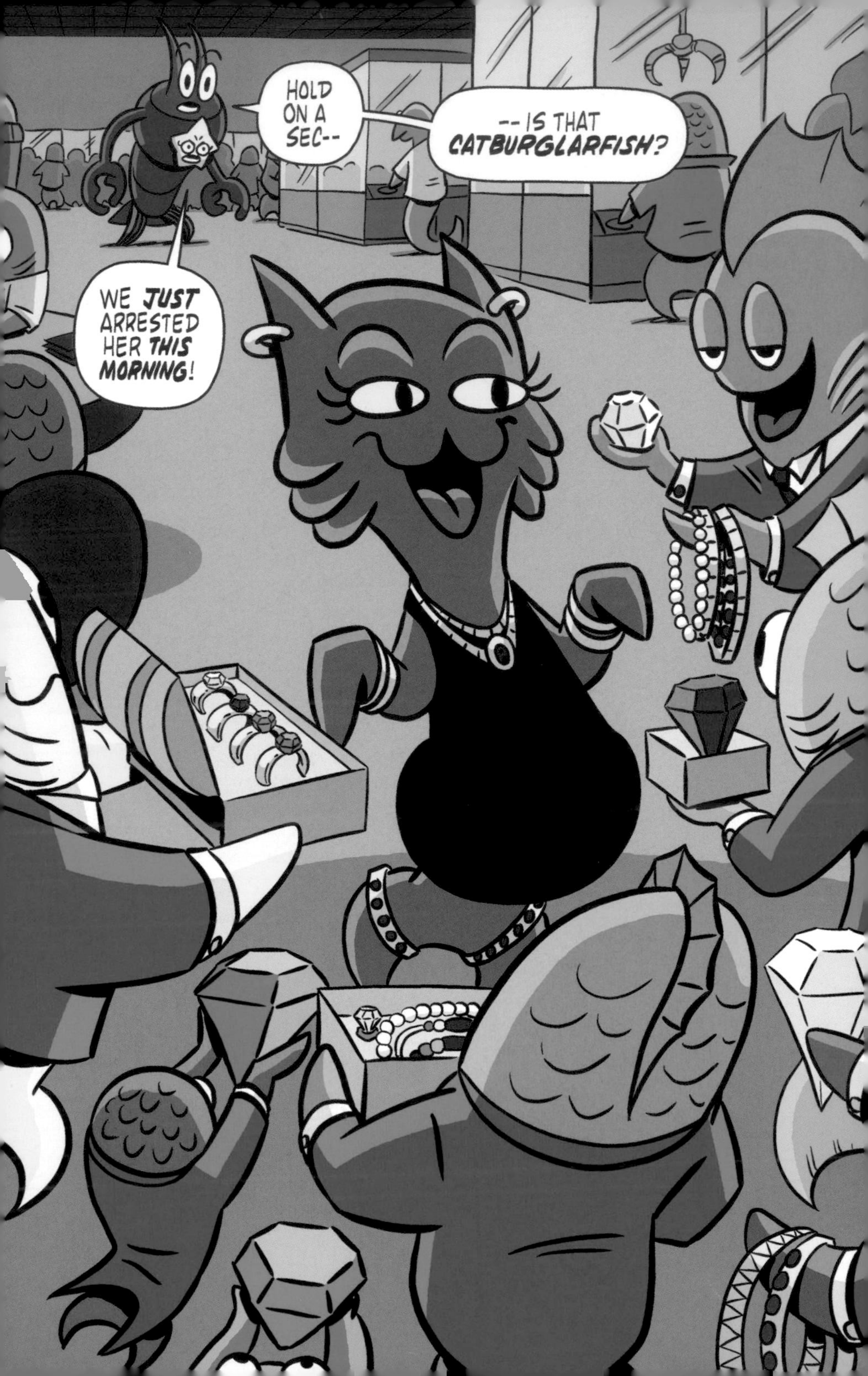
HOLD ON A SEC--
-- IS THAT CATBURGLARFISH?
WE JUST ARRESTED HER THIS MORNING!

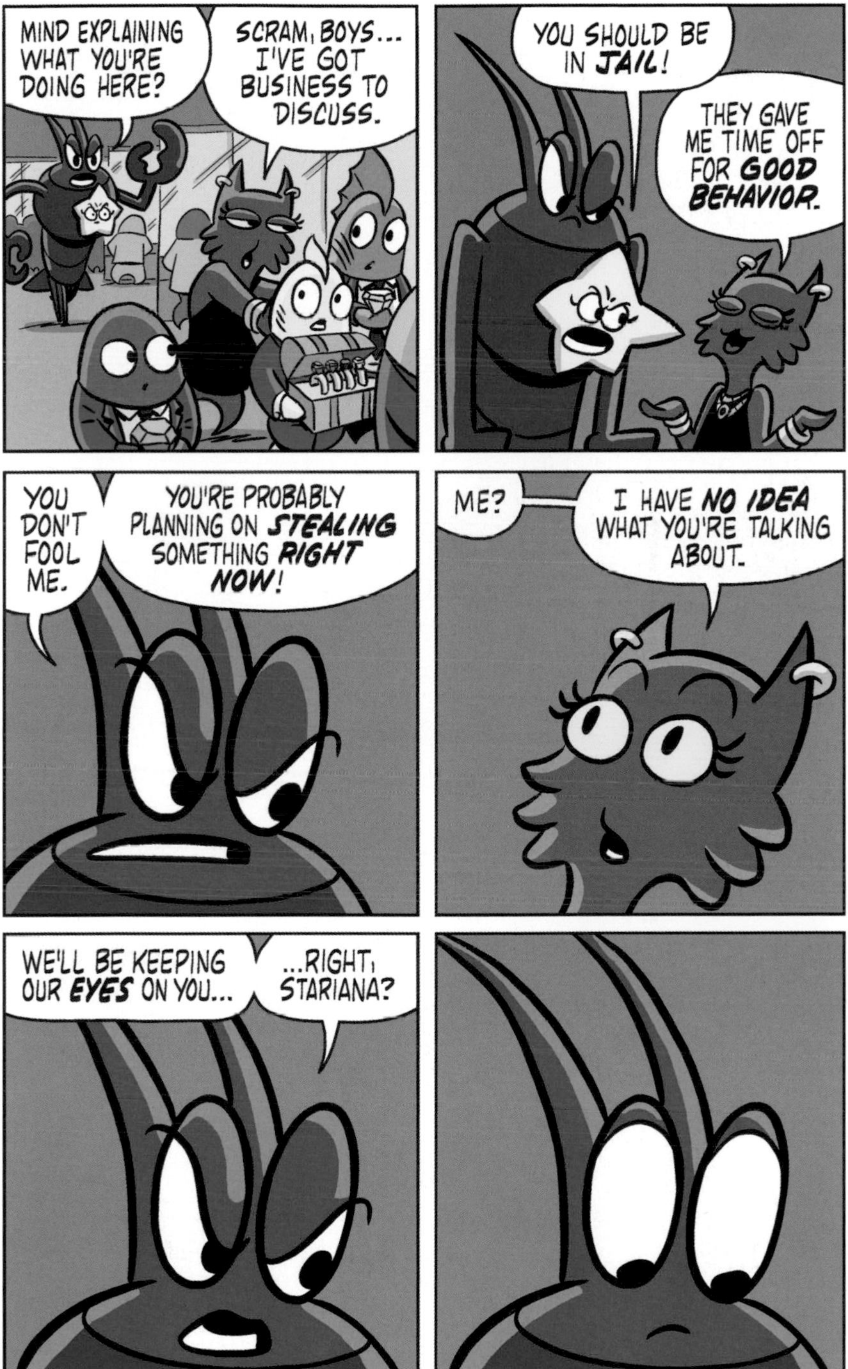
MIND EXPLAINING WHAT YOU'RE DOING HERE?
SCRAM, BOYS... I'VE GOT BUSINESS TO DISCUSS.
YOU SHOULD BE IN JAIL!
THEY GAVE ME TIME OFF FOR GOOD BEHAVIOR.
YOU DON'T FOOL ME.
YOU'RE PROBABLY PLANNING ON STEALING SOMETHING RIGHT NOW!
ME?
I HAVE NO IDEA WHAT YOU'RE TALKING ABOUT.
WE'LL BE KEEPING OUR EYES ON YOU...
...RIGHT, STARIANA?

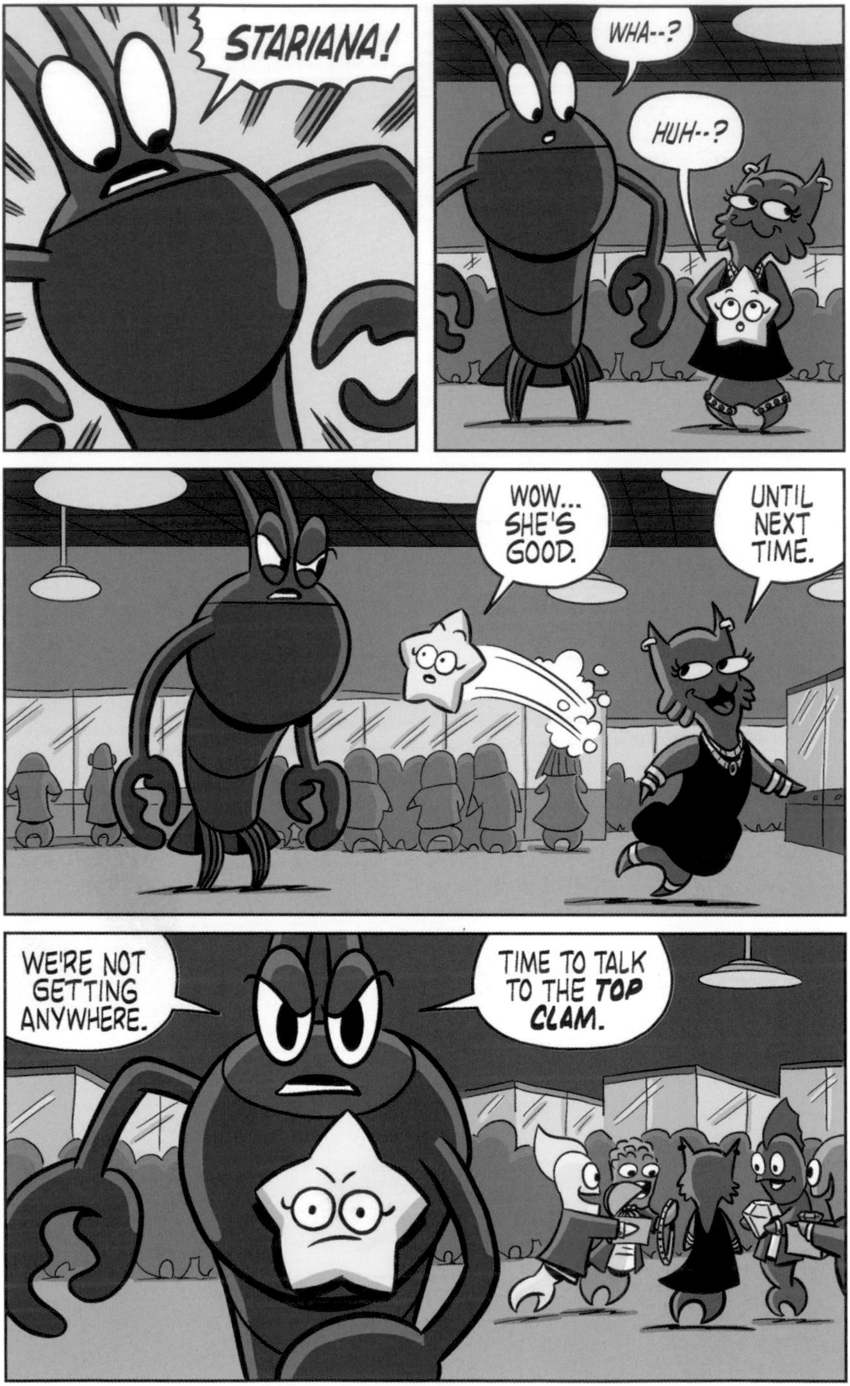
STARIANA!
WHA--?
HUH--?
WOW... SHE'S GOOD.
UNTIL NEXT TIME.
WE'RE NOT GETTING ANYWHERE.
TIME TO TALK TO THE **TOP CLAM**.

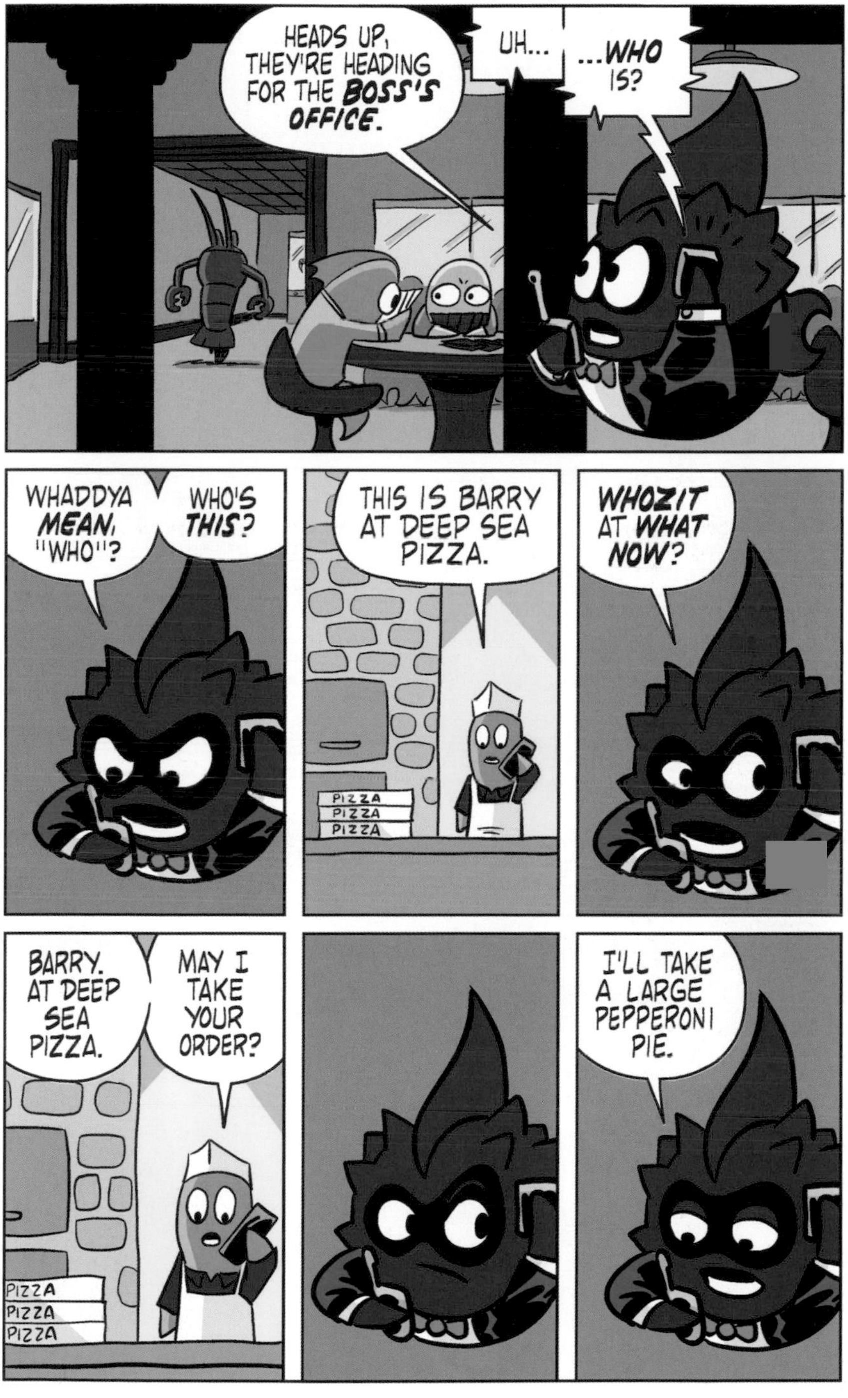
HEADS UP, THEY'RE HEADING FOR THE BOSS'S OFFICE.
UH...
...WHO IS?
WHADDYA MEAN, "WHO"?
WHO'S THIS?
THIS IS BARRY AT DEEP SEA PIZZA.
PIZZA
PIZZA
PIZZA
WHOZIT AT WHAT NOW?
BARRY. AT DEEP SEA PIZZA.
MAY I TAKE YOUR ORDER?
PIZZA
PIZZA
PIZZA
I'LL TAKE A LARGE PEPPERONI PIE.

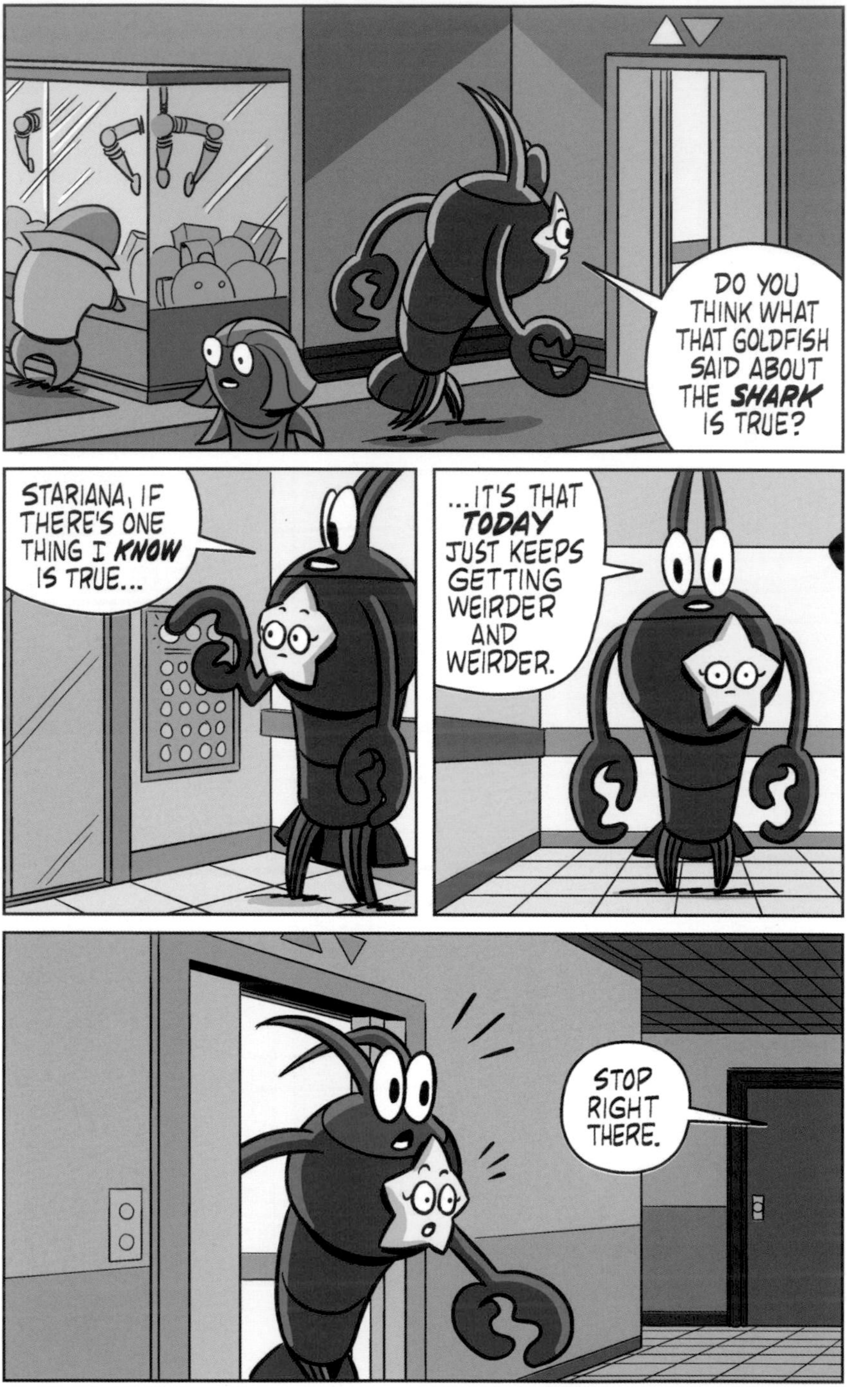
DO YOU THINK WHAT THAT GOLDFISH SAID ABOUT THE SHARK IS TRUE?
STARIANA, IF THERE'S ONE THING I KNOW IS TRUE...
...IT'S THAT TODAY JUST KEEPS GETTING WEIRDER AND WEIRDER.
STOP RIGHT THERE.

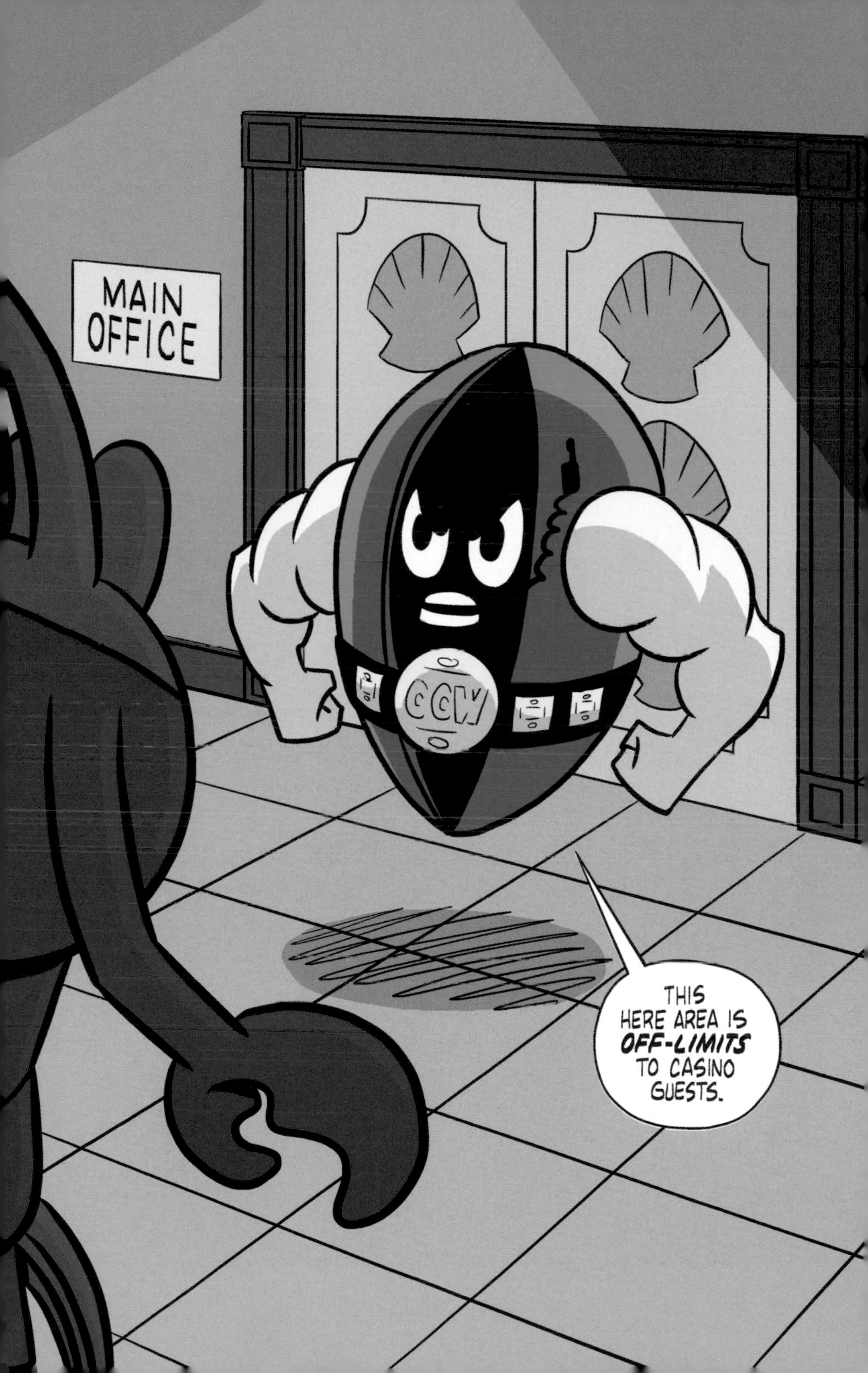
MAIN OFFICE
CCW
THIS HERE AREA IS **OFF-LIMITS** TO CASINO GUESTS.

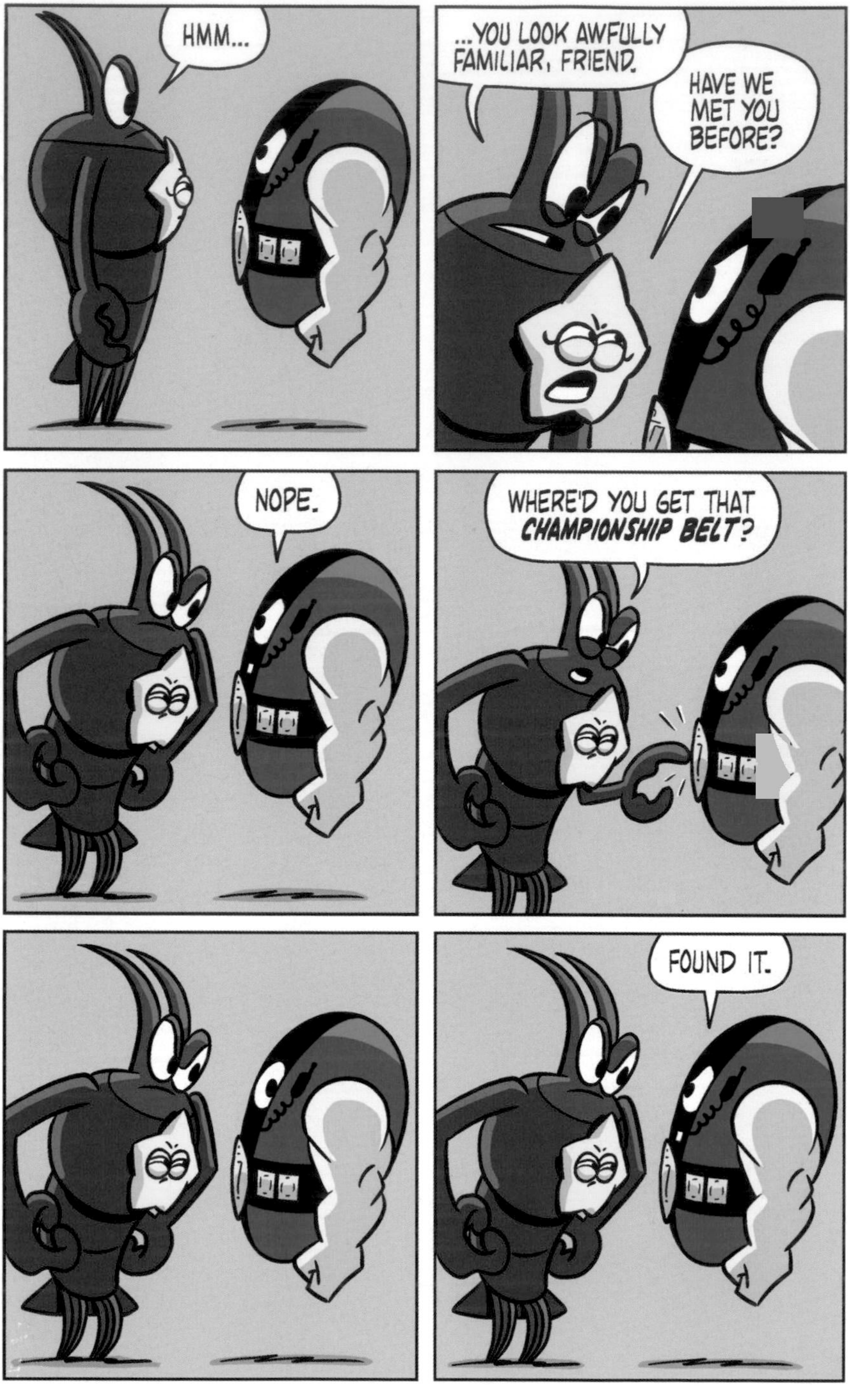
HMM...
...YOU LOOK AWFULLY FAMILIAR, FRIEND.
HAVE WE MET YOU BEFORE?
NOPE.
WHERE'D YOU GET THAT CHAMPIONSHIP BELT?
FOUND IT.

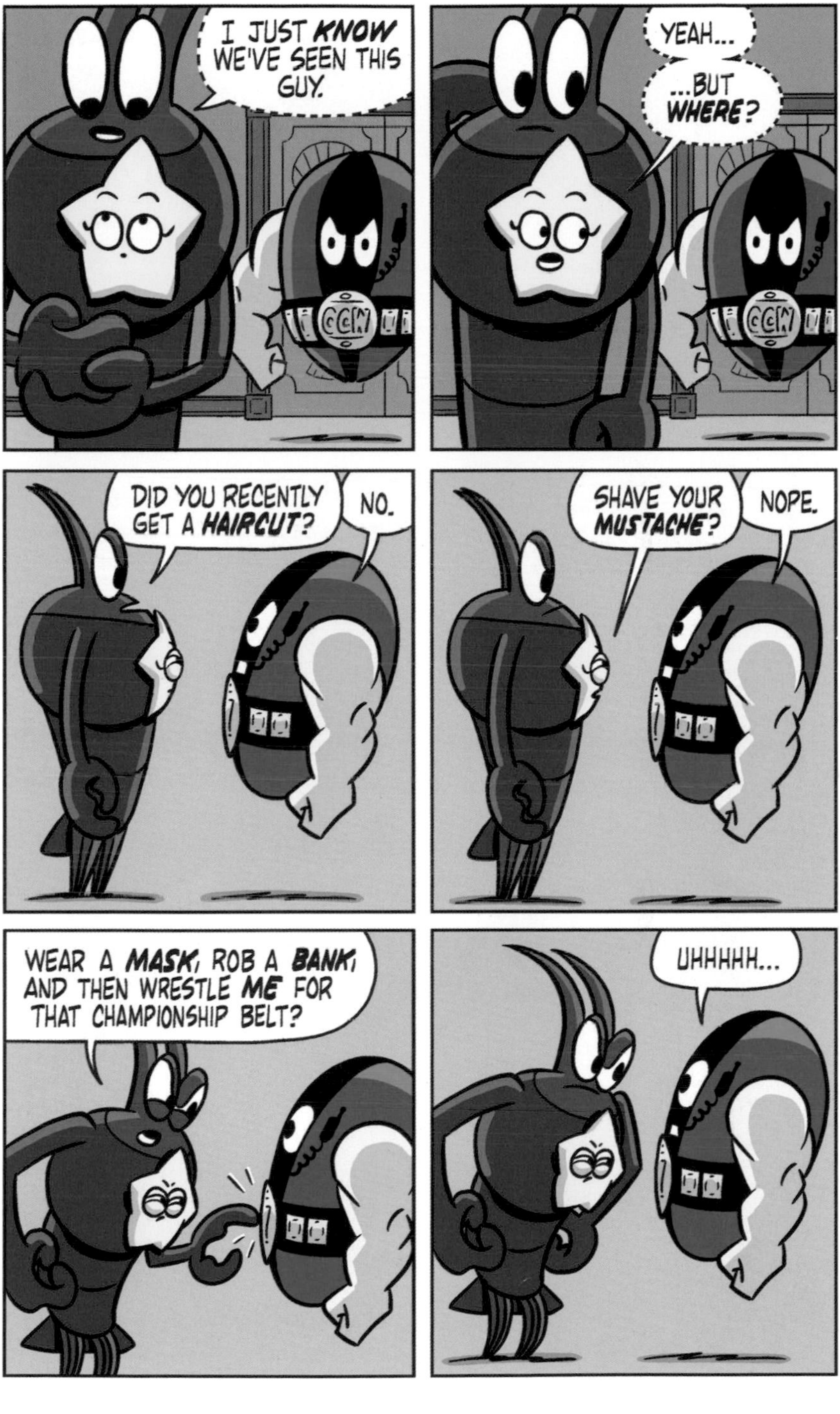
I JUST KNOW WE'VE SEEN THIS GUY.
YEAH...
...BUT WHERE?
DID YOU RECENTLY GET A HAIRCUT?
NO.
SHAVE YOUR MUSTACHE?
NOPE.
WEAR A MASK, ROB A BANK, AND THEN WRESTLE ME FOR THAT CHAMPIONSHIP BELT?
UHHHHH...

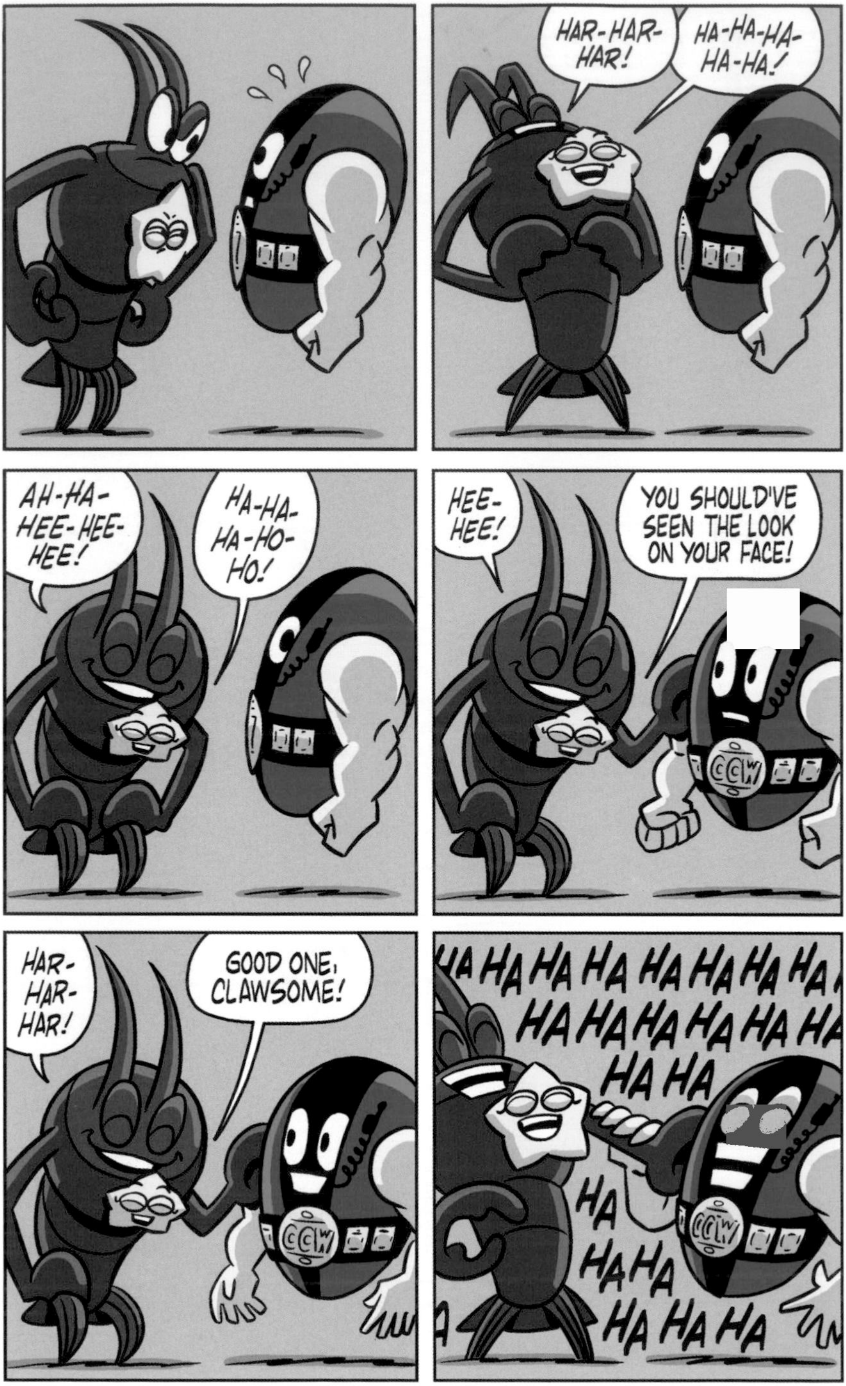
HAR-HAR-HAR!
HA-HA-HA-HA-HA!
AH-HA-HEE-HEE-HEE!
HA-HA-HA-HO-HO!
HEE-HEE!
YOU SHOULD'VE SEEN THE LOOK ON YOUR FACE!
HAR-HAR-HAR!
GOOD ONE, CLAWSOME!
HA HA HA HA HA HA HA HA
HA HA HA HA HA HA HA
HA HA
HA
HA HA
HA HA HA

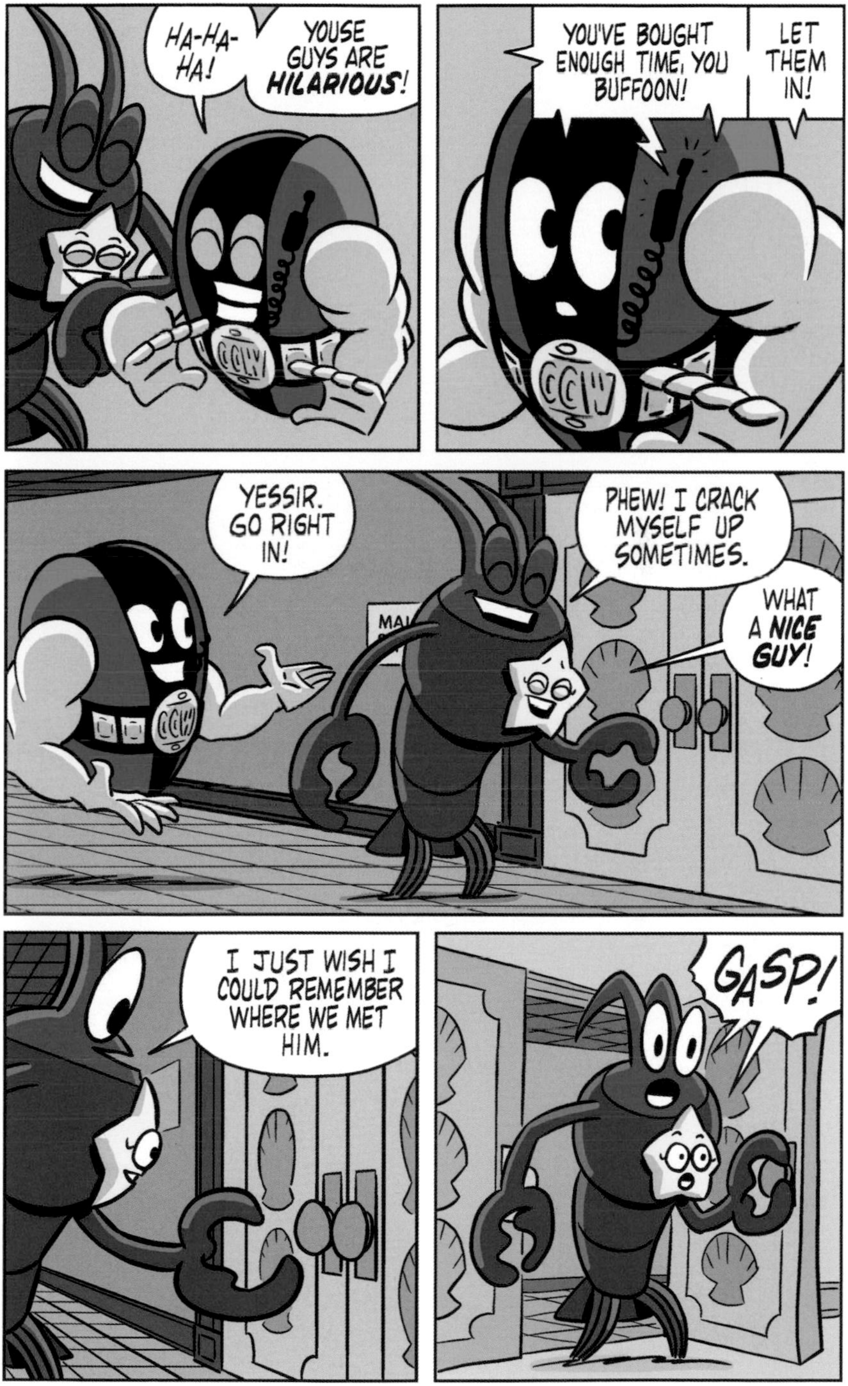
HA-HA-HA!
YOUSE GUYS ARE **HILARIOUS**!
YOU'VE BOUGHT ENOUGH TIME, YOU BUFFOON!
LET THEM IN!
YESSIR. GO RIGHT IN!
PHEW! I CRACK MYSELF UP SOMETIMES.
WHAT A **NICE GUY**!
I JUST WISH I COULD REMEMBER WHERE WE MET HIM.
GASP!

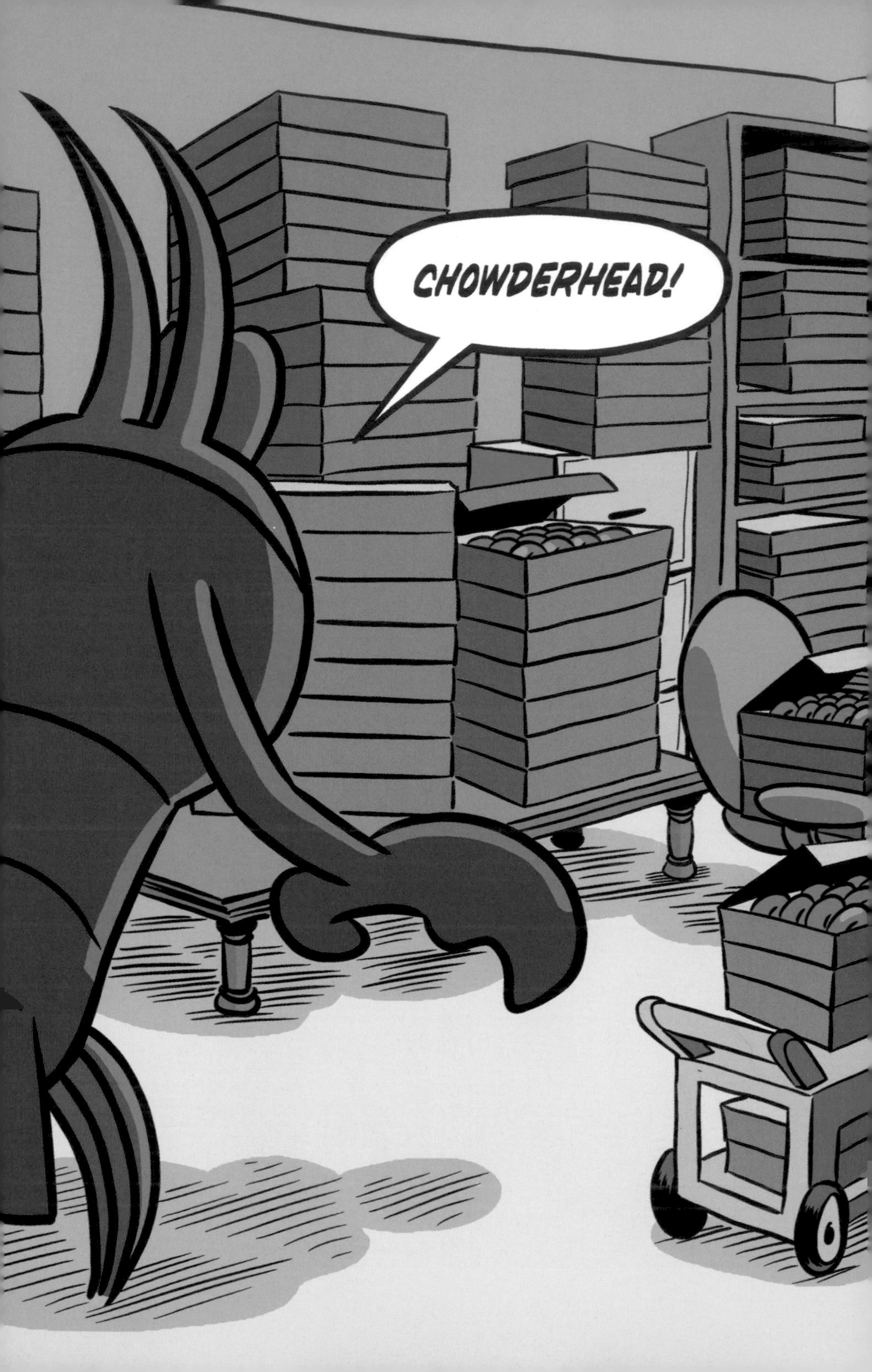
CHOWDERHEAD!

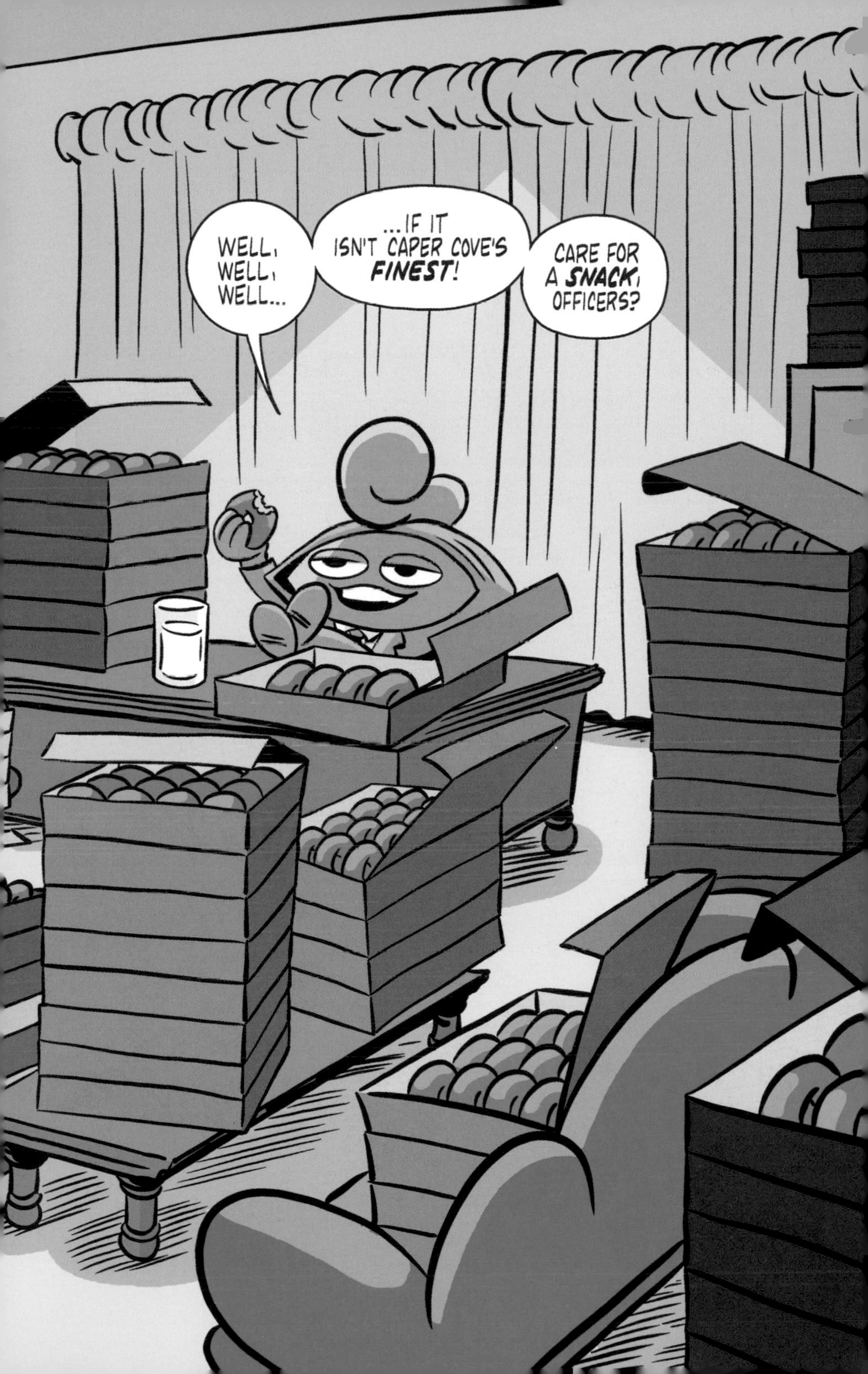
WELL, WELL, WELL...
...IF IT ISN'T CAPER COVE'S **FINEST**!
CARE FOR A **SNACK**, OFFICERS?

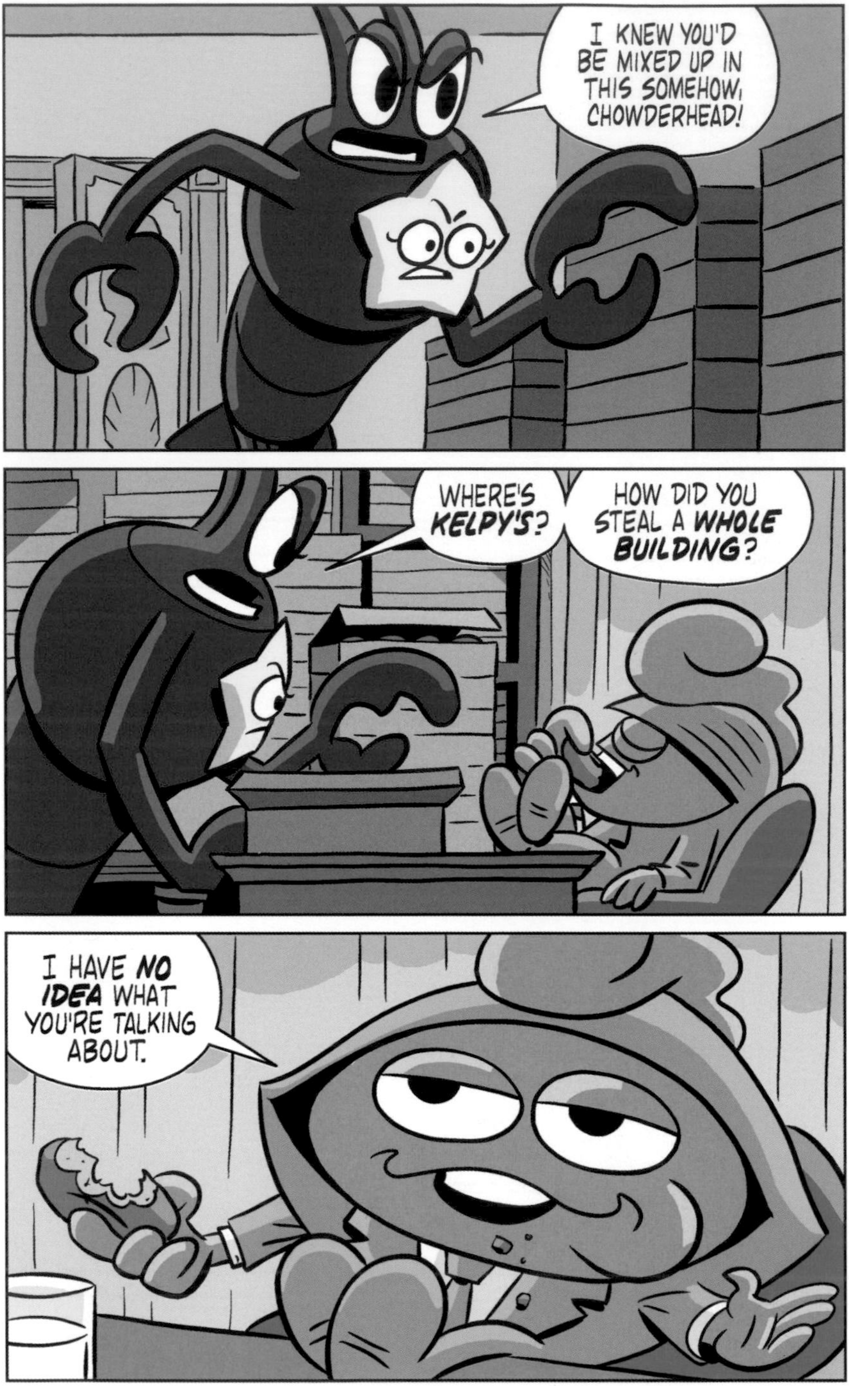

I KNEW YOU'D BE MIXED UP IN THIS SOMEHOW, CHOWDERHEAD!
WHERE'S *KELPY'S*?
HOW DID YOU STEAL A *WHOLE BUILDING*?
I HAVE *NO IDEA* WHAT YOU'RE TALKING ABOUT.

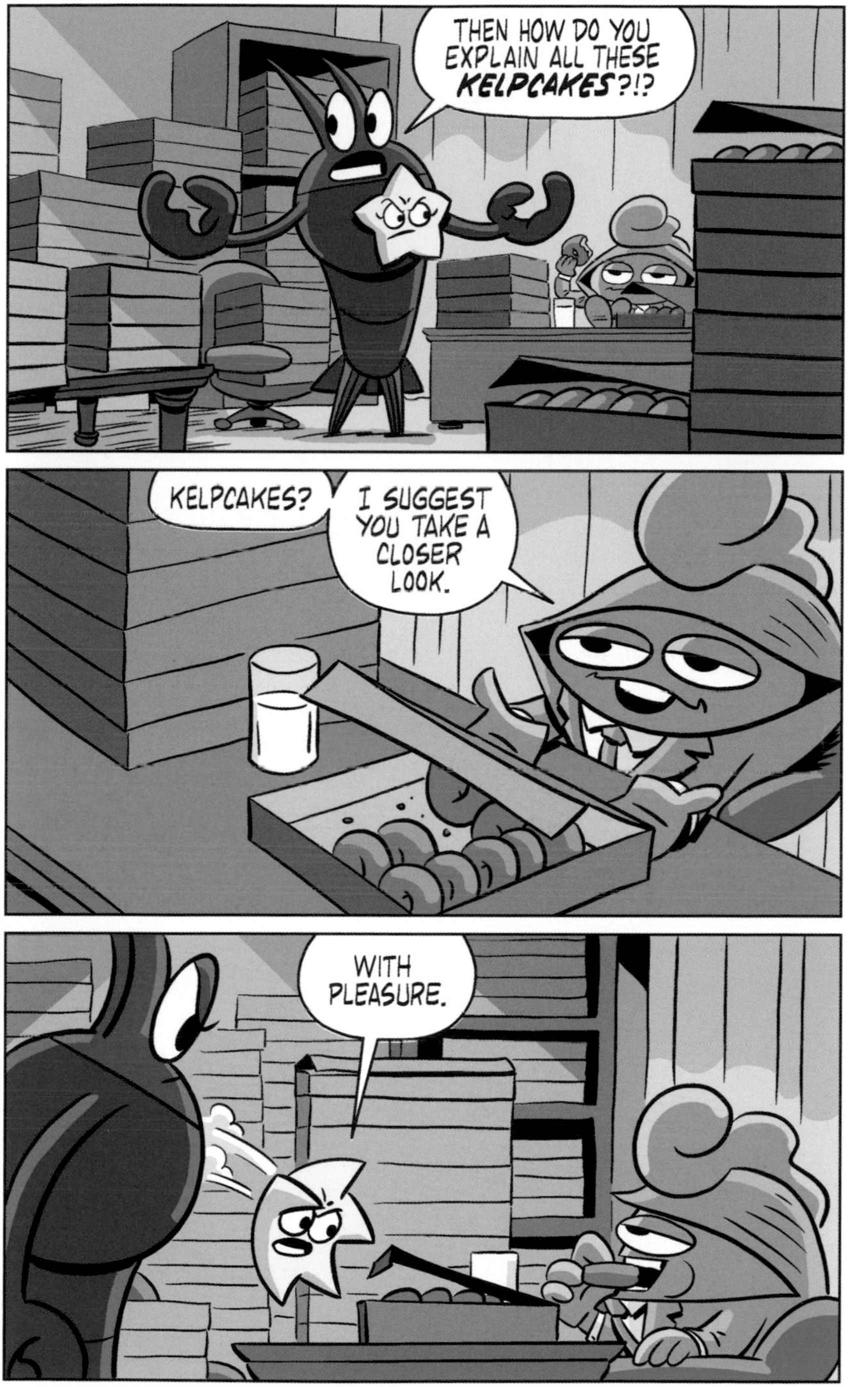
THEN HOW DO YOU EXPLAIN ALL THESE KELPCAKES?!?
KELPCAKES?
I SUGGEST YOU TAKE A CLOSER LOOK.
WITH PLEASURE.

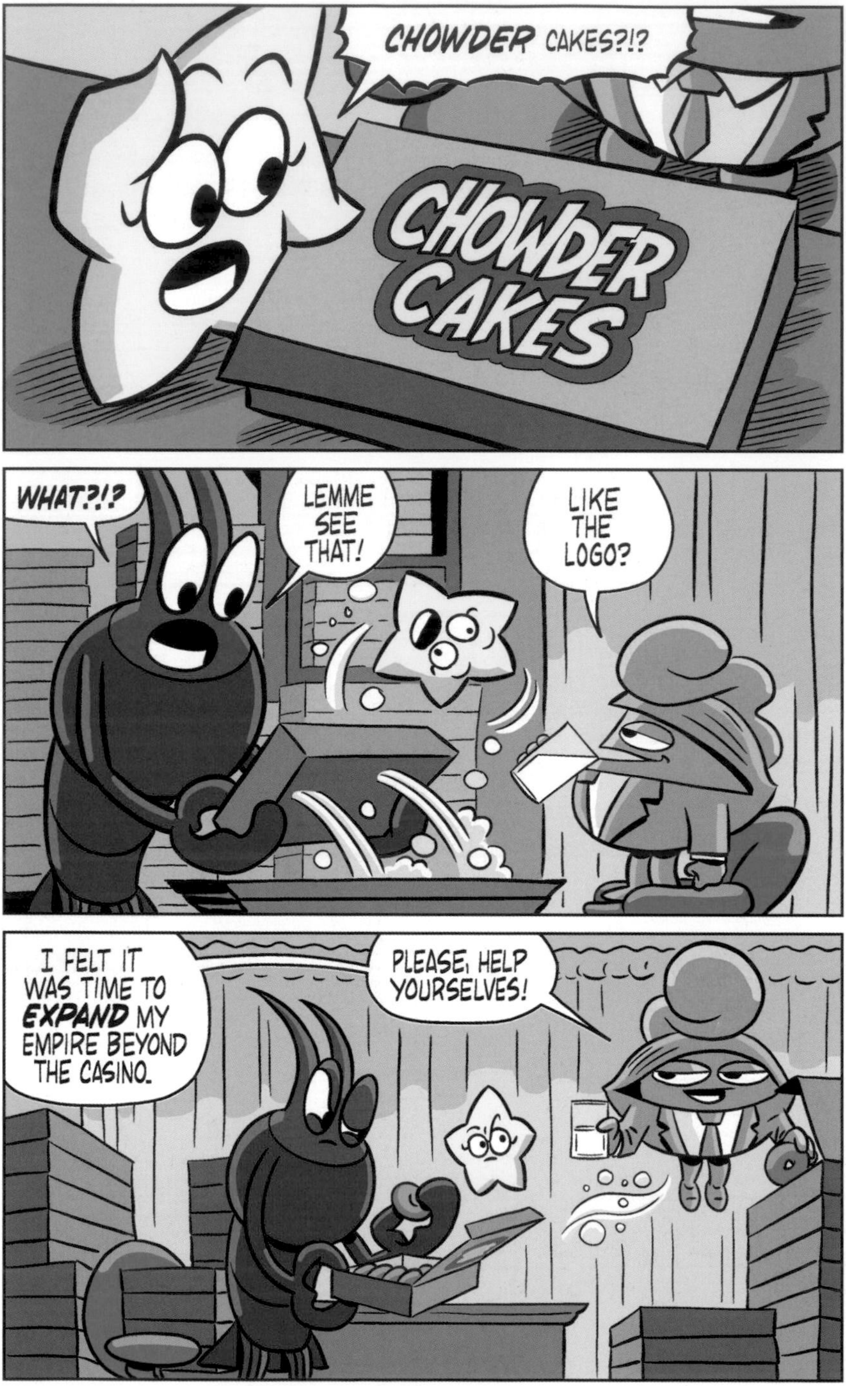
CHOWDER CAKES?!?
CHOWDER CAKES
WHAT?!?
LEMME SEE THAT!
LIKE THE LOGO?
I FELT IT WAS TIME TO EXPAND MY EMPIRE BEYOND THE CASINO.
PLEASE, HELP YOURSELVES!

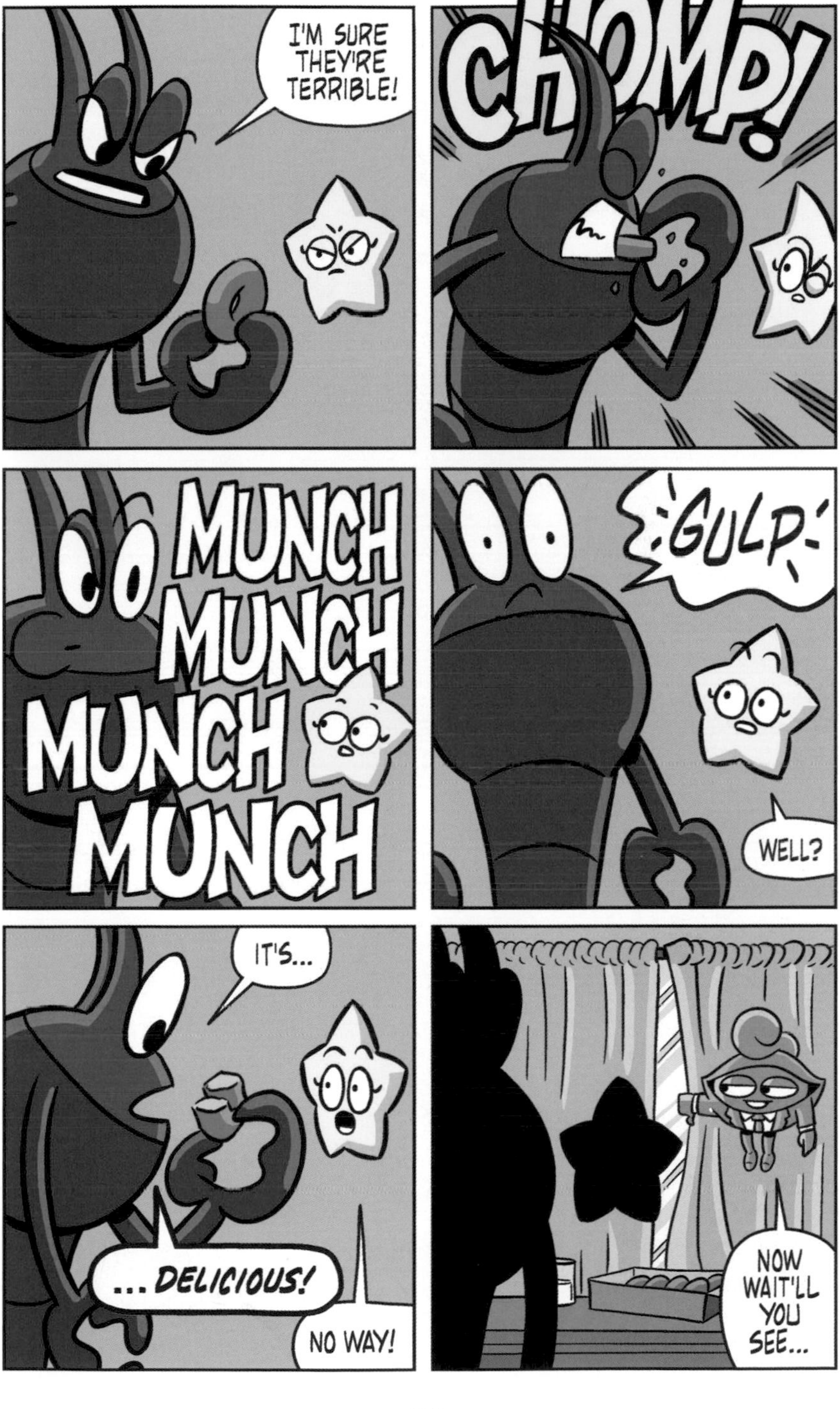
I'M SURE THEY'RE TERRIBLE!
CHOMP!
MUNCH MUNCH MUNCH MUNCH
GULP
WELL?
IT'S...
...DELICIOUS!
NO WAY!
NOW WAIT'LL YOU SEE...

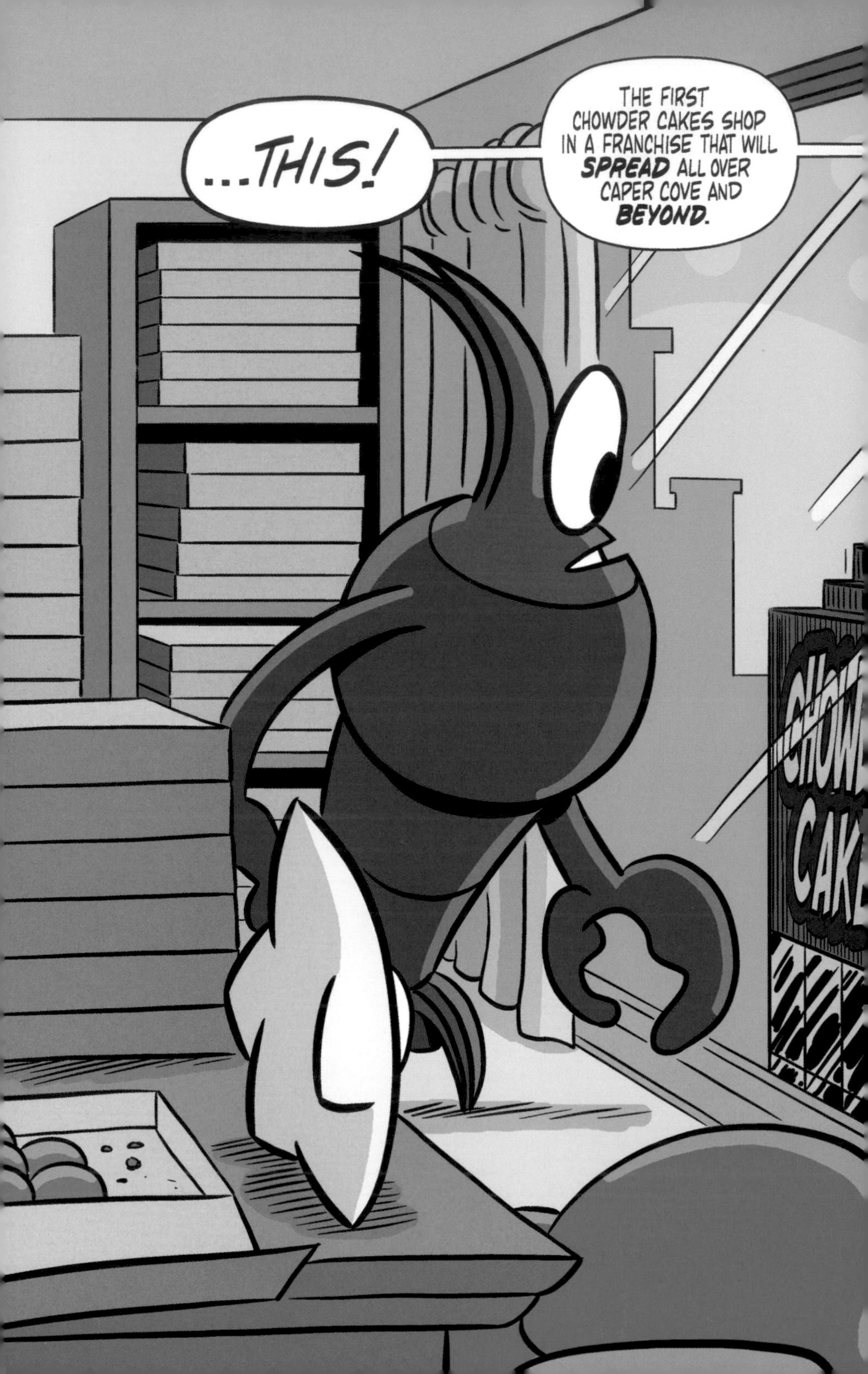
...THIS!
THE FIRST CHOWDER CAKES SHOP IN A FRANCHISE THAT WILL SPREAD ALL OVER CAPER COVE AND BEYOND.

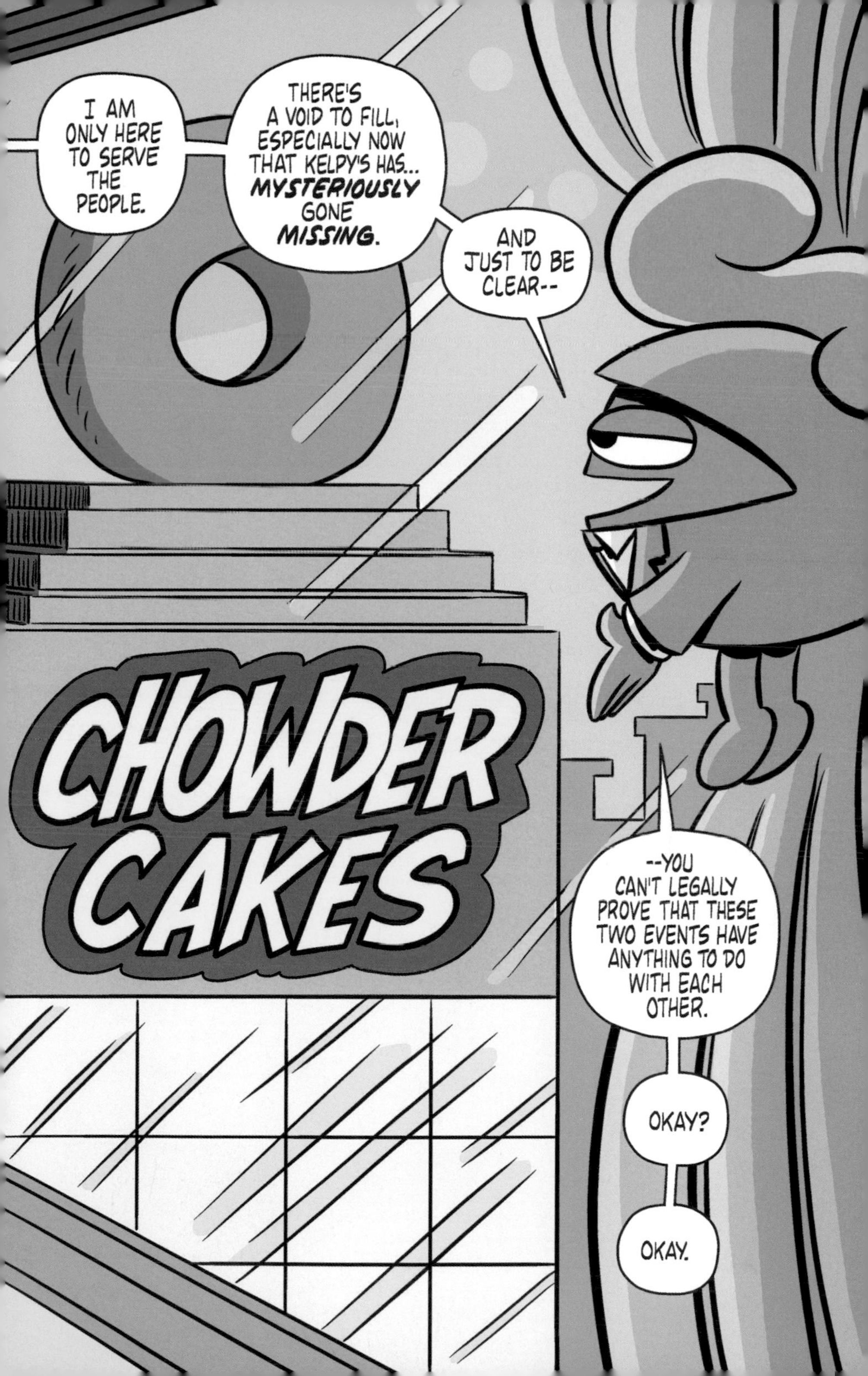
I AM ONLY HERE TO SERVE THE PEOPLE.
THERE'S A VOID TO FILL, ESPECIALLY NOW THAT KELPY'S HAS... ***MYSTERIOUSLY*** GONE ***MISSING***.
AND JUST TO BE CLEAR--
CHOWDER CAKES
--YOU CAN'T LEGALLY PROVE THAT THESE TWO EVENTS HAVE ANYTHING TO DO WITH EACH OTHER.
OKAY?
OKAY.

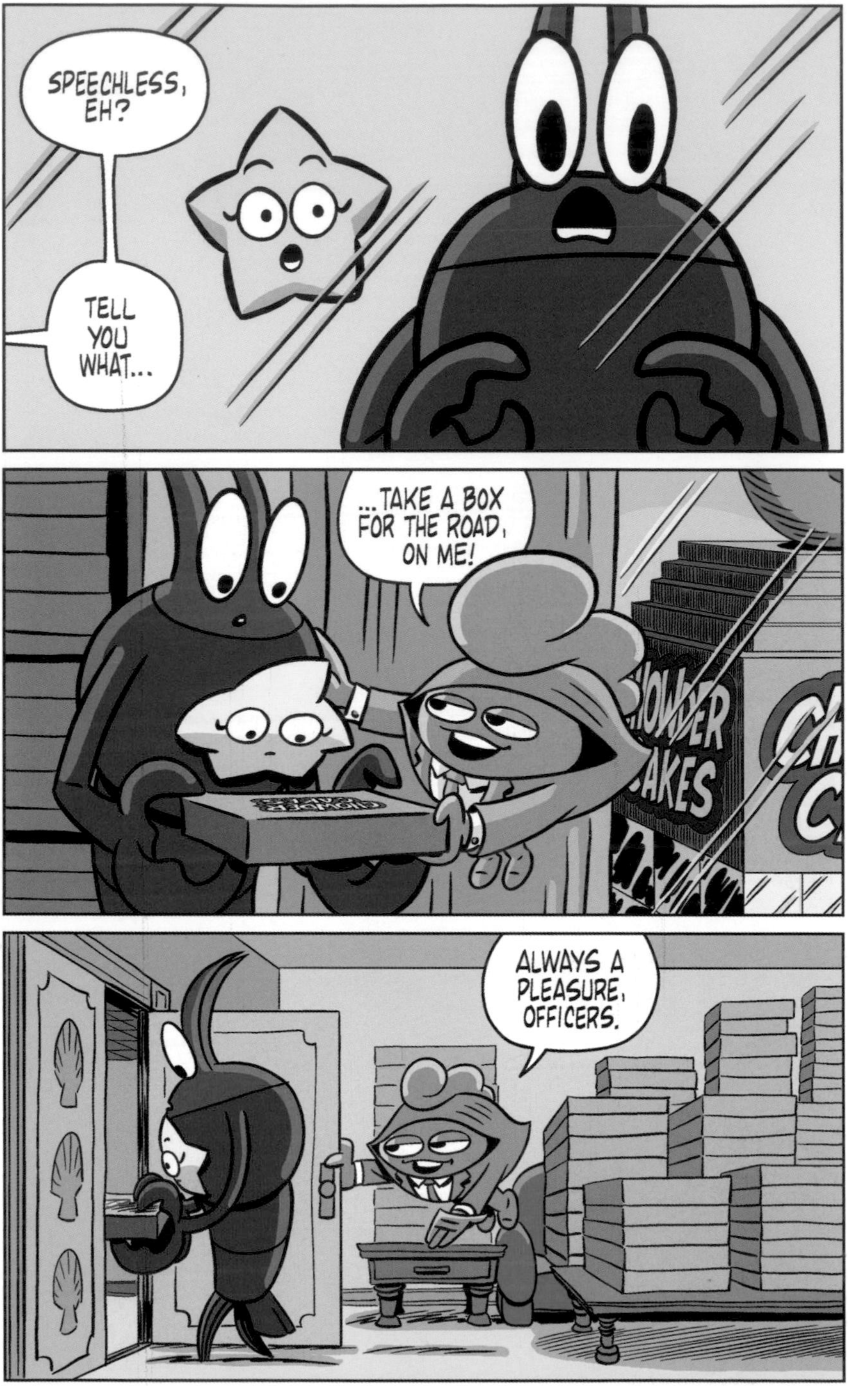
SPEECHLESS, EH?
TELL YOU WHAT...
...TAKE A BOX FOR THE ROAD, ON ME!
CHOWDER CAKES
ALWAYS A PLEASURE, OFFICERS.

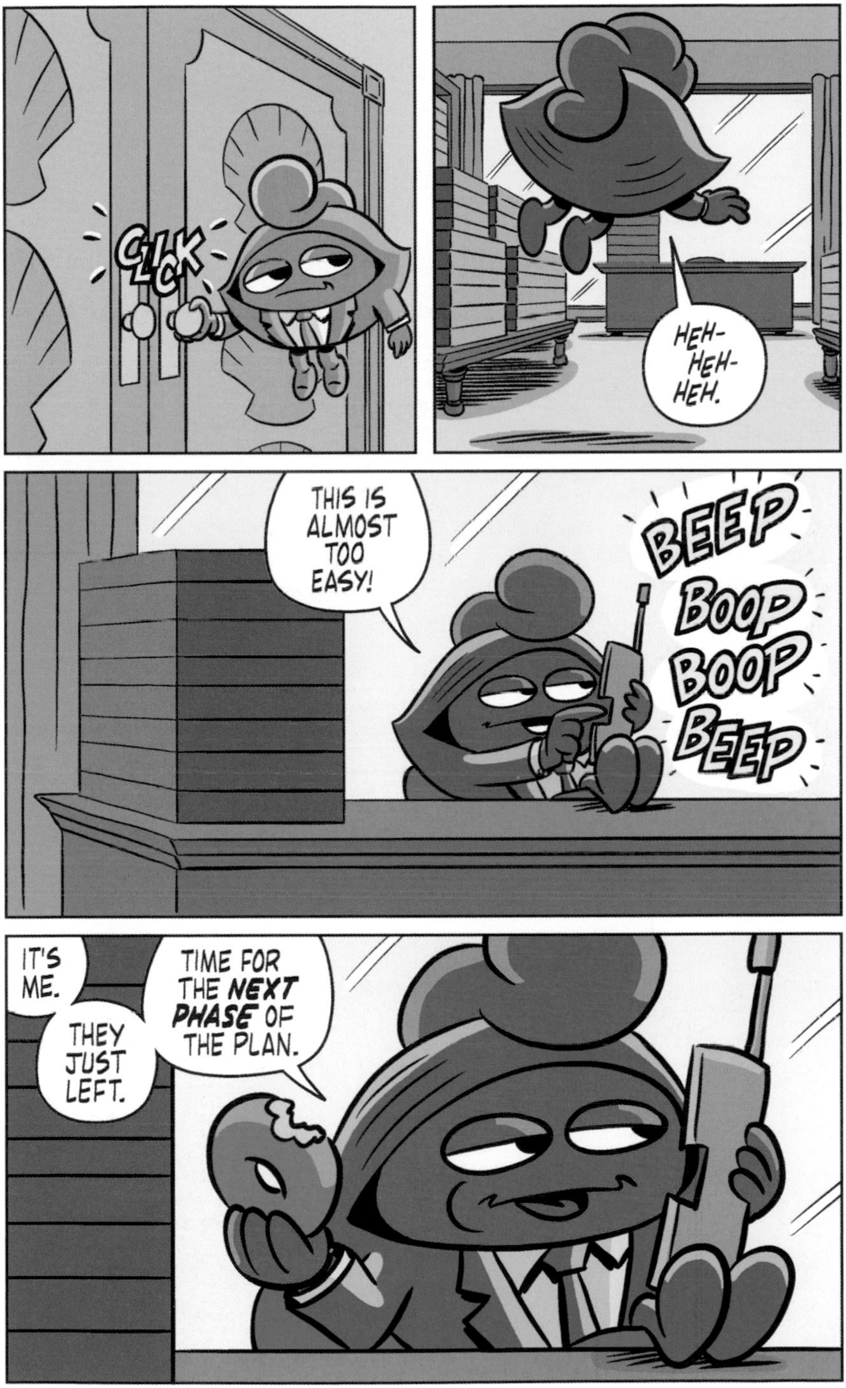
CLICK
HEH-HEH-HEH.
THIS IS ALMOST TOO EASY!
BEEP BOOP BOOP BEEP
IT'S ME.
THEY JUST LEFT.
TIME FOR THE NEXT PHASE OF THE PLAN.

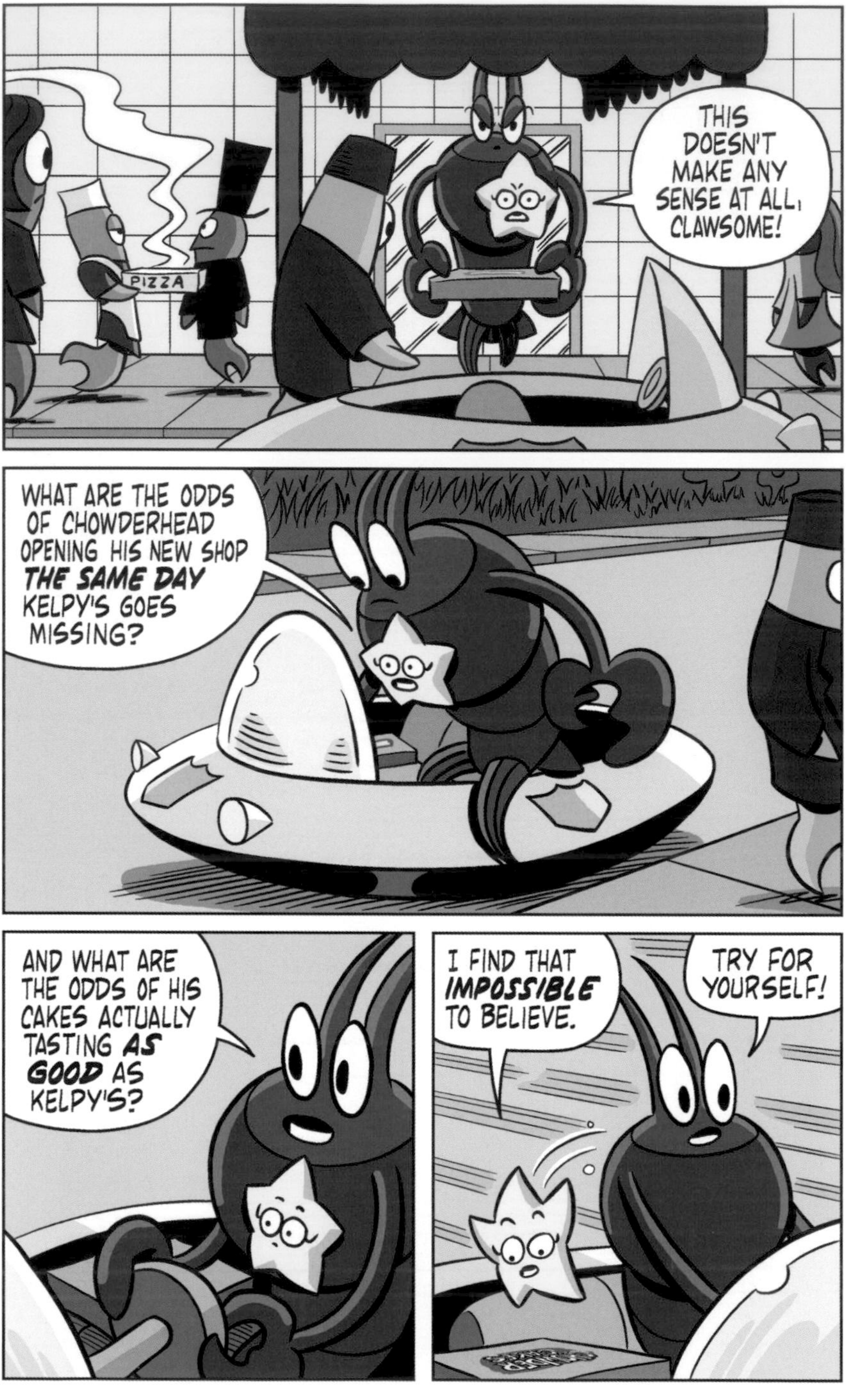
THIS DOESN'T MAKE ANY SENSE AT ALL, CLAWSOME!
PIZZA
WHAT ARE THE ODDS OF CHOWDERHEAD OPENING HIS NEW SHOP **THE SAME DAY** KELPY'S GOES MISSING?
AND WHAT ARE THE ODDS OF HIS CAKES ACTUALLY TASTING **AS GOOD** AS KELPY'S?
I FIND THAT **IMPOSSIBLE** TO BELIEVE.
TRY FOR YOURSELF!

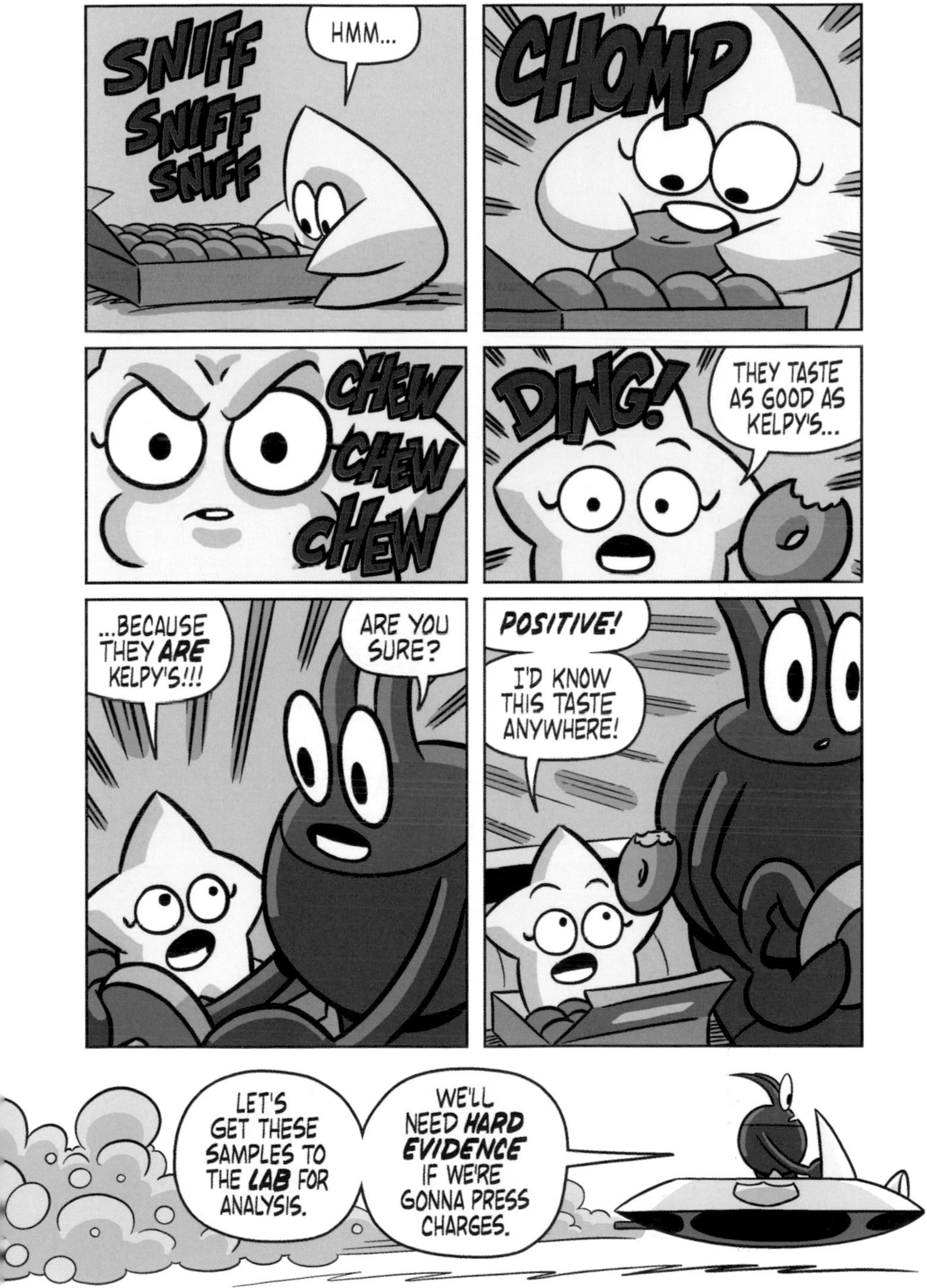
SNIFF
SNIFF
SNIFF
HMM...
CHOMP
CHEW
CHEW
CHEW
DING!
THEY TASTE AS GOOD AS KELPY'S...
...BECAUSE THEY **ARE** KELPY'S!!!
ARE YOU SURE?
POSITIVE!
I'D KNOW THIS TASTE ANYWHERE!
LET'S GET THESE SAMPLES TO THE **LAB** FOR ANALYSIS.
WE'LL NEED **HARD EVIDENCE** IF WE'RE GONNA PRESS CHARGES.

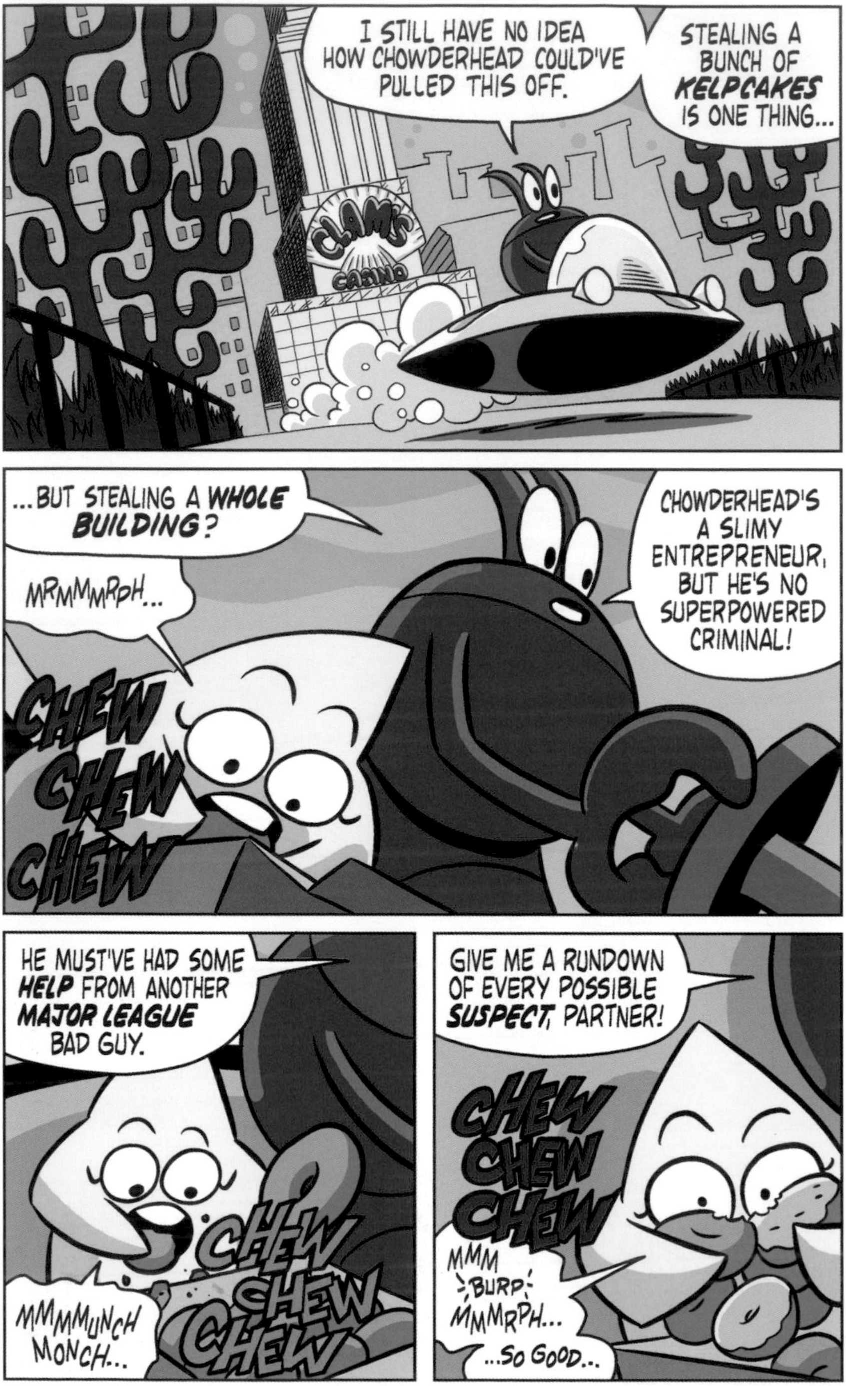
I STILL HAVE NO IDEA HOW CHOWDERHEAD COULD'VE PULLED THIS OFF.
STEALING A BUNCH OF ***KELPCAKES*** IS ONE THING...
CLAM'S CASINO
...BUT STEALING A ***WHOLE BUILDING?***
MRMMMRPH...
CHEW CHEW CHEW
CHOWDERHEAD'S A SLIMY ENTREPRENEUR, BUT HE'S NO SUPERPOWERED CRIMINAL!
HE MUST'VE HAD SOME ***HELP*** FROM ANOTHER ***MAJOR LEAGUE*** BAD GUY.
CHEW CHEW CHEW
MMMMUNCH MONCH...
GIVE ME A RUNDOWN OF EVERY POSSIBLE ***SUSPECT,*** PARTNER!
CHEW CHEW CHEW
MMM BURP MMMRPH...
...SO GOOD...

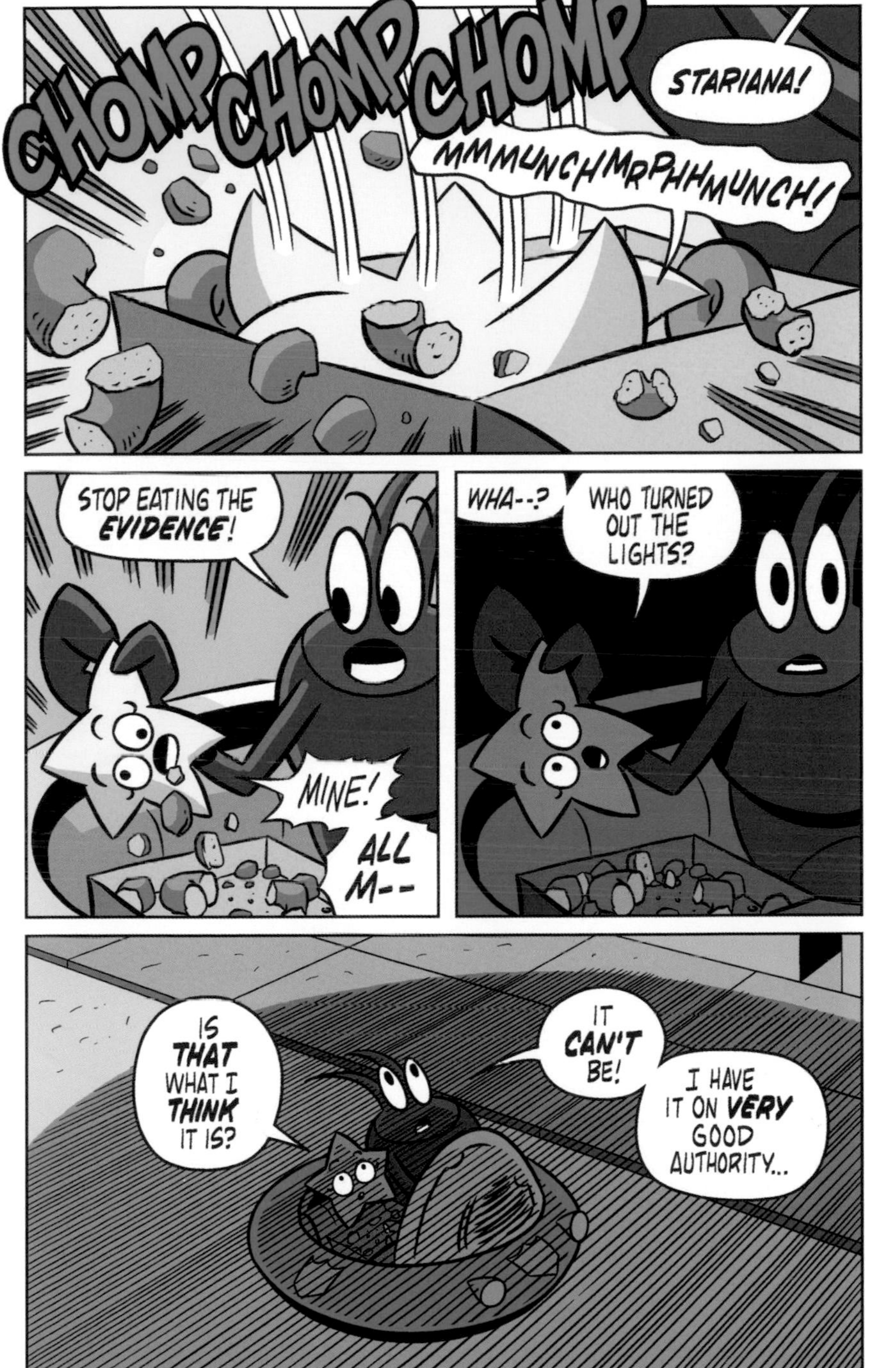
CHOMP CHOMP CHOMP
STARIANA!
MMMUNCHMRPHHMUNCH!
STOP EATING THE EVIDENCE!
MINE!
ALL M--
WHA--?
WHO TURNED OUT THE LIGHTS?
IS THAT WHAT I THINK IT IS?
IT CAN'T BE!
I HAVE IT ON VERY GOOD AUTHORITY...

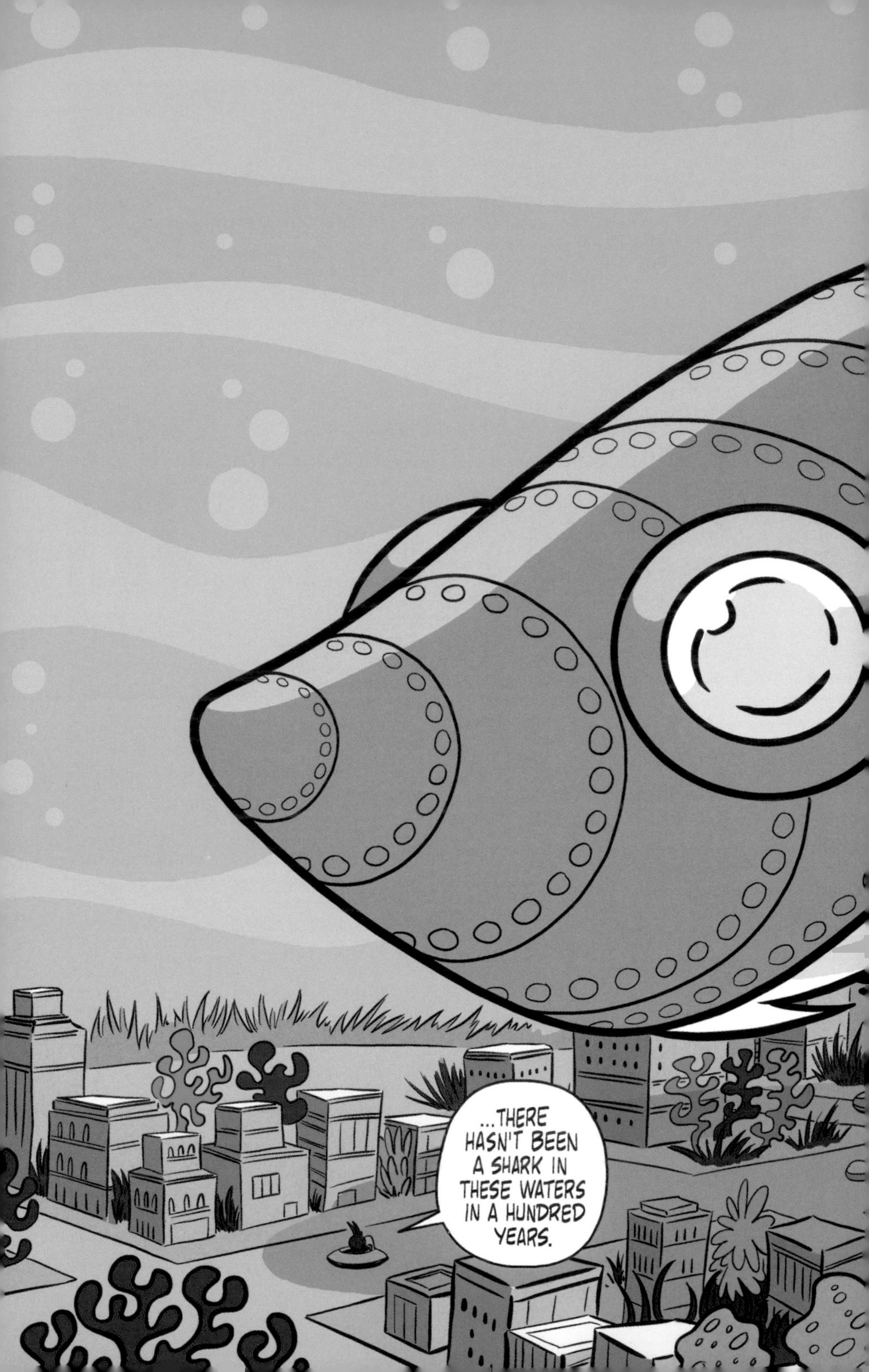
...THERE HASN'T BEEN A SHARK IN THESE WATERS IN A HUNDRED YEARS.

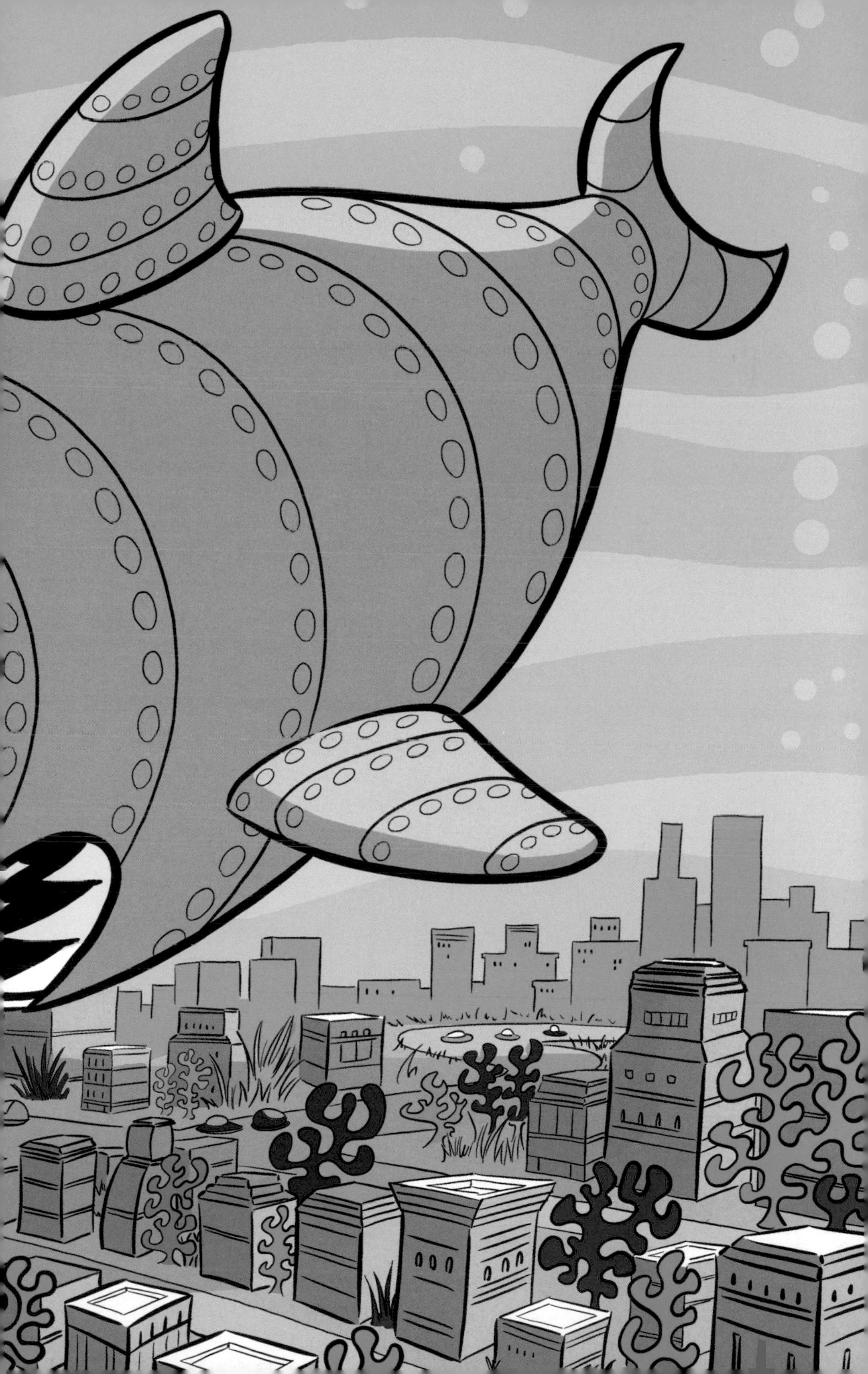

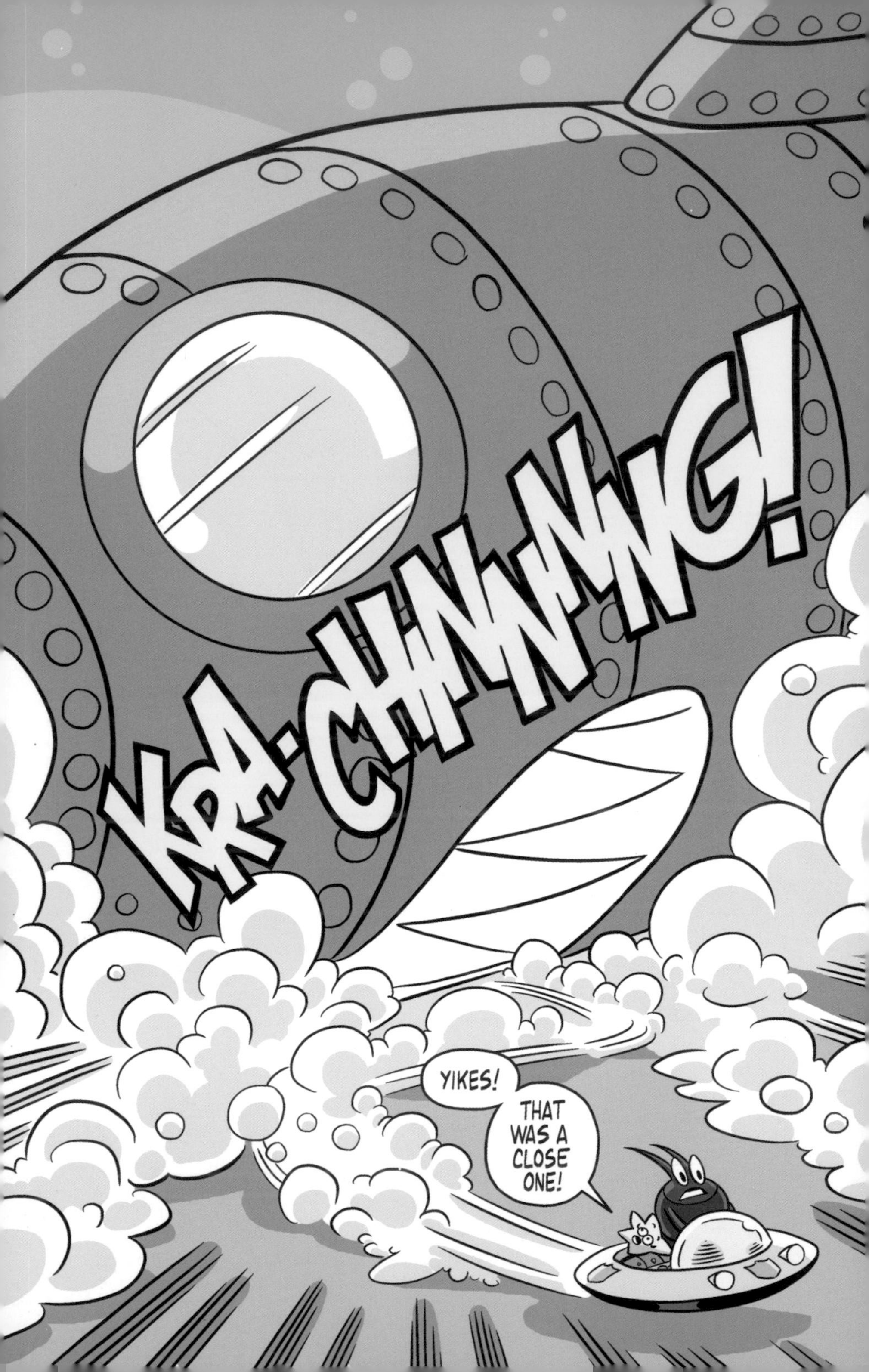
KRA-CHINNNNG!
YIKES!
THAT WAS A CLOSE ONE!

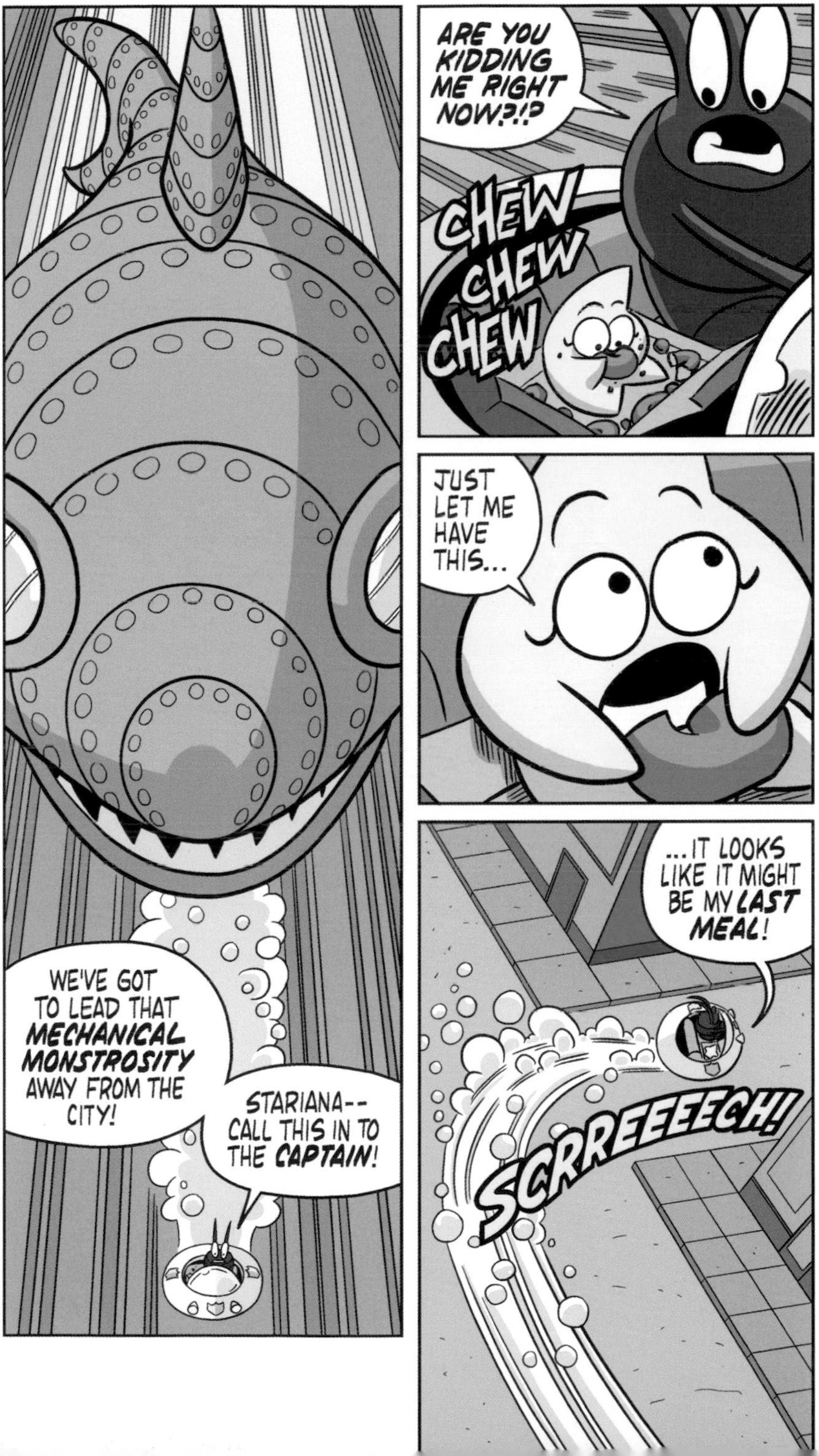
WE'VE GOT TO LEAD THAT MECHANICAL MONSTROSITY AWAY FROM THE CITY!
STARIANA-- CALL THIS IN TO THE CAPTAIN!
ARE YOU KIDDING ME RIGHT NOW?!?
CHEW CHEW CHEW
JUST LET ME HAVE THIS...
...IT LOOKS LIKE IT MIGHT BE MY LAST MEAL!
SCRREEEECH!

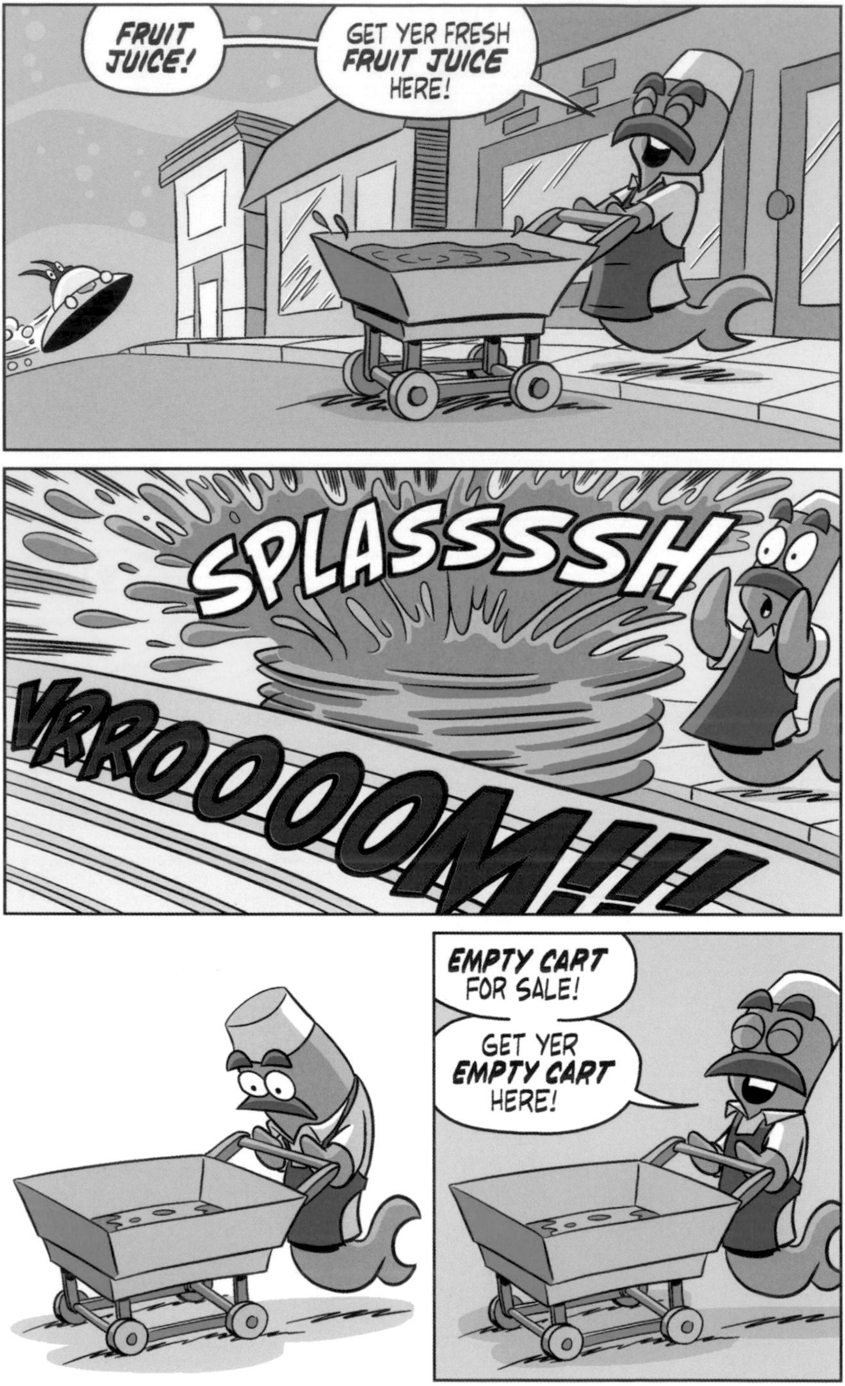
FRUIT JUICE!
GET YER FRESH FRUIT JUICE HERE!
SPLASSSSH
VRROOOOOM!!!
EMPTY CART FOR SALE!
GET YER EMPTY CART HERE!

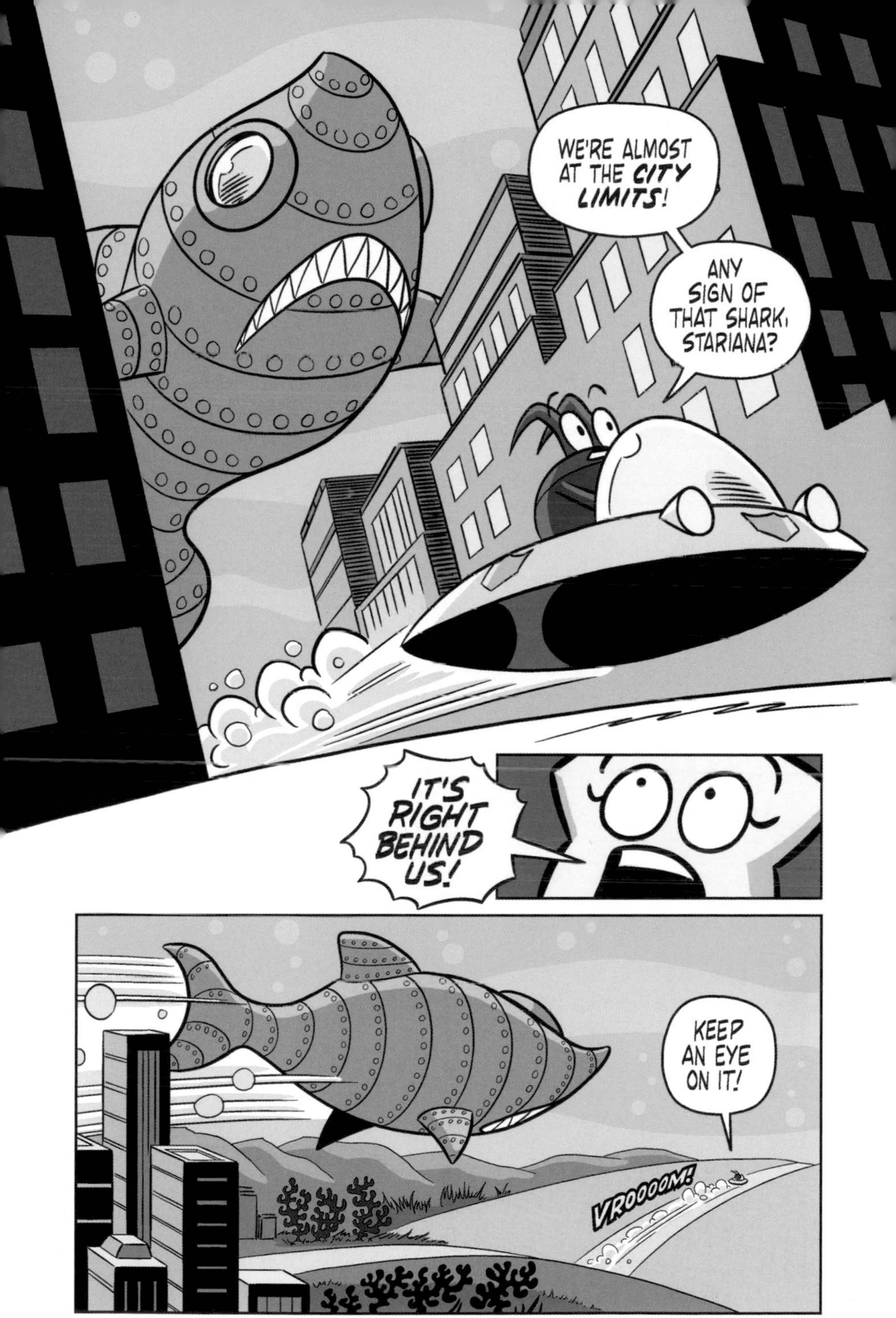
WE'RE ALMOST AT THE CITY LIMITS!
ANY SIGN OF THAT SHARK, STARIANA?
IT'S RIGHT BEHIND US!
KEEP AN EYE ON IT!
VROOOOM!

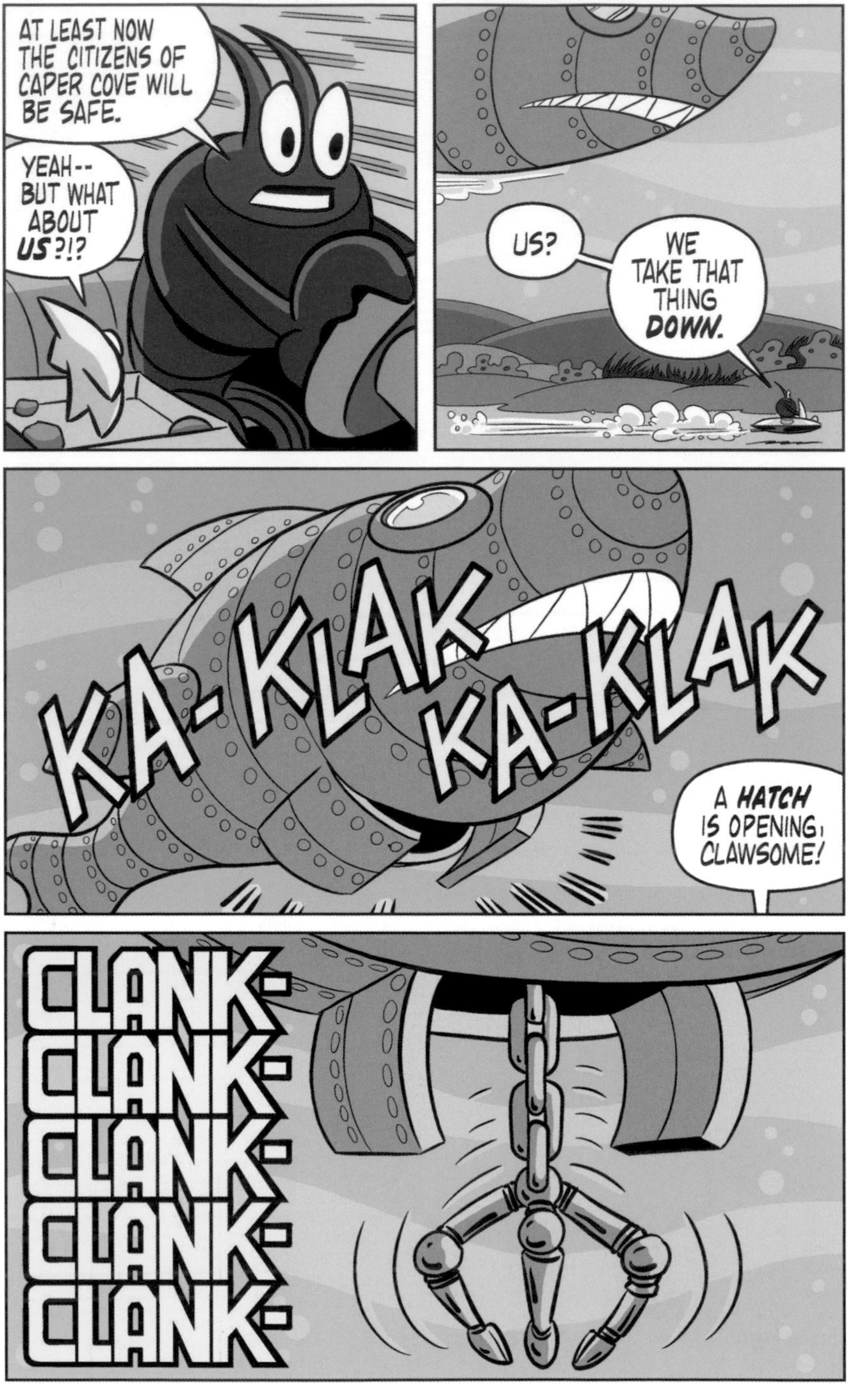
AT LEAST NOW THE CITIZENS OF CAPER COVE WILL BE SAFE.
YEAH-- BUT WHAT ABOUT **US**?!?
US?
WE TAKE THAT THING **DOWN.**
KA-KLAK KA-KLAK
A **HATCH** IS OPENING, CLAWSOME!
CLANK-CLANK-CLANK-CLANK-CLANK-

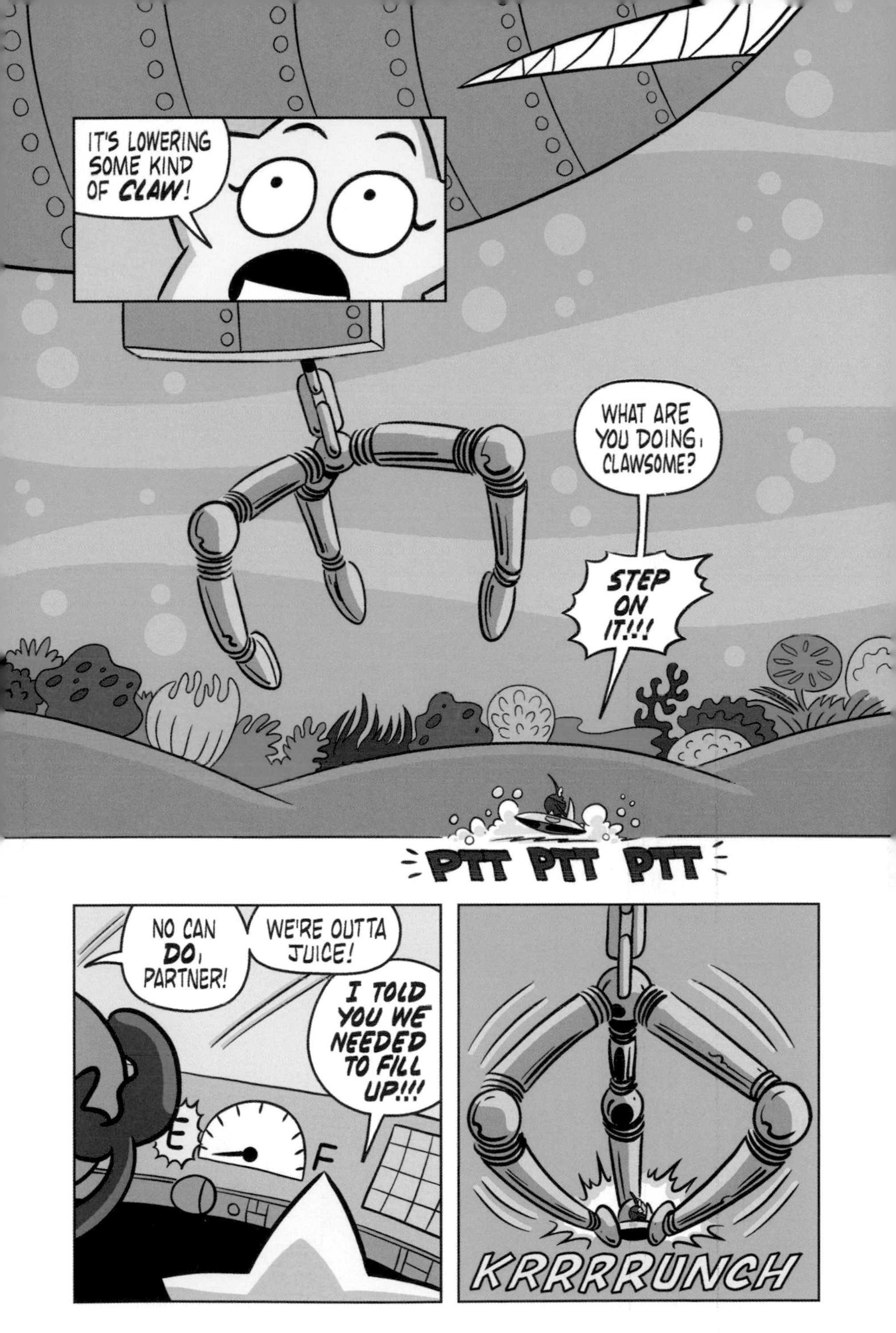
IT'S LOWERING SOME KIND OF CLAW!
WHAT ARE YOU DOING, CLAWSOME?
STEP ON IT!!!
PTT PTT PTT
NO CAN DO, PARTNER!
WE'RE OUTTA JUICE!
I TOLD YOU WE NEEDED TO FILL UP!!!
E
F
KRRRRUNCH

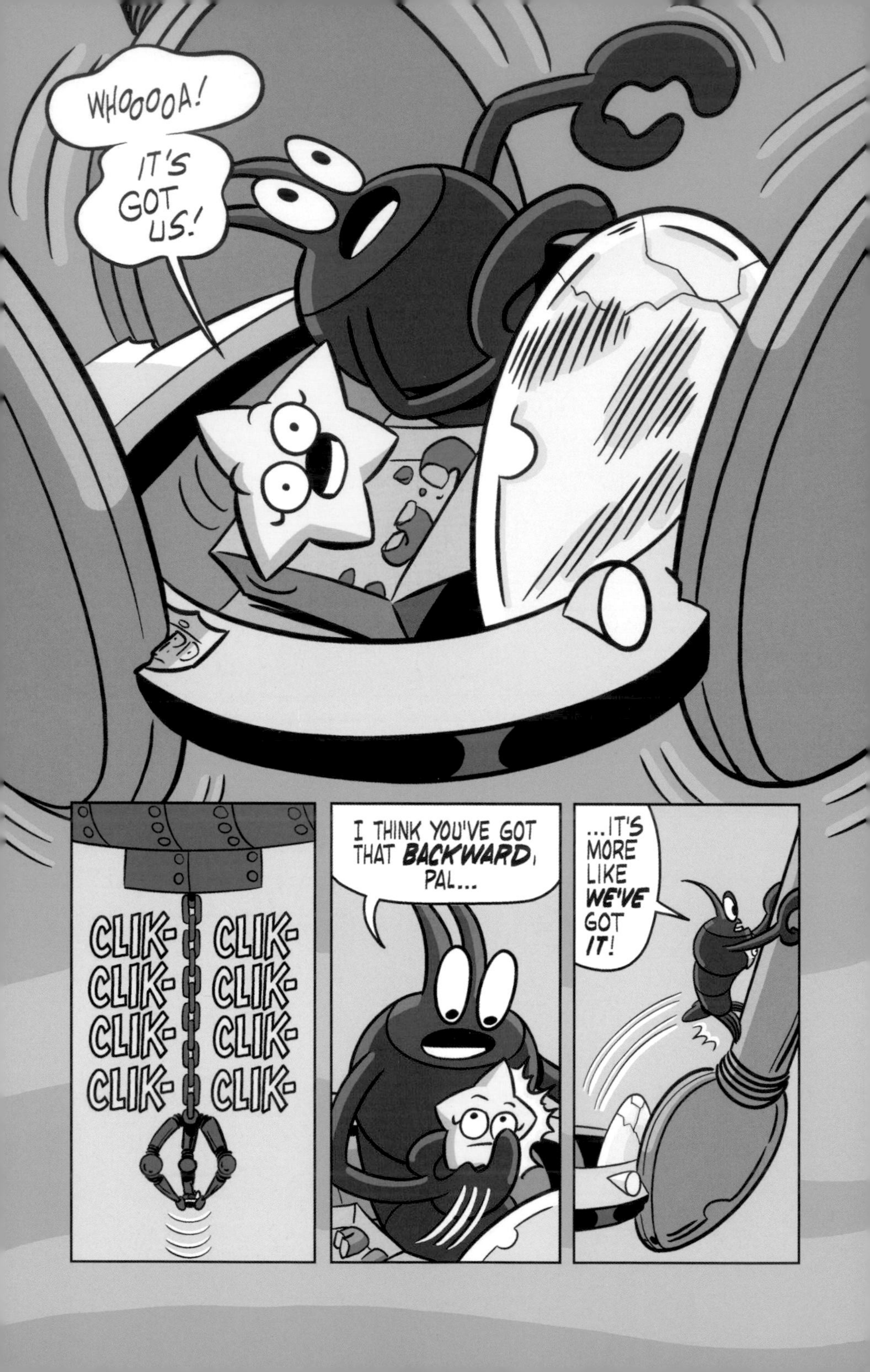
WHOOOOA!
IT'S GOT US!
CLIK- CLIK- CLIK- CLIK- CLIK- CLIK- CLIK- CLIK-
I THINK YOU'VE GOT THAT **BACKWARD**, PAL...
...IT'S MORE LIKE ***WE'VE*** GOT ***IT***!

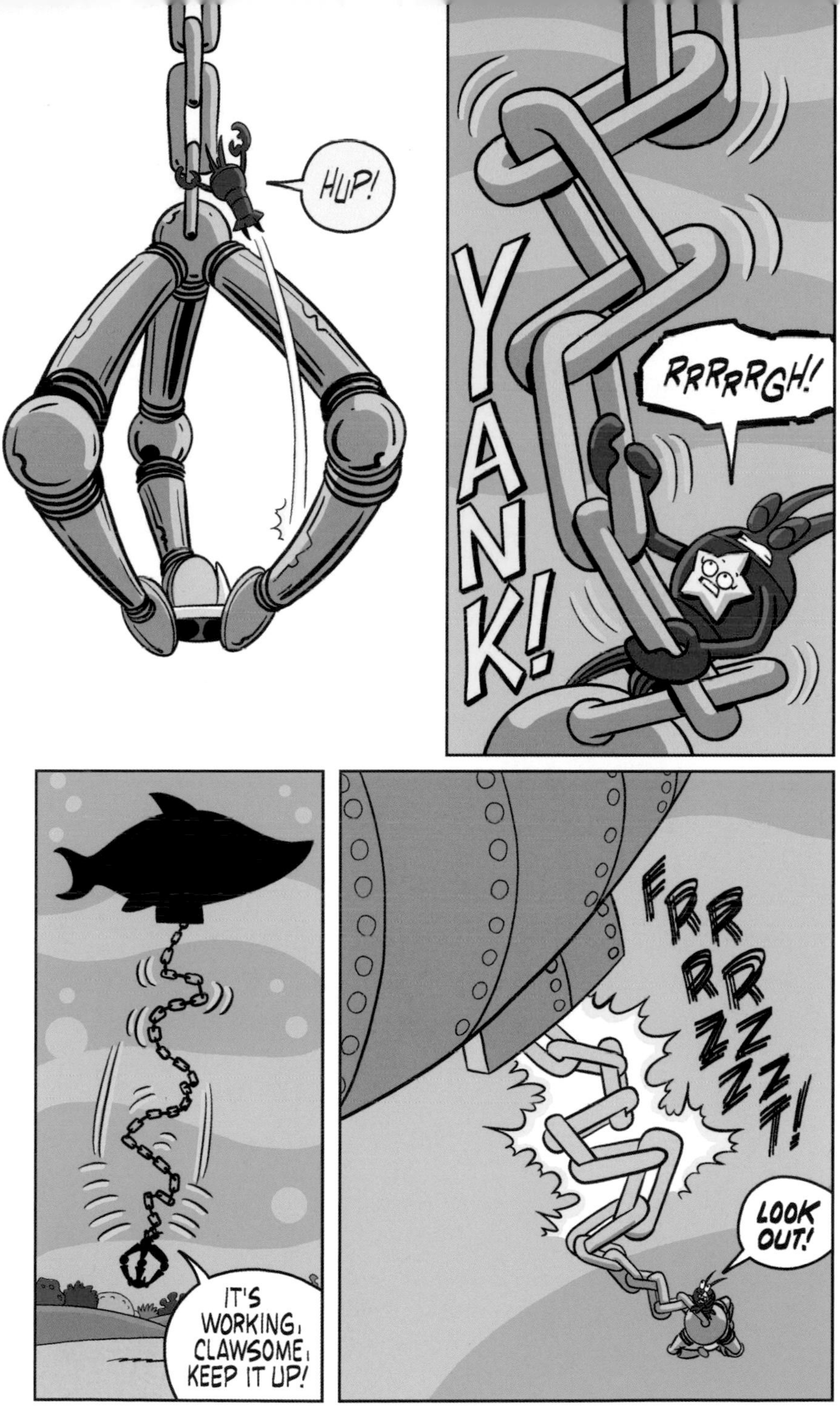
HUP!
YANK!
RRRRRGH!
IT'S WORKING, CLAWSOME, KEEP IT UP!
FRRRRRZZZZZT!
LOOK OUT!

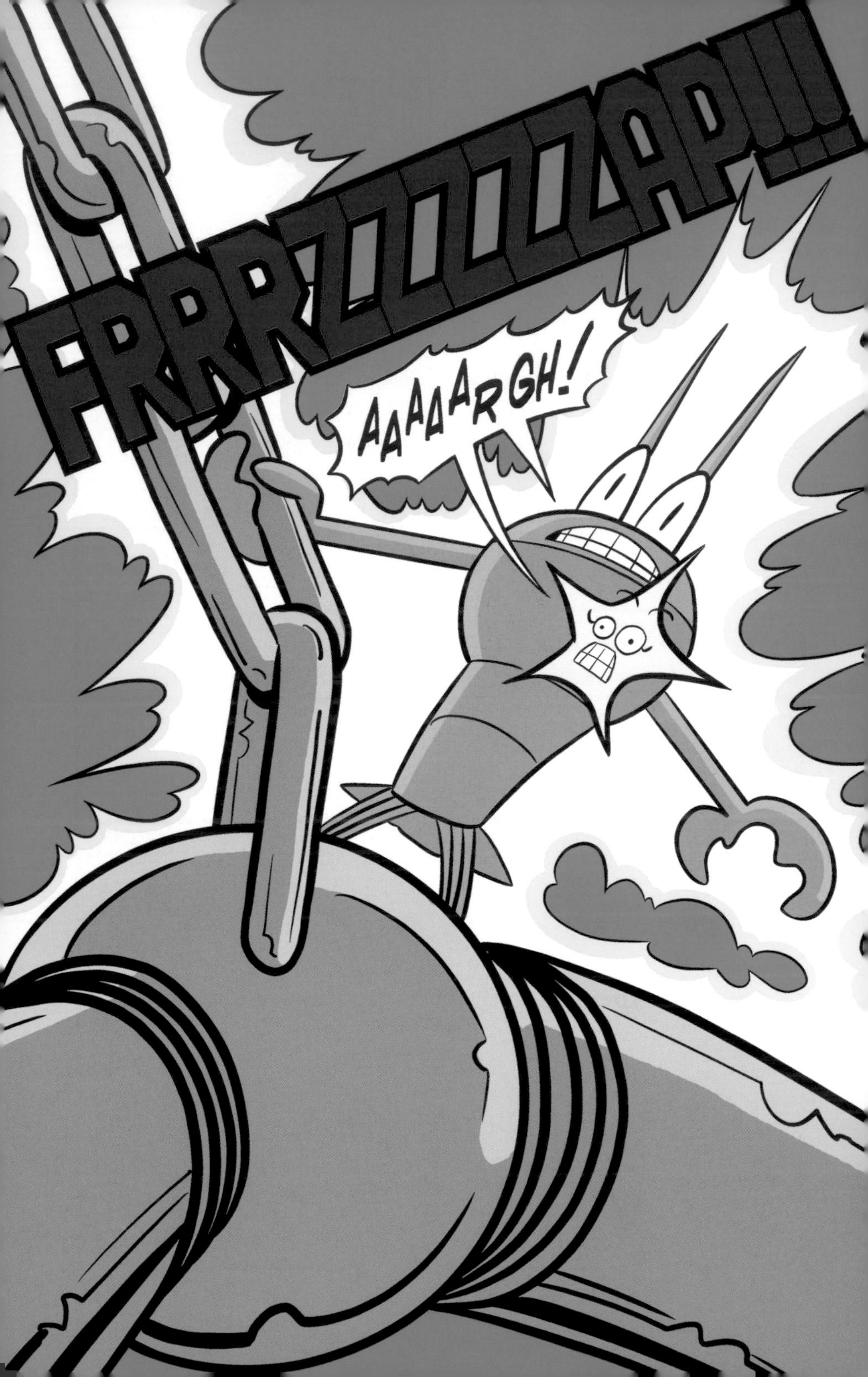
FRRRZZZZZZAP!!!
AAAAARGH!

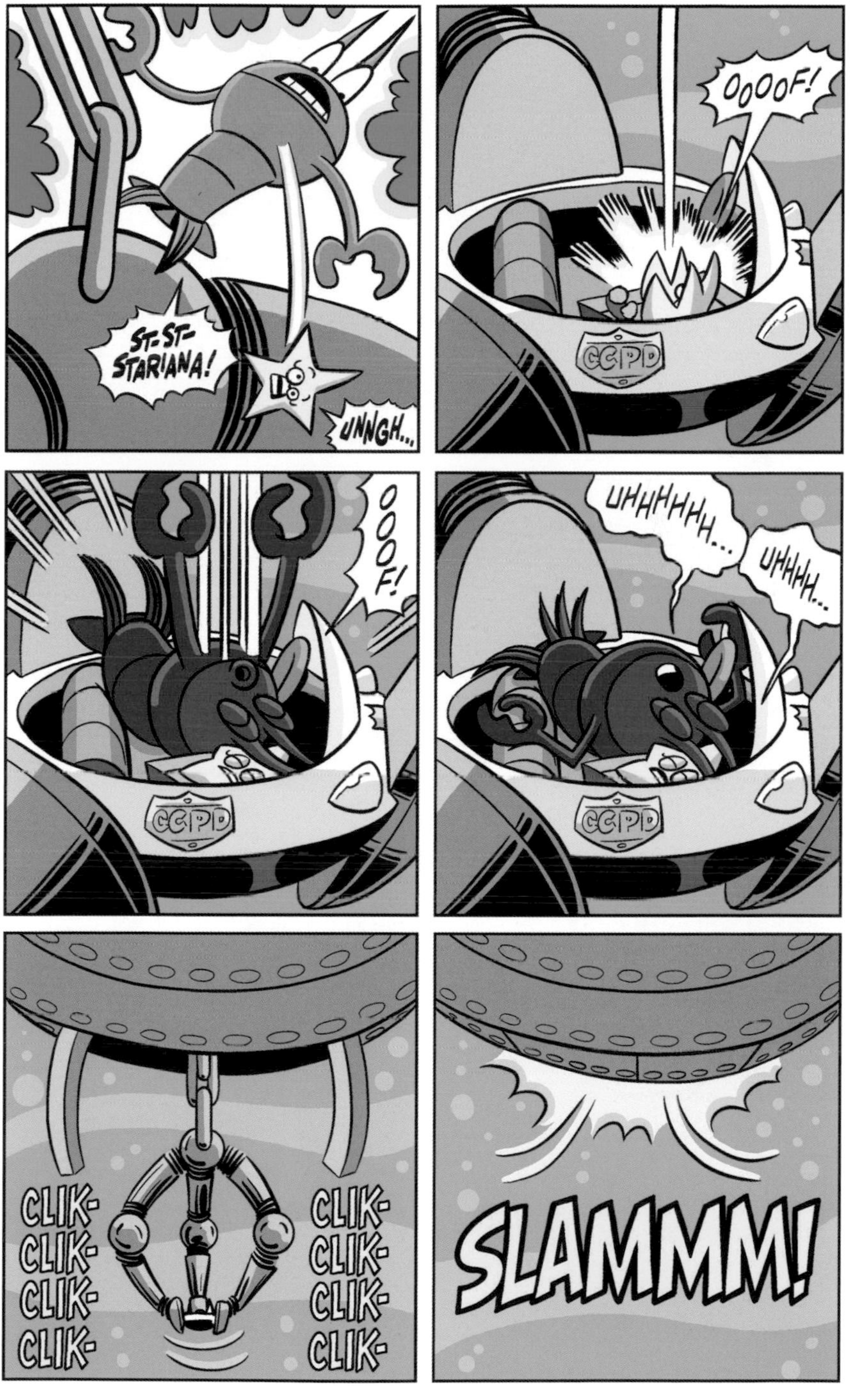
ST-ST-STARIANA!
UNNGH...
OOOOF!
OOOOF!
UHHHHHH...
UHHHH...
CLIK-
CLIK-
CLIK-
CLIK-
CLIK-
CLIK-
CLIK-
CLIK-
SLAMMM!

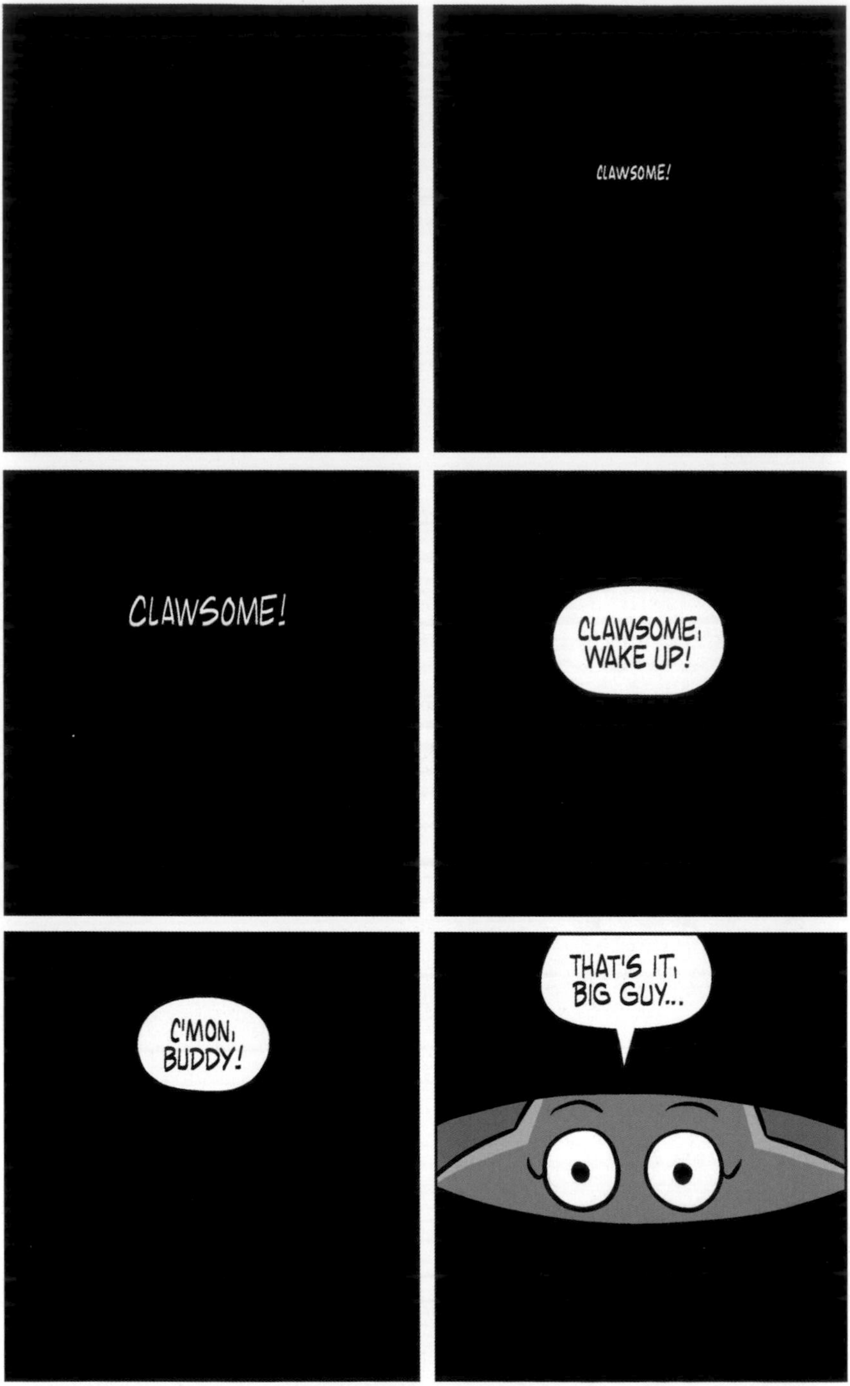
CLAWSOME!
CLAWSOME!
CLAWSOME, WAKE UP!
C'MON, BUDDY!
THAT'S IT, BIG GUY...

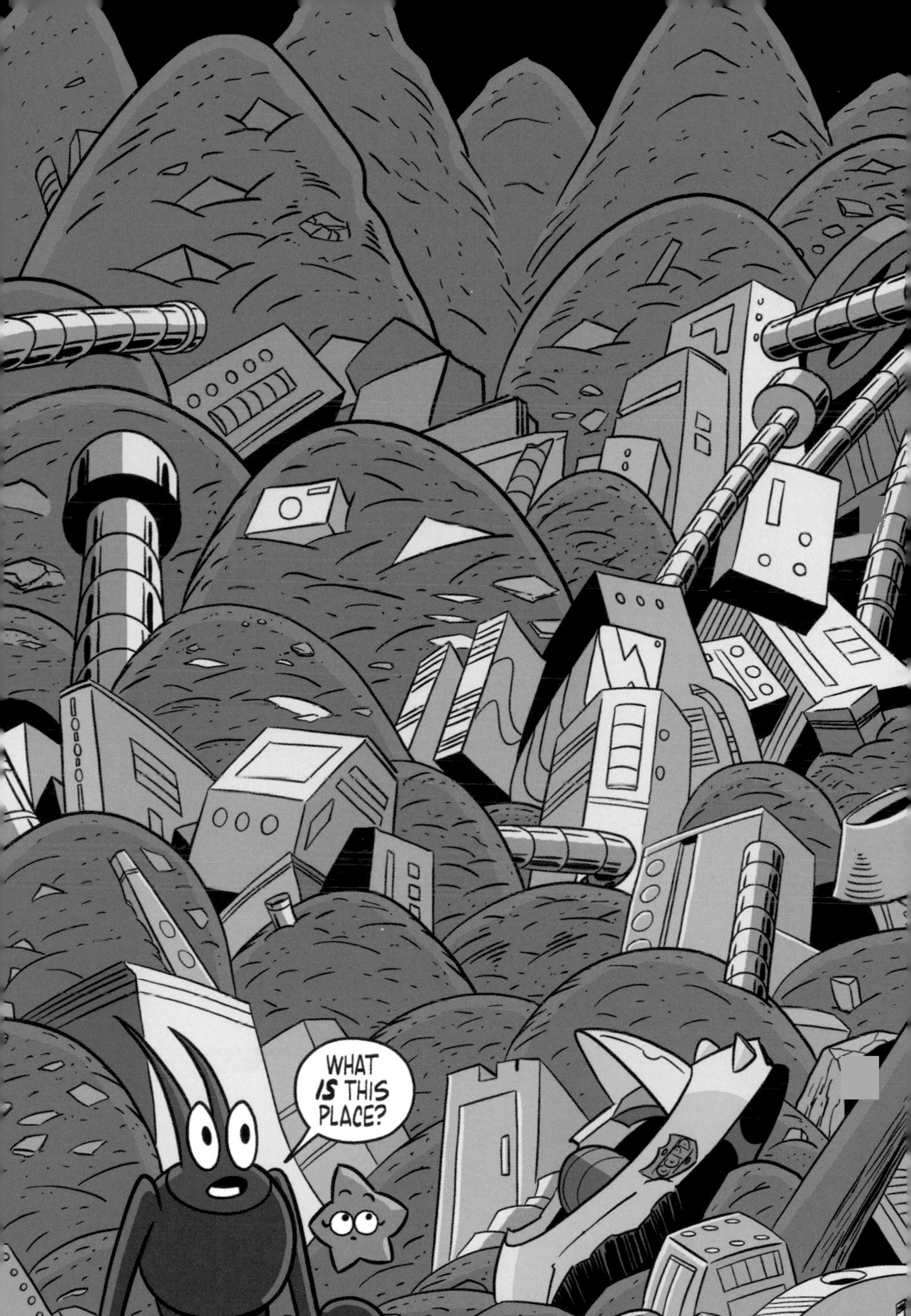
WHAT
IS THIS
PLACE?

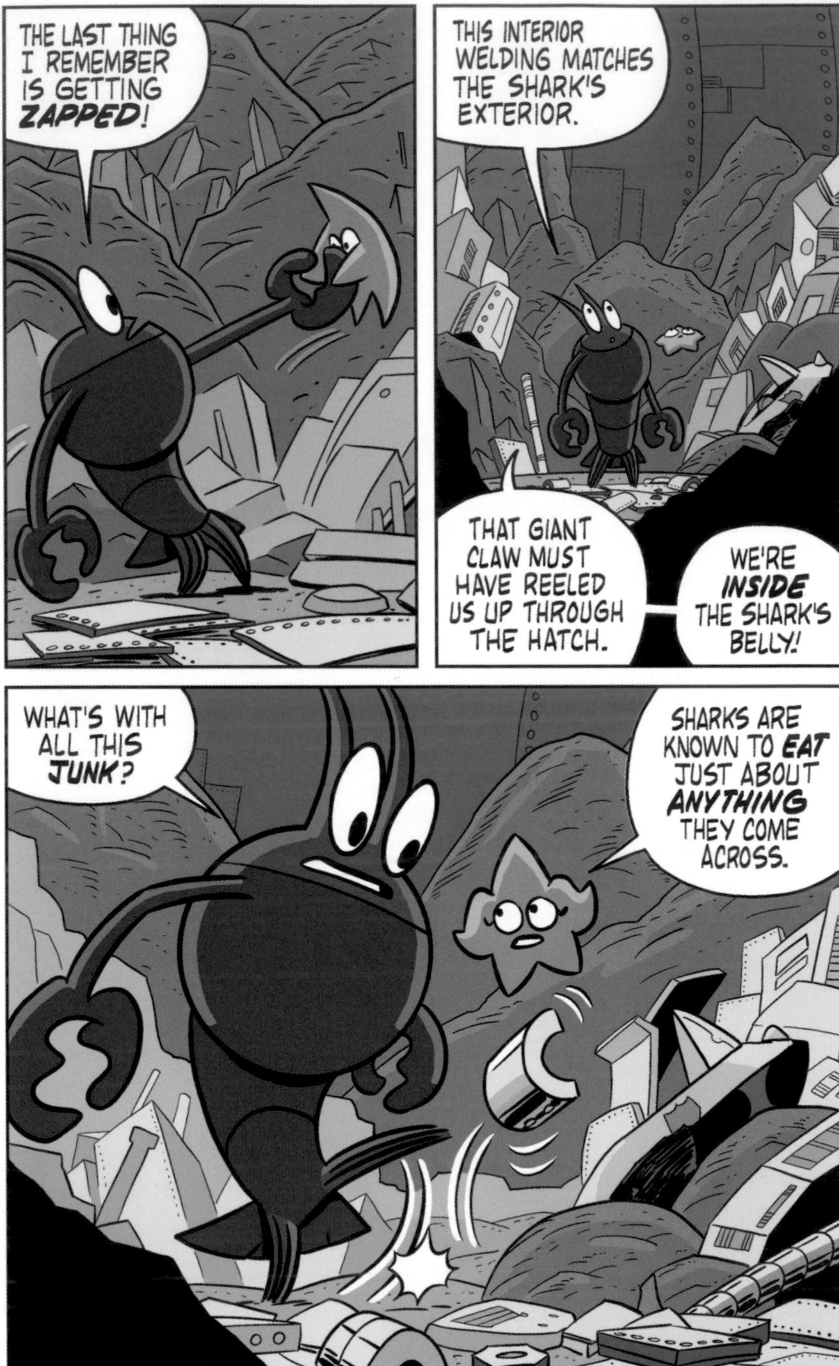
THE LAST THING I REMEMBER IS GETTING ZAPPED!
THIS INTERIOR WELDING MATCHES THE SHARK'S EXTERIOR.
THAT GIANT CLAW MUST HAVE REELED US UP THROUGH THE HATCH.
WE'RE INSIDE THE SHARK'S BELLY!
WHAT'S WITH ALL THIS JUNK?
SHARKS ARE KNOWN TO EAT JUST ABOUT ANYTHING THEY COME ACROSS.

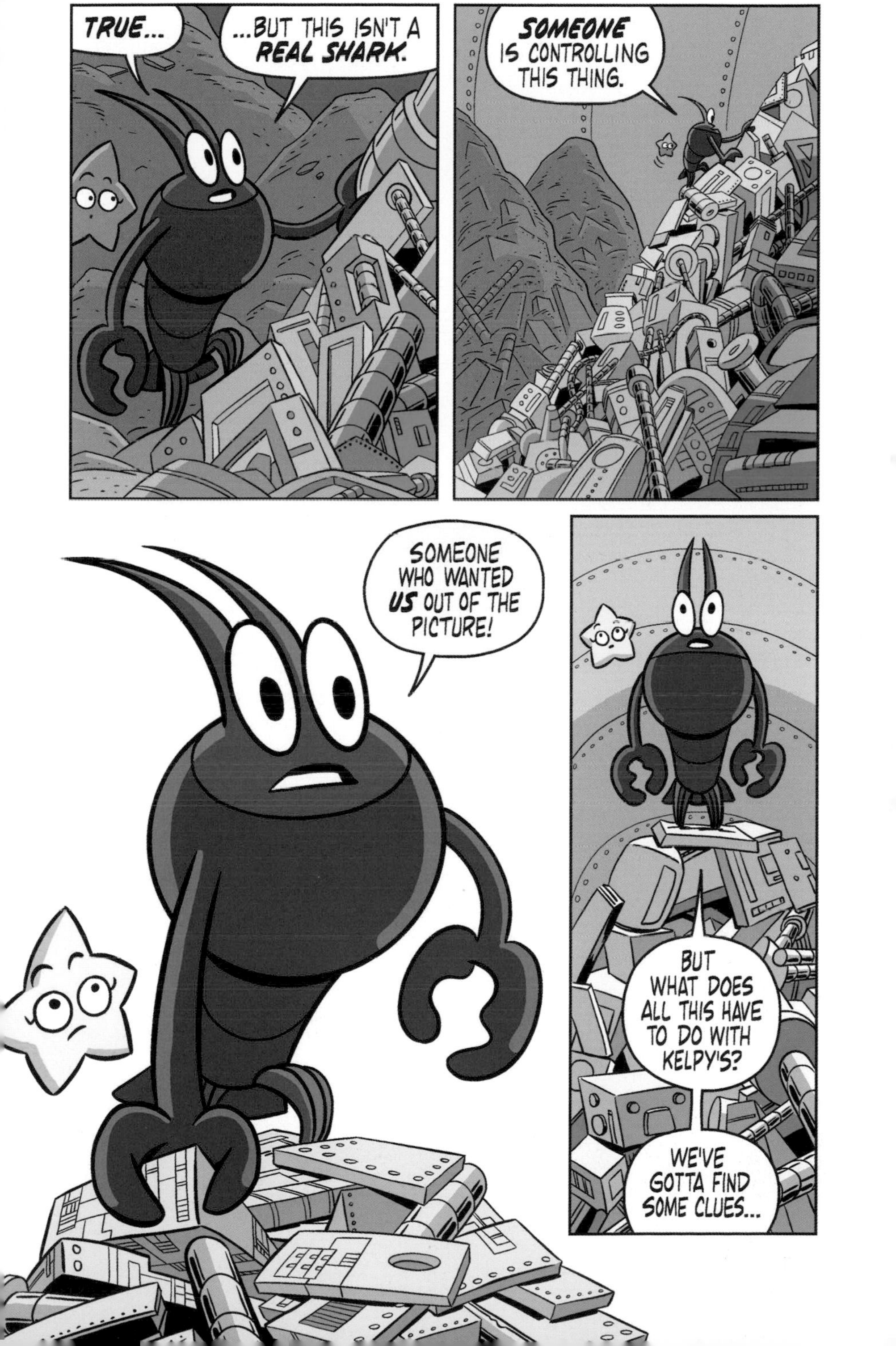
TRUE...
...BUT THIS ISN'T A **REAL SHARK.**
SOMEONE IS CONTROLLING THIS THING.
SOMEONE WHO WANTED **US** OUT OF THE PICTURE!
BUT WHAT DOES ALL THIS HAVE TO DO WITH KELPY'S?
WE'VE GOTTA FIND SOME CLUES...

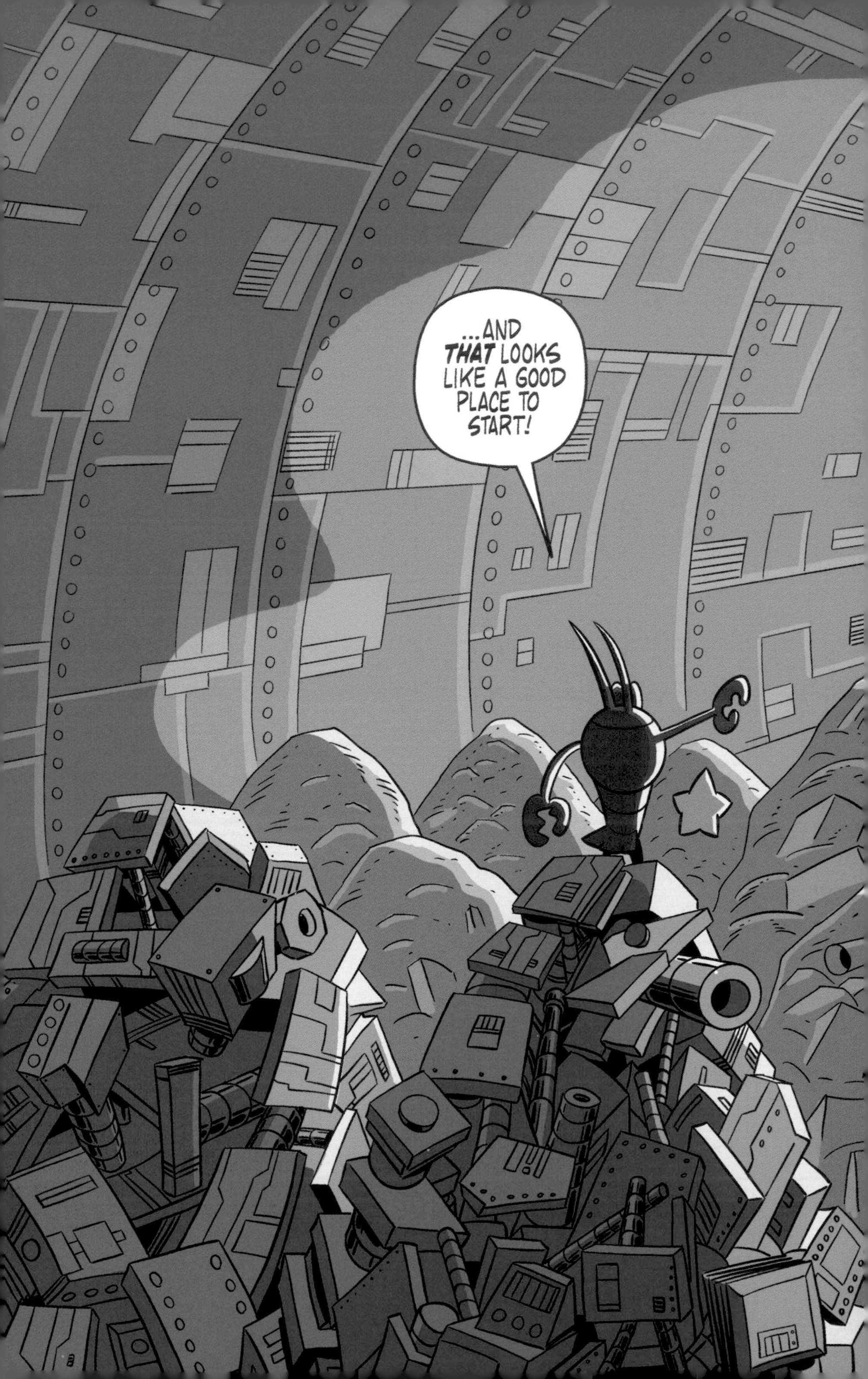
...AND *THAT* LOOKS LIKE A GOOD PLACE TO START!

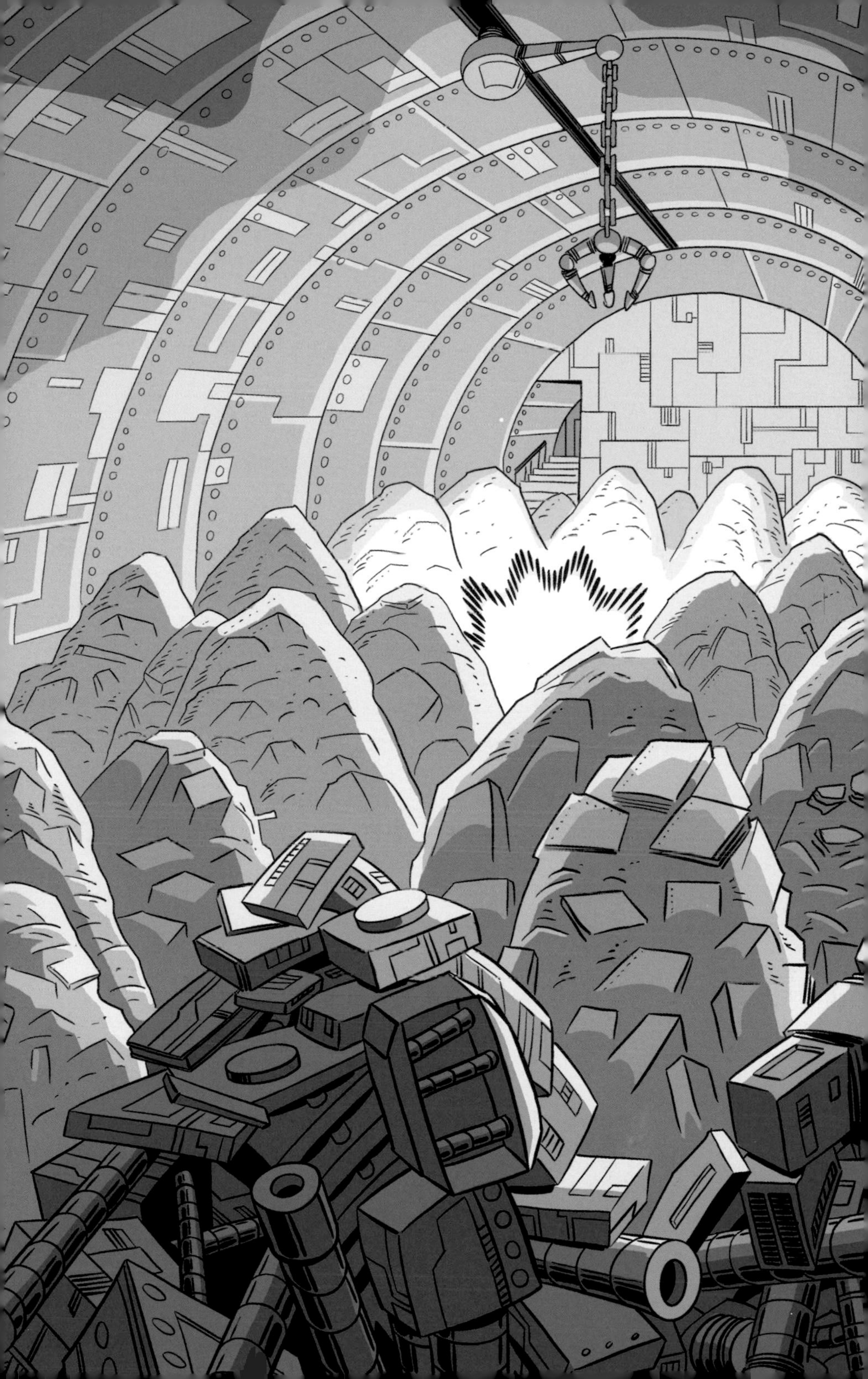

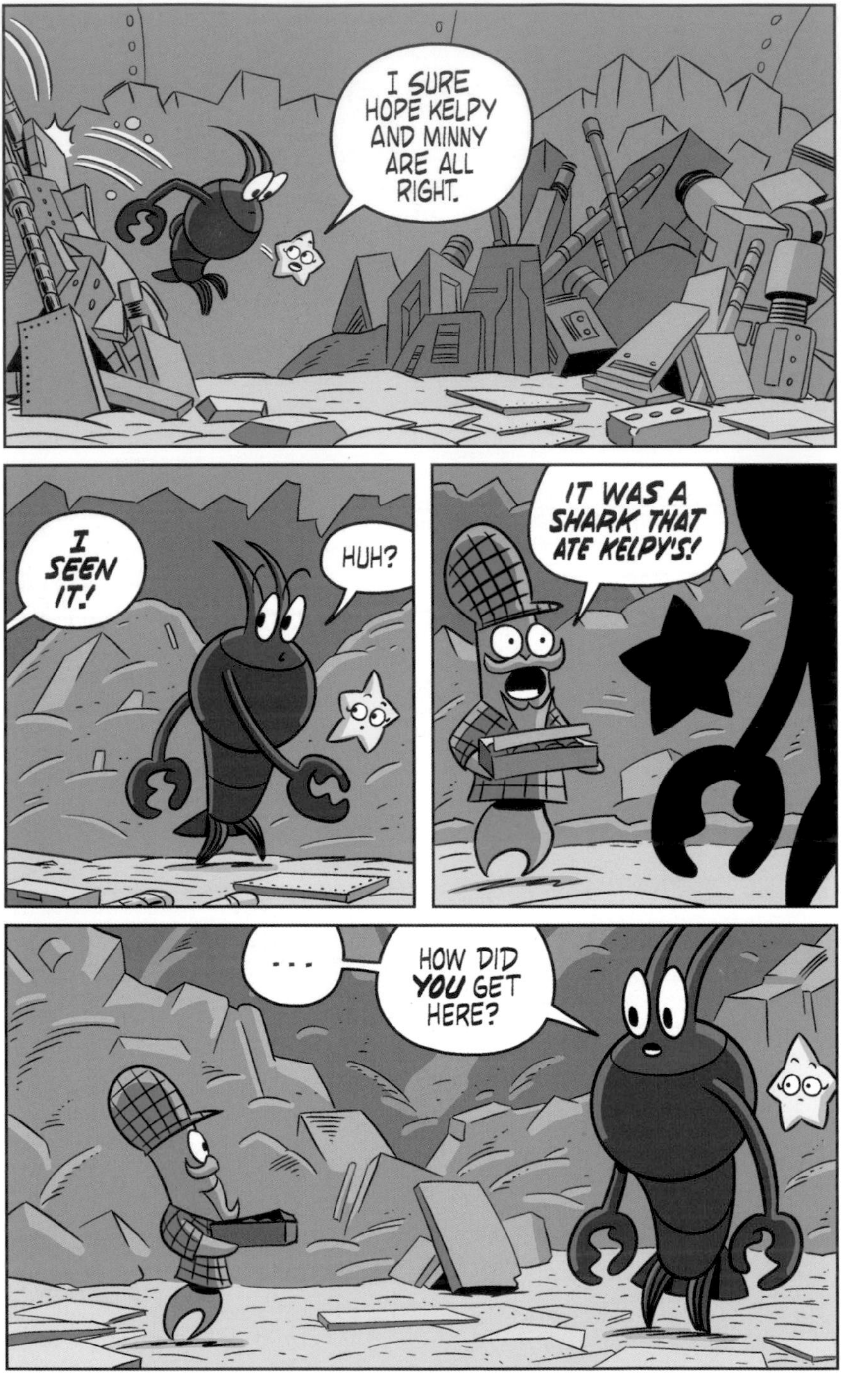
I SURE HOPE KELPY AND MINNY ARE ALL RIGHT.
I SEEN IT!
HUH?
IT WAS A SHARK THAT ATE KELPY'S!
...
HOW DID *YOU* GET HERE?

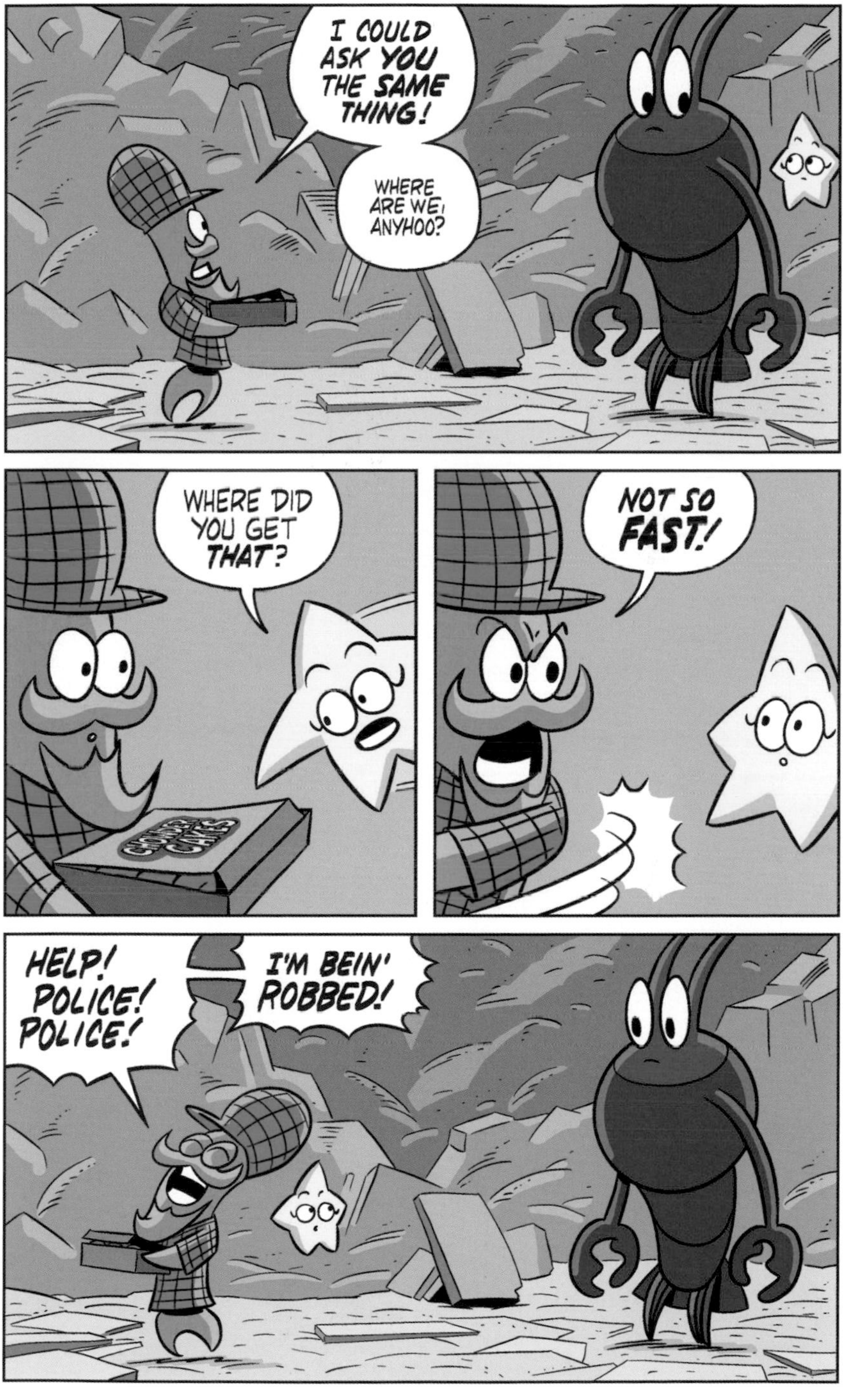
I COULD ASK YOU THE SAME THING!
WHERE ARE WE, ANYHOO?
WHERE DID YOU GET THAT?
CHOWDER CAKES
NOT SO FAST!
HELP! POLICE! POLICE!
I'M BEIN' ROBBED!

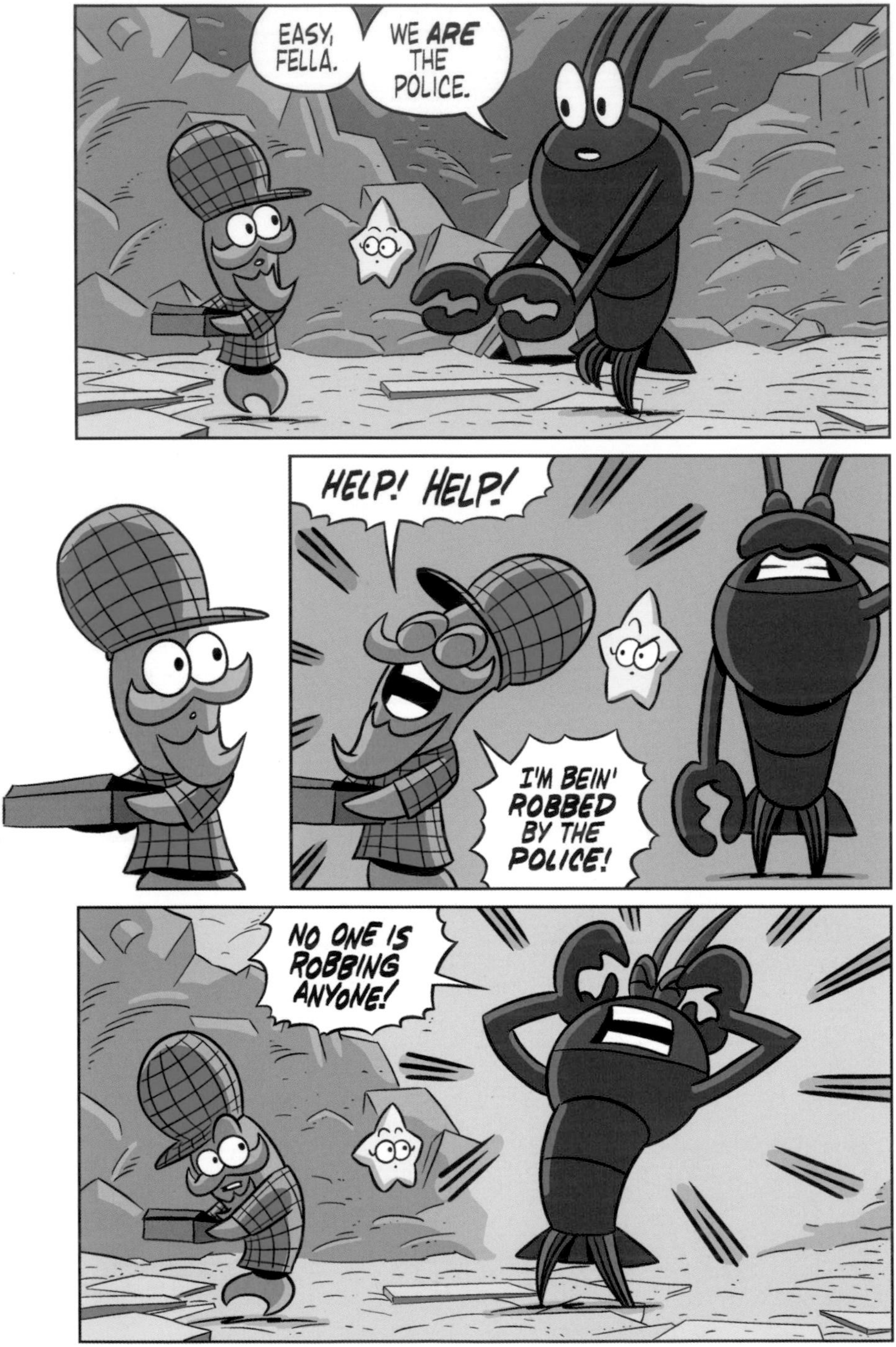
EASY, FELLA.
WE ARE THE POLICE.
HELP! HELP!
I'M BEIN' ROBBED BY THE POLICE!
NO ONE IS ROBBING ANYONE!

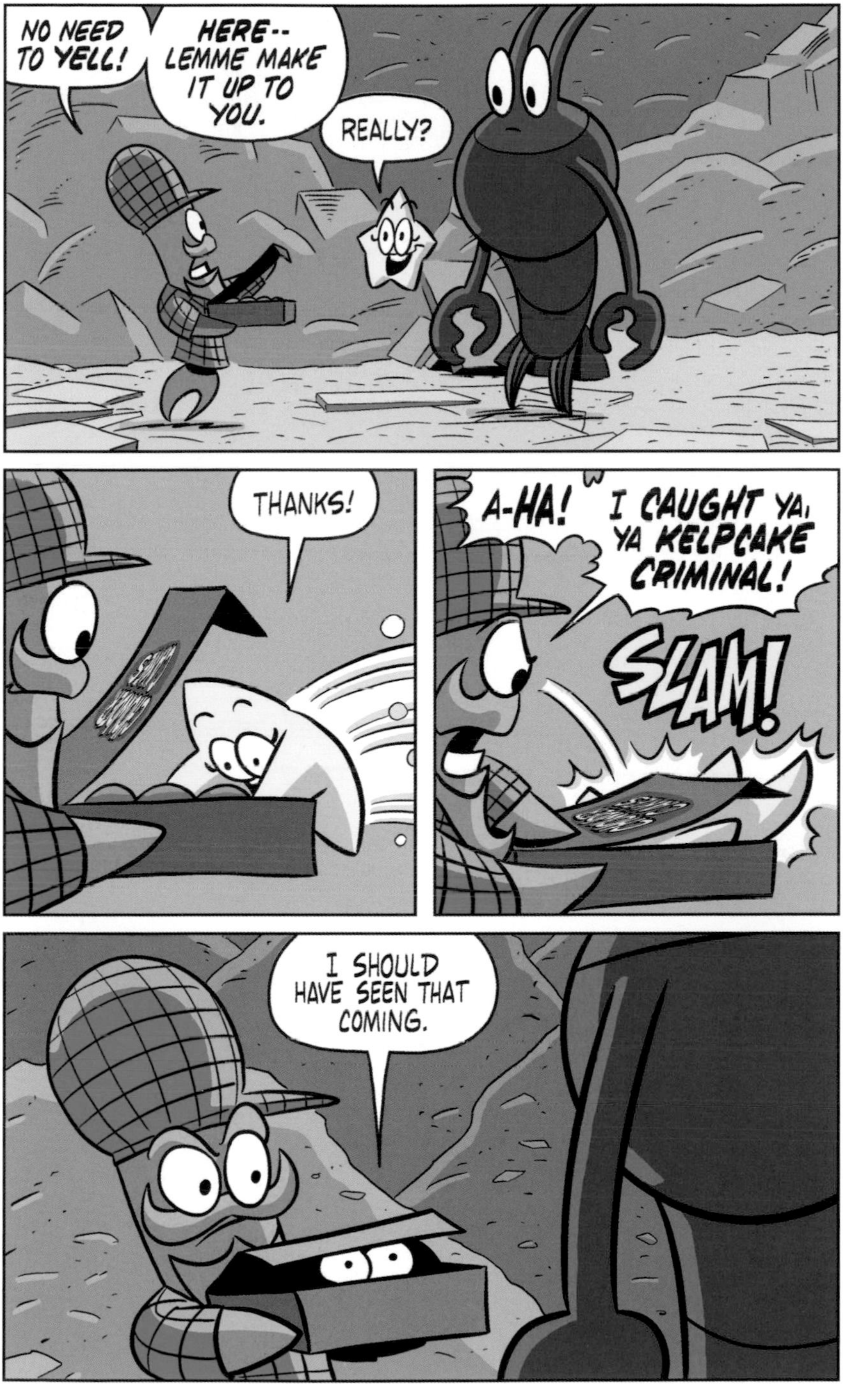
NO NEED TO YELL!
HERE-- LEMME MAKE IT UP TO YOU.
REALLY?
THANKS!
A-HA! I CAUGHT YA, YA KELPCAKE CRIMINAL!
SLAM!
I SHOULD HAVE SEEN THAT COMING.

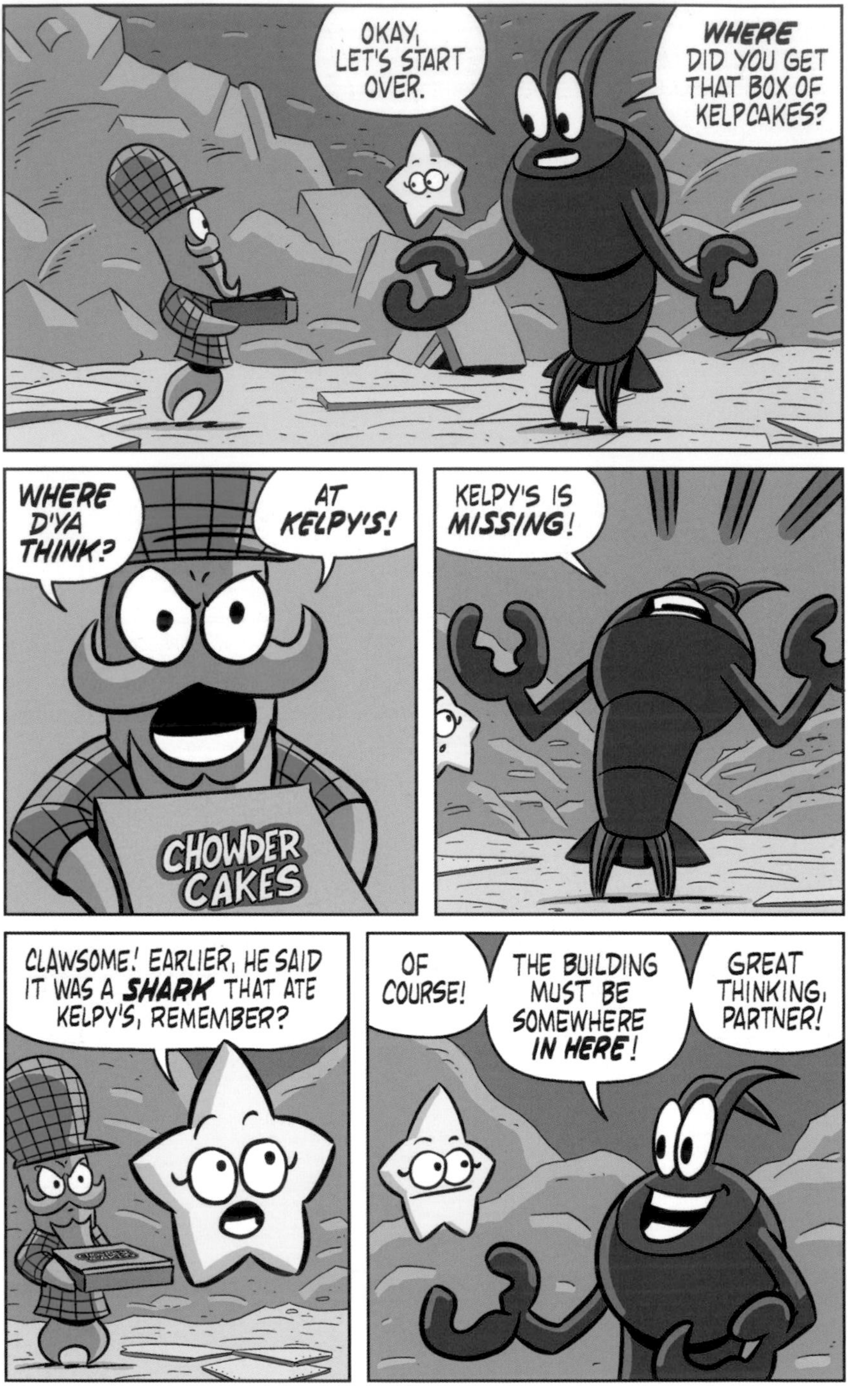
OKAY, LET'S START OVER.
WHERE DID YOU GET THAT BOX OF KELPCAKES?
WHERE D'YA THINK?
AT KELPY'S!
CHOWDER CAKES
KELPY'S IS MISSING!
CLAWSOME! EARLIER, HE SAID IT WAS A SHARK THAT ATE KELPY'S, REMEMBER?
OF COURSE!
THE BUILDING MUST BE SOMEWHERE IN HERE!
GREAT THINKING, PARTNER!

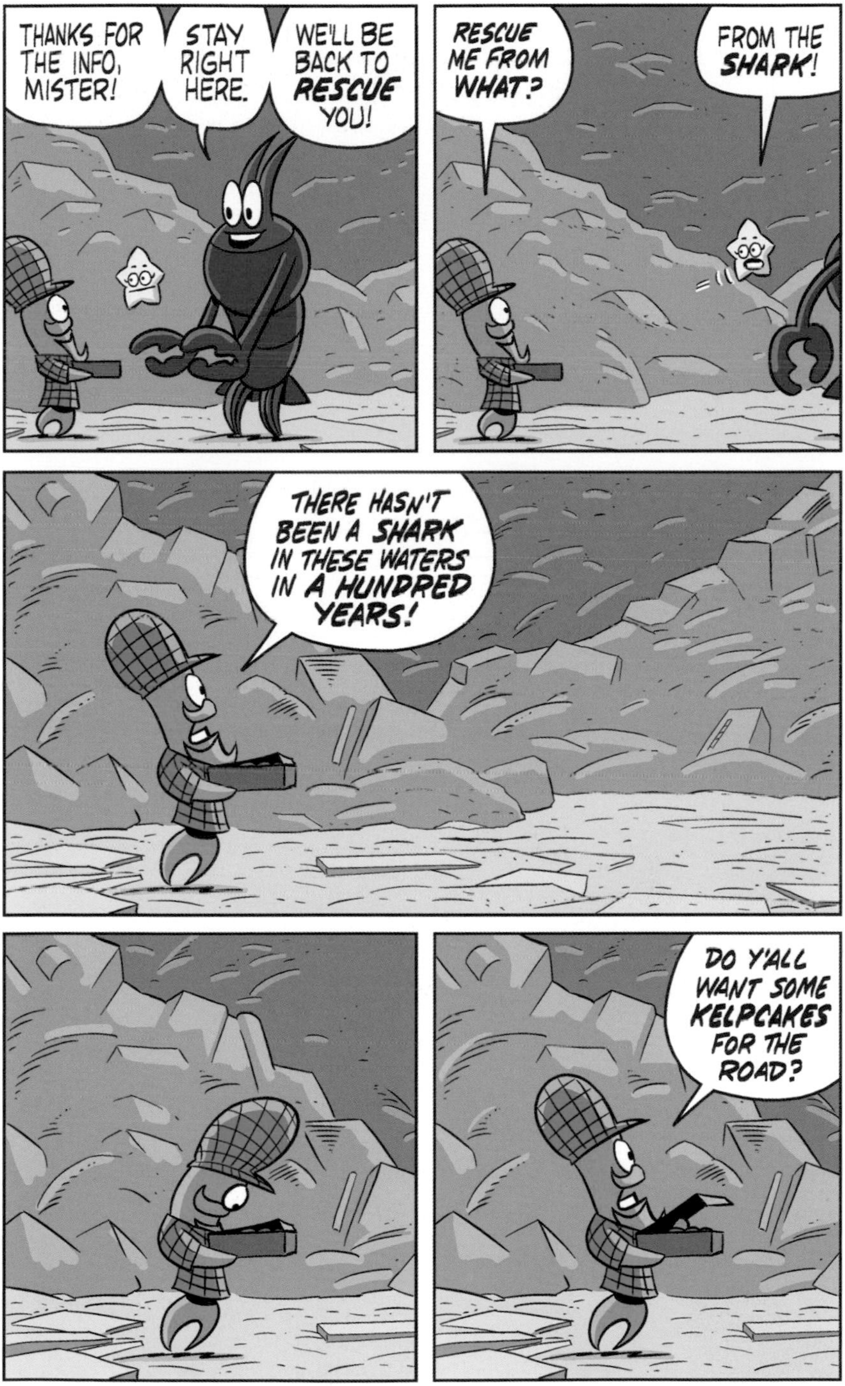
THANKS FOR THE INFO, MISTER!
STAY RIGHT HERE.
WE'LL BE BACK TO RESCUE YOU!
RESCUE ME FROM WHAT?
FROM THE SHARK!
THERE HASN'T BEEN A SHARK IN THESE WATERS IN A HUNDRED YEARS!
DO Y'ALL WANT SOME KELPCAKES FOR THE ROAD?

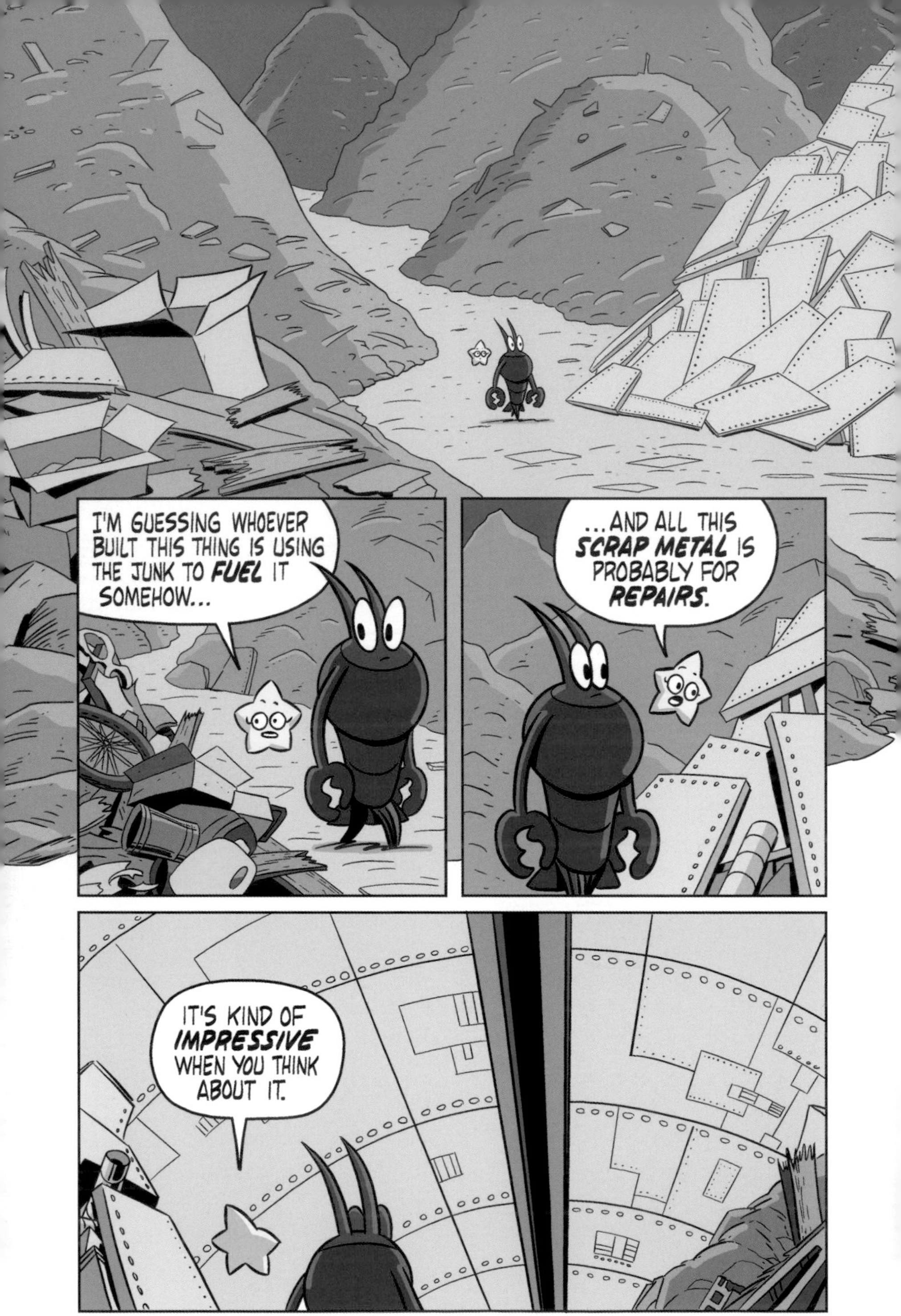
I'M GUESSING WHOEVER BUILT THIS THING IS USING THE JUNK TO FUEL IT SOMEHOW...
...AND ALL THIS SCRAP METAL IS PROBABLY FOR REPAIRS.
IT'S KIND OF IMPRESSIVE WHEN YOU THINK ABOUT IT.

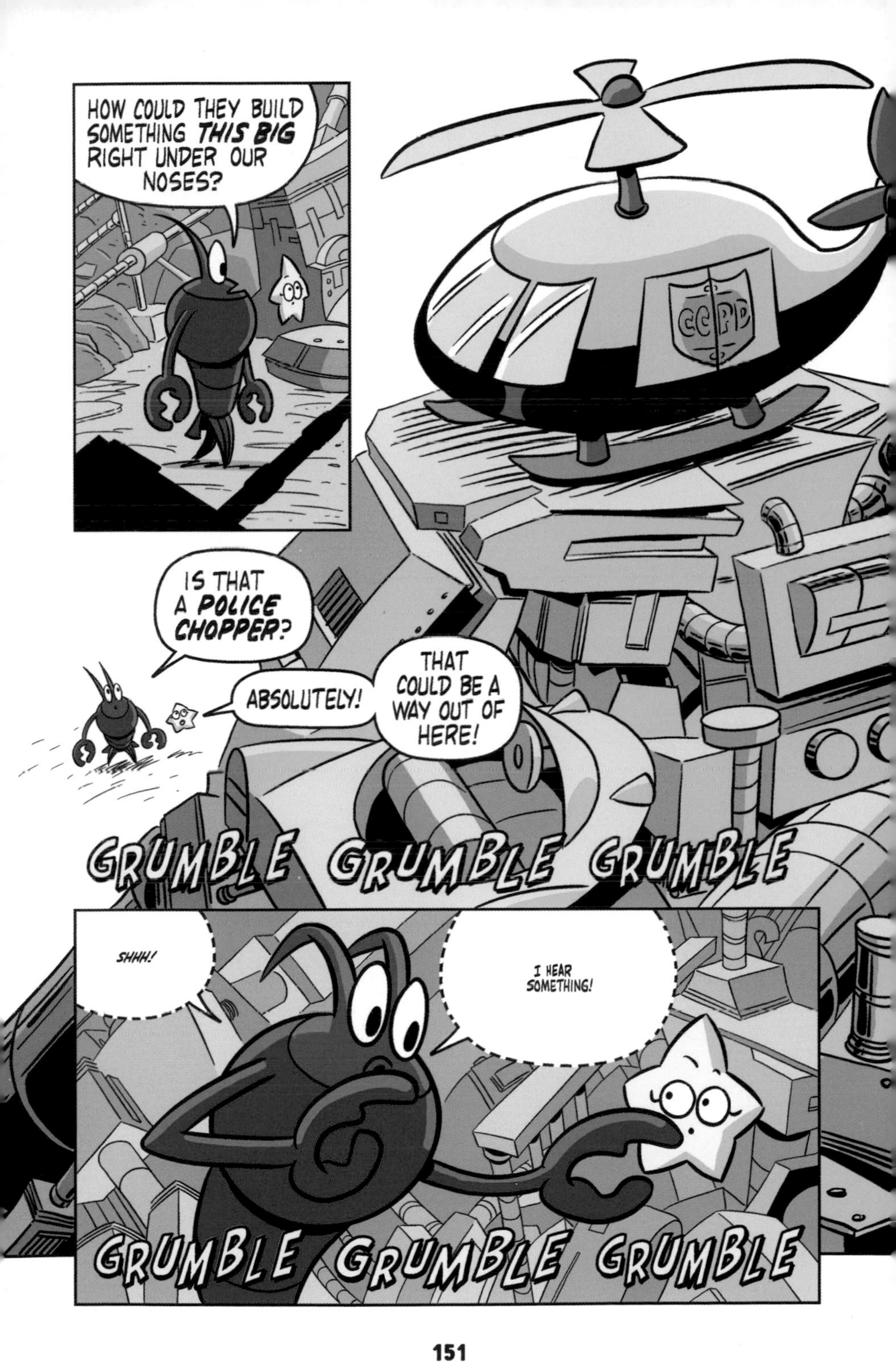
HOW COULD THEY BUILD SOMETHING THIS BIG RIGHT UNDER OUR NOSES?
CCPD
IS THAT A POLICE CHOPPER?
ABSOLUTELY!
THAT COULD BE A WAY OUT OF HERE!
GRUMBLE GRUMBLE GRUMBLE
SHHH!
I HEAR SOMETHING!
GRUMBLE GRUMBLE GRUMBLE

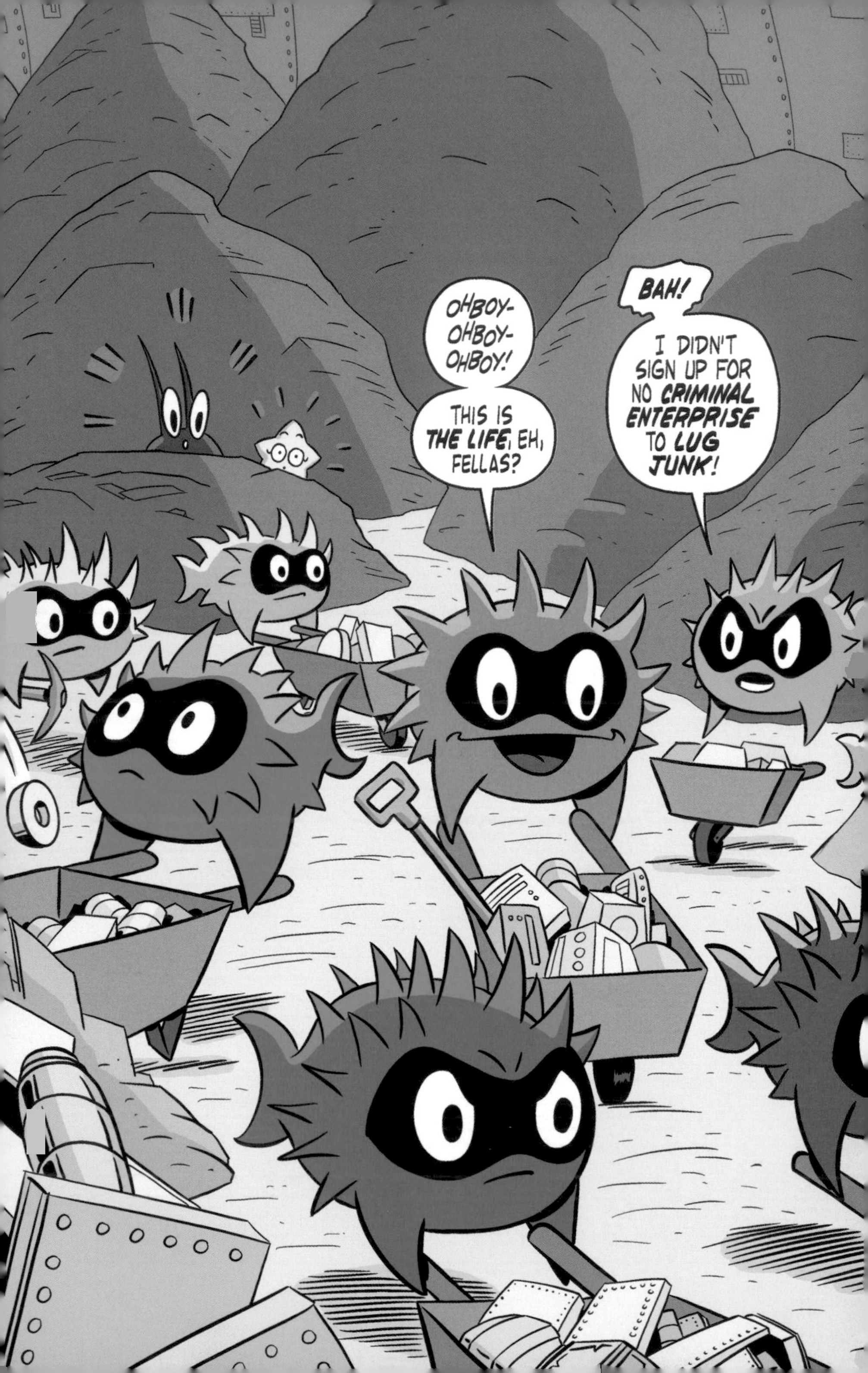
OHBOY-OHBOY-OHBOY!
THIS IS THE LIFE, EH, FELLAS?
BAH!
I DIDN'T SIGN UP FOR NO CRIMINAL ENTERPRISE TO LUG JUNK!

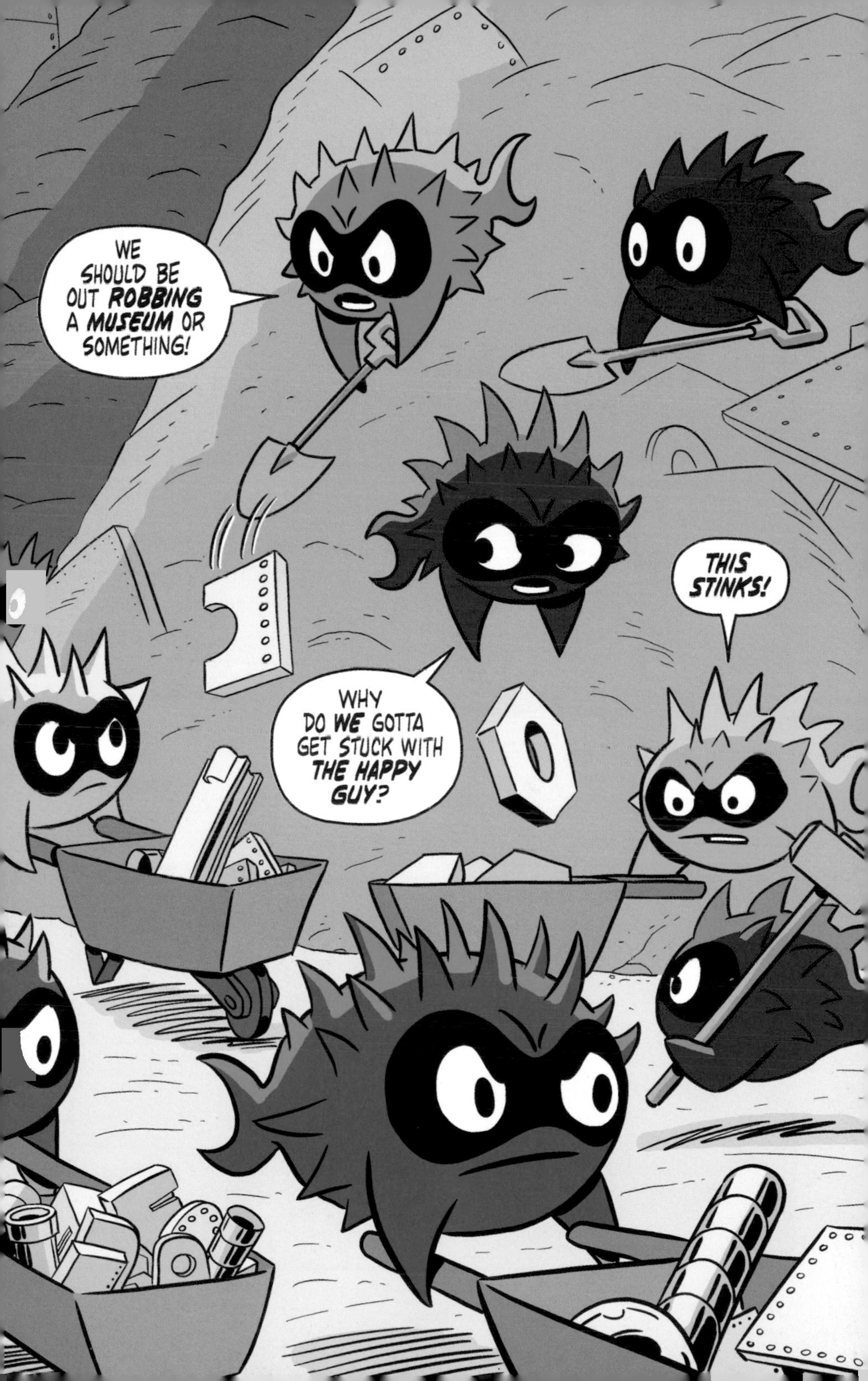
WE SHOULD BE OUT ROBBING A MUSEUM OR SOMETHING!
THIS STINKS!
WHY DO WE GOTTA GET STUCK WITH THE HAPPY GUY?

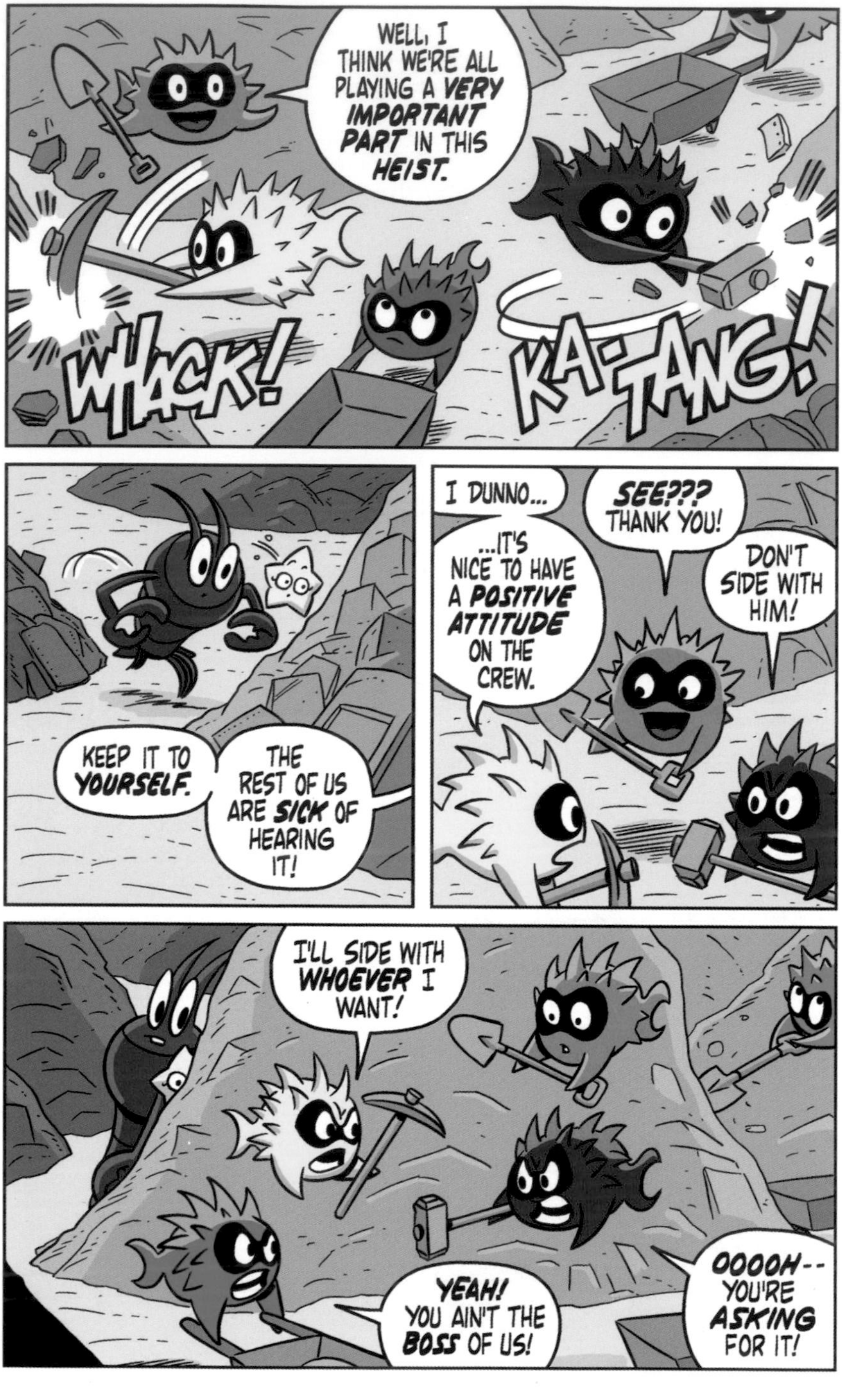

WELL, I THINK WE'RE ALL PLAYING A VERY IMPORTANT PART IN THIS HEIST.
WHACK!
KA-TANG!
KEEP IT TO YOURSELF.
THE REST OF US ARE SICK OF HEARING IT!
I DUNNO...
...IT'S NICE TO HAVE A POSITIVE ATTITUDE ON THE CREW.
SEE??? THANK YOU!
DON'T SIDE WITH HIM!
I'LL SIDE WITH WHOEVER I WANT!
YEAH! YOU AIN'T THE BOSS OF US!
OOOOH-- YOU'RE ASKING FOR IT!

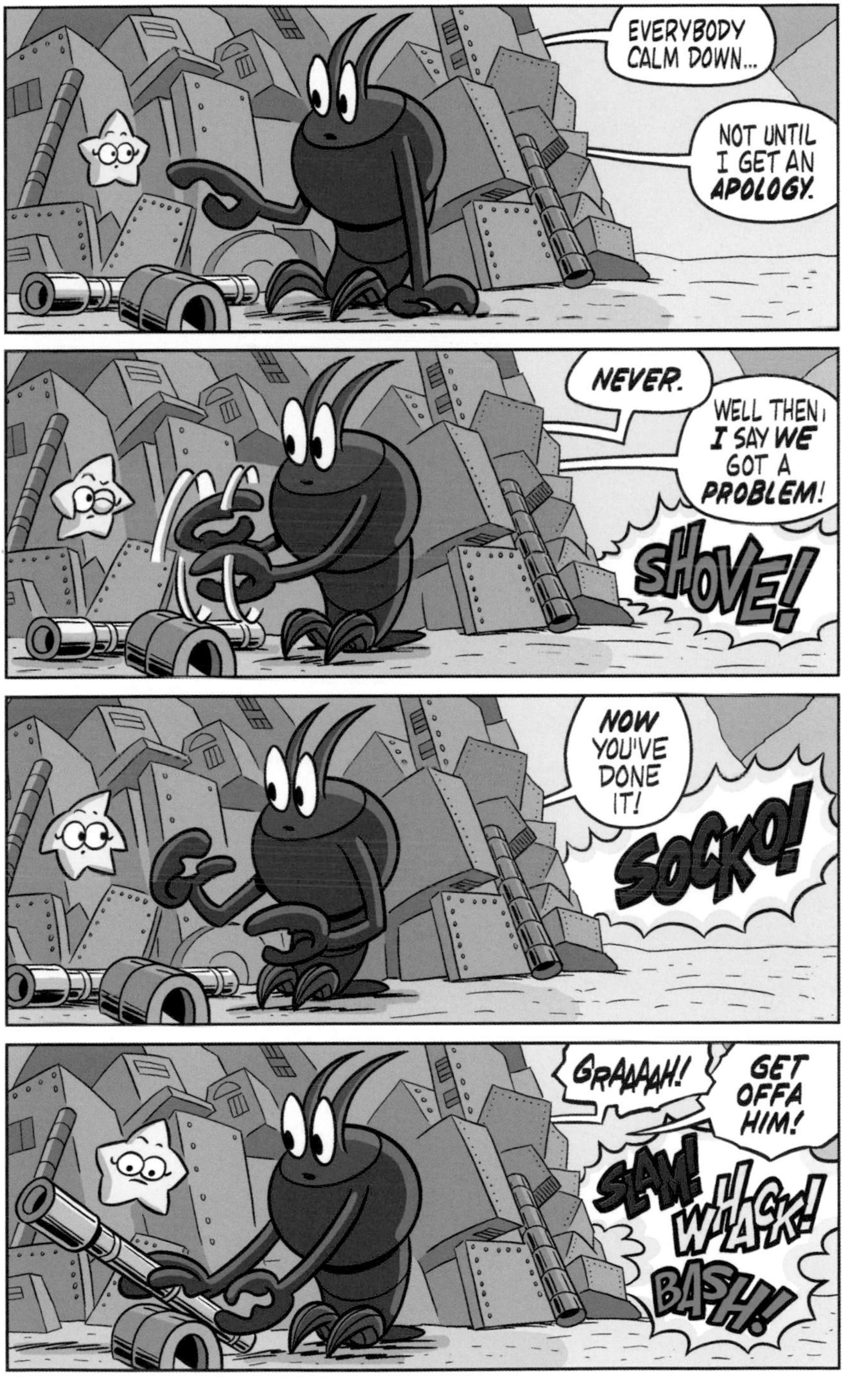
EVERYBODY CALM DOWN...
NOT UNTIL I GET AN APOLOGY.
NEVER.
WELL THEN, I SAY WE GOT A PROBLEM!
SHOVE!
NOW YOU'VE DONE IT!
SOCKO!
GRAAAAH!
GET OFFA HIM!
SLAM!
WHACK!
BASH!

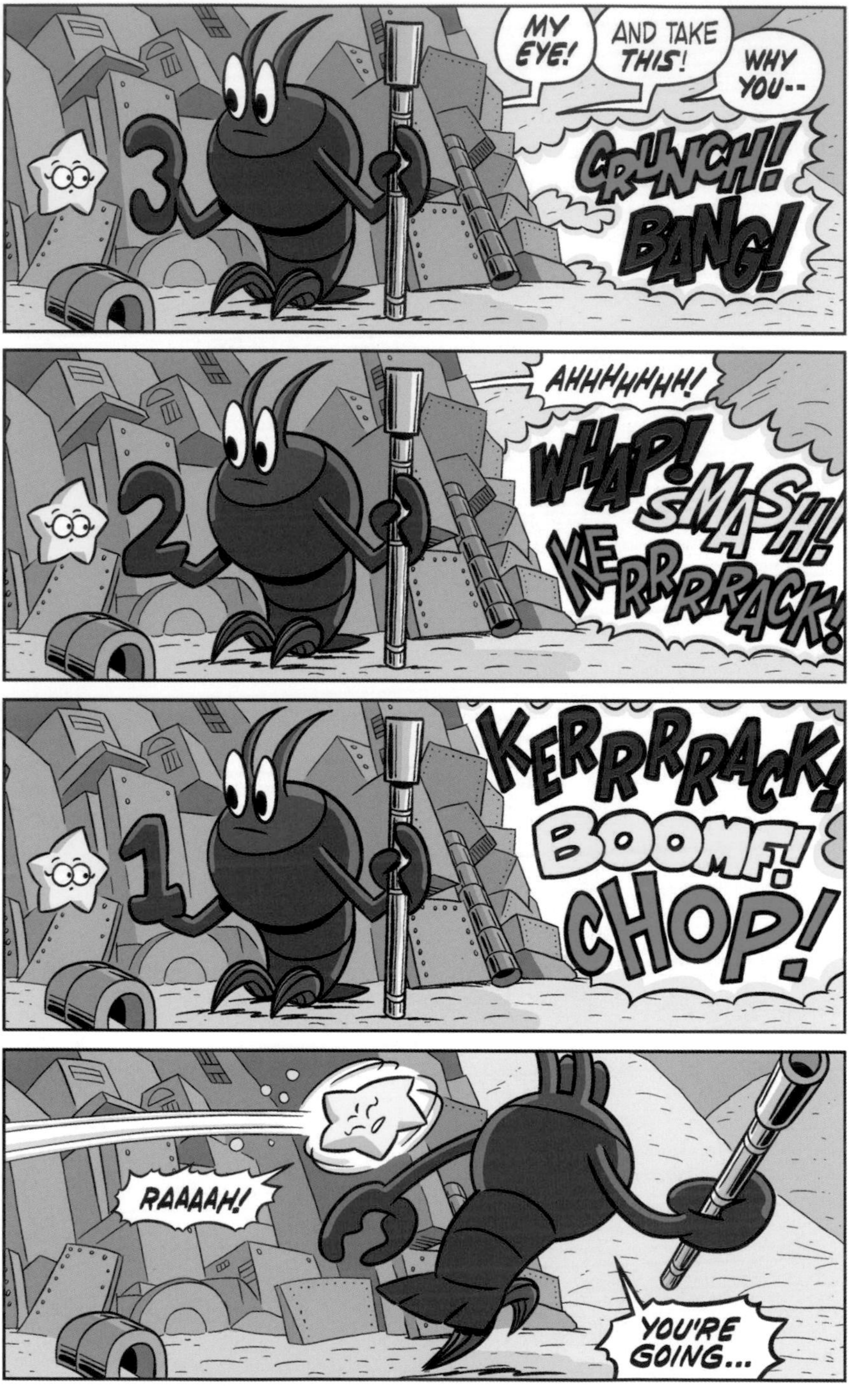

MY EYE!
AND TAKE THIS!
WHY YOU--
CRUNCH! BANG!
AHHHHHHH!
WHAP! SMASH! KERRRRACK!
KERRRRACK! BOOMF! CHOP!
RAAAAH!
YOU'RE GOING...

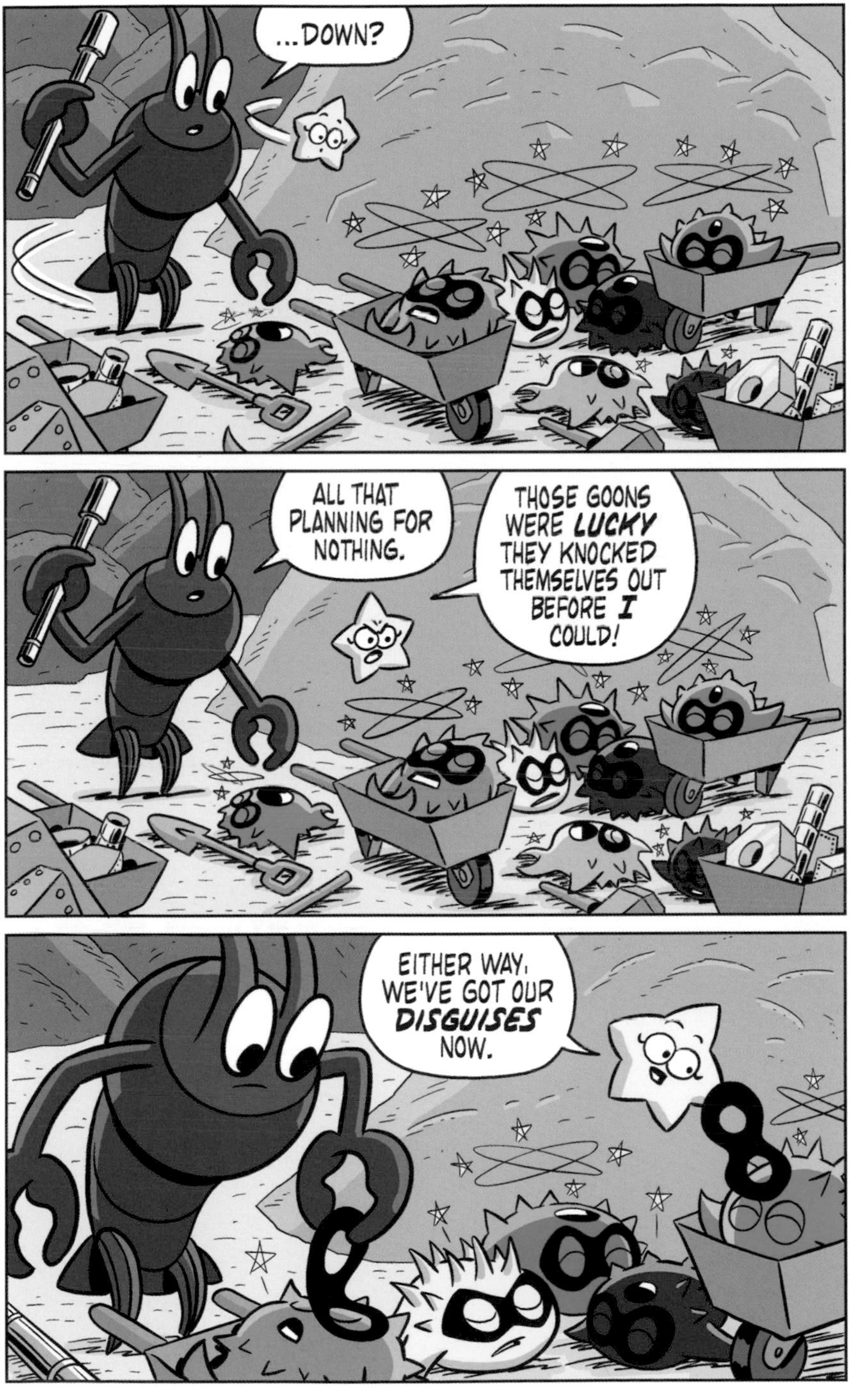
...DOWN?
ALL THAT PLANNING FOR NOTHING.
THOSE GOONS WERE LUCKY THEY KNOCKED THEMSELVES OUT BEFORE I COULD!
EITHER WAY, WE'VE GOT OUR DISGUISES NOW.

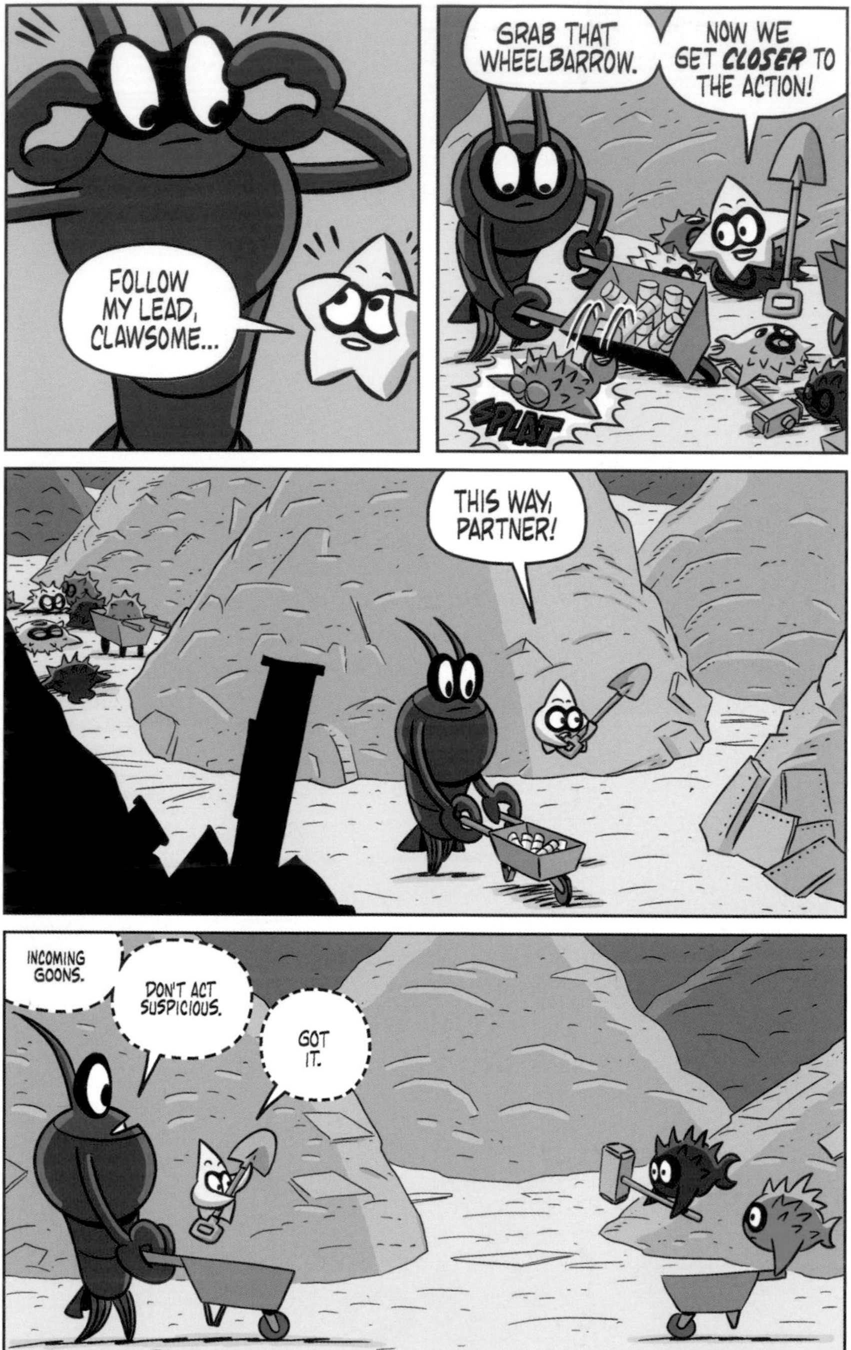
FOLLOW MY LEAD, CLAWSOME...
GRAB THAT WHEELBARROW.
NOW WE GET CLOSER TO THE ACTION!
SPLAT
THIS WAY, PARTNER!
INCOMING GOONS.
DON'T ACT SUSPICIOUS.
GOT IT.

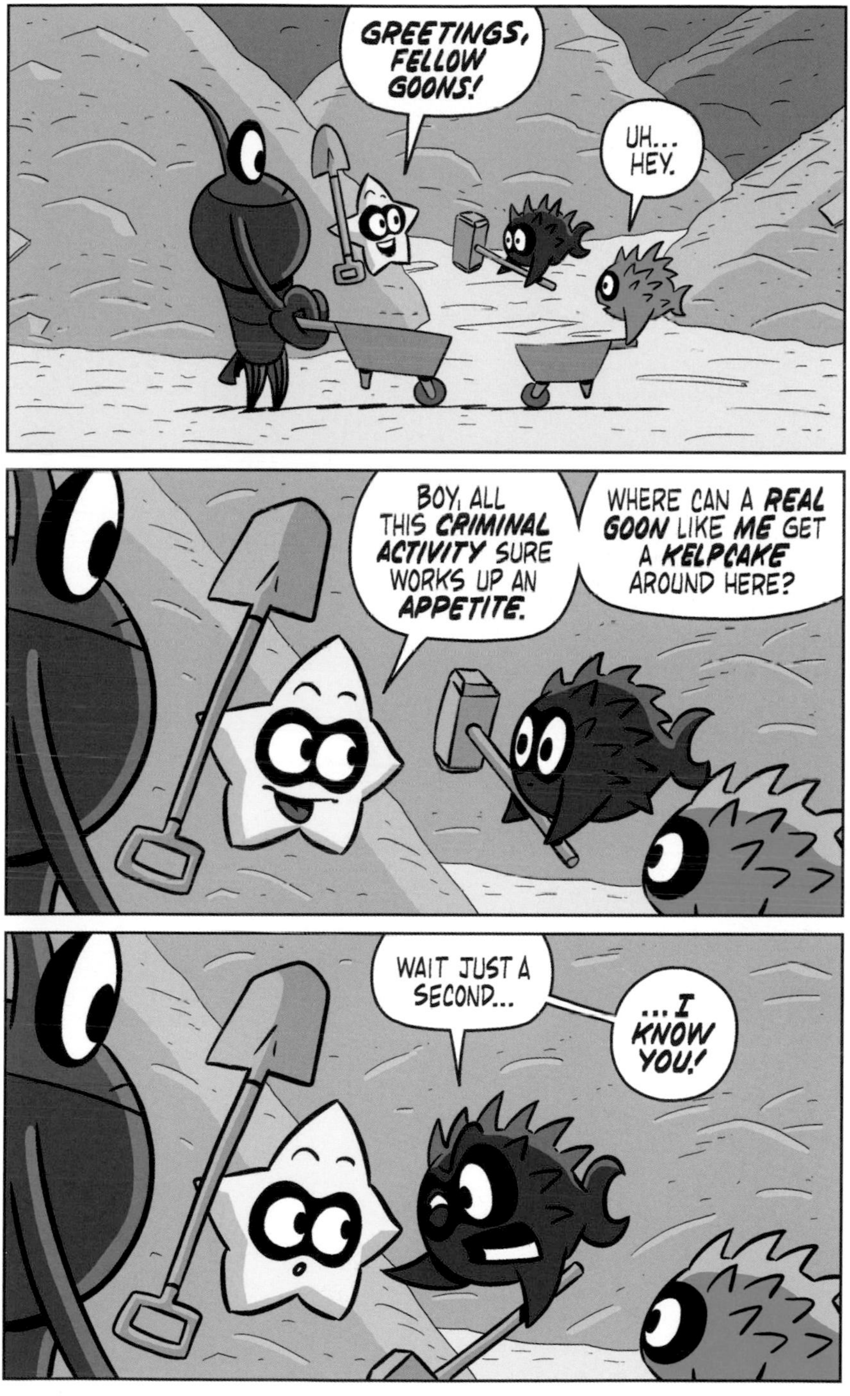
GREETINGS, FELLOW GOONS!
UH... HEY.
BOY, ALL THIS CRIMINAL ACTIVITY SURE WORKS UP AN APPETITE.
WHERE CAN A REAL GOON LIKE ME GET A KELPCAKE AROUND HERE?
WAIT JUST A SECOND...
...I KNOW YOU!

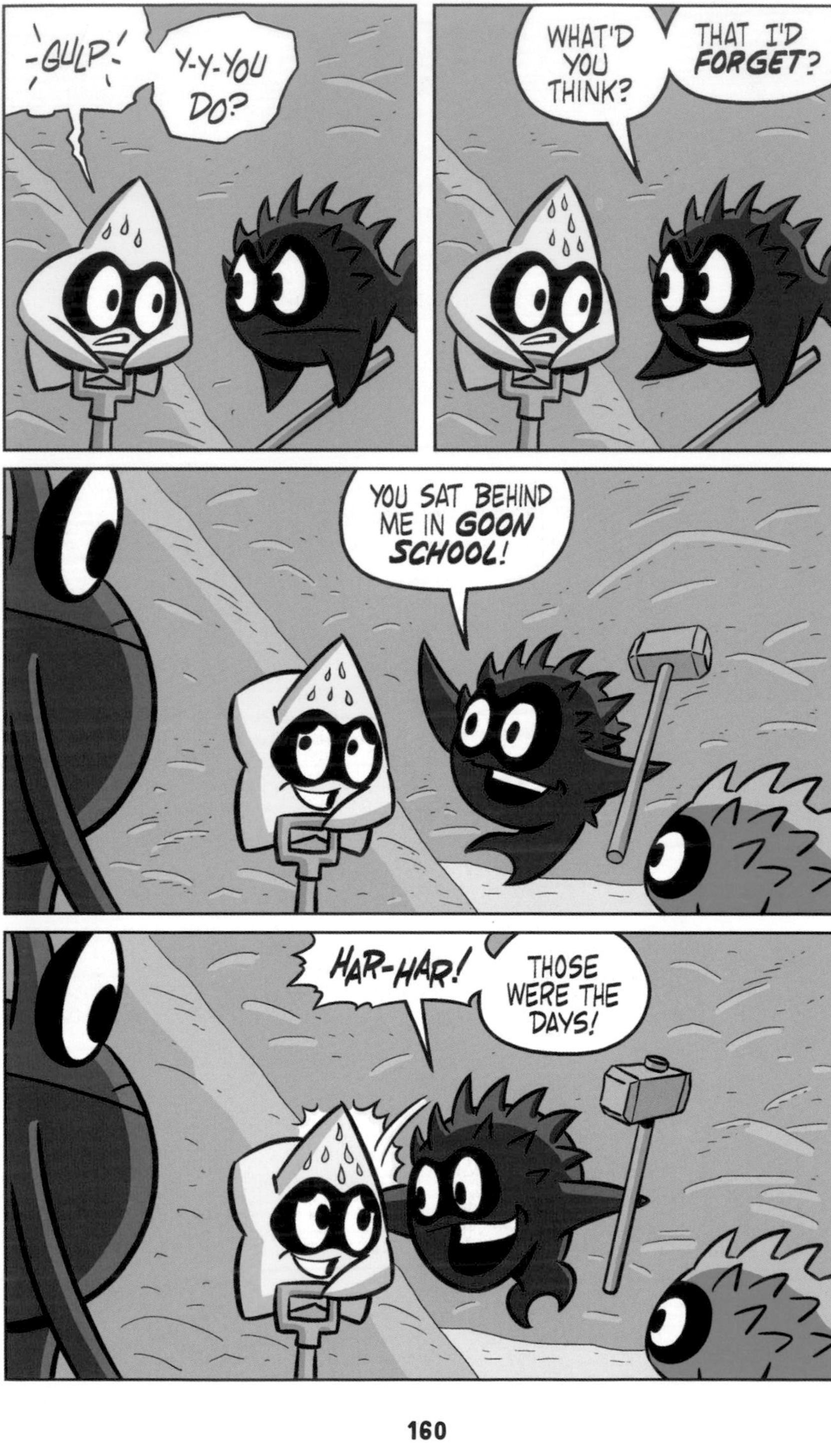
-GULP!-
Y-Y-YOU DO?
WHAT'D YOU THINK?
THAT I'D FORGET?
YOU SAT BEHIND ME IN GOON SCHOOL!
HAR-HAR!
THOSE WERE THE DAYS!

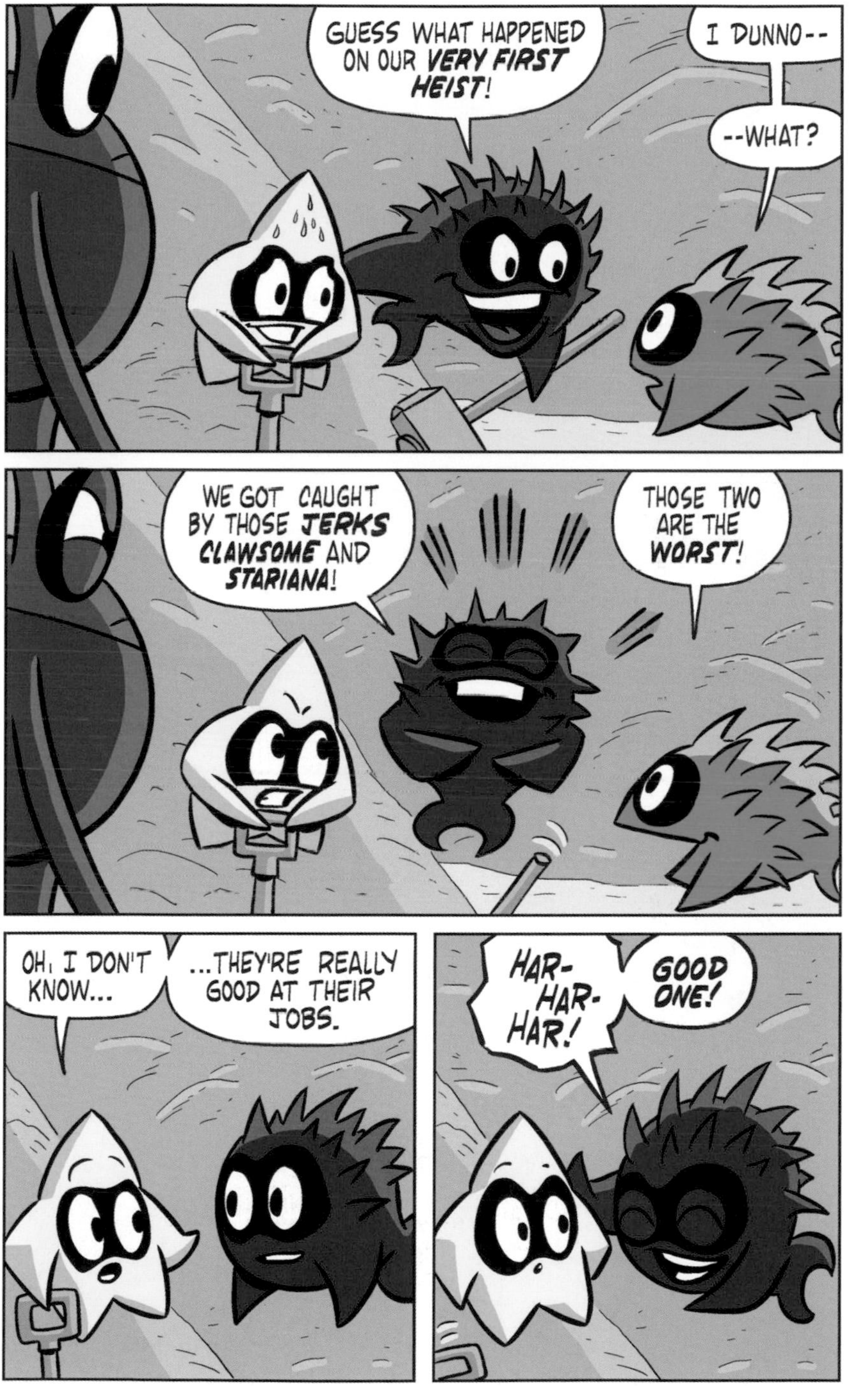
GUESS WHAT HAPPENED ON OUR **VERY FIRST HEIST**!
I DUNNO--
--WHAT?
WE GOT CAUGHT BY THOSE **JERKS CLAWSOME** AND **STARIANA**!
THOSE TWO ARE THE **WORST**!
OH, I DON'T KNOW...
...THEY'RE REALLY GOOD AT THEIR JOBS.
HAR-HAR-HAR!
GOOD ONE!

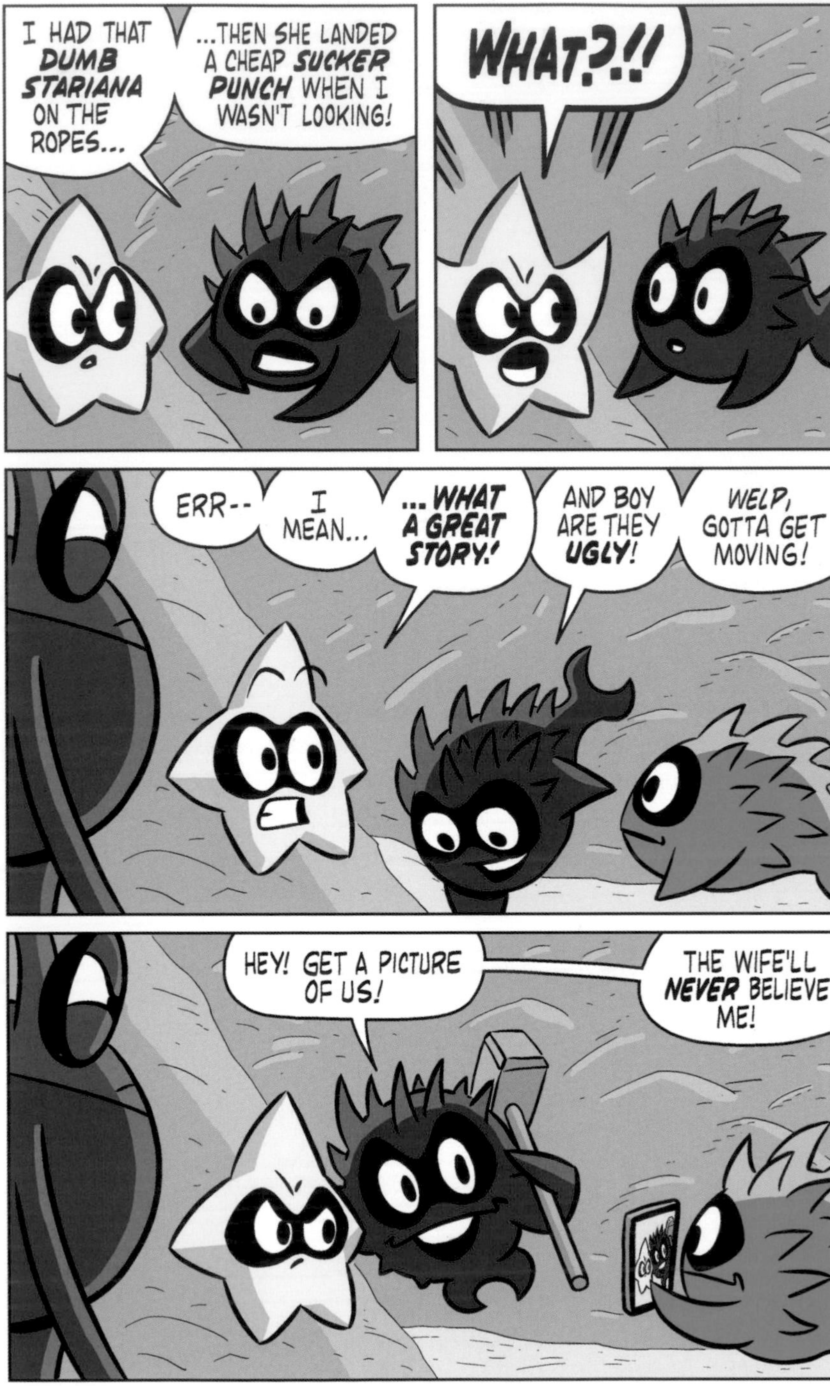
I HAD THAT DUMB STARIANA ON THE ROPES...
...THEN SHE LANDED A CHEAP SUCKER PUNCH WHEN I WASN'T LOOKING!
WHAT?!!
ERR--
I MEAN...
...WHAT A GREAT STORY!
AND BOY ARE THEY UGLY!
WELP, GOTTA GET MOVING!
HEY! GET A PICTURE OF US!
THE WIFE'LL NEVER BELIEVE ME!

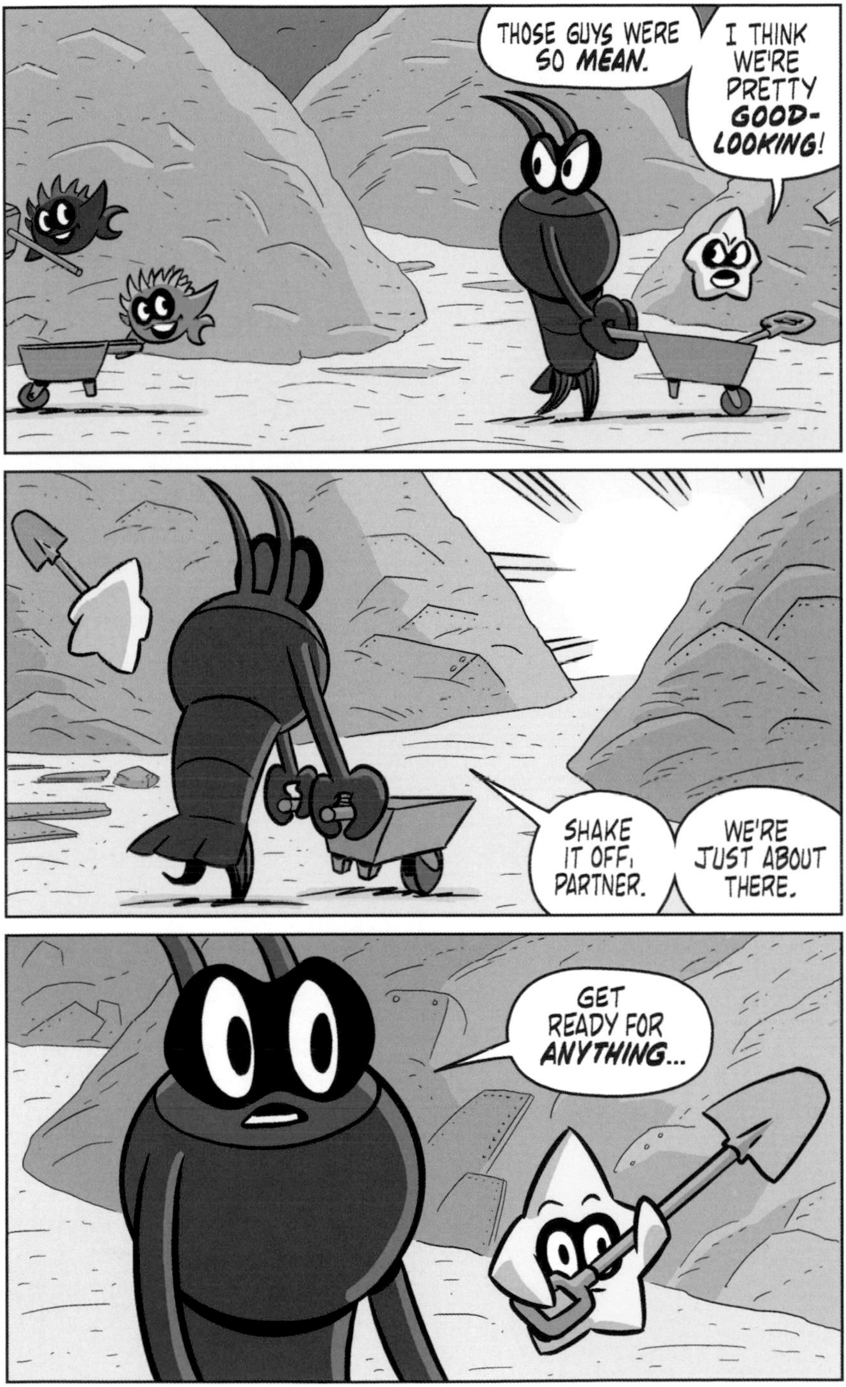
THOSE GUYS WERE SO MEAN.
I THINK WE'RE PRETTY GOOD-LOOKING!
SHAKE IT OFF, PARTNER.
WE'RE JUST ABOUT THERE.
GET READY FOR ANYTHING...

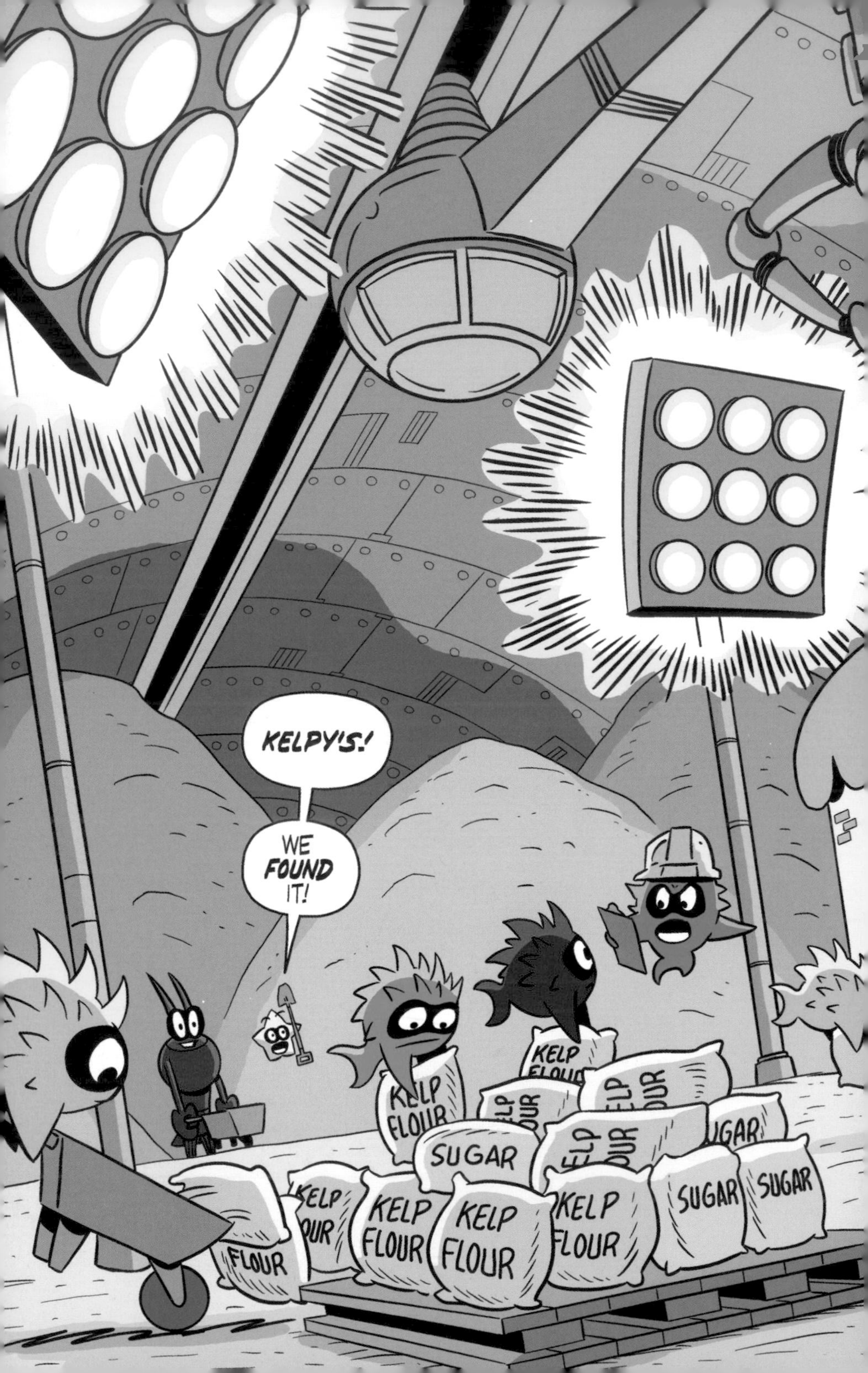
KELPY'S!
WE FOUND IT!
KELP FLOUR
SUGAR
KELP FLOUR
SUGAR
SUGAR
KELP FLOUR
KELP FLOUR
KELP FLOUR
FLOUR

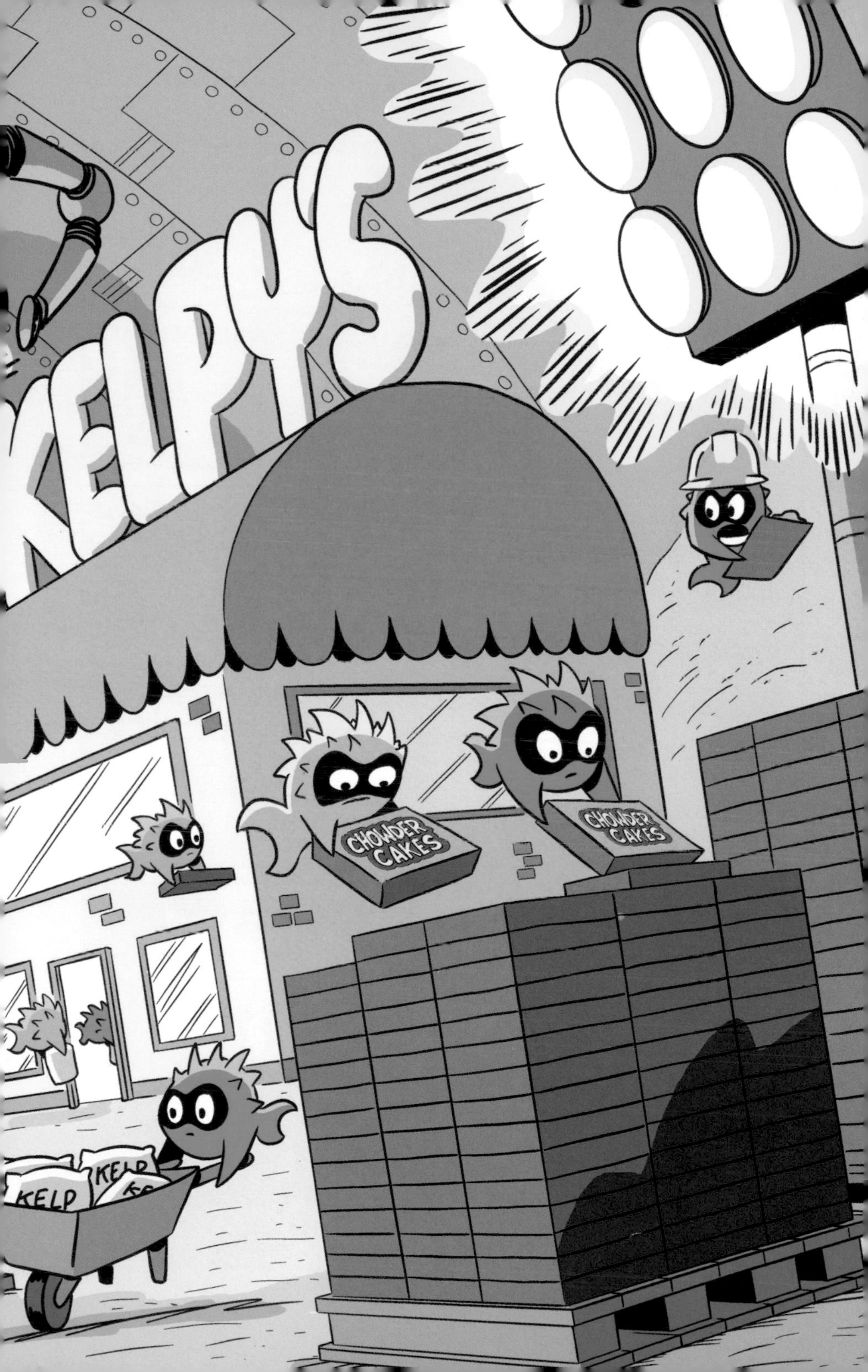
KELPY'S
CHOWDER CAKES
CHOWDER CAKES
KELP
KELP

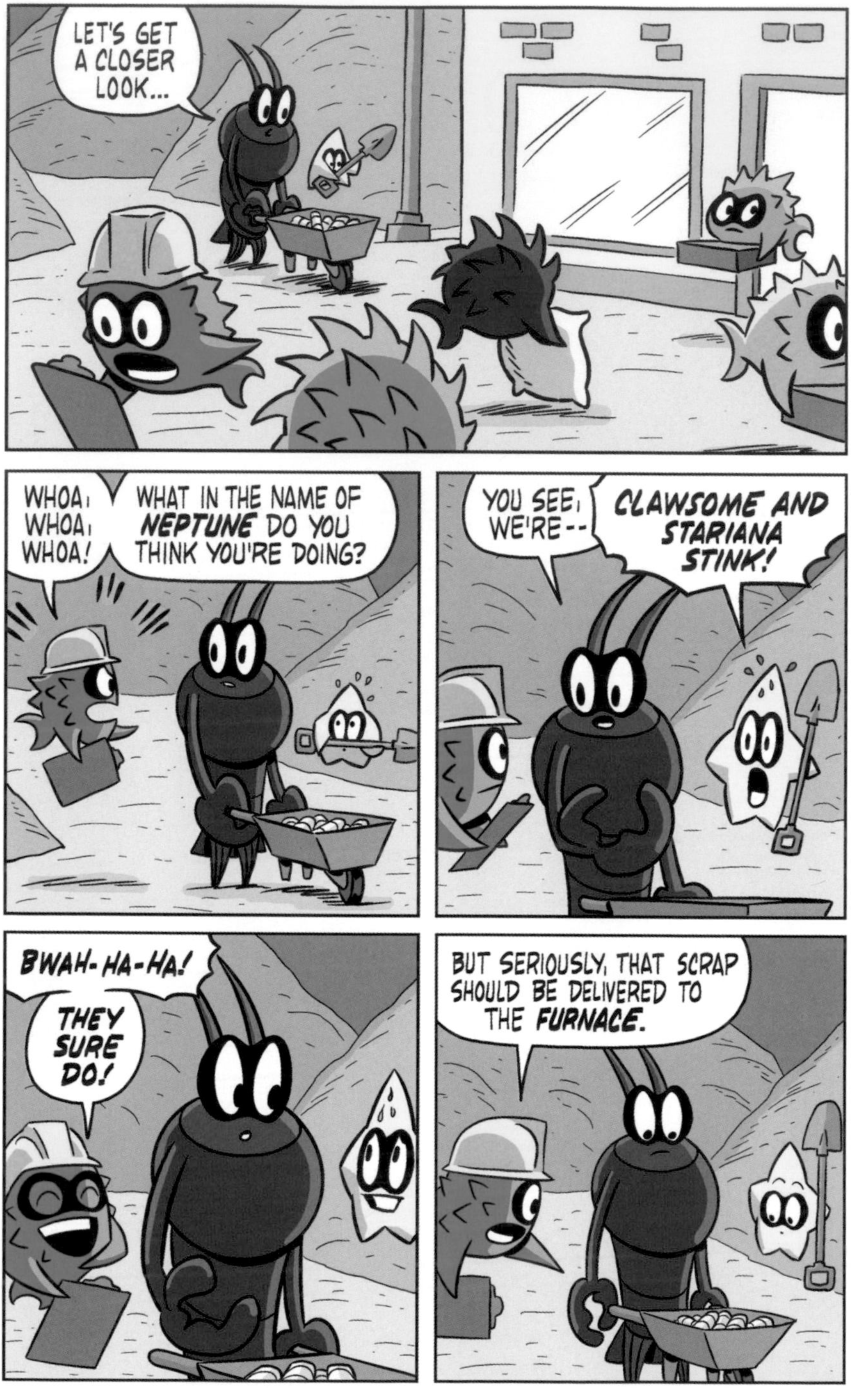
LET'S GET A CLOSER LOOK...
WHOA, WHOA, WHOA!
WHAT IN THE NAME OF NEPTUNE DO YOU THINK YOU'RE DOING?
YOU SEE, WE'RE--
CLAWSOME AND STARIANA STINK!
BWAH-HA-HA!
THEY SURE DO!
BUT SERIOUSLY, THAT SCRAP SHOULD BE DELIVERED TO THE FURNACE.

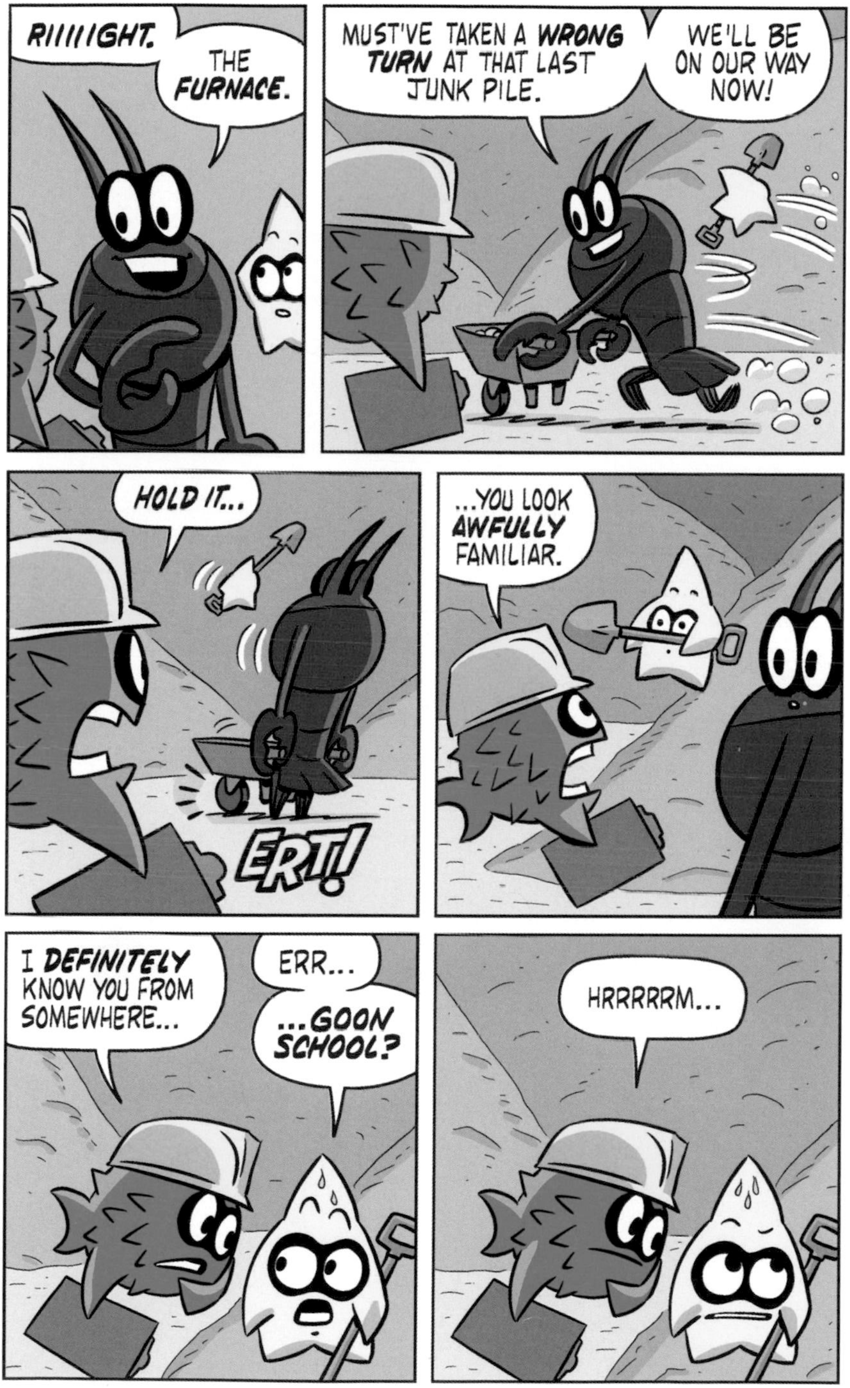

RIIIIIGHT.
THE FURNACE.
MUST'VE TAKEN A WRONG TURN AT THAT LAST JUNK PILE.
WE'LL BE ON OUR WAY NOW!
HOLD IT...
ERT!
...YOU LOOK AWFULLY FAMILIAR.
I DEFINITELY KNOW YOU FROM SOMEWHERE...
ERR...
...GOON SCHOOL?
HRRRRRM...

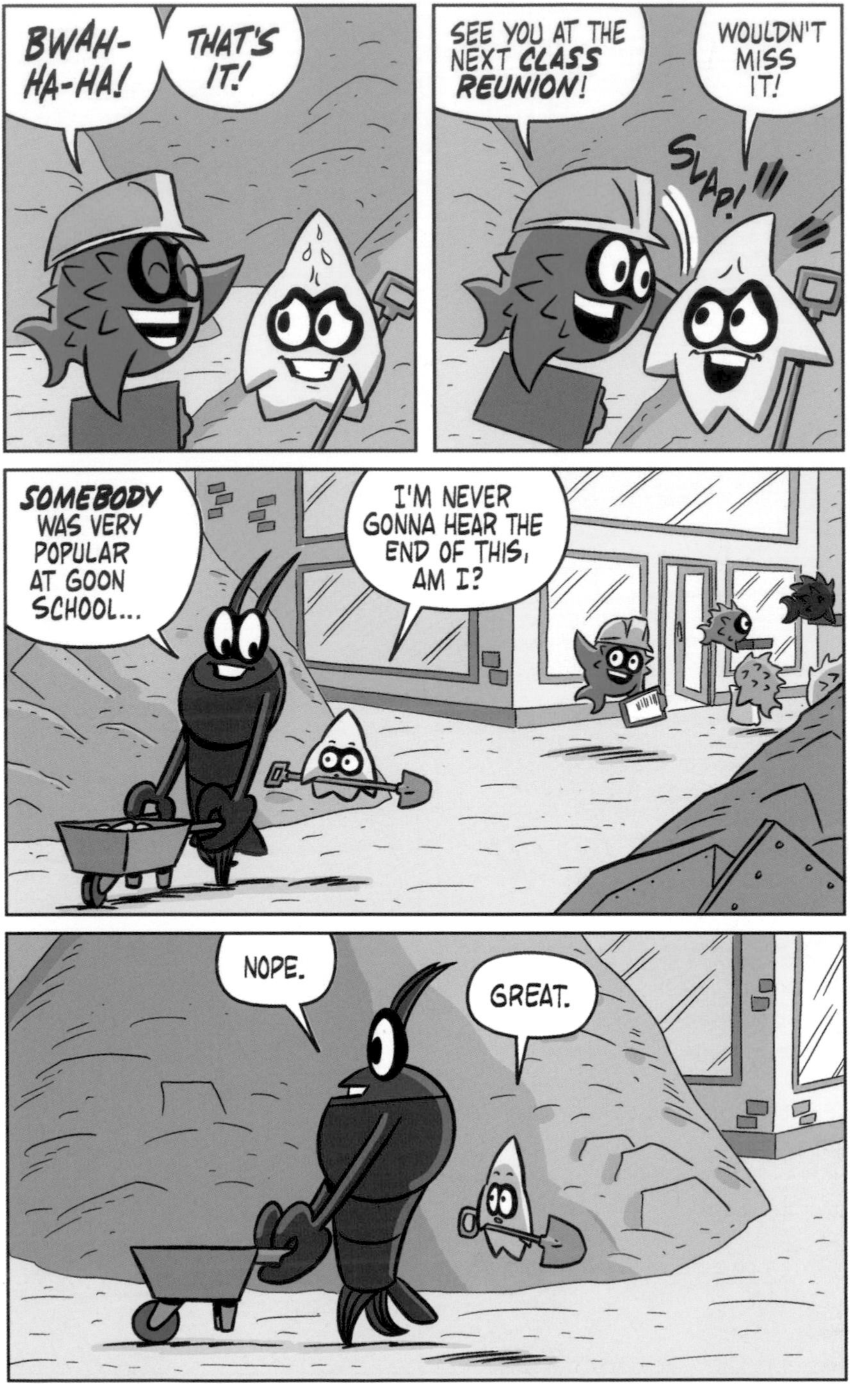
BWAH-HA-HA!
THAT'S IT!
SEE YOU AT THE NEXT CLASS REUNION!
WOULDN'T MISS IT!
SLAP!
SOMEBODY WAS VERY POPULAR AT GOON SCHOOL...
I'M NEVER GONNA HEAR THE END OF THIS, AM I?
NOPE.
GREAT.

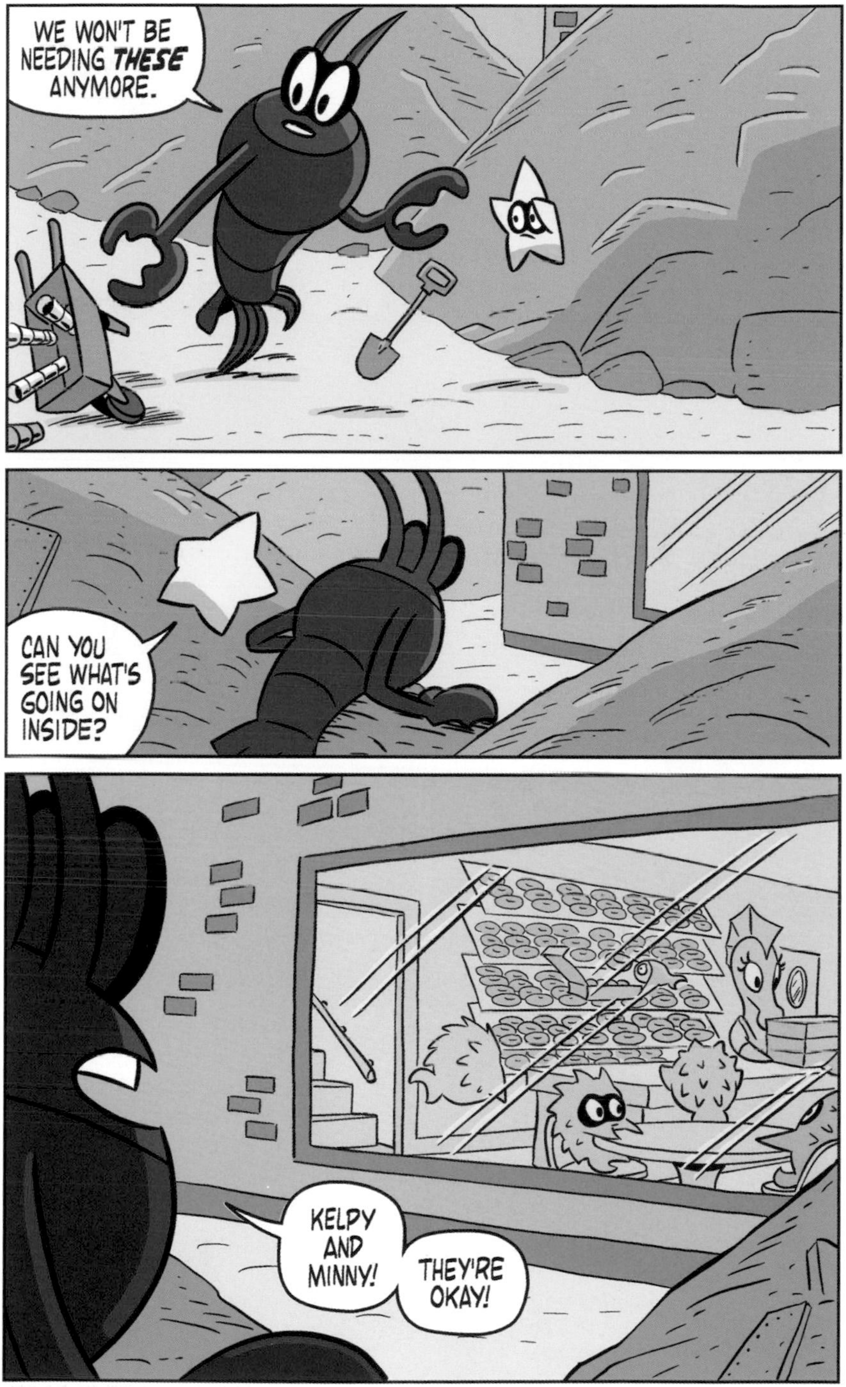
WE WON'T BE NEEDING ***THESE*** ANYMORE.
CAN YOU SEE WHAT'S GOING ON INSIDE?
KELPY AND MINNY!
THEY'RE OKAY!

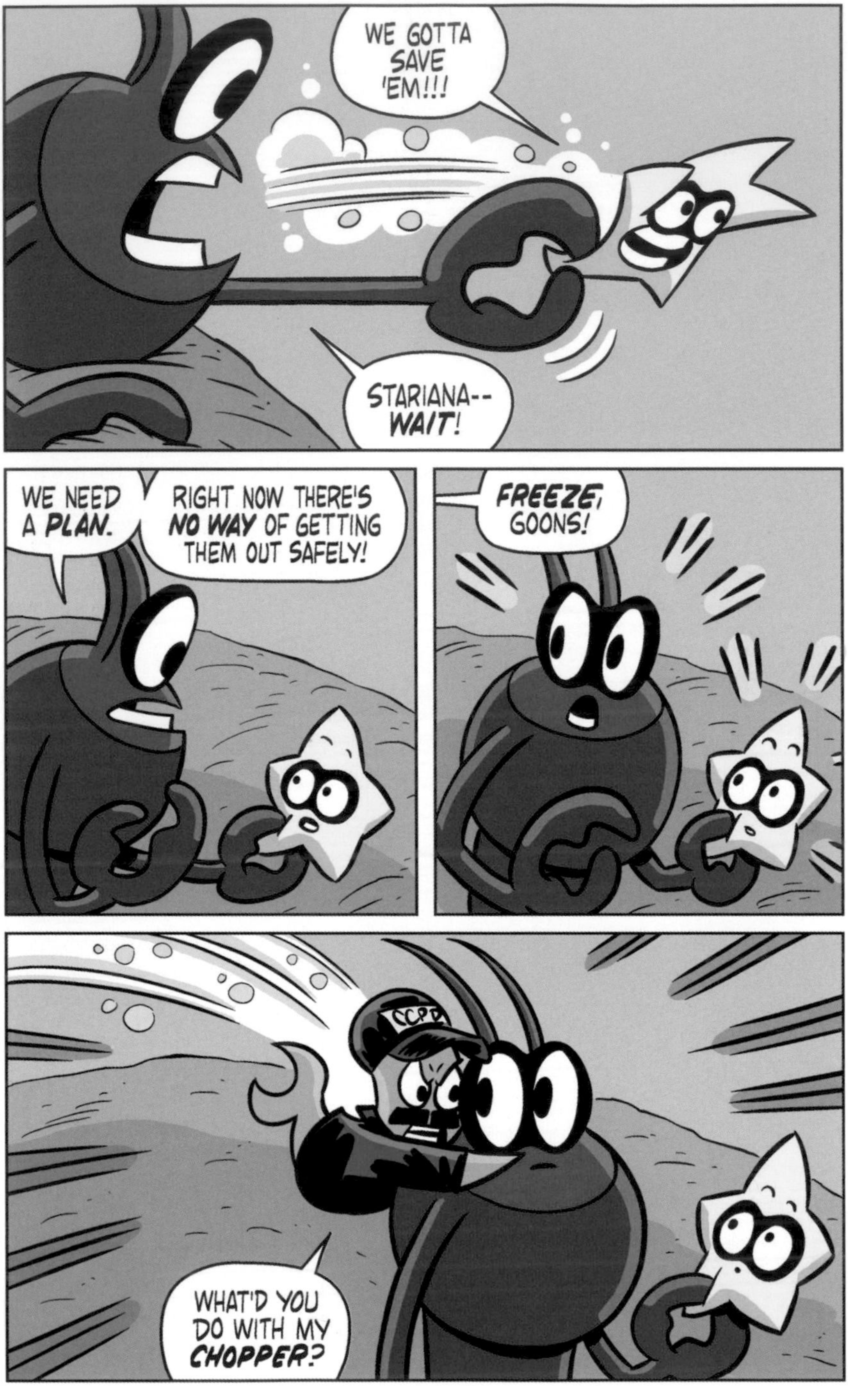
WE GOTTA SAVE 'EM!!!
STARIANA-- WAIT!
WE NEED A PLAN.
RIGHT NOW THERE'S NO WAY OF GETTING THEM OUT SAFELY!
FREEZE, GOONS!
CCPD
WHAT'D YOU DO WITH MY CHOPPER?

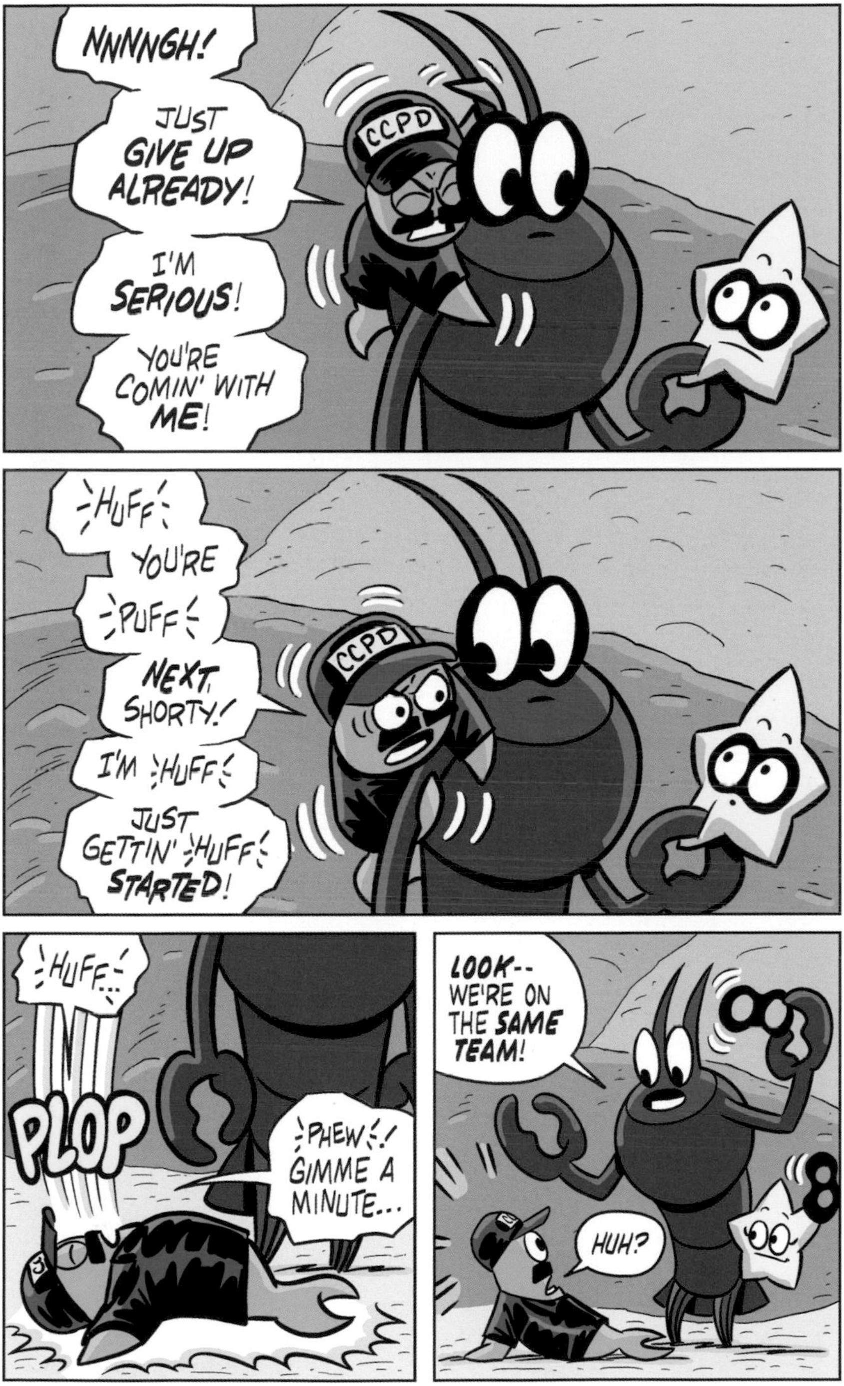
NNNNGH!
JUST GIVE UP ALREADY!
I'M SERIOUS!
YOU'RE COMIN' WITH ME!
CCPD
HUFF
YOU'RE
PUFF
NEXT, SHORTY!
I'M HUFF
JUST GETTIN' HUFF STARTED!
CCPD
HUFF...
PLOP
PHEW! GIMME A MINUTE...
LOOK-- WE'RE ON THE SAME TEAM!
HUH?

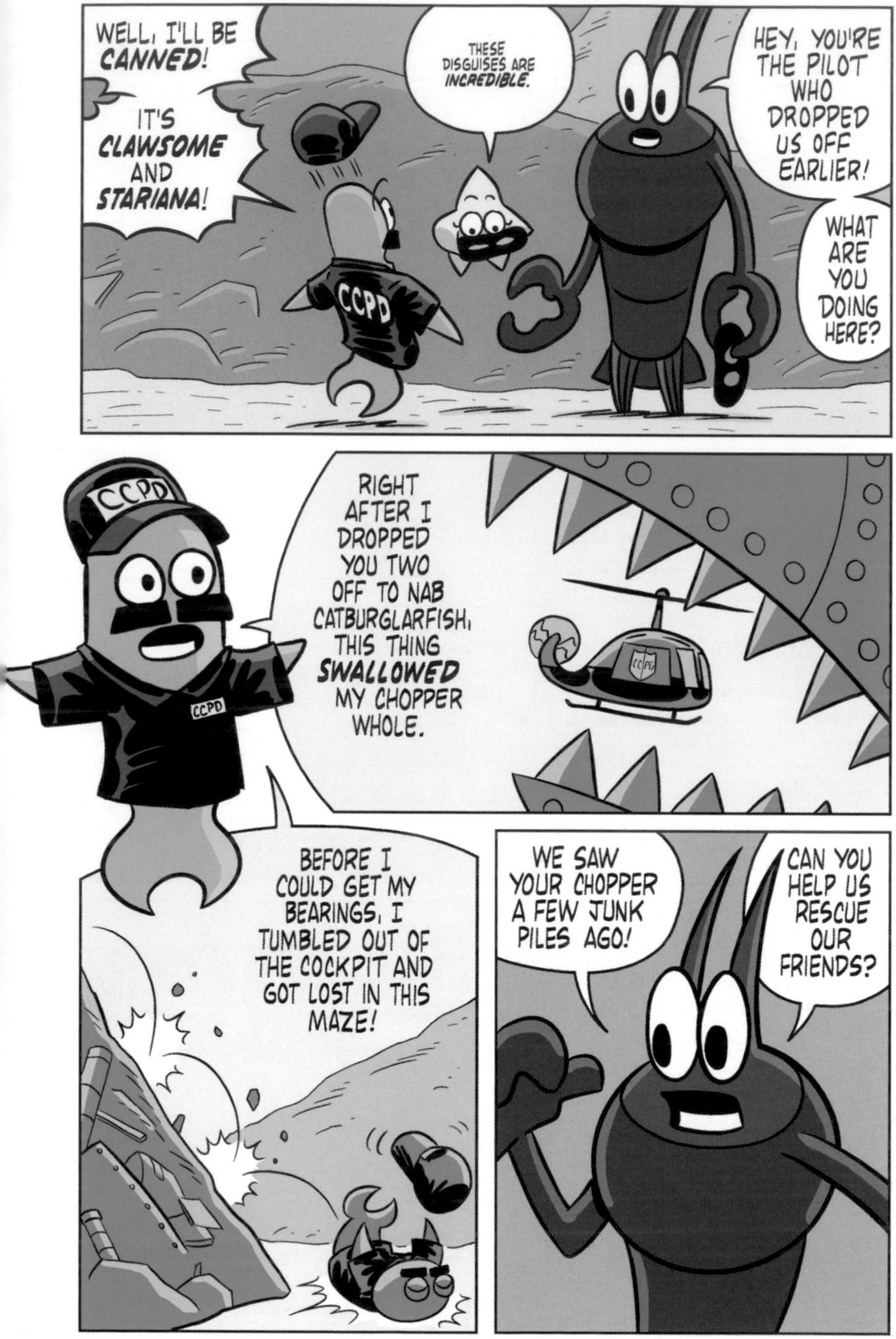
WELL, I'LL BE CANNED!
IT'S CLAWSOME AND STARIANA!
THESE DISGUISES ARE INCREDIBLE.
HEY, YOU'RE THE PILOT WHO DROPPED US OFF EARLIER!
WHAT ARE YOU DOING HERE?
CCPD
RIGHT AFTER I DROPPED YOU TWO OFF TO NAB CATBURGLARFISH, THIS THING SWALLOWED MY CHOPPER WHOLE.
BEFORE I COULD GET MY BEARINGS, I TUMBLED OUT OF THE COCKPIT AND GOT LOST IN THIS MAZE!
WE SAW YOUR CHOPPER A FEW JUNK PILES AGO!
CAN YOU HELP US RESCUE OUR FRIENDS?

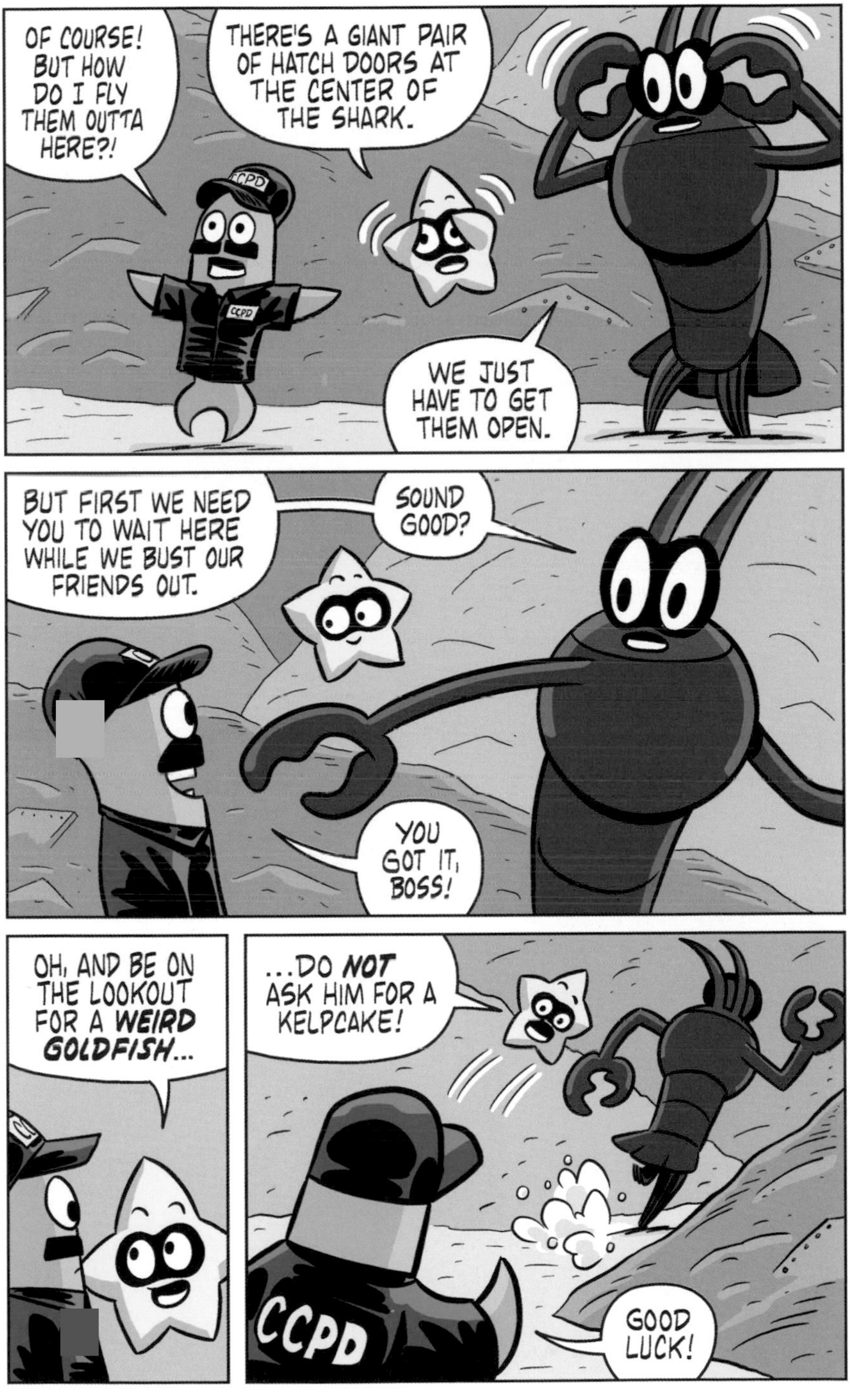
OF COURSE! BUT HOW DO I FLY THEM OUTTA HERE?!
THERE'S A GIANT PAIR OF HATCH DOORS AT THE CENTER OF THE SHARK.
WE JUST HAVE TO GET THEM OPEN.
BUT FIRST WE NEED YOU TO WAIT HERE WHILE WE BUST OUR FRIENDS OUT.
SOUND GOOD?
YOU GOT IT, BOSS!
OH, AND BE ON THE LOOKOUT FOR A **WEIRD GOLDFISH**...
...DO **NOT** ASK HIM FOR A KELPCAKE!
GOOD LUCK!

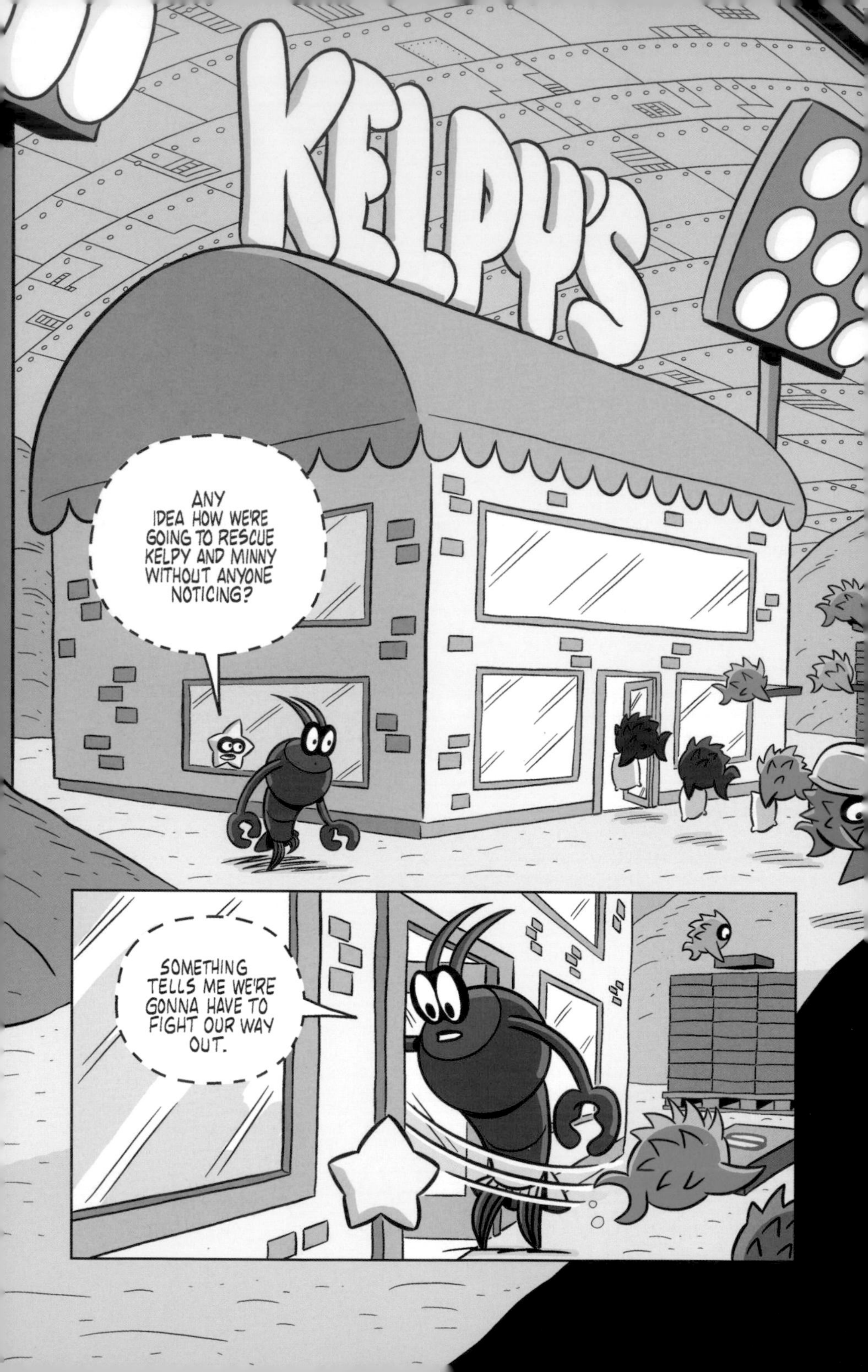
KELPY'S
ANY IDEA HOW WE'RE GOING TO RESCUE KELPY AND MINNY WITHOUT ANYONE NOTICING?
SOMETHING TELLS ME WE'RE GONNA HAVE TO FIGHT OUR WAY OUT.

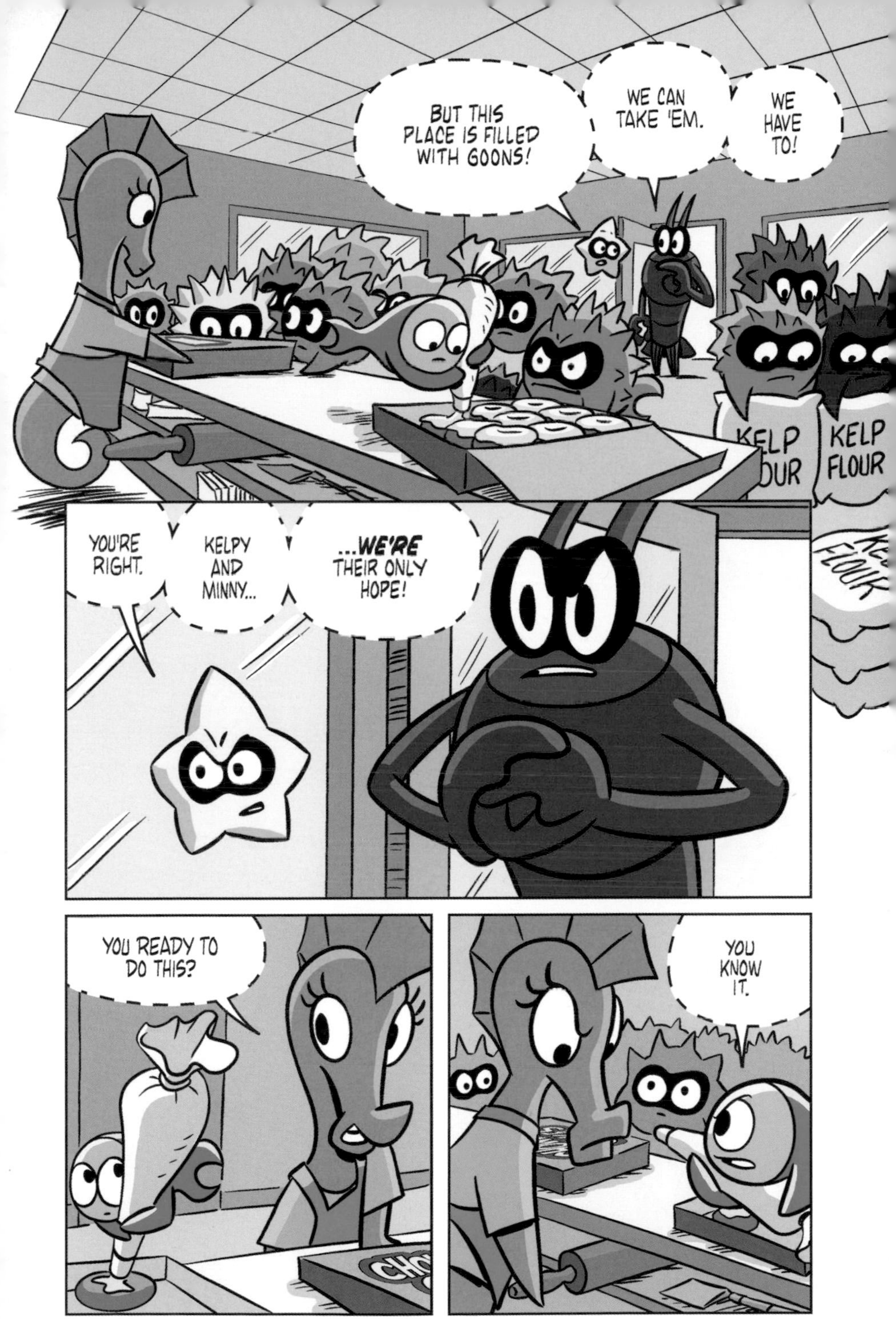
BUT THIS PLACE IS FILLED WITH GOONS!
WE CAN TAKE 'EM.
WE HAVE TO!
KELP FLOUR
KELP FLOUR
YOU'RE RIGHT.
KELPY AND MINNY...
...WE'RE THEIR ONLY HOPE!
YOU READY TO DO THIS?
YOU KNOW IT.

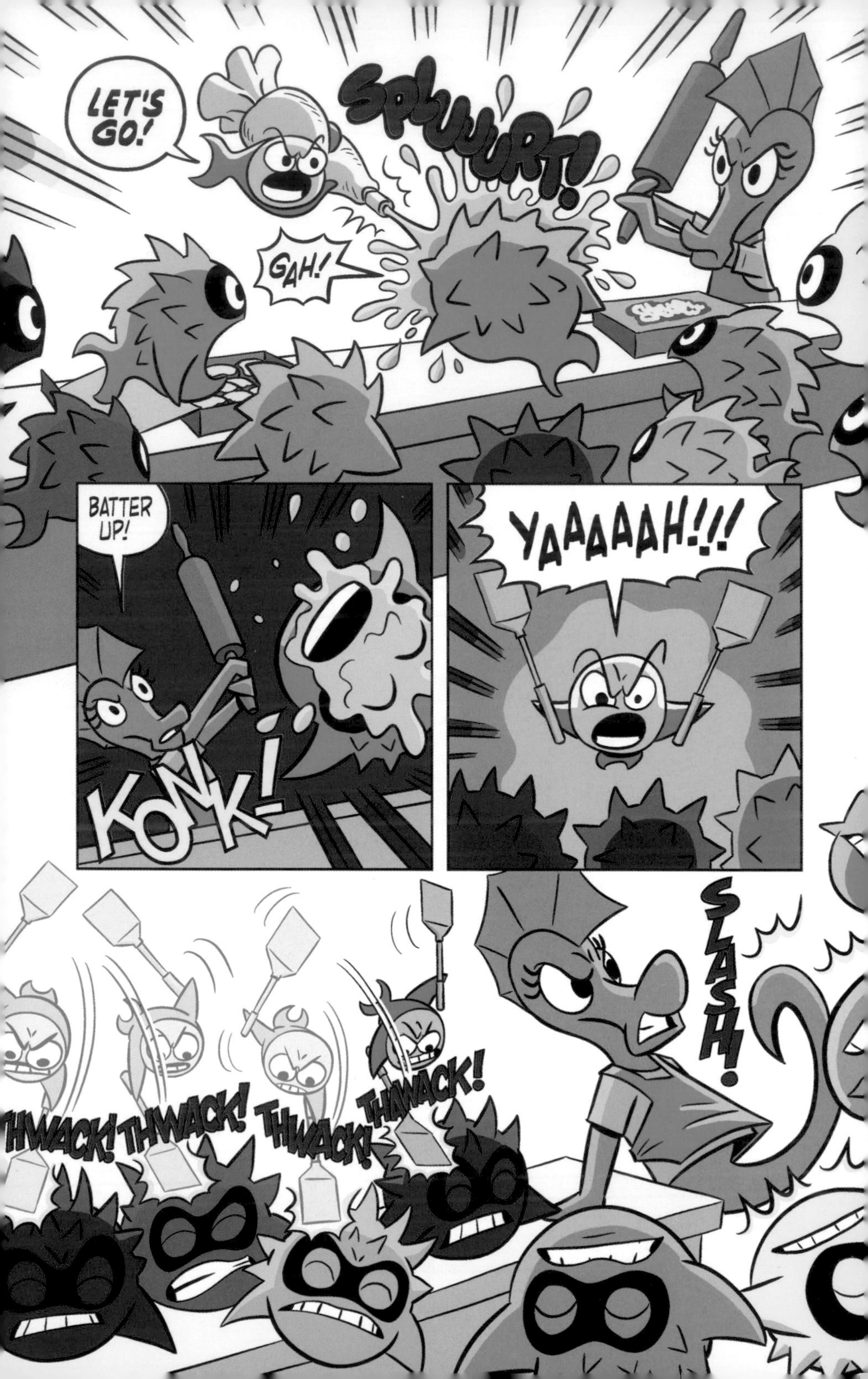
LET'S GO!
SPLUUURT!
GAH!
BATTER UP!
KONK!
YAAAAAH!!!
THWACK! THWACK! THWACK! THWACK!
SLASH!

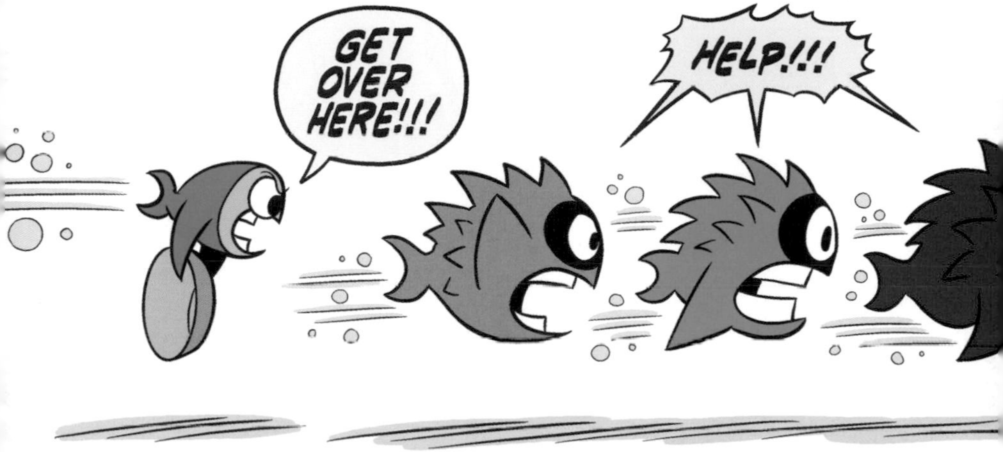
GET OVER HERE!!!
HELP!!!

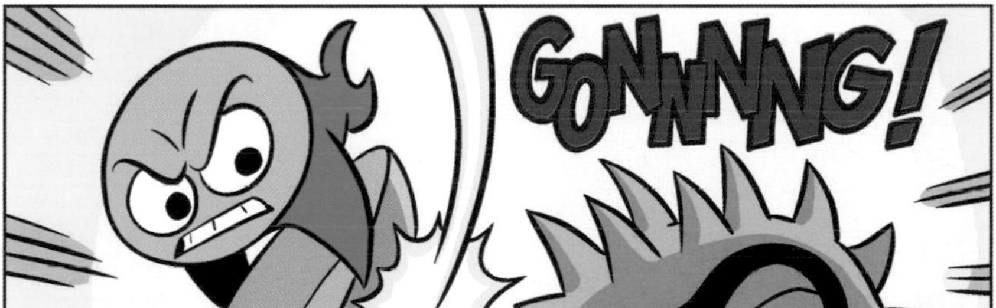
GONNNNG!

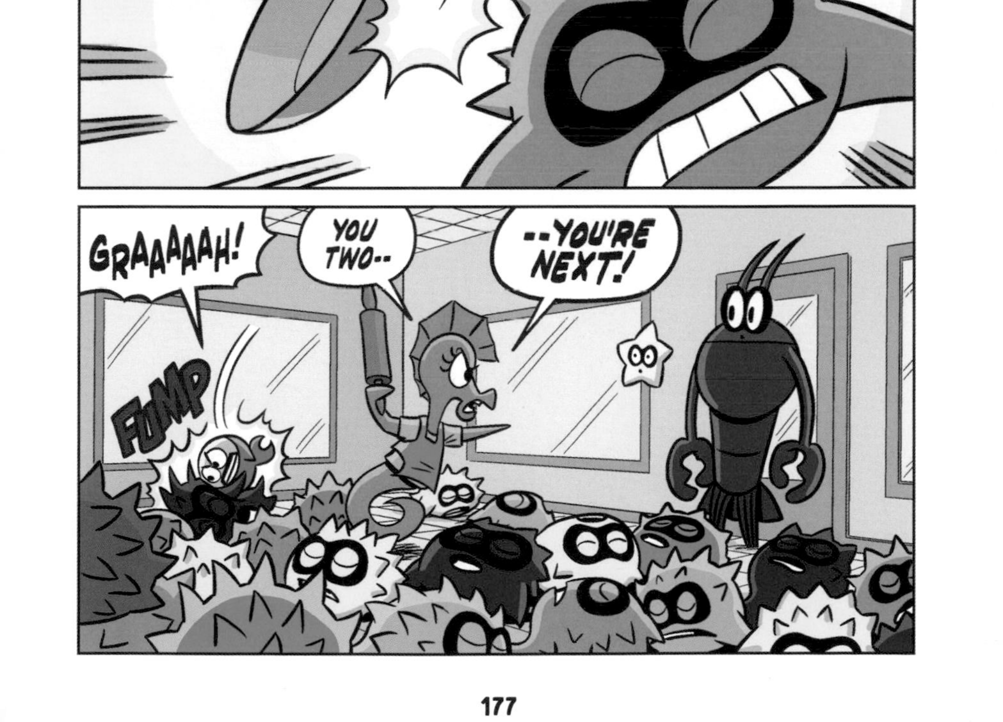
GRAAAAAH!
FUMP
YOU TWO--
--YOU'RE NEXT!

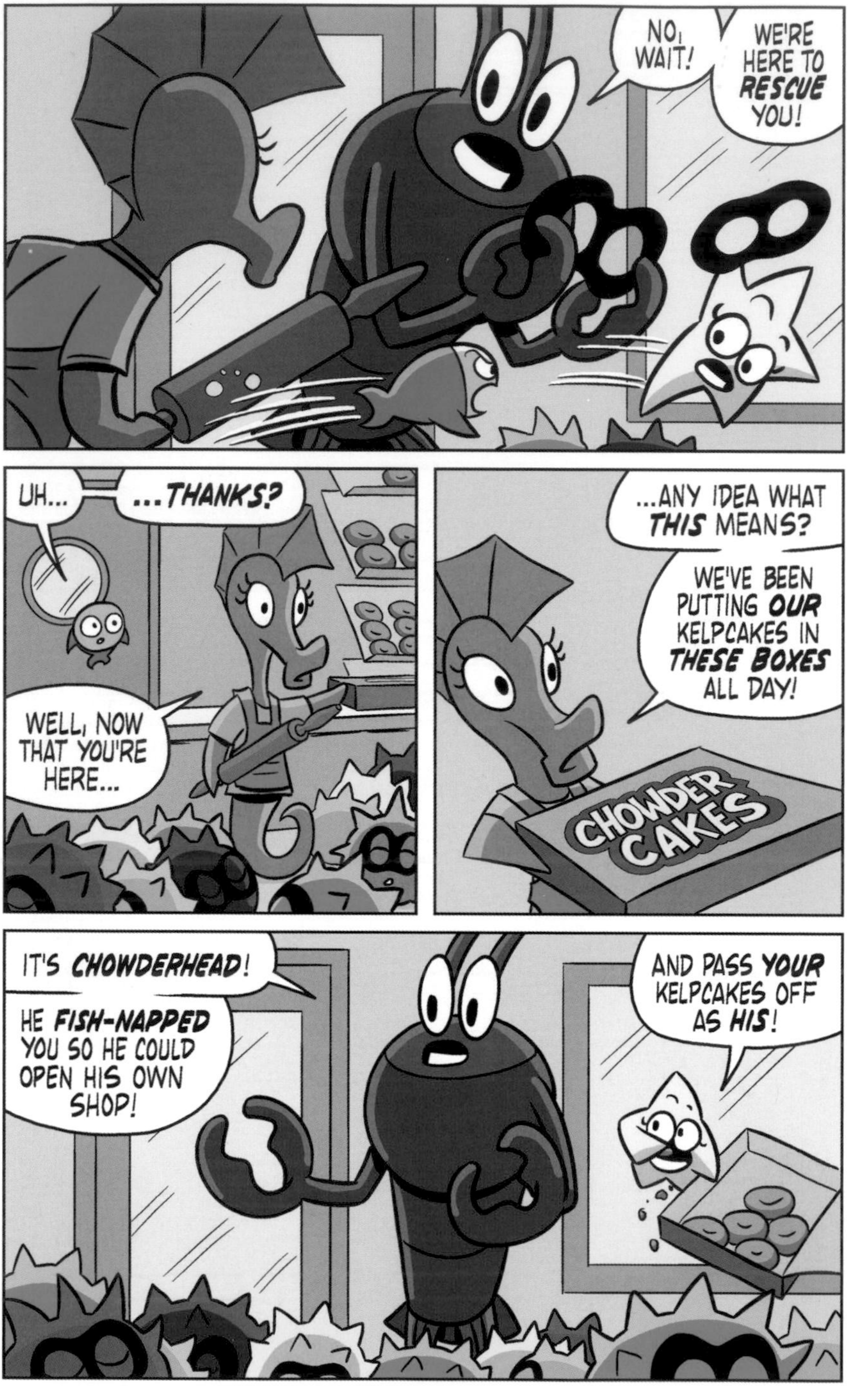
NO, WAIT!
WE'RE HERE TO RESCUE YOU!
UH...
...THANKS?
WELL, NOW THAT YOU'RE HERE...
...ANY IDEA WHAT THIS MEANS?
WE'VE BEEN PUTTING OUR KELPCAKES IN THESE BOXES ALL DAY!
CHOWDER CAKES
IT'S CHOWDERHEAD!
HE FISH-NAPPED YOU SO HE COULD OPEN HIS OWN SHOP!
AND PASS YOUR KELPCAKES OFF AS HIS!

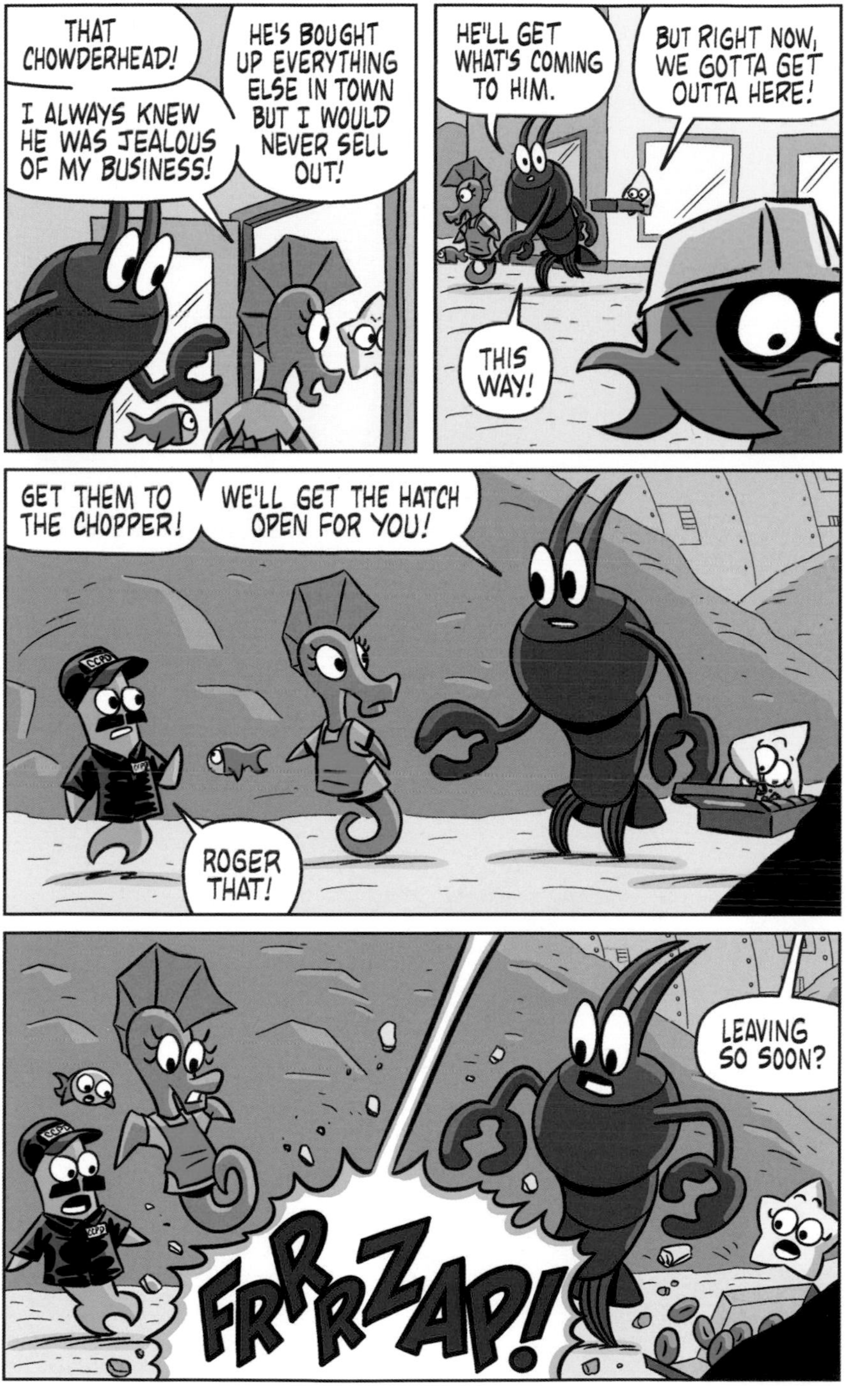
THAT CHOWDERHEAD!
I ALWAYS KNEW HE WAS JEALOUS OF MY BUSINESS!
HE'S BOUGHT UP EVERYTHING ELSE IN TOWN BUT I WOULD NEVER SELL OUT!
HE'LL GET WHAT'S COMING TO HIM.
BUT RIGHT NOW, WE GOTTA GET OUTTA HERE!
THIS WAY!
GET THEM TO THE CHOPPER!
WE'LL GET THE HATCH OPEN FOR YOU!
ROGER THAT!
LEAVING SO SOON?
FRRRZAP!

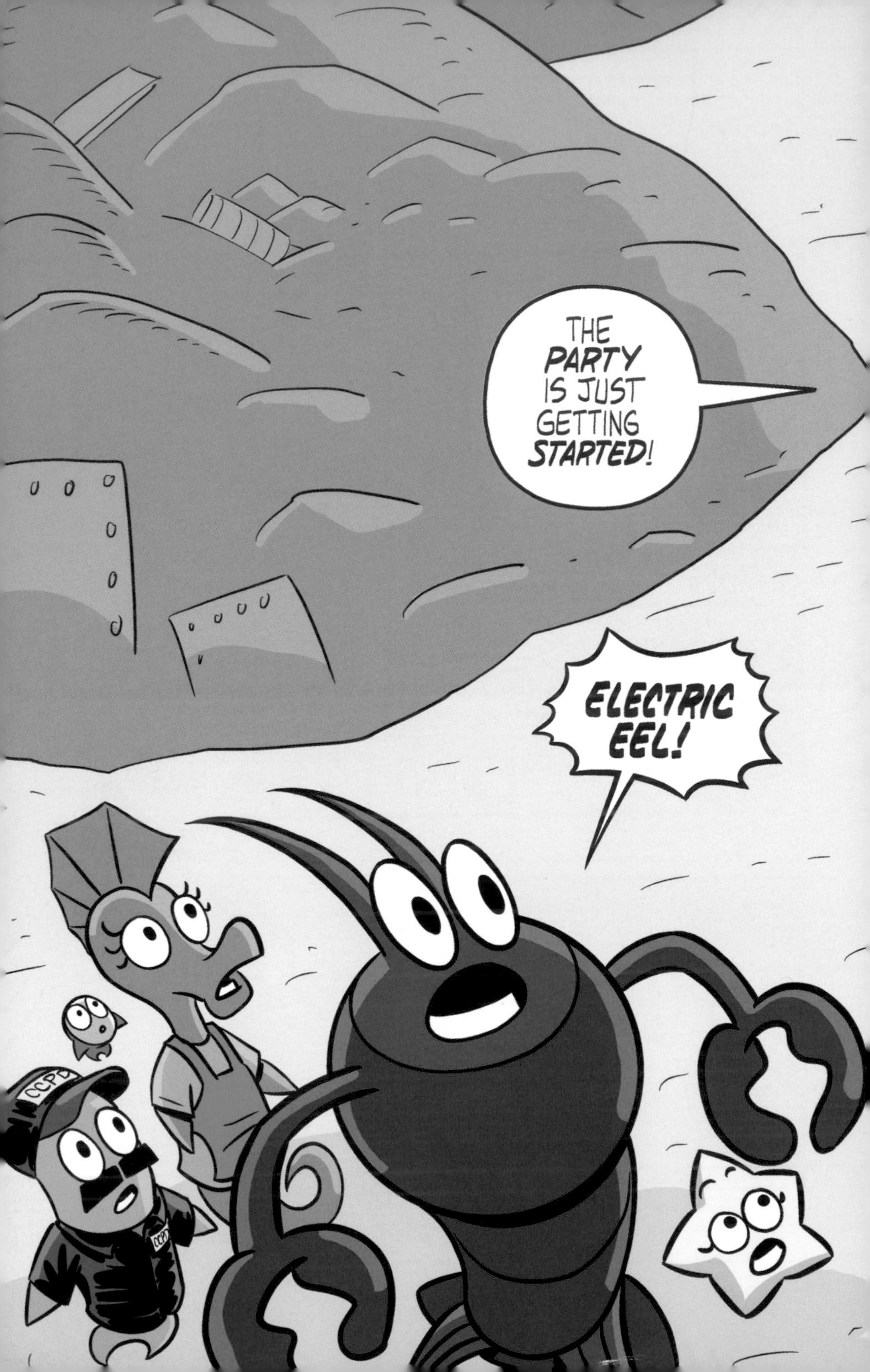
THE *PARTY* IS JUST GETTING *STARTED*!
ELECTRIC EEL!
CCPD
CCPD

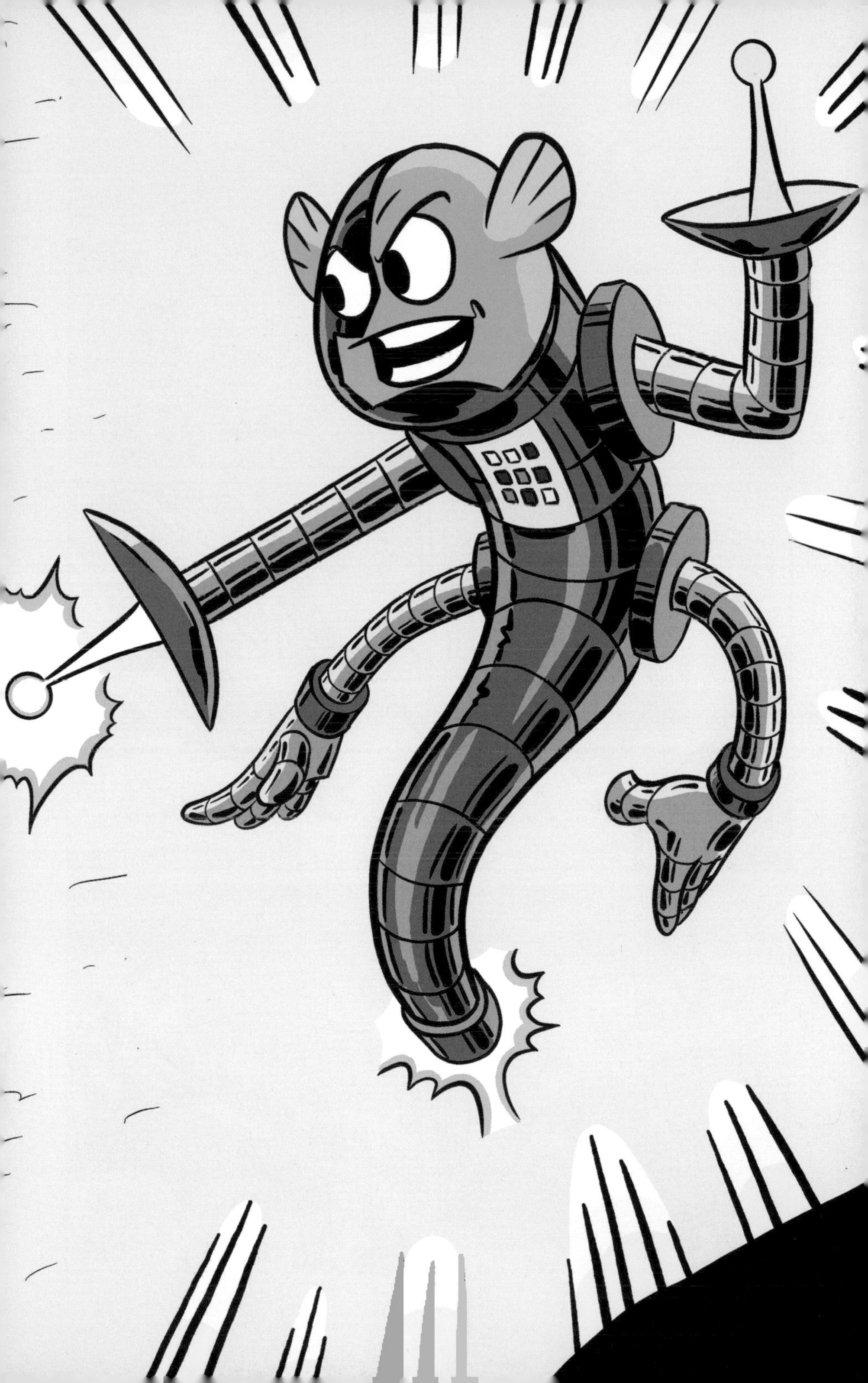

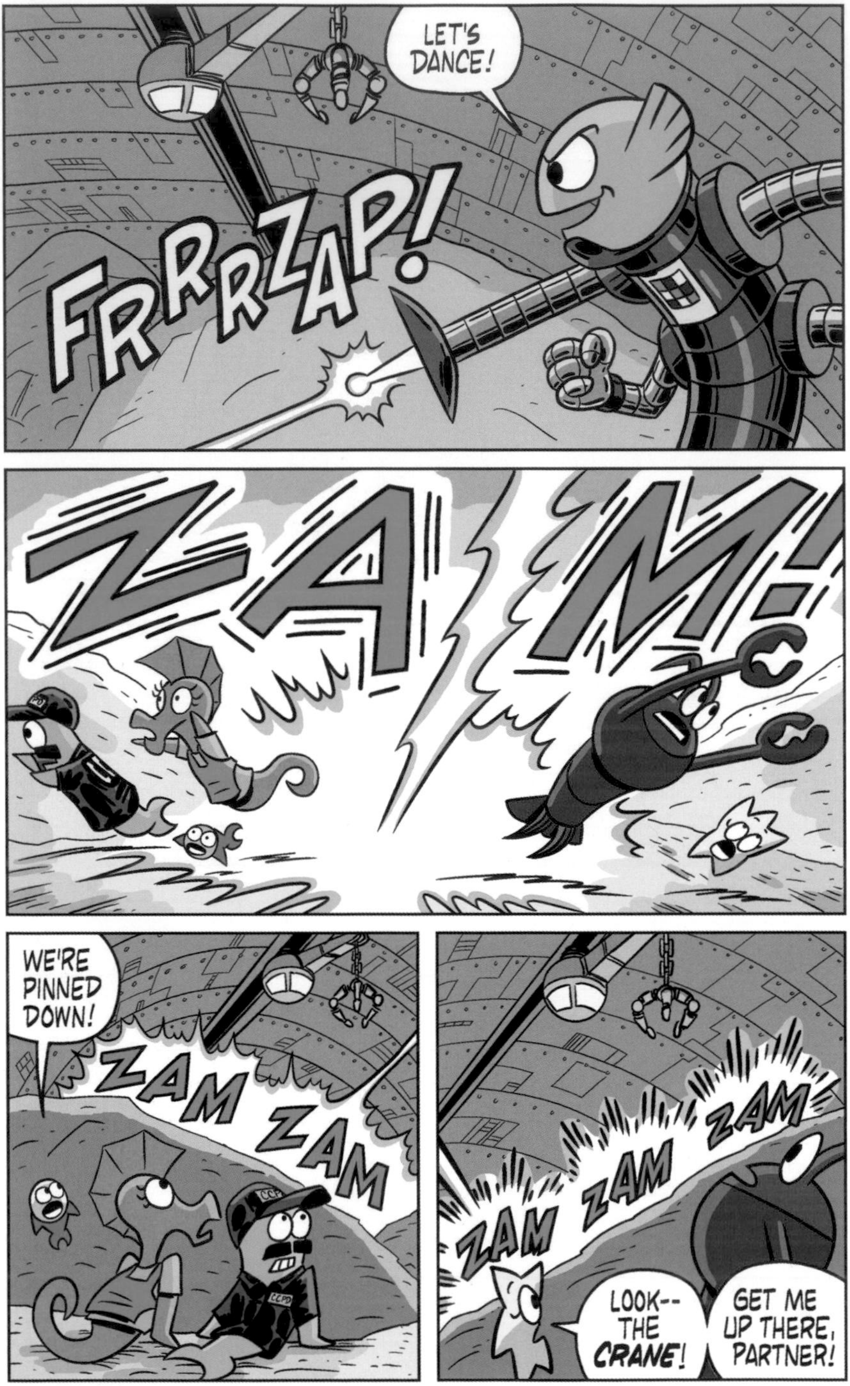
LET'S DANCE!
FRRRZAP!
ZAM!
WE'RE PINNED DOWN!
ZAM ZAM
ZAM ZAM ZAM
LOOK-- THE CRANE!
GET ME UP THERE, PARTNER!

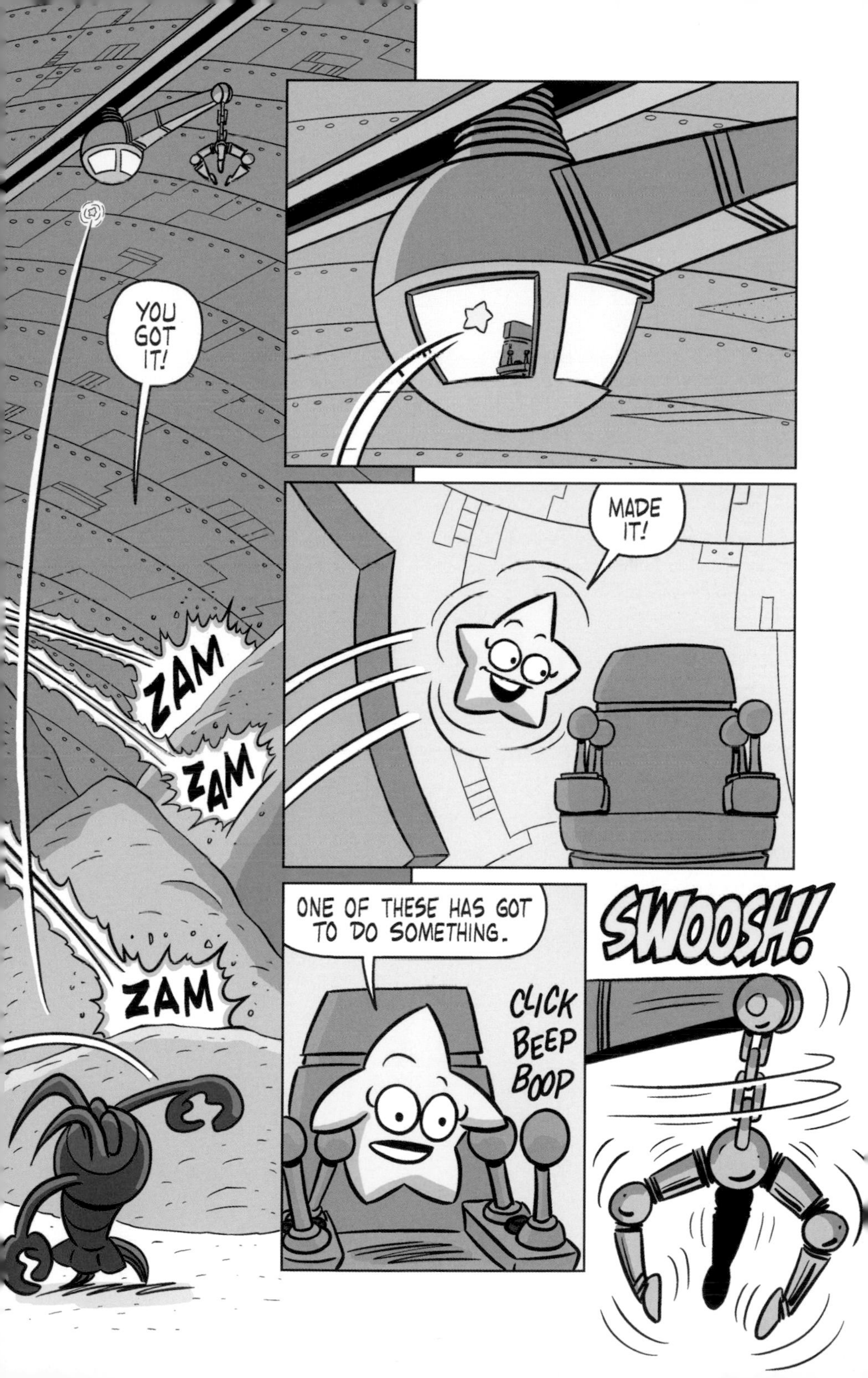
YOU GOT IT!
ZAM
ZAM
ZAM
MADE IT!
ONE OF THESE HAS GOT TO DO SOMETHING.
CLICK BEEP BOOP
SWOOSH!

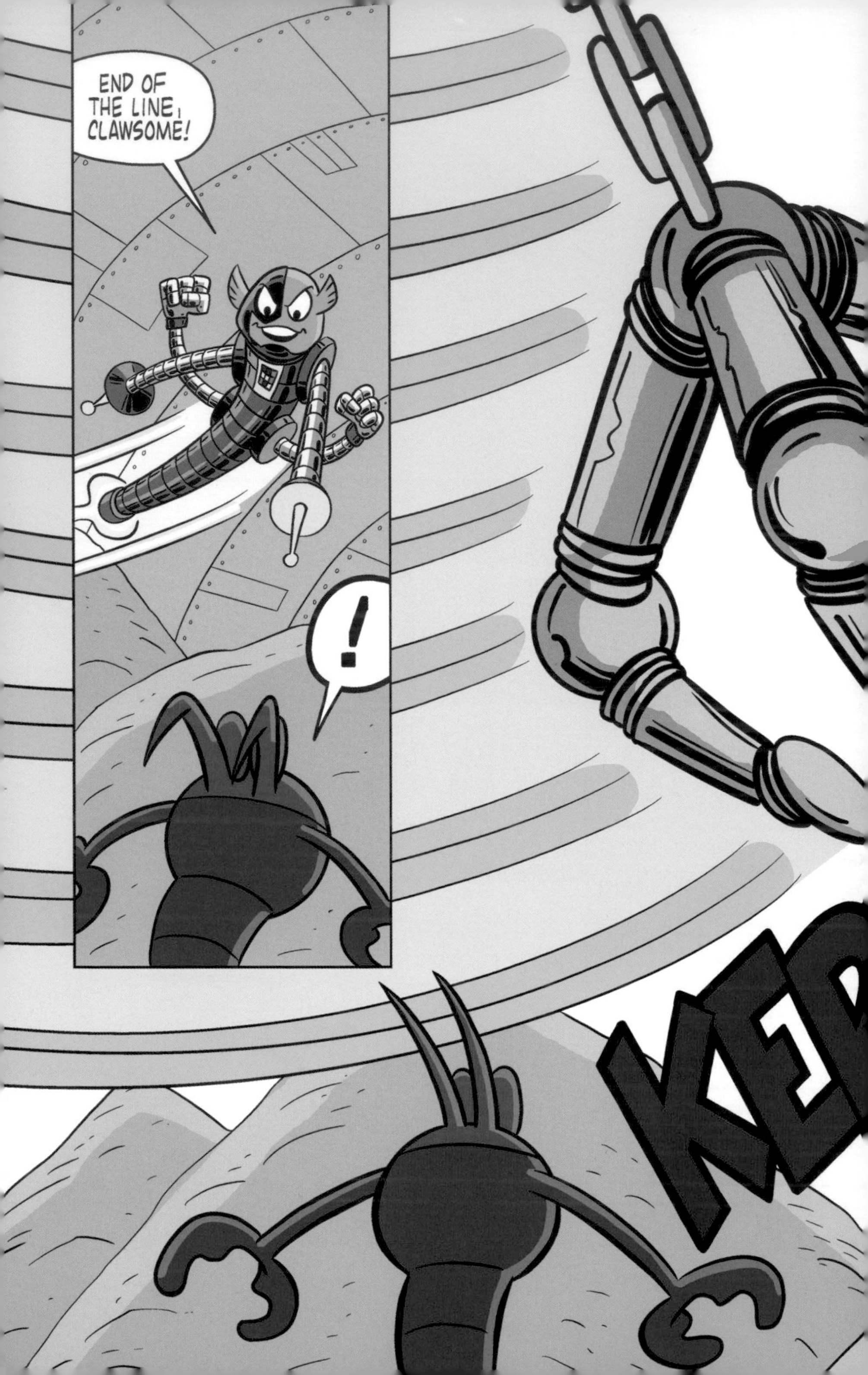
END OF THE LINE, CLAWSOME!
!
KER

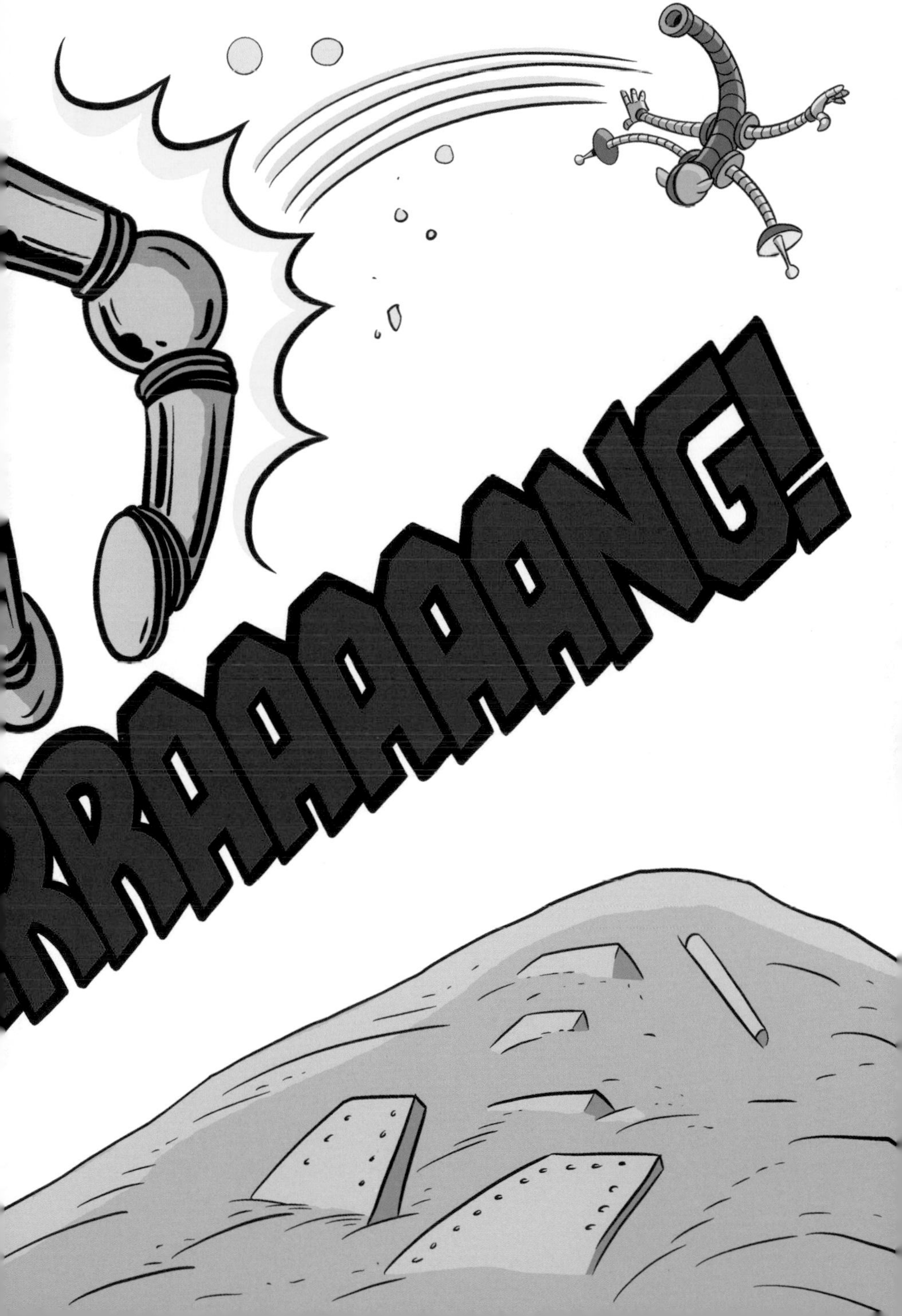
RAAAAANG!

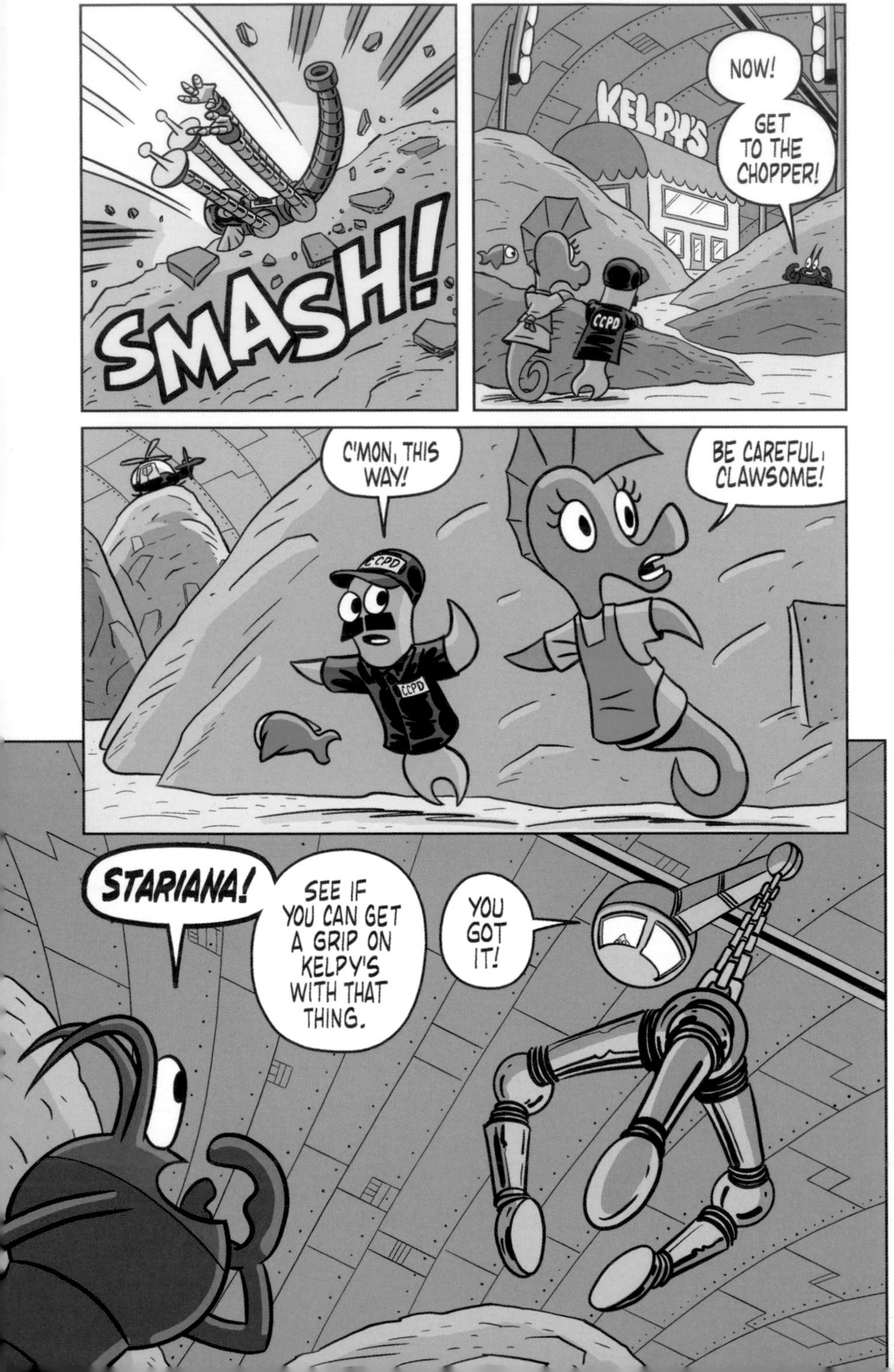
SMASH!
NOW!
GET TO THE CHOPPER!
KELPY'S
CCPD
C'MON, THIS WAY!
BE CAREFUL, CLAWSOME!
CCPD
STARIANA!
SEE IF YOU CAN GET A GRIP ON KELPY'S WITH THAT THING.
YOU GOT IT!

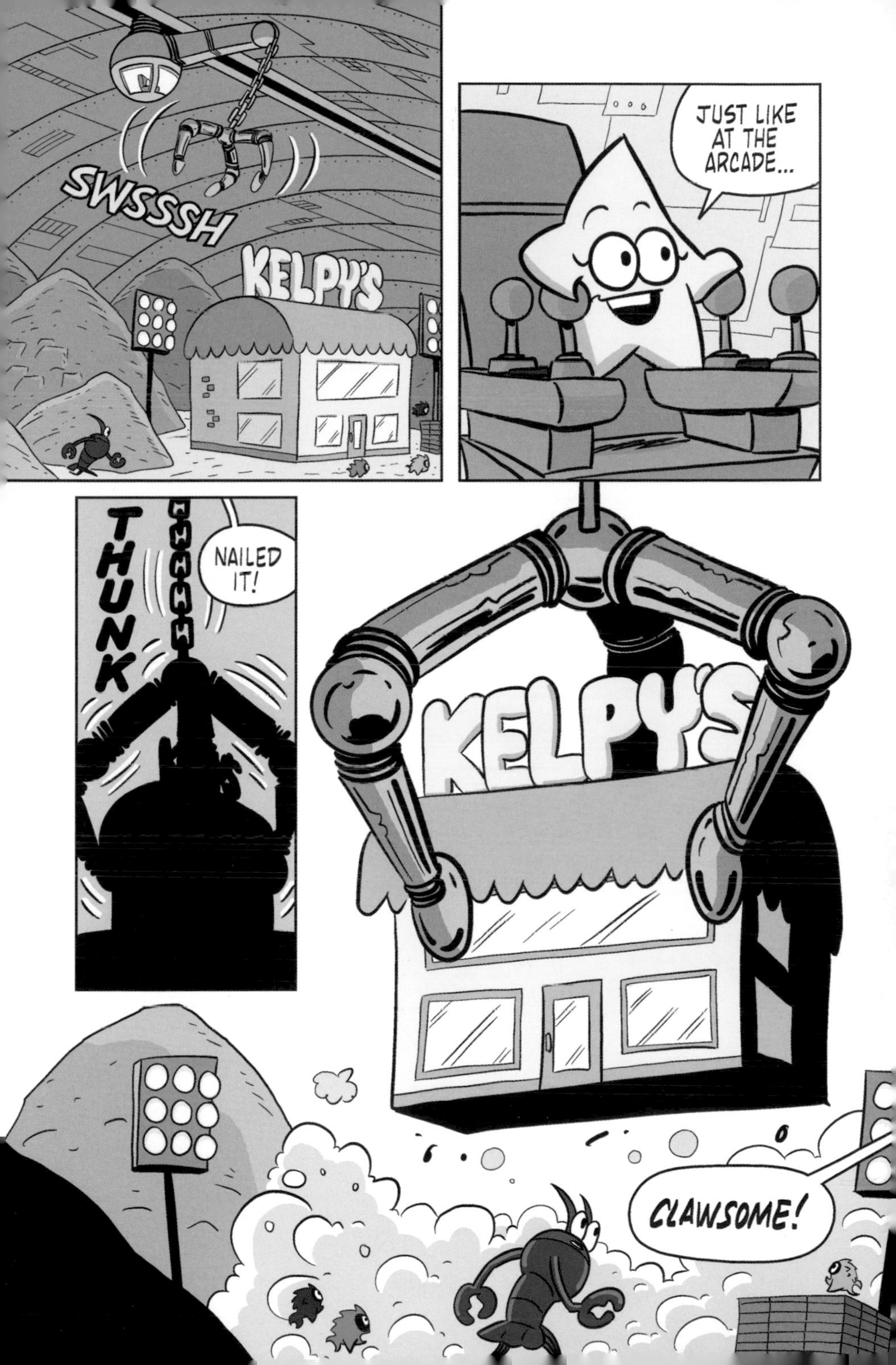
SWSSSH
KELPY'S
JUST LIKE AT THE ARCADE...
THUNK
NAILED IT!
KELPY'S
CLAWSOME!

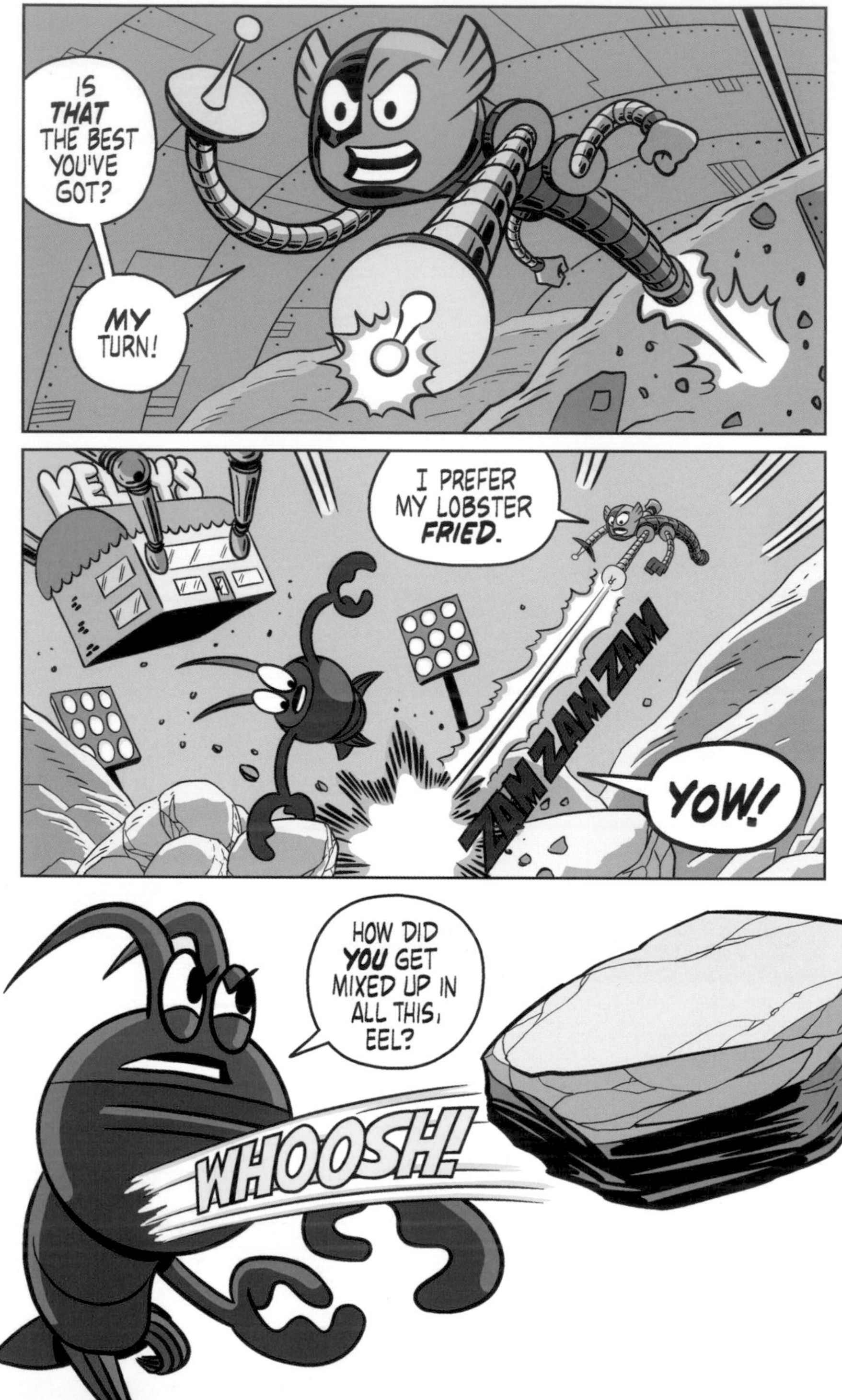
IS THAT THE BEST YOU'VE GOT?
MY TURN!
KELLY'S
I PREFER MY LOBSTER FRIED.
ZAM ZAM ZAM ZAM
YOW!
HOW DID YOU GET MIXED UP IN ALL THIS, EEL?
WHOOSH!

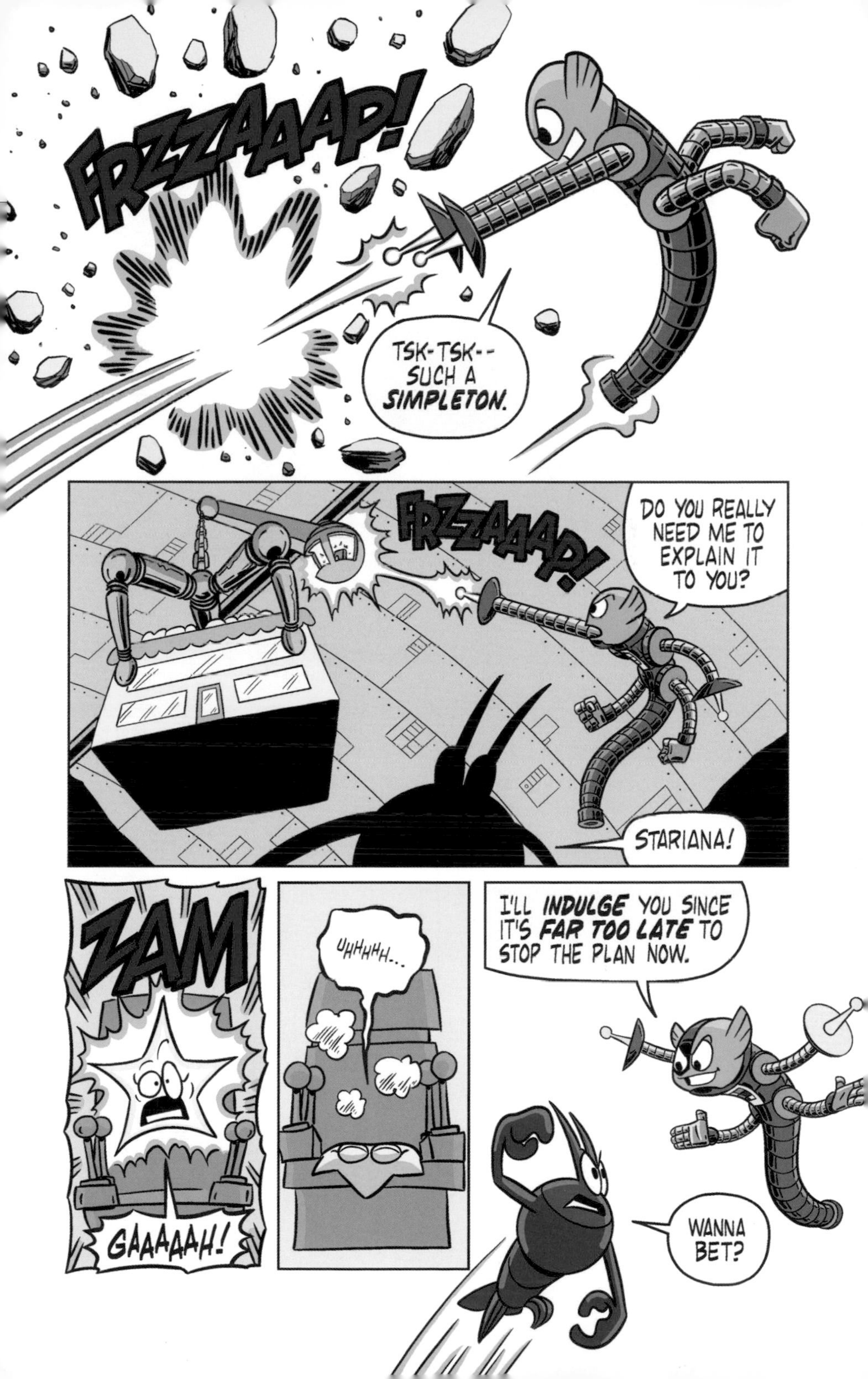
FRZZAAAP!
TSK-TSK--
SUCH A
SIMPLETON.
FRZZAAAP!
DO YOU REALLY
NEED ME TO
EXPLAIN IT
TO YOU?
STARIANA!
ZAM
GAAAAAH!
UHHHHH...
I'LL INDULGE YOU SINCE
IT'S FAR TOO LATE TO
STOP THE PLAN NOW.
WANNA
BET?

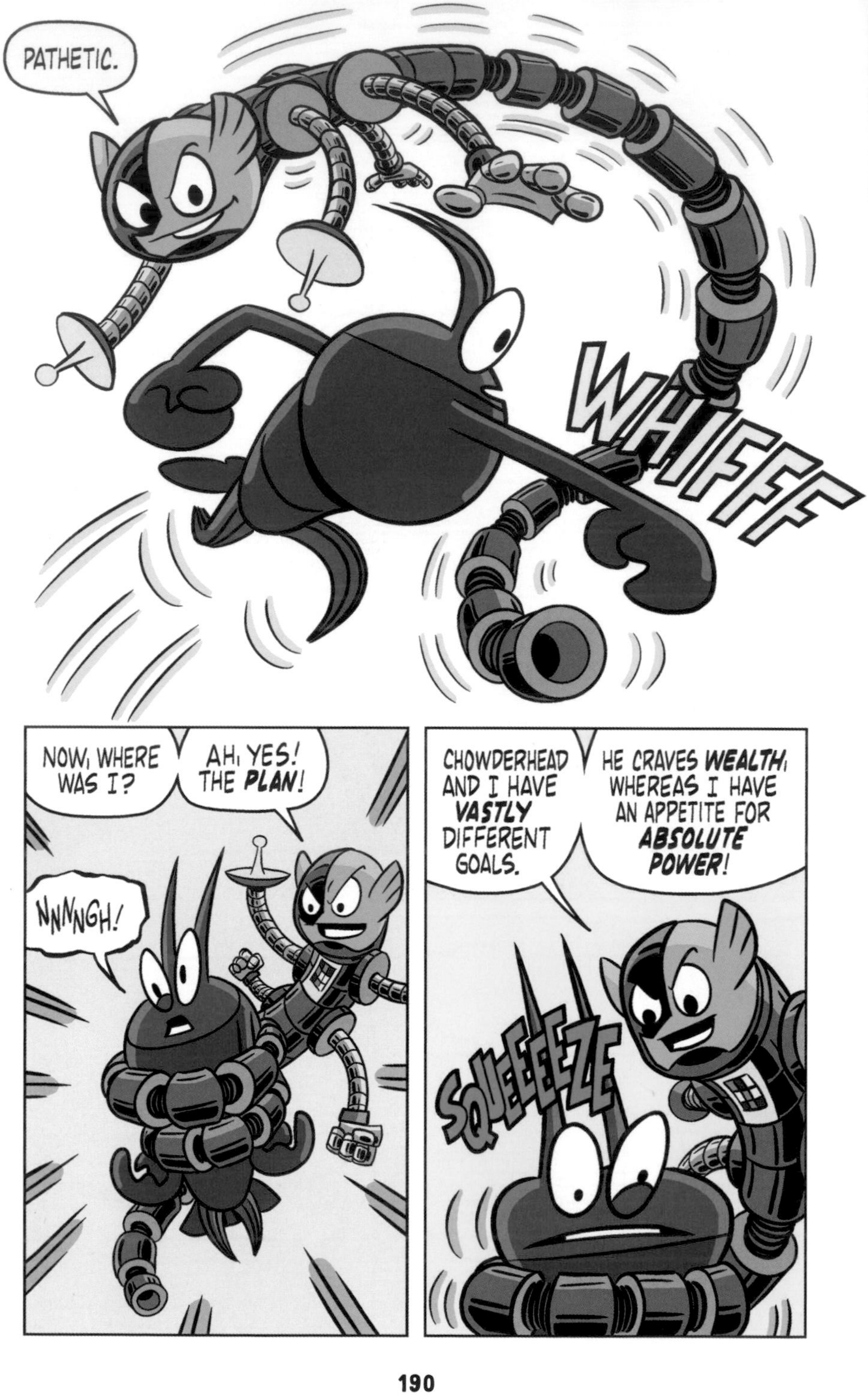
PATHETIC.
WHIFFF
NOW, WHERE WAS I?
AH, YES! THE PLAN!
NNNNGH!
CHOWDERHEAD AND I HAVE VASTLY DIFFERENT GOALS.
HE CRAVES WEALTH, WHEREAS I HAVE AN APPETITE FOR ABSOLUTE POWER!
SQUEEEEZE

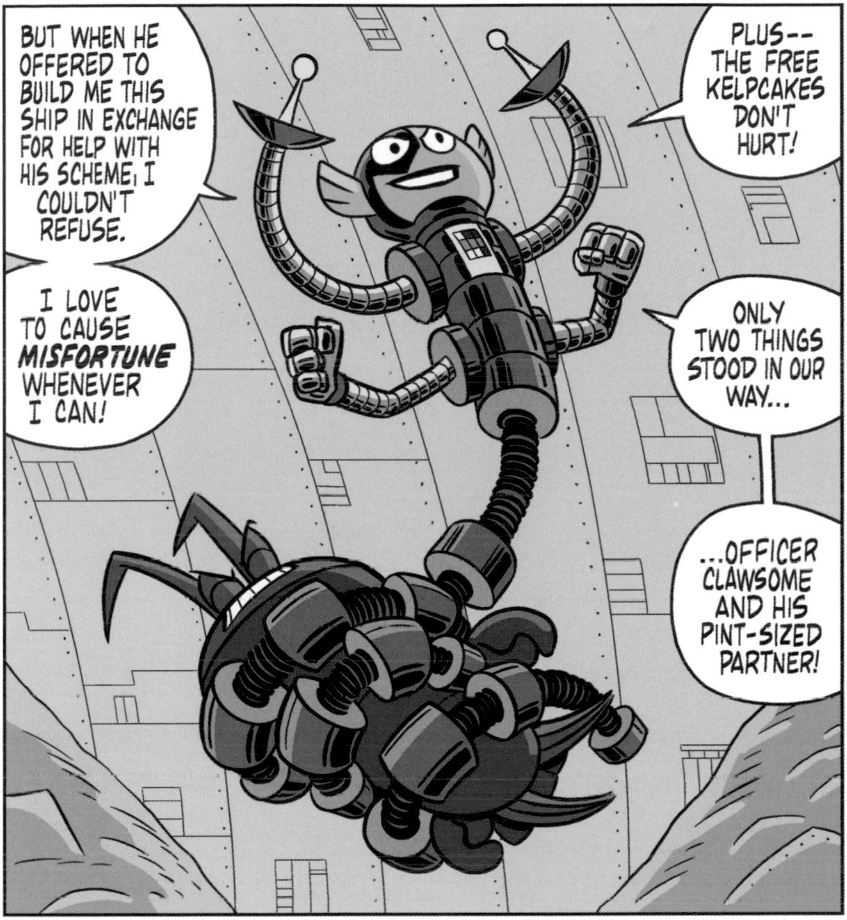
BUT WHEN HE OFFERED TO BUILD ME THIS SHIP IN EXCHANGE FOR HELP WITH HIS SCHEME, I COULDN'T REFUSE.
PLUS-- THE FREE KELPCAKES DON'T HURT!
I LOVE TO CAUSE MISFORTUNE WHENEVER I CAN!
ONLY TWO THINGS STOOD IN OUR WAY...
...OFFICER CLAWSOME AND HIS PINT-SIZED PARTNER!

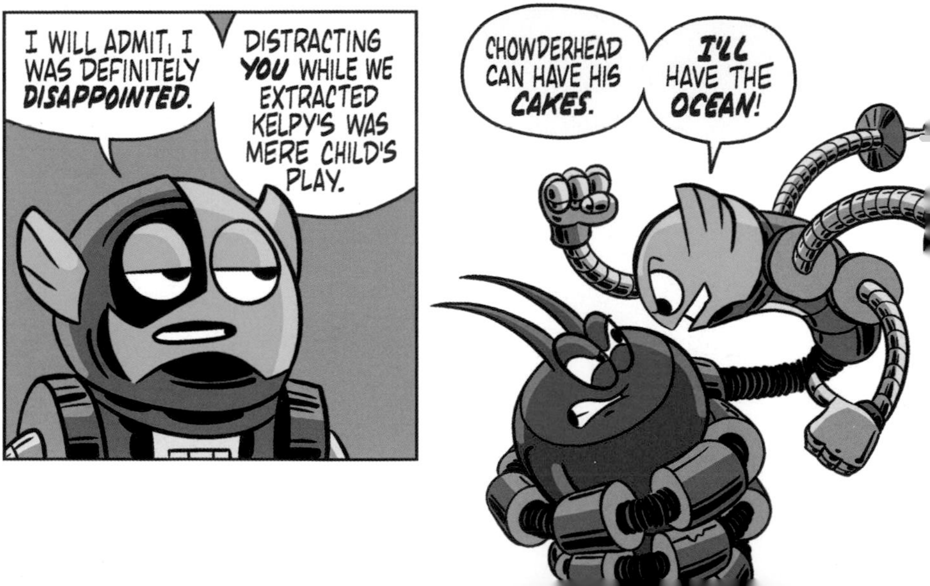
I WILL ADMIT, I WAS DEFINITELY DISAPPOINTED.
DISTRACTING YOU WHILE WE EXTRACTED KELPY'S WAS MERE CHILD'S PLAY.
CHOWDERHEAD CAN HAVE HIS CAKES.
I'LL HAVE THE OCEAN!

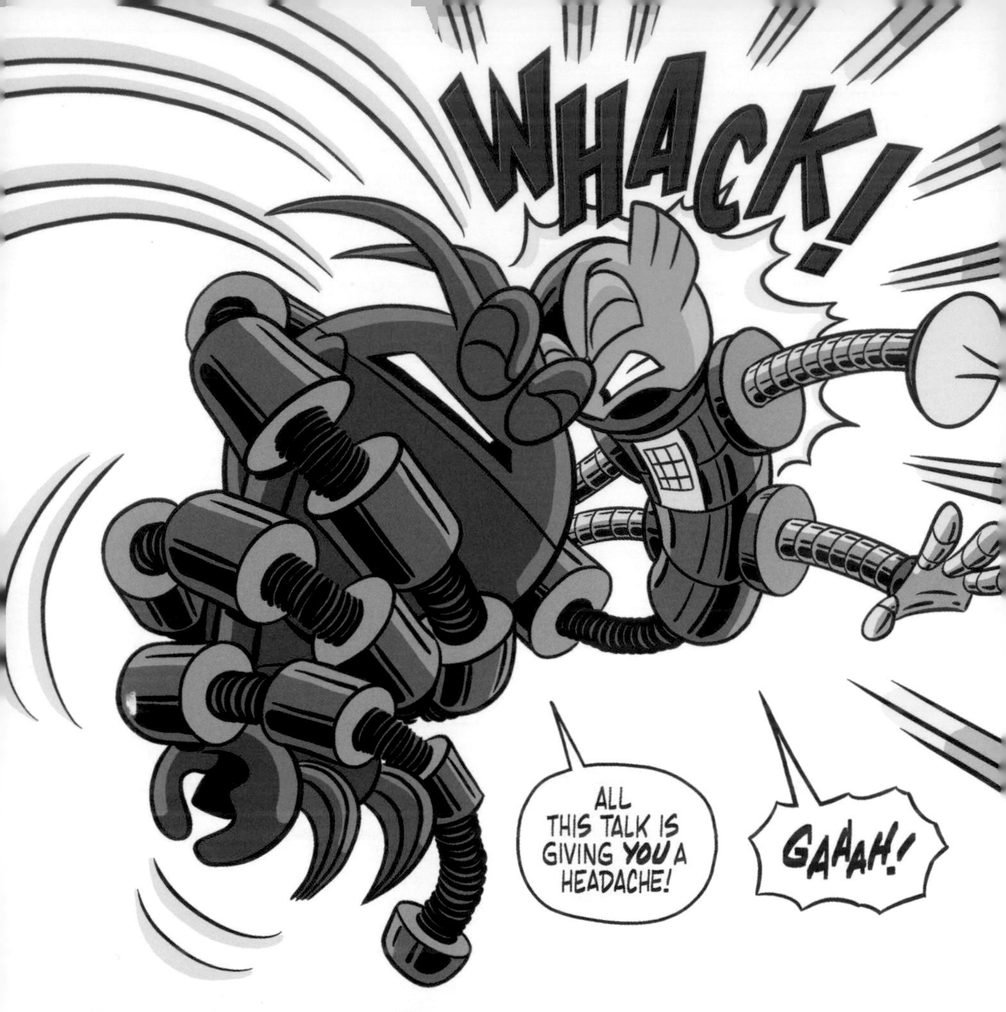
WHACK!
ALL THIS TALK IS GIVING YOU A HEADACHE!
GAAAH!

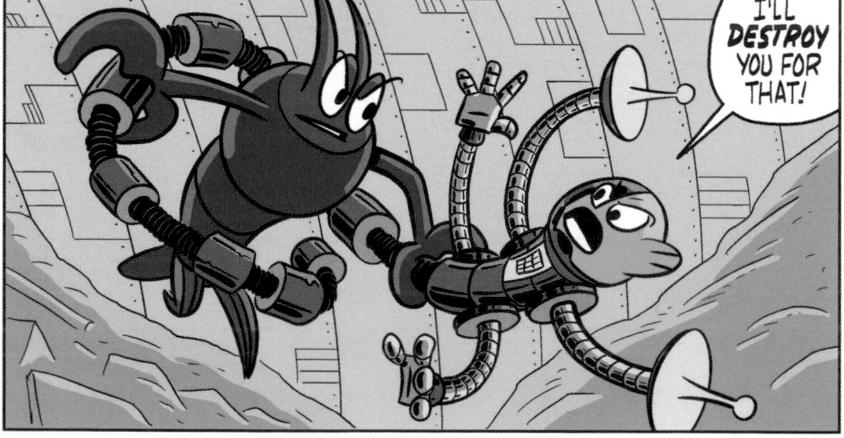
I'LL DESTROY YOU FOR THAT!

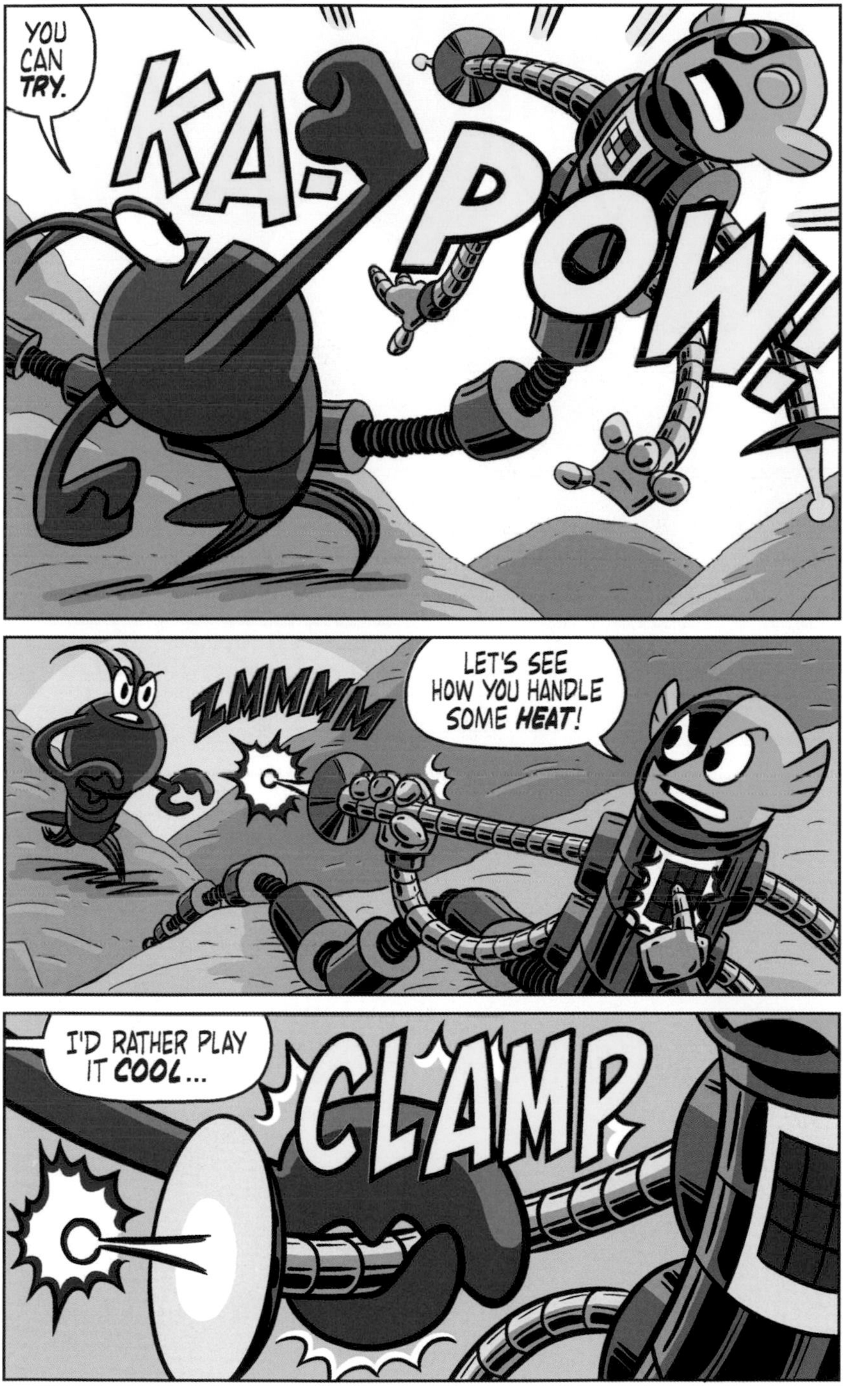
YOU CAN TRY.
KA-POW!
ZMMMM
LET'S SEE HOW YOU HANDLE SOME HEAT!
I'D RATHER PLAY IT COOL...
CLAMP

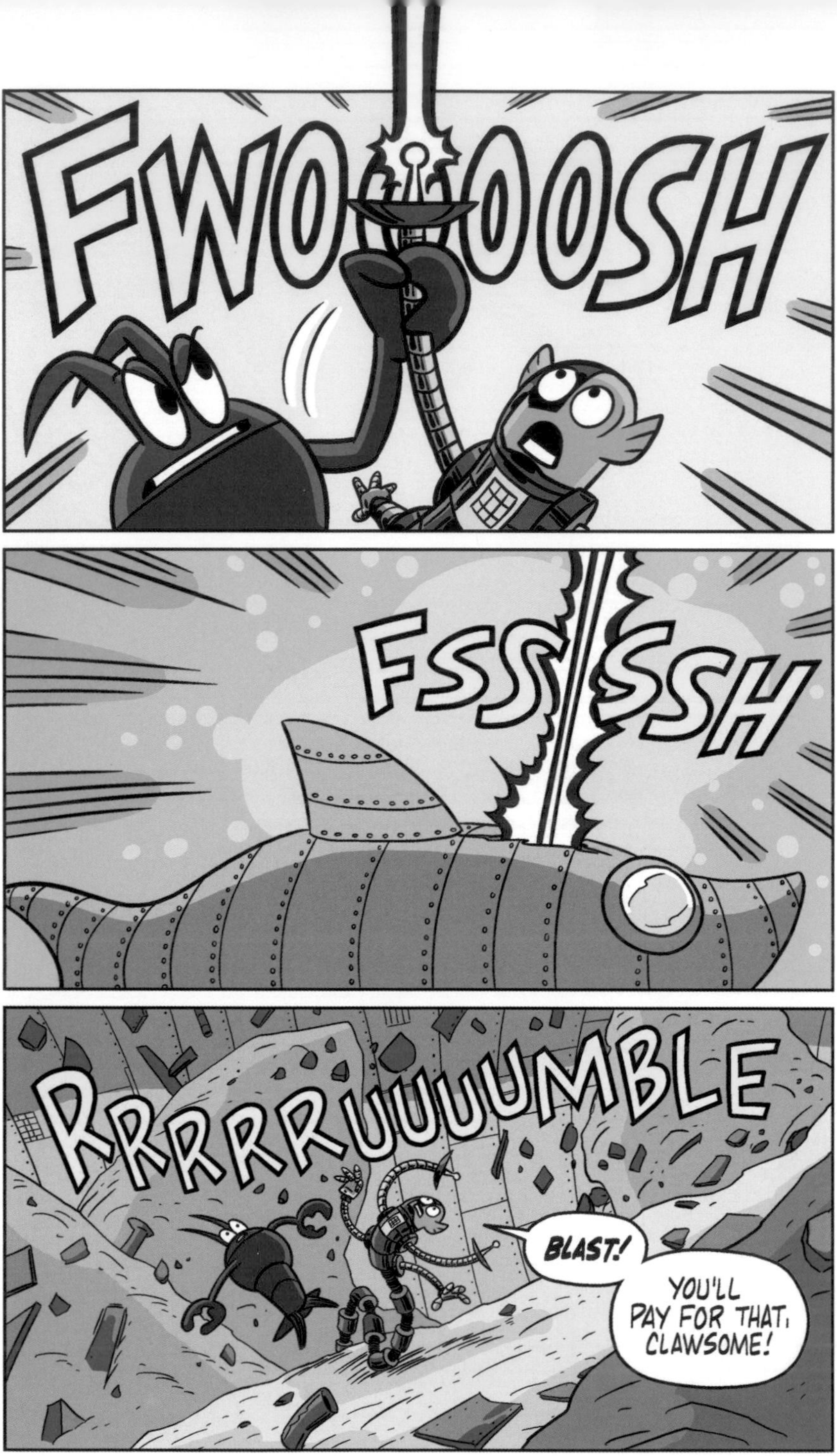
FWOOOOSH
FSSSSH
RRRRRUUUUMBLE
BLAST!
YOU'LL PAY FOR THAT, CLAWSOME!

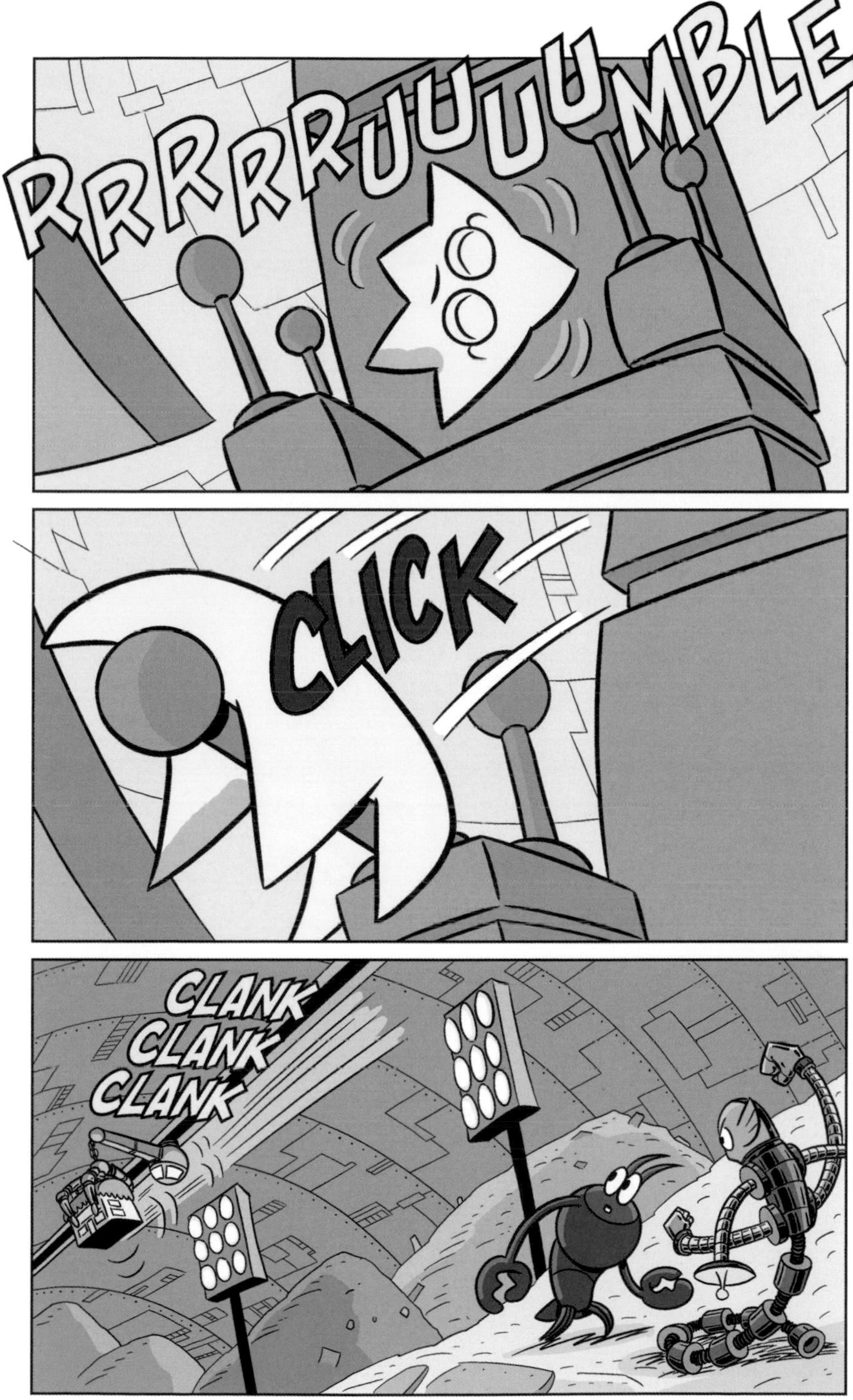
RRRRUUUUMBLE
CLICK
CLANK
CLANK
CLANK

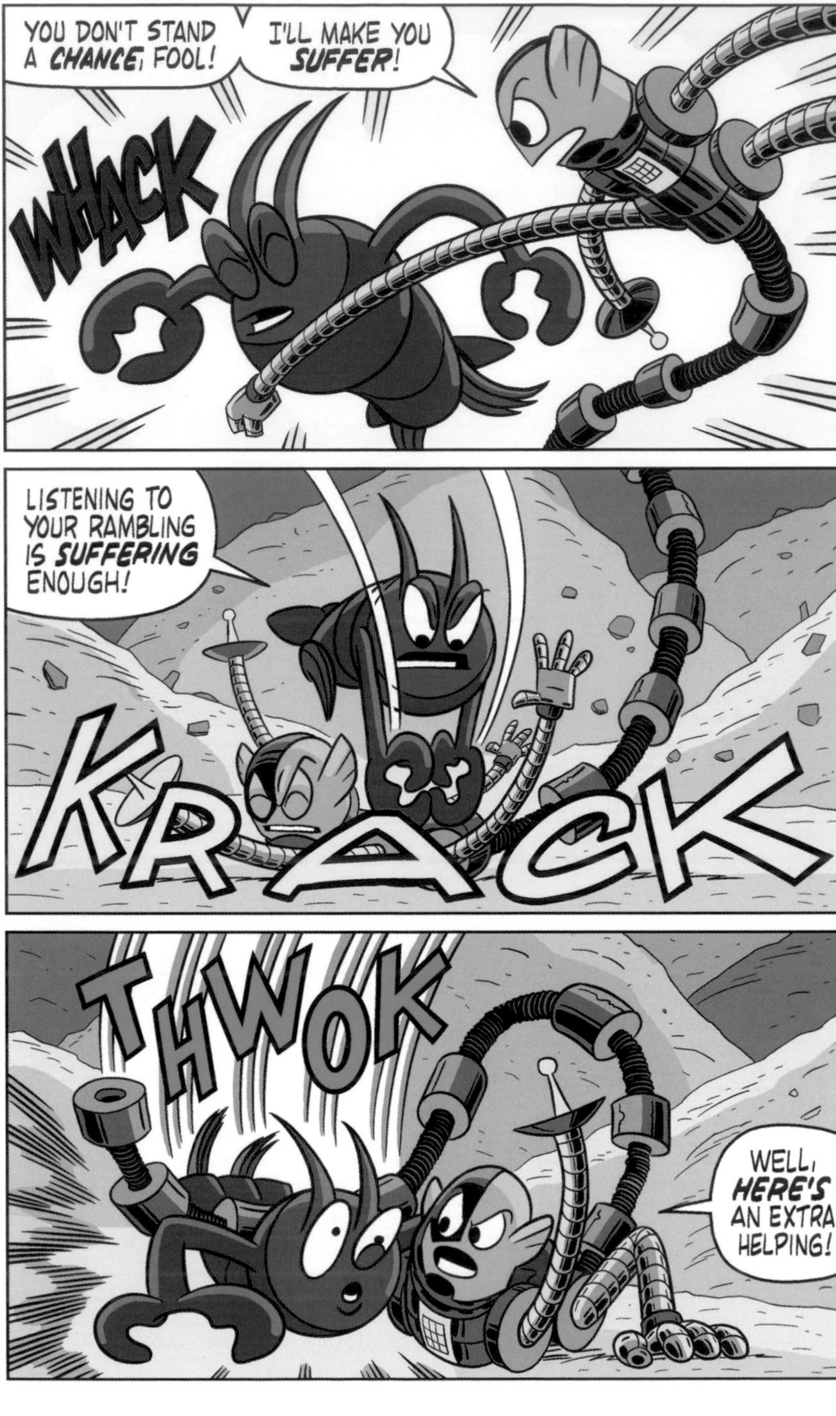
YOU DON'T STAND A CHANCE, FOOL!
I'LL MAKE YOU SUFFER!
WHACK
LISTENING TO YOUR RAMBLING IS SUFFERING ENOUGH!
KRACK
THWOK
WELL, HERE'S AN EXTRA HELPING!

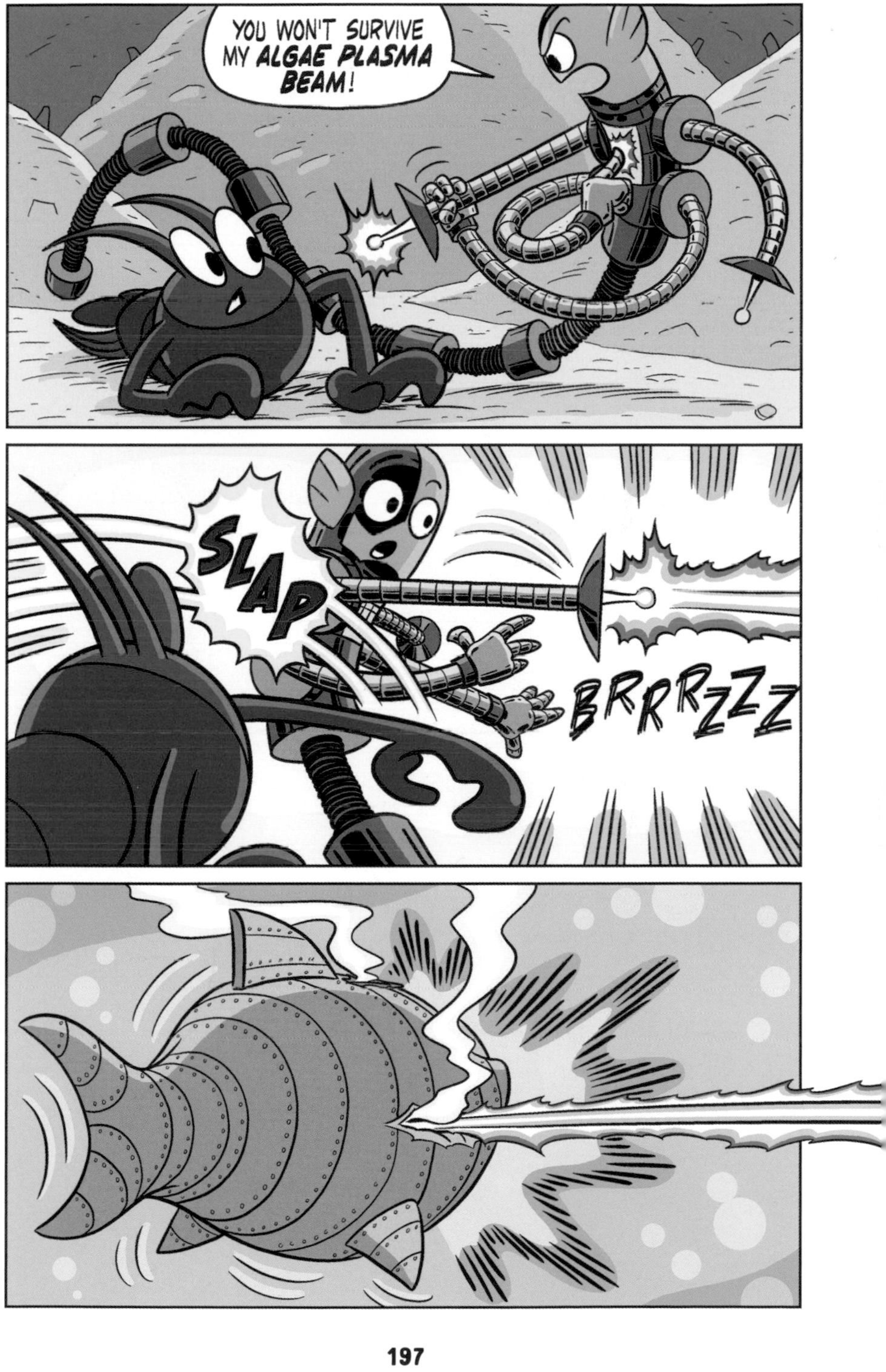
YOU WON'T SURVIVE MY ALGAE PLASMA BEAM!
SLAP
BRRRRZZZ

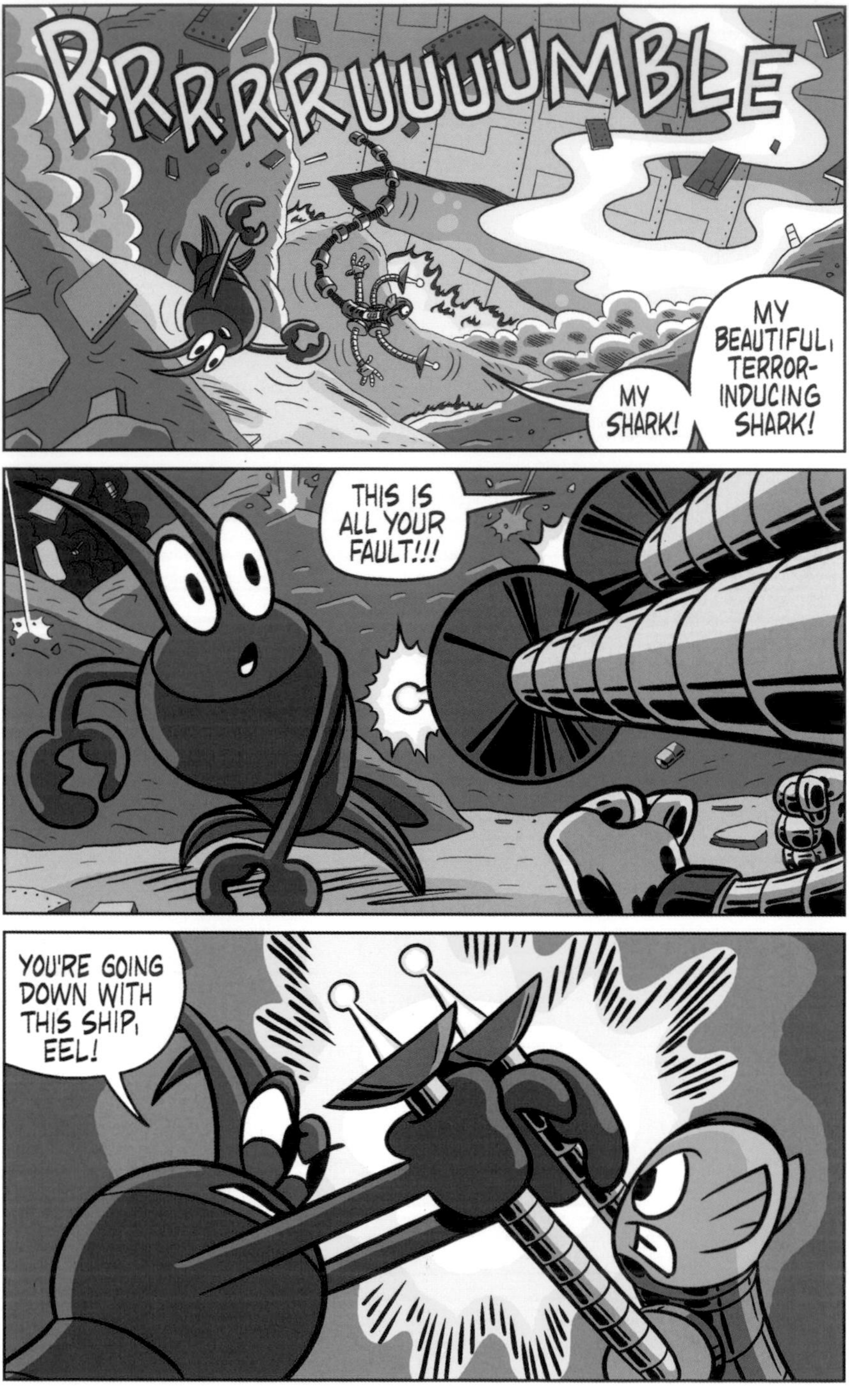
RRRRRUUUUMBLE
MY SHARK!
MY BEAUTIFUL, TERROR-INDUCING SHARK!
THIS IS ALL YOUR FAULT!!!
YOU'RE GOING DOWN WITH THIS SHIP, EEL!

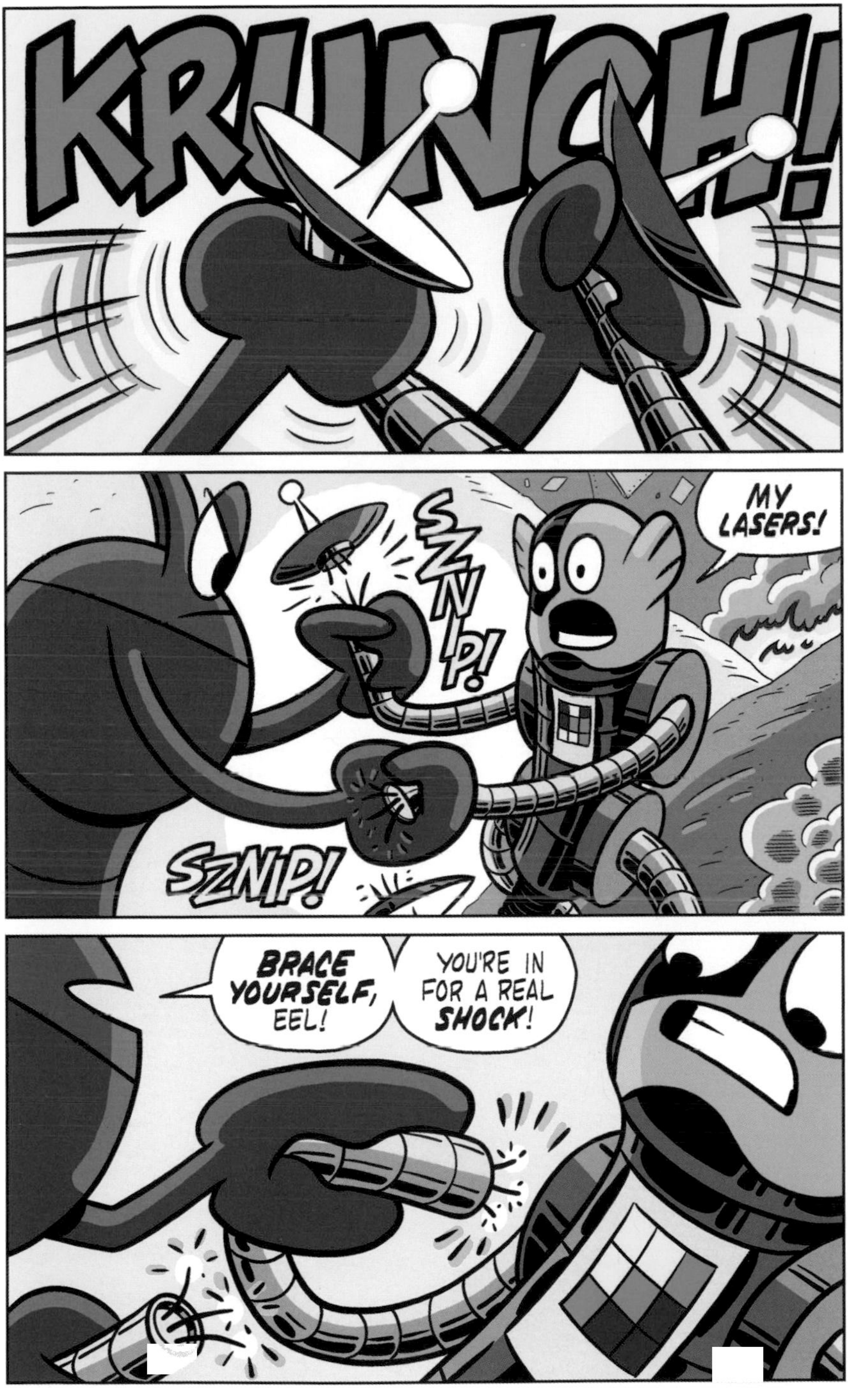
KRUNCH!!
MY LASERS!
SZNIP!
SZNIP!
BRACE YOURSELF, EEL!
YOU'RE IN FOR A REAL SHOCK!

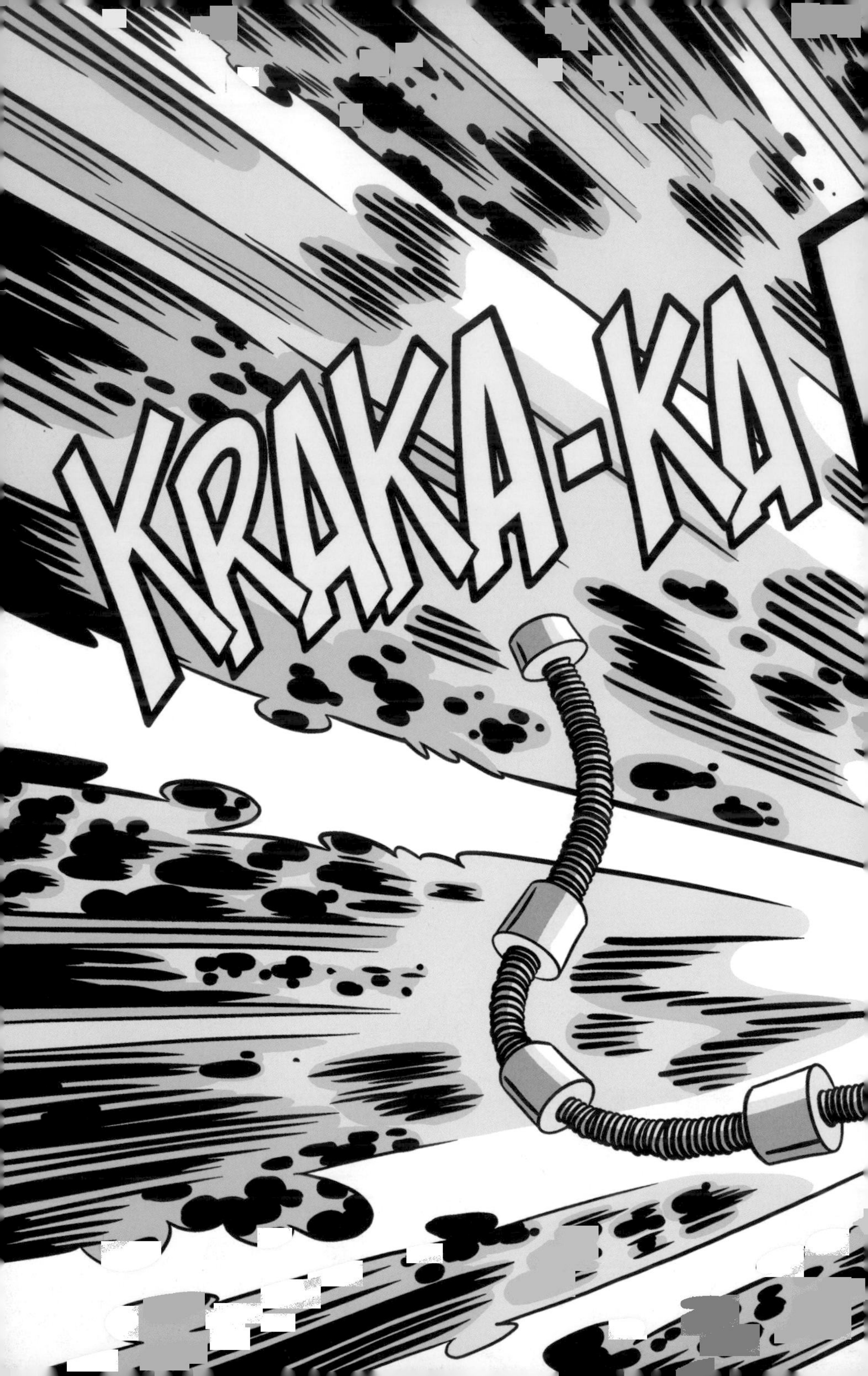
KRAKA-KA

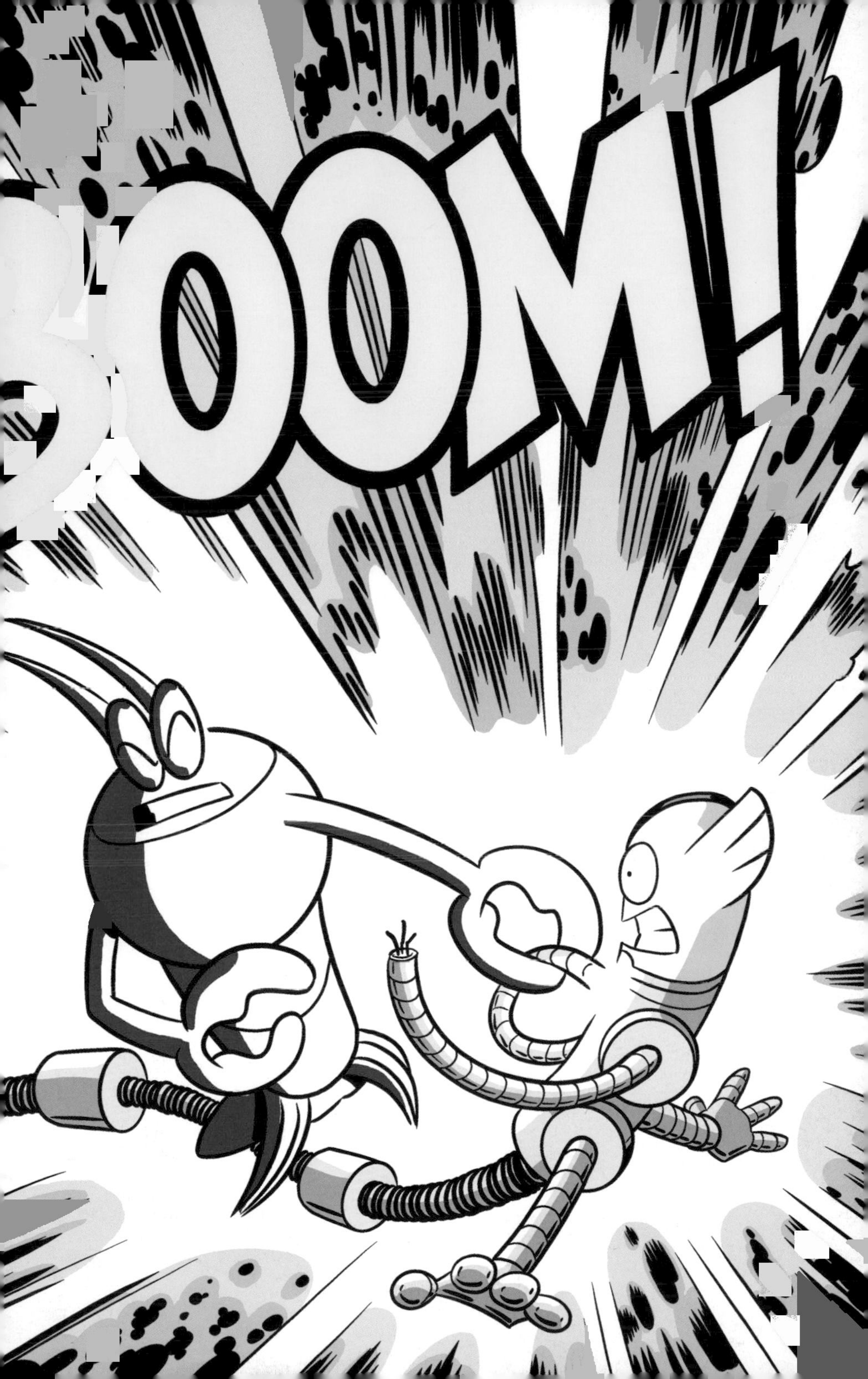
BOOM!

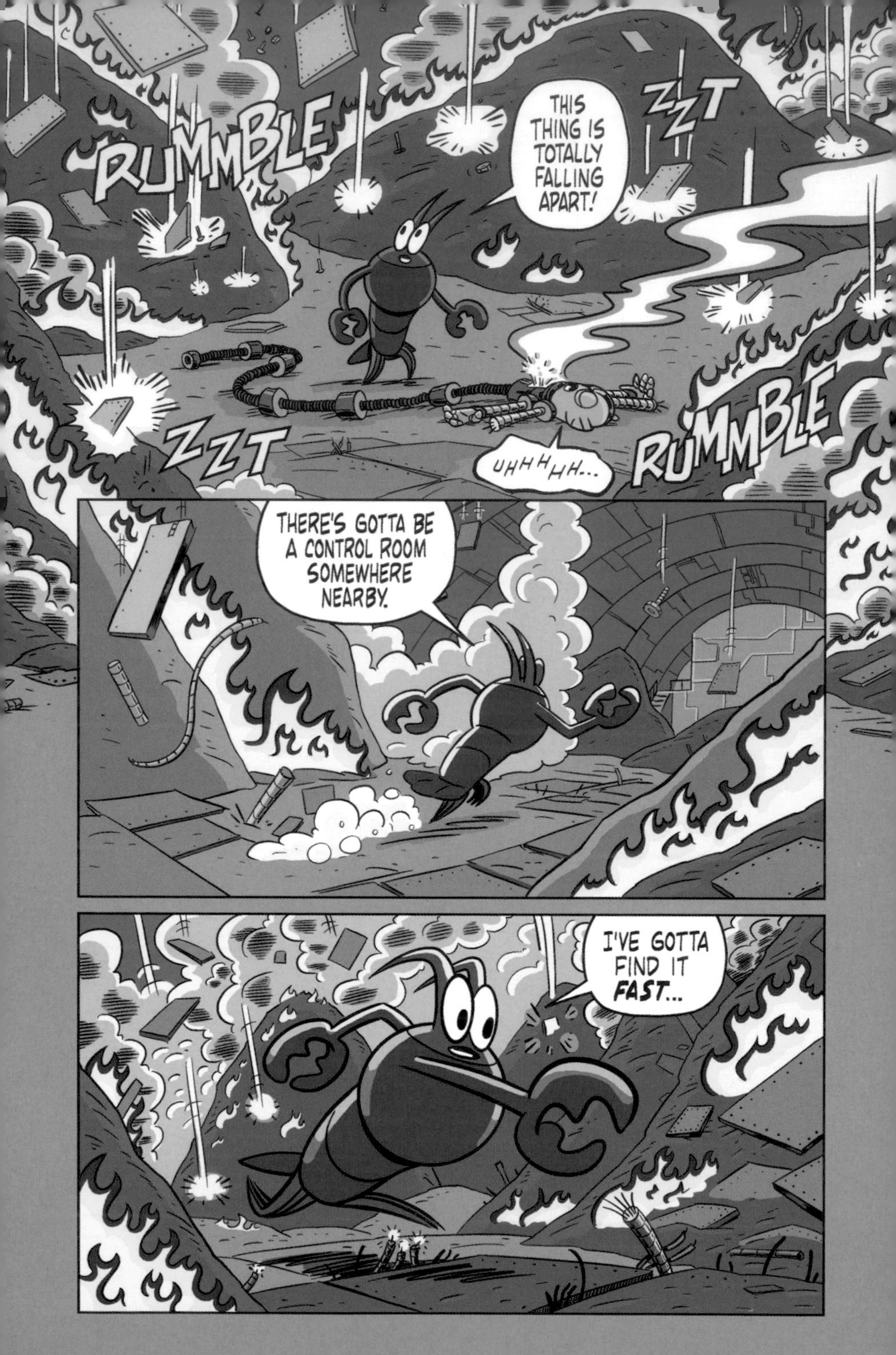
RUMMBLE
THIS THING IS TOTALLY FALLING APART!
ZZT
ZZT
UHHHHHH...
RUMMBLE
THERE'S GOTTA BE A CONTROL ROOM SOMEWHERE NEARBY.
I'VE GOTTA FIND IT FAST...

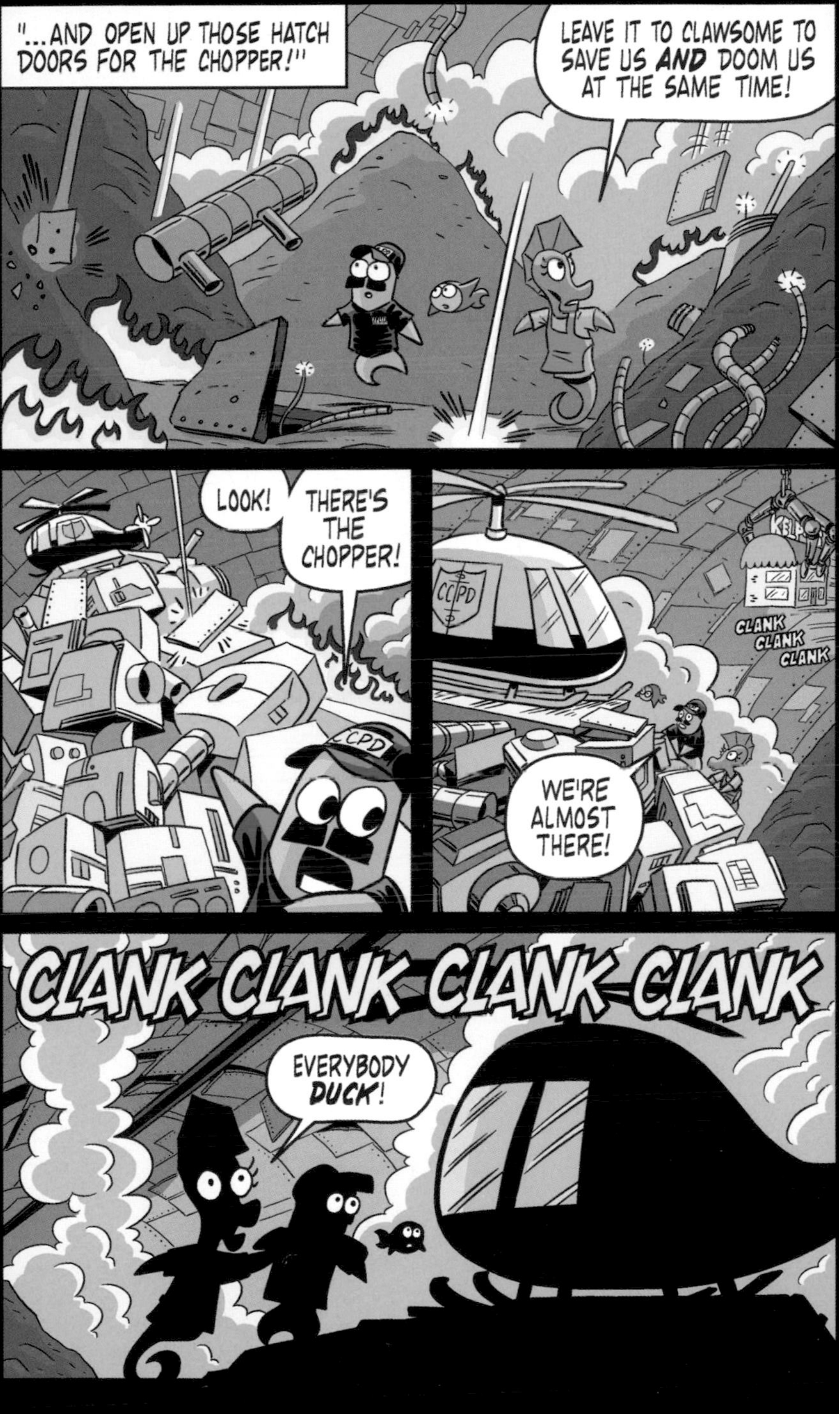
"...AND OPEN UP THOSE HATCH DOORS FOR THE CHOPPER!"
LEAVE IT TO CLAWSOME TO SAVE US AND DOOM US AT THE SAME TIME!
LOOK!
THERE'S THE CHOPPER!
CPD
CCPD
CLANK CLANK CLANK
WE'RE ALMOST THERE!
CLANK CLANK CLANK CLANK
EVERYBODY DUCK!

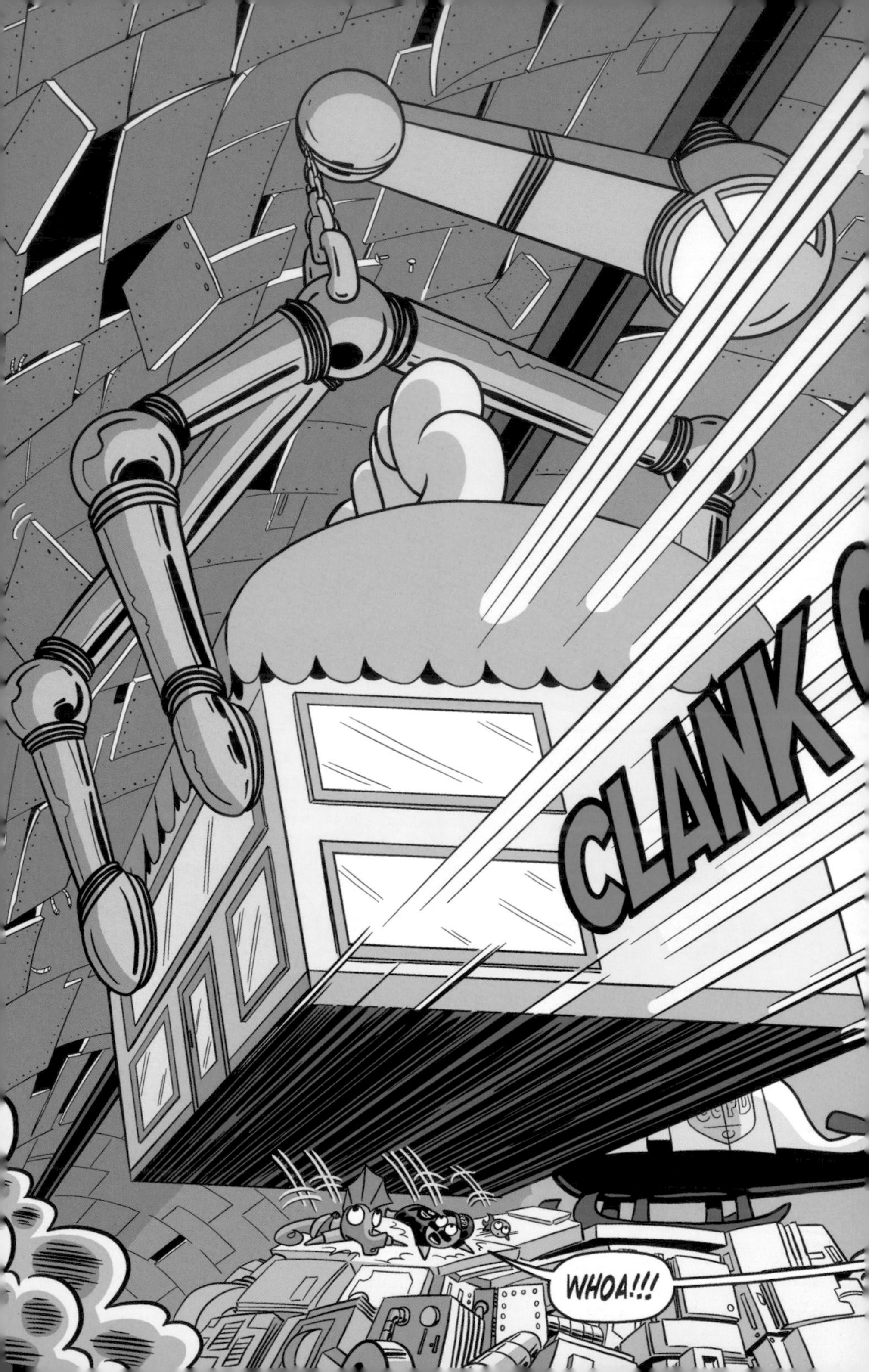
CLANK
WHOA!!!

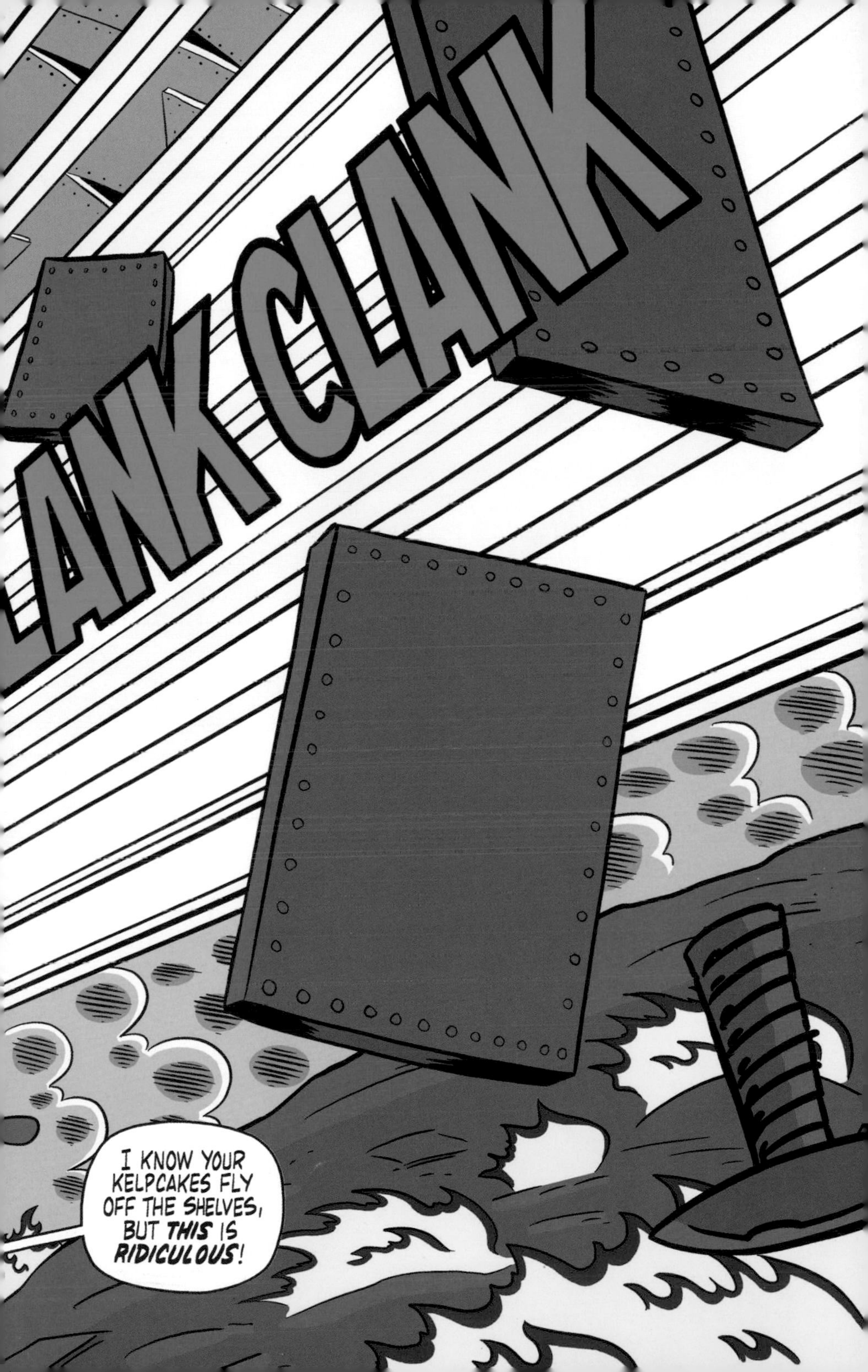
ANK CLANK
I KNOW YOUR KELPCAKES FLY OFF THE SHELVES, BUT *THIS* IS *RIDICULOUS*!

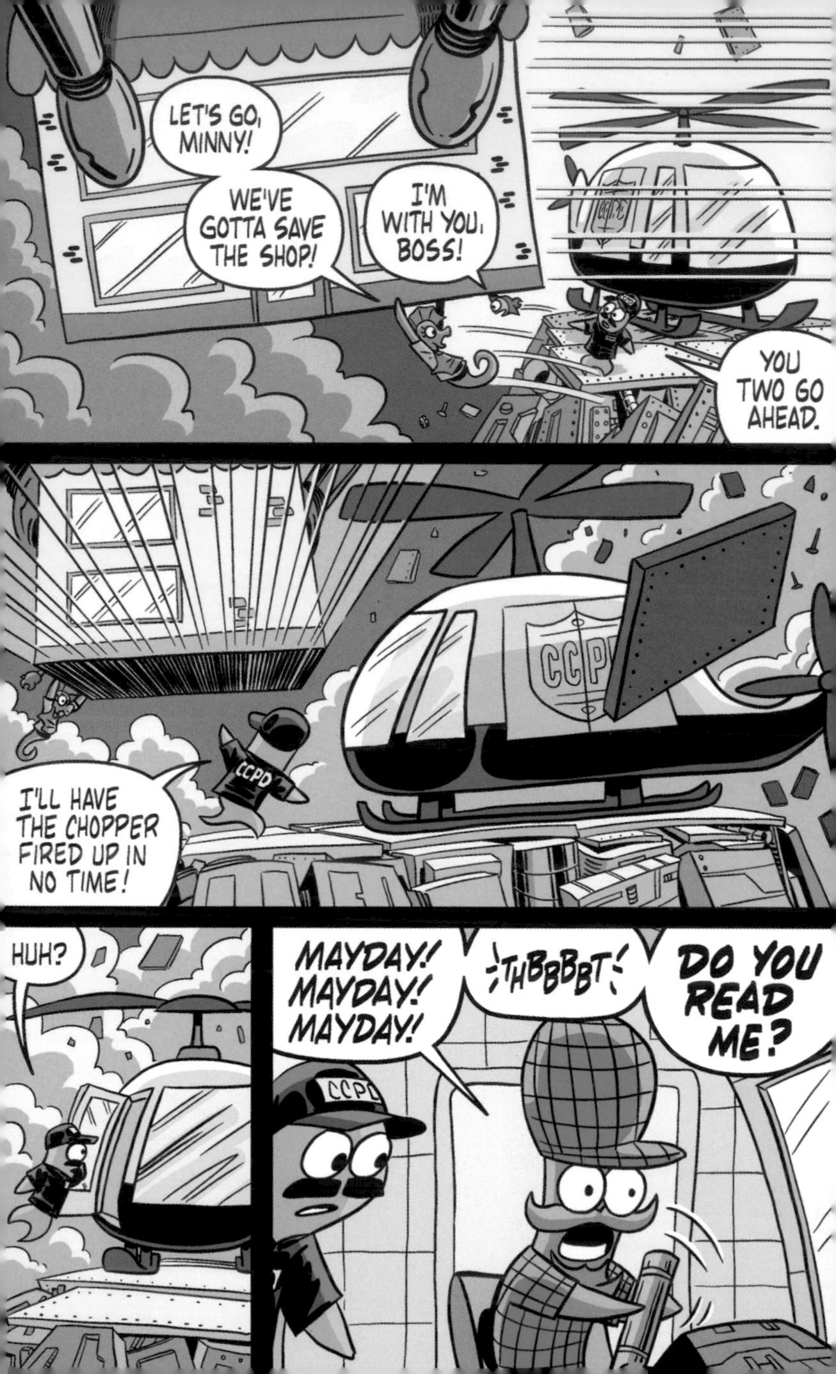
LET'S GO, MINNY!
WE'VE GOTTA SAVE THE SHOP!
I'M WITH YOU, BOSS!
YOU TWO GO AHEAD.
CCPD
I'LL HAVE THE CHOPPER FIRED UP IN NO TIME!
CCPD
HUH?
MAYDAY! MAYDAY! MAYDAY!
THBBBBT
DO YOU READ ME?
CCPD

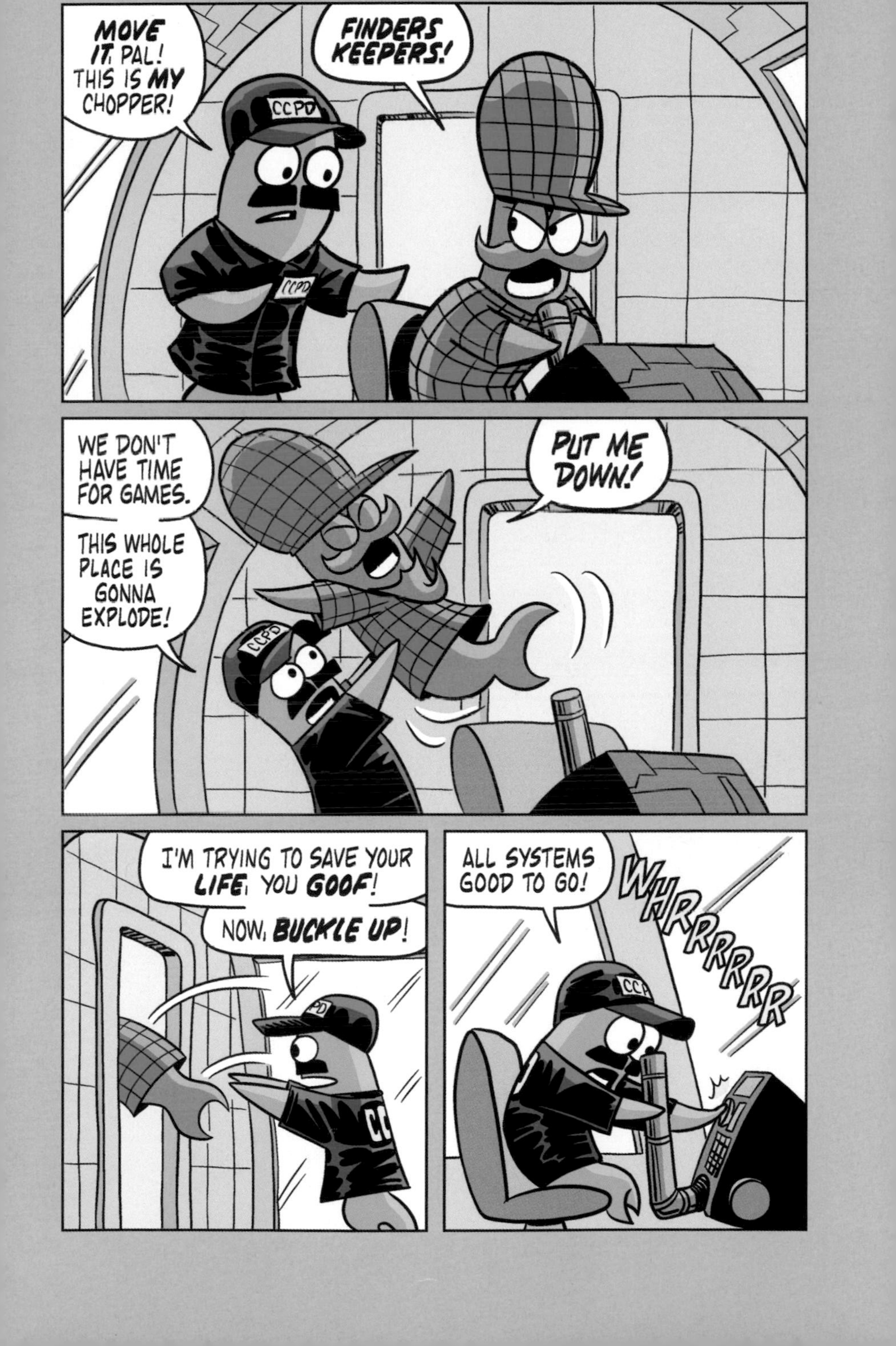
MOVE IT, PAL! THIS IS MY CHOPPER!
FINDERS KEEPERS!
CCPD
WE DON'T HAVE TIME FOR GAMES.
THIS WHOLE PLACE IS GONNA EXPLODE!
PUT ME DOWN!
I'M TRYING TO SAVE YOUR LIFE, YOU GOOF!
NOW, BUCKLE UP!
ALL SYSTEMS GOOD TO GO!
WHRRRRRRR

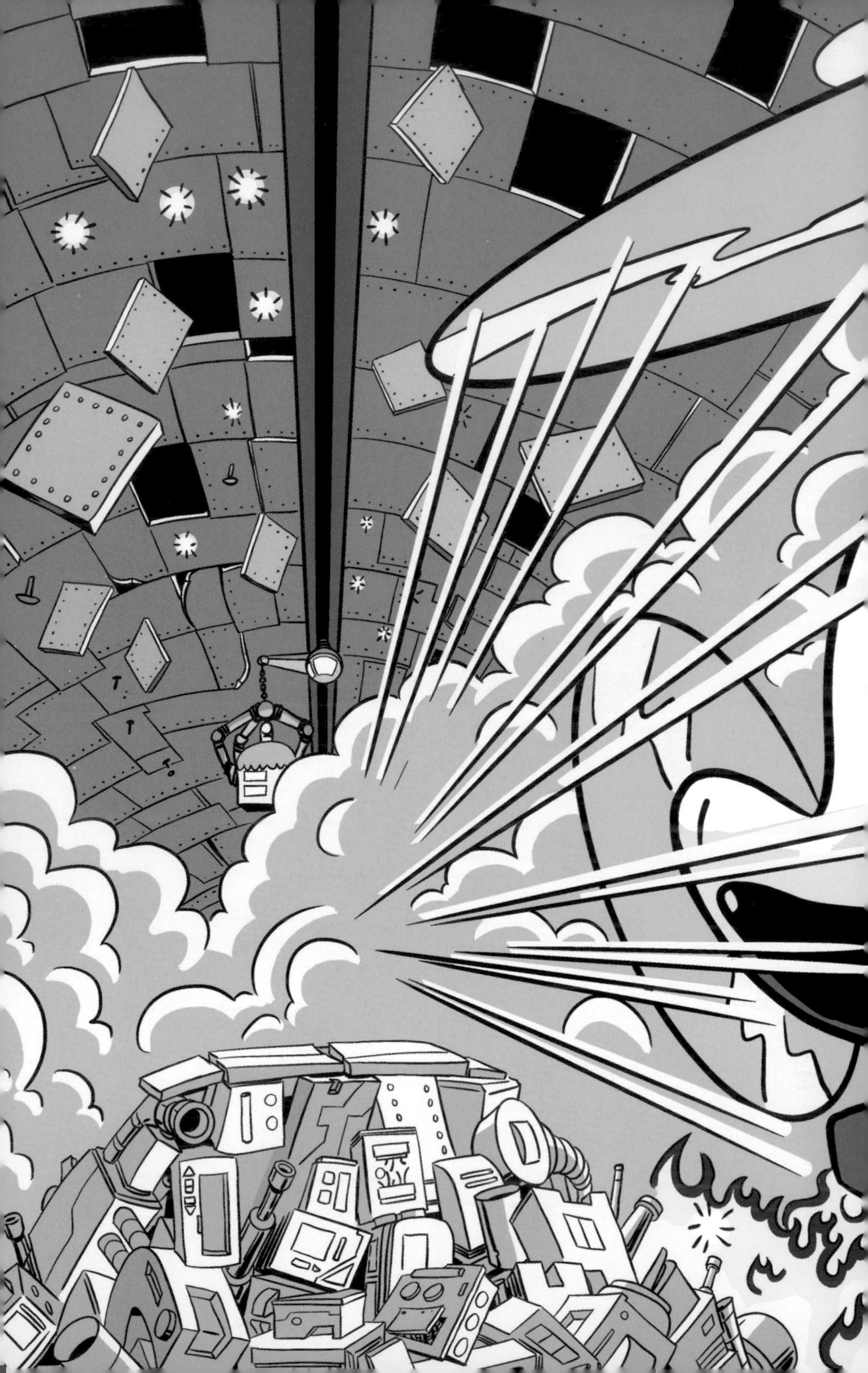

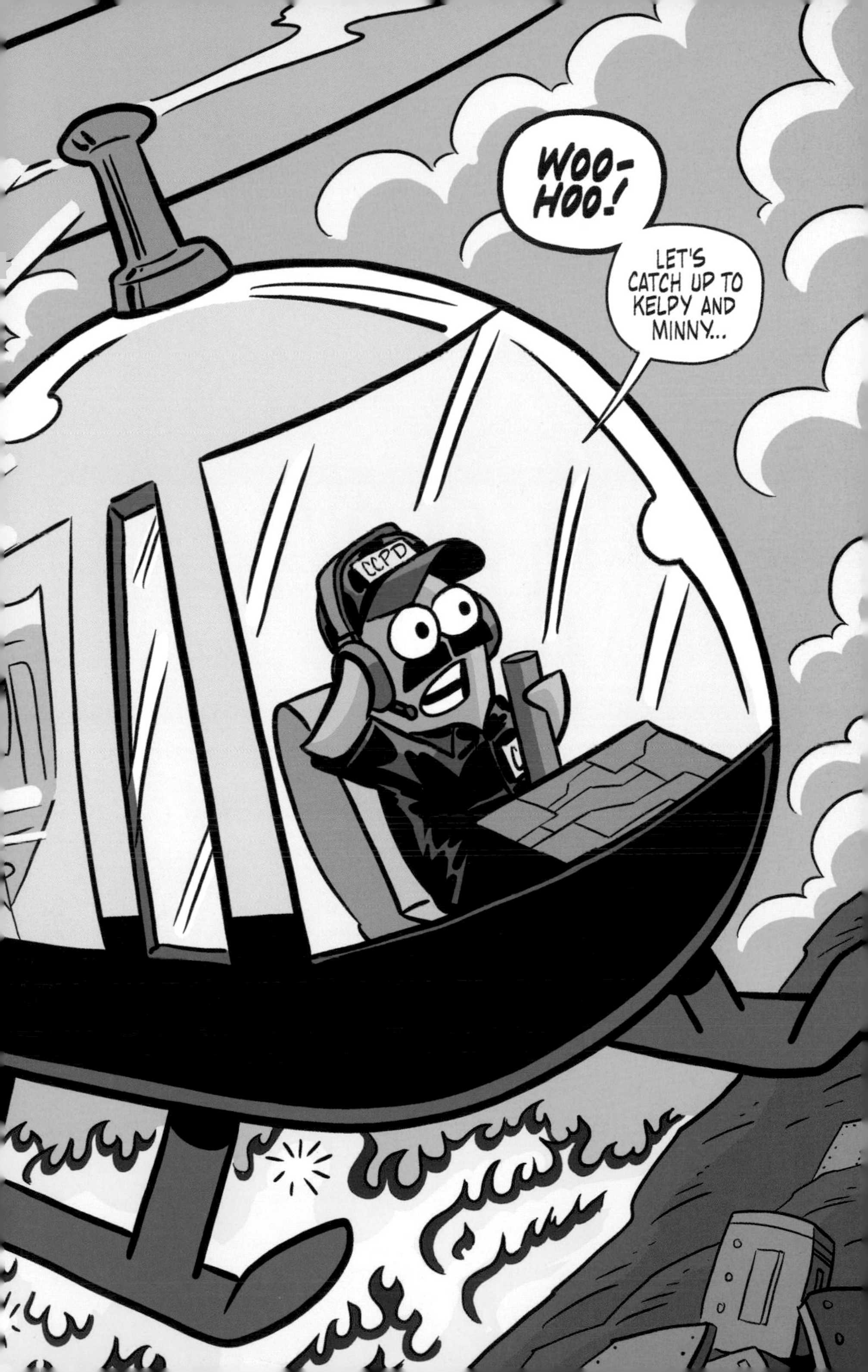
WOO-HOO!
LET'S CATCH UP TO KELPY AND MINNY...
CCPD

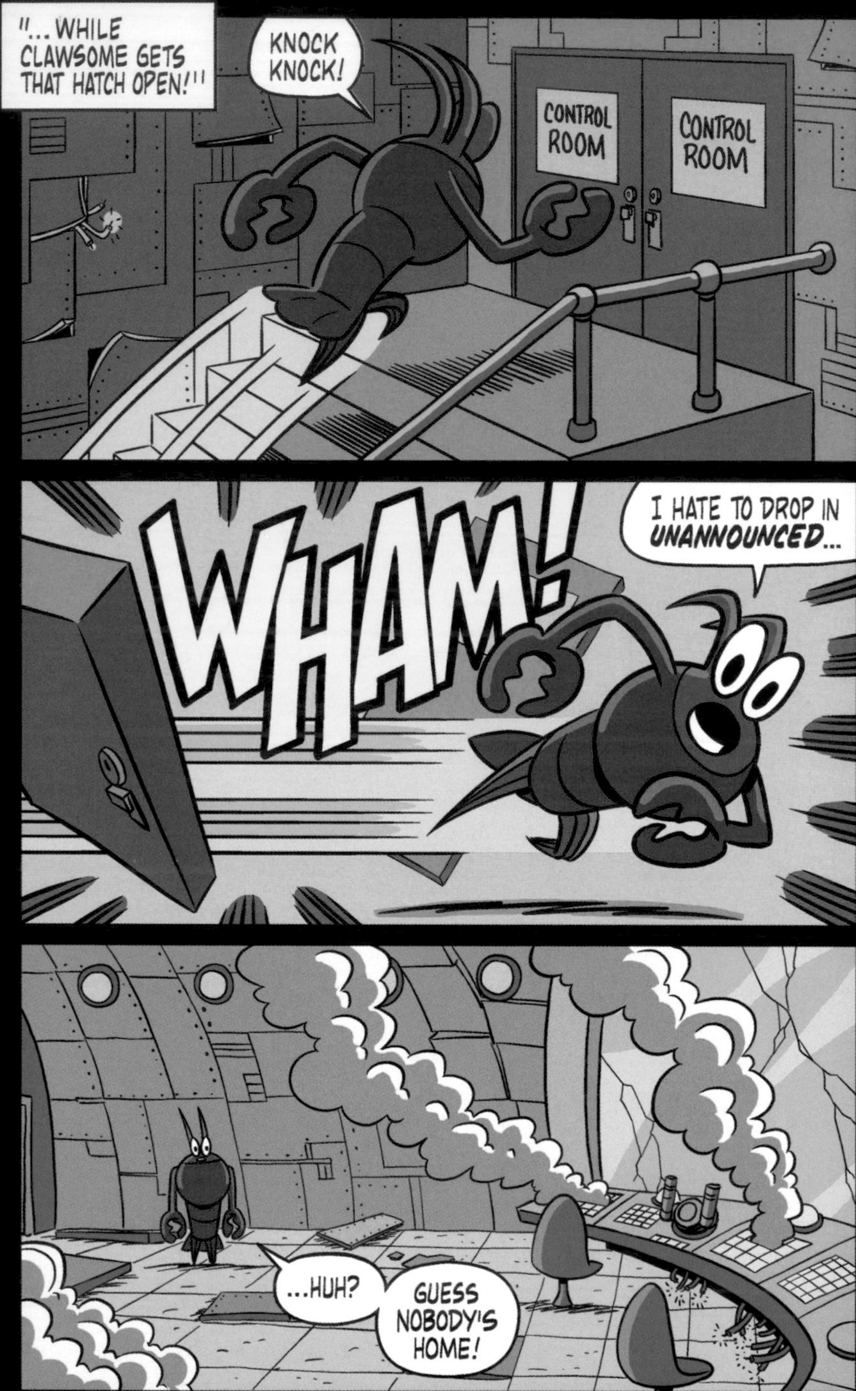
"... WHILE CLAWSOME GETS THAT HATCH OPEN!"
KNOCK KNOCK!
CONTROL ROOM
CONTROL ROOM
WHAM!
I HATE TO DROP IN UNANNOUNCED...
...HUH?
GUESS NOBODY'S HOME!

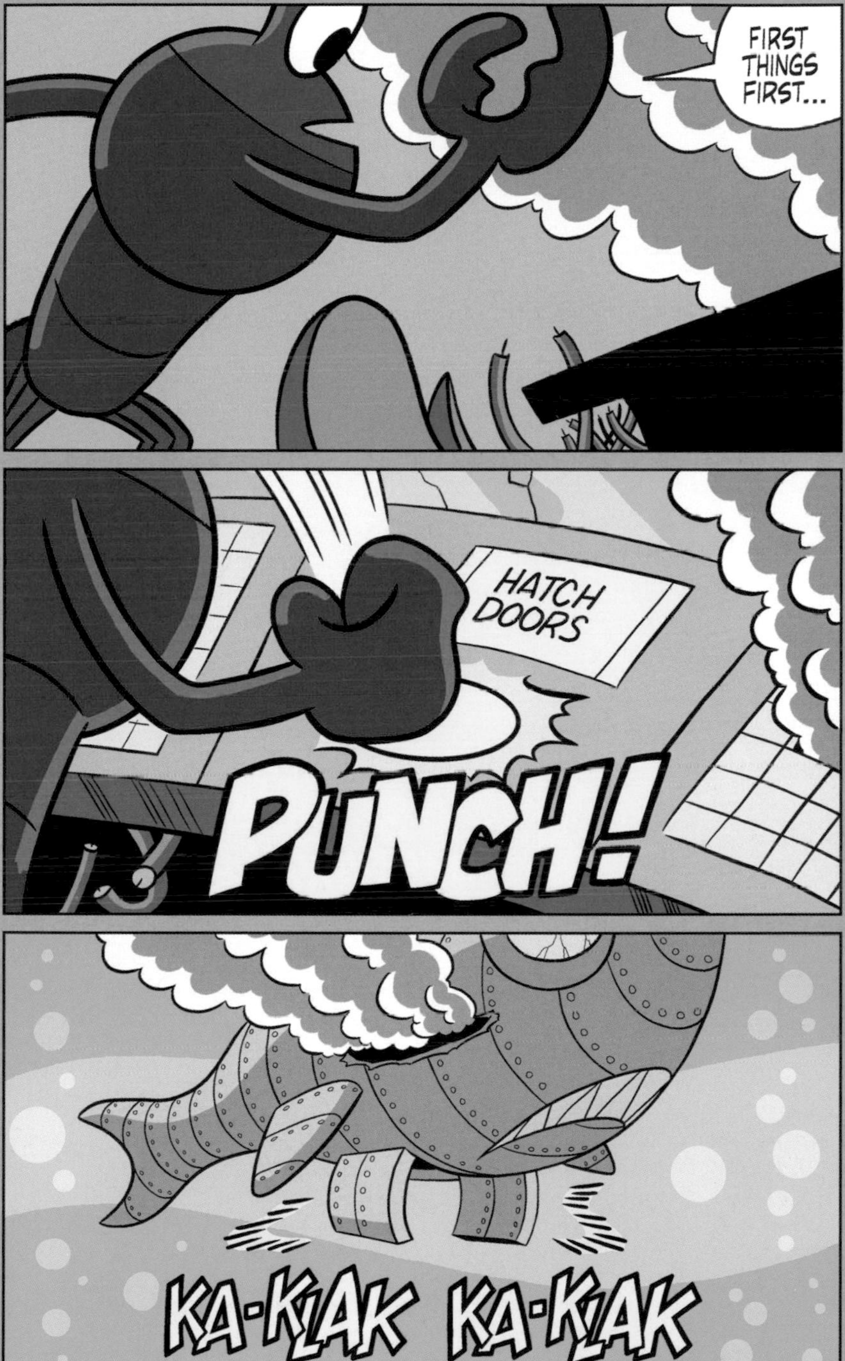
FIRST THINGS FIRST...
HATCH DOORS
PUNCH!
KA-KLAK KA-KLAK

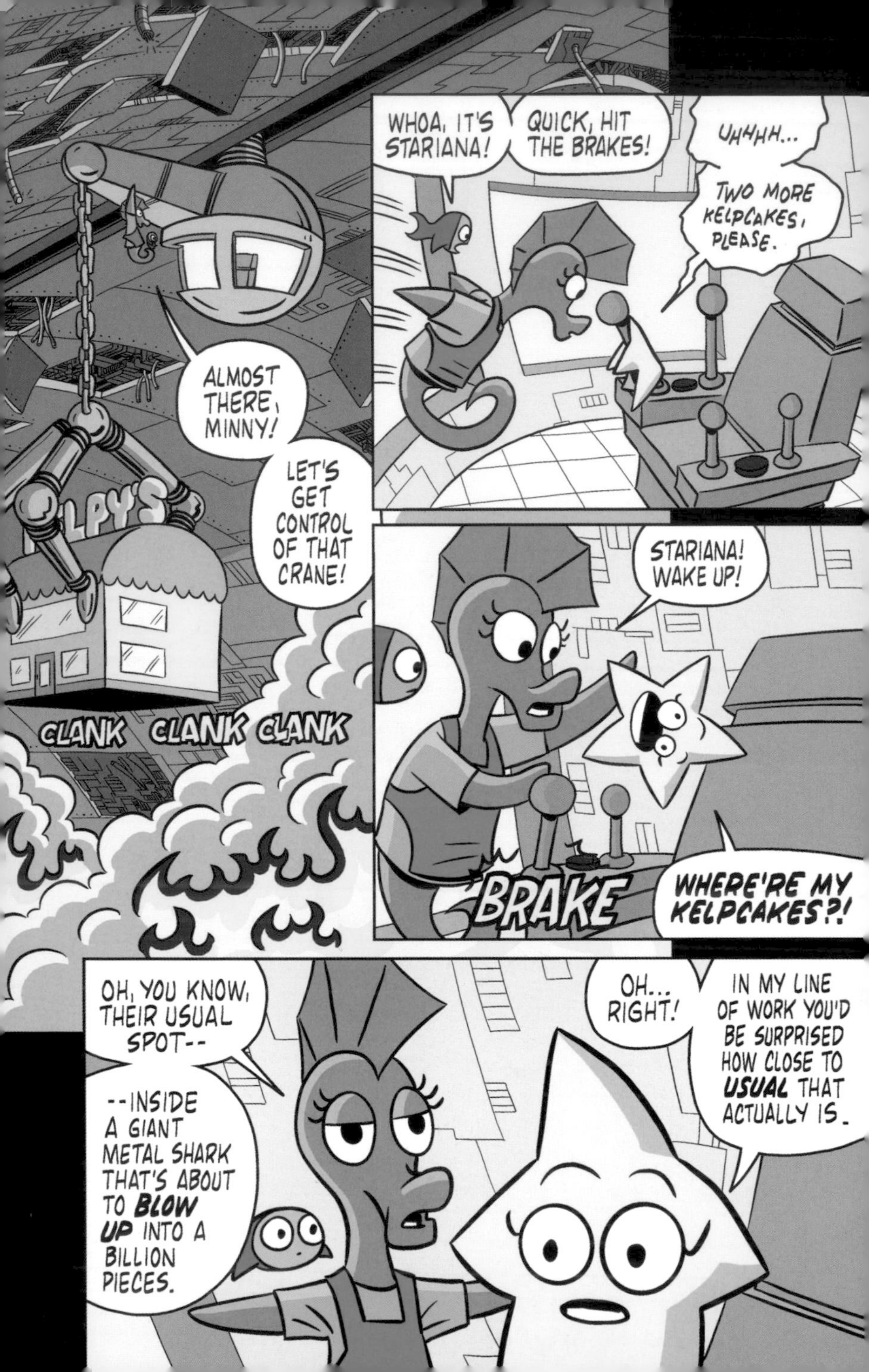
ALMOST THERE, MINNY!
LET'S GET CONTROL OF THAT CRANE!
CLANK CLANK CLANK
WHOA, IT'S STARIANA!
QUICK, HIT THE BRAKES!
UHHHH...
TWO MORE KELPCAKES, PLEASE.
STARIANA! WAKE UP!
BRAKE
WHERE'RE MY KELPCAKES?!
OH, YOU KNOW, THEIR USUAL SPOT--
--INSIDE A GIANT METAL SHARK THAT'S ABOUT TO BLOW UP INTO A BILLION PIECES.
OH... RIGHT!
IN MY LINE OF WORK YOU'D BE SURPRISED HOW CLOSE TO USUAL THAT ACTUALLY IS.

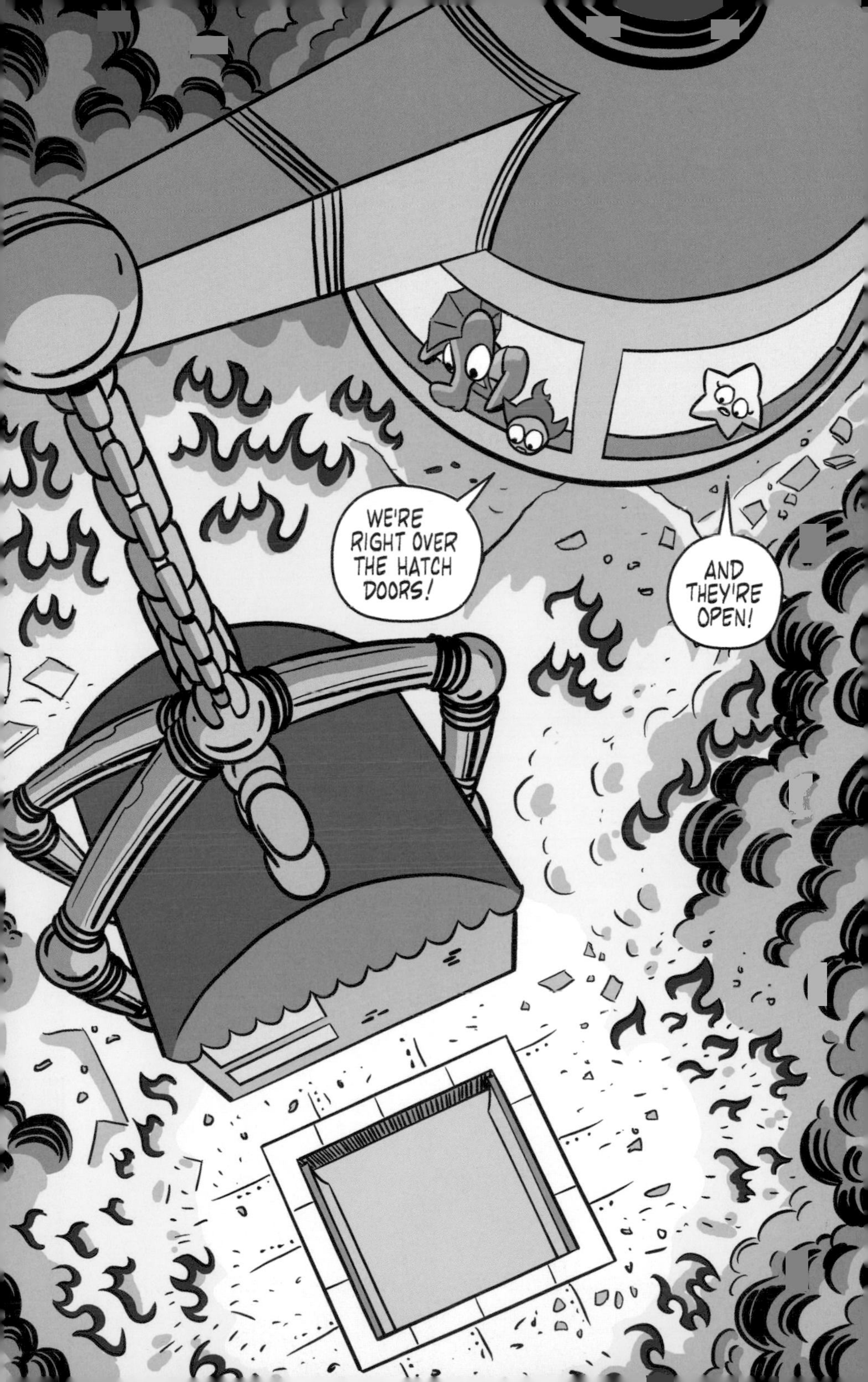
WE'RE RIGHT OVER THE HATCH DOORS!
AND THEY'RE OPEN!

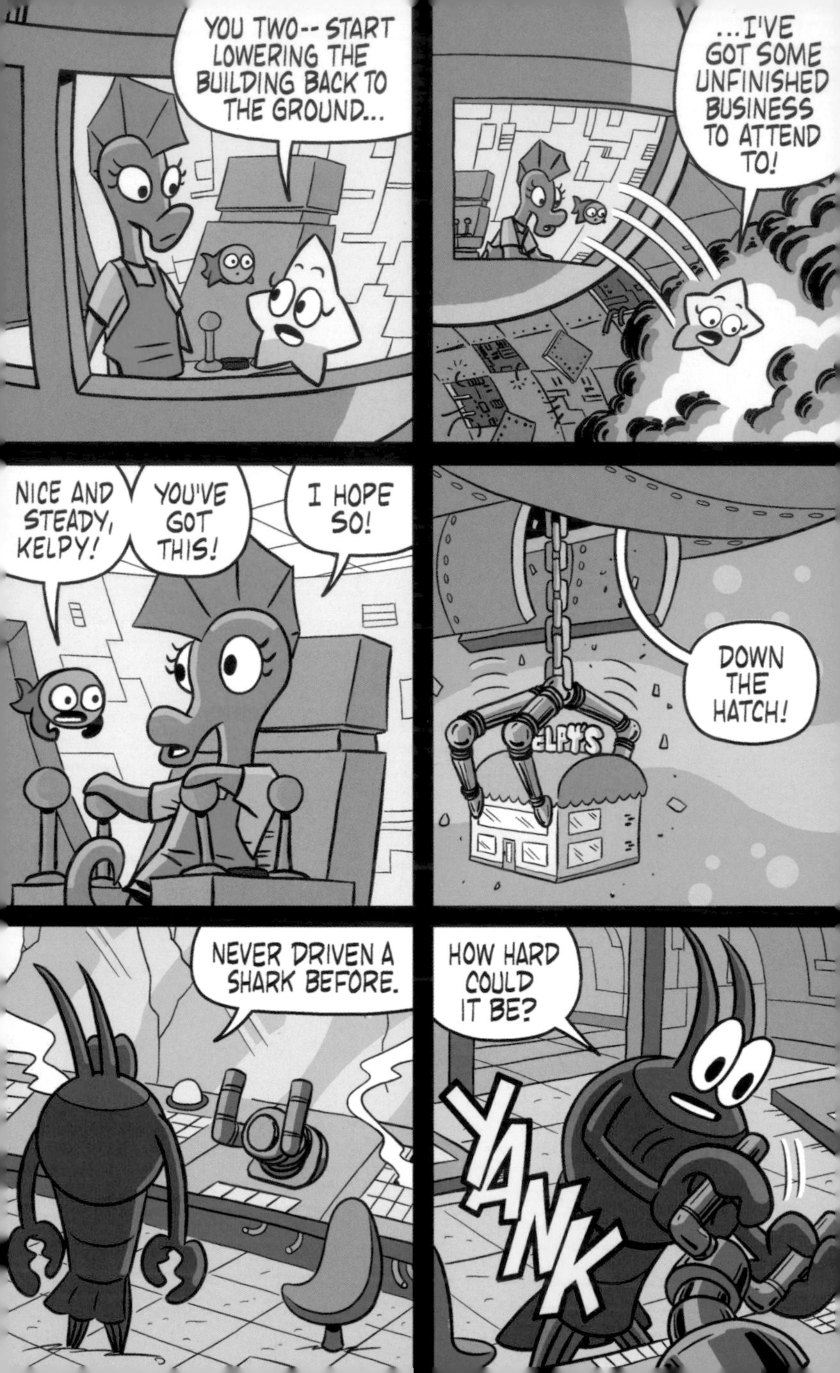
YOU TWO-- START LOWERING THE BUILDING BACK TO THE GROUND...
...I'VE GOT SOME UNFINISHED BUSINESS TO ATTEND TO!
NICE AND STEADY, KELPY!
YOU'VE GOT THIS!
I HOPE SO!
DOWN THE HATCH!
NEVER DRIVEN A SHARK BEFORE.
HOW HARD COULD IT BE?
YANK

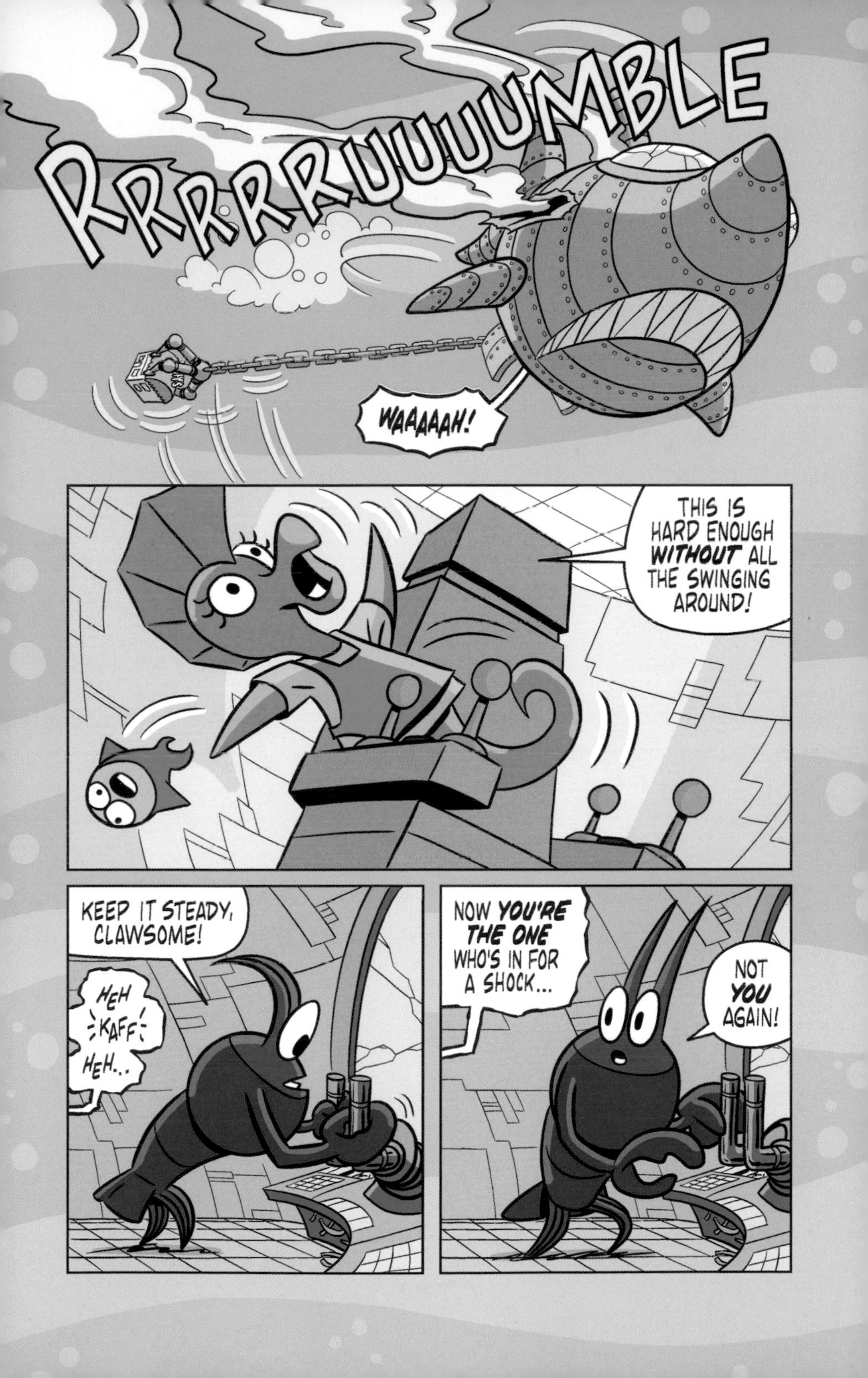
RRRRRUUUUUMBLE
WAAAAAH!
THIS IS HARD ENOUGH WITHOUT ALL THE SWINGING AROUND!
KEEP IT STEADY, CLAWSOME!
HEH KAFF HEH...
NOW YOU'RE THE ONE WHO'S IN FOR A SHOCK...
NOT YOU AGAIN!

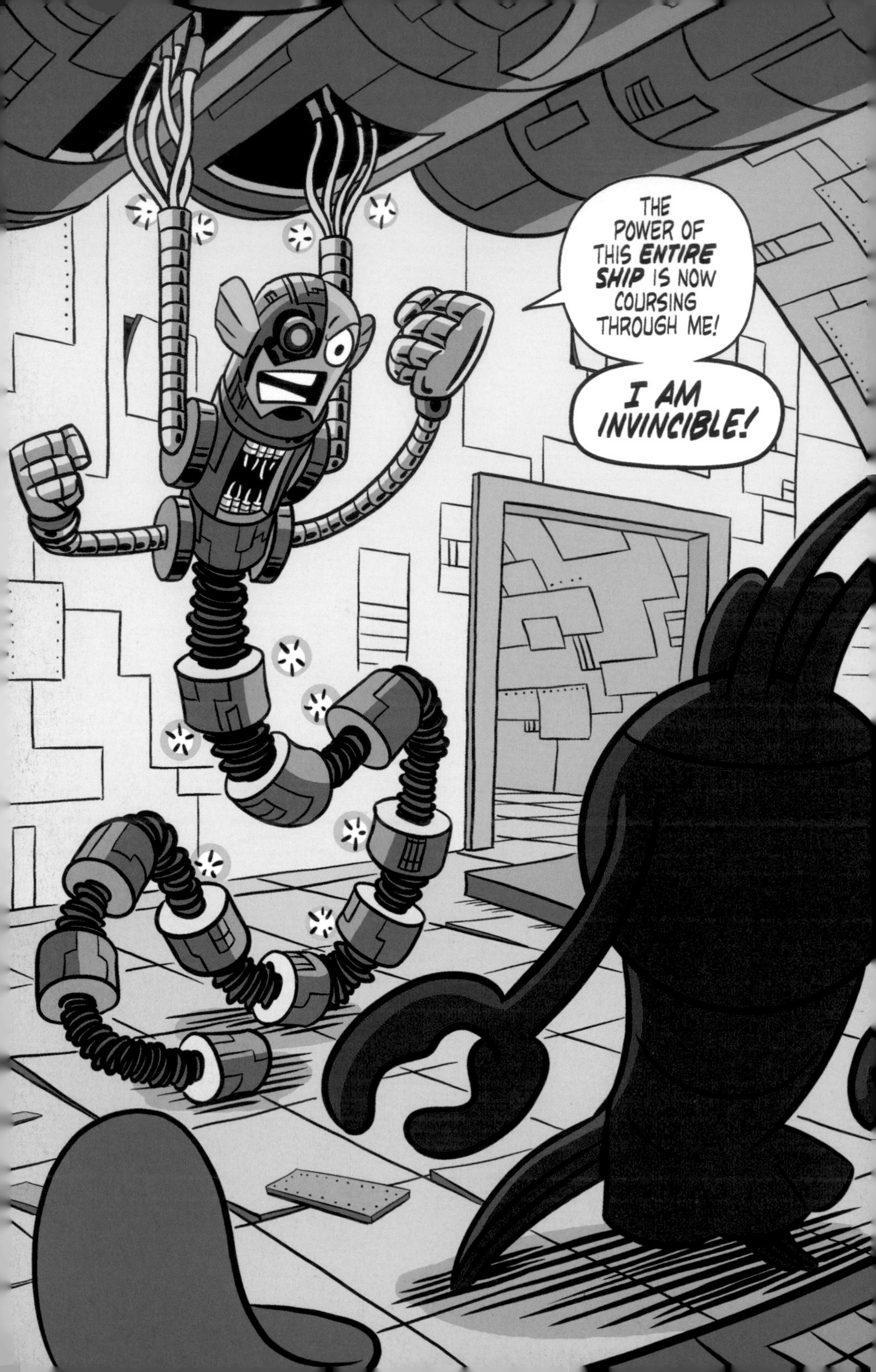
THE POWER OF THIS ENTIRE SHIP IS NOW COURSING THROUGH ME!
I AM INVINCIBLE!

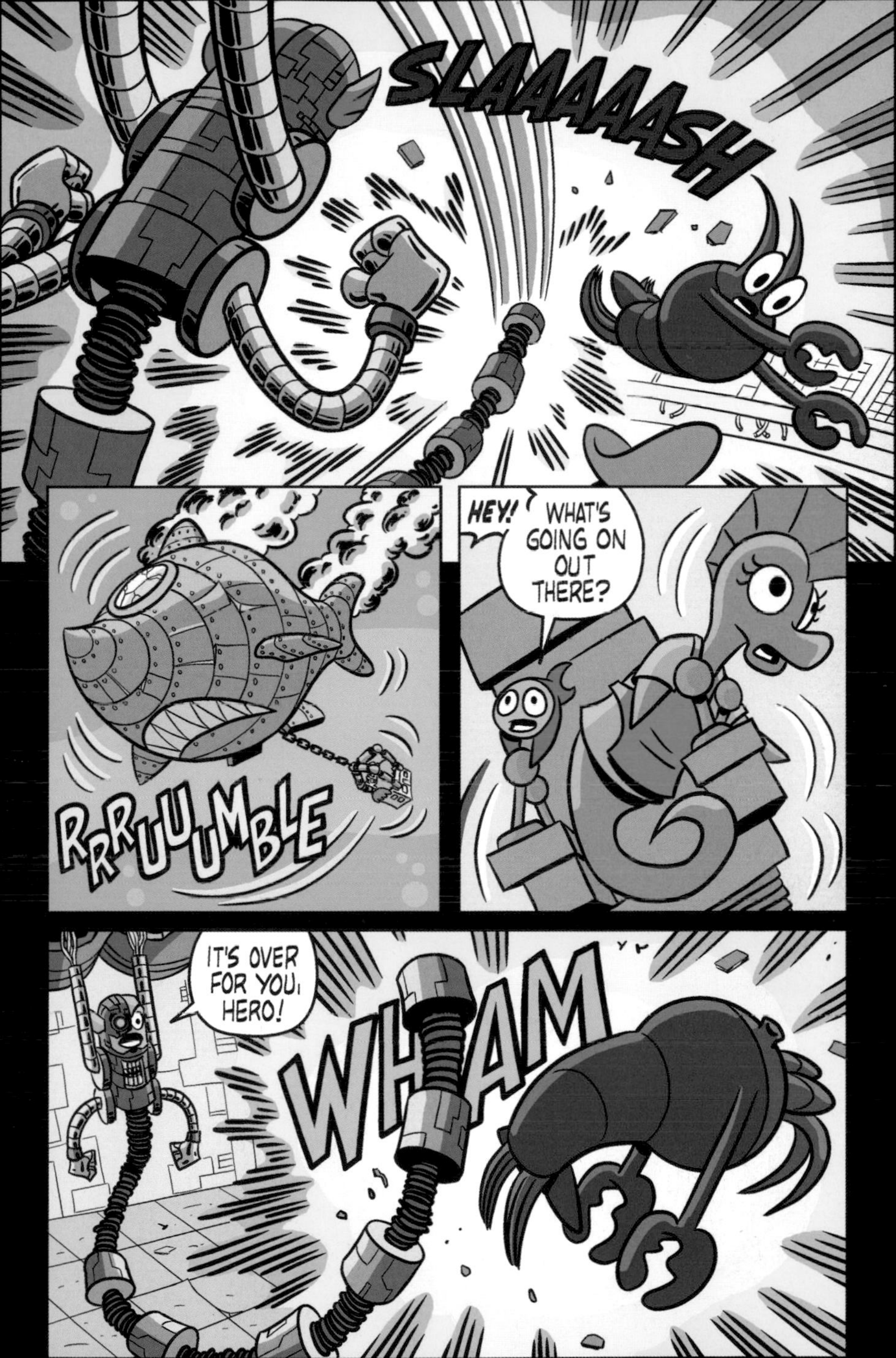
SLAAAAASH
RRRUUUMBLE
HEY!
WHAT'S GOING ON OUT THERE?
IT'S OVER FOR YOU, HERO!
WHAM

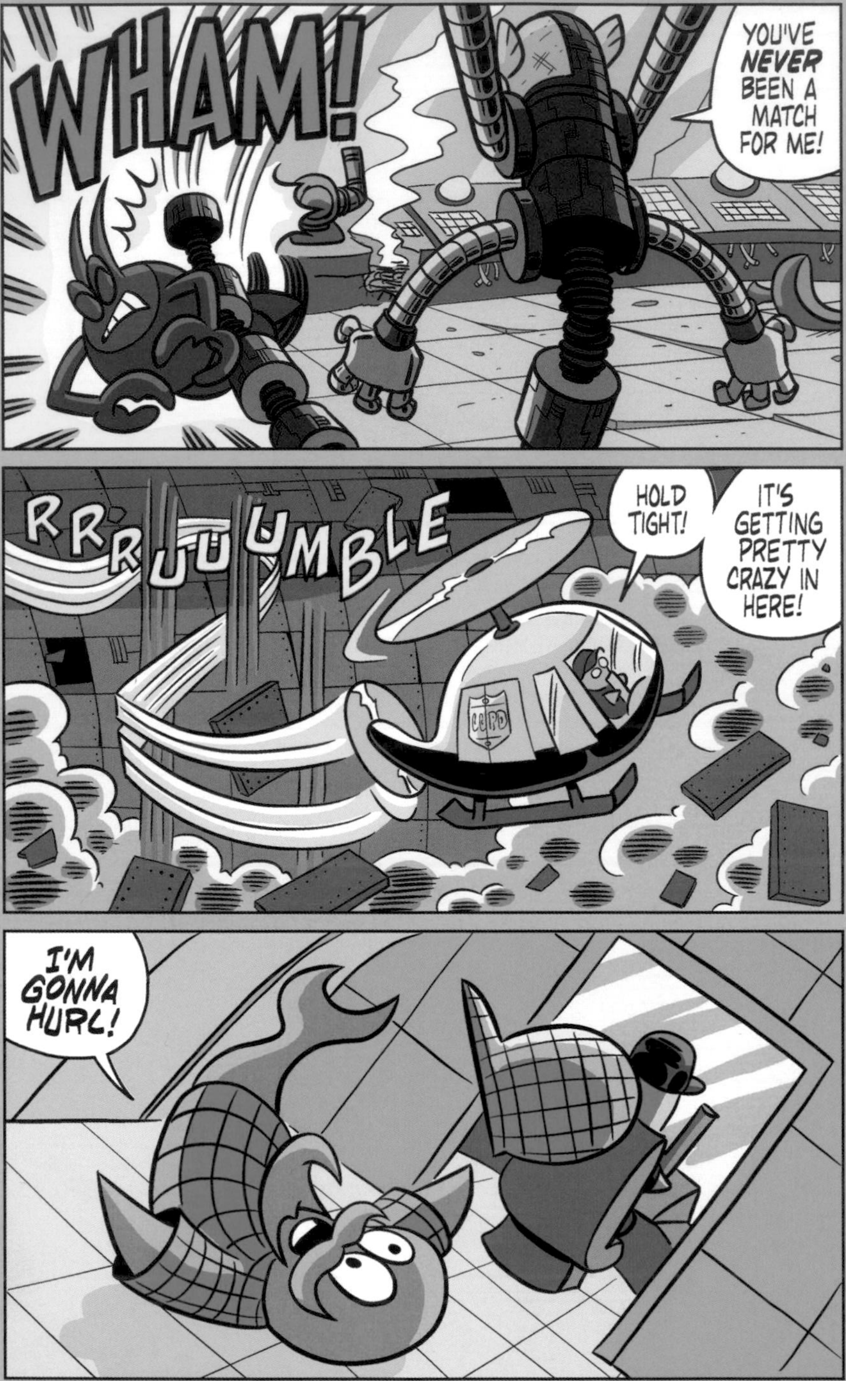
WHAM!
YOU'VE NEVER BEEN A MATCH FOR ME!
RRRUUUMBLE
HOLD TIGHT!
IT'S GETTING PRETTY CRAZY IN HERE!
I'M GONNA HURL!

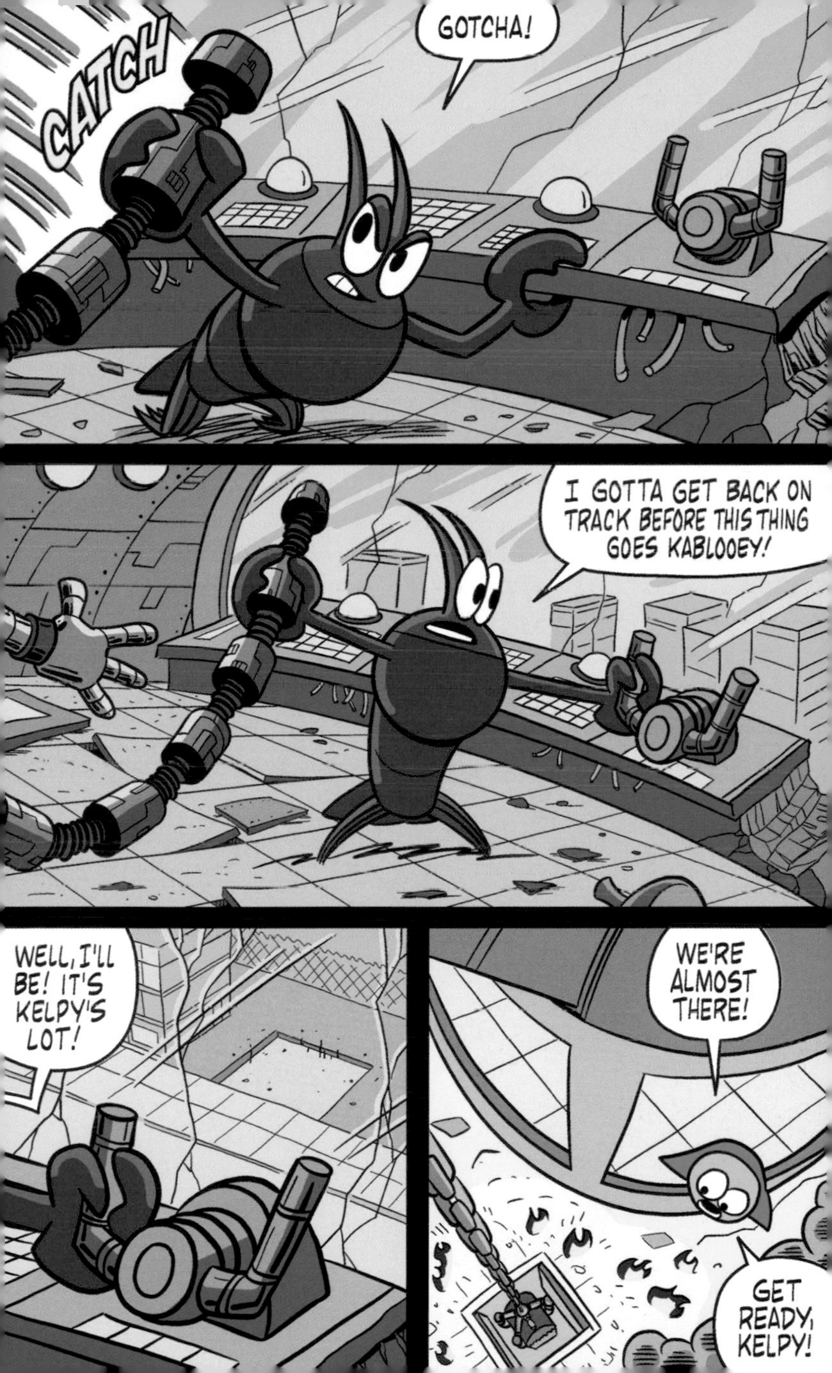
CATCH
GOTCHA!
I GOTTA GET BACK ON TRACK BEFORE THIS THING GOES KABLOOEY!
WELL, I'LL BE! IT'S KELPY'S LOT!
WE'RE ALMOST THERE!
GET READY, KELPY!

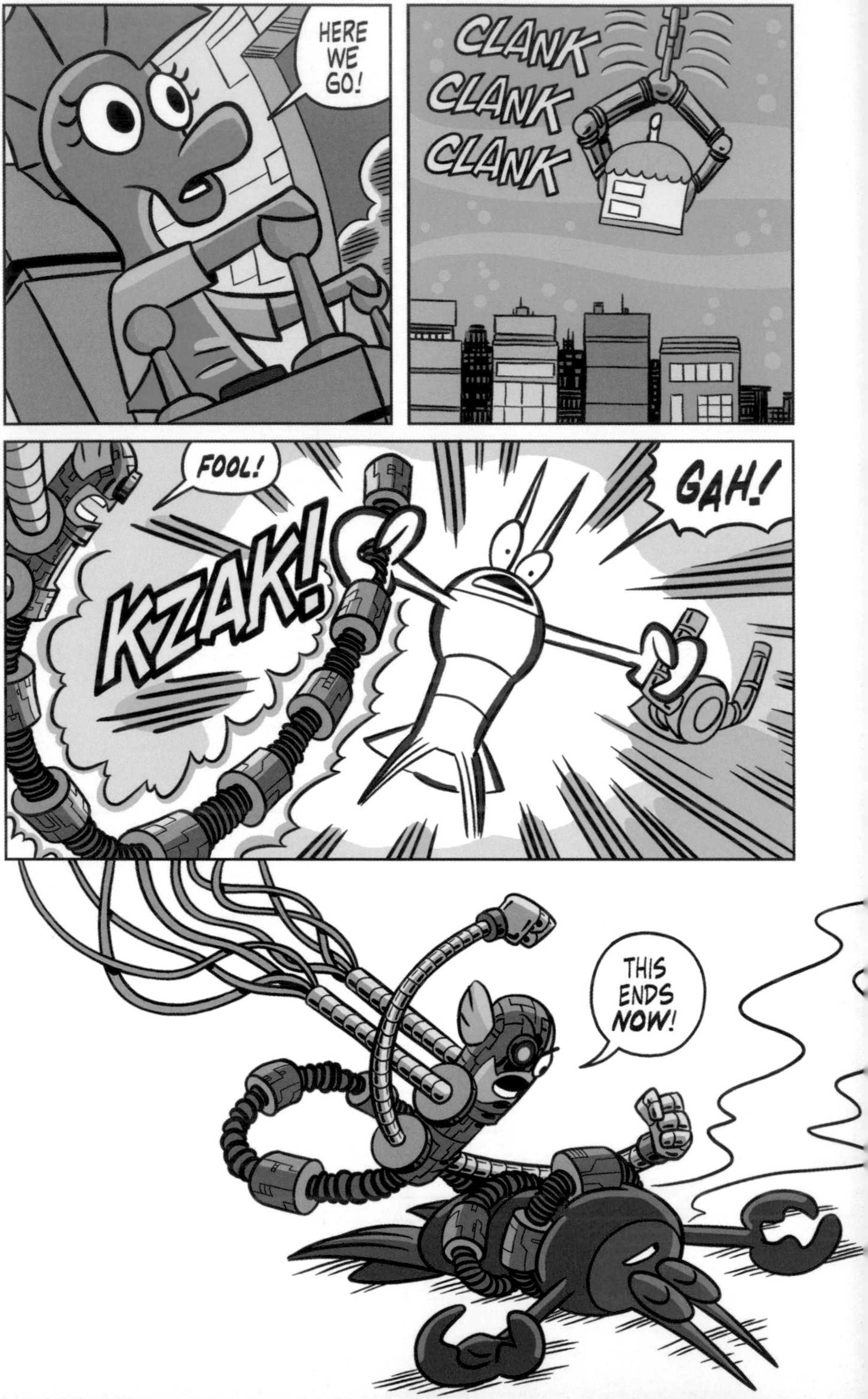
HERE WE GO!
CLANK
CLANK
CLANK
FOOL!
KZAK!
GAH!
THIS ENDS NOW!

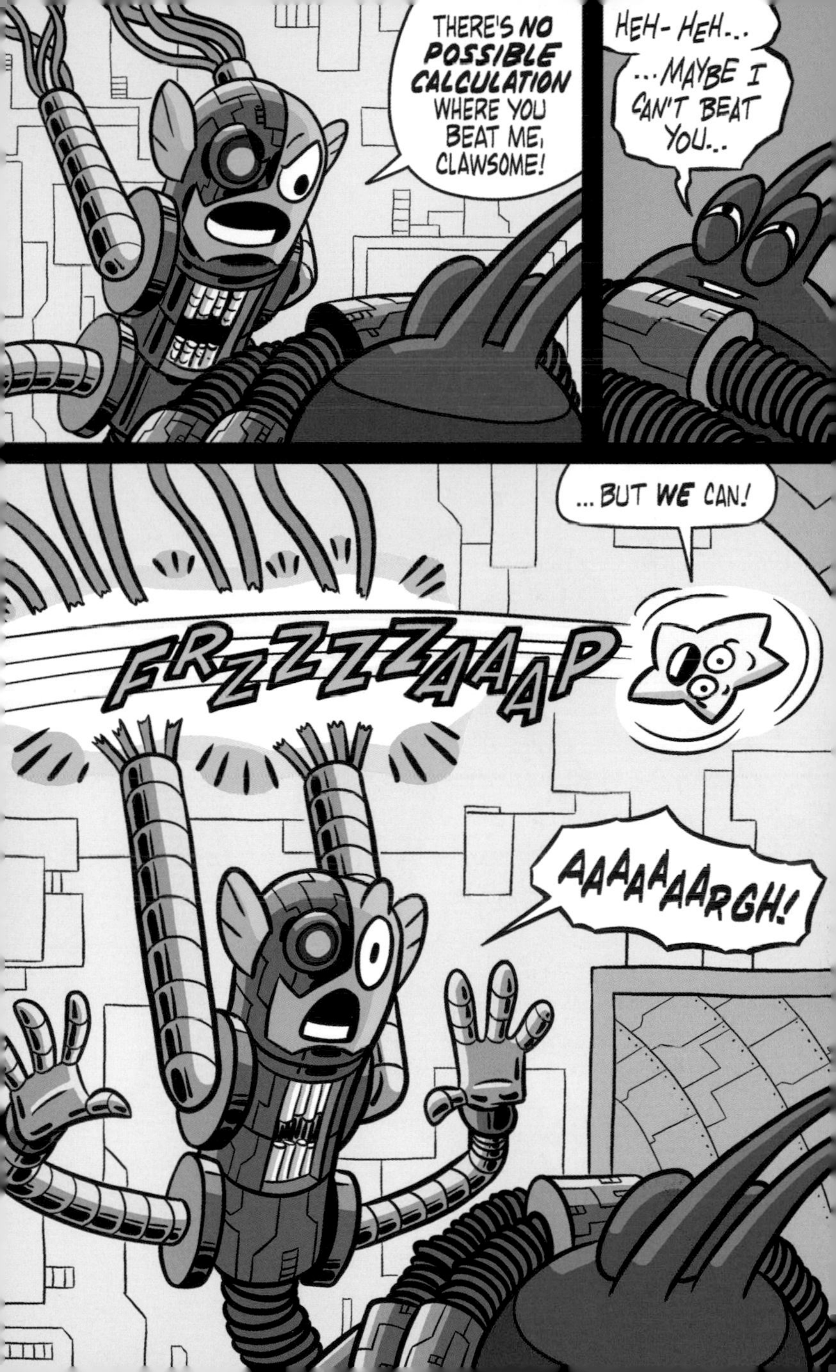
THERE'S NO POSSIBLE CALCULATION WHERE YOU BEAT ME, CLAWSOME!
HEH- HEH...
...MAYBE I CAN'T BEAT YOU...
...BUT WE CAN!
FRZZZZZAAAAP
AAAAAAARGH!

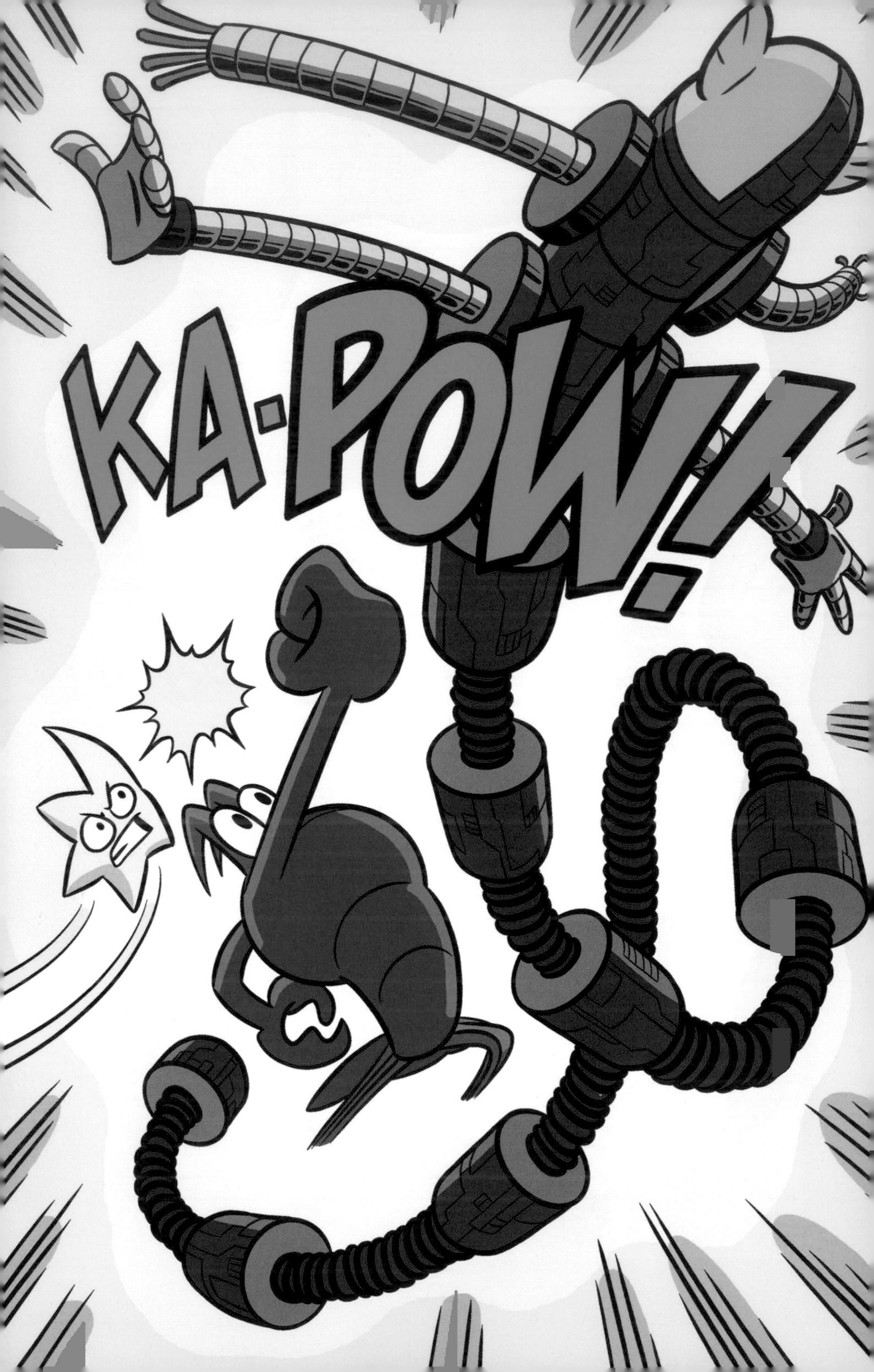
KA-POW!!

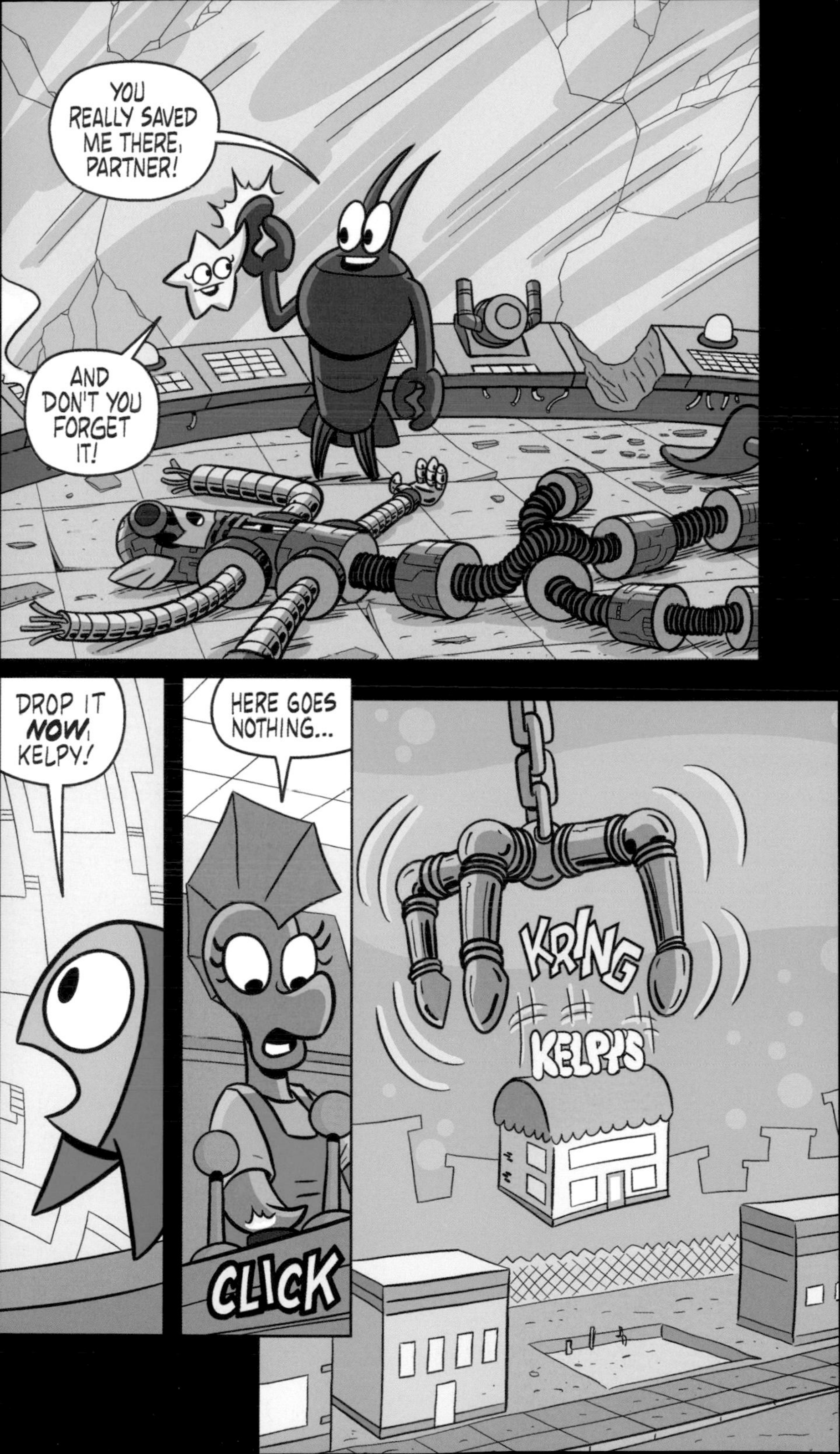

YOU REALLY SAVED ME THERE, PARTNER!
AND DON'T YOU FORGET IT!
DROP IT NOW, KELPY!
HERE GOES NOTHING...
CLICK
KRING
KELPY'S

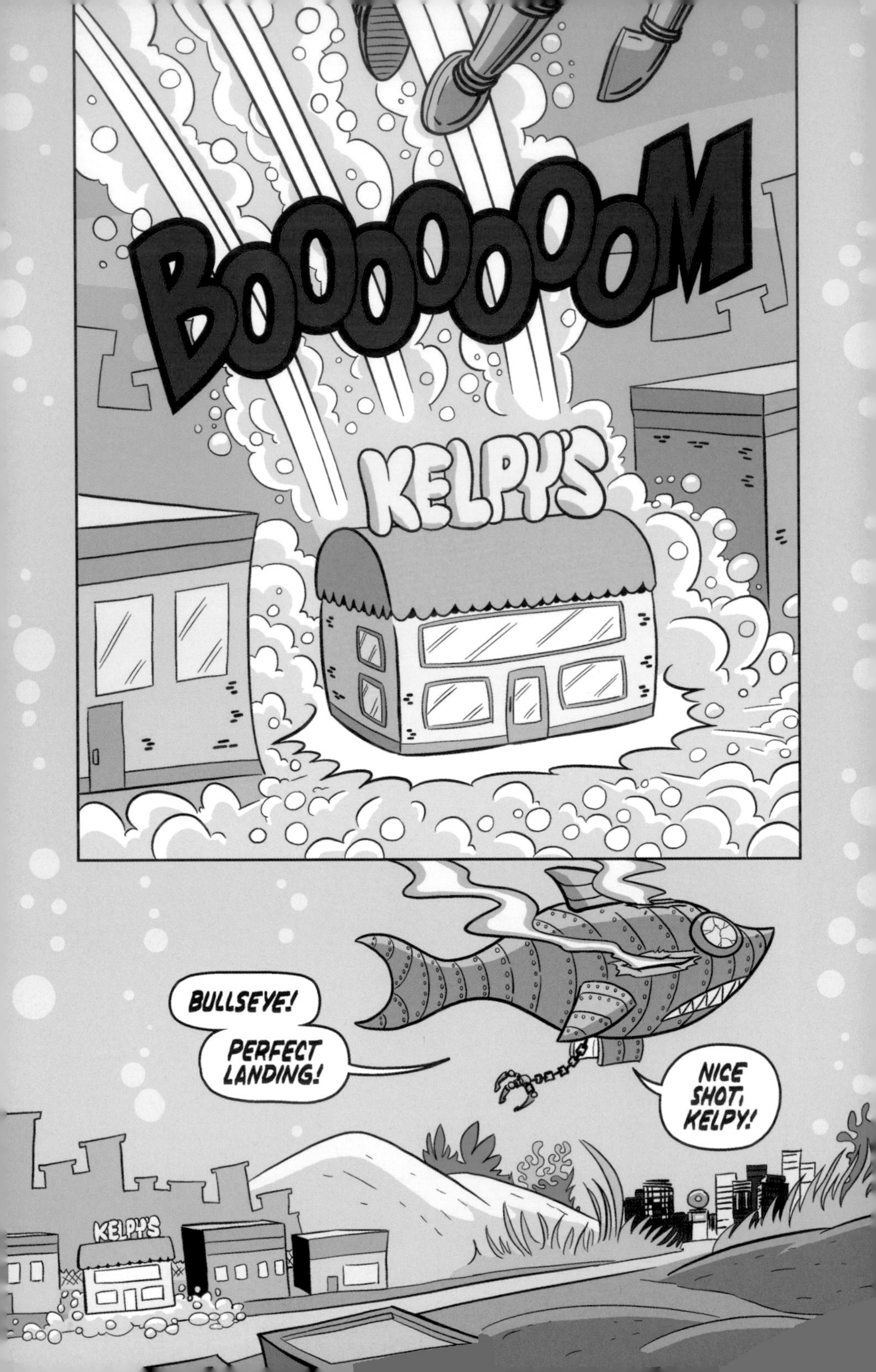
BOOOOOOOM
KELPY'S
BULLSEYE!
PERFECT LANDING!
NICE SHOT, KELPY!
KELPY'S

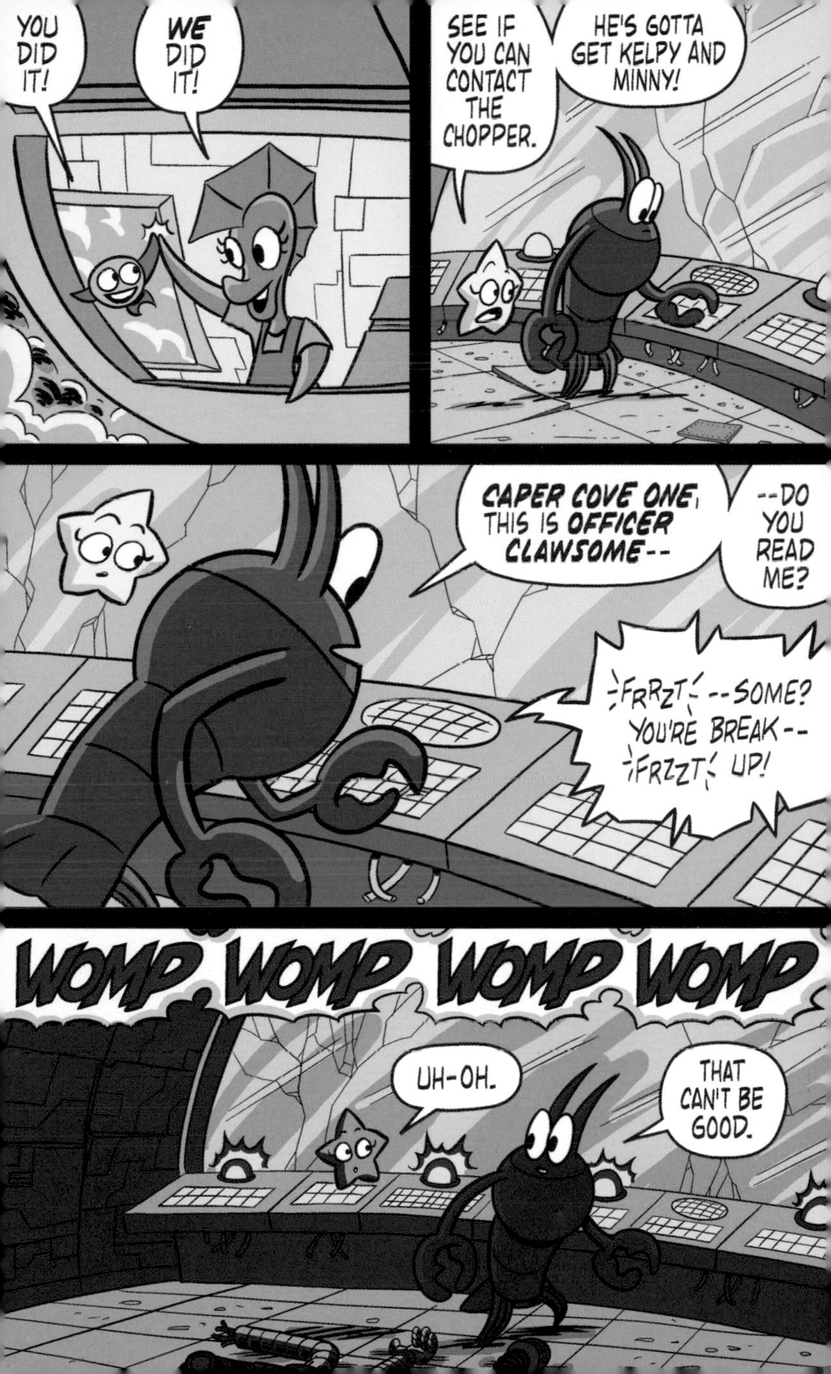
YOU DID IT!
WE DID IT!
SEE IF YOU CAN CONTACT THE CHOPPER.
HE'S GOTTA GET KELPY AND MINNY!
CAPER COVE ONE, THIS IS OFFICER CLAWSOME--
--DO YOU READ ME?
FRRZT --SOME? YOU'RE BREAK-- FRZZT UP!
WOMP WOMP WOMP WOMP
UH-OH.
THAT CAN'T BE GOOD.

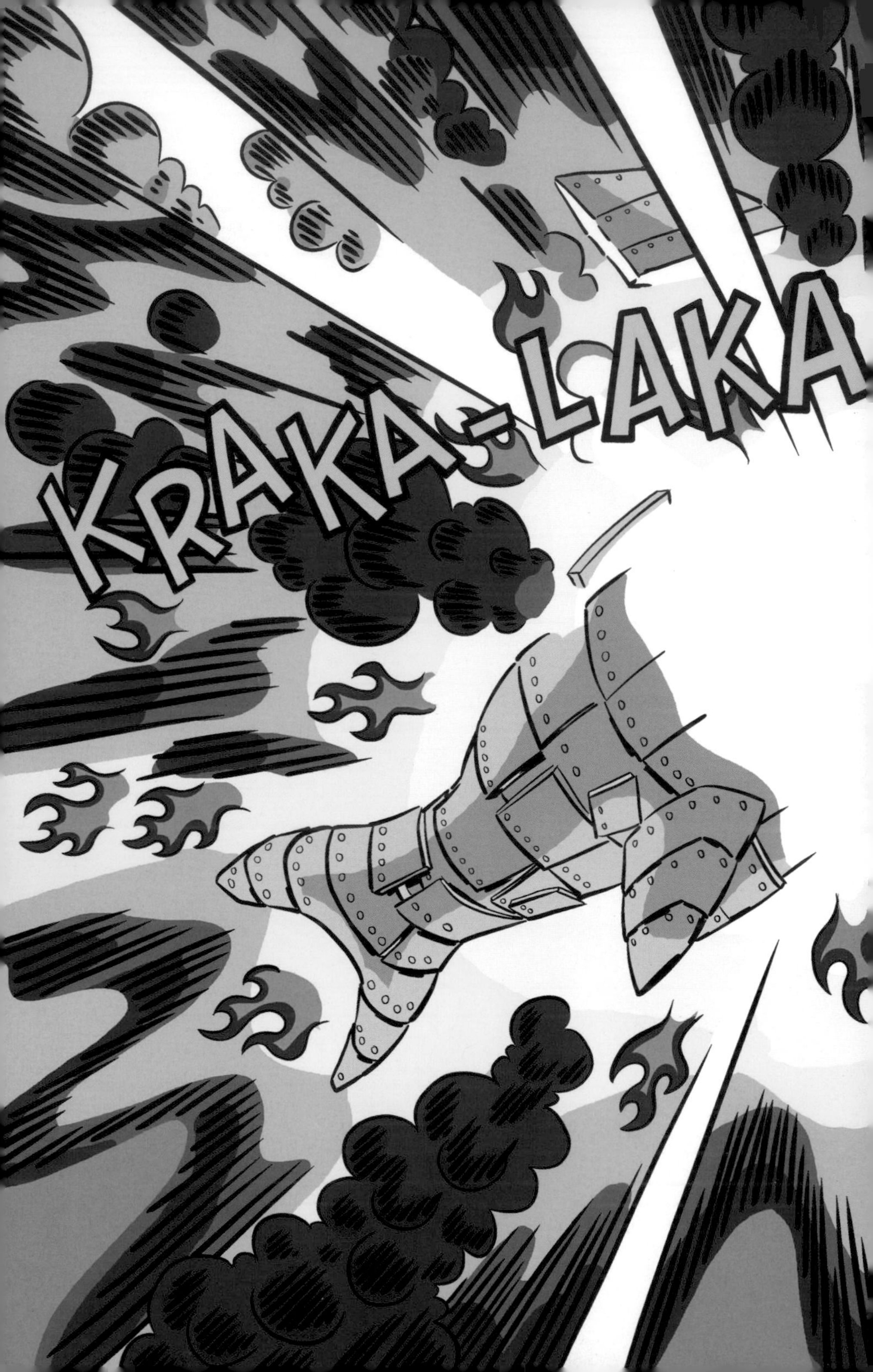
KRAKA-LAKA

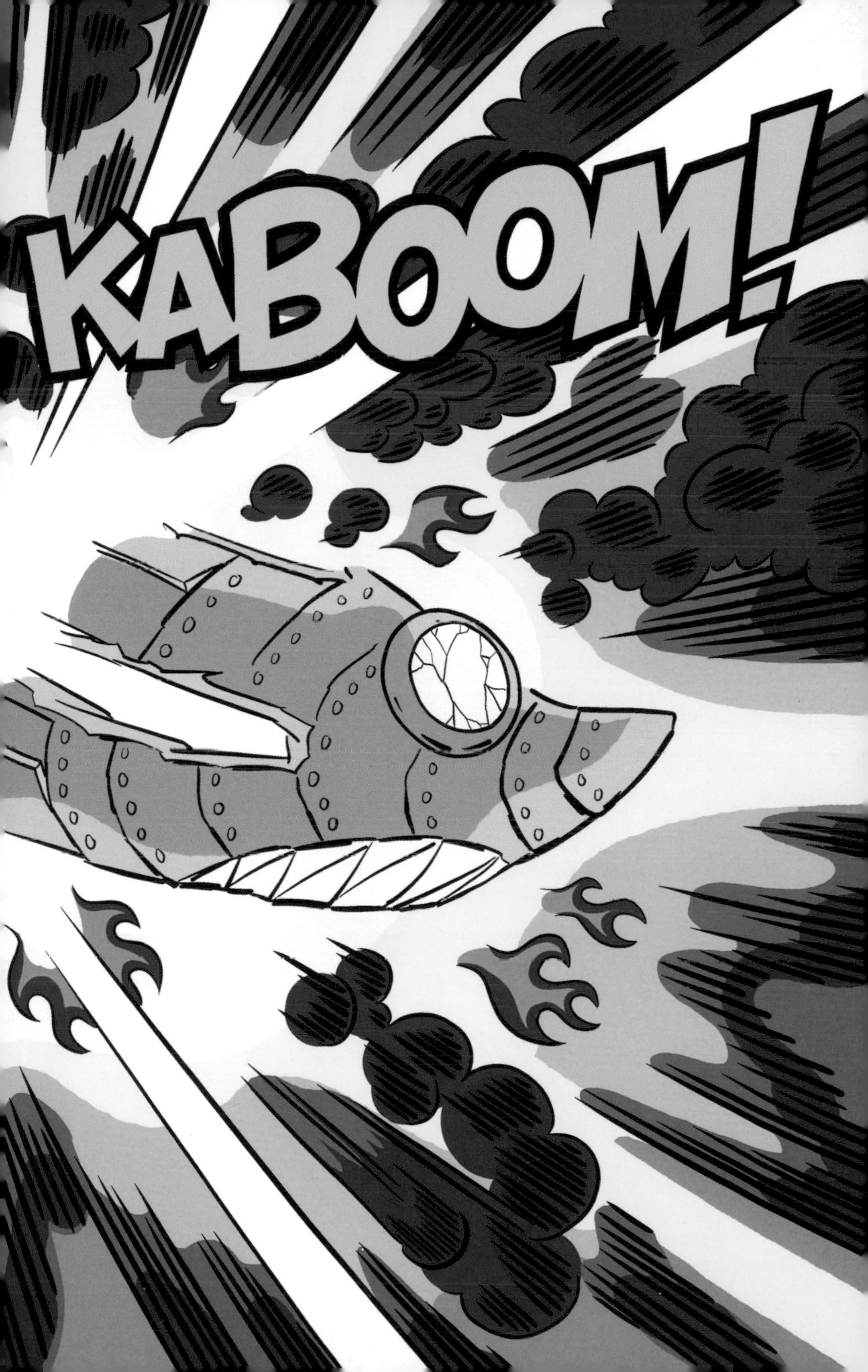
KABOOM!

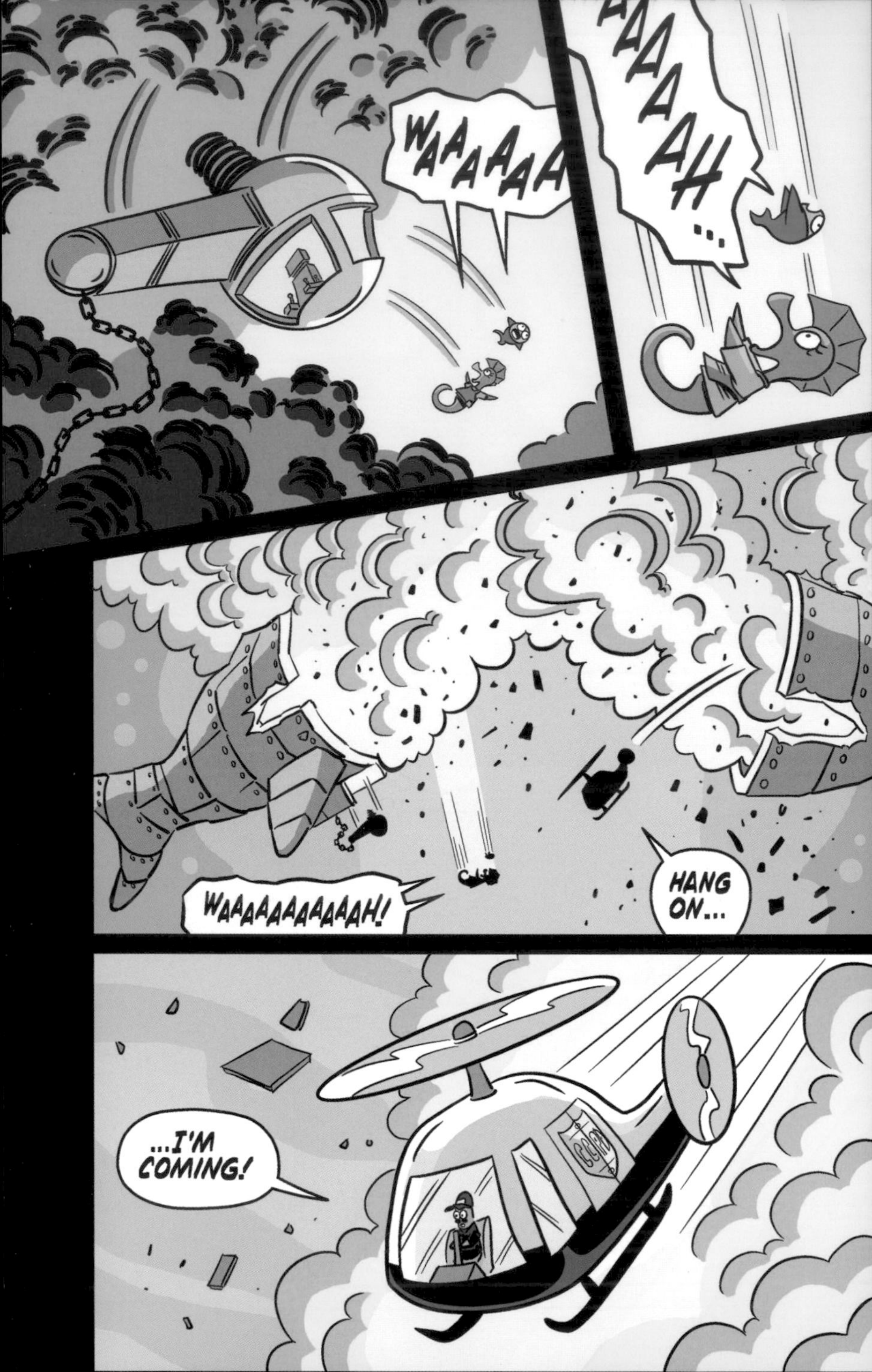
WAAAAAAA
AAAAAAH...
WAAAAAAAAAAAH!
HANG ON...
...I'M COMING!

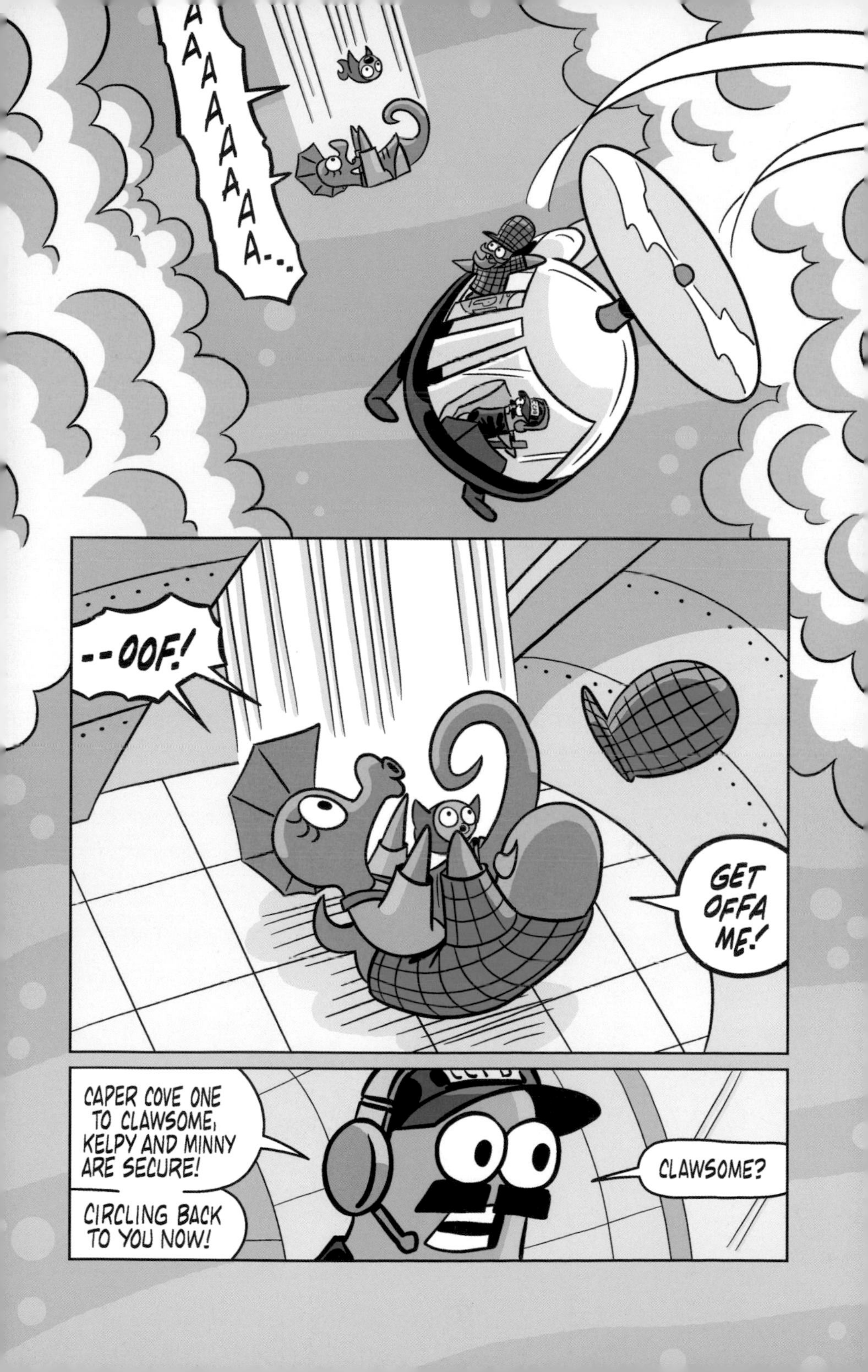
AAAAAAAAA...
--OOF!
GET OFFA ME!
CAPER COVE ONE TO CLAWSOME, KELPY AND MINNY ARE SECURE!
CIRCLING BACK TO YOU NOW!
CLAWSOME?

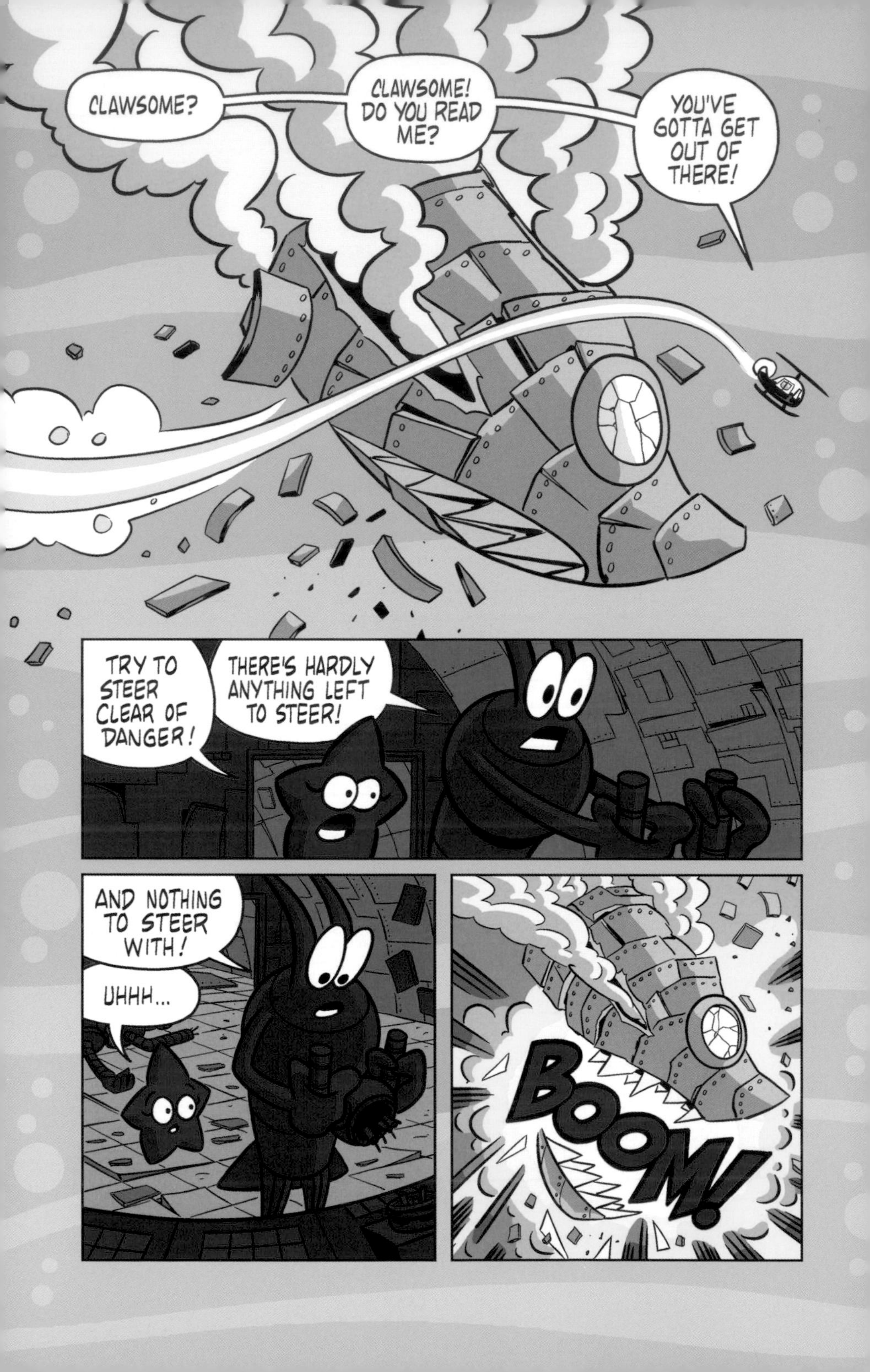
CLAWSOME?
CLAWSOME! DO YOU READ ME?
YOU'VE GOTTA GET OUT OF THERE!
TRY TO STEER CLEAR OF DANGER!
THERE'S HARDLY ANYTHING LEFT TO STEER!
AND NOTHING TO STEER WITH!
UHHH...
BOOOM!

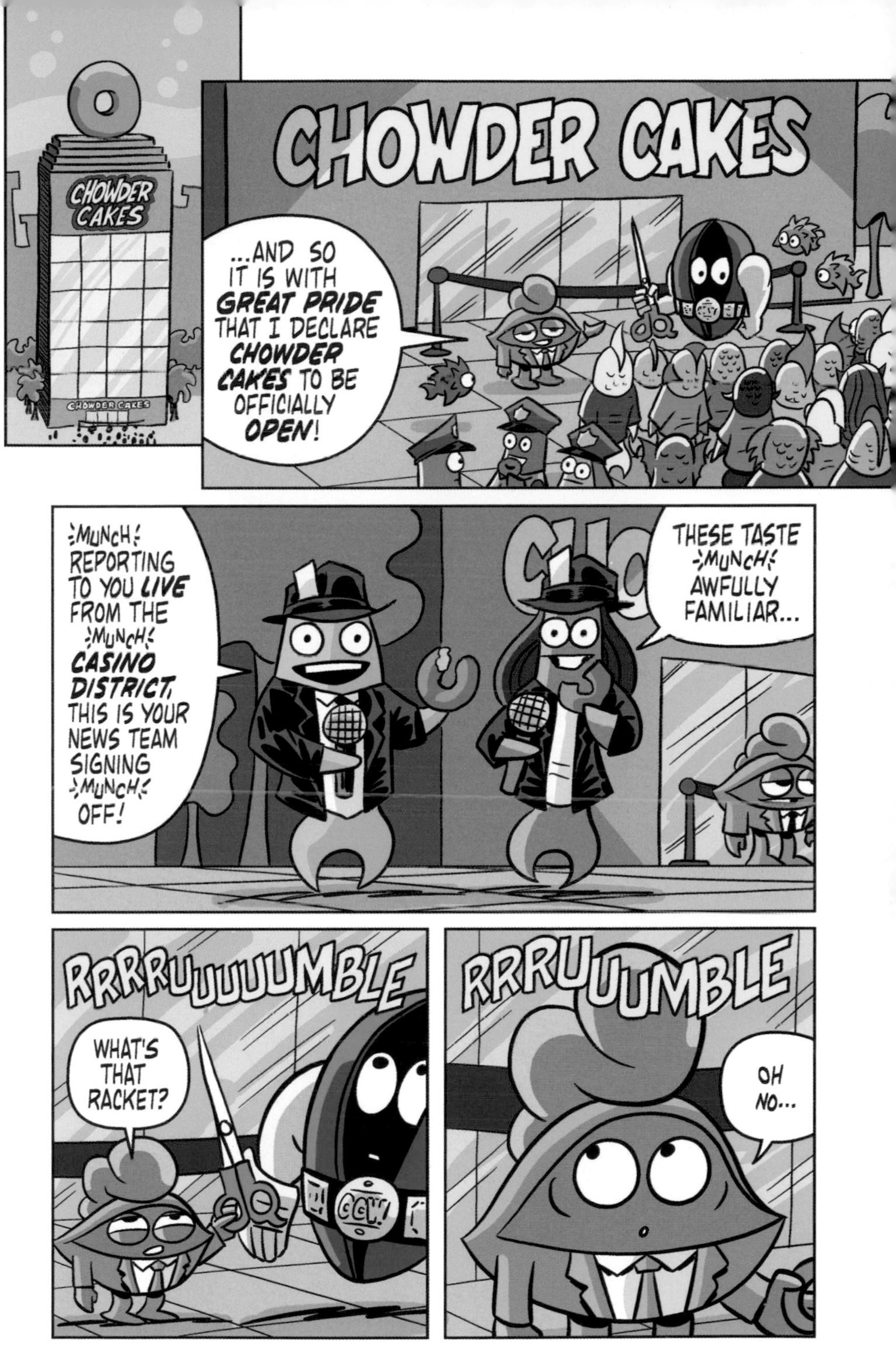
CHOWDER CAKES
CHOWDER CAKES
CHOWDER CAKES
...AND SO IT IS WITH **GREAT PRIDE** THAT I DECLARE **CHOWDER CAKES** TO BE OFFICIALLY **OPEN**!
MUNCH REPORTING TO YOU **LIVE** FROM THE MUNCH **CASINO DISTRICT**, THIS IS YOUR NEWS TEAM SIGNING MUNCH OFF!
THESE TASTE MUNCH AWFULLY FAMILIAR...
RRRRUUUUUMBLE
WHAT'S THAT RACKET?
RRRUUUMBLE
OH NO...

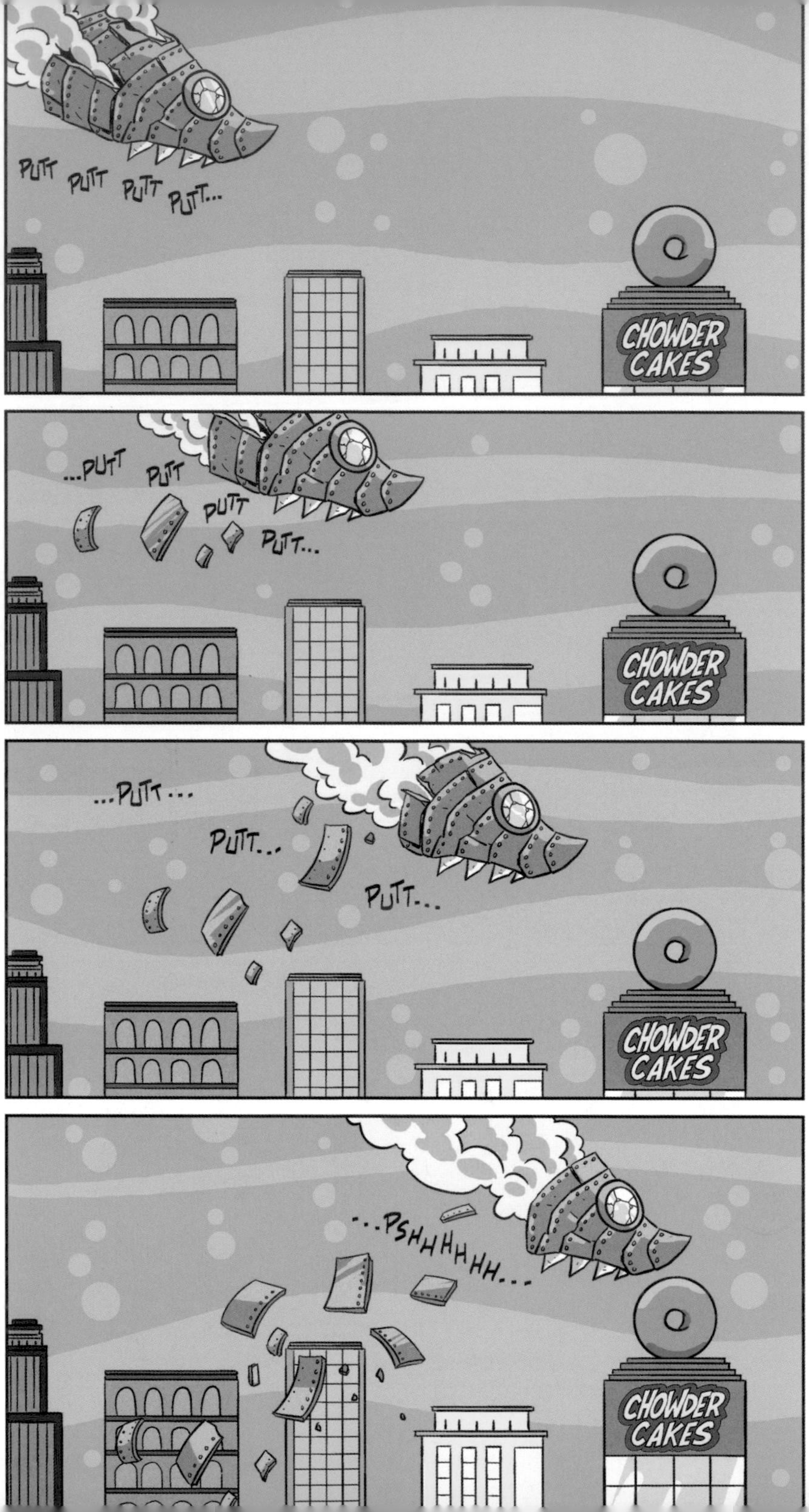
PUTT PUTT PUTT PUTT...
CHOWDER CAKES
...PUTT PUTT PUTT PUTT...
CHOWDER CAKES
...PUTT...
PUTT...
PUTT...
CHOWDER CAKES
...PSHHHHHH...
CHOWDER CAKES

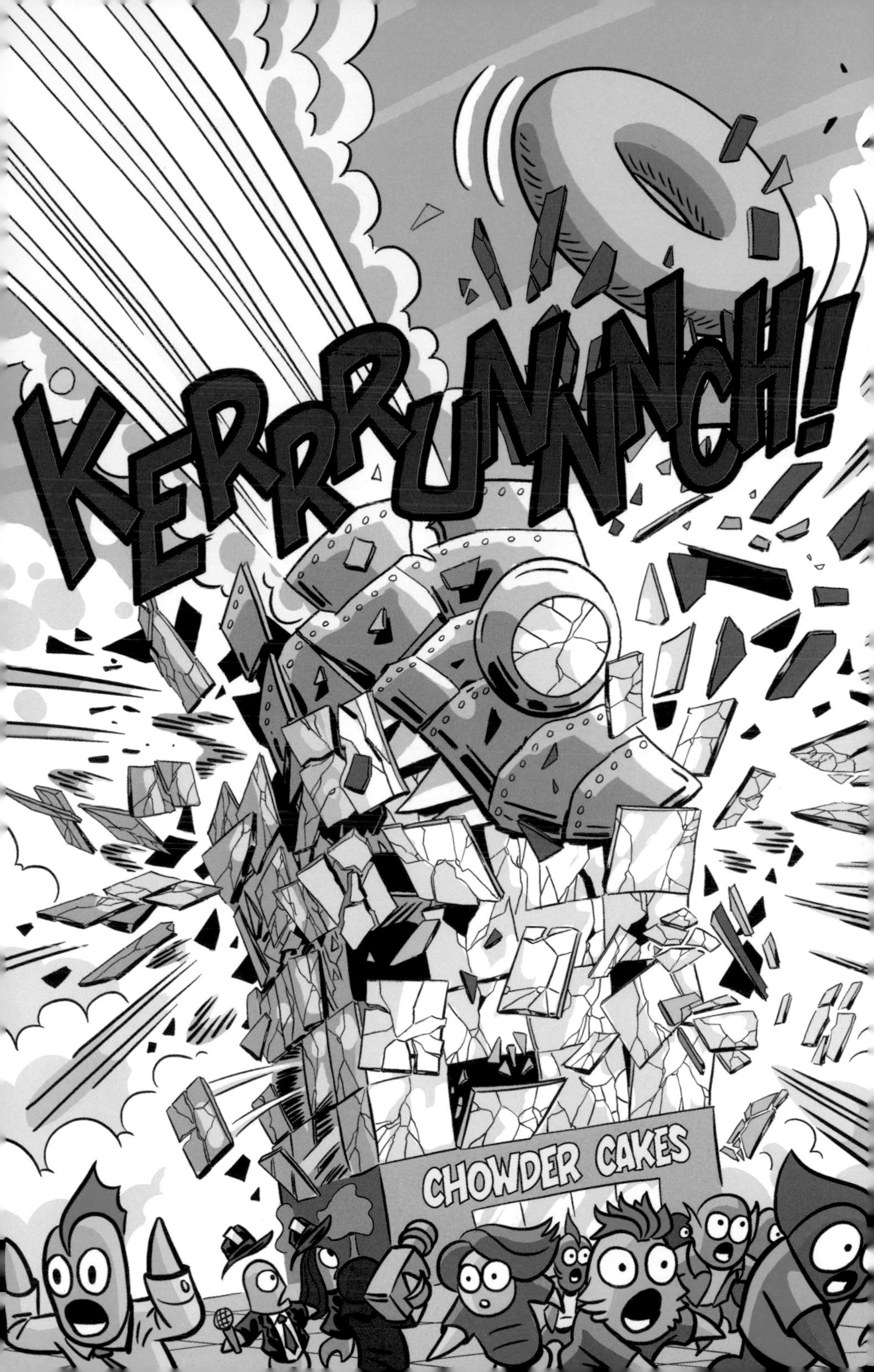
KERRRUNNNCH!!
CHOWDER CAKES

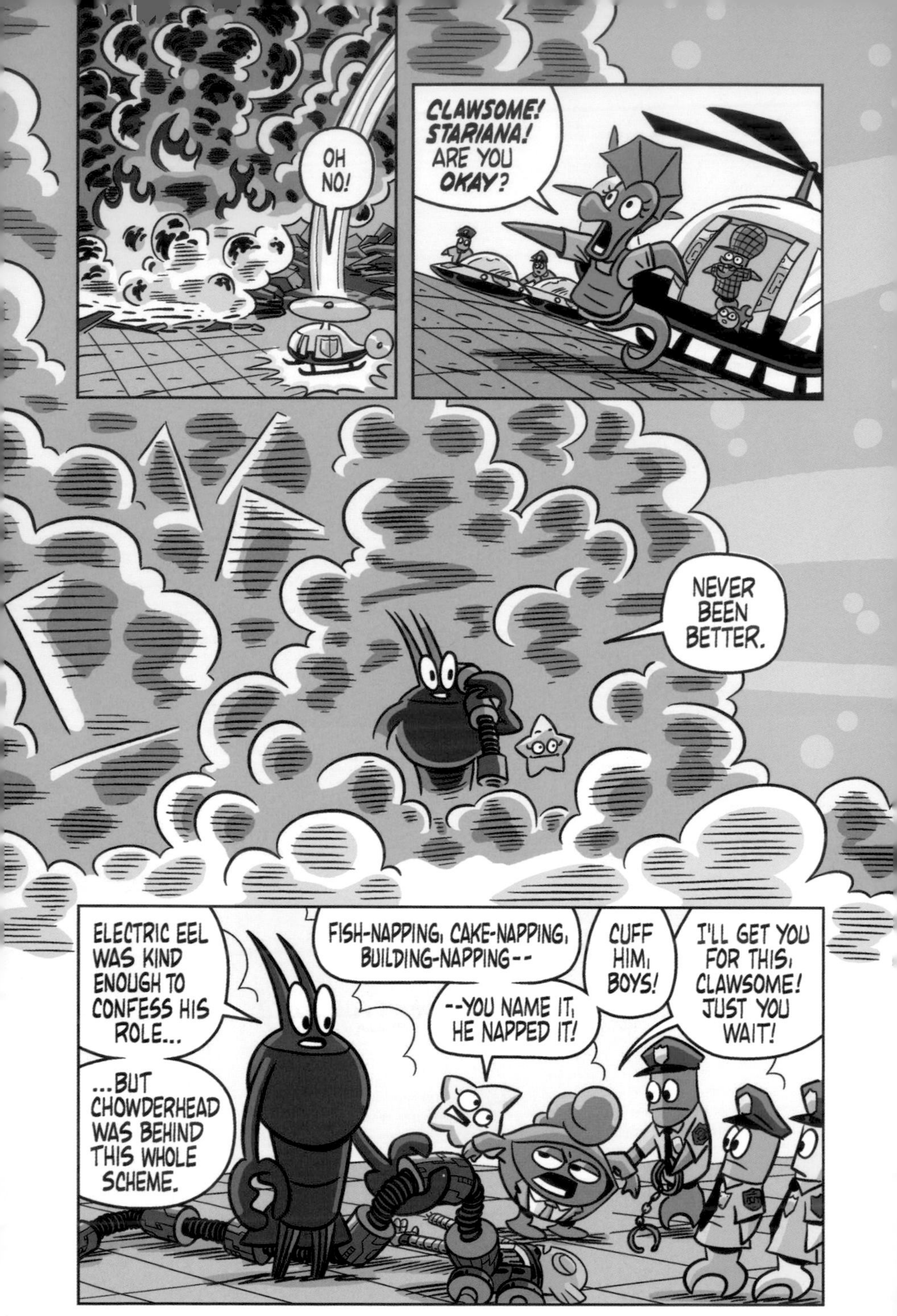
OH NO!
CLAWSOME! STARIANA! ARE YOU OKAY?
NEVER BEEN BETTER.
ELECTRIC EEL WAS KIND ENOUGH TO CONFESS HIS ROLE...
...BUT CHOWDERHEAD WAS BEHIND THIS WHOLE SCHEME.
FISH-NAPPING, CAKE-NAPPING, BUILDING-NAPPING--
--YOU NAME IT, HE NAPPED IT!
CUFF HIM, BOYS!
I'LL GET YOU FOR THIS, CLAWSOME! JUST YOU WAIT!

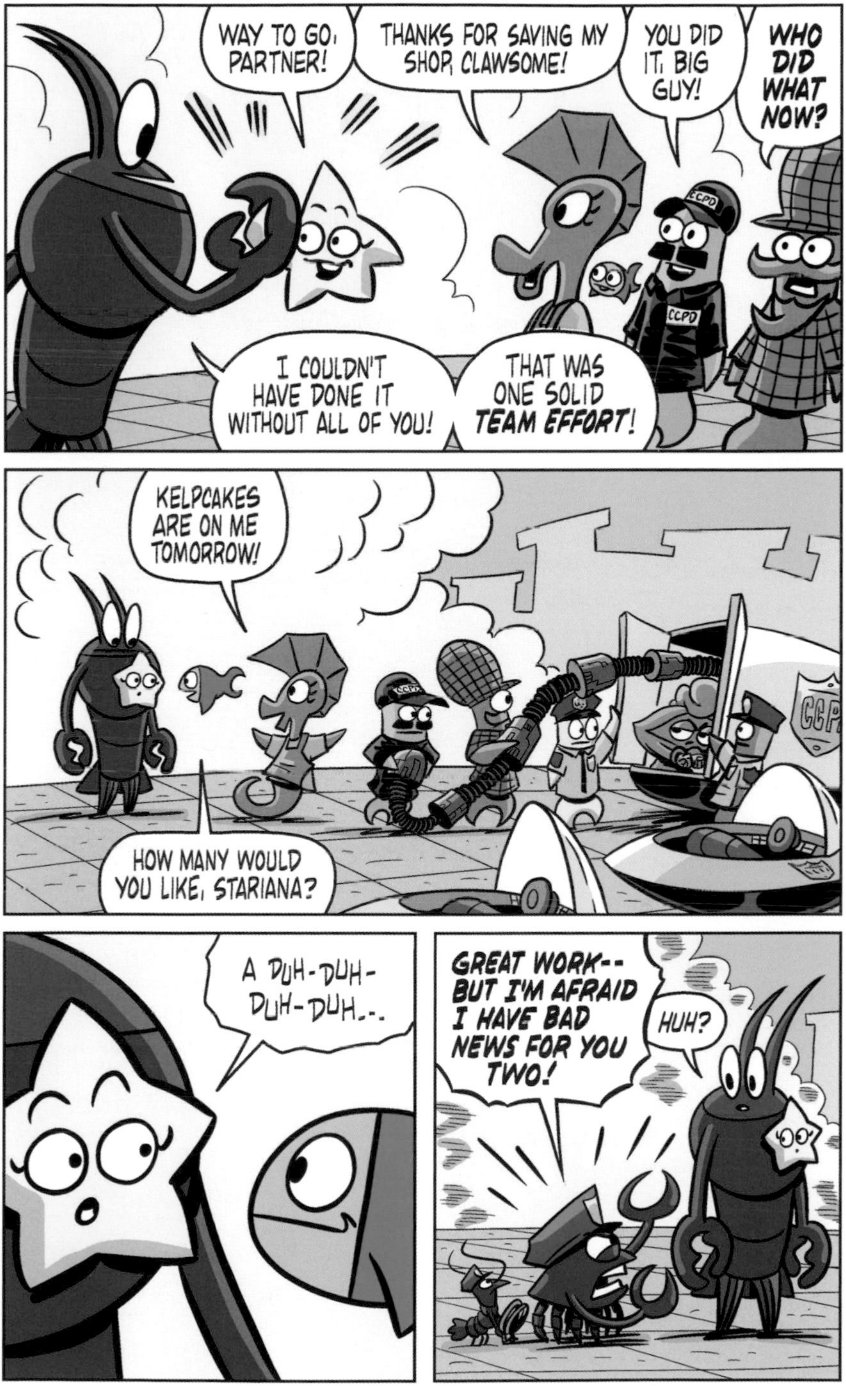
WAY TO GO, PARTNER!
THANKS FOR SAVING MY SHOP, CLAWSOME!
YOU DID IT, BIG GUY!
WHO DID WHAT NOW?
I COULDN'T HAVE DONE IT WITHOUT ALL OF YOU!
THAT WAS ONE SOLID TEAM EFFORT!
CCPD
CCPD
KELPCAKES ARE ON ME TOMORROW!
HOW MANY WOULD YOU LIKE, STARIANA?
A DUH-DUH-DUH-DUH...
GREAT WORK--BUT I'M AFRAID I HAVE BAD NEWS FOR YOU TWO!
HUH?

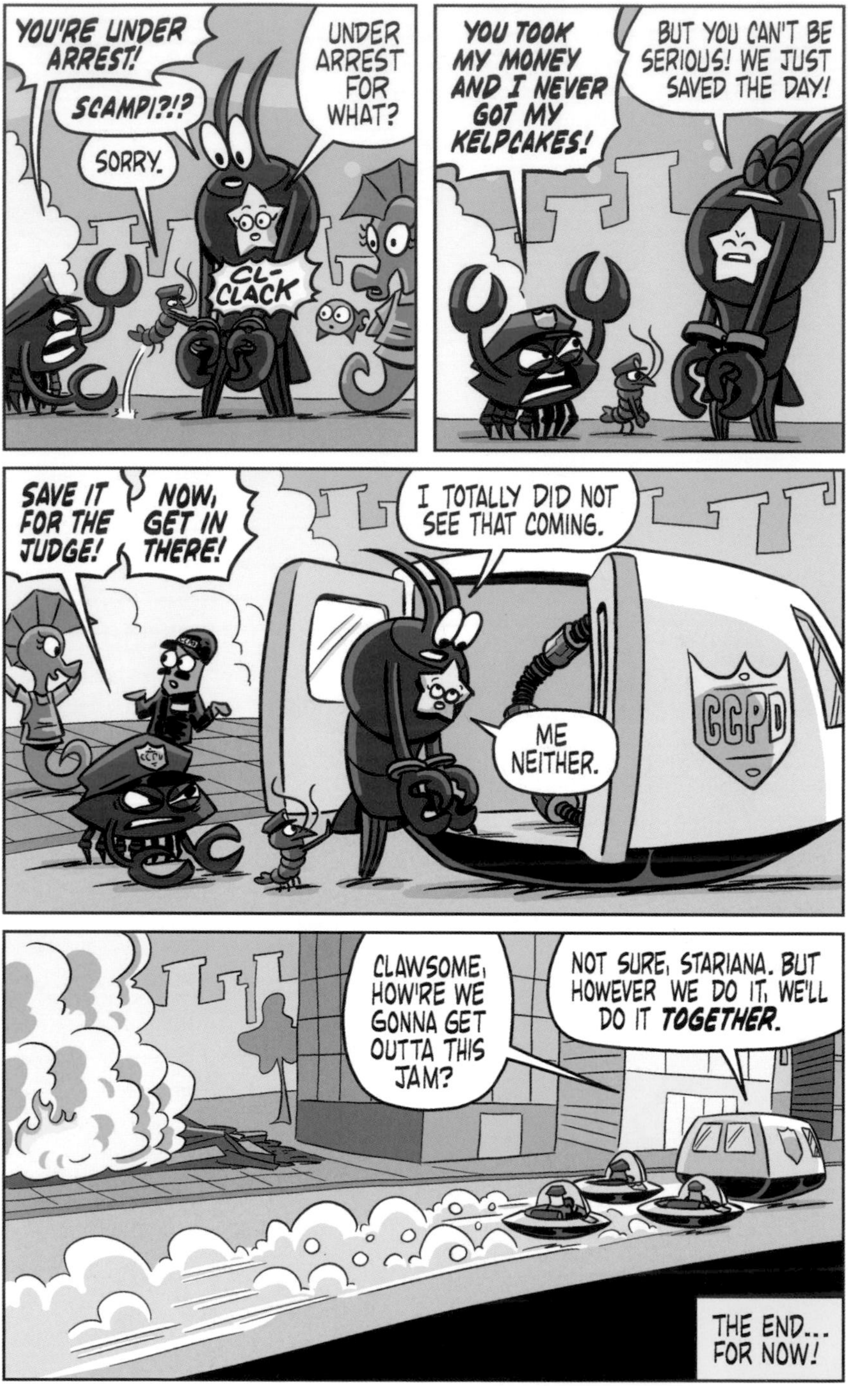
YOU'RE UNDER ARREST!
SCAMPI?!?
SORRY.
UNDER ARREST FOR WHAT?
CL-CLACK
YOU TOOK MY MONEY AND I NEVER GOT MY KELPCAKES!
BUT YOU CAN'T BE SERIOUS! WE JUST SAVED THE DAY!
SAVE IT FOR THE JUDGE!
NOW, GET IN THERE!
I TOTALLY DID NOT SEE THAT COMING.
ME NEITHER.
CCPD
CLAWSOME, HOW'RE WE GONNA GET OUTTA THIS JAM?
NOT SURE, STARIANA. BUT HOWEVER WE DO IT, WE'LL DO IT **TOGETHER**.
THE END... FOR NOW!

For Mom & Pop

—Smitty

Special thanks to Dave Giarrusso,
Stephen Mayer, and Michole Miller

—Chris

HarperAlley is an imprint of HarperCollins Publishers.

Officer Clawsome: Lobster Cop
Copyright © 2023 by Brian "Smitty" Smith
All rights reserved. Manufactured in Italy.
No part of this book may be used or reproduced in any manner
whatsoever without written permission except in the case of brief
quotations embodied in critical articles and reviews.
For information address HarperCollins Children's Books, a division of
HarperCollins Publishers, 195 Broadway, New York, NY 10007.
www.harperalley.com
Library of Congress Control Number: 2022940756
ISBN 978-0-06-313636-6

The artist used Procreate and Adobe Photoshop to create the
digital illustrations for this book.
Typography by Chris Giarrusso and Maddy Price
22 23 24 25 26   RTLO   10 9 8 7 6 5 4 3 2 1
First Edition